# COLLECTED STORIES of JESSAMYN WEST

Books by Jessamyn West

*The Friendly Persuasion*
*A Mirror for the Sky*
*The Witch Diggers*
*Cress Delahanty*
*Love, Death, and the Ladies' Drill Team*
*To See the Dream*
*Love Is Not What You Think*
*South of the Angels*
*A Matter of Time*
*Leafy Rivers*
*Except for Me and Thee*
*Crimson Ramblers of the World, Farewell*
*Hide and Seek*
*The Secret Look*
*The Massacre at Fall Creek*
*The Woman Said Yes*
*The Life I Really Lived*
*Double Discovery*
*The State of Stony Lonesome*
*Collected Stories of Jessamyn West*

# COLLECTED STORIES *of* JESSAMYN WEST

WEST, JESSAMYN

HARCOURT BRACE JOVANOVICH, PUBLISHERS

SAN DIEGO      NEW YORK      LONDON

B-2

Requests for permission to make copies of any part of the
work should be mailed to: Permissions, Harcourt Brace
Jovanovich, Publishers, Orlando, Florida 32887

Library of Congress Cataloging-in-Publication Data
West, Jessamyn.
    Collected stories of Jessamyn West.
    I. Title.
PS3545.E8315A6 1986     813'.54     86-12031
ISBN 0-15-119010-0

Some of the stories in this collection, a few in different
form, originally appeared in *Harper's Bazaar, Harper's
Magazine, Ladies' Home Journal, Mademoiselle, The New
Mexico Quarterly, The New Yorker, The Saturday Evening
Post,* Grinnell College *Tanager, Woman's Day,* and *Wom-
an's Home Companion.*

Designed by Julie Durrell

Printed in the United States of America

First edition

A B C D E

# Contents

# By Way of Introduction

IN 1979 Robert Kirsch, the respected and seasoned critic, concluded his review of *The Life I Really Lived* by declaring that it was time to recognize Jessamyn West as one of the treasures of this nation's literature. He was referring to the totality of her work, which includes novels, short stories, memoirs, poetry, essays, reportage, screen plays, and an opera.

Before she died in 1984, Jessamyn West received a generous measure of recognition. In addition to the doctorate in English literature she earned as a graduate student at the University of California, she was awarded nine honorary doctorates in humane letters and literature. She was sought after as a lecturer at colleges and universities and accepted a few of the many invitations to take short-term posts as teacher and writer-in-residence. As her reputation flourished over more than forty productive years, she undertook thirty-five commissions for articles from periodicals ranging from the popular to the scholarly.

She is herself the subject of an analytical biography, a briefer critical study, a film for students on the writing experience, and some twenty examinations of her writing. Short stories and extracts from her other works have appeared, and continue to appear, in more than one hundred anthologies. Public acclaim has come through occasional bestsellerdom and book club selections. In all editions, her nineteen published books have sold more than six million copies, an impressive record. It leaves no doubt of the deep and lasting impress Jessamyn West has made on American literature.

The relationship between certain of the novels and short stories, insofar as it pertains to this collection, requires brief notice. Three of the novels—*The Friendly Persuasion*, its companion, *Except for Me and Thee*, and *Cress Delahanty*—are composed of chapters that can stand easily as short stories, and, indeed, the majority of them were initially published as such in periodicals. Arbitrarily, no parts of those novels appear in this book; they remain available in their final, more cogent form as chapters in their larger contexts.

*Collected Stories of Jessamyn West* contains all of the independent short fiction that she wished preserved. It is intended to be representative rather than definitive. The dozen or so stories omitted are, as the author stated, "not wayward offspring, to be hidden or denied. But in the chilly wind of re-appraisal, it seems to me they might be more warmly dressed. If I ever have enough time to knit them some scarves and mittens, I'd let them out to play." There wasn't enough time.

Her first published work, the story titled "99.6," *is* included and is noteworthy on two nonliterary counts. First, it derives from her near-fatal battle with bilateral tuberculosis, which confined her to a sanatorium for several years; was followed by a long, physically difficult and psychologically draining convalescence; and profoundly influenced her future. Second, it affirms the enduring support of her husband, Harry Maxwell McPherson, whose persistent urging finally caused a diffident author, then thirty-six years old, to submit her work for publication, thus launching a career that was to prove superlative.

I have had the joy of being Jessamyn's friend and editor for almost a quarter of a century. I am spared the hopeless venture of a short summing up, personal and literary, of her life; the task has been accomplished brilliantly by Jessamyn in her memoirs—*Hide and Seek, The Woman Said Yes, To See the Dream*, and *Double Discovery*. Taken together they reveal this extraordinary human being in shining honesty and comprehension.

More needs to be said of Jessamyn—of her fortitude, generosity, and gentleness; her loveliness and femininity; her fierce devotion to truth as she perceives it; her delight in kindly laughter; her sense of beauty; her startling ability to pierce the light and dark veils of human conduct; her deep affinity with nature; and her abiding humanity—but that awaits another day.

No guide is necessary to her novels and stories. They have an intense clarity that speaks to any reader willing to listen. This introduction serves only as an invitation to discover some of the worlds of Jessamyn West. Her others beckon.

More than once, Jessamyn said to me, "Writing fiction is an almost certain way of making a fool of yourself." If that is so, Jessamyn is the wisest fool I have known.

Julian Muller

# COLLECTED STORIES *of* JESSAMYN WEST

# Probably Shakespeare

THOUGH THE AIR in the vacation cottage was swooningly hot, the sea sent into the heat its occasional needle pricks of salt freshness, so that Melinda experienced that peculiar glancing, shifting awareness the shore gives.

Reading and weeping, she heard nothing: not the sea itself, nor her mother, who was shouting. She sat upon her bed and, holding her book before her, let two tears—like pearls or moonstones, she thought—fall on its green binding. Then she put her book carefully down on the white honeycomb bedspread, so that the two tears would not be disturbed, and once more lay back against her pillows and wept.

"Love is like that," she whispered. "That's what I feel for Leonard."

She licked up the unfallen tears—which smarted her cracked and sunburned lip—and thought about Leonard . . . brown, in his bathing trunks . . . surrounded by girls, regarding them carelessly . . . evasive when her eyes found his. Yet in every tangle of sound she listened for his voice, searched every assemblage for his face.

" 'Sword strong,' " she quoted from the green book, " 'tender as dusk.' "

"Melinda," called her mother.

Melinda, wiping away her tears with the back of her hand, sat up.

"In the name of heaven," her mother asked, "why don't you answer me? I've shouted myself hoarse."

"I didn't hear you," Melinda answered truthfully.

"I don't wonder. Why don't you open things up? This room's an oven. A fiery furnace."

She picked up the book. "Merciful Father," she said. "In all this heat. Where'd you find this, Melinda?"

"In the closet," said Melinda defensively.

Her mother flipped the pages. "It's twenty years since anyone read this."

"Did you?"

Her mother nodded, her eyes busily scanning a page.

"Did you like it?"

"It's a mess," her mother said briskly, continuing to read. "Nothing's like this. Sickening," she said, closing the book on a finger. "Melinda, you need to get out. Think of coming to the beach for a vacation—then mooning about all day in a stifling house. I want you to take Brother for a little walk. You can walk down the pike. You'll just have time before supper. I'll give you a dollar to spend."

"I don't like to take Milton for walks. He embarrasses me. He runs under saloon doors and the men laugh at me. He talks to people."

"Well, there aren't any saloons here," her mother said, "and what's wrong with a boy of five talking to people?"

"If I have to be a nursemaid," said Melinda, "I wish you'd get me a uniform and cape. It's humiliating—going on this way. People don't know what I am."

"Nonsense," said her mother. "Of course they do. A big sister taking little brother for a walk. And a very pretty picture too." She turned another page.

"You like it, don't you?" Melinda asked.

"It's not Shakespeare."

"Shakespeare," said Melinda scornfully. "All that seeing ghosts and jumping into rivers and getting smothered . . . Where does that get you?"

"That's literature," said her mother dreamily.

"It's not love," said Melinda, but her mother didn't hear her. She was busy reading.

The sea was just in front of them as they walked away from the house. It lay out from the land like a purple petal reaching toward a center on the far horizon. Where it broke, green and white on the shining sand, it was like the mottled foliage some flowers have. It was like a flower; it was like a cavern too, Melinda thought, for its constant muffled roar arched overhead, built a hiding place where one could be alone. But even the sea was not sufficient to shut out the presence of Milton.

"Pull up your pants," Melinda told him, eying his drooping sunsuit with distaste.

No wonder Milton runs under saloon doors, Melinda thought morosely; he looks like a saloonkeeper—fat, red hair, pugnacious nose. All he needs is a white apron. Or a big brewer; he looks like a big brewer bending over a vat . . . Or a big brewer's horse, she decided, getting more and more bitter over Milton's clomping matter-of-fact presence and his noisy chewing on something he'd picked up coming through the kitchen.

"Swallow that," she commanded sharply.

Milton swallowed.

"What was it?" Melinda asked.

Milton was looking astonished. "String," he said.

"Crazy," Melinda told him. "You shouldn't swallow string."

"I can pull it up," said Milton.

"Hush up," said Melinda. "You make me sick. You can just digest it."

Milton swallowed some more—which was almost as noisy as his chewing.

Why was it? Other girls had sweet little brothers with curly hair and blue eyes and dimpled legs. Little boys you wanted to hug. Milton had legs like a brick wall and you'd as soon think of hugging a cement mixer, and his dark eyes stared up at you as if he knew your worst thoughts.

What must people think? They'd reached the pike now and were paralleling the sea: not the pike of shops and hot-dog stands, fortune tellers and men who guessed your weight, but a boardwalk filled with people, bound like themselves toward the real pike; or people tasting the spray and stretching their legs after the day's heat.

What would they think? Why, what could they think except that in spite of her slenderness, her fine ankles, her delicate even spiritual face, there was something definitely coarse and earthy about her?

Unless . . . of course . . . they thought . . . perhaps, they did. Melinda, dreaming, wondered. Very delicately, she put her own sad case to herself, scanned the passing faces, hunting for compassion. Her own face became thoughtful, overcast with memories, weighted with concern. They must be thinking that the boy took after his father. . . . She put a remorseful hand on Milton's shoulder—poor fatherless child. It was her fault entirely . . . the man had been horrible,

horrible. How could passion have so blinded her? She lifted her pure (in spite of everything—or perhaps purified by suffering) face to the great sea and found there forgiveness and understanding. Would she find as much in the child? The child who bore the stigma? Melinda closed her eyes and opened them wet with tears. An erring woman . . . and her blameless child, alone at evening, pacing the shores of the ancient sea.

Melinda's hand pressed more heavily on Milton's shoulder. She felt as if she might sob. She murmured quite brokenly, "Poor little fatherless bastard."

Milton looked up, but all he said was, "You're pushing me over, Lindy."

Melinda took her hand off Milton's shoulder and watched the sea that lifted ships and stirred old bones and separated lovers.

They had come to the booths and shops and stands; the many eyes hunting customers, the many voices shouting wares. Melinda looked at the faces, lined, puffed, waiting.

"Milton," she said, "I'm not really your sister."

Milton walked unconcernedly on.

"Did you hear me, Milton?"

"Not my sister."

"A long time ago. Long, long ago . . ."

Milton listened. It sounded like a story.

"Mother and Father—I've always called them that," she explained, "to make things easier for you—adopted me. D'you know what adopted means, Milton?"

Milton's small dark eyes looked interestedly up into Melinda's.

"Yes," he said.

"I was a foundling," Melinda told him.

"What's a foundling?" Milton asked.

"Somebody who's found. I was found on a doorstep. A baby no one wanted—so your father and mother just took me in. To work. A kind of slave," she explained. "To take care of you, to run errands, to do whatever no one else wanted to do. But I'm not your sister. Just an outcast. On the face of the earth," she said reflectively, "just an outcast and a dreamer."

She looked down at Milton. "You mustn't call me sister any more, now," she said kindly.

Milton was unimpressed. "You're my sister."

"I've just told you," Melinda repeated patiently, "that this happened many years ago. Before you were born, Milton, dear."

"You're my sister," Milton persisted.

"You were always taught to believe that . . . poor child. They started the fantasy," she said, "almost as soon as you were born."

"I heard Mama tell about when you were born," Milton said. "You took three days to come."

Melinda was silent for a while. Presently she said, "That was just a fairy tale I was telling you, Milton."

"I knew you were lying," Milton said placidly. "Let's spend the dollar."

"O.K.," said Melinda, "but first, let's hunt. Let's not spend it for the first thing we see. Let's find a tremendous bargain."

"What d'you want?" Milton asked suspiciously.

"Why, Milton, I said, let's hunt." But Melinda had an idea.

Toward the end of the pike was a striped tent and a sign that said: "Madame Rose, $1.00. Learn the Future. Secrets of Love Life Revealed. Arts of Attraction Amplified."

She had planned going there before, but always at the last minute had been unable to expose her love for Leonard so conspicuously. For that was what it would be: enter and say, "Will Leonard ever love me? Will his eyes ever search for me, his ears listen for my voice?" But perhaps if she kept her mind off it, really hunted bargains with Milton, she could, when she came to that tent, step in, put down the dollar, say, "Tell me . . . will he ever . . . ?"

It was nearly evening now. Beyond the breakers, whitecaps flashed angry heads; farther out the roiled waters took on a steely sheen. The tide was high, and spray from the heavy rollers was carried by the wind to the boardwalk and dashed like rain across their faces.

"I'm hungry," Milton said.

"O.K.," said Melinda, "let's hunt bargains in hot dogs."

"Or sea-foam candy," said Milton.

Two doors more was Madame Rose's. Melinda, talking fast, said,

"Or pickled pig's feet. Did you ever eat a pickled pig's foot, Milton? No, it's not really a pickled pig's foot. It's a pig's pickled foot. See, Milton? See the difference? They're wonderful, Milton. They're the ice cream of meat."

Suddenly she grabbed his arm. "You stand right here, Milton. You take hold of this flap and don't move and don't you talk to anyone until I get back. I won't be gone five minutes. You hear me, Milton?"

Milton nodded, and she closed his hand on a piece of canvas that folded back from the door of Madame Rose's tent . . . and walked in.

Madame Rose lay on a dirty couch, and her flat dark eyes moved up and down Melinda like a smudge. Her voice curled around Melinda like a damp tongue.

"You like to know about love?" she asked when Melinda had given her the dollar. "You like to know about men? Yes?"

"Yes," Melinda said, the word almost a whisper. She wished she were outside—eating a hot dog, hunting for sea-foam candy, counting the waves to see if the seventh would be the largest. "Do you see . . . any . . . romance . . . ahead for me?"

Madame Rose took her hand. "Romance," she said. "Men. Many men . . . many lovers. You like to hear about them?"

Madame Rose's hand was very soft, but it was a strong hand: it seemed not to notice Melinda's outward pull.

"Leonard?" Melinda asked.

"Ah," said Madame Rose. "A special one? You want to know about one special one?"

"Yes," Melinda said.

"Now . . . he does not notice you. He has eyes for someone else. But you, you, imagine his kisses, yes?"

Melinda got her hand away, "Will he ever . . ."

"There are things I could tell you. For five dollars," said Madame Rose, "for five dollars only," and she took Melinda's hand again.

"I haven't got five dollars," said Melinda, and as Madame Rose's grip became at once softer, and more enveloping, she pulled herself free and ran outside the striped tent with a panicky feeling of escape.

Twilight had come while she was inside; the streetlights were on.

"Milton," she said, "Milton." But he wasn't there. There was the flap of canvas, just as it had been, but Milton was gone.

There were tiny flecks of phosphorescence on the incoming waves, and the crash of their breaking set the boardwalk to vibrating beneath her feet. People thronged the pike now, coat collars up against the cold wind, buying hot dogs, drinking cups of steaming coffee.

"Milton," Melinda called, "Milton," but her voice was lost among the many voices, muffled by the sound of the surf.

Still, she wouldn't be afraid yet. Milton was talking to somebody . . . a boy was buying him a hot dog . . . an old man had taken him to watch the sea-foam-candy girl. Melinda made herself walk slowly, look carefully, but in her heart she knew what had happened.

Milton had stood by Madame Rose's tent watching the great waves rear up like walls of glass, then fall, shatter into something soft and hissing like snow and he had done what she had often wanted to do. He had climbed down from the boardwalk, gone out across the sand to touch with one finger the scalloped edge of the surf; and while he was bending over, one great wave had crashed landward and picked him up as easily as if he were a feather or a leaf. He had called her name, had said, "Lindy, Lindy," but she hadn't heard him. She had been in that sickening tent, thinking of Leonard . . . saying, love, love.

"Have you seen a little boy? Red hair, blue sunsuit?" A whisper was all she could manage.

"Kinda late for a kid to be out, sis."

"My little brother . . . red hair . . . blue sunsuit?"

"Pretty cold in a sunsuit this time of evening."

"A fat little boy . . . red hair?"

"Didn't keep your eye on him, eh?"

She was sure of what had happened; still, she felt as if her remorse and sorrow were strong enough to restore Milton, to let her suddenly see him sitting on a stool at some counter, dry and cozy, drinking root beer . . . see him standing with a sailor in a shooting gallery . . . see him . . .

"Oh, God," she said earnestly, "now I know what love is." Not Leonard! She loathed his very name now. But for Leonard, she and

Milton would be home now, and Milton would not be lost forever, drowned.

She could scarcely bring herself to look out toward the dark rolling water for fear she would see something light and small, aimlessly tossed about there. She walked back to Madame Rose's tent and took hold of the canvas flap Milton had held.

"This is the last thing Milton touched," she said and resolutely jumped off the boardwalk onto the sand and gazed across the surf. "Milton," she called, though she knew calling was hopeless. "Milton! Milton!"

"Lindy," Milton answered close at hand. "It was longer than you said. It was more than five minutes."

"Oh, Milton," cried Melinda. "I've looked everywhere. I've searched and searched."

There he was, sitting under the boardwalk, dry and cozy, sand piled over his legs.

"I thought you'd call me," said Milton, "when you were through. I was cold."

"I looked everywhere. I thought you were lost, Milton. I thought you were . . . maybe drowned. Oh, Milton, I've been a bad sister, but I do love you, and I'm going to devote the rest of my life to you, Milton," she said in a voice that quavered.

They walked homeward together, Melinda's arm around Milton's shoulders to keep him from being cold. Uplifted and transfigured, purged of illusions by suffering, she felt as she supposed a saint must feel after long fasting and praying.

"There's that boy," said Milton.

Melinda looked up. There under the corner light stood Leonard, no girls around, alone except for a stooge of his. Leonard was raising his arm in salute.

"There's that boy," said Milton again, but Melinda had not the slightest idea of recognizing Leonard, of playing traitor to her new, purer vision of love. She had seen where love like hers for Leonard could lead. This was renunciation, and it hurt cruelly, but the pain that filled her chest was clean as well as sharp. She passed Leonard, unseeing, her gaze fixed on the lights that led toward home.

Leonard's arm dropped awkwardly. His stooge didn't bother to lower his voice. "She didn't look eager and willing to me," he announced.

Leonard's voice was loud and weary. "At that age they're unstable. Still adolescent."

Melinda, unstable adolescent, walked disdainfully past him down the pike. How blind she had been . . . and how clearly she could now see. Love was holy and domestic: mother, father, and dear little pudgy brother. She rested her hand on Milton's soft thick hair. At the far end of the pike, bars of light reached out from the cottage windows like warm fingers. Warm scents of cooking food were all around them, and the sea had a sleepy lulling sound.

"Bastard," said Milton reflectively but quite clearly, "poor little bastard."

Melinda was wrenched from her pensive and reposeful mood. Her ears throbbed. "Milton," she said, "you musn't."

"You said I was," Milton repeated with satisfaction. "Poor little . . ."

Melinda squatted down on the boardwalk, her face level with Milton's. "Maybe what I said was buzzard. Poor little buzzard? Maybe you just got mixed up, Miltie. That's it, you got mixed up."

" 'Not your brother,' " said Miltie. " 'Poor little bas—' "

"I told you that was a fairy tale."

"Bast—" Milton began.

"Look, Milton," said Melinda. "I've got a dollar. If you forget it—that word—and not say it to Father and Mother—or anyone—I'll give it to you."

Milton appeared to be thinking. "You spent all that dollar."

"All right, Miltie," said Melinda wearily. "You know my red stuffed horse, the one you want? You can have it. And it cost one seventy-five. Not a dollar. Seven quarters," she said persuasively.

"Okey doke," said Milton.

"And what do you do?"

"Not say you called me a little—"

"Just forget it," Melinda told him. "Just erase it away. Like a word from a blackboard. It just doesn't exist any more."

"O.K.," said Milton.

Melinda stood up, but she didn't put her arm around Milton's shoulders again. She walked with arms severely folded across her chest. The sea still lifted and fell, with all its earlier mystery and force, but it was powerless now to move her.

Melinda felt very tired and longed intensely to be in her own room, reading again in her own book. Or perhaps not that book. Perhaps something much sterner. Probably Shakespeare.

# A Time of Learning

EMMETT MAGUIRE, hitching Old Clay to the buckboard, was suddenly convinced of folly. He became too sorrowful to slide the thin tail through the crupper, too pensive to buckle a hame strap. He stood in the sallow, early morning light gazing about the farmyard. Fool, he asked himself, where'll you find anything like this?

Just then, as he renounced it, the whole landscape so altered that he felt that for the first time in his nineteen years he was seeing it truly. All the familiar paraphernalia of the farm seemed suddenly to detach themselves from their background, move nearer him, become luminous and significant.

Amos, the blue-nosed mule, stood out against the sulphur-colored sky like sculpture. Emmett could not take his eyes from him. Now he was leaving—he had, in fact, moved heaven and earth to get away— and what did he really know of Amos? He had consigned himself to dabbling and traveling when he might have stayed home and learned, got to the bottom of mules. Against the morning sky, streaked now like a ripening Baldwin, Amos's head hung more heavy and knowledgeable than the rock of ages. Would there be any wisdom in the next county equal to what Amos had?

In the moment of leave-taking Emmett doubted it. Leaving, what could he expect? Girls and fritterings. No doubt sleep with the swine at the last, too, he supposed. But he felt as bound to move on as the prodigal himself, and for a better reason.

A sign and house painter soon paints himself out in his own neighborhood. All who incline toward paint and have money to pay for it come finally either to the end of the houses and sheds and outhouses needing a new coat or to the end of their money. All who care to have their fences decorated with signs for Hi-John Compelling Powder have them so decorated. Then the painter moves on or puts down his brush.

"Having trouble?" Emmett's father came from behind the buckboard, where with Emmett's mother he had been stowing away a round leather box of clean collars.

"No trouble," said Emmett, pulling the long switch tail on through. "I was thinking."

He was thinking, if they shed a tear, I'll have to unhitch, unpack, stay forever. But he was mistaken. Had his father laid a hand on the bridle, or his mother clung to him, he would have been off, as determined and set in his leave-taking as he had been in his preparation to go. But the leave-taking was seemly, no tears shed or protestations made. As he drove away, the known objects continued to move toward him, become big with the brightness and urgency of the willfully rejected.

His parents saw him depart, untransformed: their dear son, artist and thinker, Emmett. Though those were words they had never been permitted to say to him.

Once, in the barn, his father had come upon a picture of Emmett's painting. He had stared at it a long time. It was a big, empty picture with great reaches of unoccupied cardboard. Except for the front of a house, an expanse of white siding dazzling in sunlight, there was almost nothing in the picture at all: shallow wooden steps ascended to a partially open door; beyond the door on the dark floorboards and deep in shadow lay something crumpled, a piece of goods, a ribbon perhaps, and beyond that a naked, retreating heel.

Emmett's father would have enriched the picture with many more objects: set pots of flowers on the steps, put a window next the door and a face at the window. Still empty and unembellished as the picture was, it had a certain power. He had found himself wondering about it: about that heel, more yellow than pink, about its haste, its alarm. Then he had noticed that there was a shadow across the steps, that near the house someone, stock-still, stood and watched. Listened, too, perhaps.

But when he had said to Emmett, who came in and found him staring, "Son, you're an artist," Emmett had taken the corn knife he had in his hand, and cut the picture to shreds.

"Don't call me that," he told his father. "Never say that. I can't learn. I'm a house and sign painter."

\*          \*          \*

He was a house painter, or a barn or shed painter when he could find houses and barns and sheds to paint; but in Bucklin County he was treading upon the heels of a competitor. Emmett regarded with scorn the wash of murky green that marked the man's progress. A color not fit to set to the side of a henhouse, he thought, not good enough for any privy I'd paint. He thanked God for his contract and painted signs.

He had known for some time that he was being watched. That didn't trouble him. It was almost as if the eyes that followed the movements of his hand gave it added force. It was talk that troubled.

"What's 'Crossing and Un-Crossing Powder?' "

"I don't know," Emmett said, painting on.

"Would you make a sign for what you don't know?"

"Yes," said Emmett, "I would."

"I wouldn't."

Emmett said nothing.

"What's 'David the Fearless Floor Wash?' "

Emmett set his brush in the can of linseed oil, turned away from the granite rock on which he was lettering freehand.

"What's a kid who stands asking questions while you're trying to work?" he asked.

The boy was big but round, round as an apple, and his round black eyes were swallowing the lettering like quagmire.

"A nuisance," Emmett told him, shortly.

"What's the sign for?" the boy asked, as if he hadn't heard.

"Make people buy the stuff."

"How can they buy it if they don't know what it is?"

"You couldn't buy if you knew. You haven't got any money."

The boy's pants were tight, his pockets taut, his hands fat; still he managed to squeeze a quarter up to the air.

"All right," said Emmett. "Read that and be quiet." He tossed him the Occult Supplies Catalogue, turned back to his painting.

"Bat's Blood Oil," the boy said and Emmett could hear him moistly swallowing.

"Shut up," said Emmett, "or I'll take it away from you."

The boy shut up. Except for the swallowing he didn't make another sound until the sign was finished. The minute Emmett stepped away from the boulder to judge his completed work, he began again. "Which would you buy," he asked, "Graveyard Dust or Oriental Lover's Powder?"

"Graveyard Dust," said Emmett.

"Not me," said the boy. He pushed his quarter to the surface again. "I'll take three packages Oriental Lover's Powder."

"I don't sell the stuff," Emmett told him. "I just paint the signs. You write them," he pointed to the catalogue, "to get the powders."

"Have you got a pencil so's I could write it down?" the boy asked.

Emmett tore a sheet from the little notebook he carried, handed it and a pencil to the boy.

"What do you figure to do with it?" he asked, watching the boy, who wrote with his tongue as well as his fingers.

The boy looked up, but a sudden film came over his eyes. "None of your business," he said.

"That's right," said Emmett, "It isn't."

He took back the pencil and began to collect his gear.

"That your horse and rig by the bridge?"

"Yes," said Emmett.

"I'll help you carry your paints."

Emmett handed him a bucket. "Watch your step," he advised. "That's valuable."

The boy planted his bare feet as carefully as if walking through nettles. He looked over the amount of material in the back of the buckboard. "Takes an awful lot of paint to paint signs," he said.

"I paint houses, too," Emmett told him.

"Barns?" asked the boy.

"Sure," Emmett said.

"We got a barn to be painted."

"Who's we?"

"Us. My father. He wanted the other man to do it but Ivy said his paint looked like scum on a frog pond."

"Who's Ivy?" Emmett asked, thinking she'd picked the right word for it.

"My sister. But Ma said, 'There's things worse than scum, Miss Ivy.' "

"Don't your mother want the barn painted?"

"Oh, sure."

"I'll apply for the job." Emmett said. "You want to ride on home with me?"

They went by the river road. Red dust clung to the lush green growth that arched above their heads and Old Clay methodically lifted more of it to their faces. Even in the gloom of red dust and green shadows the boy bent over the catalogue, reading or rereading, Emmett didn't know which, the wondrous items. Emmett himself was rehearsing a sales talk; reassuring himself, before he tried to convince others, that he was the man for the job.

When they turned away from the river, made for the open, rolling farmlands, Emmett asked the boy his name.

"Oral," he said, not looking up from his reading.

"Oral," Emmett repeated. "How do you spell that?"

Oral spelled it. "I'm named for a bird," he said, keeping his place in the catalogue with one finger. "A yellow, singing bird that sang where my mother used to live."

Emmett looked at the cannonball boy, his black eyes and white hair. "You're not very yellow, Oral," he said. "Can you sing?"

The boy didn't smile and he closed his catalogue. "No," he said, "nor lay eggs, neither."

"Excuse me, Oral," Emmett said.

There was no more talk for a time. Finally Oral said, "You're not very big for a man."

"Big enough," said Emmett.

"You ain't bad-looking, though."

Emmett nodded his thanks.

"You got a girl?" Oral asked.

"No girl," Emmett said. "I'm off girls."

"Not me," said Oral. "I got two."

"You don't look very old to be having girls," Emmett told him.

"Old enough," said Oral and went back to his reading.

He roused to point out his home before they got there. It and its outbuildings were planted on a gentle rise of land, visible, as they approached, from every hilltop: a substantial brick house and a big weather-beaten, two-story barn. Three-story, it proved to be when they arrived, the hillside on the back having been scooped away to make room for stalls for the animals.

Oral's father, who was Oral expanded and coated with hoarfrost, heartily welcomed Emmett.

"I'm C. B. Lish," he said after Emmett had stated his own name and business, "and I'm pleased to make your acquaintance. The barn needs painting the worst way."

Emmett then delivered the rehearsed speech, speaking, as he thought right, of the quality of his paints: linseed base, lead content, color, time a coat would last; of his own work, skillful, experienced, painstaking. But C. B. Lish was reading.

"Candle Powder," he said wonderingly. "Now the way I always heard that was candle *power*."

"This is something different," Emmett explained, wishing the catalogue had never fallen into Lish hands. "This is a powder."

"Now, how," said C. B. Lish, "do you recken they go about getting a Candle Powder? Grind 'em up?"

"I don't know," Emmett said. "I just paint the signs."

"Bible Bouquet Oil," he said reading on and sniffing as he read. "There's a concoction ought to be mighty sweet. You sell this, boy?"

"No, sir," Emmett said. "I don't. I'm a painter. I'd like to get the job painting your barn."

C. B. Lish was turning the pages. "Jinxers. Four inches tall."

"I don't sell that stuff," Emmett reminded him. "I paint."

C. B. Lish nodded, but didn't look up. "That's what you told me before. You walk on up to the house and talk to Emma and Ivy. They're the ones to decide."

Emmett never forgot the room he stepped into. After the summer dust and heat it was as if he had plunged into water, shadowed and cool. He closed his eyes once or twice as he would have done under water, to feel the coolness on his eyelids. The bricks, he supposed, were what made the room cool, the pulled blinds kept it dim.

The room was a kitchen because it had a stove in it: unlit, cool-looking, even, black and shiny like a stoat fresh from a shady wallow.

But besides the kitchen furniture—the safe, the cabinet, the set table—there was much else in the room. There was a sofa, a small bird in a big wooden cage, a secretary whose space was about evenly divided between books and dishes, a diamond-shaped mirror with pegs for hats and coats at each corner. Beneath one of the pulled blinds, Emmett guessed, a prism was hanging, for onto the bleached floorboards fell shafts of multicolored lights.

And there was a girl in the room. Emmett saw her last of all. She stood in the darkest corner of the room, leaning against the sink, grating nutmeg on a pudding of some kind. Emmett could smell the vanilla, sweet and sharp, above the sweet muskiness of the nutmeg.

The girl looked up at Emmett, then grated away, not saying a word. Emmett prepared to speak, but could not for a minute. He knew what a beautiful girl should look like; he had often thought about it; he knew exactly what it took. So far as he could see, nothing was missing.

The girl had on a white dress. She curved in and she curved out. Her waist went in to a span as narrow and supple as a grapevine; elsewhere she had the fullness of the clusters. Her hair was like Oral's, but her eyes when she had looked up at Emmett were like the best milk-agates he had ever owned. O God, Emmett silently prayed, I thank thee for not letting me stay home and study mules.

She was a calm-looking girl, but seeing Emmett, she dropped the nutmeg, and the sound it made rolling along the bare floorboards brought him back to speech.

"Your nutmeg, Miss," said Emmett, getting it before it stopped rolling.

"Thank you," said the girl.

"I'm Emmett Maguire, house painter," Emmett told her.

"I'm pleased to meet you," said the girl. "I'm Miss Ivy Lish."

That night in the south upstairs chamber, a hot little room where a full-leafed chinaberry tree shut all the air from the single window, Emmett lay in a kind of trance. Sometimes he slept but more often he was awake, and every time he awakened he rejoiced as though he were Lazarus newly come to life. Sleeping, he dreamed of Ivy, but awake he thought of her. And, since he reckoned thinking to be one step nearer reality than dreaming, he hated to lose time in anything as second-hand as sleep.

He would awaken, wonder for a minute where he was, hear the leaves of the chinaberry tree moving outside his window with a watery ripple, say, "Ivy, Ivy." Inside himself he would feel a happiness so great it made him a little sick: a feeling like that he had tobogganing each winter on Sugar Slide, when at the final curve he always thought, I'll die this is so wonderful—joy and pain being at that point so delicately balanced.

Once he got out of his bed and laid the palms of both hands first against the west wall of his room, then against the east, telling himself as he did so, one inch of wood may be all that separates us. But all he heard as he stood, hands pressed to either wall, was a serene snoring: too delicate for Oral, probably C. B. Lish himself.

He had been in love before but always unlucky, and never able to do much but suffer. Once with a girl who was engaged, who had bent down and kissed him twice on the eyelids, but would have no more to do with him; once with a girl whose father had promised to shoot any man or boy who came on the place, and Emmett, after hearing the first load of buckshot whistle past his legs, had never again been able to feel the same about her; the last time had been with a girl in Mercer, but before he had a horse of his own, and in the weeks when he had not been able to see her, she had met and married a coffee salesman.

But now he was lucky: in love and beneath the same roof with the girl he loved. And going to be beneath the same roof with her for two more weeks at the least. For the barn painting, if he did a good job, would take that long; and he intended doing not only a good job, but a job so wonderful people for miles around would marvel at it. He intended to paint the Lish barn as if it were a miniature, with every brush stroke being set on ivory.

The last time he awakened the summer night had ended. The air in the room had cooled and outside in the chinaberry tree the awakening birds were whetting their bills and stretching their throats.

I could paint her, Emmett thought. I see just how to do it, where she should stand, how turn her head. I would paint her in her white dress, full length, a shadow at the base of her throat. In his hand he already felt the brush and the strokes it would make so that Ivy would stand curving in, curving out, alive upon cardboard. Alive with a reality beyond life because to her store of realness he would add all of his own.

There was nothing in the next week he did not do well. He was so filled with power and sureness he walked about his scaffolding as if gravity were a force from which he was exempt. He laid the brush against the barn each day in strokes so solid that the barn rose up clear and bright again, rebuilt, it almost seemed, as well as repainted.

At night, untired after the day's work, he washed first in turpentine and then in water, and talked with the family.

Privately, he said to C. B. Lish, "I'll paint the toolshed free if I can borrow your buggy, Sunday."

"What you want of the buggy?" Mr. Lish asked.

"I want to take Ivy to church."

Mr. Lish whistled. "So that's the way the wind blows."

"Yes, sir," said Emmett, "it is."

"Ivy's no churchgoer," Mr. Lish told him.

Emmett was taken aback. He had supposed all nice girls were churchgoers. He had no idea where else he could take a girl on Sunday, or what other entertainment she could want. Though he would never have denied that for himself coming and going would be the best part of it. Still this was Bucklin County, not home, and he hated a man who was set in his ways.

"Wherever she wants to go, I'll take her."

"The novelty of it," her father admitted, "might appeal to her."

Ivy said yes when he asked her, as if novelty had nothing to do with it.

Upon himself, upon Old Clay and the buggy, Emmett had done an amount of polishing just short of abrasion. A stroke or two more and varnish and hide, human and horse alike would have given away. Tender and glittering, they drove churchward.

There was nothing Emmett could think of to say which did not seem too personal for words. His mind was filled with Ivy: her sweet, flowery smell, which it was probably wrong even to notice, let alone mention; the blue vein in her forehead; the way a fold of her full skirt lay across his shinbone, where its lightness weighed upon him like a burning glass.

They drove through heat waves rippling like lake water. Already the leaves hung downward, giving the sun only their sharp edges to taste. Old Clay was discolored by sweat and on the fence rails the birds rested with lifted wings.

"Ivy," said Emmett, "will you let me paint your picture?"

"Can you paint people, too?" Ivy asked. "Besides barns, I mean?"

"Yes," said Emmett, with sudden knowledge, "I can," and he used the word he had forbidden his father, "I'm an artist."

"Perhaps you would make me look funny," said Ivy.

"Funny," repeated Emmett. "What do you mean, funny?"

"Queer," Ivy told him. "Not pretty. Maybe you don't know how to paint well enough. Maybe you would make my eyes look funny. Eyes are very hard to paint."

"I know how to paint eyes," Emmett said. "I know how to paint all of a person. I would make you look the way you are, Ivy."

"How am I, Emmett?" asked Ivy.

"Beautiful," said Emmett, trembling with frankness.

From there on, the drive to church went by in a flash, the church time, too, though Ivy was unable to attend the services with Emmett. In the churchyard Arod Johnson had awaited her. His mother was sick, pining to see Ivy, and with Emmett's permission he would drive Ivy to his place, have her back by the time church was over. He was considerably later than that, and Emmett was sorry for Ivy cooped up with a sick old woman while he sat in the shaded churchyard. Still, he had been so deep in thought about his painting of her that he had not had time for much pity.

"Let's go home the long way," Ivy said when she got back.

They went home the long way through the hot afternoon.

"Tell me about my picture," Ivy said.

"I will paint you," Emmett said, "in the parlor bay window. I will push the lace curtain back so that on each side of the picture will be just their ripple. You will stand in your white dress before the clear glass and behind you will be the mock orange."

"How will I look?" asked Ivy.

"You will look," Emmett said slowly, seeing her like a white column budding for flowers—"fine."

"We came home the long way," Ivy told Oral, who was in the barnyard when they drove in. "We came home the long way and had to go slow because of the heat." She gave Emmett both her hands when he helped her from the buggy and walked at once to the house.

Oral helped with the unhitching.

"I reckon you seen Old Arod," he said.

"Arod Johnson?" asked Emmett.

"You know any other Arods?"

"No," said Emmett, "I don't. His mother was sick."

"She seems to be a mighty weak old lady," Oral told him, he himself leading Clay to the barn.

In the second week Emmett began work on the barn each morning at sunup. In that way he made time for his painting of Ivy. He had never supposed hand and brush could work so well together. It was as if the lines of Ivy's body flowed downward of themselves, through his arm and hand, and onto the cardboard; it was as if her colors stained his fingers and he had only to touch his brush for them to be left where and as they should be.

"What do you think of while you paint?" Ivy asked.

He thought of very little. Then he was lost in the work; in the brush strokes, in the leaf-shaped shadows on the white dress, on the way Ivy's roundness and solidity were transferred by means of his skill so that in thin paint and upon a flat surface, still she was round and solid.

Afterward, when he was not painting, he thought: in later days the picture will hang in a special place in the house and I will say to visitors, that is my beautiful wife, Ivy Lish Maguire; and to the children I'll say, that is the first picture I ever painted of your mother. And I will never part with it, no matter what I should be offered for it.

"I would like my eyelashes made longer," said Ivy.

"No," said Emmett, "that would be wrong."

"Wrong?" said Ivy. "They are longer."

"But not looking at you," Emmett told her, "this way against the light."

If someone had told him, you have never said the word love, he would have been surprised. Everything he did said the word, every look, every tone, every gesture. He himself heard no other sound.

"Is it finished?" asked Ivy.

"One more day," said Emmett. "Do you like it?"

"The eyelashes should be longer," said Ivy, but Emmett could tell by the way she stood looking at the picture, turning her head, smiling, that she liked it.

That night he worked until late on the barn and went early to bed. He lay in his upstairs bedroom listening to the chirr of summer insects, and thought, tomorrow night the picture will be finished and I will put, in one corner of the picture, my name, in the other, hers.

He was still awake when Oral came in, noisy in his unaccustomed shoes, and sat on the edge of his bed. Oral moved his feet back and forth across the floorboards, the bed squeaked as his weight shifted, a bird sang a note or two as if, awakening suddenly, it had mistaken the moonlight for dawn.

"Well, Oral?" asked Emmett.

"I got me a date with one of my girls," said Oral as if answering the question.

"Which one?" Emmett asked sleepily, not caring, thinking, he's got no one else to talk to about his girls.

"The best one," Oral said.

Emmett yawned silently, shut his eyes. The moonlight here in the corner, he thought, isn't strong enough for him to tell whether my eyes are open or shut.

"Two's too many," Oral said, "if you've got one good girl."

"One good girl's enough," Emmett agreed, smiling at Oral's wisdom. "How's the other one taking it?" he asked.

"She's down in the mouth," Oral admitted, "but she'll get over it."

"Sure," Emmett echoed out of his drowsiness, "they all get over it."

"Emmett," Oral asked, "who's that picture belong to, you or Ivy?"

"Ivy," Emmett said, wanting to say her name, though he had thought of the picture as theirs together.

"That's all right, then," Oral said getting off the bed.

"It's Ivy's and mine together," Emmett amended.

"She's given away your half too, then," Oral told him. "Both halves together to Arod Johnson."

Emmett sat up in bed. Oral was standing where the moonlight from the window fell across his broad and sorrowful face.

"I could've told you," he said, "but there wasn't ever a time when you'd hear to it."

"It's gone," he assured him, as Emmett got out of bed. "Wrapped in butcher paper and given away."

Emmett sat down again.

"My girl's waiting for me," Oral said. At the door he turned back. "Ivy's a born two-timer. You ain't the first."

For a long time after Oral left, Emmett sat on the edge of his bed. He felt numbed, beyond feeling anything, but when he stood up his hands and face were wet, and he saw that without knowing it he had been crying.

The thing to do, he decided, is to get out, pack and leave. Get gone before I have to look on any of their faces again.

Outside, his carpetbag in his hand, he stood for a time in the barnyard. He could see that it was still early, a moonlit summer night, cooling off now so that the river mists were flowing up into the draws. He could hear the soft, slow movements of the animals in their stalls and once in a while, as the air freshened, a slight fluttering of leaves.

Old Clay came quietly to the fence, hung his head across the top rail, and, with eyes glassy in the moonlight, looked at Emmett.

"Let's get out of here," Emmett said.

But when he saw the ladder and scaffolding still against the barn, and the unpainted section around the haymow door, he determined, stubbornly, to finish the job. "I'll not go and leave a stroke undone," he told Old Clay, as if his horse had argued with him about it.

Once he was on the scaffolding, brush in hand, another idea came to him: she took my picture and gave it away. I'll leave another here that can't be given away, and I'll paint her this time as she really is, so no eye can miss it.

He went down the ladder and brought up his other paints, and while he was doing this he was filled with hate and scorn, thinking

I'll put her on the barn so that everyone can see what a slut looks like. But he could not do it.

He did not know which way it was: whether he was unable to paint and hate at the same time, or whether actually he would never be able to hate Ivy, no matter what she might do. Whichever way it was—whether the brush strokes took away his hate, or he was without real hate to begin with—he was painting a picture not much different from his first. And better, too, he knew; though whether on that surface, with the paints he had, it would show as much, he couldn't tell. There would be no rippling lace curtains in this picture because it would be Ivy herself, unobscured by any of his imaginings. He remembered what he had thought: a tower of white. And budding; and remembering, spat with disgust over the edge of the scaffolding.

From below someone whispered, "Look out for me," and there in the moonlight, gazing upward, was Oral.

"What you doing out this time of night?" Emmett asked.

"Getting home," Oral whispered, so that Emmett, answering, whispered too—though the house was far enough away to keep anyone from hearing. "You better get on to bed. You'll catch a strapping, staying out all night this way."

"Strapping," Oral scoffed. "I'm not sleeping in the house anyway," he said. "I'm sleeping in the haymow." He stood, stocky legs far apart, head thrown back so that his white hair shone in the moonlight like dandelion fuzz.

"What you painting her for again?" he whispered scornfully. "Whyn't you paint something nice for a change? Whyn't you paint something pretty up there? A big sunflower or a rooster?"

"Be quiet, can't you?" Emmett said. "This makes me feel better."

Oral went inside the barn and Emmett could hear him mounting the ladder into the haymow, then rustling about as he hollowed himself a place to sleep.

Long after Emmett had supposed him to be sleeping, he heard Oral's voice very near at hand as if he were speaking with his mouth close to a knothole or crack.

"Emmett?"

"What you want now, Oral?"

"Whyn't you get some of them powders, Emmett?"

"Powders?" asked Emmett.

"The ones from the catalogue. They work good, Emmett." Oral's voice was filled with kindness.

"I didn't know they'd come."

"Oh, sure, they came. They're strong and good. I wish you'd try some, Emmett."

"No," Emmett told him, "they wouldn't work for me. No powder'll do me any good. I've just got to learn."

"Don't waste any more time on her," urged Oral. "Paint something nice. Paint a picture of a field of punkins."

"When I finish this," said Emmett, "I will."

The moon was still bright when he finished, but the stars had begun to dim and the sky's darkness was fading. He hitched and loaded his stuff into the buckboard, but before he drove away he stood looking up at his work.

"I can paint," he said looking at his picture of Ivy, forgetting Ivy herself.

He had driven down the slope from the house and up the first little rise when he heard a clear but controlled halooing behind him. Turning about, he saw that Oral had opened the door of the haymow so that his picture of Ivy was cut in two: a head, then where the upper part of her body should have been, the empty space of the open door, and below that the swelling white skirts.

"Emmett," Oral halooed quietly.

Emmett waved to show that he heard.

"You forgot your catalogue, Emmett."

"Keep it," Emmett called back. "You keep it, Oral, I can get another."

Their gentle voices carried on the quiet morning air. The late stars had faded and the river smell was fresh and sharp.

"Good-bye, Emmett," Oral called as Emmett, waving, drove on.

For as long as Emmett could be seen, Oral stood in the open doorway, not waving, himself, but following the buckboard with his eyes until finally it topped a distant rise and dropped from sight.

# The Mysteries of Life
## in an Orderly Manner

I T WAS initiation night, a candle-lighting ceremony, a big night in the lodge, and through the spring twilight of the California hill town, past the parking meters and the street-corner loungers, the matrons carrying their candles unlit drifted like moths. Not moth-like certainly in their plumpness but varicolored, fluttering, and pleasure-bent.

Emily Cooper (Mrs. W. H. Cooper—William H. Cooper, Inc., Insurance—"See Us B 4 U Burn") sat with her husband in their car, parked at the curb. Across the street from them, and a little way down, was the Vasconi Building, where the initiation was being held. Emily was herself to be initiated that night, but she didn't know the Pocahontas women very well and she was sitting for a time with her husband, gathering up courage from his matter-of-factness and checking the suitability of her dress against what she could see of the evening dresses of the other initiates, passing in the fading light. Only the initiates wore evening dresses (formals, formals, Emily reminded herself to say). The established lodge members, the Pocahontases in good standing, went to their meetings in Indian regalia. Emily watched them go by in the twilight, coats thrown back, because the evening was warm, fringes swaying, beaded headbands gleaming, moccasined feet silent on the sidewalk. Emily was proud to recognize some of them.

"There's Mrs. Asta Bell," she said to her husband. "She's Keeper of the Wampum."

"Keeper of what?" asked Mr. Cooper, himself no lodge man. Emily got into Pocahontas because of her father, Clement McCarthy, a long-time Redman, though not a resident of the state. "Join, join," her father had always urged her, but Emily would not as long as the children were little.

"Wampum," said Emily. "Indian for money. She's treasurer."

Mrs. Edna Purvis went by, black-haired and straight, most Indianlike of all, and Mrs. Wanda Turner, married to the county sheriff, and Ruby Graves, married to no one at all, the only unmarried Pocahontas in the lodge. When Emily had remarked on this to some of the other lodge members, she had been told, "Most single girls are too frivolous for lodge work. Can't concentrate on ritual and memorizing, let alone beadwork. Spend their time mooning about, thinking of . . ."

Emily, anxious to appear quick-witted before her sisters-to-be, had suggested in this pause "men," and her informer had repeated the word, but it had seemed not quite to fill the bill. "Yes and no," she had told Emily. "Yes and no." But Ruby Graves was an exception— no mooner, they said, and, though maiden, as brisk in ritual and beadwork as any married lady.

More officers, some of the most important, passed by on the sidewalk. "Look, look," said Emily, whispering, "but not right away. Now, that's the Grand Prophetess."

Mr. Cooper looked. "Couldn't tell her from an ordinary prophetess," he said calmly.

"Oh she's full of authority," said Emily. "A power in the lodge, believe me."

It was exciting for Emily to sit in the car with her husband, pointing out to him the town's leading ladies. It was a novelty, too, for it was he who had usually known everyone and done the pointing. But they were new in Los Robles, the insurance office had been open only a couple of months, and Mr. Cooper's work in opening it had kept him too busy for getting acquainted with the Pocahontas ladies.

"That's Mrs. Pleasant Jones," said Emily. "She's First Scout, and the one with her, the tall one with the red headband, I can't remember her name but I know she's the Second Runner."

Following the Second Runner were the Guards of Tepee and Forest, and Pocahontas herself—Mrs. Virginia Smiley—with feathers in her headband. Emily knew all three of them and pointed them out as they went by carrying their candles and squares or oblongs of home-baked cake. They passed on foot, by twos and threes, or alighted, singly, from cars driven by their husbands. They were laughing and talking, but their voices were low; an initiation by candlelight was solemn and secret; it was spring, it was almost night.

"They shouldn't have candles, really," Emily explained to her husband.

"No candles?" said Mr. Cooper, who had been watching the Second Runner. "Why not?"

"It's not in the Ritual. But the Grand Prophetess says we're so far off the beaten track here in the hills that we can plead ignorance in case of criticism."

"Why, sure," said Mr. Cooper. "Sure you can. Why not?"

"We shouldn't be hit-or-miss," explained Emily. "The lodge treats of the mysteries of life in an orderly manner."

Mr. Cooper looked at his wife inquiringly.

"That's what I was told," she said. "And the candles aren't part of that order."

"Maybe they're part of the mystery," suggested Mr. Cooper.

Emily supposed that her husband was smiling, but no, he was serious, looking intently into the creamy blooms of the laurel trees that lined the sidewalk, and listening to the birds that were singing on into the night because of the springtime.

"It's the second spring," said Emily.

In California, the first spring is in November. March only echoes it. In November the first spring is brief and sharp after the early rains. Then the grass flares up like fire; dry streambeds, as dead to the eye as old snakeskins, revive, all their bends and shallows filled with the curve of bright water; quail call; mushrooms push their blunt heads through the sodden leaves under the valley oaks; and at the end of the town's short streets, early sunsets and winter barley, alike green, meet. Spring is sharp in November—a slap, a blow, a kiss, soon over, soon forgotten, colder weather to follow. In March it is easy, gentle, nothing to wonder at, it will last a long time. Summer will come, the hills be brown and faded, no one able to say just when the rains stopped or the grass withered.

"Counting November, it's the second spring," said Mr. Cooper.

"I *was* counting November," said Emily, dangling a hand out the car window to test the air. It was still warm, though the sun was down, no color left behind, the sky as drab as a cast-iron skillet. Emily pushed her feet, slim in pointed satin slippers, up the incline of the floorboards until they cleared her full, white marquisette skirt.

She reset the white daphne she had pinned in her hair and redampened her handkerchief from the bottle of Hoyt's perfume she had in her purse.

"Do I look all right?" she inquired anxiously of her husband.

"Fine, fine," said he. "Couldn't look better."

"Do I smell too strong of cologne?"

"Look fine, smell fine."

With sudden energy, Emily gathered her coat about her shoulders, grasped her candle, prepared to depart. "I always look fine," she said irritably. "I always look fine and I always smell fine to you. You don't give me any confidence."

Mr. Cooper leaned over, detained her with his hand on her arm. "But you do," he said. "You always do. What do you want me to say? Want me to be a liar?"

"No," said Emily, "but if I knew you were critical, it would give me more confidence."

"Oh, critical!" said Mr. Cooper, surprised. "Why, I'm critical, critical as all getout. That Second Runner, now. She's bandy-legged. I criticized it in her first thing. They'd ought to have given her the wampum job. Something she could do sitting down, not put her to running."

Emily opened the car door, jumped out, and banged it behind her. It was dark enough for the first stars to show, not distinctly, a little blurred in their outlines, as if the moist spring air had caused them to run a bit. The birds were still rustling and chirping in the laurel trees, unwilling for this day to end. Down the street the neon signs said "Eat," said "Drink," said "Short Orders," said "Church of the Open Door." There were no Pocahontases in sight and Emily felt a little strange, on the street after dark in her long white dress. A man paused under the "Drink" sign to look at her before pushing the swinging doors apart. She lingered at the car side.

"Don't joke about serious things," she said fiercely. "It makes me nervous. And I'm already nervous to begin with."

"Don't be nervous," said Mr. Cooper. "I'm critical and you look fine and smell fine and you are going to see the marvels of life in an orderly manner."

"Mysteries," said Emily, "*mysteries*," and she turned away without so much as a good-bye and started toward the Vasconi Building. But before she had taken two angry steps, Mr. Cooper had caught up with her.

"Mysteries was what I meant," he said contritely, and they walked on together arm in arm, past the birds and the trees and the plate-glass windows and the men going in for a drink. "The mysteries of life in an orderly manner," he said, "was what I fully intended to say."

# Love, Death, and
# the Ladies' Drill Team

EMILY COOPER, the newest member of the Pocahontas Drill Team, was the first to arrive at the Burnham Building, where the morning practice, called by their drillmaster and team captain, Mrs. Amy Rotunda, was to be held. She stood for a while enjoying the wind—California's warm, dry September wind—before starting up the stairs to Burnham Hall. Burnham Hall was less pretentious than its name, being no more than the drab, unfurnished second floor of the building that housed, on its first floor, Burnham's Hardware, but the only other hall available in the small town of Los Robles was, though its rent was lower, unfortunately located above Sloane & Pierce's Undertaking Parlors.

Emily was halfway up the stairs when she was hailed from the sidewalk below by Mr. Burnham himself, holding a key aloft. "You one of the Pocahontas girls?" he called.

Emily turned about on the stairs and gazed down at the wide-shouldered old man. The wind was lifting his coattails and tossing his white hair about in tufts, like those of the bunch grass she had known as a girl in the Dakotas. She hesitated for a moment before answering. She was a Pocahontas, all right, but "girl" was a different story. She was thirty-six years old, had been married half her life, and had only an hour ago started her youngest off to his first day of school. Then, left without a child in the house for the first time in fifteen years, she had told her passing image in a mirror, "This is the beginning of middle age for you, Emily Cooper." Now "girl."

Mr. Burnham, as if understanding the reason for her hesitation, smiled as she came back down for the key. "My youngest is fifty," he said. Then, perhaps fearing that she might consider such confidences too personal, coming from a stranger, he spoke reassuringly of the weather. "Nice blow we're having—nice touch of wind." He faced about for a second after saying this, to get the full force of the

31

warm, lively agitation, which had everything movable in Los Robles moving.

Actually, this talk of the wind was far more personal to Emily than Mr. Burnham's remark about his children. When he put the key in her hand, she said, "It's wonderful weather. I love the wind." Then she, too, was overtaken by a conviction that there was something unseemly in so much openness with a stranger, and she said a quick thank you and started back up the stairs. As she was unlocking the door, Mr. Burnham called, "Throw open the windows, will you? Modern Woodmen used the hall last night and they're a smoky lot."

Mr. Burnham was right about the Woodmen. Emily felt as she were stepping into the bowl of a pipe still warm and filled with fumes. There were windows across the entire front of the hall, which faced on Los Robles' Main Street, and she opened them all. Then she pulled a chair up to the middle window and sat down to await the arrival of her teammates. There was not much to be seen on the street below her. Ten o'clock on a Monday morning is not an hour for shoppers, and the children who yesterday would have been out in the wind, shirttails lofted for sails, diving and swooping like birds, but much noisier, were behind closed doors, with shirttails tucked in, and speaking only when nodded to by Teacher. She thought of her own Johnny and hoped he was finding school the wonder he had imagined it. He had left her without a tear, without even a backward look, declaring, with the pleasure of a man who has arrived at a goal long deferred, "Now I am a scholar."

Emily leaned out the window to watch a tumbleweed, blown into town from one of the surrounding barley fields, across Main at Brown, traveling west swiftly and silently. In the vacant lot across the street, the tall, switch-stemmed dust flowers were bent down almost as low as grass. Beneath the window, the Burnham Hardware sign was swinging, and the awning was bellying and snapping with the sound, she supposed, of a ship under full sail. A few merchants were beginning to go up the street to the Gem for their midmorning cups of coffee. Merchants, the wind revealed, had bodies. Inside their usually unyielding tubes of serge and herringbone, their legs were astonishingly thin. As if in restitution for this exposure, the wind parted their coattails to display their firm and stately bottoms. A black cat passed below, its blackness not even skin-deep, for its hair, wind-blown, exposed a skin as white as that of any butcher-shop rabbit. Emily thrust her hands out across the windowsill, feeling through her outspread fingers the full force and warmth of the blowing—as if I were the one true gauge, she thought, the one responsive and harmonious harp.

She was leaning thus, and by now almost half out of the room, when Mrs. Rotunda, the drill captain and coach, and Miss Ruby Graves, the team's star performer, arrived. Emily was new not only to the drill team but to the town of Los Robles, and was still able, she thought, to see people as they really were, unlabeled by a knowledge of their professions or reputations. But "Miss" and "Mrs." are in themselves labels, and Mrs. Rotunda's gray hair, elaborately waved and curled, with a fancy off-center part at the back and sculptured bangs arranged with all the finality of marble, said widow, said woman without a husband, filling in an empty and lonesome life with what, in the old, rich days, she would never have wasted time on. While, somewhat contradictorily, Miss Graves's black hair, long and innocent of the slightest ripple, said spinster, said woman without a husband and reconciled to the idea that her hair, curled or uncurled, was never going to be a matter of moment to any man. But without that "Miss" and "Mrs.," without her knowledge that Amy Rotunda was Fred Rotunda's widow, and Ruby Graves was Milton Graves's unmarried daughter and housekeeper, would she have had all this insight about hair? Emily couldn't say.

It was the same with Opal Tetford and Lacey Philips, who arrived next. Mrs. Tetford's husband was an official in the local Bank of America, while Mrs. Philips's husband owned and operated a big grain ranch out on the edge of town. Knowing this, Emily thought Mrs. Tetford's soft opulence was suited to the protection of vaults and burglar alarms, while Mrs. Philips's rawboned frame was right in its austerity for a background of endless barley fields and rolling, cactus-covered hills.

Mrs. Rotunda said, "I am going to demand that the Woodmen do something about this tobacco smoke. Do they think they're the only ones who use this hall?"

Miss Graves, who prided herself on being unprejudiced about men, though with every reason to justify prejudice, said, "I expect they are chain-smokers, Amy. One cigarette after another all evening long."

Mrs. Rotunda, who had no need to conjecture, said, "Well, they could at least use a little Air-Wick afterward." She went to a window and leaned out for a breath of uncontaminated air. The other ladies drew up chairs at the windows. Beneath them, Mr. Sloane, of Sloane & Pierce, passed by on his way to the Gem for his midmorning cup of coffee. Mr. Sloane, like many undertakers, was the picture of rosy durability, an evidence to mourners that though one life had ended, life itself endured.

Mrs. Rotunda withdrew her head from the window and began to pace up and down behind her seated teammates. "No," she declared. "I could never bring myself to do it. Not for a mere two-fifty, anyway."

Emily looked inquiringly at Lacey Philips, who was seated next to her. "The Sloane & Pierce hall rents for two-fifty less than this one," Mrs. Philips explained.

"Save two-fifty at the price of drilling back and forth, quite possibly, over the body of your own dead mother? Not I," said Mrs. Rotunda firmly. "It would take a lot more than two-fifty to reconcile me to that."

Ruby Graves, who, in the manner of maiden ladies, combined extreme idealism on some subjects with extreme matter-of-factness on others, said, "If your mother passed away, Amy, wouldn't they hold the services for her down in Anaheim?"

Mrs. Rotunda replied with patience. "Ruby, I was speaking hypothetically. Mother has owned a plot at Rosemead for I don't know how long, and will, of course, be laid to rest there—not be brought up here to the Sloane & Pierce funeral home to be marched across by Odd Fellows and Knights of Pythias and others for whom such things don't matter. But I only mentioned her as an example. I would have exactly the same scruples about marching over *your* mother."

Ruby turned away from the window. "Mother passed away a year ago Labor Day, Amy," she said in a voice that forgave the forgetfulness.

Mrs. Rotunda put her hands to her head. "Ruby, I could bite my tongue out!" she cried. "My point was—anyone. I'd have too much fellow feeling to be willing to meet above the remains."

Emily said, "I think Sloane & Pierce is a good place for Jehovah's Witnesses to meet, though."

"Do they meet there?" Mrs. Tetford asked. Mrs. Tetford had a reputation for asking questions—trained, they said, by Mr. Tetford, who was a man who liked to supply answers.

Emily nodded.

"Why?" Mrs. Tetford asked.

"I don't know," Emily said.

"I mean why do you think it's a good place for them to meet?"

"Oh. Well, that's one of the things a church is for, isn't it?" Emily asked, and, thinking of her children, seeing them already grown and scattered, and herself and John left alone with their memories, she added, "To remind us that all earthly things pass away?"

Mrs. Rotunda, at the words "pass away," stopped her pacing, and the hall had the silence of a room in which a clock suddenly ceases ticking. The women turned toward her and she extended her arms as if about to ask some extraordinary favor. "Oh, girls!" she cried. "My dear girls! Let's not be morbid. Let's not dwell on the inevitable or we'll have no heart for our practice."

Her life is drilling, Emily thought, smiling. The lodge is her husband and we are her children. She admired Mrs. Rotunda and hoped that, should she ever be left alone, she could be as sensible. Mrs. Rotunda came to the window before which Emily and Lacey sat, and perched between them on the windowsill. Gazing down into the street, she shook her head. "Poor girl. Poor, poor girl," she said.

"Imola Ramos?" Emily asked, though there was not, at the moment, anyone else in sight who could possibly be called a girl. Imola was a black-haired, brown-skinned woman of about her own age. Her red-flowered dress, which looked as if it might have started life as a window curtain or a tablecloth, was cut like a Mother Hubbard and belted in closely with what appeared, from the second story of the Burnham Building, to be a piece of gray, frayed clothesline. It was plain to be seen that she wore no brassière—and not much else, for the wind plastered the big red flowers as close to her thighs as if they were tattooed there.

"Ramos!" Mrs. Rotunda said. "Why, Emily, Imola's name's no more Ramos than yours is. Her name's what it's always been—since she was married, anyway. Fetters. She married LeRoy Fetters so young it's hard to remember that she was born a Butterfield. But it's Fetters now. That Mexican never married her. Couldn't, to do him justice, since LeRoy would never divorce her. And anyway why should he have married her? She was willing to live with him."

"Live with him as man and wife," Ruby explained.

"I never knew they weren't married," Emily said. "I've always heard her called Mrs. Ramos."

Mrs. Rotunda excused this. "You haven't been in Los Robles very long. It takes a little time to catch on to these things."

Imola, who was carrying two shopping bags heavy enough to curve her square shoulders, stepped off the sidewalk and into the vacant lot opposite the Burnham Building. There she set the bags down amidst the blue dust flowers, and while the disturbed cicadas one by one ceased shrilling, she hunted in her purse for her cigarettes. By the time she had her cigarette lighted, the cicadas were once again filling Main Street with their country cries, and Imola, her head on one side, appeared to be listening with pleasure to the sound.

"Why did she leave her husband?" Emily asked.

"That is the mystery," Mrs. Rotunda admitted. "There never was a better man on earth, to my mind, than LeRoy Fetters."

"LeRoy used to wash Imola's hair for her, regular as clockwork, every ten days," Mrs. Philips said.

"Why? I always wondered," Mrs. Tetford asked.

"Pride," Ruby said. "Pure pride in that great mane of black hair."

They were all watching Imola, standing at her ease in the vacant lot, the wind outlining her sturdy body—a woman obviously well and happy.

Disagreeing with Ruby, Mrs. Tetford answered her own question. "In my opinion, LeRoy did it to save the price of a beauty parlor."

Contradicted about motives, Ruby took a new tack. "They say, Mrs. Cooper, that this Mexican manhandles her."

Mrs. Rotunda sniffed. "They say," she said. "I *saw*. Just a week ago today, I saw them having breakfast at the Gem, and Imola had black-and-blue spots the size of quarters on her arms."

Ruby said, "Poor Imola."

"What were *you* doing down at the Gem at breakfast time, Amy?" Mrs. Tetford asked.

"Who said anything about its being breakfast time? As a matter of fact, it was three in the afternoon, and I was having a root-beer float. But those two were having fried eggs and hot cakes, bold as brass, not making the least effort to deceive anyone."

"Why?" Ruby asked. "Why were they having breakfast at that hour?"

"You may well ask, Ruby," said Mrs. Rotunda shortly.

"I feel sorry for Imola," Mrs. Tetford said.

"They live out near our ranch, you know," Mrs. Philips told them. "They're on the edge of the irrigation ditch, in one of those three-room shacks that the water company furnishes its Mexican workers. Two rooms and a lean-to, really, is what they are. Mattress on the floor, in place of a bed. Old, broken-down, rusty oil stove. Chesterfield with its springs half through the upholstery."

"I wonder how Imola's mother *bears* it," Mrs. Rotunda said.

"Do you ever see them?" Mrs. Tetford asked Mrs. Philips.

"Many's the time. Manuel doesn't seem to have any regular working hours, and in the summertime they do a lot of sporting around together, in and out of the water. And the shoe's on the other foot this time so far's washing is concerned. Imola's the one who does the washing now."

"His hair?" asked Ruby.

"Well, just generally," Mrs. Philips answered.

"A Butterfield washing a Mexican! Sunk that low! It doesn't bear thinking about," Mrs. Tetford said.

"I expect he's pretty dark-skinned?" asked Ruby, who evidently could bear thinking about it.

"They both are," Mrs. Philips explained. "After they finish swimming or washing, whichever it is, they lie around in the sun, sun-tanning. And, like as not, Manuel will play some music for Imola on that instrument of his. That banjo or guitar—I never can tell the two of them apart."

"Fred used to play the clarinet," Mrs. Rotunda said. "He had a natural ear for music and could play anything he'd heard once."

"Is it flat-backed or curved, Lacey?" Mrs. Tetford asked. "This musical instrument?"

"I never did notice."

"Big or little, comparatively speaking?"

"Big," Lacey Philips said.

"It's a guitar, then. I thought it would be. That's the Spanish national instrument."

"He is dressed, I suppose, by the time this music-making starts?" Ruby Graves said.

"Dressed!" Mrs. Philips exclaimed. "Why, Ruby, he sits there strumming out melodies and flinching off flies as innocent of clothes as a newborn babe!"

"And Imola?"

"Naked as a jay bird. Lying in the grass kicking up her heels. Sometimes silent, sometimes singing."

Mrs. Tetford shook her head. "The poor girl."

"Play to her, hit her. I guess Imola runs the full gamut with that man," Ruby speculated.

"Speak of the devil," said Mrs. Philips, motioning with her chin up the street.

Emily, who had been watching Imola as she listened to the talk about her, saw her throw away the stub of her cigarette and wave at the man coming up the street toward her. Ramos was a short, stocky man with a strong, toed-in walk and, when he reached Imola, a quick, white smile. Imola stooped down when he turned in at the vacant lot and brought up out of one of the shopping bags an enormous bunch of purple grapes.

"Isabellas," said Mrs. Philips. "First it's a feast, then it's a fast with them, I guess."

"He's a big, burly fellow," Mrs. Rotunda admitted.

"Naked and singing by the irrigation ditch," Ruby marveled as Imola popped grapes alternately into her own own mouth and into that of the Mexican.

"LeRoy Fetters was a registered pharmacist," Mrs. Rotunda told Emily. "A very responsible man. He always took a real interest in whether his prescriptions helped."

"Breakfast at three o'clock," Ruby murmured as the feeding below continued, interspersed with considerable affectionate horseplay. "I wonder what it tastes like at that hour."

"Not a thing in the world to keep you from finding out, is there, Ruby?" Mrs. Rotunda asked.

"I doubt it would be the same alone," Ruby said.

Across the street, the grapes finished, Imola, there in the broad daylight of midmorning and in the middle of Los Robles, first kissed the Mexican full on the mouth, then put a cigarette between his lips and, while he shielded it with his hands, lighted it for him.

The ladies were silent for quite a while after this. Finally, Mrs. Tetford said, "Poor Imola! Where is her pride?"

Imola now lighted a cigarette for herself. Emily, watching the two of them at their ease amid the weeds and dust flowers, the wind carrying their cigarette smoke streaming away from them in transparent plumes, said, to her own surprise, "Pride? Why, Mrs. Tetford, pride doesn't enter in. She loves him."

There was another long silence in the hall. A number of additional members of the drill team had arrived, and Emily felt that her unconsidered word was settling among them like a stone in a pond of still water. But just at the moment when she supposed the last ripple had disappeared, Mrs. Rotunda repeated the word, in a voice that lingered and explored. "Love?" she asked. "Love?"

Is she asking me, Emily thought. But evidently she was not, for before Emily could answer, Mrs. Rotunda had turned her back on the window and was calling the team together. "Girls, girls!" she cried. "Let's not moon! We won't wait for the others. Now, hands on shoulders, and remember, an arm's length apart."

Mrs. Rotunda turned them away from the windows and got them linked together. They reversed by eights, went forward by twos, and formed hollow squares. Emily, still thoughtful, still lingering by the window, saw Imola and the Mexican pick up the shopping bags and proceed, together and equally burdened, down the street. She saw Mr. Sloane return, refreshed, from the Gem to his work. She saw Mr. Burnham out on the edge of the sidewalk, face uplifted as if searching the wind for scents of some lost place or time. She saw how the wind, swooping down off the dry, brown hills, wrapped the soft prints of her drill mates' dresses about their varishaped bodies, so that they moved through the elaborate figures of Mrs. Rotunda's planning like women in some picture of past days. And Mrs. Rotunda's brisk commands—"To the rear by twos!" or "The diamond formation!"—were like a little, inconsequential piping, the way the wind, veering, shrills for a second or two through a crack before resuming its own voice, deep and solemn and prophetic.

# *Homecoming*

H ENDRICKS LIFTED HIMSELF on his elbow. He thought he knew all the sounds that were to be heard at that time of night: the soft relaxed coughs of those who coughed without awakening: the hard bitter coughs of those who had no hope of sleeping longer, and who sat up in bed and held their sputum cups in straining fingers; the distant muffled clink and thud of the night nurse as she started her final rounds in Culbertson; the heavy sighing groans of Kurtz as his two o'clock codeine began to wear off; and far above in the hills the crying of the last coyotes before dawn.

Hendricks was accustomed to listening to these sounds each morning, as his own procaine lost its effectiveness. Only a few moments before, the hearse had crept down the hill with that silence which the management hoped minimized for those who remained the import of its journey. The velvety throb of its engine still pulsed in his ears, and he had to wait until that echo had faded before he could be sure that he had heard anything else.

As he strained forward in his bed, supporting himself on arms that quivered a little from the unusual effort, he heard, not a continuation of the light gritty sound to which he had been listening, but the first cocks crowing below on the valley ranches.

He slumped back on his pillows. Sometimes he forgot that other world where men left their beds in the morning and went to work, and he was happier when this was so. He could manage to live in the abnormal and isolated world in which he found himself only by dint of forcing himself to forget that another existed. When he thought of the men on the ranches below plunging out of their beds into the gray morning coolness with responsive bodies, he hated them, as though their health was the result of some thievery from him.

He grinned to himself at this warped fancy and wondered which young rancher pulled on his pants with extra force that morning, because to his energy had been added all that he, Hendricks, had

41

lost. Pull 'em on with a will, Buddy, he thought, for God knows how soon you may have to shed them permanently. He felt his own limp pajamas, still damp from his heavy night sweat, with bitter distaste. Better rivet them on, Buddy, then they'll never get you in a joint like this.

He turned his face unconsciously toward McRae's bed. This was only the second morning McRae had been gone, and after seven months of hearing him say at this hour, "Well, Hendricks, another day, another bug," he missed him. It was a ritual with them, a TB-er's salute to the dawn: "Another day, another bug," McRae would say.

Hendricks would answer, "What do you mean, kid? Another bug manufactured?"

And McRae would answer with scornful conviction, "Hell no, Rick, another bug *dead!*"

Somehow Hendricks was always comforted by the assurance of McRae's voice. He liked to think that his early morning depletion was the result of a nightlong struggle with a bug, who at morning light was in worse case than he.

McRae's conviction seemed to have some basis in fact, for two days ago the doc had said he could go home. Not that his fibrosis really warranted it—he should have had another six months in the san— but McRae was a level-headed guy and he had a wife whom he missed and who clamored for his return. Hendricks had seen her a couple of times, and listened through many a twilight to McRae talk of her.

No TB-er had a higher color or more transparent skin than McRae's wife. She was always late when she came to see McRae, and bubbling over with a pretty breathless penitence, which tried to say, Hendricks thought, "Darling, I've come to you in spite of really ghastly difficulties." McRae ate it up and didn't even notice that her act was as much for Hendricks's benefit as his own.

After her first conversational bubble had burst she hadn't much to say. She sat there and let McRae entertain her. Hendricks could feel the poor kid go taut with the effort to convert the dreary tragic routine of their days into something sprightly and amusing for her. That cockroach on his tray, which had really ruined a meal for him when meals were important, became simply a funny story for Nella, and his eyes were anxious and bright until she smiled.

And he gave her that horrible story of Kurtz's signing his name in his hemorrhage blood mockingly and lightly as if he had not been aware that many of them in just such blood would sign their final signatures.

McRae gave her everything he had; all the energy he had conserved through weeks of discipline and denial he drained off now recklessly for Nella. Hendricks supposed he wanted her to feel that he was no invalid, not really sick, washed up, but just a guy taking a little time out and amused and a little touched at what was going on around him.

He'll have to take a triple dose of Amytal tonight, Hendricks would think. Why in God's name doesn't she tell the kid something? Tell him how a streetcar looks, or what the fellow in the drugstore said when he mixed her frosted chocolate, or whether the peach trees are in bloom yet. All the sights her eyes see and all the sounds her ears hear that are denied McRae. Why doesn't she bring them to him? Why doesn't she tell him that the guys at the plant miss him? Why doesn't she tell him what Martin said to Lewis in the show last week, or how the air smells outside these antiseptic halls?

Then he'd think, Oh hell! This isn't the way McRae looks at her. And he'd try to see her through McRae's eyes. She wasn't hard to look at through his own eyes. Pink and clean, and plump in all the right places, and wearing her clothes so that all of the right places showed. And smelling sweet and fresh, too. If he could remember sleeping with her, as McRae could, he'd probably be sending his own temp up in an effort to keep her interested.

Hendricks looked out at the morning, gray now like a mouse, or a skillet, night's blackness completely gone. He reluctantly put his hand out for his temp stick, shook the bichloride solution from it, and slid it under his tongue. He was unconcerned over this ritual. The morning subnormality didn't faze him; it was the afternoon's horrible upper oscillation that made his chest heavy and tight as he waited to see how high the mercury had risen, to gauge again the heat of that fire which consumed him.

So, with his temp stick in his mouth, he lay over on his side, happy to have the dark uncharted night behind him, to be caught up, once more, into that ordered and methodical routine which made his days tolerable; a routine in which he lost his identity and became simply a cell in the great sanatorium organism.

He looked down the slope of the hill toward the administration building where a clump of eucalyptus was just moving, gray-green, in the gray air. The thud of a closing door made him drop his eyes, and he saw a man emerge from the administration building. Someone on the way out, he thought, if they're getting relatives here at this time of the morning. Some poor kid up to see his wife off. Agony and relief all in one. He's thought of her as dead for so long that it will rest his mind not to have the contradiction of her live eyes looking at him from the pillow. He raised himself to have a better look at the young husband.

"McRae," he called, half swallowing his temp stick.

McRae heard him, gave a little gesture, half of recognition, half of warning to be quiet, and came on, slowly, up the path.

Hendricks looked at his temp stick, saw the usual 97.4, and put it back in the glass, irked that not even McRae's appearance had jarred his egocentric interest in his body's heat.

McRae was at the door. "I hope I didn't send it up a couple of degrees."

"Kid, what are you doing here?"

McRae eased himself onto his old bed, and lay face up as if dead beat. He shut his eyes, and pulled his coat around his throat.

"Come on, McRae, get out of your clothes," Hendricks urged. "You'll freeze there. Get on a pair of my pajamas. Take it easy, but get into them, and get in bed. I thought I heard something a half hour or so back. Was that you? I'll ring for Samuels to help you; you're all in."

"Samuels is busy. It was me you heard, all right. I was going to come up and just slide in, but Samuels saw me, made me wait while she phoned the doc if it was O.K."

"Why didn't she come up and help you?"

"A girl's hemorrhaging down in Ballard."

"Samuels can smell arterial blood a mile off. She's like a fire horse smelling smoke. I've seen her flanks heave when a hemorrhage call went through. She lives on blood like a vampire."

"Cut it, Hendricks."

"Did you spit some rubies while you were gone, kid?"

"Nothing like that."

"Come on, McRae, get out of your clothes. I'll get my pajamas for you myself."

McRae sat up, his eyes still closed, as if the effort to open them was beyond what he could endure. He pulled off his tie, got out of his coat, stumbled over to the chest of drawers where Hendricks's clothes were kept.

"The middle drawer, Mac. The flannel ones are there on top."

Hendricks watched McRae get out of his clothes with pitying and speculative eyes. He's lost weight, he thought, in the last forty-eight hours. Lord, how his phrenic scar shows up when he's cold. Looks like something tattooed on him.

"Don't be a fool, Mac. Let 'em lay. Samuels can put them away. What's she paid for?"

McRae got into bed with the jerkiness of fatigue and cold. Hendricks tossed him his warm pad. "Put this on your belly. It'll warm you up quicker than putting it on your feet. Now shake down, kid, and take it easy. Breakfast will be here in an hour or so, and some hot coffee will put you right."

McRae said, "Rick, it's swell to be back. I didn't know."

"Sure you didn't, kid, but you'd better catch some rest before breakfast."

"You going to sleep?"

"Hell no. I finished two hours ago. Go ahead and talk if you want to. How'd you come back?"

"Bus."

"You weren't fool enough to sit up all night on a bus? What for, Mac?"

"I wanted to get back. And I was afraid to wait."

"What do you mean, afraid? Afraid of what?"

"Afraid of myself, afraid I'd never do it if I waited."

Hendricks looked over at McRae, who was getting warmed up, los-

ing his bluish pallor. He supposed he might as well let him talk—
better perhaps. God knows what had happened to him, but it had
something to do with that pink-and-white Nella.

"You know, Rick, I'd been counting the days until I could leave
here. Had 'em marked off on my calendar like a schoolgirl. There are
a lot of things here I thought I'd like to get away from."

Hendricks knew: the deaths, the smells, the sounds; the specula-
tion about your own durability; the mechanical care; the pork and ice
cream every Sunday; the feverishness of weighing day; the sound of
bedpans being emptied—and filled; and above all the sense of being
shut off from the world, confined, like one from whom all humanity
has fled. Sure, Hendricks knew.

"Well, kid, you got away, didn't you? When did you get into Fresno?"

"Tuesday morning at eight. I felt like a convict on the train, Rick.
Thought everyone could tell I'd just got out of a san."

Hendricks knew about that, too.

"Did you have breakfast with Nella in Fresno?"

"I ate there, but she had eaten already. It's hot down in the valley.
She had on a white suit. You know she's been selling real estate
since I've been here, with her brother. She had a big deal on. She
told me about it while I ate."

"So you listened to the 'big deal' on your first morning out, kid?
You hadn't planned on that, had you? Thought you'd as well be back,
with Samuels giving you theosophy with your breakfast tray?"

"We went out to go to the car. It was burning hot already. Have
you forgotten how the people walk along on hot summer mornings
before they're tired, Rick? Stepping along on the balls of their feet,
and their eyes proud because they feel so strong and fresh? Nella
was like that. She pulsed and glowed when she walked. I tried to
match her but I couldn't do it. How could I? I haven't walked for a
year. The heat and walking along so fast made me feel damned queasy.
I thought I'd lose my breakfast.

"Then Nella met a man who was in on this real-estate deal and
they stopped to talk. They talked for a long time—maybe a half hour.
At first I tried to be knowing about real estate—be the little woman's
husband come home to help. But I was too sick standing in that sun.
I didn't know where the car was and Nella was too busy to tell me.

All I could do was lean against a building and hope I wouldn't slide down.

"After a while Nella finished. She was good, all right. Plenty good. But she wasn't proud of me, gray-green and hanging on to a wall.

"Well, we started home, and I thought everything would be all right. We had fifty miles to go, and I thought we'd get to talk at last. That things would be like I used to imagine them—here. But Nella had to stop at Ralston to see the banker, and she had to think how she'd put her case to him. We left Ralston about one o'clock."

"Nothing to eat since breakfast, Mac?"

"No, but it was the heat that made me sick. Well, we got home. Lord, how I've longed to see it. I planted a lot of things there, you know. And my dog was still there. But all I could see was a string of cars in front of the house. I began to think the heat was making me see things. I'd always thought of me coming home to just Nella, and a quiet house.

"When we got out of the car a lot of people came out on the porch: mostly people from the real-estate office. They yelled all together, 'Welcome home to the invalid,' and Nella took my arm and said, 'See, I've planned a party for you.' "

"My God, kid," Hendricks murmured, "that Nella of yours is some planner. And then you had to shake hands, and say you felt swell, and how good it was to be home. And you had to stand up some more, or thought you did."

"There was a cake, Rick. It had printed on it in red icing, 'East, West, Home's Best.' I had to cut it like a bride at a wedding. I sliced that home in two with the first cut. They all looked at me."

"Yeah, I know kid." They all looked at you, Hendricks thought. They got in corners and whispered that you looked a little feverish. They wondered if you'd ever had a hemorrhage, and some said you wouldn't be much good for Nella. And you felt it all. What they had to say closed in tight about you so there was no place to turn. And you had to play up to Nella. Be gay. Celebrate. Drink some wine you didn't want. Hell, kid, don't tell me.

"They left after a while. Said they knew Nella and I would want to be alone."

"Well, that was what you wanted, wasn't it? You used to spoil your days here thinking of Nella. Now you had her, you didn't want her, eh? You thought of rest period before supper, and Blaise plumping up the pillows for you, and the towhees chirping a little, but no other sound; and you wished you were back."

"No, I didn't want to be back. Not then. This was the first moment I'd had with Nella. Sure, I was dead beat, but have you forgotten how beautiful Nella is? She put on a kimono—long and soft, and pink. Not like these damned stiff white uniforms. Thin, you know. It was still blazing hot."

"Mac, I'm not sure I like reunion scenes. Husband and wife together at last. So you took her in your arms. You're done in, Mac. Why not cut it? Breakfast's about due. What you need's food, not confession."

"I need to explain myself to myself. Why I'm back here. You don't need to listen. No use telling you TB doesn't make a female any less desirable."

Hendricks watched Mac put his arm over his eyes. No use telling me, he thought. Makes you concupiscent as hell. Funny thing, for a disease to make you want what will kill you quickest. Nature double-crosses you every chance it gets. He regarded the boy with the pity of remembrance.

"Well, Mac, looks to me like the perfect setup. Boy meets girl. All legal and everything. Where's the hitch? What're you doing back here?"

"I came back because I wasn't ready to die yet. I could die for some things—but not that. Nella—I didn't mean a thing to Nella, Rick. Not a thing—or only one thing. I thought she'd been counting the days and hours, as I'd been. I thought she'd be proud of what I'd done. Pulled out of this business when no one thought I could."

I'd ought to told you, kid. They don't wait for you like that. They've never had the measure of their life taken on a temp stick. They've got, without turning over a finger, what we've had to work for like hell. It's like asking a millionaire to understand how a kid feels about a penny.

Hendricks saw, for a minute, both sides. Oh God, the sick and well were never meant to be together. They only hurt each other. The well could take it; but the sick died two deaths. First, the soul's death at being misunderstood; then, until its release, the sick body must go burdened with a dead soul. He watched Mac trace with his forefinger, by the feel of the ridges alone, the pattern in the bedspread. His Nella had more than health's indifference; she had health's cruelty and arrogance.

"There's no use kidding myself, Hendricks. Trying to believe now that what I felt then was the result of being upset and overwrought. God knows that's what I want to do. But it's no use. Nella has found she's as good a man as I was when it comes to making money. She's no more need for me—that way. Oh, she still had a use for me, but I didn't figure in it. She didn't love me." McRae sat up in bed. He turned to Hendricks in bitterness. "She used me, Hendricks, she used me. There was no love nor pity in her. She didn't give a damn if I died when she finished with me. When I coughed, she laughed and said, 'Cough some more, it feels good.'"

He caught his breath in an angry sob and pressed his cheek against the iron headboard of his bed.

Hendricks eased himself out of bed and into the chair by McRae's side. It was full day now. He looked with pity on McRae's drawn face and taut body.

"Lay down, kid," he said. "Lay back and rest."

McRae sank back into the pillows. "I had to leave, Rick."

Hendricks knew how it was. You had to leave, all right—and you'd seen it otherwise up here: a world of good will, full of tenderness, and everybody hoping you'd have a negative test this time. "Sure, kid, you had to leave. Forget that gal. You're back home."

There were footsteps on the graveled walk. Hendricks got back into bed, fast. "Lord," he said, breathing hard with the effort, "here's Samuels with our hot water. It's seven already. Well, kid, another day, another bug."

McRae looked out toward the valley. "Seven o'clock," he murmured. "She's just getting into her shower now."

# The Battle of the Suits

JOE ORTIZ, the janitor at the Temple Home for Boys, in Reno, thought the Christmas decorations, even though it was three weeks past Christmas, made the tunnel-like main hall more cheerful. But Mr. Buchanan, the superintendent, said, "Take them down, Joe. They're unseasonable." Prettiness is always seasonable, isn't it, Joe thought, but he said nothing, naturally, to the boss. He got out the stepladder and went up it like a sailor or a monkey and began to unfasten the crepe-paper swags. It was a job his heart wasn't in, so he got what pleasure he could out of the climb itself, thinking that for fifty-six he wasn't such a bad specimen. He had a mouth full of thumbtacks and a dangle of crepe paper about his neck when he saw the boy they called the Senator come out of Buchanan's office at the end of the hall. Joe took the thumbtacks out of his mouth, the crepe paper off his neck, and climbed down the ladder. Then he stood, back to the wall, hands free, awaiting him.

The Senator was a fine figure of a man, from a distance—tall, raven-haired, and commanding. He was a little portly, but his round paunch was balanced by his equally round buttocks, so the effect was symmetrical. The Senator had a loud, sweet voice or a loud, scornful voice, as the occasion required. Now it was loud and sweet. Lifting a plump arm in greeting, he called, "*Salud, Papacito Ortiz!*"

The Senator always addressed Joe in this second-year Spanish, kindly overlooking the fact that the janitor was born in San Diego and spoke English, and that what Spanish he had was pure border Mexican.

"You want to see me, Harold?" Joe asked when the Senator, a slow and stately walker, finally reached him.

"*Por favor, Señor José,*" Harold said, as if they were two Castilians far from home and happily met amidst strangers.

Close up, the Senator's fifteen years showed on him. He had a big, round face, raw now with acne, a full, unformed mouth, and heavy black brows. He had a good forehead and nose, and later would be

50

handsome. Joe knew this, and the fact was not comforting. He had enough to do handling the unsightly Senator. Let the Senator grow into good looks (and the Senator would be the first to know when this happened), and Joe probably *couldn't* handle him. As it was, Joe was the only one in the Home who called the Senator by his proper name, Harold Whitehall.

The Senator didn't like to be called Harold. Hal he tolerated. But his proper title was the Senator. The name had been given him by the kids in the purest derision, as Joe well knew, and Harold had wrapped it around himself with such ostentatious pride that the Home was now impressed by what it had itself created. But not me, Joe thought. I'm not impressed.

The Senator's *"Señor José,"* his big-hearted determination to make an equal of Joe, somehow managed to push Joe into a barefoot Pancho pose, as if he were a peon who had never tasted white bread or owned a pair of shoes. Joe hated himself as well as the Senator when he was overtaken by this play-acting. He, a man with three years in San Miguel High School, was, at the moment, better educated than the Senator himself, who was now a second-year student in the Reno High School. Joe was old enough—matters accelerated a little, as is possible with Mexicans—to be the Senator's grandfather. (Though, God be praised, things had not so fallen out.) He had five grown sons, a sweet wife dead, and a sweetheart as alive as could be, and willing, any time he gave the word, to be a wife, too. He had a 1950 Chevy, two guitars (one of them electric), and a fine library of paperbacks, and he knew probably five hundred songs. So why let a kid like the Senator get under his skin?

Besides, the boy had good traits. Beautiful traits compared to some of the young criminals at Temple. What was wrong with speaking second-year Spanish, bowing from the waist, and hating dirty stories? And sing! The Senator sang like a bird. Church, bonfire programs, funerals—wherever singing was either needed or permitted—there was the Senator lifting what in an older man would have been called his whisky tenor in song. Sometimes the Senator would go to an out-of-the-way spot and sing to himself, and even when he was pointed out, singing there, he didn't stop or become self-conscious. By God, Joe thought, I hate myself for not loving that boy. He's a good kid, though unpleasant. And he resolved never again to call him Harold.

"Kid," he said, managing to keep it from becoming "keed," "what's your problem?"

"*Señor*, it is the *patrón*. He desires word with you."

"You mean Mr. Buchanan, Harold?"

"*El patrón, Señor Ortiz.* He desires word with you about the suits."

"O.K. I been expecting it. I want to wash up first. You go tell him I'll be there as soon as I've finished."

"He told me to bring you."

"O.K., bring me. But first I'm going to wash up."

Joe's room was in the basement, down a steep flight of narrow, un-railed cement stairs. With the Senator on his tail, he took it running—showing off, risking his neck to impress another show-off.

The room was a space fifteen by fifteen, walled off from the furnace, hot-water heaters, janitor's supplies, and the like by partitions of beaverboard. From the outside, no one could guess what a pretty place Joe had made of it. Sometimes he'd leave work for five minutes and come down to take a peek at it. Just open the door and, without going in, have a quick look, the way a man will pull the picture of his baby or sweetheart from his pocket to make sure they really exist. He did not care to have the Senator in his room, but now that the Senator was there, he'd let him see how good it was, how warm, orderly, and *bright*. The two guitars were hung up on the wall by red ribbons Joe had braided himself. They were as pretty in their way as any of his pictures—the Virgin excepted, of course. His paperbacks were arranged in alphabetical order, and not one stood a fraction of an inch farther out on the shelf than another. And the shelf, like the ribbons, was red. The window, being in the basement, looked out into the bottom of the shrubbery that grew around the foundation of the building. Joe had his table against this window, and he could sit there, as if in a game blind, observing intimately the habits of cats, sparrows, and lizards. He turned to ask the Senator to enter, but it was too late for such courtesies; the Senator had walked in and was busy looking around.

He continued to look around as Joe washed. In the mirror over the washbasin Joe could see him examining his books and pictures. The

Senator gave the pictures a glance that was scornful or pained or embarrassed—Joe couldn't tell which—and went on to the books. Joe hoped the Senator would not take this occasion, while he waited, to tell him sad stories of his childhood. He had heard one or two. If you were to believe them—and Joe always did—you had to hand it to the Senator for just surviving.

"What's this?" the Senator asked.

Joe shook the water out of his eyes and looked into the mirror. "Tequila," he said.

"Alcohol, *Señor?*"

"*Sí,*" Joe said, falling into the Senator's pattern in spite of himself.

"Abraham Lincoln said, 'There are many defenders of alcohol but no defense.' "

"Good man, Lincoln," Joe said. "He saved the Union."

The Senator would not be put off by such pleasantries. "You defend alcohol, *Señor?*"

Joe, in his own room, felt easily the Senator's equal. "No, I just drink it."

"It is the same thing, *Señor.*"

"No, sir. I do many things I wouldn't waste a minute defending."

"Well," said the Senator, flabbergasted, "I never heard anybody say that before."

Joe felt proud. I have the Senator on the run, he thought. "The best things I have done in my life I wouldn't defend."

A shocked darkness, like a polliwog surfacing, floated up into the Senator's bright blue eyes. "I have never done anything in my life I wouldn't defend," he said.

"I believe you, completely," Joe said.

This lack of argument discouraged the Senator. He sat down in the chair by the window and gazed out into the shrubbery. "There is a bee out there," he said aggressively.

Joe wouldn't argue about that, either. "Must've spent the winter in the basement and just got out."

"I owe my life to bees, and in spite of the fact, I hate them."

Joe resisted saying "How's that?" and said, instead, "Let's get going." He did not want to hear how a bee had saved the Senator's life. But the Senator did not budge. He still sat gazing with melancholy into the shrubbery. Joe could not see the bee, and though he warned himself not to get mixed up with the Senator's past life, the old, natural habit of courtesy, acquired long before he had entered Temple, asserted itself, and he said, "How's that, Harold?"

"When I was a baby, still drinking milk, my folks ran out of money. To save my life, my father robbed beehives of honey. My mother diluted it with warm water, and I lived on it. It saved my life. That was a fine, unselfish thing for my father to do, wasn't it? Be willing to rob to save his child's life?"

"Yeah," Joe said. "It was."

"I don't like him, though. I have a strong antipathy to him. You understand antipathy, *Señor?*"

"I understand what you mean, Harold."

"I got a strong antipathy to bees, too. Once I told my mother about this, and she said, 'Baby, bees saved your life. You should love bees.' But I said, 'Mother, what I feel is antipathy.' "

"How old was you when you said this, Harold?"

"Ten, maybe."

What Joe felt was strong sympathy for the Senator's mother, but all he said was "Mr. Buchanan's waiting for us, Harold."

The bee at that moment made a short flight, and Joe saw it. It was a battered, ragged bee and didn't look as if it had ever seen a flower or had anything to do with honey.

"The bee stands in the same relationship to me as the wolf did to Romulus and Remus. Romulus and Remus were—"

"I know about those two kids," Joe said. "A wolf nursed them."

He had studied classic myths at San Miguel High School, and he had an unpleasant picture now of the Senator, a big, fat, black-haired baby, being suckled by an oversize, hairy-legged bee. Maybe there would be a statue of it on the courthouse lawn someday. He emptied his Thermos bottle, in which he carried hot coffee when he was working out on the grounds and couldn't be bothered coming in for lunch, and began to rinse it.

"My mother really loved me, didn't she, keeping me alive on honey and water that way?"

"No doubt about it," Joe said. "She dead now?"

"No, she's alive. She's shacking up with some guy in Tucson, charming fellow. He's crazy to marry her, but she don't know if it would work out. I'd be with them now, except he's insanely jealous of me."

Startled, Joe turned, Thermos bottle in hand.

The Senator reassured him. "It's a Freudian thing," he said. Then he got up quickly. "That's a disgusting thing to do."

"What's disgusting?"

"Cleaning a Thermos that way. No scalding, no soap. That's unsanitary. All kinds of bacteria breed in warm, dark places like that. The least we can do is to be sanitary, isn't it?"

For a second, Joe was apologetic. The last thing he wanted to do was to offend anybody by being unsanitary. Then he was mad.

"Whose bottle is this, anyway?" he asked. "For thirty years I've been rinsing Thermos bottles this way. If it's so God-damned unsanitary, why haven't I been sick?"

"It makes me sick to watch you."

"Who asked you to watch me?" He grabbed the Senator's arm. "You get out and stay out. It's none of your business if I park cockroaches in my Thermos bottle."

The Senator's head dropped, but not before Joe saw the tears in his eyes.

"I'm sorry, *Señor*," he said. "Something must've happened to me when I was young. Dirt just makes me sick."

Joe let go his arm. The kid looked sick. His face between the raw spots was gray, and the tears rolled down his cheeks without losing their shape. No satisfaction, Joe thought, kicking the Senator. Kick the Senator, who needs it, and who you hurt's a kid.

"You got no right talking that way, Harold."

"I know it. But you made me feel so at home down here, *Señor*. You certainly know how to put people at their ease."

Joe, who knew a buttering-up when he got it, nevertheless responded, "I try to."

"You succeeded. You made me think we could just work our problems out together."

Joe got mad all over again. "I got my Thermos problems all worked out, kid. You just don't worry about it. You just keep your nose out of it. Now let's get going."

The Senator was once more meek. "Could I see your suit before I go?"

"You've seen it."

"Not off you."

"O.K. Look. It's there in the closet. I'm going."

He waited a minute or two at the top of the stairs.

The Senator, when he came, said in a condoling voice, "It's rather an upsetting coincidence, isn't it?"

"It don't upset me none, Harold."

Outside Buchanan's office, the Senator said, "Charming fellow, Buchanan. Regular he-man."

Joe had never thought of Buchanan that way. The Superintendent's face was veal colored and heart shaped; that is, if you turned the heart upside down, so that the pointed end disappeared amidst thin strands of dun-colored hair and the double curves of the top of the heart coincided with Buchanan's fat jowls.

The Senator ushered Joe into the office as if he were a stranger.

"Sir," he said, "*Señor Ortiz*, our neighbor from down under."

The Superintendent, to Joe's surprise, found this funny. He was seated behind his desk in a dark blue double-breasted suit. "Welcome, *Señor*," he said.

Joe nodded. "You want to see me?"

"Sir," said the Senator, "before I leave, may I just say how much we all appreciate your gesture in creating the noon music hour?"

"Thank you, Senator," Mr. Buchanan said. "Will you wait outside, please? I may want to speak to you later."

The Senator left the room, and Mr. Buchanan gazed after him. "Remarkable youngster," he told Joe. Joe agreed. "Sit down, Joe, won't you?" Mr. Buchanan pointed to a chair at one corner of his desk. "How's the world treating you, Joe?"

"I got no complaints," Joe said.

"I expect you know why I asked you in for this little chat?"

"I have an idea."

"The Senator tell you?"

"There are quite a few things I know without any help from the Senator."

"Sure, Joe. There sure are. Well, first of all, let's get this straight. I don't intend to push you around any. You've been in this institution longer than I have. In fact, you're an institution yourself around here. The kids say 'Joe the Janitor' and I truly believe, Joe, it means a lot more to them than 'Buchanan the Superintendent.' I may be the titular head, but you're the heart and guts of the place. O.K., Joe?"

"O.K.," Joe said.

"So what I wanted was for us two heads of Temple to get together and talk over a little problem that faces us."

"O.K.," Joe said again. "Here we are."

"This involves you and the Senator, Joe. One of you has to give ground."

"I don't see why."

Mr. Buchanan ignored this. "Now, you know, Joe—or maybe you don't—the Senator's had a rough life. He's been very underprivileged up to now."

"I know," Joe said. "He was brought up by the bees."

"Oh. The Senator tell you?"

"Nobody could guess a thing like that."

"No. I guess not. Now, Joe, what I'd like first of all is your version of the suits. I've never heard your version, you know."

"Version? There's what happened. How do you get versions out of that?"

"O.K., Joe. What did happen?"

"Check down at the store if you want to, about what happened. They ran this ad about their after-Christmas sale of suits, and I needed a new suit. So Tuesday noon I went down, picked one out, and bought it. They had to turn up the cuffs, like they always do, and I was to get it Wednesday. Wednesday after work, when I stopped in for it, they said, 'Which one is yours?' I said, 'What do you mean which one is mine?' And they said, 'Look. Two suits just alike and both going to Temple.' They were just kidding—they knew which one was mine, all right. The other one was the Senator's. That's the only version there is of the suits, Mr. Buchanan. The Senator and I bought identical suits. Only," he added, "we don't wear them the same."

"No, you don't," Mr. Buchanan said. "That's a fact."

"Well, that's my version. Is that all you wanted?"

Mr. Buchanan rubbed his hands together. "No, Joe, not to beat around the bush, it isn't. You're a man, Joe, The Senator's a kid. I want you to make a little sacrifice for the boy."

"What?" asked Joe.

Mr. Buchanan filled his snorkel pen, seemed dissatisfied with the job, and did it again; then, having discharged all the ink, he got up, went to the window, and there alternately exposed and retracted the mechanism. Finally, he turned around and faced Joe. "It's not easy to say this, Joe."

"Go ahead. You don't have to go easy on my account."

"You know how kids are."

"Yes, sir, I do."

"Well, they're riding the Senator about his suit."

"It don't look good on him, that's a fact. He ought never to have bought it. Big pin stripe, double-breasted. It's a man's suit."

"You're right, Joe. But that's not why the kids are riding him. You know how the Senator is."

Mr. Buchanan hesitated, but Joe didn't like to say, either.

"Kids have no understanding of the dignity of labor, Joe. You know that. So they're saying the Senator's wearing a janitor's suit."

"What can I do about it?"

"If the Senator so much as puts his head around the corner, they start telling him the furnace needs attention or a john's out of order. This humiliates the boy."

"What can I do?" Joe asked again.

"I'll tell you what, Joe. You could take your suit back and get another. I've called the store. Under the circumstances, and since you've only worn it once, they'll take it back at full price."

"If the Senator don't like to wear a suit like mine, why don't he take his back?"

"Trouble is, Joe, the Senator had to have his suit altered considerably. It won't fit anyone else."

"For a kid," Joe admitted, "the Senator's got an unusually fat tail."

"Yeah. Well, there it is, Joe. You've got a chance to make a fine gesture. Do something for an underprivileged boy."

"No, sir," Joe said. "I'm not going to do it. I bought mine first, it looks good on me, and I'm going to keep it. Couple of weeks, the

Senator and me wear our suits so different, they won't look alike anyway. The kids will forget they ever started out the same."

"Meanwhile, the boy has to suffer."

"That's up to him. It don't give me any pleasure having him wear
my suit, either." Joe wondered how to explain to Mr. Buchanan what
he felt about the Senator in *his* suit. That suit which was made to
take chances, to go a few unexpected places. The Senator made it
look like a uniform of some sort. "The Senator contradicts that suit."

"I don't get it," Mr. Buchanan said.

Joe shrugged. "I'm keeping my suit. If you think the Senator's suffering too much, you buy him another."

He had perhaps gone too far. Mr. Buchanan retracted his snorkel,
capped it, put it in the desk drawer, and sat down.

"Joe, take the afternoon off. Go downtown. Ride out toward the
mountains. Get some perspective on this. As I see it, this is an opportunity for you to make a magnificent gesture to a young person. Give
yourself a little time, and I'm sure you'll come up with the right decision."

As far as Joe was concerned, he had already come up with the right
decision; but he didn't have anything against an afternoon off.

"O.K., Mr. Buchanan," he said, and left the office.

He met the Senator halfway down the hall. The Senator lifted his
arm in his usual salute. *"Vaya con Dios, Señor,"* he said.

Go with God! Joe's skin prickled. As if God himself were a gift the
Senator could hand out or withhold as the fancy struck him!

He didn't say a word, but he went down the stairs to his room,
immediately undressed, and put on his new suit. Then he stood before the mirror looking at himself.

By God, he thought, the Senator's wrong. It don't look like a janitor's suit. What it looks like is a gambler's suit. It looks like the suit
of somebody who don't know all the answers but is willing to take a
chance. "Yes, sir," he told his suit. "You stand up for me, and I'll
stand up for you. The way I've been doing."

Since his mind was all made up about the suit, there wasn't any
point in going out and looking at the mountains. There wasn't any
point in going out into the raw January afternoon at all. He and his

suit would just stay in here and celebrate a little. The Janitor's suit wanted to defy the Senator's suit. He saw the Thermos bottle, and though he'd never had anything in it but coffee before, and though it was a little unhandy to drink from, he felt he'd enjoy having his drink from it now. That way, he could defy the Senator twice, be unsanitary and alcoholic at the same time. He poured some tequila into the Thermos bottle, and when a few drops fell onto his suit, he didn't try to wipe them off. "Share and share alike," he said.

His first sip quieted his anger, and as his anger left him, he felt apologetic toward his room. He hadn't really looked at it since he came in. It could've been a jail cell or a comfort station, for all the attention he had paid it. He went over and stretched out on his bed. By God, he thought, I have made myself a pretty room—warm, lively, and bright colored as a woman. Not that a room could take a woman's place. A man who thought that would never have bothered to put up the pictures he had: telephone girl, girl wearing chaps, girl blowing soap bubbles. Though the girl pictures weren't all; besides his holy pictures, he had pictures of his five sons, his dead wife, his live sweetheart, a lonesome coyote, Segovia, and the 1950 Chevrolet. He had an eye for anything that was beautiful, he told himself— human or animal, vegetable or mineral. He sloshed the tequila around in his Thermos and drank a toast to the beauties in his room, and to beauty generally, and to the poor Senator, who had no eye for beauty and who, though he loved himself, must be repelled when he looked in the mirror to see the face of the one he loved best so disfigured. The only thing about the Senator that's really a thing he can take any pride in is his suit, Joe thought. And me laying here on my bed of riches depriving the poor kid of his one pride.

He took another sip and thought about it some more. I'm not going to take my suit back, he decided, but what I will do is tell Buchanan I'll never wear it here at the Home. Here in my room if I want to, Reno if I want to, but noplace where any of the kids can see me. The Senator's got his world and I've got mine, and there's no use trying to mix the two.

Having made his decision, he wanted to tell Buchanan at once, so he finished his drink in a hurry and started up the stairs in a hurry.

*     *     *

It was the Senator, of course, lurking in that neighborhood to be the first to hear his decision, who found him. Before Joe could tell him his decision, his eyes closed and he lost for a while not only the problem of the suits but the whole world.

When he opened his eyes, the school doctor, the Senator, Mr. Buchanan, and Father Jiménez were standing by his bed. He was evidently in a bad way. Their faces were very serious.

Father Jiménez said, "Are you feeling better, Joe?"

"Am I going to die, Father?" he asked.

The doctor didn't give Father Jiménez a chance to answer. "Die?" he said, and chuckled. "Don't be silly, Joe." Then, to Buchanan, "I told you there was going to be an accident on those stairs if you didn't put up a handrail."

The Senator poked the Thermos bottle under the nose of the doctor, who was bending over Joe. "Sir," he said, "it wasn't the stairs. It was the liquor."

"Poor kid, raised by the bees!" Joe cried. "What can you expect? Father, if I die, bury me in my suit." He pulled the coat up under his chin. "It's my last request." Then, pressing his hands to his bandaged head to hold it together while he spoke, he said, "What'll you do then, Harold? You'll be wearing a dead man's suit, not a janitor's suit. How are you going to like that?"

The Senator drew himself up proudly. "*Señor*," he said, "in that case, I have no choice. I'll walk the earth in a dead man's suit."

Joe could see him doing it, could see his chance-taking gambler's suit walking the world and beginning each day to look more like the Senator. He gave a groan and fell back across the pillows, one arm across his eyes. In that case, *he* had no choice at all but to get well. He shut his eyes and prepared to continue the struggle.

# Tom Wolfe's My Name

THE FIRST TIME I ever saw Sterling was four years ago in April at a place called Babe's. Babe's is a nice little tavern just outside of Burley. I'd gone up to Burley to sell an order of books to Tidy Smith, the principal of the high school there. Burley isn't very big, couple of thousand people maybe, but they've got a good-sized union high school and Tidy's been sold on Bonn and Company texts for a long time.

There wasn't anything to it—no salesmanship, no high pressure—nothing. Tidy just checked what he needed against the Bonn and Company list and that was that.

"I like the Bonn and Company line," Tidy said, "but the names you're giving schoolbooks nowadays set my teeth on edge." He flicked through one of our catalogues. "All the arithmetics are *Adventures with Numbers*. Here's a biology called *The Mystery of Life*, a history, *The Romance of Civilization*. Adventure, mystery, romance." He spat out the words as if he'd got something nasty in his mouth by mistake.

I picked up a sky blue book spangled with stars. "What difference does the name make, Smith?" I asked. "They've got good stuff inside—the kids like 'em, and they sell."

"Don't fool yourself, boy," Tidy said. "Names are damned important. You're so glad to have a job, you'd sell books that taught kids that two and two made five if they paid you for it."

"Don't be so conservative, Mr. Smith," I said. "I'd sell books teaching kids that two and two made seven—if they paid me for it."

"Nice to meet an honest salesman," Tidy said, "but the world wouldn't be in such a hell of a shape today if people gave things their right names."

I tried to defend the titles on our list, but I guess I was pretty weak. Tidy cut me short. "OK, Madden," he said, "I see you've got just the romantic touch they're looking for in schoolbooks today. You ought to try your hand at a geometry. Call it 'Adventures with Angles.'"

"I don't have adventures with angles, Smith," I said.

By the time Tidy'd talked himself out the school was empty except for a couple of janitors whose brooms you could hear thumping against the walls—and a bunch of kids waiting in the hall for their folks to pick them up. There was a lot of rain coming down and the wind that blows up the Burley Valley off the bay was smacking it against the windows. If there's anything drearier than an empty school building I don't know what it is. And that goes double when it's raining. I was watching the runoff wash out their new track when Tidy said to me, "Let's go out and have a drink."

I didn't know Tidy then the way I do now. I don't suppose there's another high-school principal like him in California—probably not in the United States. He's a little fellow with a pointed bald head that looks like some kind of a mushroom or tulip pushing up through the grassy fringe round his ears. He's a south of Market Street Mick— same as me—and he's come up the hard way. Now that he's cashing in on the years he spent getting an education, he likes it plenty. Snappiest dresser not in vaudeville—and if there's anything in Burley he doesn't do I don't know it. Sings at the funerals, talks to the garden clubs, plays Joseph in their Christmas plays. But I didn't know all that then, and being asked to take a drink by a high-school principal gave me a turn. I decided he must mean a cup of coffee.

I guess I must of showed my surprise. "What's the matter, Madden?" Tidy asked. "You on the wagon? If this isn't the weather for a Tom and Jerry I never saw the weather for a T and J."

"It's sure the weather for it," I said, "and I'm not on the wagon." I hated to ask him what the town was going to think of its high-school principal tossing down a quick one. The fellow was a stranger to me then—wasn't my place to be looking after his job—but Judas, any other town in California and he wouldn't have had a job next morning. Besides, teachers, the male ones anyway, give me the jumps. I'd rather go out and have a drink with a nun. You can understand what a sister's doing with her life—got her eye on God and the life everlasting. But a guy choosing of his own free will to sit down opposite a bunch of empty-faced kids every day for the rest of his life—nope, that's got me licked. So I figured it would be better for me to have my drink alone. I'd be more comfortable and Tidy'd have his job next morning and the *dinero* to buy more of those fancy clothes of his.

I guess Tidy read my mind. "Come on, Madden," he said, "they let teachers be human beings in Burley."

So we drove down to this place called Babe's, he in his car and I in mine. It was a darned nice-looking spot, even in all that rain. An old whitewashed brick building set under some peppers out on the edge of town. And it was just as nice inside. Big wood fire, stone floor, old-fashioned heavy round tables. There were seven or eight men in the place—mostly looked like ranchers killing time until the rain was over. A couple of fellows at a table by the stove were playing cribbage and their counting, fifteen-two, fifteen-four, and so on, was about all the talk you could hear above the rain.

Tidy spoke to some of the men, who called him professor. We ordered our drinks, and sat down and stretched our legs out under a table. Jeez, that's a good minute—when you've sold a big order, the day's over, and you've got a drink coming up. And it was a good drink, too.

I was just ready for my second one when another guy came in and Tidy Smith got a kind of pleased look in his eye. The look a guy gets when he thinks he's going to let you in on something special. Of course I'm writing with hindsight now, but I think I noticed it—even then. Anyway Tidy called out, "Hi, Sterling, come over and join us."

The fellow he called Sterling got out of a big yellow raincoat, banged his hat against the door a few times to get the water out of the crown, and came over to our table.

Tidy said, "Sterling, I want you to meet a book drummer, name of Madden." We said the usual howdys, and this Sterling ordered his drink, a glass of dry sherry.

To be saying something, I told Sterling wine drinking, when you could get anything else, had me beat.

"Well, Mr. Madden," he said, "I own a vineyard. The very grapes that went into this glass," and he held the leather-colored stuff up so's the light went through it, "may have been grown on my land. Beneath my soil, their million-footed roots, into my sunshine their million-fingered tendrils." He took a drink and set his glass down.

That kind of talk before a guy's got his drink down him—after, even—well, it makes you sit up and shake your ears. And this Sterling was enough to make you sit up, even without any of this "million-footed, million-fingered" stuff. He wasn't any fullback—short and slight, though he was plenty wiry looking. What made you notice him first was his hair. I guess it was lemon-colored hair—kind of a mixture of yellow and silver and green. And instead of looking fine and kind of brittle the way most blond hair does, it looked soft like fur. It was smoothed down on top, not a ripple, but around his neck, where it was too long, either because he liked it that way, or hadn't bothered to have it cut, it went into curls.

But what really got you were his eyes. If they were any color they were air colored—or maybe water colored or ice colored. Anyway they were transparent and they were bottomless. You got the same feeling looking in them you get looking down an empty elevator shaft. It's only your eyes that travel the length of that shaft, when you lean over, but your body follows somehow and you have the sensation of falling. It was the same way looking into that fellow Sterling's eyes. They gave me a sensation of falling, so I decided to concentrate on my drink.

Just then the phone rang somewhere in the back of the room, and the fellow who ran the place called, "Professor, somebody wants to speak to you." Sterling and I drank and watched the rain while Tidy was gone.

When he came back he said, "Couple of my kids are mired down out by Lodi Lane. Guess I'll have to pull them out."

Sterling said, "Why don't their folks do it?"

"That's just the trouble. They don't want their folks to know it happened. Nope, I'll have to go. You two entertain each other. Remember Madden's a book salesman, Sterling," Tidy said, and I kind of got the feeling that that meant more to Sterling than it did to me. "You two ought to have a lot in common."

I didn't know what I could have in common with that platinum-haired grape grower, but it was still pouring and Babe's place was a damned sight more pleasant than a hotel bedroom. So I was willing to stay and find out.

When Tidy finally took off, this Sterling said to me, "What kind of books do you sell?"

"Schoolbooks," I told him.

"So," he said, "books for children."

"That's right. Kid stuff. Algebras, histories, and so forth."

"Do you ever see any authors?" he asked.

"Sure," I told him. "I've seen the author of *Our Eskimo Cousins* and *Our Mexican Cousins*, and the author of *The World We Live In*, and the—"

Sterling cut in. "You've never met any of the big authors, then?"

"You mean the best sellers?" I asked.

"No, no," he said, "the authors of the best books—regardless of how they sell. The books the critics praise."

"Nope," I said. "That lets me out. I've never even seen Kathleen Norris, and they say she's in and out of San Francisco all the time."

This all sounded right sane to me—the usual questions I get from people who hear I sell books—and don't know authors are the same tissue of artificial dentures, overdrafts, and unrequited love as the rest of us. Well, as I said, this talk about authors sounded sane to me—and I decided that "root and tendril" stuff had been just a passing flight. So I chanced another look at the fellow—but jeez, his eyes were still empty and you still fell.

Anyway I decided it was time for a little reciprocity. He'd asked me about my bookselling. Time for me to ask him about his grape growing. "This late rain doing your grapes any harm?" I asked.

"No, no," he said. "It feeds them. At night I hear not only the rain falling, with a sound of bells in the darkness, but I hear the thirsty vine roots drinking. I lie awake these spring nights and hear the sounds their throats make swallowing—and no other sound, unless perhaps far off in the Napa Valley the clank of great wheels pounding on a rail, and a long whistle like a cry of sorrow across the hills, cutting the night air."

I sure wished I'd let reciprocity alone. But there wasn't much I could do—except to order another drink. I figured that to be an earpiece for this guy you needed to be a little tight.

Sterling emptied his third glass of sherry. "No, there's more to be heard than that. If you listen long enough on a wet night you can hear the feet of the rain on the surface of the little creeks: the Napa, the Feather, the Yolo, the Rio Hondo. And you can hear the voices of the little creeks deepen as they lose themselves in the mighty plunge and welter of the Sacramento, the San Joaquin. In the nighttime, while we sleep, immortal rivers flow by us to the sea."

He stopped speaking, looked out into the rain, kind of self-consciously. "Forgive me," he said. "It's very easy for a writer to start quoting himself."

"You write?" I asked. That relieved me some. The guy was just a writer then—not screwy the way he sounded.

"Yes," he said. Then he swung around from looking out into the rain. "My name's Thomas Wolfe."

I tell you that stopped me—stopped me cold. I couldn't think of a think to say. I just sunk my face in my Tom and Jerry and gave that guy's hair and build another look over the top of my mug. Well, you can only spend so long drinking a Tom and Jerry.

So I put my cup down and said, "The author of *Look Homeward, Angel?*"

"That's right," he said.

"Thomas Wolfe," I said.

"Yes, that's right."

I didn't see any use in our going through that again.

"I understood Tidy to say your name was Sterling."

"You did—you did." The fellow was smooth as soap. "It's the name I use here in Burley. Intelligent men, men like you and Tidy can accept a writer—his differences and limitations. But if it were generally known here in Burley who I am, it would set me apart—keeping me from being one of the people—as I wish to be. No, Tidy was right. Here in Burley I'm known as Tom Sterling, but Tom Wolfe's my name."

When a fellow tells you a thing like that, blank out, it gives you a damned funny feeling. You know that little blond cornstalk can't be Thomas Wolfe, but jeez, when that guy said, "Tom Wolfe's my name," his eyes changed. They filled in—focused. Something moved in behind the cellophane. You didn't fall any more.

But I decided to put it to him straight. "Your talk sounds like Wolfe," I said, "but you sure don't look like him. Look the opposite I should say. He's a big, dark fellow."

"You've seen pictures of him?" he asked me.

"Sure," I told him. "Who hasn't? He's a big black fellow, looks like a wrestler or a truck driver."

"That's just the reason I chose those pictures for my publicity releases," Sterling said. "I don't think my appearance suggests or is in harmony with my writing. And I feel it is important for the reader's singleness of mind that the author's face suggest his writing. You do agree, don't you?"

I told him I supposed it helped.

"Of course it helps. You were shocked just now to think that a man of my appearance should write as Thomas Wolfe writes, weren't you?"

"Yes," I said. I'd been shocked all right.

"And you do feel, don't you," he urged, "that the face I chose does represent my writing? That it has a dark October quality?"

"Yes," I said, "particularly around the mouth." And then, right away, I was damned sorry for that. I was a little tight by then, but that's no excuse for hitting a guy where he lives, and Sterling was sure living in that Thomas Wolfe fantasy. When I made that crack his eyes got empty again.

To make up for it I said, "Who is this fellow whose picture you use, Mr. Wolfe?"

My calling him Wolfe integrated him—gave him back his core curriculum so to speak.

"I don't know," he said. "I've never wanted to know. The publicity department simply furnishes the pictures for me—produces a new pose when I need one for a new book."

By that time this Sterling-Wolfe had me going. I wanted to ask him a hundred questions—just to see how he managed the practical side of impersonating a famous author. Because I was damn sure it was an impersonation. But jeez, there's so many screwy things going on in the world it could be the way he said. It would be an outside chance, but it could be. I wanted to ask him some questions but I didn't want to hurt him—so I asked the questions straight—I didn't farce them.

"Mr. Wolfe," I said, "your publicity material says you live in the South—and in New York—and your novels are about the South."

"That's right, Mr. Madden," he said. "This is more or less my hideaway. But I intend to be more than a sectional writer. I hope to speak for all of America. To do that I must know all of America. So for a part of each year I grow grapes in Napa County. But I'm not here as often as it seems to the people in Burley. Genius has a protean quality that makes it seem more omnipresent than it is."

I never expected to meet a guy who looked less like Proteus—but no use mentioning that, I figured. Besides I had a lot more questions to ask him. I wanted to see if I couldn't trip him up. No—that wasn't it exactly. I didn't think I really could—he made you feel he had the answers to all the questions. But anyway I wanted to hear a few more answers. When he finished his fourth or fifth glass of sherry, though, he said he had to leave—had a dinner date.

"I've enjoyed talking with you, Madden," he said. "Look me up next time you're in Burley. Tidy'll tell you how to get out to my place. I might be away, but I've a feeling I won't be. I've a feeling you and I will meet again."

As soon as he'd left I tried to get Tidy on the phone. I wanted to find out what he knew about this Sterling-Wolfe. But I couldn't raise Tidy. So, when I paid for my drink I asked the wop who ran the place, an old fellow with a pair of sad mustaches, about him.

"Who's the guy who was tucking away the sherry?" I asked.

"That's Mr. Sterling," he said.

"What's he do?"

"Grows grapes, like everybody else here."

"He a newcomer?"

"Nope," the wop said. "He been here before me."

"How long you been here?"

"Eleven years."

Tidy was out all evening, and I had a date with a principal in Petaluma next morning at eight. So I didn't get to talk to him about Sterling until the next April. I didn't make my usual September trip to Burley that year. I was out in the Islands then on that promotion junket.

But the first thing I did when I saw Tidy this April was to ask him about that guy. "Say," I said, "who's this fellow Sterling you introduced me to last year? Corn-silk fellow who says he's Thomas Wolfe?"

Tidy kind of laughed. "So you remember him?"

"Hell, yes. Who is he?"

"His name's Thomas Sterling. The Sterling family's lived over by Santa Rosa for the past sixty, seventy-five years."

"How long's he been saying he wrote Thomas Wolfe's novels?"

"Ever since the first Wolfe novel was published."

"You don't think he writes 'em?"

"How could he? He spends all his time growing grapes. He's got forty acres of grapes up there on the mountain, and he does most of the work himself. Besides, we never heard any of this Tom Wolfe talk until about six months after Wolfe's first novel was published. And when the newspapers were carrying accounts of Wolfe's being in Europe Tom was right up there tractoring his vines."

"How'd he explain that?" I asked.

"Promotion stunt by the publicity department. 'People like to think authors get around,' he said. 'I write the books. My publishers can do anything they like in the way of promotion.' "

I asked Tidy if he figured the fellow was crazy.

"I figure," Tidy said, "that on the subject of Wolfe he's touched. Pretty definitely touched. But he's smart as they make 'em when it comes to growing grapes."

"I'm going up to see him," I said. "He asked me to."

"OK," Tidy said. "You do that. It's a beautiful drive and you can't miss his place. It's the last vineyard on the mountain. But seeing his place, Madden, isn't going to settle your mind any."

Tidy was 100 percent right—about the drive—and about my mind. The drive was beautiful—lupine and poppies in bloom and the vineyards just uncurling. I didn't have any trouble locating the Sterling place. A house painted white up there among the trees couldn't be missed. It was the neatest, prettiest little place you ever saw. Green shutters on the house, flowers in beds, bricked paths. Outside it looked like a retired lighthouse keeper's heaven.

There was a fellow down the slope a ways doing some pruning, and I knew it was Sterling from the way his hair shone in the sun—like a mirror. I gave a whoop and the fellow—it was Sterling—came up to the house.

I told him I didn't suppose he remembered me. That my name was Madden and that I'd had a drink with him a year ago down at Babe's. I called him Mr. Wolfe, too.

He was as pleasant as possible. "Of course I remember you. I don't forget people who like my books. Come in and have a drink and a chat."

"Sure I won't be interrupting your work?" I asked.

"No, no," he said. "When an idea doesn't take shape I go out and prune for a while, and there, thinking only of the vines and their needs, the solution of my problem comes to me."

He took off his gloves and opened the door for me. The room we stepped into gave me quite a shock, it was so different from the yard. But in a second I realized it was just what I should have expected. I remembered the Tom Wolfe legend—shirts and socks thrown into a corner until they were all dirty. Writing done by the pound instead of the page in big ledgers. Place a jumble of frying pans and papers.

That's the room I stepped into. That's the legend Sterling was living. The dirty shirts were right there in the corner where they should have been. I don't know which there was most of on his table—books or milk bottles. And the ledgers you read about were right there in an open packing case. I walked over and put my hand on them.

"These will all be in the Library of Congress someday," I said. I didn't suppose there was a word written in a one of them. I thought they were stage properties—duds. Sterling smiled modestly.

"*Look Homeward, Angel, Of Time and the River*, all those famous and eloquent words," I said, "here in longhand."

I let my fingers open a book, flick a few pages, but I kept my eyes on Sterling. I expected to see him wince, show some strain, suggest I look at something else. But he stood there easy and smiling.

"Every word in longhand," he said. "Terribly silly, but I can't seem to write any other way."

OK, fellow, I thought, you asked for it. So I lifted out three of the ledgers, took up the fourth one and opened it—the pages were filled. A heavy angular hand, the hand of a guy who writes fast with his mind on what he's saying. I looked at half a dozen books. I saw the familiar words. Believe me, I felt plenty funny. This guy was a phony. He had to be. But he had sure gone to a lot of trouble to be a phony. It's bad enough when you look at something that's not what it seems— but it's a hundred times worse when you get a load of something that seems to be what it's not. I guess that's just the same thing put backward. Anyway, here was this guy who talked Wolfe, lived Wolfe, who even wrote Wolfe—but he wasn't Wolfe.

I gave up trying to get him on anything. There he stood, his face shining like a kid's at my speaking of his "famous words." OK, fellow, I decided, you can put on your act for me. You sure spent plenty of time working it up. I've got an hour to play audience for you.

In lots of ways it wasn't a bad hour. It was a good hour, lot of ways, except for the times I got a kind of sick feeling as if I was living in a dream and might fall through any minute and hit myself hard on a hunk of reality somewheres.

He fixed me a lunch, slices of ham, steak-thick, stewed tomatoes, black coffee, a bakery cake. He stowed it away like a teamster and talked about the good food he'd eaten—and where. And he talked about his books. What he'd written and was going to write.

"I'm just a funnel through which America can pour," he said. "It has to come out the way I saw it and the way I felt it, but it will come out America, not me."

I think he smoked a pack of cigarettes while he was talking.

"When I finish writing," he said, "when I'm all through, the last book filled, the last word written, all of America will be down in print, there for anyone to sample: the smell of America—her million smells: the sweat of the Negroes, the dry smell of leaves, the autumn smell of chrysanthemums, the fish frying on a summer evening, the wind off our thousand miles of ocean, the smell of new rubber on the roads, and of asphalt, and of printer's ink wet on the evening papers, and the petunias freshly watered, and the damson plums boiling up in the little lean-to kitchens, and the girls sprinkling Hoyt's cologne on their hair."

Oh, he sure ticked them off. I didn't know America had so many smells and sights and sounds. He had them all on his tongue—in his heart, too, I guess. Before I left I went out to the car and got a copy of *Look Homeward, Angel* I'd brought with me, and asked him to autograph it. It was half a trick to catch him out, and half wanting to please him.

"I don't autograph my books," he said. "It gives books a false value too often. I want mine liked for what they say. But I'd be glad to write your name in it." He stood staring out the window for a minute, then he gave me a kind of amused look and wrote, "For Mike Madden who values good writing." But he didn't sign his name.

That was in April—and I thought about that guy off and on all summer. When I'd be talking textbooks to some principal I'd be thinking about that Sterling—what'd he get out of a racket like that— what was there in it for him? I still figured he was a phony and I still wanted to catch him out—but somehow I'd got to respecting the guy. He was sure going to a lot of trouble to be what he'd dreamed about. He must have spent half his nights after he was through working on his grapes copying Tom Wolfe in those big ledgers. He was kind of like a religious, I figured. A real religious. Not one of these dames who go to prayer meeting and sing "I Want to Be like Jesus," and let the matter drop there—this Sterling set right out to be the guy he wanted to be like. I was ready to hand it to him for doing what he was and handling it the way he was—never letting himself be cornered.

In September, just after the schools had reopened, I was back up north, checking over the spring orders with the principals, seeing if enrollments had picked up, new classes been added and so forth. On the sixteenth I was in Ukiah. It was a hot dry morning and I was having breakfast in the William Tell Hotel where I always stay, and hating to go out of the air-conditioned grill into the heat, so I was reading the *Chronicle* through pretty thoroughly, postponing the minute. Otherwise I probably would have missed it—a little article saying Thomas Wolfe had died the day before, in Baltimore I think it was. Dead. It didn't seem possible. That big, black fellow, so in love with all that had to do with living—food, women, the sound of trains in the night, the oceans washing against the shores of America, the names of our rivers. Dead and gone to dust—no more words to write. I looked out into the sunlit street with a sad, empty feeling in the pit of my stomach.

Then I remembered Sterling, the phony Wolfe. Say, I thought, how's he going to explain this? Ukiah's only about twenty miles from Burley—so I got right in my car and drove over to find out. On my way over there I had it doped out what Sterling was going to say—that he had decided he'd written himself out in the vein of Thomas Wolfe— that he wanted to begin again—not to be saddled with Wolfe's fame or manner. That he'd told his publishers to announce that he was dead so he could start over—be a new and different funnel through which America could pour. Then, I thought, after a while he'd identify himself with the first guy who published a promising novel. I didn't think he'd say this last—but that's the way I thought he'd have it planned.

I kept an eye on the vineyard as I drove up to Sterling's place. It was picking season and I thought he might be at work. But there wasn't any work going on at his place, so I drove straight to the house. Nobody answered my knock and I figured he'd probably taken a load of grapes down to the winery. I tried the door anyway. I wanted another peek at that Tom Wolfe stage set.

I got it—and I got more than I'd figured on. There was Sterling himself stretched out on the studio couch. Opening the door turned a whole shaft of light on him. I thought he was asleep, until I walked over to him, laid a hand on him. He was dead—stone dead, and cold as a stone, too.

Believe me, I didn't lose any time putting in a call for the coroner and the county sheriff. While I was waiting for them I had a good look around. Looked to see if there wasn't a morning paper there with a notice of Wolfe's death—but I couldn't find a thing.

On the floor by the couch Sterling was on was one of the big ledgers—face down, and on top of it Wolfe's *The Story of a Novel*, and a fountain pen. It looked like the fellow had been copying the stuff when he died.

I stayed in Burley until the autopsy was over. I had to—since I'd found the body, but I wanted to anyway. I supposed the guy had killed himself—couldn't stand the letdown of not being Wolfe. But the coroner said "no"—"death by natural causes."

Tidy and I talked it over afterward in Babe's. Tidy said, "You hear the coroner says he'd been dead approximately twenty-four hours when you found him?"

"Judas Priest," I said, "you mean he died about the time Wolfe did?"

"I figure it was about the exact time," Tidy said.

"What do you make of it, Tidy?" I asked. I expected him to ring in his old line about the importance of words and so forth. But Tidy just shook his head. He just wrinkled up his long Irish lip and looked far away. "I dunno," he said. "I wouldn't know. How about having a glass of dry sherry?"

What I wanted in that heat was a beer, but I said, "OK, dry sherry for me." Maybe this was just a case to remember, not explain.

Tidy lifted his glass and said, "Their million-footed roots, their million-fingered tendrils."

# Learn to Say Good-bye

JOHN THOMAS had awakened thinking of Curly—or, rather, when he woke up, he did not stop thinking of Curly, for all night he had been with the young steer, encouraging him, patting him on his curling forelock, leading him before the admiring judges. The boy was wide awake now, yet Curly's image was still as strongly with him as in the dream—the heavy shoulders, the great barrel, the short legs, the red coat shining with health and with the many brushings John Thomas had given it. And Curly's face! The boy's own face crinkled happily as he thought of it, and then turned scornful as he thought of the people who said one baby beef was just like another. Curly looked at you with intelligence. His eyes weren't just hairless spots on his head, like the eyes of most baby beeves. They showed that Curly knew when eating time had come and that he understood the difference between being told he was a lazy old cuss and a prize-winning baby beef. You had only to say to him, "You poor old steer," and he put his head down and looked at you as much as to say he knew it was true and not to kid him about it. John Thomas remembered a hundred humors and shrewdnesses of Curly's, and lay in bed smiling about them—the way he had of getting the last bite of mash out of his feed pail, and his cleverness in evading the vet, and how he would lunge at Wolf when the collie barked at him.

"This is the day!" John Thomas said aloud. "This is the day!"

Across the hall came a girl's sleepy voice. "Johnny, you promised to be quiet."

John Thomas didn't answer. No use arguing with Jo when she was sleepy. He sat up and slipped his arms into the sleeves of his bathrobe, and then stepped onto the floorboards, which were so much cooler than the air, and walked slowly, because he wanted so much to walk fast, to the window.

There Curly was, standing with his nose over the corral fence look-

76

ing up toward John Thomas's window. Curly acts as if he knows, the boy thought. I bet he does know.

"Hey, Curly!" he said softly. "How you feel this morning? Feel like a prize baby beef? Feel like the best steer in California? First prize for Curly?" Curly swished his tail. "Don't you worry, Curly. You *are* the best."

John Thomas knew he was going to have to go in and talk to Jo, even though she'd be mad at being waked so early. If he stood another minute looking at Curly—so beautiful in his clean corral, with the long blue early-morning shadows of the eucalyptus falling across it—and listening to the meadow larks off in the alfalfa and remembering that this was the day, he'd give a whoop, and that would make both Jo and Pop mad. He tiptoed across the hall, opened his sister's door, and looked at her room with distaste. Grown-up girls like Jo, almost twenty, ought to be neater. All girls ought to be neater. The clothes Jo had taken off before she went to sleep made a path from her door to the bed, starting with her shoes and hat and ending with her underwear. Curly's corral's neater, he thought, and said, "It's time to get up, Jo!"

Jo rolled over on her face and groaned. John Thomas stepped over Jo's clothes and sat down on the edge of the bed.

Jo groaned again. "*Please* don't wake me up yet, Johnny," she said.

"You're already awake. You're talking."

"I'm talking in my sleep."

"I don't care if you don't wake up, if you'll talk. I've seen Curly already. He looks pretty good. He looks like he know's it's the day."

"He's dead wrong, then. It's still the night."

John Thomas laughed. If he got Jo to arguing, she'd wake up. "It's six o'clock," he said.

Jo, still face down, raised herself on one elbow and looked at her wristwatch. Then she whirled onto her back, stuck one leg out from under the sheet, and gave her brother a kick that set him down on the floor with a thud. "Why, John Thomas Hobhouse!" she said indignantly. "It's only five-fifteen and Nicky didn't get me home until two. You're so kind to that damned old steer of yours, but you don't care whether your own sister gets any sleep or not."

John Thomas bounced back onto the bed. Jo looked at him sharply and he knew what was to come.

"What have you got on under that bathrobe, John Thomas Hobhouse?" she demanded. "Did you sleep in your underwear last night?"

"I slept in my shorts."

"That's a filthy thing to do."

"You say it's filthy if I don't wear them in the daytime and filthy if I do wear them at night. What's daylight or dark got to do with it? Now, if I—"

"Look, Johnny, let's not get started on that. There are some things you're going to have to do that aren't reasonable. Once school starts, you'll be spending some nights with the other boys, and their mothers will be saying I don't look after you, and let you sleep in your underwear."

"I don't do it away from home, Jo, but it was so hot last night. You tell Mrs. Henny to do my ducks up special for today? Boy, wait till you see me and Curly go by the grandstand! Wait till you see us in the ring when Curly wins!"

"When Curly wins! Maybe he won't win, Johnny."

"Maybe the judges *won't* see he's best—but they will if they're any good."

John Thomas lay on his stomach, hanging his head over the edge of the bed until his long pompadour spread out on the floor like a dust mop and his face was out of Jo's sight. "I prayed about today," he said.

"Did you, Johnny?"

"Yep, but I didn't think it was fair to pray for Curly to win." He heaved himself up and down, so that his hair flicked back and forth across the floor. "A lot of kids probably did pray they'd win, though."

Jo regarded him with tenderness and amazement. "I never would have thought most of the kids who go to the fair had ever heard of praying," she said.

"Oh, sure, they all heard of it," Johnny said. "And when it comes to something important like this, they all think you ought to try everything. But I didn't ask for Curly to win. I just prayed the judges would be good and know their stuff. If they do, Curly will get the blue ribbon, all right. With everyone else asking to win, I thought maybe that would kind of make an impression on God."

It made an impression on Jo. Lord, she thought, I'm a heathen. "What do you care whether or not Curly wins, if you know he's best?" she asked.

John Thomas heaved his head and shoulders up onto the bed and lay on his stomach with his face near Jo's. "How can you wear those tin things in your hair?" he asked. Then he answered her question. "I know for sure Curly's best, but *he* don't. He knows he's good, but he don't know he's that good. I want him to win so he can have the blue ribbon on his halter and walk up in front of the people while all the other baby beeves watch him."

"You going to walk with him, kid?" Jo asked.

"Yep, I got to."

"Kinda nice to have the other kids watch, too."

This slyness tickled John Thomas and he laughed. No use trying to fool Jo about anything. "Anyway, it's mostly Curly," he said.

Jo started taking the curlers out of her hair. She tucked them, one by one, into Johnny's bush of hair as she took them out. "Remember when Curly got bloated?" she asked. "You weren't much help then. You cried and didn't want the vet to stick him."

"Yeah, but, Jo, it looked so awful. To take a knife and stick it inside him. And Curly was so darned scared." He spoke dreamily, with the satisfaction and relief of dangers past. "He looked like he was going to have a calf, didn't he? And I guess it hurt more."

"Yep, Johnny. A cow's made to have a calf, but a steer isn't made to have gas. Hand me my comb. Top left-hand drawer."

John Thomas got up and stood looking at himself in the mirror. His hair was thick enough to keep the curlers from dropping out.

"You look like an African Bushman," Jo said. "Come on, get that comb."

When John Thomas handed it to her, she began loosening her sausagelike curls. He watched her turn the fat little sausages into big frankfurters.

"Time to get dressed, kid," she said. "Jump into your ducks. They're all done up fresh and hanging in your closet."

"Do you think I've been giving him too much mash, Jo?" Johnny asked. "Does he look kind of soft to you? Too fat?"

"He looks just right to me. But it's all over now. No use worrying any more. This time tomorrow, he'll be someone else's problem."

John Thomas sat down on the windowsill and looked out at the tank house. The sunlight lay on it in a slab as heavy and yellow as a bar of naphtha soap. There was already a dance of heat out across the alfalfa fields. White clouds were boiling up from behind purple Tahquitz. The morning glories were beginning to shut themselves against the sun. This was the day all right, but he could not think ahead until tomorrow, when Curly would have been sold.

The boy made the width of the room in three jackrabbit hops, and banged on the door behind him.

Jo swung herself out of her bed and her nightgown in a single looping movement and stood before her mirror. I guess it's hell to be thirteen and not have a mother, and to love a steer that's going to be beefsteak in forty-eight hours, she thought somberly. I ought to take better care of Johnny, and Dad ought to wake up from remembering Mother. He's been that way ever since she died.

But the air flowed like liquid silk about her naked body, and she lifted her arms and tautened her body, thinking no longer of John Thomas but of Nicky. She regarded her image with affection and pride. I don't know where I would change it, she thought. The sound of Johnny's leaps down the stairs—four house-shuddering thuds— and his cracked voice calling out to Mrs. Henny made her look at her watch. Almost six. Jo grabbed fresh underwear from the drawer and ran for the bathroom.

When Jo came downstairs, ten minutes later, all dressed except for putting on the scarf and belt that were hanging over her shoulders, she saw her father seated at the table on the screened porch where they ate breakfast in summer and reading the morning paper. She was fond of her father, but in one respect he was unsatisfactory: She didn't like his appearance. He didn't look fatherly to her. There wasn't any gray in his black hair or any stoop to his shoulders, and her girl-friends exasperated her by saying, "I could go for your old man."

He called to her now, "Tell Mrs. Henny we're ready to eat."

Jo went through the porch door into the sunny kitchen, where Mrs. Henny was slicing peaches for breakfast. She was already dressed for the fair, in a lavender dotted swiss with a lavender ribbon through her bobbed gray hair. "Hello, Mrs. Henny," Jo said. "Dad says let's eat. Gee, you look swell!"

"I thought I'd better wear something light," Mrs. Henny said. "It's going to be hot as a little red wagon today. Take these peaches out with you. Time you've finished them, everything else will be ready."

Jo stopped to buckle on her belt and tie her scarf. Then she took the peaches out to the porch. Her father put the Los Angeles *Times* under his chair and took his dish of peaches out of her hand. "Well, Josephine," he said, "considering you only had three hours' sleep last night, you don't look so bad."

"You hear me come in?"

"Nope, but I heard that fellow drive away. He ran into everything loose and bangable on the place. What's wrong with him?"

"Blind with love, I guess," Jo said lightly.

Her father held his third spoonful of sugar poised over his peaches. "I take it that you have no impairment in your eyesight," he said.

"Things look a little rosy, but the outline's still plain, I think."

Mrs. Henny came in with the eggs and bacon and muffins. "I don't want to hurry you," she said, pausing, on her way out, at the kitchen door, "but it's not getting any earlier."

"Where did Johnny go?" Jo asked. "He ought to be eating. He'll be sick this afternoon if he doesn't eat." She took two muffins, buttered them, and put them on Johnny's plate.

"He's out talking to Curly. You'd better call him."

"Dad, what's Johnny going to do about not having Curly any more after today?" Jo asked. "You know he acts as if Curly were a dog—or a brother."

"Oh, Johnny's all right. He knows what the score is," her father said, with his mouth full of muffin and scrambled eggs. "But call him, call him. We've less than an hour to eat and load the steer. I ought to have taken him down last night, but John Thomas was afraid Curly would look peaked today if he spent a night away from home."

"Remember John Thomas's kitten?"

"Kitten?" said her father grumpily. "He's had a dozen."

"This was the one he had when he broke his leg. Don't you remember? He said, 'Let's never let her see herself in a mirror, and then she'll think she's just like us, only smaller.' He's that way about Curly now, you know. He never lets Curly know there's any other difference than size between them."

"Doesn't he know where Curly'll be tomorrow?"

"He *must* know it, but he hasn't felt it yet."

"Well, call him, call him," her father said. He got up from the table and stood with his back to her. "He can't learn to say good-bye any earlier."

He's thinking of Mama, Jo thought, and walked slowly out through the screen door and down the steps into the sunshine, eating a muffin-and-bacon sandwich as she went. She stopped at the foot of the steps to pick up the cat, and balanced him, heavy and purring, on her shoulder, and let him lick the last of the muffin crumbs from her fingers. "Oh, Nicky, Nicky," she murmured, pressing her face close against the cat's soft, furry side. Then she saw Johnny, sitting hunched up on the top rail of the corral, looking at Curly. "Well, Bud," she called out, "he looks like silk!"

"He's kind of rough on the left flank," Johnny said as she came and stood beside him. "Been rubbing against something. Can you notice it? I been working on it."

"Can't see a thing," Jo said. "Now, look here, John Thomas, you're going to make him nervous, sitting there staring at him—give him the jitters before he ever gets to the fair. You'll spoil his morale. Dad let you keep him here till this morning when he didn't want to, so don't you gum things up now."

John Thomas slid to the ground. "So long, Curly," he said. "I got to eat now." And he ran for the house.

A little before eight, they all drove into Verdant, the county seat—Mr. Hobhouse and Mrs. Henny and Jo and Johnny in the car, and Curly in the trailer behind them. "Awnings up early this morning," said Mr. Hobhouse as they moved slowly forward in the already long line of cars. "Going to be a scorcher, I guess. Flags look dead when there isn't any wind, don't they?"

Jo, who was riding beside her father in the front seat, nodded, but nothing looked dead to her. She loved the beginning-again look of a town in the morning—the sidewalks sluiced down, the vegetables fresh and shining, the storekeepers in clean shirts, the feeling that nothing that had been spilled or broken or hurt or wronged the day before need be carried over into the new day. The heat made her sleepy, and because she wouldn't be seeing Nicky until evening, the day seemed dreamlike, unimportant. She would move through it, be kind to Johnny, and wait for evening and Nicky again. Her father swerved sharply to avoid hitting a car that had swung, without signaling, out of the line of cars heading for the fair.

"Hey, Pop, take it easy!" John Thomas yelled anxiously from the backseat, where he sat with Mrs. Henny. "You almost busted Curly's ribs then."

"John Thomas ought to be riding back there with that steer," declared Mrs. Henny. "Or else I wish I could have rid in the trailer and the steer could have set here with John Thomas. The boy hasn't done a thing since we started but put his feet in my lunch basket and squirm, till I've got a rash watching him."

"Hold out five minutes longer, both of you, and we'll be there," Mr. Hobhouse said.

Jo roused herself, lifted her eyelids, which seemed weighed down with the heat, and turned around. "Hi ya, Johnny," she murmured.

As soon as they were well inside the fairgrounds, her father maneuvered out of the line of cars and stopped. "Jo, you and Mrs. Henny had better get out here," he said. "It'll take me and Johnny some time to get Curly unloaded."

As Jo climbed out, John Thomas touched her arm. "You'll sure be there, won't you, Sis?" he asked.

"Where?"

"In the grandstand for the parade at ten-thirty. All the baby beeves."

"Johnny, where'd you think I'd be then? Looking at the pickle exhibit, maybe? Of course I'll be there. Just you and Curly listen when you go by the stand. You'll hear me roar."

"Hurry up, you two," said her father. "It's getting late."

"When's the judging, Johnny?" Jo asked.

"Two-thirty. Front of the Agriculture Pavilion," he replied.

"I'll see you then. Don't worry. I think the judges are going to know their business." She poked a finger through the trailer's bars and touched Curly. "So long, Curly. You do your stuff!"

Her father edged the car and trailer back into the line of traffic. Mrs. Henny lumbered off, with a campstool on one arm and the lunch basket on the other, and Jo was left alone. The day was already blistering and she was glad. She took no pleasure in a moderately warm day, but a record breaker, one that challenged her ability to survive, elated her. She went into one of the exhibition buildings and walked through acres of handiwork, wondering if she would ever find life so empty that she would need to fill it with the making of such ugly and useless articles. Children whimpered as mothers jerked them doggedly through the heat. Oh, Nicky, I promise you never to be like them, Jo thought.

She was in the grandstand at ten-thirty when a voice from the loudspeaker announced, "Ladies and gentlemen! The Future Farmers of Riverbank County and their baby beeves will now pass in front of the grandstand for your inspection. At two-thirty, the final judging will take place in front of the Agriculture Pavilion, and after that the steers will be auctioned to the highest bidders. I'm proud to announce that there isn't a first-rate hotel in Los Angeles that hasn't a representative here to bid on one or more of these famous Riverbank beeves. There they come now, ladies and gentlemen, through the west gate. Let's give them a big hand—the Future Farmers of Riverbank County!"

Jo craned forward to watch the long line of steers and boys move proudly in review before the grandstand. The steers were mostly Herefords, shining like bright-russet leather in the blazing sun. Jo had not realized how thoroughly John Thomas had convinced her of Curly's superiority. She looked down the long line, expecting Curly, by some virtue of size or spirit, to be distinct from all the others.

A woman leaned heavily against her to nudge a friend in the row below them. "There they are!" she said excitedly.

Jo followed their glances before it occurred to her that they were not talking about John Thomas and Curly. Finally, she saw them, well along toward the end of the line, the steer like the other red steers, the boy like the other white-clothed boys. But unlike, too, for surely no other boy walked with the sensitive, loving pride of her brother. Then she saw that Johnny was the only boy who did not lead his animal by a halter or rope. He walked beside Curly, with only a hand on his neck. Idiot, thought Jo, he's put something over on somebody; he ought not to be doing that.

She stood up and, to fulfill her promise, shouted, over and over, "Hi, Johnny! Hi, Curly!" until a man behind her jerked her skirt and said, "Sit down, Sis, you're not made of cellophane."

After the boys and the steers had circled the grandstand and passed through the west gate again and out of sight, Jo closed her eyes and half slept, hearing as in a dream the announcement of the next event. She fully awakened, though, when someone wedged himself into the narrow space that separated her from the stair railing on her right.

"Dad! Where did you come from?" she exclaimed.

"I was up above you," her father said. "Well, the boy's having his day. You're half asleep, Jo."

"More than half. Where's the car? I think I'll go and sleep in it until the judging. I've seen all the Yo-yo pillows and canned apricots I can take in one day."

"I don't know whether you can find the car or not," her father said. "It's over in the first nine or ten rows of the cars back of the dining tents. Here's the key, and don't forget to lock it when you leave."

Jo slept for a long time, doubled up on the backseat of the car, and then awakened with a sudden sick start. She seemed to be drowning in heat, and the velours of the seat she was sleeping on were a quicksand that held her down. She looked at her watch and saw with consternation that it was after four o'clock.

She had a long way to go to reach the Agriculture Pavilion, and because she was so angry with herself and still so sleepy, she ran clumsily, bumping into people. I'm so full of fair promises, she accused herself bitterly, and now I've let poor Johnny down. She wanted to hurt herself running—punish herself—and she finally reached the Pavilion with a sick, cutting pain in her side and a taste of sulphur in her throat. A deep circle of onlookers stood around the judging ring, laughing and talking quietly. At last, she saw Johnny and her father in the front line of the circle, a little to her left. Paying no heed to the sour looks she got, she pushed her way to them. John Thomas saw what she had done and frowned. "You oughtn't to do that, Jo," he said. "People'll think we can get away with anything just because we own the winner."

"Has Curly won already?" Jo asked.

"No, not yet," Johnny said. "Couldn't you see the judging where you were?"

"Not very well," Jo said. "No, I couldn't see a thing."

She looked now at the animals that were still in the ring, and saw that Curly was there with three other Herefords and an enormous black Angus. He was wearing a halter now, and one of the judge's assistants was leading him. Unless one of the five steers had a cast in his eye or a tick in his ear, Jo did not see how any man living could say that one was an iota better than another. She knew the points in judging as well as Johnny himself; she had stood by the corral many half hours after breakfast while Johnny recounted them for her, but while she knew them well, her eye could not limn them out in the living beasts.

"Why're you so sure Curly will win?" she asked Johnny.

"Higgins said he would."

"Who's Higgins?"

Johnny shook his head, too absorbed to answer her question. The judge, an old, bowlegged fellow in a pale blue sweater, had stopped examining the animals and was reading over some notes he had taken on the back of a dirty envelope. He walked over for another look at the Angus. Seemingly satisfied by what he saw, he took off his gray felt hat and with the back of his hand wiped away the sweat that had accumulated under the sweatband. He set his hat on the back of his head, stuffed his envelope in a hip pocket, stepped to the edge of the ring, and began to speak.

"Ladies and gentlemen, it gives me great pleasure to be able to announce to you the winner of the Eighteenth Annual Riverbank Baby Beef Contest."

There was a hush as the spectators stopped talking, and Jo tried to find in her father's face some hint of what he thought the decision would be. She saw nothing there but concern. Johnny, though, had a broad and assured smile. His eyes were sparkling; the hour of Curly's recognition had come.

"And I may say," continued the judge, enjoying the suspense he was creating, "that in a lifetime of cattle judging I have never seen an animal that compares with today's winner."

The fool, thought Jo, the damn fool orator! What's got into him? They never do this. Why can't he speak out?

But Johnny looked as if he enjoyed it, as if he knew whose name would be announced when people's ears had become so strained to hear it that it would seem to be articulated not by another's lips but by their own heartbeats.

"The winner, ladies and gentlemen, is that very fine animal, John Thomas Hobhouse's Hereford, Curly!" said the judge.

There was a lot of good-natured hand clapping. A few boys yelled "Nerts!" but the choice was popular with the crowd, most of whom knew and liked the Hobhouses. The judge went on to name the second- and third-prize winners and the honorable mentions. Then he called out, "I would like to present to you Curly's owner, John Thomas Hobhouse himself. Come take a bow, Johnny!"

Jo was proud of the easy, happy way Johnny ran over to his side. The judge put out a hand intended for the boy's shoulder, but before it could settle there, Johnny was pressing his cheek against Curly's big, flat jowl. The steer seemed actually to lower his head for the caress and to move his cheek against Johnny's in loving recognition. This delighted the spectators, who laughed and cheered again.

"Now, ladies and gentlemen, the show's almost over," said the judge. "Only one thing left—the auctioning of these animals—and, believe you me, the enjoyment you've had here is nothing to the enjoyment you're going to have when you bite into one of these big, juicy baby beefsteaks. Now if you'll all just clear the ring. Ladies and gentlemen, may I present that silver-tongued Irish auctioneer, Terence O'Flynn. Terence, the show is all yours."

The non-prize winners were disposed of first and in short order. They fetched fancy prices, but nothing like what would be paid for the prize winners. The big Los Angeles hotels and the Riverbank Inn liked to be able to advertise "Steaks from Riverbank's Prize Baby Beeves." Jo felt sick at her stomach during the auction. This talk of club steaks and top sirloins seemed indecent to her, in front of animals of whom these cuts were still integral parts. But Johnny seemed unaffected by the auction. "Bet you Curly will get more than that," he said whenever a high price was bid.

"He'll fetch top price," his father answered him shortly. "You'll have a big check tonight, besides your blue ribbon, Johnny." The prize winners were auctioned last. All of them except Curly went to Los Angeles hotels, but the Riverbank Inn, determined not to let outside counties get all the prize winners, bid Curly in for itself.

"I'm not a Riverbank citizen," boomed O'Flynn, "but I don't mind admitting, folks, that I'm going to come back the day my good friend Chef Rossi of the Riverbank Inn serves steak from Curly. I know that baby beef is going to yield juices that haven't been equaled since Abel broiled the first steak. If *I* was young Hobhouse, I'd never sell that animal. I'd barbecue it and pick its bones myself."

Most of the animals had already been led into slaughterhouse vans and trucks, and the rest were being quickly loaded. A van belonging to Mack's Market, the Riverbank Inn's butchers, backed up to the ring, which now held only Curly and the Angus. As O'Flynn finished speaking, two young fellows in jumpers marked "Mack's" leaped out and came over to give Curly a congratulatory pat before sending him up the runway.

"Well, kid," one said pleasantly to John Thomas, "you got a fine animal here."

Johnny didn't hear him. He was looking at O'Flynn, hearing those last words of his.

Now it's come, thought Jo. Now he's really taken in what he's been preparing Curly for. Now he knows for the first time. Don't look that way, Johnny, she pleaded silently. Oh Johnny, you *must* know you can't keep Curly—you can't keep a fat pet steer.

But Johnny didn't smile. He walked over and stood with one arm about Curly's neck, staring incredulously at O'Flynn. "Nobody's going to pick Curly's bones," he said to the auctioneer. Then he turned to the steer. "Don't you worry, Curly. That guy hasn't got anything to do with you."

There was a sympathetic murmur among the bystanders. "The poor kid's made a pet of him," one man said. "Too bad. Well, he can't learn any earlier."

The men from Mack's Market tried to take the matter rightly. "Look here, Bud," said one of them. "Get yourself a canary. This steer don't want to be nobody's pet. He wants to be beefsteaks." And he put a hand on Curly's halter.

Johnny struck it down. "Don't touch Curly!" he shouted. "He's going home, where he belongs! He's won the prize! That's all he came here to do!"

The circle of onlookers came closer, augmented by passers-by whose ears had caught in Johnny's voice the sound of passion and hurt. The buzzards, Jo thought. She saw Johnny press himself still more closely against Curly, keeping his eyes all the time on O'Flynn. She gripped her father's arm. "Dad, do something!" she cried. "Let Johnny take Curly home. There's plenty of food and room. Johnny wouldn't feel this way about him except for you and me. It's our fault!" She was half crying.

"Yes, this nonsense can't go on," her father agreed, and went quickly over to Johnny.

Jo couldn't hear what he said or see his face, for he stood with his back to her, but she could see Johnny's face, and its anguish and disbelief. At last, the boy turned and threw both arms around Curly's neck and buried his face against the steer's heavy muscles. Jo saw his thin shoulder blades shaking.

When her father turned and came toward her, eyes to the ground, she found she could not say to him any of the bitter things that had been on her tongue's tip.

"Dad," she said, and put her hand out to him.

"There's no use, Jo."

"But he loves Curly so."

"Oh, love!" her father said, and then added more quietly, "It's better to learn to say good-bye early than late, Jo."

"I'm going to the car," Jo said, and she turned and ran blindly through the crowd. Because Dad's had to learn, why must Johnny, she thought bitterly.

She got into the front seat and leaned across the wheel, without any attempt to stop crying. Then, as the sobs let up, she pounded the wheel. "No, sir!" she said aloud. "I *won't* learn! I refuse to learn! I'll be an exception."

# A Little Collar for the Monkey

IT WAS THURSDAY, the day the fish wagon came by, so old Mrs. Prosper shouted from her bed to her daughter in the room next to hers, "Thursday, Lily, fish day!"

The strength of her shouting lifted her momentarily above her pillows, and she sank back pleasurably, awaiting a reply. The sun was just up but it was not rising on a world in any way strange to it. It was rolling back into its own heat, heat left over from the day before. It was moving across the sky in a blaze of its own redness, mounting a streak of crimson spread out above it like a length of welcoming carpet. Outside in the growing light the birds, who for two hours had been whetting and sharpening their already thin, sharp little voices, now cut the air with razor strokes of sound.

"Poor fools," wise old Mrs. Prosper addressed them, "poor fools."

Two more hours and sparrow and linnet, towhee and mockingbird would be sitting in the umbrella tree's deepest shadow, wings extended, mouths gaping, and tongues—dry from singing and heat— shrunk to the size of little black basting threads. They would then drop down to the hydrant, dripping inside the circle of ferns, to lick up a warm drop or two.

"Poor fools," said Mrs. Prosper. "Not the least idea in the world what's good for you. Screeching now because the sun's up—and in two hours it will have you parched to the bone. Poached like eggs, and willing to pay money to be rid of your feathers."

Mrs. Prosper, herself old, thin, and unfeathered, enjoyed the heat. She let one foot dangle out from under the single sheet which covered her until it touched the uncarpeted floorboards. The floorboards were still warm from yesterday's heat, and the feel of that lingering warmth excited Mrs. Prosper. A small ripple shook her, as if she had been some variety of electrical mechanism suddenly enjoying the shock of a propulsive voltage. Be a scorcher today, she thought, be a record breaker—but probably not, she concluded. Nature continually disappointed Mrs. Prosper. It seemed capable of so much variety and actually was so repetitious. Mrs. Prosper was always searching for a wildness, a violence, nature never provided. A strangeness which any day might by very simple means provide: let only the sun reverse itself, or flowers fly; let fish sing or rain fall upward. That would do it. The possibilities were endless. Life might easily be exciting, strange, and awesome; as it was, everything was in a rut. Spring, summer, winter, fall. First the bud and then the blossom. First the egg and then the bird. And then the song at sunup. "Poor fools," said Mrs. Prosper, listening.

Mrs. Prosper wasted very little time wondering about who was at the helm of the world, who ordered matters thus tamely. That someone was there she took for granted; she wasn't a fool, only imaginative. But she had long ago concluded that it was someone either dozing or unaware of the possibilities; someone, at least, totally unlike herself.

She herself, limited as she was, had gone out one spring, when the apricot trees were smaller, and had broken from one of the sturdiest trees every single bud and blossom. Painstakingly, every one. Then, when the trees all about it had been heavy with fruit, she had been pleased to stand beside it noting its peculiarity and bareness: full of heart-shaped, shining leaves, a perfect bower of greenness, but no fruit. Looking at it, she had felt full of power and accomplishment.

"What do *you* make of it?" she would inquire, addressing it, her tree, her handiwork, turned in a direction quite opposite from what nature had intended.

Her husband, then alive, had also looked at her tree, though with no notion it was hers. "An odd business," he had said. "Gopher at the roots, maybe. Possibly gum disease."

"Possibly," Mrs. Prosper, not then old, had replied. "But it looks healthy, doesn't it? Green and flourishing."

Mr. Prosper had laid a hand on the puce-colored bark, like a father testing his child's temperature. "It does," he agreed. "It does for a fact. I can't figure it out."

"Can't you, Enos?" asked Mrs. Prosper.

"It's a mystery to me," he said, feeling and touching.

"A mystery," said Mrs. Prosper.

She liked her husband well enough, considering she despised him. But then, whom did she not despise? She could have respected only a man capable of looking at her and saying, "You don't for a minute fool me." And there had never been anyone to say that. And for her, a woman alive in a world in a rut and among men without insight, Enos Prosper was as good a man as any other and better than many.

They had walked back to the house together. "Next year I'll make it bloom and bear," she had said.

Her husband took her hand. He kissed the fingers that had broken off the buds. "I believe you could," he said. For Mrs. Prosper, who lived on irony, that was a dainty mouthful.

"Fool, fool," she said now, coming near enough the edge of her bed to rest the whole of her foot upon the floorboards, whose warmth, retained from yesterday, promised still greater heat for the coming day. The words she spoke recalled her to the present, and she listened for a sound from her daughter's room. There was none.

"Thursday, Lily," she shouted again. "Fish day. Time to curl and primp." Again there was no answer, but there were now other sounds. A car down the road. A cock crowing. A faraway tractor. Bees in the Gold of Ophir rose which had laced itself among the limbs of the umbrella tree at the corner of the house.

"Get up," shouted Mrs. Prosper. "Rouse yourself, Lily, and make yourself pretty for the fishmonger."

Mrs. Prosper got out of her own bed and walked to the front window. She unlatched the hinged screen, swung it open, and leaned out into the morning air. "Be a furnace by noon," she speculated; but the rest of the world was disappointing. With the help of a half dollar and a matchbox a child could draw it; rounds, squares, and rectangles, that was the whole of it. Round sun, round sky, and apricots and their leaves nearly round. The road itself, in front of the house, a half circle, a tunnel of green under the wholly round umbrella trees: trees round as upturned green basins and chinked only enough to let sufficient light travel through. The ranches she looked out on were squares or rectangles, separated by a road or a row of standpipes. A world for a child to draw. But she herself, she thought, too complex for any such picturing.

She spread her unbleached muslin gown across the foot of the bed to air, walked to the old bureau, and saw herself in the mirror which was blurred with constellations and sunspots, pocked with moonlike craters. Gone sallow, gone stringy, but not flabby; tight in buttock and neat in breast; no one with a matchbox and a half dollar could draw her. She gave herself a smart slap and put on her wrapper. She lived inside herself as precisely as a walnut in its shell, nothing rattling, nothing wasting, rich and orderly, too tough a nut for time to crack.

"Get up, Lily," she called again in the hall, on her way to the bathroom. "Get up and slick yourself up for your fish peddler." But as she waited for a reply she heard Lily, already downstairs, bustling about in the kitchen.

Mrs. Prosper went down to breakfast, smooth and shiny as a beetle in her coal black; her gold brooch and earrings as many faceted as a beetle's eye in the morning light. She found the table already set in the breakfast room, and curtains already partly drawn against the heat. From beneath the curtains, bars of yellow light slanted down onto the rag rugs; but this light was only ankle deep; above the ankles the room was dusky. Hodge, the cat, lay on a windowsill, one ear cocked to follow the buzzings of a fly, self-conscious with being watched. Hodge was a fly trap more certain than Tanglefoot, more deadly than a Daisy Fly-Killer; and this lone survivor, having witnessed since sunup the engulfment of all his kind in the breakfast room, buzzed now a nervous swan song.

"Good morning, Hodge," said Mrs. Prosper. The marmalade-colored tom closed his yellow eyes.

In the dusk of the upper room Mrs. Prosper saw white sweet peas in a glass bowl on the center of the table, coffee already poured, dishes of strawberries, and a fringed napkin, covering, she knew, a plate of Lily's fine-grained scones.

Mrs. Prosper appreciated the scene, all of it, even the buzzing fly. It looks like a home, she thought. She imagined herself a stranger standing outside the windows and peering through the glass with a stranger's eyes. She saw how pleasant the surface was. It does look like a home, she thought, it looks like a nice breakfast, I look like a nice old lady come down to eat my breakfast; and Lily, there, pulling out my chair, looks like a daughter.

Only Mrs. Prosper had never been able to think of Lily as a daughter at all. She thought of her as a female relation, connected, but distantly, through Mrs. Prosper's mother's people. A niece or possibly a cousin of her mother's. Indeed, Lily looked so like Mrs. Prosper's mother that Mrs. Prosper sometimes had the feeling that she had spent her entire life with her mother, knowing her first as a mature woman and then, in Lily, as a child and a girl. Now, at forty, Lily was her mother as Mrs. Prosper best remembered her: the same soft, dun-colored hair looped back in the same aimless way; the same light brown eyes, faintly pink lips, and teeth that, curving inward, gave the mouth its peculiarly childlike look. Well fleshed, as her mother had been, but no muscles beneath the flesh, so that she was as soft to the touch as a handful of yarn. Always neat, always the same flowered dresses, white aprons, and black oxfords; shoes sensible of heel but so fancifully cut about the vamp that they contradicted everything else Lily wore.

"Good morning, Lily," said Mrs. Prosper seating herself in the chair that Lily pushed carefully in for her.

"Good morning, Mother," said Lily.

"I called you early this morning, Lily," said Mrs. Prosper. "Several times. At the top of my voice. No answer."

"I didn't hear you, Mother," said Lily. "I came downstairs early this morning."

"Then you did remember," said Mrs. Prosper. "Good. I didn't want you to oversleep."

Lily said nothing, but took the napkin from the scones and held the plate for her mother.

"Courted by a fish peddler," said Mrs. Prosper helping herself. "How does that seem?"

Lily put the napkin back over the scones and said nothing.

"Ah, well," said Mrs. Prosper, "it's an intimate subject. I don't blame you for not wanting to talk of it. What's his name again, by the way? I know, but I keep forgetting it."

"Olav," said Lily, "Olav Duun."

"Sounds like an owl hooting," observed Mrs. Prosper. "An old owl in the dead of night. He a foreigner?"

"He's Swedish," said Lily.

"He don't look it. Black. Black as soot and long mustaches like a catfish. I've heard that people who live a long time in China begin finally to look like Chinamen and that people in charge of the crazy begin after a while to look crazy themselves. Do you reckon if you sell fish long enough, you begin to look like a fish?" asked Mrs. Prosper.

"Olav hasn't sold fish for so very long," said Lily.

"He's made progress, then," declared Mrs. Prosper. "Whiskered like an old catfish already."

Lily, undisturbed, insofar as Mrs. Prosper could see, buttered a scone. "Courted by a Swedish fish peddler, name like an owl in the night! Has Hodge been fed this morning?" she asked, suddenly tiring of Lily's unresponsiveness.

"No," said Lily.

Mrs. Prosper took the saucer from under her coffee cup and half filled it with yellow cream. She handed the saucer to her daughter and Lily placed it on the sill beside the cat.

"Kit, kit, kit," said Mrs. Prosper. "Cream for breakfast."

Hodge turned his eyes for a moment away from the bemused fly, buzzing just now against the hot windowpane above his head.

"Cream," said Mrs. Prosper. "Thick cream!"

Hodge turned back to the window, with a sudden soft slap killed the sunstruck fly, and, negligently chewing it down, settled himself for sleep beside the untasted cream.

Mrs. Prosper laughed and struck her hands together. "Wonderful animals," she said, "wonderful Hodge." She glanced up at Lily and it was her mother who regarded her.

"The sugar, please, Lily," she said. She sprinkled sugar thickly over the big, deep red berries. "I remember picking strawberries once, when a girl. A day about like this."

"Yes, Mother," said Lily.

"I and a friend, a hulk of a girl, twice my size and a year or two older. Her name was Rose. Rose Vawters. Our mothers sent us over to a Jap's who had berries for sale. The berries were cheaper if you picked them yourself. It was a hot muggy day with gnats and the ground had been newly irrigated and wasn't nice to kneel on. 'You'll pick mine too,' I told Rose. 'Why?' she asked. 'My mother only

wants . . .' 'Don't talk,' I said. 'Pick.' She began to pick. 'Faster,' I
said, and she picked faster. I only nudged her with my toe now and
then, never kicked her or really hurt her. She was twice my size and
considerably older, but she picked all my berries. A bucket for each
of us. And she carried them home. 'Walk in a ditch,' I would say, and
she walked there. 'Hide,' I would say, 'you've stolen the berries,' and
she would hide. 'Lie flat on your stomach, they'll see you,' and she
would flatten herself in the slime of an empty irrigation ditch. 'Run,'
I would tell her, 'run, you're being chased,' and she would run. Pretty
fast too, though the berries were heavy and she wasn't slim herself.
I can still see her pounding down the road ahead of me, a berry jolt-
ing now and then out of the two full buckets she carried."

Mrs. Prosper finished her berries. "I never eat berries but I remember that morning. I've forgotten a lot of things that happened when I
was a girl . . . not that morning and how I felt. But I've told you
before, haven't I, Lily?"

"Yes, Mother," said Lily.

Mrs. Prosper noticed that her daughter had pushed her own berries aside and was looking at nothing, or possibly a crack in the floorboards or a spot on the wallpaper. "But you don't listen, do you, Lily?"
she asked.

After the breakfast work was finished Lily and her mother sat in
the shadowy, still-cool living room. Tightly closed as it was against
the heat, it smelled of furniture polish, of the acacia branches which
Lily put in the fireplace in summer to hide its reminder of heat and
burning, and of Hodge, the cat. The smell of Hodge was remarkably
like that of the Shasta daisies which, like spokes from a wheel, rayed
out from a bowl on the center table: a smell Mrs. Prosper had been
sampling since her youth, unable to decide whether it was good or
bad. On each side of the daisies were candles, which were not reminders of heat or burning since they had never been intended for
lighting. They were candles by reason of their being placed in can-
dlesticks. Actually, encrusted as they were with deep swirls of blue
and green paint, they more nearly resembled stalagmites rising upward from the gloom of the center table.

In this pleasant darkness Lily sat tatting, Mrs. Prosper buffing her
nails, Hodge watching the pendulum of the clock on the mantel-

piece, with its movement so like that of something which might be crushed and eaten. Lily's bobbin, as the thread left it, made a very light tick, the clock echoed it on deeper note, Mrs. Prosper's buffer went over the ridges of her old nails with a dry swish. Only Hodge was silent, his eyes following the pendulum, which he believed would sooner or later forget he was there, fly out from behind the glass that housed it, and finally slide, a round juicy mouthful, down his throat.

As the clock struck ten, Mrs. Prosper put down her buffer and listened. Within a few minutes, so faint that any other sound would have drowned it, came the tootle of a horn blown three times.

"There he is," said Mrs. Prosper. "The fishman. Right on time."

Lily paused for a minute in her tatting. Then her bobbin flew again.

"Ladies a quarter mile in each direction freshening themselves up," said Mrs. Prosper, "in order to be ready to buy a half pound of halibut."

"He blows it so they can have their money ready," Lily said, "and a pan to put the fish in."

"He tell you?" asked Mrs. Prosper.

"Yes," said Lily.

"Money and pan ready don't seem to speed him any here."

"He's polite," said Lily. "He thinks of more than selling. He likes to pass the time of day. He don't rush."

"No, he don't," said Mrs. Prosper. "Why don't you walk down a ways to meet him, Lily? He goes clear round the section before he gets here. You could ask him which fish were most tasty this week. Inquire if the sand dabs are up to par."

Lily's shuttle went perhaps a little faster but she said nothing.

"I will, then," said Mrs. Prosper. "I'd like a little ride. I'll catch him at the corner, ride round the section with him, ask him about his wares."

Mrs. Prosper put her buffer on the center table. "How is it exactly you say his name, Lily?"

"Duun," said Lily, "Olav Duun."

"Mr. Duun, I'll say, I've come to ride a ways with you."

That was what she did. She walked down the tunnel of green under the umbrella trees and caught Mr. Duun at the Burneys'. Mrs. Burney had just departed with her change and fish for the house. Mr. Duun stood at the back of his wagon, wiping out his scales.

"Mr. Duun," said Mrs. Prosper, "I've come to ride a ways with you."

"Duun's the name," said Mr. Duun without turning about.

"Duun," repeated Mrs. Prosper.

Mr. Duun gave his cleaver a final swipe, placed it in its rack, and closed the heavy doors of the truck upon his stock of fish.

"Hop in," he said.

Mrs. Prosper walked around to the right side of Mr. Duun's fish truck, climbed up and in, and closed the door behind her.

Mr. Duun, for whom the height of the running board had been less of an impediment than for Mrs. Prosper, was already in the cab, writing down his sales, when she got there. Without looking up he said, "Slam your door, otherwise it rattles."

"Slam it yourself," said Mrs. Prosper, settling comfortably back.

Mr. Duun did so. He reached across Mrs. Prosper, pencil still in hand, and banged the door. Then he went back to his totting up.

Mrs. Prosper watched him as he worked. In age, he was a man halfway between Lily and herself. It was untrue, what she had said about his mustache. The hairs about the mouth of a catfish are sparse, gray, and stiff. The hairs about Mr. Duun's mouth were thick, soft, and black. There was only something in the angle of their growth, their curve being long and downward, which had put her in mind of a catfish. There was no gray in either his mustache or his hair, which he wore roached back in an unstylish pompadour. From its bridge his nose ran along straight enough for two-thirds of its length, then splayed out, became thumb shaped. His eyes, Mrs. Prosper knew, were black; now, because he was looking downward and because they scarcely bulged his eyelids, they seemed very flat. He was olive skinned and smooth contoured, the smoothness being broken only by his cheekbones and full Adam's apple. He looked a good, craggy man to Mrs. Prosper, wearing a white apron and woven straw gauntlets on his wrists, as a fish peddler ought. His hands, busy with his writing, were perfectly clean except for a splash or two of fish blood.

"You wouldn't think fish peddling would take so much book work," said Mrs. Prosper.

"You know much about fish peddling, Mrs. Prosper?" asked Mr.

Duun closing his book and placing it in a little rack above his left shoulder.

"I know what I think," said Mrs. Prosper.

"Ah," stepping on the starter.

"Do you write down, five cents for a quarter of a pound of smelts sold to Mrs. Butts's cat on Thursday?" asked Mrs. Prosper.

"Sometimes less, sometimes more," said Mr. Duun swinging out onto the road.

"More?"

"A word about Mrs. Butts herself, and now and again a word about the cat."

"Have you ever put down a word about—us?"

"About your daughter."

"What did you say?"

Mr. Duun looked full at Mrs. Prosper, and she saw that his eyes were less flat than she had thought. "It slips my mind," he said.

Mr. Duun then picked up his horn, an ordinary cow horn it looked to Mrs. Prosper, silver tipped at the blowing end. Neatly parting his mustache with the tip, he blew three blasts, two short and one long.

"That like to burst my drums," said Mrs. Prosper.

"They tell me it'll carry a mile if the wind's right," Mr. Duun agreed.

While Mr. Duun sold fish at his next stop to the O'Toole sisters—two plump maiden ladies who brought him iced lemonade and warm spongecake to stay his midmorning hunger—Mrs. Prosper took a look at the cab of Mr. Duun's truck. It was thoroughly decorated. There were flowers painted on the glass of the dome light and a little vase in a bracket, the vase now filled with some wilting lop-headed fuchsias. There were tacked-up picture postcards, mostly of boats and harbors, and some oddments, unfamiliar to Mrs. Prosper but connected, she supposed, with either fishing or fish selling. There was even a motto of some kind, in a language Mrs. Prosper could not read, above the rearview mirror.

When Mr. Duun and the O'Toole sisters had concluded their considerable visit, and after Mr. Duun had written down whatever it was he did write down after such sales, Mrs. Prosper asked him about the motto.

"What language is that?" she asked.

"Swedish," replied Mr. Duun, putting his account book in its rack and his pencil behind his ear.

"It's a peculiar-looking language," said Mrs. Prosper.

"Not to Swedes," said Mr. Duun.

"So you're Swedish," said Mrs. Prosper.

Mr. Duun, busy backing his truck out of the O'Toole driveway, nodded.

"You don't look it."

Mr. Duun, now in the clear, replied, "The Lord must've thought so, otherwise he wouldnt've set me down among Swedes."

"The Lord makes mistakes."

Mr. Duun did not contradict this.

"How did you happen to come to America?"

"My ship put in here at a time when I'd decided I'd had enough of the sea. Time to learn something about the land."

"You a sailor?"

"I was."

"How'd you come to take to fish peddling?"

"Nearest there is to sailing. You move about and you move with fish. Nothing lacking but water and that was what I wanted to get away from."

Mr. Duun turned into the Smedleys' palm-lined driveway.

Mrs. Prosper, looking at the drawn blinds, the closed garage door, said, "No one home here."

"Home or not," said Mr. Duun, "every Thursday I put a lobster in the Smedley icebox."

When Mr. Duun returned from delivering this lobster, Mrs. Prosper handed him a silver-inlaid leather circlet, which she had lifted from a hook that also held a calendar, a good luck medal on a chain, and two brown shoelaces braided together.

"A nice piece of work," she said, "a pretty bracelet for a plump arm."

Mr. Duun turned the leather circlet about in his hands a time or two; then, lifting up his apron, he vigorously polished the silver work on his pants leg.

"It's a collar," said he.

"It'd take a skinny neck to fit that little circle."

"I made it for a skinny neck," said Mr. Duun, "and it fit to a T."

"You a silversmith, too?" Mrs. Prosper asked. While Mr. Duun's hands looked skillful enough to handle a fish knife, the silver work on the collar was fine and intricate—something beyond a mere fish carver.

"My father did the silver work. He was a farmer, and in the winters, when work was slack, he made collars—first for his own dogs and then for the dogs of all his neighbors, until finally he was as much a maker of dog collars as a farmer."

Mrs. Prosper took the collar from Mr. Duun and ran her fingers around its circumference. "Tiny little dogs you have in Sweden," she said.

"That was never made for a dog—it was made for a monkey."

"Where's the monkey?" asked Mrs. Prosper.

"You're ahead of the story," said Mr. Duun. "When I was twelve I got a piece of leather—that piece of leather," he said touching the collar Mrs. Prosper now held. "And I cut it just that size. When my father saw it he was just like you. 'Well, boy,' he said, 'what toy neck you planning to span with this collar, what lady's lap dog?' 'It's not for a dog,' I told him, 'it's for a monkey, a little collar for a monkey.' 'A monkey!' said my father. 'So you're going to sea,' for every sailor who came home to Göteborg, which was a port town, had his monkey with him."

"You were forehanded," said Mrs. Prosper. "A monkey collar at twelve."

"So my father said. But he helped me with the collar, set in all the silver work himself, though he was against my going and needed another hand on the farm. And when the day came for leaving—I was seventeen then—I was so excited I forgot all about my little collar. My father went up to my room, and fetched it down. He opened my bag, already strapped shut for my journey, and laid the collar inside. 'There's your little collar, son,' he said, 'And I hope you find a good little monkey to wear it.' "

"Did you?" asked Mrs. Prosper.

"No," said Mr. Duun. "I found a bitch of a monkey, a regular she-devil, the devil in monkey form maybe."

Mr. Duun reached over, took the collar out of Mrs. Prosper's hands,

and hung it once again on its peg. Then he started his motor and
backed out of the Smedleys' palm-lined driveway.

The fish truck, because of the amount of ice Mr. Duun carried,
was cooler than the air outside, but even so it was hot. Mrs. Prosper
could no more sweat than a stone, but she saw that Mr. Duun's olive
skin had become ruddy and that among the black hairs of his mustache fine beads of sweat glistened like little brilliants.

He turned left and right, and then into the green tunnel under the
umbrella trees. The little monkey collar swung back and forth with
the momentum of his turning.

"It doesn't appear to have been much used," observed Mrs. Prosper, watching it swing.

"Two weeks," said Mr. Duun. "We were two weeks out of Monte-
video when I took the collar off her neck and tossed her into the sea."

"Drowned?" said Mrs. Prosper.

"She asked for it," said Mr. Dunn. "She was vicious. She had bad
habits."

"So you drowned her," said Mrs. Prosper. A monkey's dying by
drowning seemed somehow stranger than if it had come to its death
from a blow on the head or a knife thrust.

"She drowned herself, I reckon," said Mr. Duun. "I only tossed her
over the rail. She clung to the rail, she clung to me. She knew what
was coming and she was suddenly loving. I threw her over and she
looked like a big black spider there on top of the water. She cried out,
too. Pitiful to hear, I suppose, if you hadn't known how she had asked
for it."        ·

Mr. Duun's recital was calm enough, like that of a law-respecting
judge summing up a case, but Mrs. Prosper's heart was beating faster.
She could see it all, very clearly. Mr. Duun, large, young then, handsome; though he was handsome now, for that matter. She could see
him take the collar from the monkey's neck and hand it to a fellow
sailor. And she could see the look in the monkey's eyes as he did
that, the foreknowledge, and the thin black hands on the rail, and
the little hands torn off, and the unbelief in the eyes as it fell, and
the desperate flailing as it tried for a time to regain the ship.

"Did you ever get another?" asked Mrs. Prosper.

"One was enough," said Mr. Duun.

Mrs. Prosper reached out and touched the collar. "But you kept the collar."

"So far I have," said Mr. Duun. "To remind me."

"Did you think as you watched it drowning," asked Mrs. Prosper, "Your monkey—did you think—monkey, you were born to live in a tree, but I've changed all that for you?"

"I did not," said Mr. Duun, who was now turning into the Prosper driveway.

"It would have been an interesting thing to see," Mrs. Prosper said as Mr. Duun brought his truck to a stop at the back steps of the Prosper house, "a monkey drowning in midocean. I wish I had been there."

Mr. Duun took his hands from the wheel and turned sideways so that he squarely confronted Mrs. Prosper. Sitting thus, he gave Mrs. Prosper the glance she had never before encountered, but which, now that she had received it, she felt she had spent a lifetime looking for. It was a glance of recognition. It took her all in. It missed nothing. Mr. Duun sat for quite some time in this way, gazing at Mrs. Prosper; then, slowly, he turned away, and after a few seconds or a few minutes—Mrs. Prosper was too shaken by the complete reflection and recognition she had seen in Mr. Duun's eyes to keep track of time—he spoke.

"What will you have today?" he asked in the same matter-of-fact tone he had used to describe the drowning of the monkey.

"Have?" repeated Mrs. Prosper, somewhat bewildered.

"What fish?" asked Mr. Duun. "I've got some nice halibut. Sea bass. Salmon. Barracuda."

Mrs. Prosper recalled herself. "No fish today, Mr. Duun," she said.

"No fish! Don't tell me, Mrs. Prosper, you ladies have lost your taste for fish!"

"Not I," declared Mrs. Prosper. "Not I. But Lily's never cared for them and she's finicky. She says that in this hot weather the smell of so much as a fish frying would turn her stomach."

Mrs. Prosper unlatched the door on her side of the cab.

"You might ask your daughter, when you go in," said Mr. Duun, "if she'd like a little ride with me out San Jacinto way. She'd find it cooling, I think."

Mrs. Prosper let the door—which she had been holding open—come to, but not latch. "It would be better not," she said. "Lily's my daughter, Mr. Duun, but it's my duty to tell you she's at the age an old maid's likely to reach. The age when it's her pleasure to think every man has his eye on her. For harm, you understand. The milkman, a Mexican come to clean out the henhouse, an agent with magazines, it's all one to Lily, so he wears pants. She's going to make trouble for some man someday. And I wouldn't want it to be you."

Mrs. Prosper looked upward, once again searching Mr. Duun's glance for that shock of recognition—for that reflection of her whole self.

It was there. It was fully there. While Mrs. Prosper was using it, making up for what she felt to be a lifetime's lack, Mr. Duun suddenly opened his own door and stepped out.

"It would be better, I see, for me to ask her myself," he said, and went into the house without a knock at the door or even a pause. Mrs. Prosper climbed slowly down out of the fish truck—and stood for a minute in the driveway, enjoying the sun, now almost at its height, and thinking about what might be going on in the house. Whatever it was, it was soon over. Before she had turned about the screen door slammed, and there was Lily—her white apron off, her Milan straw hat on, Mr. Duun with his hand on her elbow, and, at Mr. Duun's heels, Hodge.

"I'm going for a little ride with Mr. Duun, Mother," said Lily, and Mrs. Prosper watched Mr. Duun hand her up into the truck like an honored guest. When he had done that and closed the door he walked on around to the back of the truck and got out a smelt for Hodge. Then he climbed up into the cab with Lily, and slammed the door after him. He didn't at once start his engine, however, but sat leaning out of his window, looking at Mrs. Prosper. Mrs. Prosper thought he intended speech. Instead he reached across Lily, took down the little collar, and tossed it at Mrs. Prosper's feet.

"A gift from the groom," he said.

"Groom?" asked Mrs. Prosper.

"Groom-to-be," said Mr. Duun.

Mrs. Prosper stooped and picked up the collar. "A gift to the bride's mother in memory of her that wore it," said Mr. Duun; then he started his engine, and he and Lily drove on around the house and out the driveway on the other side.

Mrs. Prosper, who lived on irony, had her cupful then, pressed down and running over: the "bride's mother," and that collar, and known as she was; those three, all together and at one time. Mrs. Prosper stood for some time in the dry, burning sunlight without moving. Then she laughed. Not silently, but loud enough to cause Hodge, busy with his fish, to look up.

"Come, Hodge," said Mrs. Prosper, quickly stooping, "you'll wear the collar." But Hodge was faster than Mrs. Prosper. In one snake-like curve he was out of her arms and under the oleanders, carrying what was left of Mr. Duun's gift. So Mrs. Prosper had to enter the house without him, empty-handed except for the monkey collar.

# Public-Address System

A NUMBER OF people are blaming Bill Hare for what happened
to Leonard Hobart. They say he's responsible. Bill Hare doesn't
have to depend upon hearsay for this information. He's president of the Tenant Building and Loan Association and is in his office
on the main street of town eight hours a day. That's a public place,
every Tom, Dick, and Harry feels free to go in—and does. They go
in—Bill hasn't any way of telling a client from a busybody since they
look pretty much the same and oftentimes are—and say, "Bill Hare,
don't your conscience hurt you the way this Leonard Hobart business
has turned out?"

It doesn't. But Bill is getting tired of saying so. He'll say something
else soon. Mrs. Hobart comes oftenest. She'll say, "Mister Hare"—
when Nadine Hobart says a word she says *all* the letters—"Mister
Hare," she'll say, "I hold you personally responsible for what happened to my husband." She came in yesterday. "Mister Hare," she
said, "I place the blame for what happened to Leonard squarely upon
your shoulders."

Bill Hare will take a good deal from Nadine Hobart because of what
she's been through. But not everything. He watches her tear-shaped
specs tremble on her fleshy nose and notes the way she builds her
braids up into a kind of stockade on top of her head and remembers
a few of the things Leonard told him about his wife. He thinks, Mrs.
Hobart, you're a good-looking woman and you've been through a lot,
but you keep *nagging* me and I'll tell you the truth. I'll tell you for
one thing that you're responsible, far more responsible for what happened to your husband than I am.

From first to last, what Bill Hare did was done to help Leonard. He
was more Quixotic than anything else—had far more to gain, personally, by letting the softball committee do what it wanted to do: that
is, go into Los Angeles and buy a public-address system from a Los

Angeles firm. But no. Not fair-minded Billy! "We must play ball with the local merchants," he told them. "We must give Leonard Hobart his chance." And since Bill Hare was chairman of the committee to buy the public-address system he was naturally listened to.

"You mean Hobart's Electric Shop?" asked Aldo Mattutzi. Bill said he did.

"Why waste time on Old Leonard?" asked Aldo. "I move we go right into L.A. where we can see the stuff at its source and in quantity."

"No sir," said Bill Hare. "The success of softball in Tenant depends upon the goodwill of the townspeople. We've got to play ball with them if we want them to play ball with us."

"Oh hell!" said Aldo. "In the first place, Leonard probably don't carry the equipment. In the second place, even if he does and we bypass him he'll be the last person to raise a squawk."

"Mattutzi," Bill said reasonably, "you know that's not the way to handle this."

"Hobart's your next-door neighbor, isn't he?" Aldo asked, insinuating that Bill's reasons for going to Hobart's might be personal.

"He is," Bill said. "I've lived next door to Leonard Hobart for ten years but as far as I'm concerned he'd just as well not be there."

That was the truth. And it wasn't because Bill Hare was a big wheel in Tenant and Leonard Hobart a practically invisible cog. It was the truth because of time and silence and Nadine. Time: twenty-four hours in the day; eight or ten for business. Eight for sleep. Six left for his family (Bill has a wife and three children), for softball, for taking a drive, for tuberous begonias, for fishing, for the Royal Arch. Where was there any time for Leonard? Silence: Leonard was silent. Not even his shoes squeaked. In a room full of furniture he looked like furniture. When he was outdoors he appeared somewhat leafy. Leonard was a vacation for the eye and for the ear an intermission. Nadine: Bill heard *her*. In the morning he heard her tell Leonard which tie to put on. At lunch she told him what groceries to pick up on his way home. At night she reminded him to wash his hands before he ate.

"As far as I'm concerned," he told the committee, "Leonard doesn't exist. And if he hasn't got what we want I'll be the first to say let's go in to Los Angeles. But we ought to see him first and find out what he does have."

Bill naturally was given the job.

Leonard had a small shop, dark, and crowded with radios. Amidst them he seemed somewhat varnish colored himself. Bill looked this way and that trying to find him and saw him, finally, at the back of the shop taking the insides out of somebody's portable.

"Hi, Leonard," he said.

Bill saw Leonard look up, then quickly look downward, pretend in fact that he had not seen him nor heard his greeting. Bill walked down the narrow alleyway between radios to the back of the shop. Unconsciously he kept step to "Doing What Comes Naturally," sung by the Nightingales. That's a chorus of twenty girls and one of the radios was tuned in on their program.

"Hi, Leonard!" he called again. But still Leonard didn't reply.

Arrived at Leonard's workbench he said, "Hard at it, eh?"

Leonard then looked up. "Good morning, Mr. Hare," he said. "Radio's making such a racket I didn't hear you come in."

That was a lie. Bill knew it, then; and afterward Leonard told him so. Afterward Leonard told him almost everything.

"Remember the day you first came into the shop?" he asked Bill, afterward.

Bill didn't very well. "Yeah, I guess so," he said.

"I resented you that day, Bill."

"Resented me? I was just a poor customer."

Leonard disregarded this. "You were a big wheel in Tenant, Bill. And you had lived beside me for ten years and paid no more attention to me than if I were a stray dog."

Afterward, Leonard could say things like that to Bill and laugh. They were friends then and Leonard could tell Bill things he had never told anyone else and in most of what he had to say Bill was interested.

"I thought to myself when you walked in that first morning," Leonard said, "here comes Bill Hare, who'll expect me to drop everything the minute he says, Hi, Leonard."

Bill laughed. "Why hell, Leonard, didn't you want to make a sale?"

"Sure I did. But it was a pleasure to make you say hi twice to get my attention."

Leonard didn't have any trouble making the sale. He could get the softball committee just as good a public-address system as any Los Angeles firm and he quoted them an even better price. Bill placed the order with him then and there, Leonard agreeing, of course, to install the system at the softball field.

Leonard was very pleased about the sale. Pleased to have made the acquaintance of Bill Hare and to have the prospect of working with and getting to know the committeemen. He went home happy that evening. He told Bill about it afterward.

It was raining as Leonard walked homeward from work that night, the first rain of the season, a sort of practice downfall, very slow and easy. On the empty lots the summer dust was cratered by the big drops. When the first autumn rain comes down the tiny shreds and particles of a long summer's grinding, the bits of leaves and cellophane and dried flower petals, the flakes of tobacco, hairs from bird feathers, horse's tails, lipstick brushes, the grape seeds, dried cherry stems, broken off thumbnails, all these things, pulverized, leap upward, an inch or so off the earth as the big drops hit them. Leonard watched this happen on his way home that evening. He had done so before, but he had never before had anyone to whom he could speak of it.

The whole town of Tenant seemed interesting to Leonard as he walked home that evening. First a building, then a vacant lot. Everything mixed. Loops, garlands, tendrils, lamp posts, swinging signs. Foothills at the end of streets. Frequency modulation beneath the lacy pepper boughs, empty bottles glittering in a clump of farewell summer. Beautiful uphill dream breasts behind the plate-glass windows. Busts, he corrected himself.

"Does your wife insist on busts?" he asked Bill.

"What?" asked Bill, who hadn't been listening very closely.

"As a part of your vocabulary," Leonard explained.

"Sally leaves my vocabulary pretty much alone," Bill said.

Leonard reached his own front porch that night and stood there, reluctant to go in: fall, the first rain, home town, big sale, acquaintances, friends! Next door was Bill Hare's house. Bill a neighbor of his, a business associate. A friend! Leonard closed his hand gently on a spattering of raindrops as if afraid he'd crush them. Why not go in, he thought, and lead the kind of life you've always dreamed about? What kind of a life is that? he asked himself. Why loving, he answered himself, lead a life of loving kindness. He went inside and it seemed possible.

Sometimes the furnishings of his living room disturbed him. There was a wicker settee in which the wickerwork strands seemed too numerous and to be traveling in too many directions. Sitting across the room from it he would find himself trying to follow one particular strand: discover where it began and where it was going. His eyes would hurt with the intensity of his concentration and still the pattern would elude him.

One evening, his eyes following, then failing to follow, the design of the wickerwork in the settee's arm, he had gone over and tried to trace the design with his fingers. Piece out the pattern by touch if sight were not enough. But Nadine had said, "Leonard for heaven's sake what are you doing? Creeping around the settee that way. And patting it."

"Patting it!" he had protested. "I'm not patting it. I'm just trying to feel out the pattern."

"Feel out the pattern? That's just as bad. What do you want to feel its pattern for?"

"I want to see if it *has* a pattern."

"Leonard Hobart," said Nadine, "are you crazy?"

"No," said Leonard. "No, I don't think so."

If he sat on the wicker settee the problem of its pattern escaped his eyes. But then he saw and worried about the picture on the wall opposite the settee: the picture of a vast, midocean welter of green-gray swells. At the picture's lower edge there was one wave, poised, ready to break. Only it never broke. That was the trouble. There it hung, a white lip, threatening but stationary. Once he had run into the dining room to the wall behind the picture. But arrived there he had felt foolish. A painted wave cannot be made to break by getting behind it and pushing.

Tonight, however, neither the stationary wave nor the wickerwork settee troubled him. In fact, he didn't even see them. "Nadine, Nadine," he called. From the kitchen there came sounds of supper being prepared, but no answer.

"Nadine," he called again, "I'm home."

Nadine came to the kitchen door, her coronet of braids lustrous and her eyeglasses shining.

"Hello, Nadine," Leonard said. "Beautiful evening, warm, with a drizzle of rain."

"What are you saying?" Nadine asked.

"Raining," Leonard replied. "Beautiful evening, warm and raining."

"Is it?" said Nadine. "Well, I wish you'd speak up, Leonard, so I could hear you the first time. I wear myself out trying to find out what you're saying."

"And not worth the trouble half the time," Leonard agreed pleasantly.

To this Nadine did not reply, but observing his empty hands she asked, "Where are the rolls?"

"Rolls!" Leonard exclaimed clapping his hands to his pockets as if they might be there. "Rolls. I forgot them. Do you need them for supper?"

"Not if you don't mind stale bread."

"*I* don't," said Leonard turning back toward the living room and the evening paper, but Nadine told him, "Wash your hands. Supper is ready." So he had no time to read.

He was first at the table, even so. He and the stuffed pork chops and the creamed celery and the stale bread waited together. The children were not there and Nadine was calling them, calling up the dark stairs to young Nadine, aged sixteen, out into the rainy evening for Tom, aged twelve. Finally they were all at the table and the pork chops were passed, rich little pockets filled with food. Like a squirrel's cheeks, Leonard thought, then tried not to think as he cut into one.

"I had a piece of luck at the store today," Leonard told his family after the eating had started.

Young Nadine turned eagerly to her mother. "Timmy's coming. I told you he would. I'll have to have new sandals and a bag to match."

"Who's Timmy?" Tom asked.

"You wouldn't know, dear," his mother told him.

"Bill Hare stopped in. He wants—"

"If *she* gets new sandals *I* get a new football. Mine leaks so it's got to be pumped up every five minutes," Tom said.

"Good! Pump it up every five minutes. You can't be kicking it into people's faces if you're pumping it up."

"Do your face good to have a ball kicked—"

"Tom, dear," said Nadine. "You can have the ball. Now let your sister alone."

"They're installing a new public-address—" Leonard began again but Nadine had an idea. "I could dye that scarf for you," she told her daughter, "so that it would match your sandals and bag."

It wasn't until after the children had finished eating that Leonard had a chance to tell his wife about the sale.

"You seem pleased," said Nadine.

"I am. Bill could just as easy have gone into L.A."

"So it's Bill, now."

"Well, he calls me Leonard," Leonard defended himself. "We had a nice chat. I appreciate his swinging the sale to me."

"So he told you that, did he?"

"No, he didn't. But he's chairman of the committee. And whatever Bill Hare says in this town you can bet goes."

"You don't think Bill Hare's thinking about anyone but Bill Hare, do you?"

"What are you driving at, Nadine?"

"Bill Hare's buying the system of you so he'll have someone on hand to service it. You'll take care of it. Gratis, too, or I miss my guess. You'll spend your summer at the softball park. Any little flutter in the thing and they'll be calling on you."

"I like baseball," said Leonard. "That won't be much of a hard-ship."

"Baseball and servicing a public-address system are two different things. You'll be doing the latter. You mark my words."

*          *          *

Nadine and Leonard were both right. Leonard did spend a good deal of time at the park. And it wasn't, for him, a hardship. The system didn't go in until just before the opening of the softball season in late May. Leonard not only installed it but he went with Bill and Bill's committee for a number of nights after it was in to make sure that the loudspeakers were exactly where they should be, that the announcer's booth was properly and handily equipped, the connections dependable and so forth. Leonard was as anxious as Bill that both patrons and players be convinced that nothing out of Los Angeles could have been better.

Leonard enjoyed himself on those May evenings. The air was mild and soft. The grass (the softball diamond is located in Goodman Memorial Park) after its mowing and watering earlier in the day gave the place a fresh, country smell. Troops of kids followed the committee about; and in the midst of all the technical talk Leonard was the authority.

Leonard intended, of course, to be on hand for the opening night. He was an enthusiastic baseball fan in any circumstances and with a public-address system of his own installing receiving its first official tryout, he could not have been kept away. The game—the Tenant All Stars were playing the San Benito Champs—was not scheduled to begin until eight o'clock but Leonard planned to be at the field by seven-thirty.

At six-thirty, however, Bill Hare stopped in to ask Leonard to ride down to the park with him. "I thought it might be a smart idea to go down early and make a few tests," Bill said. "Just be certain everything's clicking."

The Hobarts were still at the dinner table and Nadine, at this request of Bill's gave her husband a look which said plainly enough, What did I tell you? Bill caught the look and asked Nadine somewhat apologetically if she'd like to ride to the game a little later with his wife.

"Thank you, no, Mr. Hare," said Nadine. "Softball's a little outside my province."

When Bill and Leonard reached the diamond Bill said, "Maybe Burt's already here. If he is we'll get him to call out a few over the loudspeaker. Just to see if she's still got the power."

*          *          *

Burt Gaynor was the announcer for the evening, a professional from Los Angeles hired to add éclat to the opening game. But Burt hadn't showed up yet, so Bill told Leonard, "I'll go out in the stands. You go up there and give her a tryout. Say the multiplication table if you want to. It don't matter *what* you say."

Bill still had the idea, at that time, that Leonard was a silent man for the lack of anything to say. Later, he realized, of course, that Leonard had been a silent man for the lack of anyone to listen to him. Bill walked up into the stands at the southwest corner of the field where tests had proved the acoustics to be bad and waited for Leonard's voice. What he expected to hear was, "One—two—three—testing."

Instead, what he heard was, "Tonight, ladies and gentlemen, the Tenant All Stars play the San Benito Champs in what promises to be a sizzling spine-tingling history-making softball classic. While we're waiting for the teams to put in their appearance on the field let me tell you something about the players.

"On the mound for the Tenant All Stars will be Al Tuck, big two-hundred-pound side-wheeler. Al's a spot pitcher, the boy who holds the league record for strike-outs, a southpaw who's got control as well as steam. Give Al a low ball hitter and boom, upstairs the old apple comes. A high ball hitter and it's down in the basement."

Bill stopped, turned around, faced the announcer's booth. He stood stock-still, squinting across the twilit diamond, as the talk about Al Tuck continued. It wasn't what Leonard was saying so much—that was the spiel of a man who knew the Tenant team, all right, but who had read more baseball than he'd played it—it was Leonard's voice that impressed Bill. The voice of Leonard, the silent man. It had the authority of a natural phenomenon: of a cataract, or a thunderstorm, or a glacier, Bill climbed quickly down from the grandstand, then ran back across the field to the announcer's booth. He felt very excited, somehow.

After the game Bill took Leonard home. (The All Stars had won, Al Tuck, the spot pitcher, holding the Champs to six hits, one run.) They talked about Burt Gaynor, the announcer for the evening, who had not arrived until the fourth inning, and who had then been incompetent.

"Burt would've done a lot better," Leonard defended him, "if he hadn't been nervous."

"Nervous," said Bill. "Was he nervous, too?"

"A cop stopped him in Belvedere Gardens on suspicion of drunk driving. It upset him."

"Suspicion!" Bill exclaimed. "Well, I'm glad he was stopped. Five innings were more than enough for Burt."

"I thought he got better as he went along," Leonard said. "As it wore off."

"Look, Leonard," said Bill. "Burt Gaynor is no problem to softball in Tenant. Drunk or sober. You know that. Tenant got itself a new announcer tonight."

To this Leonard said nothing. It was eleven o'clock and in about half the houses they were passing the lights were still on, and in half of these the blinds were up so that they could see what was going on inside.

"Lots of card players," observed Leonard.

There were. Tables of four, two men and two women for the most part. High-school girls slamming cards at each other in a violent game of double Canfield. Solitary players, middle-aged men, moving cards from the top of a deck to the bottom. The wanted card never seeming to turn up.

"Lots of hair combers," said Leonard.

One hair washer. A man painting the ceiling of his kitchen. A woman ironing. A boy cleaning his rifle.

"You know who he is, don't you?" Bill persisted. "Our new announcer?"

They passed more card players, hair combers, workers, talkers, lovers.

"You'd want the job, wouldn't you, Leonard?"

Leonard replied reluctantly, as if talk might make the whole evening fade out like a dream.

"My voice was quite a surprise to me, Bill," he said.

"Me too," Bill replied.

"I'm not used to having people listen to me."

"How'd it seem, Leonard?" Bill asked.

Leonard tried to say. Out there, far out in the field *his* voice echoing against the stands. Bringing the heads of people about from their companions to face *him*. Drowning out lesser sounds: birds, wind in the park's trees, a kid's crying. *His* voice: the breath out of his own lungs, the vibrations given his breath by his own muscles. A part of him going where he could not go, doing what he could not do.

"Why, it's power," he told Bill.

"Sure, it is," Bill said, smiling. Then he had an idea. They had stopped at Leonard's place and Bill could see Nadine silhouetted against an upstairs window. "Maybe you'd like to talk this over with Nadine before you commit yourself to the job."

"No," Leonard said. "There's no need to do that. I'll accept it right now."

As the season went on Leonard's announcing got even better. Not his voice. That couldn't be improved, but his manner and what he had to say. There was talk of his being invited to be the official announcer in other leagues. Bill was naturally proud of him and when softball fans dropped into the Building and Loan office to hash over the games, Bill would tell them the story of Leonard's debut as a broadcaster and of the part he had played in it.

"I lived next to him for ten years," he would tell his listeners, "and I never heard him speak. Didn't know if he *could* speak. Now listen to him."

Every one marveled at Bill's astuteness in discovering in such unlikely material a softball announcer, and Bill was willing to accept a fair share of the credit for Leonard's success. Then, when the criticism began to come in, he had to accept his share in that, too. It was natural that it should come to him, since he had been chairman of the committee that bought the public-address system. The criticism, at first was unorganized and sporadic and Bill paid little attention to it. Then Mrs. Florence Delia came to see him.

Mrs. Delia was president of the Goodman Park Neighborhood Association and as such came bearing an official protest. To her, Bill listened. He sat her down as formally as if she had been a stockholder, folded his hands on his desk and gave her his undivided attention.

"What's on your mind, Mrs. Delia?" he asked.

Mrs. Delia had several things on her mind. First of all she wanted Mr. Hare to know that the Neighborhood Association enjoyed the softball games. They enjoyed the broadcasts. They were proud of the Tenant All Stars. They were proud of Leonard's success as an announcer. Only, and here Mrs. Delia was both firm and warm as only an Italian matron can be, there was too much of it.

"At six o'clock, two hours before a game starts Mr. Hobart is out there at the field yelling balls and strikes," Mrs. Delia said. "Even when there is to be no game at all he does this. We are no longer able to hear ourselves think in the Goodman Park neighborhood. Mr. Hobart has a very fine, big beautiful voice, but we are getting too much of it."

Bill had heard all this before. He had even heard *it*, Leonard's practicing, Leonard's voice carrying as it did. He knew he would have to put a stop to it sometime and meanwhile he tried to placate Mrs. Delia and defend his protégé.

"Mrs. Delia," he said, "you can understand that a man needs to practice, can't you? Mr. Hobart is new at broadcasting. It's only natural that he should feel the need of practicing."

"He practices at the top of his voice," protested Mrs. Delia. "He makes the china rattle on our shelves. That is not natural, Mr. Hare."

Bill tried another tack. "Mrs. Delia, you are an Italian and you Italians understand artists. Your Caruso—for instance—rehearse, rehearse. Isn't that true?"

"Our Caruso," Mrs. Delia said, "sang. Mr. Hobart bellows. Bellowing is not a pleasant thing to listen to, Mr. Hare."

Bill Hare is an honest man. "I agree with you, Mrs. Delia," he said. "I'll speak to Mr. Hobart about it. I'll put a stop to it."

This was all Mrs. Delia asked. She left Bill with some compliments for Leonard's regular broadcasts. "Those we enjoy," she said. "It sounds like something very great going on when Mr. Hobart broadcasts. It makes my spine tingle like the late war and the sadness of good men dying."

This confused Bill but he said, "Thank you. Thank you, Mrs. Delia. I understand how you feel. I'll see Mr. Hobart at once."

By at once Bill had meant in a day or two. But he went to see Leonard that very afternoon, for hard on Mrs. Delia's heels came Nadine Hobart. She would neither sit, shake hands, nor speak of the weather. She was in a hurry, she told Bill, and what she had to say was painful to her.

"Mr. Hare," she said, "you are breaking up my marriage."

Bill was aghast. The last thing in the world he would willingly do was to interfere in any way with Nadine Hobart's marriage. "Mrs. Hobart," he faltered, "what do you mean?"

"Leonard," she said. "Before you got him started in this broadcasting business he was a good husband. Punctual, sympathetic, helpful. Now all that is changed. And above all Leonard is never at home any more. Broadcasting or practicing to broadcast! You must have heard him."

"Yes," said Bill, "I have."

"Well," said Mrs. Hobart, "put a stop to it. Besides my personal situation the neighbors are complaining."

"I know," said Bill. "To me, too."

"You're responsible for it, Mr. Hare."

"I'll do what I can," Bill said.

"Do what you can? You started it. Now you stop it."

Bill closed his office about four that afternoon and went around to Hobart's Electric Shop to have a talk with Leonard. Leonard, as on the first time he had called, was at the back of his shop doing some repair work. But this time he replied at once to Bill's "Hi, Leonard."

"Hi, Bill," he said, put down his work and came to meet his friend. "What's new, Billy-boy?" he asked.

"Well, Leonard," said Bill, without any beating about the bush, "we've been getting some complaints about the broadcasts."

"You mean about the practice broadcasts, don't you?"

"Yes," said Bill. "About the practices. The Goodman Park Neighborhood Association objects."

"Well, that's all fixed up, Billy," Leonard said. "I was going to tell you. The Association won't complain any more. I'm putting in a public-address system of my own."

Bill pushed his hat to the back of his head, then took it off. "At your house or the shop?" he asked.

"My house. It's already arrived. I'll connect it up this evening. It's a thing I've had in mind to do for some time. It'll be a great help to Nadine for one thing, calling the kids in to meals and so forth. And I'll find uses for it, too, no doubt. I've discovered that I enjoy using the darned thing, believe it or not. Over the public-address system, I don't mind admitting to you, Bill, I feel like a different person. Amplification—well, I don't know—it just seems to suit me, somehow."

"Are you planning to practice your broadcasts at home?" Bill asked doubtfully.

"I wasn't," Leonard said, "unless you think I ought to, Bill. I kind of had the idea that my softball technique was okay now."

"I think so, too," Bill said heartily. "Rehearse and you're liable to go stale. The broadcasts are just about perfect as they now stand."

"Perfect!! They're not perfect yet by a long shot," Leonard said, "but I have noticed one interesting development in them recently."

"What's that?" Bill asked.

"I don't know just what to call it—anticipation's maybe the word."

"Anticipation?" Bill repeated.

"Most announcers call out the plays a little after they're made, don't they?"

"Sure."

"I call them a little before."

"You what?"

Leonard repeated what he had said. "I call them a little before they're made, Billy. Haven't you noticed it?"

"No," said Bill. "I haven't."

"Not very much before, yet; less than a second, probably. I call ball, and *after* I say it the pitch turns out to be a ball. Inside curve, low, I say, and inside curve, low, it is. You've never noticed?"

"No," said Bill, "I never have."

"Watch tomorrow night's game, Billy. You'll see what I mean. They move when I give them the word. Not vice versa as with other announcers. It'll be an added attraction, when people catch on."

Bill felt uneasy and embarrassed. He knew Leonard was full of whimsies, he *liked* it in him, but this seemed carrying a whimsy pretty far. He left Leonard and went immediately home. He had no appetite that evening and couldn't keep his mind on what his wife said. There was an old hollow feeling under his breastbone, not quite a pain, but unpleasant enough to send him to bed as soon as dinner was over. About midnight his wife awakened him. She had leaned over from the twin bed next to his and grasped his arm.

"Bill," she said, shaking his arm. "Bill. What in the world is that noise?"

"What's what?" Bill asked, only partially awake.

"That sound. What is it?"

It seemed to Bill more like a subterranean force than a sound. It was strong enough to be felt in vibrations along the headboard of his bed, against which he had pushed his shoulders in his hurried wakening. Then he realized what it was.

"It's Leonard," he said. "He was going to install a public-address system at his place this evening. He's testing it."

"Go on back to sleep, Nadine," Leonard said, the words issuing from the Hobart house like thunderclaps.

"Why is he shouting?" Sally Hare asked. "Why doesn't he turn it down?"

"I'm not shouting," said Leonard, as if answering *her*. "This is my normal voice."

At that Sally scurried over into Bill's bed. There was something frightening about that voice in the middle of the night, the more frightening because the voice was Leonard's. It suggested that there was no more dependence to be put on reason. It was not reasonable for such a sound to issue from Leonard Hobart's mouth. So quiet a man.

"I guess he doesn't realize how much he's being amplified," Bill said.

"Doesn't he realize it's the middle of the night, either?" Sally asked.

"I don't believe time means much to Leonard," Bill said.

\*          \*          \*

Next evening Bill went early to the softball field. It was Saturday, the sixteenth of August, a warm, still night. Although it was a half hour before game time the stands were already three-fourths filled and Leonard was in the midst of his regular pregame talks. Listening to him Bill lost all the uneasiness that he had felt the night before. Leonard's introductory remarks were calm and factual, Leonard at his best. And his voice, or the voice which was the union of Leonard and the amplifying mechanism, it, too, had never been better.

"Tonight, friends," Leonard was saying, "we are to see the play-off for the Tenant softball championship, Elks versus Tavern Keepers. Battery for the Elks will be Kitto and Patrick. Battery for the Tavern Keepers Eby and Eldridge."

Bill, in his seat behind first, relaxed completely. I must've somehow misunderstood Leonard yesterday, he thought as he listened to him soberly relaying statistics to the crowd: batting averages, gate receipts, league standings. People were still pouring onto the field through the turnstiles and those already in the stands were discussing the coming game with animation. As one of the persons responsible for softball in Tenant, Bill looked about with pride. After the record-breaking crowds they had had all season they would be able to afford another piece of equipment for the field next year. Bill speculated a little as to what it should be. The lines past the turnstiles had dwindled, had ceased to be lines at all. The Elks team was in the field. Kitto their pitcher was warming up, and in the announcer's booth Leonard was telling the fans about Ben Woodford, Tavern right fielder and first man at bat.

"Ben's batting average for the season," he concluded, "has been .294, good but not sensational. On deck for the Tavern Keepers is Jim Lazarus. In the hole, Al Bailey."

Kitto finished his warm-up, the Elk fielders went out deep, for Woodford, when he connected, was known to take the ball for a ride. Kitto sent a final toss over to second, the umpire called, "Play ball," and the game started. Bill settled back to enjoy himself. Kitto was an amusing pitcher to watch, a tall lanky boy with an involved windup which took him, at its midpoint, right down to the earth.

"Here comes the crank-up," said Leonard. "Kitto's starting off the game with his Sunday pitch. It's a fast one, it barely cuts the outside corner of the plate and Big Ben watches it go by. Strike one on Big Ben Woodford."

"He called that before the umpire, didn't he?" Bill's neighbor, a man in a yellow T-shirt asked him.

"I couldn't say," Bill answered.

"Did *you* hear the ump call it?" the man persisted.

"We probably couldn't hear the umpire for the loudspeaker. He was probably drowned out," Bill said.

"The ump didn't even have his hand up yet, did he?"

"I don't know," Bill said uneasily. "I wasn't watching the ump."

Whatever had happened, the umpire evidently did not object, for Leonard's magnificent commanding voice continued.

"Patrick, Elk catcher, is signaling Kitto for a repeat and he gets it, a knee-high sizzler right over the plate. Woodford swings but misses. Two strikes on Woodford."

"What'd I tell you?" Bill's neighbor asked.

Bill said nothing.

"Here comes another crank-up," boomed Leonard, "Big Benny is going to look this one over. He does. It's a fast peg, but it breaks wide. Ball one for Woodford. The count now stands one and two on Woodford, first man up in the first inning of the ball game, Elks versus Tavern Keepers, Elks at bat."

Down on the field umpire and catcher with masks up were having a talk. Kitto trotted off the mound to join them.

"Ump says *he* wants to call them," the man in the T-shirt told Bill. Then as the three men resumed their positions he added, "Ump says he'll give the announcer one more chance."

"Kitto gets back on the firing line," Leonard announced to his listeners and Kitto, as if he had received an order, walked slowly back to pitcher's box. "Here comes the windup," Leonard continued, "it's another fast ball, a hummer dead over the plate but high. Woodford swings, he really leans on the old stick this time, but he misses. He misses by a mile. That's three strikes and out for Big Benny Woodford."

In the echo of Leonard's encompassing voice Woodford swung and connected, drove a liner deep into right field. Tate Pierce fumbled the pickup, finally made it, then in his hurry, overthrew. Woodford was safe on first with plenty of margin.

Leonard's amplified voice, mighty and reverberating, was undaunted by this fact. As if to compensate for the discrepancy between what had happened and what he had declared would happen, his voice became even louder, even more commanding. It vaulted over the grandstands, spiraled skyward, then hardening in an arc of solid sound settled just above the heads of the spectators, a weight beneath which they all sat, silent and unmoving as prisoners.

Bill had never suspected that the mechanism which he had selected and helped install was capable of so much power. It—or Leonard's voice amplified by it—not so much split the air with sound as filled it. The voice which had arched above their heads settled lower and lower. It became a yoke on their shoulders, a weight, a gravestone pushing them nearer and nearer the earth. The words Leonard had been saying, "Three strikes and you're out," he continued to say. But through repetition the words lost their meaning and finally, as words, they disappeared all together. The sound of Leonard's voice, amplified, became nothing but power, nothing but brute force. Bill could feel it belaboring him across his shoulders, thundering against his eardrums, and finally, pummeling him inside his head, in the innermost private and vulnerable recesses of his mind.

Bill never knew, no one ever knew, how long it went on nor why they all sat there numb, unmoving for however long it did go on. Bill himself was the first to do something. Next was the man beside him in the yellow T-shirt. To him Bill whispered—it was impossible to shout *above* the horrible din of that great, amplified voice, the only way to be heard was to get *under* it—"The poor fellow is out of his mind."

Together Bill and the man in the yellow T-shirt scrambled down through the crowded stand, then reaching the ground ran at full tilt toward the broadcasting booth. Leonard wept when he was separated from the amplifier.

They took him to Norwalk that night.

At the time no one blamed Bill for what happened. Now they have begun to talk. They come into the Building and Loan office and say,

"Except for you I guess Leonard Hobart would still be here selling radios."

Bill doesn't pay much attention to them. Nadine is different. She came in yesterday. She was in again this afternoon.

"I hold you responsible for what happened to my husband."

Up to now Bill has listened with patience to these tirades. Now he says, "Madam, *you* are responsible for what happened to your husband."

"I?" Nadine's usually firm glasses wobbled upon her fleshy nose.

"I, you, all of us," says Bill. "But especially you."

"What do you mean, Mr. Hare?" asks Nadine.

"Poor Leonard," Bill says, "we forced him—" He begins again. "No one listened to Leonard—" But suddenly he is tired of explaining. It is useless, he feels, to explain anything to anybody—particularly to Nadine.

"Good day, madam," he says and walks Nadine right through the doorway of the Building and Loan office and out onto the street. "What do you mean, Mr. Hare?" insists Nadine but Bill puts the plate-glass door between them and locks it.

"What *do* you mean, Mr. Hare?" Bill asks himself, ironically, imitating Nadine's demanding voice. He walks over to his desk, sits down, and begins to think about Leonard.

He puts his hat on his head, his feet on his desk. "What do you mean, Mr. Hare?" he asks himself, but flatly now and without irony.

# Foot-Shaped Shoes

THE KNOCKING at her door continued and Kass reluctantly opened her eyes. There was such a dazzle of brilliant August light and bitter August heat in her room that she thought it was midmorning, that Rusty had given up his crazy five o'clock trip. But no, the clock said five and it was her brother's red head that came cautiously around the slowly opening door.

"Kass," he whispered. "Kass, you awake?"

"Sure," she answered jauntily, then added, "I guess so."

"It's five."

"I know."

"But you don't have to get up for fifteen minutes. I said five to give you fifteen minutes extra before you had to get up. I remembered how you hated to get up the moment you opened your eyes."

"Well, thanks, chum," she answered drowsily.

Her brother came into the room. "Kass, you going back to sleep?"

She shut her eyes. "I am asleep."

"Kass, Kass."

She opened her eyes and smiled at him. He was shirtless, in skin-tight jeans. "Gosh, you've grown. What're your dimensions now?"

"Dimensions?"

"In space and time?"

"Oh. Six one, a hundred and eighty."

"Wowie! A heavyweight. The age?"

"Fourteen."

"Fourteen? How come fourteen? The last time I saw you I distinctly remember you were thirteen."

"That was six months ago. That was the night you got married. I'm older now."

"Well, me too, for that matter. *You* haven't gotten married since then have you? Or anything like that?"

Rusty laughed. "Father's the only one who's gotten married. I don't even have a girl."

"Why not?"

"I'm going to. I just haven't got around to it yet. I've been pretty busy."

Kass reached for her brother, pulled his cheek down to hers and hugged him. "You're my baby," she said.

The word *baby* seemed to make Rusty self-conscious. He backed away from her without returning her hug or snuggling, puppylike, as he would've done six months ago.

"I know you didn't really want to get up early and go out to the ranch on your first morning home," he apologized. "I expect you're used to sleeping real late now."

He had backed half across the room and stood looking down at her, round-eyed, as if she were a patient critically ill or someone who'd just run the mile in four minutes. She supposed he had been suddenly hit by some speculations about her as a married woman, as opposed to the mother-sister he had always known. What was it like for a man and woman to sleep together? Was she perhaps going to have a baby? She had no idea how much a fourteen-year-old boy knew about marriage. And of course Rusty was no average fourteen-year-old. With his brain, there was no telling whether his silences meant he knew all there was to know about sex or whether he had been too busy, up to the minute, figuring out how to get to the moon on a rocket to know there *was* such a thing. It could be either way. *She* knew, though, and his stare made her self-conscious.

"Sleep late? A thing of the past. Bob goes to work at seven-thirty and I have to be up at dawn to put the toast on."

Rusty laughed. "OK. See you in twenty minutes. Want to go out in your car?"

"Sure. Why not? It's brand-new, bright red, and will go one hundred and twenty miles an hour. You wouldn't mind that, would you?"

"No," Rusty said, smiling, and tiptoed out.

She could dress in ten minutes, easy, so she lay back and looked at her old room, which was exactly the same, but as strange to her as if she'd never seen it before. As a matter of fact she never *had* seen it before. Had these shifting shadows cast by the jacaranda tree ever flowed in the same instantaneously flowering, instantaneously dissolving patterns across her blue rug before she was married? Had there been a maned horse in the knotty-pine ceiling? Rainbows in the mirror's beveled edge? A delicious crack in the footboard of her bed? Never, never! She had never seen anything before, in itself, but only as stage dressing for the imagined drama of being in love, of being courted and married.

Nothing in that unborn time had been an end in itself, all was means: Would it help? Would it hinder? Would a girl whose room had chintz curtains, a white enameled desk made by her father, and a Roman-stripe afghan which had once belonged to her mother be as appealing—to a man, that is—as a girl with her books on shelves supported by bricks, and a studio couch instead of a bed? If not, she had been prepared to change in a flash. She had been conscious throughout her girlhood of the eyes of all the potential lovers and husbands upon her, approving, disapproving. For those eyes, not knowing a thing about either lovers or husbands, she had brushed her hair dramatically, eaten daintily, written lush descriptive passages describing sunsets and bird song in her Five Year Diary. She had lived a hypothetical life. Nothing real, and the unreality she had conjured up was not really suitable, as it turned out, for the life she had been imagining.

But that was all past. She was alive, and through acting. No more dramatized hair strokes or faked nature loving. Bob had made her a real person and to a real person the world is real. She picked up one of her moccasins from the floor by the bed, seeing for the first time that it was made of separate pieces of leather skillfully sewed together so that the whole affair was not only soft but strong, and that—most remarkable of all—it was foot shaped. She turned it round and about. I couldn't make one in a thousand years and this is the first time I ever gave it a glance—as a thing in itself. She threw it into the air, caught it, kissed it, said, "Bob, I adore you," then closed her eyes, shoe to cheek, to think of Bob for a minute.

A pebble on the window aroused her and, knowing who it was, she jumped out of bed, went to the window, and tossed the shoe to Rusty.

"A hostage," she said, "until I arrive."

\*         \*         \*

Rusty went back to Kass's car, shoe in hand. She had left the car parked in the driveway—August nights in Hemet are bone dry—and he walked round it admiringly. If Kass had turned up with a ten-year-old broken-down Chevy it would have been all right with him, but a big red convertible was more like Kass, and he smiled at the image of her, small and blond, behind the wheel, like the white-hot nub of a red-tailed comet. Besides looking right for Kass, it meant something else more important: it meant that lack of money wouldn't keep her from helping Alfred.

He had lifted the hood, when she came running out of the house, tough-footed enough not to mind the absence of one shoe. He put the hood down and said, "We go now."

"No," she said. "Not me. I've changed my mind. I'm not going."

Her face was wet; sweat, he guessed, not her shower, because her hair was dry. It didn't occur to him to say to her, "But you promised" or "But Alfred expects it" or anything like that, because what good was any act done just because it was promised?

He said, "Why not, Kass?"

"I don't want to see this Mexican kid."

"You would like him."

"That's just the trouble. I don't want to like him."

"You could decide before you went, so that liking him wouldn't . . ."

"I have decided."

"What I was going to say was that you could decide you weren't going to have anything to do with him—just go out and see him for the fun of it."

Kass went, "Hmmmph."

"You sound like Father."

"I feel like Father, like I'm getting a little sense. There is no place in my life for a nine-year-old Mexican kid. I'm sorry I let you think there was. But I got carried away, my first night home and everything. Father said no and he was right. I say no, too."

"Father's got his new wife. He's got to pay attention to what she wants."

"What she wants is very sensible. And if being newly married cuts any ice I'm practically a bride myself. I want to do what Bob wants.

And I'm sure adopting a nine-year-old Mexican kid is the last thing that ever crossed his mind."

"You wouldn't have to adopt him. You could just take care of him."

"And even if Bob's one goal in life *was* to adopt a nine-year-old Mexican, there isn't room in a three-room apartment."

"I told you he was only the size of a six-year-old."

"No."

"He's used to sleeping on the ground."

"We don't have any ground for him to sleep on. We don't even have a hole in the ground."

"Did I tell you about the first time I ever saw Alfred?"

"You certainly did. He was up in that tree. What I'd like to know is, why is a Mexican kid called Alfred? Why isn't he José or Juan or Chico? If I were going to adopt a Mexican kid I'd at least want him to have a Mexican name. Not be Arnold or Albert or . . ."

"His real name's Alfredo. You could call him Alfredo if you wanted to. It was the umbrella tree in the backyard. It was the Fourth of July and Father had some of the Mexicans in for a picnic. Alfred climbed to the top of the branches, then he crawled out across nothing but leaves really and sat there in the center of the tree on nothing but leaves really. . . ."

"Must've looked like a hen on a nest."

That wasn't the way he had looked. Rusty could see Alfred now, floating there in the crown of the tree, upheld only by faith and leaves, shiny and thin boned as a cricket; but he didn't contradict Kass. What she thought Alfred had looked like didn't matter.

"What he sang up there was 'Columbia the Gem of the Ocean.' There were more verses than anyone had dreamed of and he knew them all."

"Oh Lord," Kass said.

Rusty defended Alfredo. "He's got a sweet voice. People like to hear him sing. What *they* worried about was his safety, sitting up there on practically nothing but leaves. Everybody yelled at him to come on down. And he yelled back, 'Caramba.' That's a Mexican swear word."

"I know, Rusty. I get around."

"He yelled, 'Caramba! Who wants to live forever?' "

Kass answered this vigorously, "Me! I do. I want to live forever. I want to live forever in my three-room apartment with Bob, and with no little Mexicans climbing up things, sitting on leaves, and yelling 'caramba' at me."

"I like it, though," Rusty told her.

"Like what? Singing, or what?"

"I like being willing to take a little chance. I like that. It appeals to me."

"It takes all kinds, I understand," Kass told him. "Some want to live dangerously and some want to live."

Rusty ignored this. "He's an awfully bright kid. He does arithmetic with the seventh grade."

"This family's lousy with bright kids. One more genius and we're sunk."

"He can play the guitar."

"That does it. Climbing chandeliers, yelling caramba, and playing the guitar. Oh no, Rusty. Oh no."

"Nobody mentioned chandeliers, except you," Rusty reminded her. "His mother doesn't take any care of him, cook for him or anything. He just lives on scraps and sleeps on rags."

"Where's his father?"

"He doesn't have any father. I mean around," Rusty explained. "Also, I think his mother's a whore."

"Hore," Kass snapped.

"Like wrestle, and so on? The *w*'s silent?"

"That's right. If you're really going to get in there and mix with the underworld, you'd better learn how to pronounce them."

"Alfred doesn't have anything to do with the underworld. You know that."

"OK. I'm sorry. I know he doesn't."

"His mother might, though, for all I know. She goes out every night with some different man. I mean stays out. She'd be glad to get rid of Alfred. She'd probably even pay us. He could just disappear and she wouldn't say a word. Unless maybe hurrah. Tonight's the dance and tomorrow all the Mexicans are leaving and if Alfred just wasn't around she'd go without him. It isn't as if anybody wanted him."

"No," Kass said, "no. I won't do it. I can't do it. Don't ask me any more, Rusty. OK. So he may really be the brightest, best little kid in the world. If you say so, I don't doubt it. I'm sorry his mother's a whore. I'm sorry he has to live on scraps and sleep on rags. I love you for loving him. I'll give you some money for him. I'll help you get him into an orphanage."

"No. He doesn't want to be in an orphanage—and his mother would take the money. He'd never see it."

"All right, then. That finishes it. You go on. Take my car and go out to see him. But don't talk to me about him any more. He's not my problem. I can't do anything about him and I don't want to hear about him any more. Or think about him."

She ran back to the house, her run a little lopsided because she'd forgotten her shoe, which was still on the seat of the car where Rusty had put it. Rusty drove the ten miles to the ranch slowly. He felt calm because he knew now what he could and couldn't do. He was on his own now and he had thought he might be and was prepared. He had only to find Mrs. Campos, if she was home, tell Alfred, and he would have given everybody a fair shake.

He turned into the ranch road, drove between the apricot trees, bare now of fruit, and parked beside the deserted cutting shed. The apricot season was over. A couple of the Mexican families were staying on for another week to help scrape and stack trays and to store the dried cots; but the others would pull out in the morning after the evening's farewell dance. Already, up in the last few tree rows at the base of the foothills where they had camped, the Mexican families were preparing to leave. What he saw and heard up there was somehow different from the sights and sounds of mornings when everybody had to be at work by seven.

Though Mexicans, contrary to all he had ever heard, were early risers, work or no work. And when they got up they took over exactly where they had left off the night before: singing, talking, fighting, playing the harmonica. They didn't seem, as Americans did, to go away from their daytime selves during the night. They didn't need a kind of decontamination period of orange juice, coffee, and radio news before they could start being their daytime selves. They seemed to stay the same, night or day, awake or dreaming. They awakened revved up, slid into high gear, and were off until the heat of midafternoon slowed them down. He liked that. It seemed to him a nice way to live.

He had been at the cutting shed some mornings at five, and knew that up there on the hill they would already be singing; their fires would be burning, and the sweet-sour smoke, which always smelled to him like stewing rhubarb, would be towering upward in clear blue columns. He had hears a coyote at five, yelping from the hilltop his farewell to night and the Mexicans' chickens; and he had heard Domingo answer him in the song the Mexicans called "Señor Coyote." And it had really seemed that the Señor, up there on the hilltop, gray and foxy, the early sun at his back, had known he was being addressed, for he had waited for the pauses between stanzas to reply. All the Mexicans had stopped their work to laugh and applaud the duet sung by Domingo and the Señor; and not until the singing was over had the coyote turned and loped over the crest of the hill and out of sight.

It was too late now for coyotes. The smoke on the heated air was transparent. The voices, singing or talking, already tempered by the sun, were thin and sweet—like sharpened knives. Human voices, animal voices; domestic fires and the wild heat of the untamed sun; smoke, an autumn thing, a thing of fallen leaves and coldness, drifting upward now into the summer heat; everything at once so balanced and so contradictory, and likes and opposites so solemnly meshing, Rusty thought he might have to run up some hilltop and there, like Señor Coyote, give a great yelp of happiness. You surely weren't supposed to just walk through stuff like that doing nothing, were you? But he didn't know what to do. Not yet, he didn't. Except, he thought, to call it beautiful; which was true but somehow not enough.

He headed for the tents on the hillside, walking down the alleyway formed by the head-high stacks of drying trays on one hand and the cutting shed on the other. He took his Audubon birdcall, a spool-shaped cylinder of wood with a metal pin in its center, from his pocket. By rotating the pin properly, you could make squeaks birdlike enough to cause birds to reply. Rusty rotated the pin properly, and sure enough a bird did reply, a song so exactly like a bird's imitation of an Audubon birdcall that Rusty laughed aloud.

To reach Mrs. Campos's tent, which stood a little apart from the others at the far end of the row that made up the Mexican encampment, he passed his many friends: the Pérez, Ramos, Rodríguez, Ortiz, Padilla, and Flores families. They were packing, getting breakfast, eating breakfast, preparing for the dance, all at the same time and mostly out of doors. Domingo Rodríguez, the coyote serenader, was tuning up his old truck. Manuel Ramos was milking the family goat. Angel Flores was washing her hair. Mrs. Estobar was washing her underwear. Chico Pérez was painting a baby buggy red. They all yelled at him, asked him to breakfast, asked him for advice, gave advice.

"Hi-ya, Rusty" (they pronounced it Roosty), Chico called. "What you think? Paint the wheels red too?"

Manuel Ramos said, "You asked Angela to the dance yet tonight?"

Pablo Ortiz, sloshing stewed apricots over a tortilla said, "You gonna be ready to pull out with us tomorrow, Rusty?"

"I'm thinking about it."

"You're a good checker, Rusty."

"I like checking," Rusty said, modestly.

"We do peaches next."

"Yeah," Rusty said. "I know."

"In peaches you make a fortune, Rusty."

"What I want a fortune for?"

"Buy you a shirt, Rusty. Never seen you wear one yet. You go with us, Rusty, and you be a big shirt and pants man."

"It's an idea," Rusty said, and meant it.

"You could ride with us."

"You serious?"

"You be here tomorrow morning and see."

"I might, I really might. I'd like to."

"Okey doke," said Pablo. "You tell me no first. I don't move tomorrow till I hear from you."

Rusty felt so happy and proud about Pablo's invitation that he thought for a minute that the tears which had come to his eyes might run down his cheeks. He started on toward Mrs. Campos's place, controlled his feeling, stopped and turned back to face Pablo.

"Thank you, Pablo. I sure do appreciate the invitation." Then he hurried on.

There wasn't much to knock on at Mrs. Campos's tent, but Rusty called her name and slapped his hand a few times against the canvas. When there was no reply he opened the flap and looked in. The tent, except for the usual confusion of bedcovers, clothes, dirty dishes, and empty beer cans, was empty. The air inside the tent was blazing hot and stank with a combination of smells, all stale and heavy: beer and chili and some nasty perfume. The smell alone made him feel uneasy. It was Mrs. Campos's smell exactly, and she made him feel that way, too. With most people he could tell where he was. With grown-ups he was a kid, ignored, or advised, or liked—he hadn't had much experience of being disliked. With other kids he was an equal. With Alfred, he didn't know exactly—he was a kind of father, maybe, or whatever Kass had been to him all of the years since Mother died.

Kass can't really blame me, he thought, about Alfred. I'm just treating him the way she always did me.

Kass used to say to him, when he would tell her not to take so much trouble with him, "I'm not doing it for you, kid. I'm doing it for me. When I play mama to you I don't miss Mama so much. Besides, I like you, I have fun with you." That was about the way he felt about Alfred.

So Mrs. Campos, of all the people in the world, was the only one about whom he wasn't sure what he felt. He certainly hated her, for the way she treated Alfred and for what she was; he wasn't sure he had a right to come between mother and son, and though he knew Mrs. Campos was a bad mother he felt apologetic to her because of it. And on top of all this, in spite of the hatred and disgust and apology, he felt a strange curiosity in Mrs. Campos's presence; as if, in spite of all of his real aversion, Mrs. Campos had some deep hold on him which she knew about and he didn't and which she could exercise if she wanted to. So far she hadn't wanted to, and maybe she never would; but the threat of that power made it more difficult for him to face her about Alfred.

While his nose was still inside the tent and while he was still breathing the scents which both repelled and attracted him, Mrs. Campos herself called to him. He turned around then to face her. She had come up the back way through the orchard and was still a couple of tree rows down the hill.

"Go on in," she called. "I'll be right with you."

"No thanks," said Rusty. "I just came to see about Alfred."

Mrs. Campos stood directly in front of him now, smelling like her tent, the perfume which, Rusty thought, was like some rotting flower. She was sweating and tired, but very revved up, drunk maybe—he couldn't tell.

"You want something, Rusty?"

Mrs. Campos was dressed like the waitress in Bill's Broiler: black satin skirt, white blouse so thin you kept looking at it to see if it was really there, big fake diamond earrings in her ears, fake diamonds in the high heels of her black platform pumps. Her shoes were gray with dust, there was dust on her skirt, and her white blouse was stained brown with streaks of sweat. She stood, hands on hips, with a big white bag—streaked and dusty too—hanging from one hand. This she kept in constant motion by a little outward thrust of her knee; that bag rising and falling. The curve of her long brown neck as Mrs. Campos looked at him over one shoulder out of her flat glittering brown eyes reminded Rusty of the time he had thought he was cornered by a rattlesnake. He moved back a step or two.

"Do you know where Alfred is?"

"Ain't he in the tent?"

"No."

"Don't ask me, then, I don't know and I don't care. He wasn't here last night. Run off, drowned in the reservoir. He's big enough to take care of himself. What you want, Rusty? Want me to push him around in a baby carriage? Feed him on a bottle? You're always asking, 'Where's Alfredo?' 'Has Alfredo had supper?' 'Do you let Alfredo drink beer?' 'Does Alfredo have some clean clothes?' What's the matter with you, Rusty? You're big enough to be interested in women, not little boys. You so interested in little boys, why don't you make a little boy, Rusty?"

Rusty backed still farther away from Mrs. Campos. "I don't think you'd care if you never saw Alfred again."

Mrs. Campos faced him directly then, and her knee and the white bag stopped moving.

"I wouldn't care if I never saw either of you again, Rusty. Alfredo yelling, 'Where's Rusty?' Rusty yelling, 'Has Alfredo had supper?' Go on, beat it, Rusty. Get the hell out of here. Go find your little boy. Fall dead. I don't care. I'm going to get some sleep."

Rusty was trembling as he followed Mrs. Campos's route back to the cutting shed. He went to the rear of the shed, where the empty trays were stacked ten and twelve feet high. He looked around, saw no one, then detached from the center of one of the stacks he saw the loose side of a tray. Through this opening he was able to look down into a neat little cell formed by the removal of the bottoms from a dozen trays. On the final tray, in a room, not large, but homelike, furnished with two folded blankets, a carton of Cokes, a stack of sandwiches wrapped in waxed paper, Alfred sat cross-legged, playing double Canfield. He looked up at Rusty but played the card in his hand without saying anything.

Rusty looked at the layout and said, "You might win this."

Alfred nodded.

"You been OK?"

"Sure. I liked it."

"Well, I gave everybody a fair shake."

Alfred played a heart king and a jack of spades before answering. Then he said, "Nobody wants me?"

His voice was without feeling and he continued to look at his cards, but Rusty didn't answer his question. He couldn't. Instead he said, "I got an even better idea. I'm going to work in peaches. Pablo asked me. I'm a good checker. I can earn enough money for both of us."

Alfred put down his cards at this, and looked up. "Your folks won't let you."

"They won't care," Rusty said. "They won't miss me. They're all messed up in love. They don't want to be bothered."

Alfred played another card. "You never lived in a tent, Rusty."

"I'd like to. I'd sure like it a lot better than feeling the way I do now at home."

"I can take care of myself," Alfred said.

"I know you can. I'd be going because I wanted to and because I liked it."

He didn't know exactly how to describe what he liked to Alfred. Alfred was probably too much of a kid to understand; besides, he didn't know if he could explain it to anyone, even to himself: about the quick waking in the morning, and Domingo and the coyote, and the rhubarb smell of the smoke—and much more he had no words for, for all of them working together, moving on together.

"*I'd* like it," he said again, "but it would've been better for you, all right, if you could've lived at home, or with Kass."

"I didn't think it would work out."

"OK. Come on, now," Rusty told him. "Climb out while I'm here to help you. Your mother's not going to be looking for you. She's asleep."

"She wouldn't anyway."

"Come on, then. You'll break your neck if you try to get out alone. Come on. I got to go home and pack."

But Alfred wouldn't budge. "I can get out when I get ready to. I'm going to finish my game first. I got a chance to win."

The minute Rusty was abreast of the back door and before he had stopped the car, Kass came running out of the house. She banged the screen door behind her so loud Rusty heard it over the Porsche's motor. He stopped the car, cut off the motor, and looked back at her. She had her other moccasin in her hand now and she ran tender-footedly down the graveled path to the driveway. She was slapping the shoe against her hand as she ran, and when she reached the car she slapped the door with it. She was crying and had been crying. Her eyes were red and her cheeks blotched and scalded.

"OK," she said, "you win."

"Win? Win what?"

"I'll take that damned kid, but I hate you for making me do it."

"I'm not making you."

"You are, too. You told me about him. What did you have to tell me about him for?"

"Well, I just told you. I didn't say you had to do anything. Besides, you don't, now. I've got other plans."

Kass looked at him scornfully. "Going to kidnap Albert, I presume, and live in a treehouse with him or some such damn nonsense. Well, forget it. It won't work."

"His name's Alfred."

"OK. Alfred. That treetop singer. Alfred's going to live with us and sing 'Columbia the Gem of the Ocean,' and it'll be terrible. It makes me sick to my stomach to think about it."

She cried or hollered, Rusty wasn't sure which, in her misery.

"Don't do it then," he said.

"I've got to," she said, and then she really did cry. "Oh Bob," she said, "I hate you, I hate you! Why did you do this to me?"

This was too mysterious for Rusty. "I thought Bob was the one you loved."

"I hate him. What chance have I got when even shoes are real? All sewed together," she sobbed, "and foot shaped."

Rusty stared at her.

"Did you ever look at a shoe?" she demanded. "Did you?"

"I don't know," Rusty said. "I never thought about it especially, if that's what you mean."

"That's what I mean. Look at it." She pushed it under his nose. "It's a miracle, isn't it? And I never knew shoes existed until Bob made them real. So what chance do I have with a poor little Mexican? I'll be opening homes for stray cats next. I hate him and I hate cats. And don't you sit there gloating either, Rusty."

"I'm not gloating," Rusty said. He saw the campfires and the singing, the early waking and easy fighting vanish forever. For a little while they had been near but he didn't suppose that, without Alfred for a reason, he would ever be near them again.

"I'm not gloating," he repeated, "but I'm glad for Alfred."

"Let's go tell him then," Kass said. "Let's not leave the poor little kid on tenterhooks. Where is he now?"

"Down in a bunch of trays playing double Canfield."

"Double Canfield!" Kass cried. "Oh God, what have I let myself in for?"

But she had stopped crying. She put on the shoe she was holding, and began to hop along the hot cement of the driveway to the other side of the car.

"Here," Rusty called, and tossed her the shoe he had. She put it on and got in beside him. Two shoes seemed to restore her sanity.

"Have you had anything to eat this morning?" she asked, quite calmly.

"Couple of apricots."

"I haven't had anything and I'm starved. Let's pick up Alfred and go into town and have some strawberry waffles. If Alfred can leave his game, that is."

"He'll be finished," Rusty said, confidently. "He's a real fast player."

# Horace Chooney, M.D.

ALTHOUGH DR. CHOONEY had lived in the country for six months he was still unaccustomed to the sudden country alternations of sound and silence. He had never, as he remembered it, heard from his city apartment anything as startling as the abrupt scream and accompanying loud machinelike drilling which now filled the air just outside his bedroom window. Dr. Chooney, at once wide awake, he thought, sat up in his bed; still, before the sight of the big live-oak tree and its resplendent hardworking woodpecker had accounted for the sounds, two other possibilities had immediately come to his mind. The minute he had seen where he was, he had of course dismissed these and watched with pleasure as the industrious, systematic bird uncovered its bountiful and surprised breakfast.

At this hour of the morning Dr. Chooney missed his wife Harriet, who since their removal to the country had found it more convenient to occupy another sleeping room. Upon awakening, his mind often teemed with analogues and whimsies, and it was a real loss to have no one with whom he could share them. He always made an effort to recall them for her, but as is often the case with such imaginative sparkles, they were not quite so good when rewarmed.

The height at which the sun came through the tangle of oak and madrone trees on the slope above the house told Dr. Chooney that he had overslept. Though there was no longer any need for early rising, the old habits still held, and he stepped at once from his bed and touched the push button which rang in the kitchen below and told Harriet that he was now up and would be ready in thirty minutes for his breakfast.

From his bedroom window Dr. Chooney regarded with pleasure the remoteness and solitude of his new home. There had been nothing in a large city practice to prepare him for it, and since he had left the city without premeditation he had had no opportunity before his arrival for even an imaginative sampling of country delights. Stand-

140

ing now looking out over his own wooded acreage, he was able to see its birds, trees, and occasional small animals in all their uniqueness; to focus upon them the same absorbed attention which he would have given in the past to some unusual lesion or malformation.

While the long-legged old-fashioned tub was slowly filling (the water pressure in the second story was bad), Dr. Chooney got out of his pajamas and walked about in his room enjoying the touch of the brisk morning air upon his unclothed body. As he passed and re-passed the mirror in the combination washstand and dressing table he noted with satisfaction the unsagging firmness of his well-larded frame and its healthy mushroom color. Before he went into the bath-room, Dr. Chooney, in case Harriet when first he rang had been out-side feeding her chickens or perhaps milking the goat, once more touched the bell; then, unflinching, he stepped into his cold tub.

Dr. Chooney used for his bath a bar of yellow soap and a coarse cloth, both intended for dishwashing. Dr. Chooney was in many ways a connoisseur of sensations, and he made a real effort to slight none, not even the smallest. For bathing, an experience cleanly, of course, but neutral, he had little regard: warm water, soft cloth, mild soap. These things did not interest him. Every experience, he believed, should be made positive through either pleasure or pain. If the plea-sure itself had become an old story, all of its reality worn down into an undifferentiated smoothness, Dr. Chooney elected a flick or two of pain to teach his nerves a continued responsiveness. He relished now every stroke of the somewhat abrasive cloth; he delighted in the sensation as of a mild burn which the yellow soap left across his chest and forearms.

There had been whole weeks recently when Dr. Chooney had not seemed very real to himself: days when his personality, capable on occasion as he so well knew of the most amazing richness and inten-sification, became thin and diffused; long periods when he had felt almost completely bereft of that constellation of interests which makes a man so uniquely himself.

Red striped now as any flagellant, Dr. Chooney stepped from his bath and gently dried himself. Psychically, he supposed he had been suffering somewhat as so precise an organization as a tiger might, had it found itself forced to exist for months on end as a mollusk of some variety—impotent, but never forgetful beneath the layers of jelly of its former subtlety and power.

Dr. Chooney finished his drying before the open window of his own room. There the zestful aromatic scents of laurel and madrone leaves, dampened earlier in the morning by fog and now heated by the sun, flowed up to him, and Dr. Chooney, inhaling, made them a part of himself. Dr. Chooney was a careful and methodical dresser. He had proceeded from the top drawer which held his underwear to the third from the bottom which held his white shirts when his wife entered.

He spoke to her a little shortly, which he certainly had not intended, but he had an aversion to unannounced entrances.

"I didn't ring, Harriet," he said without straightening.

"I know, Henning, but . . ."

Dr. Chooney closed the drawer, lifted himself, and looked down at his wife.

"Horace," she amended.

"Yes?" said Dr. Chooney. He put on and buttoned his shirt, very precise buttoning, calculated to prevent the appearance of any half-filled buttonholes later in the day.

Dr. Chooney would have preferred to have been more aware of his wife. She was a small, dark cloudy woman with a tender mouth. He berated himself for his faded responsiveness. In their former life in the city, where they had been somewhat gregarious, Dr. Chooney had heard it said occasionally that he stirred up Harriet as one might a placid, quiet animal simply to see it come to life. This was not so. He had never been interested in Harriet's impetuosity or lack of it. If he stirred her up sometimes, it was only as a means of becoming aware of himself. He smiled a little now at the naïveté of his friends' conclusions. Was frost interested in the boulder it split? Or wind in the height of the wave it piled up? No, no. His friends had not studied, as he had, natural forces and did not understand, as he did, that natural forces were interested in effects only as a means of knowing and testing themselves.

Still smiling as he thought of the incorrectness of his friends' suppositions, Dr. Chooney handed his wife a small white card. "Why wasn't this burned with the others?" he asked.

His wife read the card, then turned it over as if hoping to find something upon the underside to negate what she had just seen.

"Where did you find this, Horace?" she asked.

"Under the paper in my white-shirt drawer. How did you happen to miss it?"

"I don't know," Harriet Chooney answered. "I can't imagine. I've tried to be very careful. I was sure everything had been burned."

"Perhaps you left it on purpose," Dr. Chooney suggested.

His wife's small brown hand was trembling. "Horace, you know I never, never—"

Dr. Chooney cut his wife's protesting short. "Very well, then. Let's drop it. Let's speak of it no more. It was simply a mistake and doesn't call for so impassioned a defense. It would be better though if it did not happen again and if this were burned."

Dr. Chooney's wife first bent the card double, then folded it so that the bit of pasteboard was lost in the palm of her hand.

"You have a patient waiting," she said.

"At this time of the morning?"

"It's not really early, Horace. It's past ten."

"Who is it?" asked Dr. Chooney.

"No one we know," his wife said. "A Miss Chester from the place over the hill called Oakknoll. I think you ought to see her. You should build up a practice once again."

"You think so?" Dr. Chooney asked.

"Yes, Horace, I do."

"I'll have my breakfast now," he said.

"Horace, this girl is timid and nervous. She's waited thirty minutes already. If you don't see her now, she won't be back again," Mrs. Chooney urged.

"How old is she?"

"Perhaps twenty-five," Mrs. Chooney said.

"Show her into my office," said Dr. Chooney, "and bring us two cups of coffee."

Dr. Chooney felt very large in his small office, but efficient and commanding too. His thighs still burned pleasantly from the irritation of the harsh soap, and he could smell from the kitchen the fragrance of coffee beginning to boil. The office was filled with sunlight; his well-polished desk glittered, the madrone blossoms in the bowl on top of the case which held his medical books were translucent in the strong light. With an increasing sense of integration and well-being, Dr. Chooney seated himself and faced his patient.

"Yes?" he asked pleasantly.

Miss Chester, who herself sat stiff and unrelaxed before him, was not, he saw at once, twenty-five. Twenty-two or -three at the most. Miss Chester was one of those young women who have considerable breadth but no thickness. Her shoulders were wide, her waist narrow, and beneath her light summer dress her breasts, which did not seem organically related to her broad, flat chest, were very noticeable. She was his own color with some of the murk leached out. Her hair, by which women chiefly show their awareness of themselves and their times, was in a soft and dowdy pile.

Miss Chester's dress was of a kind Dr. Chooney could not remember having seen since childhood: soft, peach colored, it did not expose the body but was a continuation of it. It appeared to have been made at home, someone saying, "A little more fullness here," or, "Does it bind now under the arms?" Miss Chester's dress gave Dr. Chooney as much pleasure as a disease. He could not have been more lingering in a diagnosis. At the neck the dress had small peach-colored frills which touched the skin and seemed almost as if they might be an extension of the flesh.

Unclothed, Dr. Chooney speculated, Miss Chester would look somewhat like a Botticelli Venus, formed not in a warm southern sea but in some cool northern pond.

"Yes," Dr. Chooney said again, agreeably.

"I am Flora Chester," the girl told him.

"Yes, Miss Chester," said Dr. Chooney.

"I haven't been well," the girl said, "or at least I've thought I wasn't well."

Dr. Chooney understood the doubt which comes over patients in doctors' offices. Unaccustomed to speaking of their ailments, they hear their own words, "I am not well," and being to wonder if their disease is not a hallucination which has made it possible for them first to imagine, then to credit their symptoms.

"Just what did you think was the trouble?" Dr. Chooney asked.

"Perhaps I imagine it all," the girl told him, with a somewhat breathless, confessional rush. "Perhaps it is just something I dream up"—she looked up at Dr. Chooney as if she had used a daring piece of slang—"to fill my days."

"Are your days empty?" asked Dr. Chooney.

"Not empty . . . but not important."

"Just what," Dr. Chooney persisted, "are your symptoms?"

"Oh, they're really nothing." The girl paused as if asking Dr. Chooney permission to continue.

"Go on," Dr. Chooney said.

"Everything tastes like pasteboard," said Miss Chester. "I can't sleep, yet I seem to be always dreaming so that when I do sleep I wake up tired. Toward evening I feel less tired, but by then my head begins to ache."

Having told her symptoms, Miss Chester at once politely disclaimed them as a woman brushes aside a compliment. "It's probably just my imagination," she insisted.

"Why do you keep repeating that?" Dr. Chooney asked. "What kind of mechanism do you think the body is? Do you suppose it sends out false reports as to its lesions and aberrations? Why should you imagine what is painful and distressing to you?"

"My father and mother imagine things," said Miss Chester.

"You live with your father and mother?"

The girl nodded.

"An only child?"

The girl smiled excitedly, as if Dr. Chooney had said something very personal to her. "Yes. Yes, I am."

"How old are your parents?"

"Sixty and seventy-two."

"What does your father do?"

"Nothing. Nothing, that is, except his hobby," said Miss Chester. "Father's a retired dentist. One day he just walked out of his office— with a man in the chair and his mouth propped open. He came home and said—this was before I was born, but I've heard my mother tell it—he came and said, 'I will never put my hand inside the mouth of another human being.'" She looked up at him as if she had just reported a revolutionary act.

"That doesn't strike me as being particularly imaginative."

"But now he really does imagine things," said Miss Chester. "For one thing, he's not really interested in anything but teeth. He listens to the radio just in order to be able to tell about the plates or bridges people are wearing. He thinks he can tell by the way they speak or sing. He writes them letters saying, 'You have never had your six-year molars removed,' and has them sign the letter if he is right and return it."

"Is he right sometimes?" Dr. Chooney asked.

"Oh yes, he is," said Miss Chester. "Almost always."

"Then he's really not imagining things, is he, Miss Chester?"

"My mother—"

"Look, Miss Chester. Let us first consider you. Your troubles, whatever you may think of your parents, are not mental nor imaginary. No little quirk is responsible for them. Turn this way, please."

"I've never been in a doctor's office before," Miss Chester said, turning toward Dr. Chooney with stiff self-consciousness.

"You should have been," Dr. Chooney told her gravely.

Miss Chester smiled as if she had been praised.

Dr. Chooney leaned forward and with his cool, heavy-tipped fingers explored Miss Chester's slender throat: first at the jawline, then lower where the throat widened above the fragile collarbones.

"It is just as I thought," he told her.

Dr. Chooney was not surprised at the brilliant, quivering look his patient gave him—as if she were hearing a declaration of love.

"You mean there really is something wrong?" she asked.

"Decidedly wrong."

Dr. Chooney's fingers continued their skilled probing. This girl had probably never before been the object of so concentrated an interest, certainly never the object of so concentrated a male interest. Her parents old, lost in their own worlds, she without friends, this was doubtless the first time anyone had so leaned toward her or expressed concern for her well-being; the first time she had been so touched—with hands professional, of course, but conveying to her inexperienced nature feelings not wholly clinical.

"Feel just here," Dr. Chooney told her. He guided the long-fingered, soft hand to a spot beneath the jaw.

"The little lumps?" Miss Chester asked.

"Nodules," Dr. Chooney corrected her. "Indications of a serious glandular affection."

Dr. Chooney saw that his patient was both pleased and frightened. "I don't really feel so very sick," she said.

"Pardon me, Miss Chester," Dr. Chooney said, "but you actually have no idea how you feel. You have had this disorder for so long that you no longer know what it is like to feel well. You have forgotten what health is."

Miss Chester put a hand to her face. "Don't I look well?" she asked.

"No," Dr. Chooney said, "to a doctor you do not look well. Lovely, charming," Dr. Chooney said, smiling charmingly himself, "but certainly not well."

The girl flushed. "Is this glandular . . . affection . . . serious?" she asked.

"Very," said Dr. Chooney gravely. He leaned back, fingertips delicately touching, and rocked gently in his swivel chair.

"Serious enough," Miss Chester asked in a low voice, "to be fatal?"

Dr. Chooney laughed, from deep in his chest. "My dear girl," he said.

Miss Chester smiled and once more leaned back against the dark chair, but Dr. Chooney was immediately grave again. "As a matter of fact," he said, "that depends entirely upon you. You can go on, as you have been doing, from bad to worse. Or, you can put yourself into the hands of a competent physician and become the girl nature intended you to be."

"It isn't too late then?" Miss Chester asked.

"Certainly not," Dr. Chooney assured her heartily. "Not if you care, not if you try. Look at this," Dr. Chooney said.

He opened a drawer of his desk and took out an envelope. "At one time I was something of an amateur photographer. I made it a practice to take pictures of my patients. They were not only helped by being shown graphic evidence of their improvement, but others with similar disorders were encouraged when they saw what had been done in the way of arresting their disease. Would you like to see some of the pictures?" he asked.

"Oh yes," said Miss Chester eagerly.

Dr. Chooney handed her a photograph. "This girl," he said, "had your affliction, though in a somewhat more advanced form."

Miss Chester gasped. "She looks dead," she whispered.

Dr. Chooney nodded in agreement. "Yes, doesn't she," he said. "Though that is largely a result of the bad lighting and her closed eyes. And as I've already told you, she was a considerably more advanced case than you.

"Now," said Dr. Chooney genially, "have a look at this." Before handing over the second picture, however, Dr. Chooney himself regarded it for some time: a really lovely study of Anne. Frail, eyes considerably sunken, but laughing. He remembered just her posture that afternoon on the lawn chair and the way she had flung up her arms as he snapped the shutter and what she had said afterward.

"Oh," said Miss Chester, "she's better, isn't she? Much better. She's lovely here."

"A very charming girl," Dr. Chooney agreed. "This," he said, "is the third. Plump, brown, playing tennis. You could scarcely ask for a healthier-looking girl than that, could you, Miss Chester?"

"Oh no," Miss Chester said. "Here she looks"—Miss Chester paused, apparently searching for a word which would describe the change that had taken place—"quite normal. As if there were nothing in the world wrong with her."

"When that picture was taken," Dr. Chooney said, "there was nothing wrong with her. Well," he asked playfully, taking back the pictures, "is seeing believing?"

"Oh yes indeed," said Miss Chester. "I'm so glad you showed them to me. I can't thank you enough. I don't want to lose a minute getting started. What am I to do first?"

"First," said Dr. Chooney, "a prescription." He scrawled one swiftly. "Have this filled, Miss Chester, and follow the directions exactly."

"Shall I come back tomorrow?" Miss Chester asked.

Dr. Chooney looked through his engagement book. "No," he said, "not tomorrow. Could you come on Thursday at three?"

"Oh yes, Dr. Chooney, I'll be here. I won't let anything interfere." Miss Chester turned back from the door. "I feel better already," she said shyly. "I thank you so much."

Dr. Chooney, who had risen and was standing now beside his desk, said, "Hope is a great restorative, Miss Chester."

Dr. Chooney was still standing when Harriet came in with the tardy coffee.

"You're a little late," Dr. Chooney told her.

"I didn't bring it sooner on purpose," she said. "I didn't think it seemed professional—serving coffee to a patient you had never seen before—and I do so want," she explained, "everything to get started properly."

Dr. Chooney sat at his desk and his wife paused, waiting for him to clear a space upon which she could place the tray she held. As she looked down, waiting, the tray sagged, then slanted, as if all strength had left her wrists, until coffee and cream together poured downward upon the three pictures Dr. Chooney had just been showing his patient. Dr. Chooney imperturbably shook the drops of scalding coffee from his hands and himself regarded the pictures, now so ranged upon his desk that the eye moved from the girl—what had Miss Chester called her?—from the normal girl to the frail one and from the frail one to that girl who, lights or no lights, had the appearance of death.

"Let me have that tray," said Dr. Chooney. He took it from his wife and put it firmly down. "Now get a dish mop of some kind and clear away this mess."

After his wife left, Dr. Chooney first took out his handkerchief and dried his hands, touching meditatively the small yellow blisters which were already beginning to form. Then he cleaned, but did not change the order of, the three pictures. Looking at them, the well-being he had begun to feel while bathing became more pronounced. He could feel quite clearly, along channels too delicate for reason to follow, forewarnings of a delicious reintegration. The tiger's outline had begun once more to assume—from his well-stored mind Dr. Chooney chose the poet's phrase—its fearful symmetry.

# The Linden Trees

FRED NORBY stood at the kitchen door with his bathrobe wrapped so tightly about his thin body that it provided him with a sort of auxiliary backbone. He had been roused early from his bed by pain beyond what he could bear, and, not wishing to awaken his wife Emily with his groans, had crept downstairs.

Now he stood at the kitchen door looking out into the bright morning. The alfalfa patch alone was not yellowed by the sun. It was too blue a green to take any gilding. But the round apricots, already beginning to turn, were as fiery as tiger eyes.

All the world outside the house was awake. The gray tomcat, who had been dozing on the steps, stirred to catch and eat a bottle fly. He munched it slowly, his eyes half shut, as if he were still occupied with thoughts of the night. The sun shone rosily through the big, ruby-veined ears of the jack rabbits who were breakfasting on the alfalfa. The four linden trees at the south side of the barn, garage it was now, were in full bloom, and Fred Norby, now that his pain had let up a little, was aware, above all else, of their scent.

It was a great relief to him to be so caught up by something outside himself that he forgot himself completely. This didn't happen often any more, and of course he wasn't aware of it while it was happening. Only afterward, after the moment had passed, and he was once more the man to whom certain things had happened—and for whom this other certainty waited—did he rejoice and think, "For a second there, maybe even longer, I escaped. I lived in that linden smell. I remembered Father's planting those trees a long time ago, and saying how they'd been thick in Iowa when he was a boy, and how there was no honey to beat that from linden blossoms. I always planned to get me a hive of bees some day—when the press of work let up—and find out the taste of linden honey for myself. Now I suppose I'll never know what it's like but I recall Father's saying it was heavier than most."

He opened the screen door and stepped outside. Though it was still very early, heat waves were already dancing over the tin roof of Harm's garage. Old Cassius, the cat, laid his warm, supple weight across Fred's instep. The old man's moment of self-forgetfulness was gone; he was identified with the linden smell no longer. Slowly, he hoisted his foot until Cassius hung across it like a furry snake, making no move to escape. He eased him carefully to the ground, and walked painfully down the steps. In the rhubarb bed he had seen some withered stalks that needed snapping off. He thought that perhaps in a little job like this he could lose himself again, be a man like his neighbors, out to do a little weeding or hoeing before breakfast; but it was no use. Such escapes did not come by seeking. He was what he was, kneeling here by the rhubarb bed, a sick man; too sick to do any job that really needed doing. "Difficult or unnecessary jobs are the only ones I have stomach for now," he thought, as he tugged at the slack, rubbery stalks. But they were too much for him. He could neither break them, nor pull them up.

Dizzy and swaying, he got to his feet and walked back to the steps across ground that seemed so yielding his feet became imbedded in it. He pushed Cassius aside and sat with closed eyes. "It's a funny thing," he thought, after the wave of weakness had passed, "that we aren't better prepared for this— It's a wonder we can't accept it quietly, not knowing anyone who's escaped it—seeing as it's touched all we know."

He buried his hand in Cassius' dry hot fur, and felt beneath his fingers the cat's heartbeat even more hurried than his own. "I believe, in spite of everything, we all half expected to escape. More than half expected, believed completely. Thought it would come to everyone else, but pass us by. Without us, without me, how's anything else to exist?"

He stretched his hand clear of the shadow of the eaves, into the sun's morning brightness. "Heat. The only heat's the heat I feel. And the only cold I've ever had is that that's made me shake. Hard to believe there's any other. Hard to believe it won't stop with me. Hard to believe I don't have to keep on existing just to keep them going."

He sank his head against his hand. "No, that ain't the trouble," he said aloud. "The trouble is they're going on—and me not here—me leaving before I've had half my fill."

He rubbed his fingers strongly together as if to imbed in the very bone some grains of sunlight—something that would last him, after the flesh was gone.

"The trouble is," he thought, "I've got no child. I've got no way of continuing. I stop here. Them with children keep on living—they survive. Eyes just like theirs go on seeing—and hands they've given shape to go on feeling. But not for me—" and he rubbed his hands together, dryly and sadly. "Eyes just like theirs," he said.

And then he thought of Norby. Little Norb. Only last week he had come up and said, "Can I take your glasses off, Uncle Fred?"

"Sure," he said. "Sure you can, Norb. Do you want to try them on? Your eyes giving you trouble?"

Norb had laughed at this—a quick little snort. "No," he said. "I wanted to look at your eyes. Grandma said I had your eyes. She said, 'Norby's got Fred's eyes.' So if I've got yours you've got mine and I want to see what they look like."

Norby had held the spectacles carefully in one hand and with the other balanced himself on the side of the bed, while he looked long and intently into his uncle's eyes.

"Well, Norb," Fred had said at last, "are they yours?"

"They're in your head," Norb said, "so they must be yours. But," he said, wagging his head seriously, "they are i-den-tical."

"I laughed then," he thought. "That was another of the times I was able to forget. I was nothing but a laugh then. It swallowed up everything else—pain, everything. Think of a little sprout like that using a word half as long as himself. Identical.

"Identical," he mused. "Identical. Well, I suppose they are. Same kind of piebald mixture of blue and brown."

He felt a little easier and leaned back against the door, cautiously, afraid to relax completely, leave himself open and vulnerable to a pain thrust.

"Those eyes of Norby's are going to go on seeing things a long time after mine're shut. He's ten now. Why, he ought to be here for another sixty years. He ought to see the year 2000. He'll see the new century—not much doubt of it. Except for me all the Norbys are long-lived. Just to think—I've looked into eyes that are going to see the year 2000."

And then the idea came to him. He struck his palms together with almost a gesture of health. "Why haven't I thought of this before?" he said. "Why haven't I?"

As he sat there, completely filled with his discovery, taken far away from his present condition, Emily came downstairs. She had awakened and missed him and hurried, fearful and foreboding, about the house looking for him.

Now she was calling his name, trying to keep the anxiety out of her voice and failing. "Fred," she called, "Fred, where are you?"

He didn't hear her until she got to the back door and pushed the screen against his shoulder trying to open it.

"Here, Emily," he said, "What are you up to? Trying to push me on my face? Taking advantage of me because I'm sick?"

Emily hadn't heard him use this bantering tone for months. It was as if the past months had been a bad dream from which she was just awakening. Oftentimes she had thought, "This will suddenly pass away and everything will be as it was before," and for a second she felt that had happened. Here was Fred, up early, sitting out in the sunshine and joking with her just as in the old days.

She wanted to believe, to carry on the conversation in the tone in which he'd started it, but she couldn't. "Fred, Fred, what are you doing out here? I woke up and you were gone and I was terribly worried."

"What do you think I'm doing, Emily? I'm enjoying the sun. Now you get me some breakfast and I'll come in and talk to you. I've got a wonderful idea. It just came to me. I can't see why I never thought of it before. It changes everything. Now you just give me a hand up and I'll come in and watch you cook."

Emily was surprised to hear him ask for help, and glad. It made things easier and happier when he'd take the help he needed without bitterness. He slid over on the steps until she could open the door and putting his thin, dry hand in hers, let her take most of his weight in hoisting him to his feet.

"You always were a husky girl, weren't you, Emily? If you hadn't married me you'da been a lady athlete. An Olympic champion in something or other."

Emily smiled a little as she helped him into the kitchen. "I used to beat all my brothers running and jumping."

"Sure you did. You could yet." Fred smiled, too. Funny about Emily. Most women liked to be praised for their looks, or their cooking, or their mending, but Emily liked to be praised for her muscles, told what an athlete she'd of made.

He eased himself down into the breakfast nook. "Now, Emily, I tell you what I want for breakfast. Fried hominy and bacon. Hominy fried until it's good and brown."

Emily looked at him pleadingly. "Fred, you remember what the doctor said? You'll just have to pay for it afterward."

He shook his head at her. "Emily, you know as well as I do, it don't matter a hoot what I eat. Nothing I eat's going to make any difference—and I got to pay for it all afterward anyway—no matter what it is. So it had about as well be something that tastes good while I'm eating it. Now you go and start it cooking. And I want coffee, too. Bacon and grits and coffee."

Emily got some cushions from the living room and put them at the end of the bench next the wall, and lifted his feet up so he was half lying down.

"This feels pretty good," he said. "Now you hustle the breakfast along."

Emily had tears in her eyes while she measured out the coffee and water and cut and chopped the bacon. It seemed at once so much like old times, and like the end.

But Fred wasn't paying any attention to her. He was talking about his idea.

"Emily, you know how everyone's always said Norby was just like me? Same laugh, same cowlick, same way of pointing one foot further out than the other? And he's got my eyes. No doubt about it.

"Of course these outside things don't matter much—but they's what made me think of it—so I naturally speak of them."

The smell of frying bacon filled the kitchen. He shut his eyes and drew in a deep breath. "That's the first time food's smelt good in a coon's age. Fry aplenty."

"But, Fred," said Emily, "what is this idea?"

"It's about me and Norby. I ain't got much longer here. No, no, Emily. We've both knowed it a long time. No use shutting our eyes to it. But look, Norby's going to be here—say sixty years more, might even be seventy. Going to see the year 2000 and maybe more. Well, I'm going to talk to him. I'm going to have a talk with him as soon as he can get over here."

Emily stirred the hominy into the browning bacon and spoke above the hissing spatter. "Fred, what can you say to Norb?" All her happiness in finding her husband up, and talkative and hungry, dropped from her. She was afraid his mind had been touched by his long sickness. "Norb's a child, Fred. What can you say to him about—" but she couldn't go on.

"About dying, Emily? No use being scared of that word. I was. I have been. No use denying that to you. You've seen it plain enough. But this idea, this thing I want to talk to Norb about changes it."

Emily slid the skillet back and forth across the gas flame. "What idea, Fred?" she asked gently.

"It's hard to put in words, Em. I'm afraid it won't sound like much in words. But it's real all right. However it sounds, you remember its real, real as fried hominy. I'm going to talk to Norb. I'm going to tell him to look at things for me—smell things, touch things. I'm going to tell him to think about me when he's doing it. Maybe he won't be able to do that—much—but when he can . . .

"The things I've missed, Em—the things there ain't time for now. I know now what's important, and I'll tell him. He can do them for me. See 'em with my eyes. And what's the odds, Emily, whether I do it myself or not. He'll do it for me.

"Then I want to tell him about the year 2000. Then, that night, January first, I want him to go out some place—away from town, some place out in the open where he can see the stars—I want him to stand in some open field where there's trees and woods about and look at the stars and say some words I got in mind. I'll write 'em out, maybe, for him. Why, Emily, it'll be as good as being there. You know right now if I had to choose between my seeing something and Norb's seeing it—I'd choose Norb. Well, I choose Norb for the year 2000.

"Then afterward I want him to come into town. Needn't be this town. Any town'll do. I want him to go some place where there are people—people all together, and shouting and happy. You know how they are on New Year's Eve? Kind of silly. But most of them full of good thoughts about the coming year. And I'm going to leave him a little sum—say fifty dollars—to buy champagne with—that's another thing I've never tasted—and he and his friends can drink it. And in a way—this is kinda hard to explain, Emily, it'll be as if I was. Why, I can almost taste it now, that champagne Norb will be drinking in 2000."

Emily put the food before him; the hominy delicately browned, the coffee black and steaming. She couldn't help being practical, even about the year 2000. "Bertha will never let Norb taste that champagne, Fred. She's strong against liquor."

"Bertha won't be here then, Emily. She'll be with me—and Norb will be a seventy-year-old. Out from under Bertha's thumb."

Emily poured herself a cup of coffee and sat down opposite her husband. The apricot tree outside the window broke the sunshine that fell across the white tablecloth into gold nuggets.

"I can't tell you, Emily, all about it. I don't want to try too much for fear if I spill it all now there won't be any left to tell Norb. But you call Bertha right away, won't you? See if Norb can't come in this morning. It may be some time before . . . I may never feel this good again."

It was late afternoon before Norb trudged into town, hot and dusty. He'd been picking berries all morning for Bertha. Emily gave him a couple of glasses of lemonade before she sent him upstairs to Fred.

"Norby," she said, before he went up, "your Uncle Fred wants to talk to you. You know Uncle Fred's not well, and maybe what he says'll sound funny to you. But you be a good child—you listen. Maybe you can't understand everything he'll say to you. But you try. You try as hard as you can."

Norb licked the last drops of lemonade from his upper lip.

"Uncle Fred and me's got the same eyes," he said.

"All right, Norb, you remember that, and go upstairs to Uncle Fred now."

Emily walked about outside while the two were talking. She was too restless to sit still. She picked three or four apricots, hard as donnickers yet, but beautifully colored, to put on the window sill over the sink to look at.

"I don't understand it myself," she thought. "I don't understand it at all, and I don't see how a child Norb's age is going to make head or tail of it."

She stayed outside as long as she could and when she went in she found that Norby had left. He had gone out the front way, closing the door so quietly behind him she hadn't heard it.

She ran up the stairs full of misdoubts, fearful that Fred would be sad, bitter again, full of pain; afraid that he hadn't been able to say what he had in mind, or that Norby had been too little to understand.

She heard Fred's heavy breathing before she'd got to the head of the stairs, and hurried to his room.

But he smiled at her. "Get the hypo, Em," he said. "It's pretty bad." She gave him the injection skillfully and, inch by inch, he eased back against the pillows.

"It's all right, Em," he said finally, seeing she was afraid to ask him how the talk had gone. "It's all right. Everything's fine."

"Did you tell him all you had in mind, Fred? Were you able to make him understand?"

"No, Em, I didn't tell him as much as I'd planned. About all I told him was about the linden trees."

"The linden trees," Emily echoed.

"Yes, about getting a hive of bees and having linden honey. My father did, and I always planned to, but I never got around to doing it. Norb's going to do it. He's going to taste linden honey."

"Did you tell him about the year 2000?"

"Nope. No, I didn't mention about the year 2000."

"Oh, Fred," Emily said, so sad for him.

"I didn't mention it on purpose, Emily. As soon as I started talking, as soon as I laid eyes on Norb, I seen how silly all that was. All that champagne at midnight. I don't have to tell him—nor nobody like him. They got my eyes, regardless of color, and they'll use 'em in my way without a word from me. See the things I missed—year 2000 and beyond, and I'll have my share without saying a word. All I needed to speak of was the honey. And the lindens."

# Breach of Promise

EVERY AFTERNOON between two and four, depending upon the amount of business or conversation he had encountered on his route, the mail carrier came by in his ramshackle, mud-spattered car. He didn't drive up the lane to the house, a lane a quarter of a mile long and crossing at one point a brook, which after heavy rains was something more than a brook, but put the mail in the wobbly tin box, set the flag, honked three times, and drove on.

Ordinarily I waited for these three honks before I walked down to the box. But now and then, because I was at that time so eagerly hoping for a certain letter, I would convince myself, in spite of the fact that I had been listening intently, that the mail carrier had passed without my hearing him. Invariably, after I had walked to the box on these occasions to find I had been mistaken, the mail carrier would be unusually late. Then, because my work had already been interrupted and because my eagerness for the letter I awaited always made me hopeful that the mail carrier would be along in another minute or two, I didn't return to the house. Instead, I paced up and down the lane, stopping usually at the brook to examine the veining in some curious pebble or to watch an island of foam, seemingly as imperishable as the pebble, float by.

At the time, I would be scarcely aware, however, of the objects I scanned. All of my consciousness would be focused in a fury of attention on the wished-for letter: imagining its size, shape, color to the eye, weight to the hand, the heavy downstrokes of the writing, even the postmark, Yorba Linda, California.

The letter, not the one which I wanted but the one of which I am writing, came on a day when I was in this manner examining pebbles at the brookside. The mail carrier saw me and honked three times but, nervous and irritated after what had seemed my long wait, I continued obstinately to bend over my pebble. He honked again. I picked up the pebble I had been admiring and with it in my hand walked down to the mailbox.

"You got another letter here addressed to that other name," he told me.

He held this letter close to his chest, as if it were a winning card in a crucial game. The mail carrier had never been reconciled to the fact that I received letters addressed in two ways: to my "own" name, and to what he called "that other name," the name I used in my writing. The letter I had hoped for would not be addressed to "that other name," so I didn't care how long he held this square white envelope to his chest.

"It's addressed care of the Seulkes," he said (the Seulkes were the people with whom I was boarding, the house at the end of the lane), "so I reckon it's for you."

He ended on a rising note and looked at me, through spectacles as blurred and spattered as some old windowpane. "It's from Persis Hughes," he said. "You know her?"

"No," I told him, though I knew that a Mr. Hughes owned a large farm, down the road a mile or so and that he had a grown daughter.

"Funny thing," he said. "Persis writing you when she don't know you."

There was no use telling him that writers get letters from people they don't know, so I agreed with him. "Yes," I said, "it's a funny thing."

"You'd think she'd just walk up the pike if she had anything to say to you and save her three cents."

"Yes," I said again.

He finally handed me the letter from Persis Hughes, but he hadn't finished with talking yet.

"I notice it takes four days for a letter from California to reach you," he said.

"If they don't airmail it," I agreed.

"You get homesick, back here by yourself?" he asked.

"I'm pretty busy working," I told him and he didn't notice that I hadn't answered his question.

"Working?" he asked, and I could see that he thought I had found myself a job of some kind in town.

"Writing," I said, and from the way he repeated, "Oh, writing," it was plain writing wasn't his idea of work. But he drove on without any more questions, leaving me standing by the mailbox, Persis Hughes's letter in one hand, my prettily veined pebble in the other. On a sudden impulse I opened the box, placed the smooth little stone in its tin emptiness and tightly closed the lid. I did this without thinking, but I suppose that bitterly, subconsciously, I was thinking, I asked for bread and you gave me a stone, and that I felt relief in thus being able to objectify my emotions, to symbolize my self-pity.

I didn't open my letter from Persis Hughes until I reached my room. Though if the letter I wanted had come I would have read it six times over before I reached the house. My room at the Seulkes' was a perfect place for reading unwanted mail. It was sad, sad: strange, unpleasant colors, peculiar furniture, odd smells, and a most distressing, a really horrifying picture.

This picture was of the Seulkes' only son Albert, aged twelve, taken three days before he died of lockjaw. After Albert's death Mrs. Seulke had had his picture enlarged, covered with convex glass, and framed. And now Albert, looking, it seemed, already swollen, feverish, and in pain, watched me the whole time I was in the room.

A marble-topped "center table," a wicker rocker with crocheted back and arm tidies, a wooden chair, one of the dinette set which the Seulkes used in their kitchen, these, together with a large brass bed, made up the furnishings of my room.

I lived on that bed like a castaway on a desert island, like a lone survivor on a raft. It was my desk, chair, filing cabinet, table, sofa, home, world. Neither of the chairs was fit to sit on and the marble-topped table was too encumbered with decorative feet, claws, and legs to permit anyone with feet and legs of her own to get near it. It was on this bed, under Albert's picture, that I read Persis Hughes's letter.


Dear Miss or Madam [*the letter began*]:

I have heard that you are married but since I do not know for sure about this and do not want to call you Madam if you are really Miss, I address you thus.

I know you are a writer. I have read several of your stories in magazines. Some of them were interesting to me, and I suppose all must
have been interesting to somebody because I do not think editors pay
money for stories unless they are pretty sure about this.

This is not a "fan" letter though, to say I like your stories, for frankly
some of them I do not because they do not seem to me to be about
real life, but about some idea you have which you think is "real life."
Or maybe you know it isn't, but write about it because you think it is
better than real life. Or maybe more interesting.

What I want to ask you is this, wouldn't you like to *do* some *good*
by your writing? That is, not just *write about* goodness. You usually
do write about good people, etc., but I don't think this does any real
good in the world and it may do harm. People may read about all
these good characters of yours and say to themselves, "Well, if the
world is such a good place a little badness from me won't do any
particular harm."

And wouldn't you like to find out more about real life, too? Not just
your own ideas about life which you think will make a good story,
but *real* life, the way a woman suffers it?

I know a writer writes for money. So what I have to ask you is, not
only wouldn't you like to do some good with your writing and find
out more about how things really are than you seem to know (judging by your stories) but also make some money?

I could have invited you for a social call, to have supper with me,
then have asked you these things. But I think that would have been
sailing under false colors, which I do not care to do. Now that you
know that my purpose is mainly not social, would you care to have
supper with me on Tuesday of next week at six o'clock? I will be
honored by your presence. Please reply.

Sincerely,
Persis Hughes


When I finished Persis Hughes's letter it was dark. I had read it a
line or two at a time, not caring about it, thinking only of my own
letter, the one which had not arrived. I remembered all those letters
in stories and novels which never arrive or rather which are, ironi-

cally, delayed or lost until their arrival means nothing. I had almost convinced myself that my own letter had been held up in a like way, that all I needed to do was to send a telegram saying, "Your letter delayed, wire contents," to have by bedtime an answering wire and the words I had awaited the past weeks.

Almost, but not quite. By the time Persis Hughes's letter was read I had given up this silly dream. Would I like to know life, "the way a woman suffers it"? This made me smile. Persis Hughes was not much over twenty, if what I had heard was true. Still, I knew I would go to see her. For the mail carrier had been right. I was lonely here, heartsick.

Mr. Seulke drove me down the pike toward the Hughes's on Tuesday evening. I didn't tell him where I was going. Persis Hughes's father was a widower and I did not care to be twitted about him, as I would have been had Mr. Seulke known my destination, for nothing so interested him as what he called "he-ing and she-ing."

Mr. Seulke was very imaginative about such things. The first time I had hired him to drive me I asked him to take me to a small stream for the afternoon and pick me up later. With a sudden downward look Mr. Seulke had asked me, "Who you meeting, sis?"

At first I didn't understand his meaning and answered quite literally that I was going only to walk along the stream because it was beautiful and to note the kinds of trees and bushes which grew by it.

"That's your story, sis," he had said. "You stick to it."

I asked Mr. Seulke to let me out a short distance from the Hughes's farm. "You needn't come after me," I told him. "I have a way home." Persis Hughes, when I accepted her invitation, had told me she and her father would drive me back to the Seulkes'.

I can't write what Mr. Seulke said then, though to him it was no more than a half-humorous gallantry and nothing that any woman in that neighborhood would have taken amiss.

The Hughes's house was a nice place to be walking toward in the dusk. Chrysanthemums, bronze and gold, though grayish in the dark, were staked up along the path which led to the front door, and light, soft and yellow from kerosene lamps, shone out through the windows. Persis Hughes herself answered my knock and asked me in.

She seemed neither nervous nor emotional, the two things I had feared. A gusty fall wind was blowing and she shut the door quickly behind me.

"Father's old-fashioned," she said. "He likes supper early, and he eats it early, so there'll be only the two of us to eat now."

She put away my coat and purse and led me into the dining room. It was a real dining room, a room planned only for eating, and there was nothing in it which did not have to do with eating or one's comfort while eating or afterward: a big, fumed-oak sideboard, six fumed-oak chairs, a china closet through whose curving glass sides cut glass sparkled. Under each of the two windows was a Boston fern in a wicker fern stand and between these was a narrow couch upholstered in red rep on which one might rest or nap after eating. The table itself was round, covered with a white cloth whose corners touched the floor and lighted by a hanging kerosene lamp. In one corner of the room the isinglass eye of a small wood stove glowed rosily and its fire made an occasional dry tick, tick.

Persis Hughes seated me opposite her at the table. Between us was a very fine meal: an old hen, baked with dressing, glazed parsnips, baked squash, gravy, a casserole of tomatoes, slaw, a sponge cake covered with boiled custard, and besides these a number of jams and relishes.

"Did you cook all this?" I asked Persis.

"Oh, yes," she said. "Who else? There'd be only my father to cook if I didn't."

"Do you like cooking?" I asked.

"Not particularly," she said, "but it has to be done and I like good things to eat. So I cook as quickly and well as I can."

She carved the hen deftly, filling my plate with dark meat, white meat, dressing, gravy. I watched her as she did this. Afterward, but not then, I tried to see Persis Hughes through a man's eyes, which is a mistake, a thing a woman can never do. A woman, summoning all the latent masculinity she possesses, focusing it like a spyglass to peer through, remembering every item of female appearance ever lovingly described by man, will still see awry, unlike a man.

No, this particular spyglass is useless, and at that time it did not

occur to me to look through it at Persis Hughes, anyway. I thought
only, as I watched her carve, that she was very pretty. Persis Hughes
was plumper, perhaps, than she should have been. She was hazel
eyed and had wavy sorrel-colored hair which she piled high on her
head in a loose knot.

It was I, who for a time, in spite of what she had said in her letter,
tried to keep the evening "social." "How long have you lived here?"
"All of my life." "Where did you go to school?" "Local high school
and the Cincinnati Conservatory." "Oh, you play?" "Yes." "What instrument?" "Piano, that is I did." "Why did you give it up?" "I can't
write music and I don't want to go through life going do-do-do to
another man's tune." I suppose I showed my surprise at this.

"Would you want to spend the rest of your life reading aloud what
other people wrote?" she asked.

"I don't know," I replied. "Perhaps if I were good at it. One likes to
really succeed at something."

She refilled our plates and as she did so she asked, "Did you ever
see yourself unexpectedly in a mirror and not know yourself?"

I had, of course, and I said, "Yes. It's an awful experience, isn't
it?"

"Did anyone," she asked, "ever see herself in a mirror, not recognize herself, but think, what a beautiful, stylish woman that is coming down the street?"

This was something I had never thought of. "I suppose not. We're
only surprised at our ugliness not at our good looks."

"Then," said Persis, "we all actually look far worse than we have
any idea we do."

"I'm afraid so."

"Writing is a kind of mirror, isn't it?" she asked.

"A mirror?" I repeated, seeing how this was at once true and not
true.

"I mean," she said, "a man might see himself truly for the first
time in his life in a story, mightn't he? See how he really was, wicked
and ugly perhaps, instead of handsome and good."

"He might, but he'd probably not recognize himself. Just as we'd
never recognize ourselves in the mirror on the street except that the

awful woman approaching us is wearing our hat, walking in our shoes, carrying our purse."

"That's just it," said Persis eagerly. "*He'd* recognize himself in the same way. He'd read the story and think to himself, why that's what I said, that's what I wore that day, that's where we went and what we ate. He'd have to recognize himself by these things. Then, seeing himself as someone else saw him he'd see how bad, how foolish he'd been. And he would be filled with remorse."

I began to understand Persis Hughes's letter—a little. "If he *did* recognize himself," I asked, "and he *was* filled with remorse, what would he do then?"

"Change," she said promptly. "Mend his ways. Do what he promised."

She left the table to get more custard for our cake and poured us both coffee. She took no more than two bites of her own dessert, then carried her coffee over to the sofa and sat there bolt upright, sipping it. "Please go ahead and eat," she said. "I'm not hungry."

I did eat. The cake and custard were very good.

"I thought perhaps you would write this story," she said.

"What story?" I asked.

"Dallas's," she said. "Dallas's and mine."

"Who is Dallas?" I asked.

"A man," she said. "The man who promised to marry me."

"I don't know him. I don't know your story."

"You could meet him," she said. "He doesn't live far from here. And I'd tell you everything about us. I've thought over everything so much these past weeks I could talk to you all night and not a word would be untrue. I see and hear it all of the time. But you wouldn't know how that is, probably."

Not know that long, never-dissolving panorama of memory? That sound track which runs on and on repeating the very words which are most painful to hear? That film which replays, even against the closed eyes, particularly against the closed eyes, the very scenes one longs to forget?

"What good would it do if I were to write this story? How would it help you or anyone else?"

"Dallas would read it. He reads a great deal. And if he didn't happen to have the magazine it was in, I'd see he got it. Then it would be like the mirror. He would say to himself, 'If that is how I really am, God help me, I will change.' "

"Why do you want him to change?" I asked.

"I want him to do what he promised. I want him to marry me." She saw that my coffee cup was empty and refilled it from the pot she had left to keep warm on the stove.

There were so many objections to her scheme that I didn't know which to point out first. "Even if I wrote it," I said, "this story, you couldn't be sure a magazine would print it."

She wouldn't believe this. "It would be so real, so true," she said, "they would have to. They could see it was nothing anyone had imagined. That it was what a real person had suffered."

"Do you like to read about suffering?" I asked her.

"Yes," she said, "I do. I don't feel so alone then."

"Editors don't think that," I told her. "They think people want to read about happiness."

"Editors!" she said scornfully. "What do they know about people? Happiness, happiness, happiness! It breaks my heart to read about happiness."

"It breaks my heart to write about it sometimes, too," I said.

"Then why do it? I didn't intend to say this, but all those happy stories of yours! They sound silly to me. Besides," she said changing her tack very swiftly, "this might have a happy ending."

"Even so," I told her, "written in the best way I know, no one might want to print it."

She had a new idea. "It might be even better to have it printed in the *Republican*. That way Dallas would be sure to see it."

The *Republican* was Lane County's weekly paper. "I didn't know the *Republican* ever printed stories," I said.

"It doesn't. But it would if I paid them. Oh, I have the money to do it all right," she said, as if I had questioned her. "My mother left me," she stopped, as if her native hill-country suspicion and shrewdness had just reminded her that she was talking, after all, to a stranger with whom reticence about money matters was advisable, "a considerable sum," she finished. "I will also pay *you*" she said, "in that case, whatever a magazine would. And this way you'd have a sure thing. Not have to take a chance on an editor's liking it."

She put her coffee cup down on the floor with a gesture of finality, as if everything had been settled.

I said there had to be more in a piece of writing than promise of pay, otherwise writers wouldn't be writing at all but doing something that paid regularly the first of every month.

"You could do good, too," she reminded me, "by writing this story. Doesn't that interest you?"

"How?" I asked.

"You will help a man keep his word. And you will help save him from being ruined. For if he doesn't marry me, I will sue him for breach of promise. And if I do I will take from him everything he has. I can do it," she assured me. "I have his letters."

She picked up her cup again trying to find a few more drops in it. I refilled both our cups. Coffee keeps me awake, but I didn't expect to sleep anyway that night.

"I know exactly what the story should be called," she said.

"What?" I asked.

" 'Breach of Promise.' "

"That isn't a very interesting title," I said, "not very pleasant or inviting."

"What do I care about that? Interesting! Pleasant! That title will catch Dallas Hindshaw's eye, because he knows very well what I will do if he doesn't marry me. 'Breach of Promise,' " she repeated. "Yes, that's it."

I said nothing. What is there to say to the naïveté which outlines and names a piece of writing for you as specifically as if the work involved were of the same order as that needed for spading a garden plot or scrubbing a piece of linoleum? Perhaps Persis Hughes saw some of this in my mind. Anyway she said rather sadly, "Doesn't our story interest you?"

I couldn't help smiling. "I don't know your story," I told her, "the story of Persis Hughes and Dallas Hindshaw."

"What do you want me to tell you about Dallas and me?" she asked.

"Whatever you like." I put my empty coffee cup on the table, pushed the table nearer the wall, turned down the wick in the lamp, pulled up a second chair for a footrest, and prepared to listen. "Tell me whatever you like."

Persis lay back against the red sofa's bulging, built-in hump. The wind had died down, but not enough to stop the rustling of some vine against the wall of the house or to end the slight movement of the overhead lamp.

"I remember it all so well . . . the train we met on . . . his first words, everything. The only trouble is that our story is so strange, so unusual, it's hard to tell you. It isn't as if it were everyone's story."

But that was exactly what it was, everyone's story . . . my story. "Dallas was already on the Seymour train when I got on." . . . Does it make any difference whether the train runs between Cincinnati and Seymour or San Francisco and Salinas, if *he* is on it? . . . "It was snowing—that made it seem so much more close, private, shut away from everyone else." . . . What difference does the weather make? In rain, in a windstorm, in a time of quiet, not a leaf stirring, if *he* is there everyone else is shut away. . . . "Dallas had such a nice way of eating. I've never enjoyed seeing other people eat, but Dallas's hands went flying around the table, helping me, helping himself, and when he chewed there was no sign of it except a kind of shadow on his cheek. It was a pleasure to watch Dallas eat." . . . Whatever *he* does is a pleasure to watch: things unbearable in anyone else, how pretty they are in him; flip, flip, two aspirin on the back of the tongue, a gulp of water washing them down, and the smooth Adam's apple momentarily jutting out under the skin, the only grace in that is *his* grace . . . Ted's grace. "Dallas loved my faults, freckles, stubby eyelashes, anger, he didn't exclude them." *He* loves the whole person, always, unites what is severed and makes what was fractional complete. . . . "Dallas says there is no one else, so why doesn't he marry me? When he wanted to so much? All I need do is wake him up, show him himself in the mirror. Wake him up from this crazy dream he's in."

This crazy dream . . . this crazy dream . . . I put more wood in the stove. They were burning apple wood. The wind came up again and the lamp's arc widened. Back in the house a clock kept striking, quarters, halves, and wholes. After the hour struck there was always a little quaver, a kind of audible tremor as if the effort of that transition had almost overwhelmed the clock's mechanism.

Persis Hughes took down her hair, wound it up again in a tighter knot, took it down and braided it. Her father came to the door, with so big a yawn I could scarcely make out his face.

"Good night, girls," he said. "I'll lay down with my clothes on for a little snooze, call me when you want me." I stopped listening to Persis Hughes and thought my own thoughts and listened again and couldn't tell where my thoughts left off and her words began, so moved back and forth between the two and mixed them up thoroughly.

"That is Dallas's and my story," she concluded, unbraided her hair, sat up, leaned forward so that her face parted her long wavy hair the way a rock parts a waterfall. "Now you know it well enough to write it."

"Too well," I told her, "to write it."

"How can you know it too well?" she asked.

I couldn't say I had lived it.

"It's like the multiplication table. I know it by heart. I wouldn't write that."

"Do it for me," she urged.

"I can't. You can only write about what you don't know, and find out about it in the writing."

"You won't do it then?"

"I can't."

"You won't!"

"Very well, I won't. Besides, it wouldn't help you any."

"All right, then, I will sue him. You like to write about good people but you won't be troubled to do good. I will sue Dallas Hindshaw, and everything he has I will take away from him."

If she could not understand writing, I could not understand suing. We were at a standstill. "Do you love Dallas Hindshaw?"

"Were you asleep?" she asked.

"Then why do you want to ruin him, make public everything that is private and sacred?"

"I am honor bound to do so," she said. "It is a terrible thing to do but I am honor bound to try everything to bring him back."

"Bring him back!" I said. "You will make him hate you."

"If he won't marry me, I hope he will hate me enough to want to kill me. I hope every morning he will wake up thinking how he could kill me, put his hands around my throat and strangle me, or open up my dress and plunge a knife in my heart."

"You are crazy," I said. But I knew she wasn't crazy. She was speaking the truth.

"All right, I am crazy. If Dallas Hindshaw doesn't love me he must hate me. He must *do* something about me."

"You will be suing him for money. It will look to him and everyone else that you care for his money. That you can be paid with money for not having his love."

"Dallas's money is part of him. He worked for it, he invented this machine, peddled it about from house to house. If I have his money I have part of him. But I do not want a part of him. I want Dallas. Write our story."

"No," I said.

"Will you go to see him then? You might change your mind."

"I won't change my mind. And how could I go see him? What excuse have I for calling on a man I've never seen?"

"Women go to see him all the time to buy this machine. It shreds up vegetables, makes them come out finer than shavings. You could go to his house to buy one."

She was suddenly exhausted and sleepy. She fell down onto the sofa as if she were boneless, her head resting on the deepest swelling of the hump so that her hair flowed backward over it, touching the floor.

"Shall I tell him you sent me?" I asked angrily. Had I moved away from the painful emotions of my own life to be caught up in a pain that wasn't even my own? Was I to become that absurd creature, a woman without a husband who knows how husbands should be handled? The childless woman, full of advice to mothers?

"Whatever you want," she said, closed her eyes, and slept. It was three. I put another stick in the fire, blew out the lamp, and settled onto my two hard chairs. In California it was one, the October air warm; those who slept were quiet in their beds and those who were wakeful had company to solace their wakefulness. Had *he* company?

Toward morning Persis Hughes turned on her side and I saw that she was no longer sleeping. I asked her the question which had been in my mind.

"What happened?"

"What happened?" she repeated drowsily.

"Between you and Dallas? Why does he no longer love you?"

Then she was wide-awake and furious. "I tell you he does love me."

"But he won't marry you? What happened?"

"Nothing happened," she said, "nothing, nothing, nothing. Don't ask me that again."

I didn't, but I knew better. Something has always happened when we deny it so strenuously. Something we cannot bear to face.

At daybreak I walked home to the Seulkes', undressed, slept till noon under Albert's accusing picture, awakened, ate a package of dried figs, spent the afternoon writing a long letter, put the California address on it, and at dusk destroyed it. Then I washed, dressed, and went downstairs to supper.

When supper was over I said, "Will you drive me over to Dallas Hindshaw's, Mr. Seulke?"

"You planning to spend the night out again, sis?"

"No," I said, "tonight I plan to spend in my own comfortable bed."

Usually I tried to keep Mr. Seulke's conversation in channels of seemliness. But as we drove along that evening I thought, you're sixty years old, Mr. Seulke, and these are matters you've had on your mind since the age of ten or younger. If you've learned anything, Mr. Seulke, if you've got any knowledge in fifty years of thinking, speak up. If experience is a lamp, turn up the wick, Mr. Seulke, light the way for stumbling feet. Shine your light on Persis and Dallas and Ted and me. Shine it on hate and love and deceit. Shine it on hope deferred, Mr. Seulke, that maketh the heart to sicken. Shine it on a wife away from home, Mr. Seulke, lost and waiting and full of pride.

But Mr. Seulke, the minute he saw nonresistance in me, was interested in nothing but the weather, spoke of nothing but the weather. It was a mild evening, the sky curded with clouds. Occasional long drops of rain like warm fingers (there was no glass on the right-hand side of Mr. Seulke's Tudor) touched our faces.

Mr. Seulke wiped the drops from his brown face. "But it won't rain," he said. "My mother could foretell the weather and I've heired enough of her gift to prophesy wet from dry." Sniffing the air and prophesying, mild as the evening itself, Mr. Seulke drove the Tudor skillfully along the narrow graveled roads toward Dallas Hindshaw's. He pointed out Hindshaw's house from a distance. As we came nearer I saw it was small, a cabin really, with an open porch extending across its front.

"Hindshaw," said Mr. Seulke, "is an interesting fellow and of an inventive turn of mind. He's made considerable, I understand, with this vegetable reamer of his. A pity he's humpbacked."

Rousing from the lull of the weather talk, I said, "Humpbacked? That must be another Hindshaw. The Hindshaw I know isn't hunch-back."

"Know?" asked Mr. Seulke. "My understanding was you'd never seen him."

"I haven't," I said, thinking of the six hours' talk in which he had seemed to be present, "but I've heard him spoken of considerably."

"Persis Hughes?"

"Yes," I said.

"Hindshaw jilted her," said Mr. Seulke, "and you can take for sour grapes anything she has to say about him."

But this fox had said the grapes he couldn't get were sweet, not sour; that had been the whole burden of Persis's story!

"See for yourself," said Mr. Seulke, pointing, "he's humpbacked," and I saw on the porch steps a figure, even in the growing darkness, plainly misformed.

"I'll wait for you, sis," said Mr. Seulke, and there was nothing for it but to walk up that long, shell-lined path toward the man who sat motionless, watching me approach.

"Mr. Hindshaw?" I asked.

The man on the porch step was smoking a pipe. One hand was buried in the long black-and-white hair of a small dog which lay beside him, the other was lifted above his head clasping the post he leaned against. He was gazing out across the countryside which his cabin, situated on a little rise, overlooked. He shifted his eyes from the landscape to me but didn't get up.

"I've come to ask," I said diffidently, "if I could buy one of your vegetable reamers."

Mr. Hindshaw then got to his feet. Except for his deformity he would have been a very tall man. As it was, he was taller than I, dark, withdrawn, much thickened and broken about the neck and shoulders.

"I'm sorry," he said. "I don't sell them here any more—only in stores."

That seemed to end the visit. Mr. Hindshaw stood, obviously willing for me to leave; the dog got up, ready to walk to the gate with me; a lean, big-faced gray cat at the other end of the porch folded her feet beneath her in anticipation of the return of solitude. Still I stood there thinking, why won't you marry her? She'd rescue you from all of this, she'd have lights in the house at this hour, a white cloth on the table, the table set, and two bowls on the back porch, one for the cat, one for the dog. She'd be willing to play a note or two for you on the piano, after you'd eaten, and lie, without talking, her hair hanging over the edge of the sofa while you smoked your pipe. She's ten years younger than you; if she's naïve you could teach her whatever it is you think she'd be better for knowing. It isn't everyone in the world who'll love you, Mr. Hindshaw, and Persis loves you, desperately. So much, to judge by her talk, she doesn't even know your back isn't straight. You loved her once, promised to marry her, and she hasn't changed. What's come over you, Mr. Hindshaw, why have *you* changed?

With all the craft and skill of a person whose own plans miscarry, I stood there making plans for Mr. Hindshaw, even thinking that he might say, "It was all a mistake," and that I might carry this word to Persis. But Mr. Hindshaw said nothing. His live pipe dying unsmoked in his hand. Mr. Hindshaw waited for me to leave.

"Persis Hughes told me about the reamer."

Mr. Hindshaw turned, knocked out his pipe on the post behind him. "That was kind of her," he said, and once more waited.

"She's very beautiful," I said.

"Yes, she is," agreed Dallas Hindshaw.

"She will sue you," I said, "for breach of promise if you don't marry her." I felt bewitched saying these things, as if I had not the power to choose what I would say, as if I were Persis Hughes herself.

"So Persis tells me," said Mr. Hindshaw.

I hoped he would sick his dog on me, throw his pipe at my head, get rid of me. I could not mention his back, say, Persis loves you, hunchback and all, where will you find another like that? I did say, "Persis loves you just as you are."

Then I ran down the steps and down the path toward Mr. Seulke's car but I heard Dallas Hindshaw say, "I'm afraid you're mistaken."

Mr. Seulke said, "You left in kind of a hurry, sis."

"Yes," I said, "I did."

"Get your reamer?"

"He doesn't sell them at his house any more."

"I could have told you that," said Mr. Seulke, "but I figured you wanted an excuse to talk to the fellow." He turned into the home driveway. "Well," he asked, "what do you make of our jilter?"

I didn't know what to make of the jilter or of Persis, or of Albert with his unanswered question, or of the empty mailbox, or of Mr. Seulke, purely a weatherman nowadays. I lived on my hard bed, did the writing and note-taking I had come to do, and was glad, as winter drew on and the trial of Hughes *versus* Hindshaw for breach of promise was announced, that I was called away. The books I had asked for were available at the state library; they didn't circulate, I would have to come up to the capital to use them. I'll go tomorrow, I thought, and not come back until the trial is over. The thought of the trial had been a horror to me, like the wreck along the highway, which the eye, knowing it will be sickened, still seeks out. I'll go tomorrow, not come back until the trial is over. And not have my mail forwarded, I thought. Since reason had not worked, I would try magic. If I made the gestures of not caring about my letter, went off without leaving a forwarding address, no longer listened impatiently for the mailman, perhaps it would come.

I lived in a hotel room near the state library, a room very high and lodged between two jutting wings of the hotel like a matchbox in a crevice of the Apennines. It was a great pleasure to be free of hoping for the letter I had no right to hope for, free of the temptation to attend the trial, and able to work on the old books. I went to the library early and stayed late, writing down much that I needed to know and much that was useless but which I could not resist. My notebooks were filled with long lists, I was happy, almost drugged, as a child becomes repeating a series of words until finally they are without meaning, nothing but a loop of sound binding him to mystery.

The wonderful names in the old newspapers; the names a writer can never achieve, names which only a loving mother can imagine: Alert Miller, Talkington Trueblood, Cashie Wade, Leadona Leahigh, Else Grin, Omer Bland.

The names of fish: bass, salmon, pike, buffalo, red horse.

Of apples: Imperial, Winesap, Baldwin, Romanite, Russet, Northern Spy, all these ripening in October.

The useless facts: A good deerskin fetched 50 cents, raccoon 37½ cents, muskrat 25 cents.

Then, coming in after lunch one day, another list, in a folded newspaper left on my table caught my eye: "Dearest, dear heart, sweet sorrel, Puss-Precious, my burning bush, long-loved, long-loving. These," the article continued, "are but a few of the terms of endearment culled from the love letters of Dallas Hindshaw and addressed by him to Persis Hughes. These letters have formed the highlight of the breach of promise suit in which Miss Hughes, daughter of Clayton M. Hughes, prominent Lane County farmer, is attempting to obtain $10,000.00 of Mr. Hindshaw in lieu of marriage, which she says he promised her." My eyes went from one list to the other, from my list, got out of the books in the state library, to this other list, the words written first in the letters of Dallas Hindshaw, and copies now in a city newspaper. They went from "muskrats, Northern Spies" to "dear heart, dear Tawny, long-loved, long-loving." Was Persis right? Walled up in a crack in the Apennines, did I avoid what she called "life, the way a woman suffers it"? Should I stop reading about the past, go back to the Seulkes', go to the trial, go down to the mailbox? Was there a letter waiting for me there? And if there wasn't, write myself? Say, "Dear husband, having no word from you these past weeks I hasten to assure you that I regret my hasty leave-taking, my long silence. It is enough that you love me. You need not also . . ."

\*               \*               \*

But perhaps there *was* a letter waiting. Was it this, instead of the trial which took me back to the Seulkes'? I don't know. There was no letter, anyway, and the trial had ended the day before I got back. Persis, who had asked for ten thousand dollars, had been given five.

"That poor fool, Hindshaw," said Mr. Seulke, on the evening I returned, "he asked to have his money taken away from him." But I was too tired, after my trip and after searching through my mail for the letter which had not arrived, to listen to him, and I went upstairs to my hard bed and wrote nothing myself—letter *or* list—but relived old scenes.

Next afternoon the mailman honked three times and I flew downstairs, but Mr. Seulke was waiting to tell me about the trial.

"That poor fool, Hindshaw!" he began again. "Wouldn't have a lawyer, and set on representing himself! And for all the good he done himself he'd better've given the girl the money in the first place and spared making himself the laughingstock of the county with all those letters of his read out loud."

"Did he say he hadn't promised to marry her?"

"In a way he did," said Mr. Seulke, "but small good it done him, letter after letter saying, 'My sweet pigeon, I can hardly wait till we are married.' Sweet pigeon!" said Mr. Seulke laughing. "Sweet vulture is what he thinks now, I reckon."

"What defense *did* he have?" I asked.

"None," said Mr. Seulke flatly. "He had no defense, only a quirk in his mind. He wouldn't marry Persis Hughes he said because she was changed. She wasn't the girl he had asked to marry him in the first place, because that girl accepted he was humpbacked, and this girl, the one he was refusing to marry, did not accept it. He called up two dozen witnesses to testify that she never would mention his hump, talked about him as if it didn't exist, and tried to make out, in her own mind, and to others, he was straight-backed. 'I've got a hump,' he said, 'and the person who don't accept my hump don't accept me.' "

"Why didn't she?" I asked. Why didn't I? *He* was made that way when I married *him*.

"Why didn't she what?" said Mr. Seulke.

"Accept his hump? Accept the fact his back was crooked?"

"I don't know *why* she didn't," said Mr. Seulke, "but I know when it started. And I know it was the cause of Dallas Hindshaw's refusing to marry her. I was there and I saw it happen."

I remembered my question that night at Persis Hughes's and her "Nothing happened, nothing, nothing, nothing."

"What was it?" I asked.

"It was a dance at Zenith and I was as close to them as I am to you. Dallas was a good dancer and a young fellow passing by clapped Dallas on the back and said, 'This frog sure can hop.' He meant it as a compliment or at most a joke and Dallas took it so. But Persis slapped the boy not once but a half-dozen times and screamed, 'It's not, it's straight.' Hindshaw grabbed her, 'My back's crooked but my mind's straight,' he said, and that was the beginning. That's what broke them up."

"Did Hindshaw tell this at the trial?"

"Not in so many words, but he said, 'I do not intend to be half wed to somebody who sorts me out and marries what suits her, only. I could sue Persis Hughes,' he says, 'with as much justice as she sues me, for she has not kept her promise to my hump. And as I was made shorter than most men,' he says, 'by reason of a horse stepping on me when I was a boy now I will not be still further whittled down by a woman marrying part of me only and maiming me beyond the first damage.'

"So it went," said Mr. Seulke. "But Hindshaw had no real defense and nobody thought the girl didn't have a legal right to the money. But nobody would've wanted to stand in her shoes to get it."

Mr. Seulke followed me out onto the porch, sniffed a few times, and said, "It's going to snow."

It was already snowing, a first, soft, downward feathering.

"What do you make of it?" asked Mr. Seulke. "You seen and talked to them both."

"I don't know, Mr. Seulke, I don't know what to make of it." I didn't want to make anything of it, meaning was striking too close.

I stood there on the porch, the big flakes blowing against my face like cold cobwebs. Mr. Seulke stood there, too, not speaking, so presently I went down the lane toward the mailbox. I remembered saying to Persis Hughes, "I understand it all too well, it's like the multiplication table," and remembered Dallas's words, "She didn't keep her promise to my hump." Do you understand that? I asked myself.

I jumped across the brook, cold now, as it ran across its pretty stones, and specked with falling snow. I hesitated, as I always did, to open the box, then did so quickly. The only letter in the box was one from Persis. In my disappointment I couldn't pick it up for a while, but stood looking at it, and the orange-veined pebble beside it. Finally, I took it out and opened it.

Dear Miss Marsden [it began]:

Though I know now that this is only your writing name, not your real name, it seems more natural to me because I used it first, so I keep on doing so. I understand that you have left the Seulkes' but trust that this will be forwarded to you.

I am sorry you did not come to the trial and still sorrier you would not write the story. But it is too late to worry about this now. I did as I said I would and as I think I was duty bound to do, that is, show Dallas Hindshaw that I was willing to do anything to get him to marry me, even sue him.

I don't regret having done this but I find I don't want his money now and I want you to know it. So will you seal up and mail this envelope which I have enclosed and addressed, after you have read what is in it? You will see I am not keeping the money.

Since you live quite a ways off I don't expect we'll see each other again and I want to wish you the best of luck in everything, and hope you understand I did what I was honor bound to do.

Sincerely and with good wishes,
Persis Hughes

I read the letter Persis Hughes had enclosed as I had been told to do, replaced it, and sealed the envelope. It was addressed to Dallas Hindshaw. All this trouble, all this sorrow, and who had moved a step forward? I, I told myself, I have moved a step forward. It was the truth. When I put the letter back in the mailbox I took the stone out, and at the brook I stooped down and laid it once more beside its brothers at the water's edge, then I walked on up to the house. "Sort him out," and make him pay for refusing the sorting—and give the money back. It made no sense.

Mr. Seulke still stood on the porch, arms folded, watching the weaving patterns of the falling snow. "Well, did you get your letter, sis?" he asked.

I had never spoken to Mr. Seulke of my letter, nor of any letter for that matter, but I felt neither evasive nor glib now.

"No," I said, "it didn't come."

"What do you figure on doing now?" he asked.

"I'm going home," I said.

"Home? I didn't know you had a home, sis?"

"I have."

"Home and husband?"

"Home and husband."

"That's more like it, sis."

"It is," I said.

I went upstairs to write and stop my waiting.

# The Singing Lesson

Liberty School is built on a piece of low, unusable, alkaline land. There are no other buildings in sight. In spring it rises like a lighthouse about great fields of ripening barley; in fall its shadow is long morning and evening across far-reaching stretches of stubble. In winter it stands solitary in the center of a pool of shallow, wind-scalloped water.

The wind always blows about the schoolhouse. It lingers there as if the school were the last building it would be able to touch before plunging over the world's edge, as if it were reluctant to trade domestic for universal architecture.

Scalloping the water, the wind spoke to the teacher in the schoolroom at the Liberty School. It said far. It said distant, strange, remote. It said someday.

"Miss McManaman," suggested Peter, "we'd ought to be practicing our singing lesson."

"I know we ought," said Miss McManaman, but she didn't move. Rain had been falling all day—slowly and dispiritedly, with none of the clatter and excitement of a storm. Elongated drops hit the gray pool of water which surrounded the schoolhouse with a melancholy plop-plop.

"Mr. Harmon," urged Peter, "will be here tomorrow."

"I know he will," said Miss McManaman, continuing to stare at the rain.

On Thursdays Mr. Harmon, the music supervisor, drove out from town to give the Liberty School its weekly singing lesson. He was a severe, talented young man with perpendicular red hair rising above a somewhat greenish face. He had a voice so high, pure, and thin that when he sang the sound of it crept between the joints like electricity—or a razor blade. But Mr. Harmon did not sing often. "I come to hear you sing, Miss McManaman," he said. By which he meant Miss McManaman's pupils, for Miss McManaman herself could not sing. She had a disappearing voice. After four or five good notes, it vanished, fell like a waterfall over a precipice and was heard no more.

"Why is this?" Mr. Harmon would ask savagely, for he was married to his music and felt his awareness of Miss McManaman's black eyes and cream-colored arms to be a kind of infidelity. "Why is it that a healthy young woman like you should have a disappearing voice? How do you account for it?"

Miss McManaman couldn't account for it—but it was a fact that she recognized. Playing the piano with one finger she taught Peter Mr. Harmon's assignments, and Peter, singing, taught the school. On Thursdays, shorn of his musical significance, Peter would sit once more at his desk, and Miss McManaman, resolutely opening and shutting her mouth, would lead the singing. But it made her unhappy: it was underhanded, and it wasn't, she felt sure, what music should be.

"Miss McManaman?"

"Yes, Cletus."

"Can I be excused?"

"May," Miss McManaman said, and nodded. With the schoolyard underwater the boys' and girls' outhouses could be reached only by wading—and everyone had to be excused often. Miss McManaman had said no at first to all this taking off of shoes, wading out, replacing shoes—but there had been an accident and now once an hour, if necessary, was the rule. And as soon as his hour was up necessity smote each pupil again and off he waded.

"Take your shoes and stockings off and leave them off," Miss McManaman ordered suddenly. "You'll be less likely to take cold with bare feet than with damp shoes and stockings. Put your shoes and stockings by the fire to dry."

The children circled the stove with their shoes and hung their stockings over the edge of the woodbox. The woodbox, in addition to wood, held three semidrowned squirrels, a family of motherless field mice, an animal no one had ever laid eyes on before, and a ground owl was assuredly dead.

Coyla, however, pleaded to keep it. "A live ground owl," she told them, "don't look very much alive. A dead one, I think, would have to look deader than this to be dead forever." So they kept the ground owl, giving it the benefit of the doubt and warming it as thoroughly as the known living.

"Teacher," called Peter, who had no shoes and stockings to dry but had made a trip to the woodbox to inspect the refugees, "come quick."

Looking out of the high windows onto the rain-pricked, gently lapping water, Miss McManaman felt dreamy, too easeful to move.

"You come to me, Peter."

Peter ran. "What d'ya think?" he asked. "The one we don't know the name of is having babies. Two already," he said with pride. "We saved it just in time."

"That's fine," said Miss McManaman dreamily. "Put something over that corner of the box. A coat or something."

"Why?" asked Peter.

"Animals don't like the light when they're having babies."

"Why?"

"Make it snappy," said Miss McManaman.

"Will we sing then?"

"Yes," said Miss McManaman, sighing, and went to the piano.

"We gotta sing that?" Peter asked, reading the words of the song over Miss McManaman's shoulder.

"Yes, we do."

"Cherries are ripe, cherries are ripe, the boys and girls all say."

Peter read the words so that even to Miss McManaman's ear they sounded fantastic.

"Listen, Peter," she said, "this is the tune." And she picked it out with one finger as spryly as she could. "Pretty, isn't it?"

"Sour," said a resonant voice behind her. "Sour as cat piss."

Miss McManaman swung about on the piano stool. That wasn't a word to be used in the schoolroom, though it was not, she knew, a word which would startle her pupils.

"Not your playing, Miss," said the little man in the doorway. "That was refreshing. Full of feeling. Ping, ping," he said. "Tum, tum. Like a gander pecking on a lard pail. Not plushed over. Simple and melodic. I was speaking of the tone of the piano. Sour," he reaffirmed. "Sour as . . ."

"Please," began Miss McManaman.

"Swill," said the little man. "Pig swill. You understand that, Miss? Or Mrs.?"

"Miss," she said, "McManaman."

"Irish. She was Irish," he told her.

"Please," began Miss McManaman again. "To whom . . .?"

"Wilbur Smiley. Smiley by name but damned melancholy by nature."

"You mustn't . . ."

" 'You mustn't swear, Mr. Smiley, before the dear little children.' "

"Well, you mustn't," she said.

"Paugh," said Mr. Smiley. "Where'd you learn the bad words you know, Miss? Right here," he said, pointing.

"In the boys. *And* the girls . . . What's the worst you know, children?"

A dozen hands went up.

"Ta ta, children," he reproved them.

"You see?" he asked Miss McManaman. "It's in 'em. Working like yeast in a barrel and frothing at the bunghole. Treat 'em like human beings," he advised. "Or cure 'em if you're a mind to. Make 'em spend a day writing bad words on the blackboard. That'll take the brimstone out of them."

"Really, Mr. Smiley," began Miss McManaman, "what *is* your . . .?"

Mr. Smiley handed her a card.

"Wilbur Smiley," she read, "Piano Tuning. Vocal Music. 276 Railroad Avenue. Evenings by Appointment."

"Fooled you, didn't I?" asked Mr. Smiley. "Sent out by your superintendent, Professor Barr. Musical outfit you got around here. Except for the piano."

Mr. Smiley, leaning, it seemed, from the ankles, reached over Miss McManaman's shoulder and with a slight flick of his hand sent a spatter of sound out into the room.

"Be a waste of money. You do all the playing here?" he said.

Miss McManaman nodded.

"Be a pure waste," said Mr. Smiley.

He walked across to the stove. "Don't get your dander up," he advised Miss McManaman.

He was a small, red-brown man with a peaked head, dusty hair, and deep-set eyes which went about the schoolroom, lapping it up: jut and cornice, chalk dust and children, Mr. Smiley took them all in.

"Mind if I stir up the fire?" he asked. "I ain't hot blooded like the rest of you here," he said eying a row of bare feet.

"We ain't hot blooded," began Cletus, believing a slight to have been put upon them, but Miss McManaman interrupted him. "They have to wade," she explained.

"Often, too, I bet," said Mr. Smiley, taking it in.

With one hand he was poking up the fire, while with the other he felt about in the woodbox for fuel.

"What's this?" he cried. He let the poker stand in the open stove and bent over the woodbox.

"Fur-bearing wood," he announced.

He lifted the coat from the corner it roofed over. "Three already," he told them, "and more expected."

He took the ground owl in his small hand and soberly regarded it. "Ashes to ashes. Dust to dust. The life cycle complete," he informed Miss McManaman. "Birth, death, and the intermediate whistle stops. Don't know, though, as life's going to hold much surprise for these kids. They'll already've seen it all in the woodbox."

Mr. Smiley filled the stove with eucalyptus chunks, unwound his green scarf, laid aside his long black overcoat, and walked to the front of the room.

Here an experienced teacher, Miss McManaman felt, would have asserted herself, said, "Would you care to hear the fifth grade spell, Mr. Smiley?" or "What can you tell us, Mr. Smiley, of the art of piano tuning?"

But Miss McManaman was not experienced. She leaned against the piano, said nothing, traversed the slight distance which separated her from pupilhood herself, listened to the wind and the rain, lifted her eyes to Mr. Smiley's face as if waiting to be asked by him to recite.

"What was I interrupting when I came in?"

" 'Cherries Are Ripe,' " said Peter. "The singing lesson."

"Ah, well," said Mr. Smiley, "this ain't cherry weather."

With no hemming or hawing, no clasping of hands or arching of his chest, Mr. Smiley began to sing. He stood before them, his face a little sad, his eyes still looking about the schoolroom as if all he saw interested him, and sang words they could not understand in a voice so beautiful Miss McManaman pressed her hands to her heart. She could not say whether what she felt was bliss or pain. Both, she thought. As if all the things of which she had dreamed and for which she had waited, without having a name for them, were now spread before her, named, shining, and palpable. And that was bliss. But at this very minute of knowing and naming, she saw also that they would vanish: melt, run away, be lost forever. And that was pain.

"Singing," she said to herself. "Singing." This, then, was what was meant by the word they used each Thursday—the meaning she had missed and struggled toward.

Mr. Smiley, his song finished, stood for a minute regarding the Liberty School pupils. Then, turning about, he stepped to the blackboard and with three or four large swoops erased Miss McManaman's silent reading lesson and drew—in the space he had cleared—two hearts.

He then stood aside so all could see. "This," he said, pointing to the first, "is your heart . . . Thomas . . . George . . . Jane . . . Henry. A fine muscle . . . empty, easy, beating free."

Then upon the second heart Mr. Smiley made with his piece of chalk the slanting dashes Miss McManaman's pupils used to show that upon a landscape they had pictured, rain was falling.

"This is my heart," Mr. Smiley said. "These are my tears. Tears," Mr. Smiley repeated quite impersonally. "My heart is full of tears."

He began to sing again. His second song was simpler than his first; it was gentle and flowing, like rain in the early morning, or a river under trees. It sounded to Miss McManaman like the beginning of things, like first days: the new key in the rusty lock, the fresh flag hoisted, the September bell tolled. It sounded like her first day at Liberty School.

Waiting for her the morning she had begun teaching was a hay wagon. It stood on the school grounds like a frigate come to rest. Three people looked down at her from its high seat: a stout old man with a flaring semicircle of white whiskers, a ruddy woman of middle age, and between them a small boy with bright eyes and a red mouth. Mother and son dismounted by means of a ladder, slowly and with dignity.

"Miss McManaman," said the ruddy woman, "this is George Washington Berryman, the fruit of our old age. We are raising him to be a great man. We want your help."

"I will help you," Miss McManaman had said, with the feeling of taking a vow.

"If he can learn," said his mother, "well and good. If he can't, train him to be holy. Or it could be both. But that's not likely," she added. "One or the other's as much as can be hoped for. Remember your name," Mrs. Berryman told her son. "Don't do anything he'd be ashamed of."

Mrs. Berryman didn't kiss her son in parting, but laid her hand for a minute on his shining, egg-shaped head. Then Mr. Berryman helped his wife to remount and drew up the ladder after her like a skipper preparing to cast off. On the plank bridge at the edge of the schoolyard he reined in his horses for a minute and Mrs. Berryman, pivoting about on the high seat, called back a farewell message to her son.

"Stay pure, George Washington Berryman," she said in a clear, sad voice. "Stay pure."

The five Rosses came unaccompanied across the fields: downy eared, round eyed, their brown cheeks frosted with crumbs.

"The first day of school," Miss McManaman chided them.

"Us Rosses," Jennie, the oldest, explained, "always eat whatever's in our lunch pails for dessert on the way to school. Then it's done with and we don't have to worry about it any more."

"Why do you worry," asked Miss McManaman, "about dessert?"

"It's not dessert," said Jennie. "It's when to eat it. Should you eat it first recess? If you do, you kick yourself. If you don't, you think about it till second recess. Should you eat it then? Second recess is awfully near to noon. At noon you got all the rest of your lunch. Maybe you should save it to eat going home. If you do, you can't enjoy it, the rest of 'em beg so. Us Rosses always eat it the minute we're out of sight of the house. That way it's done with. Don't have to worry any more about dessert all day long." Jennie brushed the crumbs from her face.

Mrs. Renzo brought Ada to school the first day. "Ada's backward," said Mrs. Renzo, "she's a little slow. But she's deep. Ada's got ideas'll surprise you. She's got strange, deep ideas," said Mrs. Renzo.

Miss McManaman had gazed at Ada's face. It had every appurtenance faces have, yet it seemed primitive: an early, trial face to which, century after century, endearing and humanizing details would be added. It was a small granite face, made by a hurried man with a sharp chisel.

"What I figure," said Ada to her teacher, "is this. God is a bird. A peacock probably and the stars is his tail."

"See," said Mrs. Renzo. "See? Deep and strange like I said."

Peter, in his green fedora, led the Mendezes across the early morning fields. Behind him, and stepping in time to the harmonica which he played, were Felicita, Pablo, Josephina, and little Fructoso.

"Good morning," said Miss McManaman to the Mendezes. "Here bright and early. Would you like to look at your new readers?"

"To hell with reading," said Peter, tapping the spit from his harmonica. "Numbers is what counts. Numbers is the way you read real things."

"Oh, I must teach him to read," thought Miss McManaman now, watching Peter's listening face—seeing it shining as though the music to which he listened were summer sunlight. "I must teach him to read. There are things numbers can never say."

Mr. Smiley finished his second song and went again to the blackboard. There he drew a human foot, narrow heeled, long toed, and with an arch like a culvert. It was a beautiful foot made to spring away, to fly, and never linger.

Mr. Smiley, from the heart, his heart, the one which was filled with tears, drew a stream, full and lapping over, which ran beneath the culvert of the high-arched foot and was lost in the far reaches of the south blackboard.

"From my heart," he said, "the tears she has no use for. They flow under her foot," he said, tracing the stream, "but never touch her. She walks dry shod."

"Is your name Agnes?" he asked Miss McManaman.

"Not Agnes," she said. "Mary."

"Her name was Agnes," said Mr. Smiley, and sang again.

Was it the tears under the arch like a culvert he sang, was it the arch which unbending carried the weight? Or was Agnes herself his song?

Whatever it was there was no sadness in it. Or, if sorrow was there, it was sorrow swallowed, digested, ruminated, until it had become bone and blood—for singing and seeing. Agnes . . . where was Agnes? Lost, gone, turned to another perhaps . . . but here was Agnes, unknown, a name only, a pallid name, alive in the rainy schoolroom, lifting it out of chalk dust, shivering the blackboards, setting all the Rosses, Mendezes, Tritonas, Hanrahans on the edges of their seats: showing Ada a nonpeacock God, showing George Washington Berryman his mama's pure dream. Sounding to Peter numbers he had never dreamed of.

Once in October when the wind off the stubble fields had been hot and dusty and the children had fought and squirmed all day, Miss McManaman had gone to the girls' outhouse and closing the door behind her had stood with her face pressed against the smooth pine boards, looking out at as much of the world as was to be seen through the crescent-shaped aperture in the door. And as she stood thus it had suddenly seemed to her that she was in one of those prisons of which she had read: a prison so small one could never lie down; so remote a human voice was never heard; a prison where for twenty years her only sight of the world would be this finger's breadth of sky and field; her only assurance that all had not vanished from the earth, the hand which slid to her each night a bowl of food.

Just at the moment when the sky had seemed on the point of closing in about her, she had flung open the door and rushed back to her pupils.

"We are free, boys and girls," she had cried. "We are free."

They were startled by her words. "Of course," they said. "What did you think?"

"Sometimes I forget it. Oh, boys and girls, let us go outside and run up and down in the wind and never forget it."

Listening to Mr. Smiley sing, Miss McManaman wanted to say to them once again, "We are free, boys and girls, we are free." Listening to Mr. Smiley's song . . . and not to his alone, she knew, but to that other one's, the song noted down a hundred, or two hundred, years before by a hand seeking to record—what? Not Agnes, who was Mr. Smiley's song, nor the light, unfaithful, springing foot, nor the tears beneath the culvert, nor Wilbur Smiley's rain-pocked heart—or was that it? Was that all there ever was to sing, whatever hand set the notes down, whatever throat swelled with the beautiful, glancing sounds? Was that all—Agnes, the beauty, the tears, the rain? . . . Miss McManaman, listening, could not be sure.

But she wanted to say to her children, "Remember boys and girls, remember. Remember today. Remember the schoolhouse half afloat and the wind and the animals who were born whose names we did not know and remember me who loved you and Mr. Smiley, a grown man, with a heart still alive and beating."

Mr. Smiley, while Miss McManaman was wondering and dreaming, had come to the end of his song and had rewound his scarf about his neck and picked up his coat.

"Say 'peach pit,'" he told the Liberty scholars, "when you get a strong longing for a dirty word. It's got an ornery ring to it, somehow. Then sing. That'll do the trick. You'll feel like you've just said your prayers."

Miss McManaman walked to the door with him. "The bill will come for piano tuning," he told her candidly.

She scarcely heard him. "Oh, Mr. Smiley," she said, "I can never tell you . . . you do not know . . ." Then she started over again. "It was so beautiful . . . and I have to teach singing. And I can't," she said. "I have a disappearing voice."

"Let it, let it," said Mr. Smiley, undisturbed. "Too many voices in the world already."

"It makes me so ashamed. Mr. Harmon expects . . ."

"Ed Harmon," said Mr. Smiley. "That musical saw."

"He knows so much, though. He can look at a song and sing it.

He looks at a note, then opens his mouth and says it, the way I would a word."

"Vacant veins, however," said Mr. Smiley. "Sound's his whole stock in trade."

"I can't sing," Miss McManaman persisted. "Mr. Harmon says . . ."

"Why, Mary," said Mr. Smiley, "don't you know you got more music in one of them little white arms of yours than Ed Harmon's got in his whole body and shock of hair? You got grace notes in your eyes, Mary, and whole ballads in your hands. You sing with them."

Mr. Smiley turned and faced his car, which, to avoid wading, he had driven astraddle the walk right up to the porch.

"Clearing a little in the west," he said.

Miss McManaman looked and in the far west saw a thin streak of clear green.

"Say her name sometimes, will you?" asked Mr. Smiley. "Say 'Agnes, Agnes.' "

"Oh, I will, Mr. Smiley," said Miss McManaman. "I promise I will say her name and I will remember singing."

"So long, Mary," said Mr. Smiley.

Miss McManaman did not leave the porch until Mr. Smiley's car was far up the road. When she went inside again Peter was standing at the head of the room.

"I'm going to teach the kids one of Mr. Smiley's songs," he told her.

"Can you, Peter?" she asked. "Do you think you can do it?"

"Sure," he said. "Different words, maybe, but the same tune."

"It's the tune that counts," said Miss McManaman.

She walked to the stove and held out her hands to its warmth. There in the woodbox, his eyes yellow and unblinking, the ground owl gazed up at her. She opened her mouth to say, "Children, the owl's come to life," but Peter had started singing. I'll tell them later, she thought, happily.

# The Calla Lily Cleaners & Dyers

I WON'T ARGUE with you any if you want to say the title of this story is misleading. It is, and that's the unvarnished truth. This story's about Frissil Thompson more than anything else, but I own the Calla Lily Cleaners & Dyers, and under any circumstances would have more interest in playing it up than in giving that expresser Frissil Thompson any publicity. And besides, these circumstances aren't *any*. They're special.

You'd 'bout as well get the guy's name straight right off. The first thing he said to me was, "Whistle."

"I can't," I told him. "I never could. I can't hold a pucker." I showed him how I couldn't. It tells you something about the fellow when you hear that wasn't what he wanted at all. Don't it?

"No," he said, "I don't mean *whistle*."

That made me mad. Here I am giving him a lift, and here he is, first handing me an order, then saying he didn't.

"Make up your mind, buddy," I told him. "Maybe I can't whistle, but I can sure set you down on the asphalt mighty quick. Where I found you," I reminded him.

"Now, Mr. Geer"—he'd seen my name on the dry-cleaning truck— "I don't mean 'whistle.' I mean, *say* whistle. Say it, don't whistle it."

That sounded screwier to me than before. There could be several reasons why a dope might want you to whistle a whistle, but I couldn't figure why he'd wanted you to say one unless he's off his nut.

Just in case he was, I said, "Whistle."

"Fine," he said. "I couldn't do it better myself. Now you can say my name."

What the hell, I thought, but all I said was, "That'll be nice." That day I had plenty to do, as you'll see later, without getting rapped on the head with a tire iron by a dimwit for not saying his name. "What is it?" I asked him as if I couldn't wait to hear.

"Frissil," he said, "to rhyme with whistle."

192

"Also thistle?" I asked, showing him I catch on.

"Yes," said he, poking his nose over between my face and the windshield, "and not frizzle. Get it?"

I got it. The guy didn't like to be called Frizzle. I don't know why. Nothing so very bad about that, but I was in a position to sympathize with him there. My own name's Geer. You can see what that leads to: High, Low, and Reverse. I even been called Intermediate. I take it as a compliment that I'm known as High most of the time. But I could see how this fellow felt. I got a pretty first name myself—Kenneth. But I never hear it. Kenny. You'd think some girl'd have sense enough to call me that, wouldn't you? With those two *n*'s together it can be drawn out real sweet and nice. Ken-ny. But no; all I get's High, Low, and so forth.

So wanting to have his name said right's not what I got against Mr. Frissil Thompson. In fact, there's nothing I got against him; he did me as good a turn as a guy can do. I don't hold with his methods, but I'm interested in him as a specimen of human nature, not as breaker of the Ten Commandments. Which he undoubtedly is, however. Us Hoosiers got more interest in human nature than most people—and I never seen so much of it as since I came to Southern California. There's more varieties of human nature per acre in Southern California than there's ears of corn per acre on river bottom land in Jennings County. Human nature, literature, and corn—that's what us Hoosiers go for. And except I couldn't get no price for my corn, I'd never have come to Belle Vista, Southern California—and never discovered either what the climate out here can do in the way of ripening human nature. Reaches a point Rush Branch never dreamed of.

I'm not too fine haired to admit I'd never have left Jennings County if corn'd been paying. But when I got word Uncle Sil had left me his Calla Lily Cleaners & Dyers in Belle Vista, I headed west with the gravy spots sponged off my vest, trying to look like a dry cleaner from the word go—though at that time I didn't know a buzzard from a bushel woman.

Belle Vista's got seven thousand people in it, and seven dry cleaners, and there's no way you can figure out enough pairs of pants, pleated skirts, and portieres among seven thousand Belle Vistans to keep seven cleaners in naphtha, let alone groceries. But I didn't know that when I left Jennings County, and I didn't know the Calla Lily Cleaners & Dyers was paying the Building and Loan $32.50 on the tenth of every month—or else. I got that paid off. I been here three years. I've watched the Puritan, the Apex, the Acme, the Plu-perfect, the DeLuxe, and the Band Box cleaners fold—while the Calla Lily's still going. To say "strong" would maybe be to say too much, but we get steam up six days a week, and you hear somebody kicking a press there eight hours a day. Of course, while those drop-in joints were folding, seven other monkeys have opened up—the Rite-way, the Model, the Spotless, the Valet, the Tony, the Magnolia, and the Bon Ton—so as far as competition goes, I'm right back where I started.

But my only real trouble's my new steam press—a Luxite—not another cleaner in Belle Vista's got one. It's the sweetest piece of machinery you ever saw, smooth as a persimmon after a frost, more power than the Wabash in the spring, dependable as Golden Bantam. It'll send live steam pulsing through the shine of Brother Woodford's Sunday serge till that piece of pure cotton cries "Mama" when a sheep goes by. Lucy—that's what we call the Luxite for short—Lucy'll take the crease out of Mrs. Elton's let-out seams so you can't tell her dress has doubled its circumference in two years. There's no use talking, though—you can't appreciate a Luxite, no matter what language I use, if you never stomped an old 7-A press. The difference between a Model T and an eight-cylinder valve-in-head, automatic-gearshift number with chromium trim won't give you any idea at all.

The only trouble is, Lucy's bought on time—bought and not paid for. There's $14.60 due on the thirteenth of every month. I was afraid of that thirteenth from the beginning. The Luxite people are hard as nails; they got no more heart than an octopus. Five days' grace you get; then out comes their truck and they start taking the screws out. That's happened twice already. Once, Emmor Aull, my presser, collected the money from his peanut vending machines, and they had to put 'em back. And once, Mrs. Ettinger, the Calla Lily's best customer and Belle Vista's richest citizen, saved the day.

The day I picked up Mr. Frissil Thompson was the eighteenth, last Thursday, and my mind was plenty occupied that morning wondering where to find $10.00 to put with the $4.60 I had to keep the Luxite octopuses from prising up Lucy. There was no use thinking of Emmor Aull again—peanuts weren't selling any better than dry cleaning, and besides, he was living on his peanut money. I hadn't paid him any salary for two weeks. I'd started out early that morning, thinking maybe I might make some collections, but you can't get blood from a turnip, as we say back in Jennings County. Oranges weren't paying for their picking, and Belle Vista's nothing but an orange town.

There wasn't anything for it but to try Eula Ettinger. She hadn't given us a ring, but we hadn't had anything from her for more than a week, and she'd ought to have a chauffeur's uniform with a spot on it by now, or a rug with a touch of dust. Eula pays in advance, and a couple of items from her would give me $14.60 and Lucy for another month.

It was along toward noon when I headed her direction, a hot day, the heat waves hopping along the pavement like ripples on the Sandusky, and the Valencias shining as pretty against the green leaves as if they meant money in the bank. I was driving slow, thinking and figuring, when this guy flagged me down. I been in Southern California three years now and I'm hardened to anything that walks the pavement with a thumb stuck out; but this Frissil Thompson gave me a turn. He had on shorts, made out of some flowered stuff, the kind Ma's kimonos used to be made of, and a yellow shirt that hung outside and covered them down to the last three or four inches. Besides outfits like that being funny to look at and undignified, they wreck the dry-cleaning business. You can wash them out in any dishpan.

This guy with the kimono-pants on came running toward the truck the minute I slowed, and there was nothing for it but to let him ride. He wasn't what we'd call a pretty fellow back in Indiana, but, from the way things have gone, I guess Mr. Frissil Thompson is a lot prettier than he looked to me. A lot prettier. He took off his dark glasses when he got in the car, and the first thing I noticed was his eyes— light blue, like colorless water reflecting a blue sky—and his face being so suntanned they were more like vacancies in his head than eyes. To me, that is. I don't like eyes like that—nor curly black burnsides creeping down a guy's face, nor— Well, it don't matter, there are those that do.

When he'd finished teaching me the way to say his name, he asked, "You in the dry-cleaning business, Mr. Geer?" I don't know what he thought I was doing riding around in a dry-cleaning truck if I wasn't, but I didn't get sarcastic. I gave him a straight answer. "Yes," I said, and handed him my card: *Calla Lily Cleaners & Dyers*; then in italics, our slogan *We clean clothes in a running stream;* and underneath, **Kenneth Geer, Owner and Proprietor**, in boldface. Let him see I was nobody's route man.

"How's business?" he asked.

"So-so," I told him. "But if everybody strips down to his drawers, like you, there won't be any business much longer."

"These were a gift to me," Frissil Thompson said, kind of apologetic. "We can't all be choosers in this word, Mr. Geer. Not everybody's an owner and proprietor." He made me feel kind of meechin. The guy had a prosperous look, but I reckon he wasn't, or he wouldn't of been thumbing rides.

"Owner and proprietor don't mean a thing but grief nowadays," I told him, "and that's a fact."

"Competition?" he asked.

"Cutthroat. There's drop-in joints in Belle Vista'll clean a pair of pants for twenty-nine cents."

"Steam-clean, pre-spot, spot, press? For twenty-nine cents?"

"Hell, no," I said, not stopping to wonder at that time how he knew so much about dry cleaning. "All they do for that price's brush the pants with a whisk broom, set a couple of clothespins on the creases for an hour, and sprinkle 'em with benzine before they go out so they'll have a dry-cleaning smell."

"Is that ethical?" Mr. Thompson asked.

"Ethical?" I inquired. "From the way you talked, I thought you knew something about dry cleaning?"

"It's been some time back," he explained.

"Bible times, no doubt," I said. "if dry cleaning was businesslike, let alone ethical, I wouldn't be doing what I am this morning."

"What's that?"

"Going out to get an order from a lady that don't need any dry cleaning done. Mrs. Eula Ettinger by name."

"Pretty name," he said. "Eula. Got a sweet ring to it." He smoothed down his curly burnsides.

"What goes with it's got a sweet ring, too."

"Meaning?"

"*Dinero.* Coin. Nothing in the world rings so pretty."

"That's the way I remember it," Mr. Thompson said. "But without a good memory, I wouldn't know. So she's got coin."

"She's got it—and she's a Calla Lily customer. To tell the truth, Thompson, Eula Ettinger is just about the difference between surviving and folding in Belle Vista as a dry cleaner. She's the margin of profit. Every month it's just about nip and tuck between her and the Luxite wolves. So far, we've always won, but if Eula don't come across with a pair of drapes today, I'll lose Lucy."

"Lucy?" he asked.

So I told him the situation.

When I finished, all he said was, "What age's Eula?"

"She's past her first youth," I told him, "but comely. That's a fact. Somehow she's got a Hoosier look about her, a kind of goldenrod and persimmon look, if you know what I mean. A look as if she'd fed on succotash and catfish when she was a girl, and caught lightning bugs and picked huckleberries. But her youth's gone, and that's a fact. She's fifteen years older than me, even if you're a shy counter."

"Widow?" Frissil Thompson asked, his blue eyes getting more of a focus in them than I'd seen so far.

"With pleasure, I calculate," I said, "knowing Horace Ettinger the way I did."

"The way I did?" Frissil Thompson queried me.

"The way a dry cleaner knows a customer," I informed him. "By what he leaves in his pants pockets."

Frissil Thompson nodded his head. "You sweet on Eula?" he asked.

I don't like loose love-nest talk like that. "I admit to a certain tenderness for Mrs. Ettinger," I answered with dignity, "but I can't help seeing that any matrimonial association between me and Mrs. E. would ruin the Calla Lily Cleaners & Dyers. And my first loyalty is to the Calla Lily."

"Ruin, Mr. Geer?" Frissil Thompson asked, astonished. "You said yourself she's all that keeps you going."

Loose talk, loose reasoning. In spite of all he did for me, Frissil Thompson's no favorite of mine. Though I figure to give him his due. "Consider," I said to him, "with Mrs. Ettinger as Mrs. Geer, what the setup would be, Mr. Thompson. I couldn't charge my own wife for dry cleaning, could I? Send her a bill the first of each month? No, sir! I'd have a wife, but my margin of profit'd be clean wiped out. I couldn't do that to the pioneer cleaners and dyers of Belle Vista, Mr. Thompson. I wouldn't have the heart."

Frissil Thompson took off his sunglasses and gave me a long look out of those sky blue eyes of his. "Where a man's heart is, there his treasure is also," he said.

"I'm glad to see you're a church man," I told him. He didn't say anything. "We're coming to her place. Eula lives on an orange ranch but her money comes from oil."

"This it?" he asked, as we come to a grove better kept than most, with a fancy iron fence round it.

"This is the Ettinger estate," I told him, and turned left off the boulevard, past the iron-grill gates, and onto the red-gravel road.

"The trees along the edge there are jacarandas, and the lawn's pure bluegrass. That rose climbing the palm tree's Gold of Ophir." But Frissil Thompson was too busy combing out his long black locks to give heed to any beauties of nature besides his own.

We rounded the curve of the driveway and the house come in view—what they call a Monterey house out here, big white pillars with a second-story piazza. The house was looking nice—nothing wrong with it, as usual. What was wrong was the vehicle parked in front of it.

There was no use Frissil Thomson's saying, "What's that in front of the house?" He could see as well as me. It was the Bon Ton delivery car, a flashy black job with silver trim. I felt my heart go down the way a cork does when a six-pound catfish swallows the hook. The driver wasn't on the porch listening to Eula's maid say, "We send all our stuff to the Calla Lily"; he was right inside talking dry cleaning with Eula herself.

" 'Bout as well get back to the plant and kiss Lucy good-bye," I said. "No use crying; got to face facts."

"The Bon Ton good?" Frissil asked.

"All the Bon Ton's got," I told him, trying not to be bitter, "is that flossy car, a three-by-four plate-glass window with a phony press behind it, and the gigolo that's in there to kick it."

"If Eula likes good dry cleaning the way you say she does, she's not going to fall for the Bon Ton, is she?"

"Not the Bon Ton cleaning," I said, "but we got to face facts. Eula's susceptible. No use denying it. Why'd you reckon she gave me ten dollars a week's worth of dry cleaning?"

Frissil Thompson looked me over careful. I could see him out of the corner of my eye. "The Calla Lily's superior work," he said finally.

I got it. "OK"—that figured. "But Mrs. Ettinger likes a sympathetic man to talk to. Well, she's got one now," I said, and headed back toward Belle Vista.

I'd had the wind taken out of my sails, to put it mildly. Never thought to see another cleaner sitting in that house talking hat blocking and perspiration stains with Eula. Farewell, Lucy, I thought. This'll be your last night at the Calla Lily.

I put the delivery truck through the heat waves like a boat. Corn or cleaning, didn't seem like I was born for luck in this world.

Frissil Thompson said, "I'd like to have a card with your reverend's name on it."

"Huh?" I said.

"A card with your reverend's name on it, so's I can drop him a line—let him know how you picked me up, fed me a real meal with trimmings—no hamburger and potato chips."

"Are you hungry?" I asked.

"Last time I ate was yesterday noon."

"Why the reverend's name?" I still didn't get it.

"I figure you're a man who'd rather stand right with your reverend than have the cash. Anyway," he said, "I ain't got the cash."

"I could do with both," I reminded him. "I got $4.60 cash only myself, saved toward Lucy's payment."

"She's a goner, anyway," Frissil said. "Ain't she?"

"Looks that way," I admitted.

"I'm feeling might wan and peaked," Frissil said. "This heat hopping around makes it worse. I'd like to write that letter saying how I was a stranger and you took me in."

I looked him over. He looked hollow all right, white around the nose and the curl coming out of his burnsides.

"OK, we'll eat," I told him. "The world's against me, but I'll turn the other cheek."

I pulled up in front of the Chili Bowl in Belle Vista, the place I always eat. I gave Frissil Thompson a dollar bill. Let him choose his own fodder and pay for it himself, not have to act beholden to me before the waitress.

He looked up at the joint from the sidewalk, as if a chili bowl didn't much suit his fancy. "This place is run by Fructoso Sanchez, the brother of my bushel woman," I told him. "He heaps it up. I always feed here."

"A Mexican bushel woman," he said. "Never heard of one. She any good?"

"She can sew a button on good as the next one," I told him, "but as a matter of fact, when it comes to letting down a cuff or reseating a pair of pants, she wavers considerable. She don't charge, though."

We went in, sat at the elbow-shined counter, the pieces of pie pointing at us like daggers, and the fan blowing the smell of chili con carne right down to the pits of our stomachs. The waitress I'd ordered lunches from for two years didn't see me. She shot right up to Frissil, asked him what he'd have in a tone of voice that said, "Where have you been all my life?" The way she bent over him put the curl back in his burnsides. The chili beans did the rest.

After a while he remembered me again. "How come she works for nothing?" he asked while Angela was filling up his second bowl. "The bushel woman."

"Josephita's in love with my presser," I told him. "She's got a passion for Emmor Aull. She'd pay just to be let work under the same roof with him."

"How's Emmor feel about that?" Frissil asked, giving Angela a tender look for the extra meat she'd put with his chili beans. "He responsive?"

"Emmor Aull has got his mind on his peanut business. He roasts them himself, with coconut oil, and services his own vending machines. He figures to make a fortune at it someday."

"How does this fit in with pressing?" Frissil asked, thinking to keep my mind off the food he was consuming, maybe.

"It don't. But Emmor says a man has to think of the future. He don't want to look forward to a life of dry cleaning. But I got to figure that if I fire Emmor I lose Josephita. As it is, I get about one and a half for the price of one. Three-quarters of a bushel woman, three-quarters of a presser. Emmor says—"

"Emmor," shouts Fructoso, running in from the kitchen, "*Madre Dios*—I forgot to tell you. Josephita phoned. Emmor had to go to Placentia. Had a big run on peanuts there last night and he has to refill."

"I'm pleased Josephita didn't go too," I said, sarcastic, thinking, Is this a business I run, or a sideshow?

"That's not why she called," Fructoso said. "Not the fundamental reason." Fructoso talks Spanish at home and high-class book English other times. "She phoned to say Sister Mary Michael called from St. Joseph's, saying would you pick up their baseball suits and altar cloths? The bishop's coming to St. Joseph's tomorrow, and they want to have a special service and an exhibition game for him. Have to have them back by two-thirty tomorrow."

"Dog it, dog it," I yelled, forgetting myself. "While I run them through the clean, who's going to do the pressing?"

"Me," said Frissil Thompson. "It's been some years back, but the hand don't forget its cunning."

"You kidding?" I asked.

He picked up the cracker crumbs around his plate and ate them. "I've kicked a press," he said firmly.

"We're off," I said. Then I remembered. "What's the use? I get the baseball suits and altar cloths run through the clean today, tonight they take Lucy, and tomorrow I won't have any way to press them."

Fructoso banged open his cash register. "I estimate," he said, "that after I pay the rent tonight, I'll be one dollar twenty-five cents on the credit side. Take it, friend. The butcher can wait."

"Thanks, Fructoso," I said. "But it ain't a drop in the bucket."

"Emmor'll bring some money back from Placentia," Fructoso said.

"Not enough."

"Don't give up this way," Frissil said. "You can't tell what'll happen by night." He tipped Angela ten cents with my money.

"Borrow of him, High," Fructoso said, watching.

"My services *and* my purse are his," Frissil said, before I had a chance to open my mouth. "Drop me at the Calla Lily. I'll start work while you pick up the baseball suits."

"What's the use?" I asked. "Sister Mary Michael won't like the boys playing baseball before the bishop with their pants not pressed. And after tonight there won't be any way to press them."

"Who knows?" Frissil asked. "You can't tell. Look what's happened already."

So I took him to the plant, showed him Lucy, showed him the specials, showed him the clothes to get a break-run, showed him the deadheads he could skip, introduced him to Josephita.

Frissil's nowhere near the man to look at Emmor Aull is, but Josephita opened up her big black eyes for him.

"You get the suits, High," she said. "I'll show Meester Thompson his job."

"One thing, before I go," I told him. "You got to put on a pair of pants. I won't have anybody kicking a press for me in a pair of flowered drawers. It'd undermine my business. Get a pair of leftovers from the vault."

"I'll get them for him," Josephita said, fluttering around Frissil like he was a prize done up in fancy paper.

So I left them and drove out to the St. Joseph School for Boys, thinking it was a wild-goose chase—no use picking up pants I wouldn't have any way to press, and even if I figured out a way to keep Lucy, I couldn't weather another month with Mrs. Ettinger gone over to the Bon Ton.

Not even Sister Mary Michael's kind smile or the twenty-four baseball suits and eight altar cloths she gave me cheered me up. I drove back to Belle Vista seeing that Bon Ton car standing in front of Mrs. Ettinger's and seeing the bare, clean spot that would be left on the cement floor after they'd taken Lucy away.

But what I saw in my mind's eye was a trifle to what hit my bona-fide peepers when I stepped back into the Calla Lily plant. Frissil Thompson had hanging on the line the sorriest collection of so-called pressed men's suits I'd seen since I set up scarecrows along the Rush Branch bottomland. The leg crease was here and there, the cuff turned up in scallops, and the rear elevation terraced.

Frissil was sweating over Lucy with a head of steam strong enough to take the crease out of a cornerstone. "I kinda seem to have lost the hang of it," he said. "It don't come back the way I thought it would."

I dumped down the baseball suits and altar cloths and got Frissil away from Lucy. A press like her that could make an upstairs chain-store number look custom-built, being used like a mangle. "You done enough damage for one day," I told him, wasting no time in word-mincing. "You just manage to keep out of the way while I do the stuff over."

Josephita came sliding and purring up, the way she has, trying to save that Frissil's hide—why, I don't know.

"Thees suit's OK High," she said. "Eet's for a man's funeral. The pants won't show. You know how the flowers go over them? Meester Thompson done thees OK?"

That riled me. Not a thought of the work I was going to have to do over. "Meester Thompson," I said, "would make a first-rate presser to a clientele of corpses."

That held her. That held both of them. They let me alone while I went to work re-pressing those suits. And re-pressing is ten times the job pressing is. You'd have thought that Frissil Thompson'd been kind of taken aback, making the mess of things he had. Wouldn't you? But far from it. He acted as if he didn't have any idea that for the bread I'd tossed him on the waters he'd sent me back a tin of rat poison. I pressed away, putting the best I had into it, even though, as far as I could see, this was the Calla Lily's last day.

Frissil Thompson ranged around, asking questions, looking at the hat blocks, shaking up the chemicals.

He came over to me bringing a package. "What's this?" he queried.

"Mammoth Moth Eradicator," I told him.

"How come you got so many boxes of it stacked up?"

"I got stuck," I told him. "It don't eradicate."

He opened a package. "Smells good," he said.

"That makes it unanimous," I said. "The moths think so, too." I set my jaw and went back to work. But that Frissil Thompson's a hard man to discourage. He kept fussing around. I'd got about a half dozen of his jobs looking like suits again when he said, "Could I borrow the delivery truck for about an hour, Mr. Geer? I'll put my own gas in it."

With my money, I thought, but he said it so meek I didn't have the heart to tell him no.

"You be back here by four-thirty," I told him. "These deliveries got to go then."

Out he went. The day was dying hotter than it began. I was kicking the press and wetting it down with sweat. Josephita was matching up, getting coats and pants together, and between times having a look out the window at every car that slowed to see if it was Emmor Aull coming back. She never gave up hope that someday Emmor was going to wake up, see her. I was really stomping them out, trying to get the day's orders up before the Luxite people came, when Josephita yelled, "*Caramba!* Here they are!"

I knew what she meant, but I never turned my head. Let the monkeys see what they were doing—stopping work, cutting down production. A man can't work without his pants, and I was providing the pants. A key industry if there ever was one.

That didn't mean a thing to the Luxite Company. In come a guy, genial as a goat. "Got your payment, buddy?"

He knew I didn't. He just wanted to rub it in. I wanted to tell him to take his so-and-so press and get out, but Lucy's not responsible for the kind of people who sell her, and I couldn't do it. Had to make a play for her, however much it galled me.

"Look at that," I said, pointing to the pile of baseball suits and altar cloths. "It's $18.50's worth of work, and the Pope himself standing behind it. Tomorrow at two-thirty, I'll have the money."

That Luxite vampire shook his head. What he wanted was blood. "Talk, talk," he said. "What I want's cash, not holy water."

"Tomorrow at two-thirty," I said, as if I didn't hear him.

"The five days' grace is up," he said. "I got a cleaner right here in town with his eye on this. Just stopped in to see him. He's got cash. Don't give me hot air, the way some do. I've had trouble collecting for this press right along. I aim to end that. You got the money?"

"No," I told him.

He gave a bellow, like a bull moving in for the kill. "Come in, Ed," he yelled, and a fellow looking less like a himan being than Lucy comes in with his screwdrivers and so forth.

There was nothing I could do. The law was all on their side. They wouldn't even let me finish pressing the mayor's pants. I sat on the spotting table with them folded over my arm and watched. I felt worse than when I left the farm. Even Josephita was sad. She forgot to keep an eye out for Emmor Aull. There was Lucy, the keystone of my business and as true a partner as a man could wish, being prised up like a hunk of machinery.

I couldn't take it. Without a right in the world, I jumped down from the spotting table and turned on those wolves. "You can't do this to me," I yelled.

"What in hell," they asked, "makes you think we can't?"

"This," said Frissil Thompson, who'd come in without us noticing, and he waved a fistful of bills under their noses.

Five fives, it was. I thought he'd likely held up a service station, but I didn't say a word. Acted as if I'd expected him.

"Give these men their money," I said, and he did. Fifteen bucks, with forty cents back in change. They went out cussing me—but empty-handed. That's what counted.

"Looky," I said to Frissil, but just then Emmor Aull erupted into the plant.

"The Bijou Theater's chain signed up to take my peanuts," he whooped, not stopping to take in the situation in which we was involved. "Seven of them in Orange County, not counting Placentia. 'From the foothills to the sea.' That's my new slogan. 'Aull peanuts from the foothills to the sea.' What do you think of it?"

Josephita was glowing her eyes at him. "Emmor," she said, "eet ees wonderful." She vibrating like a tamale before the cornmeal's set.

Emmor looked at her as if he was seeing her for the first time, though she'd been sighing down his neck for seven months hand-running.

"Thanks, Josephita," he said. "I'm glad you can see what it means to me. What you say," he asked her suddenly, "if we celebrate a little? Have supper down at Fructoso's?"

Josephita gave signs of shattering, of going up in blazes like a Roman candle, but she managed to stay in one piece, saying, "*Si, si, Emmor*—in ten minutes I be ready."

"I'll drive you home," Emmor told her, and he walked out with her, his mind full of peanuts and Josephita, not giving a thought to the fate of the Calla Lily Cleaners & Dyers—whether we was afoot or horseback.

When they'd gone, I turned on Frissil Thompson. "How come?" I asked.

"Eula Ettinger," he said, modestlike.

"Steal," I asked, "or borrow?"

"Neither," he said, with virtue in his look. "A business transaction. I contracted to de-moth her entire establishment—using Mammoth Moth Exterminator."

"It don't exterminate," I told him for the second time.

"That's OK," he said. "There's nothing there to exterminate."

"No moths?" I asked.

"Nope."

"What in crimminy's she paying $25 for?"

"Me," said Frissil Thompson, ruffling up his burnsides and rounding his pale blue eyes. "My company. My talk. My appreciation. You're dead right about Eula. She likes a sympathetic man. Right about her looks, too. The corn in full ear. Touch of frost on it, but the full ear, and no mistake."

He went right from romance to business. He handed me the extra five and said, "Can I borrow $3.60 of you? That makes $4.60 all together. I wouldn't ask for it except I got a date with Eula tonight."

"That's OK," I said. What else could I say to the man who'd just saved the Lucy for me, though I thought he had his nerve.

"I'll need the car, too," he said. "But just to get to Eula's. We're going on from there in hers."

I had my mouth open to say no, when Frissil said, "I don't think you'll have any more trouble about Eula and the Bon Ton. I let her know about them."

"I got these deliveries to make," I told him.

"I'll do it," he said.

"You don't know the town," I told him.

"I'll pick up Emmor Aull at Fructoso's," he said. "Time that guy did a little work around here."

So he took the car and the deliveries. Plus a coat from the vault to go with his borrowed pants. I even gave the coat a press for him.

Maybe I'm a sucker. I don't know—but after they'd all pulled out, and I was left alone there in the plant, I looked around me.

Everything neat and orderly, and a pile of work to do. Everything lined up the way I liked it—movable racks for the clothes, a glass case out front to hang the fancies in, and a marble-topped spotting board. The steam going ting-ting in the pipes, the baseball suits ready for the dust wheel, and the altar cloths needing a little pre-spotting.

I looked at Lucy standing there ready to go to work and the work there was to do, and I thought to myself, I don't know but what it's pretty near as good as starting the plow a spring morning along the Sandusky bottoms. And when I picked up that load of baseball suits and started for the dust wheel with them, I didn't have any envy of Frissil or Emmor Aull, out celebrating though they was.

# The Wake

THE BRASS CANDLESTICK that had been her mother's mother's she placed on a little table at the foot of the coffin; beside it she put the red geraniums her mother had loved. When the candlelight steadied, she pulled a folding chair to the side of the coffin and sat down. For a number of weeks she had been sitting by her mother's bedside and was come now to sit for a last time near her.

She had walked through the September streets of the two-street town: down Acacia, where the arch was and the official sign welcoming Captain Beaufort, Purvis's Own Hero; past the flags and the swatches of bunting and the unofficial signs painted by impetuous merchants reminding townspeople that "Tonight is Beaufort Night." She had turned left on Madrona and had seen at its far end the foothills, fluid and shimmering in the late-afternoon haze. She had passed the Coke drinkers, the sprayed vegetables, the racks of five-o'clock papers. Halfway down Madrona she had come to the Odd Fellows Hall and had entered the Macaulay Funeral Home, which occupied its ground floor.

It had been very strange to walk the warm and busy streets with her final gifts for her mother; it was still stranger to leave behind the day's warmth, the September gloss, to enter Mr. Macaulay's velvet-hung setting for eternity.

She sat, not looking at her mother, but remembering her. In the three days since her mother's death, Mary Kingham had violently oscillated between times of dreadful weeping and periods when she felt as she now did—as if a kind of communion, which had been denied them in life, was now possible between her and her mother.

The six-o'clock bell at the Ursuline Academy sounded its spaced, then clustered notes. It still rings, thought Mary. It was the first time she had noticed it since her mother's death. It had a pleasant, end-of-day sound among the flowers cut down from their living to serve sorrow, among the symbols of death and hope.

Mary looked at her mother: the strong quiet face that had so often been contorted by laughter, drawn down with anger, shattered with tears. "Darling," she said, "you had your day, as in your time, didn't you?"

A kind of real happiness filled her, remembering those days, and she sat for a long time reliving them—unnoticing, scarcely hearing, though there were frequent footsteps through the side door and up the steps to the Odd Fellows Hall.

At the sound of a voice, she lifted her head and stared through the gloom.

"You the only one here?" It was almost dark, but by the light of the candle she saw a soldier standing just inside the door.

"My mother and I," she said, gesturing.

The soldier came toward her with the delicate, balanced air of a man who has had too much to drink.

"Where?" he asked. "These lights aren't very good."

"Here," Mary said, nodding toward the coffin.

The soldier picked up the candle and held it so the light fell on the quiet face.

"Dead?" he asked.

"Yes," Mary said.

He put the candle back in place by the flowers. "I'm not used to people being fixed up so nice when they're dead," he explained. "She doesn't look dead." He shook his head.

Mary said nothing.

"Who is she?" he asked presently.

"My mother."

The man looked puzzled. "You told me that before, didn't you?"

"I'm afraid you're drunk," Mary said.

"No," he told her. "Not at all." After a time he added, "I've had a little too much to drink but I'm not drunk."

Mary's eyes went from the candle to the soldier: some analogy was there—the wavering light, the muted incandescence.

"Would you mind," he asked, "if I sat here awhile? I'd be quiet."

"You don't have to be quiet."

The soldier looked at the coffin.

"Mother loved to talk. She was a great talker. She liked to sit up late, drink black coffee, and lay her tongue to things, as she called it."

The soldier picked up a folding chair, let it slip through his fingers onto the cement floor. He got it up again, opened it, placed it by the little table, and sat down.

"My mind's clear as a bell," he said, "but my hands and feet feel a little numb." He bent his head to the bowl of red geraniums. "Nice," he said. "No smell." Waves of heavy scent from anchors, crosses, wreaths, and tablets filled the room.

"My mother liked them."

The soldier touched the flowers with his hand. It was very brown and trembled a little. "My mother likes begonias," he said.

He moved about uncomfortably on the small hard chair, then took a bottle from his hip pocket and put it on the table beside the candle and flowers. The candlelight lit jewels in it.

"I wish you could have a drink," he said. "It would do you good. My having a drink—several drinks," he amended conscientiously, "kind of separates us."

The girl shook her head.

"Would your mother care?"

"No, she wouldn't care. But I don't need it. I feel the way you do, anyway—head clear, hands and feet numb."

"It's an honorable thing to do," the soldier told her. "Drink at a wake. This is a wake, isn't it?" he asked.

"Yes," Mary said, "I suppose it is."

The soldier lifted the candlestick, brought it toward his face while he felt about in a pocket with his free hand. Mary stared at the thin, heavy-browed face the candle lighted.

"Why, you're Joe Beaufort," she said. "Captain Beaufort. You belong upstairs. They're having a reception for you upstairs."

Captain Beaufort didn't seem to hear her. He replaced the candlestick. "Not smoking, though. To drink at a wake's an honorable thing, but not smoking. That's not serious enough."

"Joe Beaufort," Mary said, "you belong upstairs. They're having a reception for you."

Captain Beaufort looked at the girl. "Who are you? I know you, don't I?"

"I'm Mary Kingham. I was in high school with you. I remember you."

"You don't remember me. I was the school nonentity—a jerk, a dope, a drip."

"I remember you," Mary said. "You wrote pieces for the school paper."

"That's the reason," he said.

"Look," Mary urged, "you belong upstairs. You're the hero."

The Captain's voice hardened. "Drop that, will you?" he asked. He unscrewed the top from the bottle beside him. "Still a four-letter guy," he said.

"They'll miss you upstairs. They'll start hunting for you."

"Not here."

"They'll be disappointed."

"It's better I'm not there. . . . What was your mother's name?" he asked.

"Mary Frances."

"This is for Mary Frances," he said. He turned to Mary. " 'This corruption must put on incorruption and this mortal put on immortality.' " He took two short drinks. "The world is rapidly being filled with incorruption and immortality," he told her.

He recapped the bottle and set it back in place. "Did you hear the six-o'clock bell?" he asked.

"Yes," Mary said. "I was right here. I was glad to hear it."

"Up to that time, everything was all right. Everything's all haywire really. What I mean is—I was set for tonight. I wasn't planning on enjoying it, but my mother was looking forward to it, and people had been working on it, so, I figured I'd live through it."

"You still ought to go," Mary urged.

"I was heading for there when I got in here," Captain Beaufort said. "I thought maybe I might go up there and make them a little speech. I might yet. You better let me stay."

"You do what you want to, Joe."

"I want to stay here. Up there they think a soldier dies the way he does in the movies, falls down for the effect and jumps up the minute the camera moves on. Down here you know better than that."

"Yes," Mary said, "down here we know better than that. You die forever."

"At six o'clock," he said, "I was lying on my bed. In my room. The door to my room was open, and a nice breeze was blowing through. The doors in my mother's house," he said, "are held open by bricks in red-flannel embroidered jackets. Did you ever hear of anything like that?"

"No," Mary said. "I never did."

"They look like pincushions," he told her, "but you can break a toe on them. As a matter of fact, I did break a toe on one of them once. OK," he said. "I was lying on my bed watching the wind blow the curtains in and out of the windows and I remembered a wish I'd made in a little shack in North Africa, about six miles outside Nefarti."

He stopped talking for quite a long time. Finally Mary said, "What did you wish?"

"You don't mind all this talking?"

"No," Mary said.

"She doesn't mind?"

"I told you," Mary said. "She'd be listening if she could."

"Maybe she is."

Mary looked at Captain Beaufort.

"The thing to do," he said quickly and with heat, "is not to be too sure. That's death—being sure. What's left then? With everything settled? The thing to do is to wonder. I'm going to spend the rest of my life wondering." He took two more short drinks.

"What did you wish?" Mary reminded him.

"The wind in Africa," he said, "has got a different sound from the wind here. That night it was kicking up a lot of sand. You could hear it hitting the side of the shack. I suppose listening to it made me say what I did. And maybe to break the monotony of guys wishing for blonds and home-cooked food. Anyway, I said, 'Boys, give me a room with white curtains at the window and a warm wind pushing them in and out.' I could sure see that room, Mary—bed, bureau, books, windows wide open, sun. But the important thing was the curtains. I'd been in a lot of rooms lately. All of them had had windows. Most of them had had beds. Some even had books. But not curtains. Not clean white curtains blowing back and forth in a warm wind. Summer, I thought. The late afternoon. The gentle wind. The clean curtains."

Captain Beaufort passed an experimental finger back and forth above the candle flame, found the level at which the heat was unbearable, held his finger just above it. "Here, it's warm," he said. "There, it burns. A hair between them. Only way of finding the safe spot's to get burned a little."

"Look," he said, "if you wanted a drink, what would you say?"

"I don't," Mary said. "I really don't."

"I know—not now—but sometime, if you did?"

"I'd say give me a Martini, I suppose. Or an Old Fashioned."

"You would, wouldn't you? Yes, you would ask for a special drink?"

"Yes," said Mary. "I would."

"If you wanted a book what would you say?"

"I'd say, 'Give me Yeats's poems.' "

"That's right." He sounded very pleased indeed. "That's exactly what you'd say. But not me. And not in the Army."

"Not Yeats?" Mary asked.

"Yeats is OK. That's not the point. The point is, nothing specific. Nothing particular. That jinxes it. That puts a hex on it."

"I don't get it," said Mary.

"It's like this. You can ask for a bed. That's general. That's OK. But no special bed. Not a feather bed. Or a twin bed. Or a Beauty Rest mattress. That jinxes it.

"You can ask for time. But nothing particular. No unique segment. Not next Monday. Not summer, not fall. That jinxes it. You get it?"

He took a long drink. "I'm still thinking of her," he said looking toward the coffin. "I'm thinking of her every minute—her and a few others. There are bodies celestial and bodies terrestrial, and the glory of the celestial is one thing and the glory of the terrestrial another. She knows that," he told Mary.

"But not me," he said. "It's just a saying with me. Just a cheerful mouthful.

"Look, I'm telling you, so you won't have to learn the hard way: when you make a wish, Something listens. Somewhere, Something takes it in.

" 'That girl,' It says, 'that particular girl. The one with the long legs? You won't get her.' " Captain Beaufort looked away from the coffin and at Mary. "Catch on? He asked for something particular. They don't like that. They penalize you.

"But you forget again. You ask for a leave in June. 'June,' they say. 'June, eh?' It won't be June.

"You can't seem to remember. You want a wizard op. 'Wizard?' they say. 'It won't be wizard. It'll be the last.' "

The tall dark boy moved his chair along the cement floor, an inch or two nearer the girl. "But if you're careful, you can fool It—or Them. Just any girl, you say, very, very casual—any room, any day, any op. 'I don't care,' you say; 'I'm not particular.' Then what do you get? Straight wizard down the line—girl, day, op.

"At six o'clock, when the bell was ringing, I was lying on my bed watching the white curtains blow in and out. Thought I'd outsmarted Them. Hadn't said a word about a particular room. Nothing geographical, nothing specific. Very, very casual. Then the phone rang, and my mother answered it.

"In the long run," he said, "you can't outsmart Them. They catch up with you every time."

He got up and walked in his precise, difficult fashion to the coffin. He looked down at the woman in it for a long time. "She has a fine face," he said at last. "The kind of face you'd be proud to be dead with. God knows," he said, running his hand across his own forehead and down his long, somewhat narrow jaw, "what mine's going to look like."

Then he stood with one hand on the coffin. "I didn't ask for any particular room. So I got my own room in my own home. And my own mother walking around downstairs getting supper.

"Yeah," he said, "but They sure foxed me. I didn't ask for a particular room, but I asked for things to be a certain way in that room, and in that house. Without knowing it, I had asked. The minute I heard my mother on that phone I knew I'd asked, and was getting the horse laugh as a result.

"My God," he said, taking his hand from the coffin and bringing it down with much force, but quietly, against his open palm, "that was going to be a house where you weren't so damned pure, any more, where you went a little easy, where you stepped light, where you listened—and, God help me, where you learned. It was a house, wasn't it, a half-million guys had died to keep going? It was, wasn't it?"

"Yes," Mary said, "it was."

"And if you lived in that house, you'd remember it, wouldn't you?"

"Yes," Mary said, "I would."

Captain Beaufort went back to his folding chair. "You want this literary," he asked, "or bald? Bald and unvarnished? I'm a literary guy, you know. I wrote pieces for the school paper."

"Just short, Joe," Mary told him. "Just plain and short."

"Plain and short," he said. "And shocking. OK. I'm on my bed. The door is open. The curtains blowing in and out in that damn sweet way. The phone rings. 'Mrs. Kingsley,' said my mother. 'So happy Corporal Jones is home. Dear Corporal Jones. However, I really do not think it would be appropriate for him to sit on the platform with Joseph. Joseph is an officer. Joseph is a hero. Not on the platform. Most unsuitable. Dear Mrs. Kingsley.' "

Captain Beaufort took a very long drink. "Do you think that amusing?"

"No," Mary said.

"I told my mother," Captain Beaufort said, "that I would not be in for supper. I told her it would be necessary for me to go out and pick up a couple of drinks. She said, 'I think it is most unsuitable for an officer to drink.' Does that amuse you?"

"No," Mary said.

"There were a number of other things said to which, unfortunately, I cannot refer, since I am making this plain and short. But after picking up a couple of drinks I thought I might go up to that shindy after all. I thought I might make them a little speech." Captain Beaufort looked in Mary's direction but his eyes were focused on something beyond her. "I planned to begin, 'Dear, dear mothers of Purvis.'

"She wasn't like that, Mary," he said, looking toward the coffin.

Captain Beaufort shook his head slightly like a man falling asleep. "I'm forgetting whose wake this is," he said. "How was she?" he asked gently.

"She didn't know all the answers," Mary said. "She walked lightly. She was full of pity. She liked sweet smells. She believed in signs. She was always wondering. And learning."

They were both silent for a time, then Captain Beaufort, without seeming to have looked up, said, "Come on in."

Mary started up. A round little man with a pale face and red hair cut as evenly as a wig tiptoed into the room wiping his hands on the heavy white apron he wore.

"Mr. Macaulay," said Mary.

"Keeping watch," said Mr. Macaulay in a soft hollow voice. "A kindly custom. Very kindly." He seemed to catch sight of Captain Beaufort for the first time. "This a relative of yours, Mary?"

"No," said Mary. "This is Joseph Beaufort. Captain Beaufort."

"Captain Beaufort," said Mr. Macaulay. "You belong upstairs. They're having a celebration up there for you."

In the momentary silence a long peal of laughter and hand clapping came down from overhead.

"They seem to be getting on without me," Captain Beaufort said.

"I stepped in awhile back," said Mr. Macaulay. "They've got a Marine up there. A corporal from Guadalcanal. But you're the man they want. You're the hero, Captain." Mr. Macaulay looked at the candle, geraniums, and bottle. "This looks mighty cozy," he said. "It adds something we don't seem to get." He sighed heavily.

Captain Beaufort got to his feet. "Sit down, won't you? Have a drink?"

Mr. Macaulay lowered himself into the offered chair. "By rights, I shouldn't do this," he said. "I'm the host here, I suppose, but it's been a hard day. And not over yet. But no drink. Thanks just the same, but no drink."

There was a knock at the door that sounded as if it would be glad not to be heard, but Mr. Macaulay heard it. "Come in, Homer," he said.

A boy carrying two wreaths came in from the entryway. "These are for Mrs. Kingham," he whispered. "We just finished them." He stared about him, at the coffin, the burning candle, the beribboned soldier.

"How many times I got to tell you not to whisper, Homer?" Mr. Macaulay asked. "Put those wreaths down. Homer, this is Miss Kingham and Captain Beaufort."

Homer leaned the wreaths against the base of the coffin and forgot to whisper. "The guy who got the medal," he said. "I couldn't go upstairs because I had to work—and here he is." Homer spoke dreamily. "The hero."

"Just drop all that crap, will you, kid?" Captain Beaufort stood very tall above Homer.

"You got the medal," Homer persisted.

"The hell with the medal," Captain Beaufort said. He took it out of his pocket. "Here, Homer," he said, "you take it. Wear it or bury it, I don't care. Frame it, if you want to, but I don't want to see it again. Come on, Mary, let's get out of here." He pushed the medal violently into Homer's hand.

"Mary's sitting up with her mother," Mr. Macaulay reminded him.

"You do whatever you think's right, Mary," said Captain Beaufort. "Whatever you want to do."

Mary stood up. "I think you should go upstairs for a while now, Joe," she said.

"I told you I didn't—"

"I don't suppose Corporal Jones did either," she said. "He's had about two hours up there now."

Captain Beaufort made a wrenched, bitter gesture. "I can't stomach those—"

"You go on, Mary," Mr. Macaulay said. "I'll sit here. I'll keep watch for you."

"She'd be up there," Mary said, going over to the coffin, "if she were alive."

The Captain straightened his hair, pulled his tunic into place and held out his hand to Mary. "Let's get outside," he said, "where nobody's celebrating anything—and no one's dead."

Homer and Mr. Macaulay watched them leave the room hand in hand.

Slowly Homer opened his hand, gazed at the bit of ribbon and the medal on it. "I can't keep this, Mr. Macaulay," he whispered. "It don't belong to me. It wouldn't be right."

"Don't whisper, Homer," Mr. Macaulay said sharply. "No, I don't suppose you can."

"What'll I do with it?" Homer asked.

"Pin it on Mrs. Kingham," said Mr. Macaulay decisively. "I don't know anyone who ever deserved a medal more, or would be more proud to wear one."

Homer shied away from the coffin. "Oh, no, Mr. Macaulay," he said, "I couldn't do that."

"No," Mr. Macaulay said once again. "I don't suppose you could. Well, give it to me, Homer. I'll take care of it. You get on home to bed."

Homer handed the medal to Mr. Macaulay. "I'm going upstairs first," he said.

"OK, Homer, you make a night of it."

Mr. Macaulay, left alone, slid farther down on the uncomfortable chair. His pale face settled into lines of sorrow. "There lies a good woman dead before her time. I don't know how it is—after all these years, and all the jokes—I don't get more used to this business."

He smoothed the sleek sides of Captain Beaufort's bottle, which still stood beside him on the candlelit table, then unscrewed the top and swallowed half of what was left. "I needed that," he said, and folded his hands across his white apron and prepared to sleep. But before he had closed his eyes, a great burst of shouting, clapping, and foot-stamping from overhead roused him again. He held Captain Beaufort's medal in his hand so that the candlelight fell on the metal and colored ribbon, then looked up sadly toward the ceiling. "Poor boy," Mr. Macaulay said, then put the medal on the table beside the red geraniums and prepared once more to sleep.

# Grand Opening

I T WAS PURDY NEWCOMB's thirtieth birthday, though none of his family seemed to be aware of it. He came in about seven from connecting-up, in preparation for irrigating, and his wife, Zenith, who had been asleep when he left the house, stuck her coppery head out the back-porch door and called, "Bring me in an armload of wood, Purdy," just as if it were the tenth or seventeenth of July instead of the twenty-fifth.

She didn't even call him Purty, the way she did sometimes when she was feeling tender about him.

"Got something special for breakfast?" Purdy asked, filling his arms.

"No," Zenith answered. "I did think a little about popovers, but then I wasn't in the mood for them." What Zenith wasn't in the mood for she didn't do, you could depend on that.

Purdy eased his armload down into the woodbox.

"Thank you, Purty," Zenith said.

"You like my looks?" Purdy asked. He threw out his chest so that his clean blue shirt opened enough at the neck to show the mat of light hair that came up flush with the indentation below his Adam's apple.

Zenith stirred away without turning around. "I like long-waisted men," she said seriously.

Purdy let his breath out, and his shirt collar closed. That was a new one. "Am I long waisted?" he asked.

"Yes," said Zenith, "and you toe in, too."

"Do you like that?" Purdy asked. "Is that OK?"

Zenith turned away from the stove. When her face was warm, as it was now, her freckles scarcely showed.

"That's the only right way for a man to walk," she said, as if it were a thing well known to everybody but Purdy Newcomb.

Purdy walked out to the back porch watching the way he planted his feet: looked straight ahead to him, though there was maybe a little veer inward. He turned the faucet on and filled the washbasin.

"Finish connecting-up?" Zenith called.

"Sure," Purdy spluttered through a double handful of water.

"When's the water coming on?"

"About eight."

The Zanchero had stopped by the night before to ask Purdy if he'd like to get the water in the morning. He would, certainly. July had been unusually hot and dry, the trees were drooping, and he was all furrowed-out; nothing to do but connect-up.

"Saw Ed Conboy this morning," Purdy said, looking at his face in the mirror over the wash bench.

"What was Mr. Conboy doing up so early?" Zenith asked. Zenith didn't approve of Mr. Conboy and always mistered him.

"Finishing his cultivating," Purdy said, scooping up another handful of water.

Before coming to the house Purdy had stood for a time looking up the long sweep of the valley toward Old Saddle Back and the sun, which already was well above it. Valley, sun, and mountain were none of his handiwork, but everything else in view mostly was. Three years ago nothing had grown here but sagebrush and cactus; nothing had moved but jackrabbits above earth, trap-door spiders below, and over them all the black, knifelike shadows of the watchful buzzards.

He had grubbed out the sagebrush and cactus, set the plowshare to earth, dug the tree holes, put the fine, burlap-balled Valencias into the ground. It was a good piece of work, it was his own, and was what he'd always planned to do. Purdy pushed the felt hat he wore summer and winter farther back on his head. Fifteen acres of budded Valencias were really better than he had dared hope for; Zenith was the only woman he had ever wanted for a wife; and three kids, while certainly more than he had planned to have at thirty, were, now that he was acquainted with them, not too many or too soon.

What then was wrong? What was missing? What else had he ever hoped to have? He stood, feet planted in the sod he had broken, scanning the eastern sky, and suddenly, out of some unnamable sense of loss, he sailed his hat across two tree rows and yelled "The hell with it!"

It was then Ed Conboy had come up, walking silently across the plowed ground.

"What you yelling at, Purdy? Or who?"

Since he wasn't able to say, even to himself, Purdy couldn't put it into words for Ed, couldn't say: Ed, I'm yelling because this is my thirtieth birthday and I got a feeling things are going by too fast for me; got a feeling that while I'm here furrowing-out, connecting-up, irrigating, other men my age are still ranging around. He couldn't say: Ed, I had a lot of dreams about myself once. Dreamed I would bite me off a pretty fair chunk of this earth and chew it; dreamed, before things were done and finished with here, I'd know the flavor of more than one kind of chaw in my mouth, and the feel of a dozen kinds of earth beneath my feet.

What he did say was, "Nothing, Ed. Just felt a yell come one. You know how it is."

Ed picked up the old felt, gave it a lick or two across his knees to knock the dust from it, and handed it to Purdy.

"Can't say as I do," he said.

Purdy set his hat back on his sun-bleached hair. "Comes over you ever so often," he said. "Strikes you all of a sudden."

"Never strikes me," Ed persisted, so Purdy changed the subject.

"What you doing up so early, Ed?" he asked.

"Figured on finishing cultivating before the wind comes up."

The two men gazed far away to where in the east a yellow cloud the size of a matchbox hung like a little gate between San Gorgino and Old Saddle Back.

"There she is," said Ed. "Blowing over by Riverside now."

And hand, all was unusually clear and precise; the diamond-sharp air, like a lens or a drop of water, magnified everything that lay in or beyond it. Jackrabbits loomed up with whiskers wide as wires, and a stand of volunteer oats left growing at the base of a tree looked as solid as and more particularized than a forest.

"Blowing by nightfall," Purdy agreed.

"Well, let it," said Ed contentedly, "let her blow."

"You got something on tonight?" Purdy asked, knowing his friend.

Ed Conboy took a couple of dance steps, supple and easy in spite of the plowed ground. "Ja-da," he sang, as mellow and romantic as if moon, not sun, had just arisen, "ja-da, zing-zing-ze."

"Jing-jing," said Purdy, "not zing-zing."

Ed asked, "How come you know these things, Purdy? You don't go to dances any more."

"I'm not deef yet," Purdy said. "Where's the dance?"

"Olinda. Oil drillers' shindig."

"Taking Frances?"

"Ah, no," said Ed. "Saving Frances for a Sunday-school picnic."

The Sunday-school picnic was no lie, whatever saving Frances was. Ed went to everything.

"New girl?" Purdy asked.

"In a manner of speaking," said Ed. Then he added reflectively, as if her newness might be qualified by it, "She's tattooed."

Purdy whistled. "Where," he said, "if I may ask?"

"Sure you can," Ed told him. "She don't make no secret of it. Thigh."

Purdy whistled again. "Something patriotic?" he speculated.

"She don't strike me as being a particularly patriotic girl," Ed admitted.

"Wreath of roses," Purdy suggested. "Flowers and hearts?"

"As a matter of fact, linked hearts is what she's got," Ed said admiringly.

"That'd be pretty," Purdy said.

"It is," Ed agreed. "Plus initials."

"Don't they get out of date?"

"Not the way she's got it worked out," explained Ed. "Only one heart's got initials tattooed in it, and they're hers. In the other she prints yours."

"You mean *yours*?" Purdy said.

"Well, no," said Ed modestly, "not yet." But he seemed hopeful. He took another dance step, plowing up the dust, snapping his fingers, singing, "Ja-da, ja-da. Ja-da. Jing-jing-ze."

"Cute idea," said Purdy, watching his friend, wondering if it really was. Wondering what Zenith would think of a woman with linked hearts and changing initials. Then he thought, Hell, here you are, a man thirty years old, and all you do when you hear a a thing like that is wonder how it will strike your wife.

"Oh, she's cute, all right," Ed said. "Cute as tricks."

"You better marry her," Purdy said, "put her in a show."

"Why, Purdy," Ed had said, looking amazed, "you're jealous."

Purdy was amazed himself. "I've got to get up to the house for breakfast," he said hurriedly. "Water comes on at eight."

"Give Zenith my love," Ed called after him. "She's a grand girl."

Purdy waggled the hoe he had laid across his shoulders to show that he had heard, but he didn't look back or answer—though certainly not because he disagreed with Ed.

From the depth of the towel, drying his face, Purdy called in to Zenith, "Ed's got a new girl."

"That Mr. Conboy!" exclaimed Zenith disapprovingly.

"She's tattooed," said Purdy, hanging up the towel and looking in the mirror at his face, which except for the white creases at the corners of his eyes was brown.

Zenith came to the screen door again. "Tattooed," she repeated, as if Purdy had said decapitated. "Where?"

Purdy was preparing to tell her where and how when Chasteen stepped into the doorway beside her mother.

"The table's all set, Mother," she said, and Zenith told Purdy hurriedly, "Never mind now, Purdy. Come right on in to breakfast."

When Purdy came in to the dining room, he saw that something special was afoot and he smiled, thinking, They haven't forgotten my birthday after all. The breakfast table itself looked as usual: in the center a very solid bouquet of zinnias, picked by Chasteen, whose idea of floral beauty ranged beyond plenty and very close to more than enough. There was the usual platter of bacon, bowl of gravy, plate of lightbread, sauce dishes of fruit—fresh peeled peaches this morning. What was unusual was that the three children were not sitting, but standing by their chairs, and that Zenith, when she brought in the coffeepot, put it on the asbestos mat beside her plate and stood too.

Purdy, feeling self-conscious but pleased, leaned against his own chair, waiting for whatever was to come next. It was nice for them to do something special for his birthday, he decided, and looked appreciatively about the table. Before he had any, Purdy had thought of his children as being little replicas of Zenith and himself: a boy, himself when young; a girl, a smaller Zenith, all coppery and shining. The three thus far, for any resemblance they had to him or Zenith, had almost as well been scooped up with a fishnet, hit or miss, from any shoal of children. Purdy loved them, but they were queer to him, and strangers.

Chasteen, at ten, Purdy considered as practical to look at as a kitchen cabinet, but trying to follow what went on inside her head made him giddy. In Purdy, Jr.'s head, nothing, insofar as his father could tell, went on. He sat and read or sat and looked, and except that he, physically more than the other two, was kin to the family, by reason of a duplication of Zenith's rangy, long-legged build, Purdy would have felt as polite with this son as with a visitor. The baby, Hogan, who had Zenith's maiden name, was five; and for him, Purdy thought hopefully of the Presidency, fearfully of the pen. This morning, the three, unbickering, washed, and, what was more uncommon, dried, were ranged around the table in an arc so seemly that Purdy had fewer fears than usual of what his next three, with this beginning, would be like.

While Purdy was still assessing his offspring and taking pleasure in the patriarchial moment, Zenith cleared her throat. Purdy waited for her to say, "Purdy, the children have a little gift for you," but what she said was, "Purdy, Chasteen thinks it would be nice for us to sing a hymn before each meal, the way the Brookses do."

Purdy felt a kind of dryness, an emptiness of disappointment, come inside him, a feeling about his birthday he would have supposed he had parted with at the age of twelve.

"Why, sure," he said quickly. "Let's sing."

Purdy had a good voice himself. At the times of the children's births, he took over the kitchen work for Zenith, and sang in a voice so resonant and happy that kettle lids trembled downstairs, and upstairs, in her bed, Zenith could feel the bed slats beneath her vibrate.

"Why, sure, Chasteen," Purdy said heartily. "What's the song?"

Chasteen gave her father a severe look. The congregation was not evidently supposed to address informal inquiries to the pulpit.

"Bow your heads, please," said Chasteen.

Purdy bowed his head and watched, somewhat sadly, the heat escaping upward from the brown bacon gravy.

"Now," said Chasteen, and led her brothers in a voice strong and unornamental as a rope:

> *How sad our state by Nature is,*
> *Our sin, how deep it stains*
> *And Satan binds our captive souls*
> *Fast in his slavish chains.*

The words were new to Purdy, and it was hard to say, as sung by Chasteen, just what the tune was. Purdy tried to get the hang of it, hummed a little now and then, but he seemed always high when Chasteen hit a low note, or accelerating when Chasteen slowed down, so he gave up, relapsed into silent worship.

He looked sidewise at Zenith, for whom all tunes were the same, and saw she was as happy singing

> *Here let me wash my spotted soul*
> *From crimes of deepest dye*

as though the words made sense and her fluty, breathless voice could distinguish one note from another.

Purdy began to feel restive. Birthday or no birthday, he'd been up since five o'clock working, and this standing and singing while the food cooled, no matter what the Brookses did, began to pall. Chasteen had strong legs, a memory of iron, and an untiring voice. If there were twenty verses, she would sing them all.

> *A guilty, weak and helpless worm*
> *Into thy arms I fall.*

Chasteen sang, the strongest worm that ever chanted, Purdy reckoned, and unlikely to fall any time soon. He himself sat.

Chasteen stopped in midnote. "Why, Papa," she said, "we're not through."

"I'm through," Purdy said, reaching for the plate of bread. "You go right on, Chasteen. I'll chew quiet."

They all sat, and Purdy, his conscience hurting to see the pleasure fade from Chasteen's face, said defensively, "Now, Chasteen, you know good and well you don't think you're any worm. Why do you want to sing a song like that?"

Chasteen lifted her green, sandy-lashed eyes to her father.

"Compared to God, I'm a worm," she said flatly.

Purdy thought they'd better leave God out of it. "Compared to me, what do you think you are, Chasteen?" he asked, and answering his own question said, "A lion or a tiger, don't you?"

Chasteen passed her father the gravy. "We are human beings," she said, "of different ages and opposite sexes."

Purdy looked at Zenith. Zenith didn't think sex was a nice word, especially at the breakfast table, and would blame him for getting it into the conversation, though nothing had been further from his mind.

"Sex" yelled Hoagy, pounding the table with his spoon. "I'm sex."

"Oh, Hoagy," Zenith said, as if her son had spoken the worst word of all.

"Five," said Chasteen calmly. "You're five now, Hoagy. You'll be six in March."

"Sex," yelled Hoagy.

June looked up from the book he was holding under the edge of the table and reading. "Five, six, sex," he said, and laughed silently.

"Purdy Junior," said Zenith, as if sex had come out of the book he was reading, "you put that book right up."

June closed the book, lifted himself a couple of inches, and slid it beneath him.

"What made you say that, June?" Purdy asked.

"Sounded good," said June frankly. "Six, sex, sax," he elaborated, then added, "Go sit on tacks."

Purdy saw that the sound was really the thing for June, but Zenith was thinking, not of sounds, but of meanings.

"Where did you learn . . . that word?" she asked.

"The dictionary," Chasteen answered for him. "It means—"

"Eat your breakfast," Zenith told her daughter shortly, "and be quiet for a spell."

Purdy was always pleased when Zenith took a strong hand with Chasteen instead of leaving her to him. Zenith didn't try to reason with her, as he did, and didn't as a result get lost and angry, deep in a morass of logic chopping and far from the disciplinary subject.

"Well," said Purdy diplomatically, trying to get as far away from sex as possible in a single statement, "Santa Ana coming up."

Zenith nodded. "We'll have a windy ride all night."

"Ride?" asked Purdy. "Who's riding where?"

"Now, Purdy Newcomb," said Zenith, "don't tell me you've forgotten what day this is?"

Ah, Purdy thought, relaxing, now we'll have it. "Why," he asked innocently, "is it any special day?"

"How could you forget, Papa?" cried Chasteen. "It's the S.Q.R. store's Grand Opening."

"We talked it all over last week," said Zenith. "You promised to go."

"What's this nonsense about a grand opening?" Purdy asked. "The S.Q.R.'s been open and doing business for a year."

"They've never been open *officially*," Zenith explained. "Tonight it's official."

"There'll be a Hawaiian band," said Chasteen, "and free samples in all departments."

The feeling of his moment of hat-sailing came strongly back to Purdy. Was this any way to celebrate thirty years of life on earth? Cooped up for an evening between tables of crockery and counters of dry goods helping a merchant sell his wares? Having a snip of this or that on a cracker and, to go with it, a pickle briney from too long a stay in the pickle barrel?

"Hell and damnation!" he said, scraping the empty gravy bowl.

"There's more in the kitchen," Zenith said, handing the empty bowl to Chasteen.

This is the way you make it memorable, Purdy thought, the first thirty years of your life. In the morning there is plenty of gravy for breakfast, and in the evening the pleasantries of the general-merchandise store. Meanwhile, outside, the wind is blowing up from the east, the new songs are being played, and the million unknown faces move by. Purdy looked accusingly around his family circle, as if they were the foes who hemmed him in, who shut him away from the beautiful, imagined, and beckoning world.

"Take your thumb out of that gravy, Chasteen," he ordered as his daughter offered him the bowl.

"I can't take it out," said Chasteen. "You can't take anything out of what it isn't in," she explained reasonably.

"You heard me," said Purdy, determined not to argue. "Take it out."

Chasteen did not move her hand. "I can't," she said. "It doesn't even touch."

"Young lady," said Purdy, "you carry that bowl back and forth between here and the kitchen until you're ready to obey me."

Chasteen carried it back and forth. No one spoke any more; the only sounds were those of Chasteen's bare feet on the uncarpeted floorboards and the occasional easy flap of the vine that grew over the dining-room door.

Purdy pushed back his chair. He had climbed from his bed that morning a happy man, he had gone out to work for his family while they slept, he had sat down appreciatively to breakfast with them. Now they had put him in the wrong, robbed him of both his birthday and his happiness.

"Send out a couple of sandwiches at noon," he told Zenith. "I'll be too busy to come to the house for lunch. And you," he said to Chasteen, "you keep moving until you're ready to do as I say."

"What about tonight?" asked Zenith.

"Forget it," said Purdy, not bothering to turn around as he went out the door.

Purdy felt a little embarrassed when Chasteen brought him his lunch.

"Well, Chasteen," he said, "I see you got your thumb out of that gravy."

"Yes, Papa," said Chasteen, without any expression.

She disappeared while he ate, and when he had finished, came back and said, "I've been suckering trees, Papa."

That was a job which needed doing and, though Purdy had an idea that each sucker pulled off was intended as a coal of fire for his head, he said, "Thank you, Chasteen."

"Would you like me to help you regulate the water, Papa?"

Purdy would, but he thought, You're fooling yourself, miss, if you figure this will get you one step nearer the S.Q.R. store.

"OK, Chasteen," he said, "you go on down the tree rows a ways and tell me how the water's coming."

Chasteen walked along at the farther end of the furrows, calling out which needed more, and which less water; and Purdy, up at the standpipes, regulated the flow. Chasteen was a good and reliable helper. When she called up, "Too much water, Papa; it's breaking over the edges," Purdy could depend on that being just the case.

Though the cloud of yellow dust in the east had moved much nearer and there were now occasional flurries of wind, the day was yet, for the most part, what it had been that morning: dry, hot, and brilliantly quiet. Purdy moved from standpipe to standpipe, the sweat drying on him as he worked. In the furrows the water glinted like little happenchance streams; and Chasteen's voice was, in the orchard's silence, clear and forthright. Without intending to do so, Purdy had begun to feel better.

Chasteen, when she had reported on the last furrow, came up to the weir box and washed the mud from her feet.

"Mama's got a new dress to wear tonight," she said.

Purdy said nothing.

"There's a program," she said. "Pieces," she explained, "songs, presentations."

Purdy dipped his handkerchief in the weir box, wiped it across his dry, hot face, but said nothing.

"I'm on the program."

"Not singing that worm song, I hope," said Purdy, startled.

"A piece," said Chasteen. She let her feet hang unmoving for a minute in the bubbling water, then in a voice loud and full of feeling said, " 'When God sorts out the weather and sends rain, why, rain's my choice.' Do you like that, Papa?"

"I don't know about Papa," called Ed Conboy above the jingle of his team's harness as he came down the strip of land between his place and Purdy's, "but I sure do. I sure wish God would sort out the weather right now and send rain. Dry, dry. Now this hot wind. I don't think God's *done* any sorting for quite a spell. Maybe you'll remind him."

Purdy laughed and asked, "You finished, Ed?"

"All done," he said. "Going to start trimming and polishing myself now. You want to ride one of the horses up past your place, Chasteen?"

Chasteen jumped down from the weir box and looked up admiringly at Ed's big team of matched bays.

"Oh, yes, Mr. Conboy," she said, "I would."

"Come around here," Ed told her, "and I'll boost you up."

Chasteen stood rubbing the dust from the shoulder of the bay with the white blaze.

"If one of your horses is a stallion, Mr. Conboy, could I ride *it*?" she asked. "I've always wanted to ride a stallion."

"I'd sure like to please you, Chasteen," said Ed in a muffled voice, "but it happens neither one of these plugs is a stallion."

"Lots of people don't have them," Chasteen said tactfully, seeming to feel there was something apologetic in Ed's tone. "It's only where people keep a lot of horses that they usually have one stallion. Stallions," she explained, "are a fiery breed, and they keep the other horses' spirits up."

Purdy could see that Chasteen was embarrassed by Ed's big laugh, and when he put out a hand for her to step onto in mounting, she slipped and fell, the dust flying up around her black sateen bloomers as she smacked the earth. She was on her feet in a minute, and if there were tears in her eyes, she blinked them aside as she scrambled without much help onto the big bay.

"Good-bye, Papa," she said, and Purdy watched her ride off sturdy and erect, making rain her choice.

"Tell your mother," Purdy called after her, "to plan to be ready to leave the house at seven."

Purdy had entered the S.Q.R. store with every intention of being a martyr, but festivity always got under his skin. It was a weakness in him. Beforehand he could appraise an event, see it for the small shakes it was, but once he was launched into it, something inside him unfolded; he felt delight, he laughed.

I'm a sucker for a party, he thought ruefully, looking about him. Or an excuse for one. One new face, or two old ones, and something inside me kindles; something inside me says, This is special, this is a letup from everyday life, a chance to see what's just around the bend, but hidden.

Something inside me says, This is the minute to be whatever it is you're always seeing yourself as being: not just Purdy Newcomb, with one wife, three kids, and fifteen acres of Valencias; something says, This is it, but, this is the chance to see what that other guy, the Purdy Newcomb who stands a little outside the whole affair, is like— and what the affair itself is like. Able to see what it means to be young and in love, but shy, like that kid there, so that all of his loving has to be done with his eyes; or how it would be to be sheep shaped like that lady there, and never once in your whole life have had a look of love.

Oh, Purdy was everybody at a party, so that in speaking to others he could say, truly, not only what he felt, but what everyone listened to hear. It showed on him, too, this ability. It lit him up, so that it was said, "All you need for a party is a pot of fresh coffee and Purdy Newcomb."

It wasn't that he was loud or boisterous, though Purdy could let out a yell or swing himself from a doorjamb on occasion; it was another thing entirely, a feeling he had about himself, and about you, so that for once in your life you felt yourself to be involved in a situation worthy of the decorations, best clothes, and special refreshments a party brought forth.

Purdy stood alone beside a rack of fringed silk sweaters, only a little soreness about his forgotten birthday left inside him, a feeling as if a small object, the size of a marble, perhaps, was still lodged against some sensitive spot.

"Hi, Julius," he said.

Julius Stern, the S of the S.Q.R. store, a man who looked like a boulder lightly coated with caramel, stopped to straighten a sweater.

"Glad to see you out, Purdy," said Julius. "I was afraid this wind would keep you ranchers home. What'd you think of the place?"

"Looks like a bower," said Purdy.

"It ought to," said Julius. "Twenty-seven dollars' worth of crepe paper alone in here."

Purdy believed him. The store had disappeared beneath loops and swags of silver and lavender paper.

"What do you think of the birds?" Julius asked.

Twelve canaries, in cages made to look like little white cottages, were, in the light and warmth of the Grand Opening, singing like a summer morning.

"A fairyland," said Purdy. "A pure fairyland."

Julius nodded in agreement. "Rent 'em for two dollars each an evening. Must be a hell of a life for a bird," he added reflectively.

"No reason for a bird to have an easier time than man, is there?" asked Purdy.

Julius lifted his yellow eyes from the cages. "We don't sing so pretty," he said flatly.

"It's a fact," Purdy admitted.

"The musicians are one-hundred-percent Hawaiian," said Julius.

On the little balcony, which on ordinary occasions held the S.Q.R.'s shoe and bookkeeping departments, three men, all in white and with their trousers apparently lashed on with bright scarves, had begun to play, on guitars, or mandolins, perhaps—Purdy wasn't sure just what. The music their brown hands made, softly falling onto the strings, quickly lifted away, was something between laughing and whining, a sound that prickled Purdy's scalp and pleased him.

"For half the price," said Julius, "I could have picked up a fake trio in Santa Ana, but I wanted the real thing. One of these," he said, "the one with the pink sash, can't speak English. God knows what he thinks, stuck up that way over a batch of groceries, playing the pieces he learned on that island."

Julius had spoken so much of Purdy's own thought that Purdy recalled himself, gathered himself together, as if fearful lest otherwise he might escape from beneath his own skin, begin to inhabit entirely the mind of this reflective storekeeper.

In the space directly below and in front of the balcony, where racks and counters had been cleared away, the S.Q.R. guests now began to dance, no ja-da, ja-da, jing-jing-ze, but a slow looping waltz to the sweet-sour, laughing-crying music.

"Trust Maurice," said Julius, watching, "to pick the prettiest woman on the floor."

Purdy scanned the dancers looking for Julius' son, the stately Maurice Stern, M.D.

"That's my wife," Purdy said, "that's Zenith."

Julius smiled. "You think I don't know it?" he asked. "You think I got eyes only for dry goods and groceries?"

Purdy looked at the man twice his age. "No," he said, "I never thought that."

But he moved away from Julius Stern and the rack of silk sweaters toward Zenith and the dancing. When Zenith danced, everything dropped away from her, she said: concern for the children, remembrance of housework, any worry about her freckles or whether she was too thin. "Purdy," she had said once, "when I dance, I'm afraid I'm not very far from a bad woman."

Remembering that now, Purdy smiled, watched her limberly whirl in Dr. Stern's adroit arms. How near, he wondered, would the thoughts or feelings of that one-two-three-slide take her in that direction? No nearer, he knew, than a delight in the way the scarlet accordion pleating in her split skirt flared out, and a kind of tenderness flowing upward from her heart along the graceful extended arms toward what she would regard, not so much as Maurice Stern himself, as his kindness is asking her for the first dance.

"She's beautiful, isn't she, Papa?" asked Chasteen, leaning against a counter of goods by the yard, watching too. "Her skirt's beautiful."

"Flutes out kind of like an umbrella," said Purdy.

"Oh, Papa," said Chasteen reproachfully, "that's all the style."

"Style," said Purdy.

"Papa," said Chasteen, "do you think those Hawaiian men like to play in a store?"

"Why, I guess so," said Purdy. "They get paid good."

"Do you think they see us when they play?"

"I reckon so, Chasteen," Purdy said. "If they don't shut their eyes, they'd about have to."

"Maybe they see us," Chasteen said, "and we look like their own people, and the crêpe paper's trees, and the birds haven't got any cages."

Purdy looked down at his daughter. "I suspect that's about the way it is, Chasteen."

"June was sick to his stomach," said Chasteen hurriedly, as if she had come for a minute too near her father.

"Where?" Purdy asked, knowing June's habits.

"Outside," said Chasteen with composure. "He's all right now. He's here."

"Here?" asked Purdy.

Chasteen stood aside. Extended along the shelf beneath the counter a bolt of green-checked gingham serving as a support for his head, was Purdy, Jr., calmly reading.

"What you doing *there*?" Purdy asked.

"Reading," said June. *"The Thrall of Leif the Lucky,"* he said, holding out the book. "It sure is good. She's a girl, only Leif don't know it. Eric the Red knows it, though, and he—"

"Get out of there," said Purdy.

"It makes me sick to stand up," said June, nevertheless beginning, obediently, to move.

"Mr. Stern saw him there," said Chasteen. "He doesn't care. He just said, 'Watch somebody doesn't buy a yard of him for a housedress.' "

June lay comfortably back.

"The idea," said Purdy, "of driving fifteen miles to a Grand Opening, then spending the time under a counter like a rat in a trap."

"I never did say to come," said June.

"He never did, Papa," said Chasteen. "June don't care where he is," she said proudly, "so long as he's got a book."

"Eric the Red could tell she was a girl," June said, "because—"

Purdy straightened up. He would just as leave not be seen talking to a son stretched out beneath a counter like a man at home in a lower berth.

The music was all sweet now, a sweet wash, all warm, no sour-sweet curds, no notes sent off askew to comment acidly on so much sweetness. The brown hands looped and fell, the dancers seemed not

only to have a circular horizontal motion but also to rise a little per-
pendicularly, as if the brown hands on the balcony were magnets
they could not resist. Zenith's skirt flashed red, red, like sparks sent
out from a turning wheel. Dr. Maurice Stern's spectacles were dazzling as the fixed stars, though less stationary.

"Papa," said Chasteen, "after you left I *put* my thumb in the gravy.
I had to," she said earnestly, "I couldn't take it out unless it was in.
I had to put it in first. Otherwise I would be marching till doomsday,
because you can't take your thumb out of what it's not in."

Purdy was recalled from the music to himself, the gravy bowl, the
forgotten birthday, that damn thumb. . . .

"Hoagy," he said hastily. "Where's Hoagy? You got him under another counter?"

"When June was sick," said Chasteen, "I gave him to a lady to
keep."

"Well, she's probably given him away by now," said Purdy, going
to look.

Hoagy was in the grocery department, stolidly working his way from
sample to sample. Purdy caught up with him at the minced-olive-
counter, and though he bulged considerably, there was no need to
worry about Hoagy. Hoagy was built to eat and digest.

"I was lost," said Hoagy dismally as Purdy led him back toward
Chasteen and June. "Chasteen lost me and the lady lost me."

"You weren't lost," said Purdy; "you were having a good time."

"I was lost and having a good time," said Hoagy.

By the time they had again made their way to June's counter, the
dancing had stopped and Zenith was tying and retying Chasteen's
hair ribbons, straightening her eyebrows with a dampened forefinger,
twitching her dress this way and that to make it hang better.

"I've got your piece right here, Chasteen," Zenith said. "I'll count
three, and if you stop between words longer than that, I'll prompt
you."

Julius Stern was now alone on the dance floor, his hands extended
toward his guests as if about to give them a gift.

"My dear good friends and neighbors . . ." he was saying.

"Don't forget the package," Zenith whispered, "don't, whatever you
do, forget the surprise."

                        *              *              *

The car's side curtains volleyed in the wind like sails, they popped and strained in the gusty night; in spite of them the wind whistled through the car, and the car itself creaked and groaned like a ship rounding the Horn in a gale. Occasionally a blast would hit the car full broadside, so that it careened precariously; then the wind, veering, would come at them head on, slowing them down, even threatening to move them backward toward the S.Q.R. store.

Purdy listened with pleasure to the wind and drove through it with pleasure. Driving was now more than mere guidance; in the darkness of the night there was a force to struggle with. His car contended with the slippery air, found traction, and moved ahead. With feet and hands, with the muscles of his arms and shoulders, Purdy piloted the craft that carried his family homeward, and they, full of confidence in him, spoke in relaxed voices; delighted by outward violence, they were drowsy and gentle, musing and happy.

From the back seat, Chasteen asked, "Were you terribly surprised, Papa?"

"The only time I was ever more surprised, Chasteen," said Purdy, "was once when your mother winked at me."

Zenith could not move closer to him, and even now a sudden turn of the wheel would send his elbow into her side; still, she let the weight of her body settle more completely toward him.

"I wouldn't be surprised to have her wink at me," said June.

"You're her son," said Purdy. "I wasn't any relation to her. She wasn't supposed to be winking at me."

"The Thrall of Leif the Lucky," said June dreamily, "wouldn't think nothing of a wink."

"Were you surprised," Chasteen asked, "when Mr. Stern said, 'We have a slight token of esteem from his family and neighbors for Mr. Nathaniel Purdy Newcomb on the happy occasion of his thirtieth birthday'?"

"I was surprised and taken aback," said Purdy.

"Taken aback," said June, "taken afront, taken apart, taken aside."

"I didn't get any present," said Hoagy, waking up.

"I got one for you," said Chasteen. "I saved it for you."

"What?" asked Hoagy.

"A dill pickle. Lean off me, Hoagy, while I get it out of my pocket."

"Make him chew quiet, Chasteen," said June. "I can hear him chewing clear down in the bottom of my stomach."

"I'm chewing in my mouth," said Hoagy contentiously.

"Shut up about chewing," said Chasteen. "Just do it. There's lots of things to do but not talk about."

"The Thrall of Leif the Lucky," said June, his stomach relieved of the burden of Hoagy's chewing, "was every inch a woman beneath her leathern surplice!"

"*Was* she a woman?" asked Chasteen.

"Sure," said June.

"I don't see any sense in saying that, then. She couldn't very well be an inch of anything else, could she?"

"If you had your foot blown off," said June, "and had a man's foot grafted on you, you wouldn't be every foot a woman." June squealed with laughter at this sally, and Purdy himself laughed silently.

"I'm not a woman, anyway," said Chasteen, evading this.

"What are you, then?" asked June.

Purdy could tell from the silence in the backseat that Chasteen was giving this her thoughtful attention, but Chasteen didn't know . . . she was thinking about the future.

"What I'd like to be is a musician."

"Toot, toot," said June. "Go around tooting a horn."

"I would like to play like those men tonight."

"Toot, toot," said June.

"They sounded like everything all at once. I mean you thought it was the ocean, then you thought it was flowers, and then you could smell the flowers, and then they moved and you could feel them and then they cried."

"The flowers cried?" asked June.

"It sounded like crying, but it wasn't sad. That's what," she said, "all at once. Didn't you hear it?"

"Not me," said June. "I was reading."

"My pickle's gone," said Hoagy. "It was the durndest little pickle I ever ate. Whyn't you get me a big one, Chasteen?"

"I got you two Fig Newtons," Chasteen said. "Lean off me while I get them."

Purdy turned the car off the main road and headed eastward toward home and straight into the wind. The wind was less gusty now, a great, strong, heavy blowing that hit the car like a wave of water, and though it slowed them, it no longer jerked them about as it had.

"Chasteen did real well," said Zenith.

"Yes," said Purdy.

"How'd my skirt look?"

"Fine," said Purdy. "Nothing else there to hold a candle to it."

"Did you like your present, Purty?"

"Best 'cept one, I ever got."

Purdy felt Zenith's hand go into the crook of his arm, let it pull his hand down from the wheel.

"I'll kill us all," he said, "driving with one arm in this wind."

Zenith didn't let go. "For some things," she said, "you have to trust God."

Purdy gripped the far side of the wheel with his left hand skillfully and made, single-armed, the sharp left turn.

"Still can do. Hey," he said.

Under the eucalyptus trees and just off the road a car was parked. Purdy's headlights as he swung around moved across it slowly, across the two in it, who sat entwined.

"Mr. Conboy's car," said Zenith sleepily.

Purdy straightened the car out. "Yeah," he said, "the poor cuss."

# Aloha, Farewell to Thee

IN A BLIND TIME of the California seasons, when a dripping spring would not be done with and a blazing summer, waited for since March, would not break through, a fourteen-year-old girl named Awanda Tooley did a desperate thing. With another kind of brother, and in another season, her act might have been merely selfish and heedless—or even insignificant. But Ben was her brother, and the season was what it was, and Awanda herself was the last person who would want her deed underestimated. She had thought about it for a long time, had imagined herself doing it, and had been prevented only by her own knowledge of right and wrong, and her fear of what Ben would say, or do.

What brought the act on, as Awanda saw afterward, was the failure of Melody Pike's visit. The very thing that had been planned to rescue spring vacation from utter failure had wrecked it. That and the rain. On Thursday, with spring vacation half over, there had not been a single day without rain. Southern California can always use more water, and in a season when the rainfall was below normal Awanda would not have put her own preferences ahead of the needs of the land. She was not that selfish or self-centered. But the rainfall was already twice normal, mustard was so high in the groves you could scarcely see the trees, and the brown foothills had lost their wild look and were as green as any irrigated pasture. A disgusting sight for a Californian. So Awanda, convinced that her wish, if granted, would not harm the land, wished the rain would stop. It kept on raining.

It was at about ten forty-five on Thursday morning that she decided to phone Melody and ask her to come over at four to listen to records. Awanda had, necessarily, to tell her mother her plans. Her mother was delighted. This immediately robbed the plan of some of its pleasure. She was not asking Melody over because, as her mother hoped, "it's time you stopped your studying, Awanda, and saw someone." She was asking her over because Melody was a wild, romantic, statuesque girl. Awanda didn't really know her from Adam, but they were in Biology together, and Awanda was ready for the unknown and eager to test her powers of conquest on someone besides brother Ben.

"Melody is coming at four," Awanda told her mother, "and I want you to promise that I can have the living room for two hours without people coming in and out."

"If somebody knocks at the front door," her mother said, "I don't very well see how I can pretend that we're not home. Or how would it look to have me running around in the rain from the back door to the front door to answer the knock?"

"You know that's not what I mean."

"What do you mean, then? Who are these people who are going to be coming in and out while you're entertaining Melody? Ben and I are the only ones here. And the last thing Ben's going to be interested in is you and some other girl playing records."

"Ben has no interests," Awanda said, which was not true, and she knew it. Ben was in his room at that minute deciphering cryptograms that had stumped World War II spies.

"Well, then," her mother said, "you have nothing to fear from Ben."

For some reason Awanda needed to complain to her mother about something, so she said sourly, "Ben is getting pretty unpredictable these days."

"Listen," said her mother lightly, "to the pot calling the kettle black."

This little surface altercation with her mother put Awanda in a still better mood about Melody's visit. She was looking for something, expecting something, and whatever that was, she was pretty sure it wasn't going to be found in anything promoted by her parents. It would have to be found in spite of them. There had to be, beneath the monotonous surface of the life her parents lived, some secret that justified it all. Sometimes she felt upon the very verge of hearing this secret word spoken, by the sky itself sometimes; sometimes by the stars or wind.

This search, which required a good deal of her attention, kept Awanda in a continuous shiver of nerves. She had a reputation for being brave, but she had it because her search required her to tackle so many things she feared. Melody was one of these. She was a newcomer at school, but it was perfectly obvious to Awanda that she and Melody did not occupy the same worlds. Any visiting they did, Awanda knew perfectly well, had to be done before Melody discovered this. Melody was a year and a half older than she, a half-head taller, and had a figure that made Mrs. Tooley's look undeveloped. The boys were crazy about her; Melody herself was not boy-crazy; she had a kind of tender dignity that suited her motherly bosom. It was this appearance of dignity and kindness that had given Awanda the courage to call her in the first place.

Awanda spent what was left of Thursday morning arranging the setting for the visit. The first thing that seemed necessary for a meeting that might produce revelations so far withheld was darkness—or at least semidarkness. Mrs. Tooley, on a gray rainy day, had done the natural thing, which was to raise all the blinds and part all curtains. Awanda left curtains and shades as they were while she cleaned, but the minute she was finished she intended to close them.

She had no intention of sitting there talking to Melody in full daylight. She redusted the room (which her mother had done earlier), as if she were a hostess cursed with a slovenly maid. She laid a fire of eucalyptus logs, and in case the eucalyptus scent was not sweet enough, she shook a quantity of pine bath salts over the kindling. She arranged four vases of flowers, decided that four was overdoing it, and took the hibiscus out. She made a still life on the coffee table of tangerines, brownies, and caramels.

When this was done, she set about selecting the records. This took longer than the cleaning and decorating, since each record had to be right in itself, right in the sequence in which it was played, and right as an expression of her own tastes. And, above all, right for this rainy twilight hour when a lifetime friendship might be made. And the secret word said. First of all, she would play Ponchielli's "The Dance of the Hours": because she loved it, and because it said that time, though the hours danced, was passing. Next, to offset any idea that Melody might have that she was nothing but a square (a square with a straight A at each corner, as a school wit had called her); and because it was popular again, she chose Don Ho's "Aloha, Farewell to Thee"; secretly she also loved it. She saw, when she listened to it, the brown-faced men and women in their open boats, mournfully singing as they left their sunlit island homes behind them forever. The other records were equally suitable to the hour and each other; but as things turned out, she never had a chance to get to them.

She couldn't resist, when she had finished her preparations and had pulled each blind and closed the curtains, calling her mother into the living room. "What do you think?" she asked.

Her mother unconsciously lifted a hand toward a light switch.

"Oh, no," Awanda cried. "Electric lights would spoil everything. I'm going to light the fire and have candlelight after Melody comes. The whole thing's *planned* for fire and candlelight. Well," she persisted, "what do you think of it?"

"It's certainly very nice and tidy."

"I know that," Awanda said impatiently.

"It's fine," her mother said.

"No, really, Mother."

Her mother sniffed, as if making a real effort to encompass the room with all her senses. "It has a kind of odd smell," she admitted.

This was the pine bath salts, which until the fire was lit did smell more like the bathroom than the forest. But Awanda preferred not to talk about that. "Perhaps I have too many flowers," she suggested.

"Perhaps," her mother agreed.

"Go ahead and say it," Awanda urged. "Say it looks awful. Don't just stand there condemning it silently."

"I'm not condemning it at all," her mother said. "I was just thinking how much it reminds me of myself when I was your age."

Awanda had seen pictures of her mother at her age and, personally, hated to think that there was any likeness between them. She remained silent, discouraging further comparisons.

"I used to fix up our living room at home exactly like this before your father came to call. Pull the blinds, light the fire, everything. I was every whit as romantic as you are."

"My father!" Awanda exclaimed. "When he was fourteen? How ridiculous!"

"*I* was fourteen; he was seventeen. But it *was* ridiculous," she agreed hastily. "I don't mean the room—but our going together at that age."

"I don't know what your mother was thinking about," Awanda said. "permitting it. Why, you were just a child."

Mrs. Tooley defended her mother. "Mama had five children, three of them younger than me. I think she considered me a grown woman."

Awanda did not care to discuss the age at which one became a grown woman. "Well, there's absolutely no connection whatsoever between this room and any room you fixed up to entertain father—or any other boy—in. This is just a room suitable to listen to music in. Why, I bet you didn't even own a record player. Now did you? Not even one with a horn? You didn't, did you?"

"No," Mrs. Tooley admitted, "we didn't. But I owned a ukulele. Your—"

But Awanda wouldn't let her finish. "That's totally different," she said. "The ukulele can scarcely be called a musical instrument."

"I suppose not," her mother agreed placidly.

Then, lest the conversation bog down in complete agreement, Awanda said, "Mother, do you solemnly promise me to keep Ben out of here? I don't want to go dress, then come back here and find he's made a big mess of everything."

"I probably couldn't drag him out of his room," her mother said.

This, as Awanda knew, was probably the truth. Nevertheless, she persisted in exacting the promise from her mother.

Melody, driven over by her mother, arrived on the dot of four. She wore a gray-green sweater and skirt, dyed to match, and a swinging necklace of irregularly shaped amber beads. Her hair matched her beads, and her outfit matched the rainy day. Awanda admired her greatly and wished that she had taken more pains with herself and less with the room. "You're a real water nymph," she said appreciatively.

Melody looked puzzled. "Green-gray, like the rain," Awanda explained.

"Oh, my outfit! We bought it at Robinson's."

Awanda seated her friend in the chair she had planned for her to sit in, lit the candles and the fire, and waited for the conversation to begin, for those meanings that had been escaping her behind life's disappointing surfaces to be revealed.

"Wouldn't it be easier to pull up the blinds?" Melody asked.

"Oh, easier!" Awanda admitted. "But who wants to live like that?"

"Don't you have a furnace?" Melody asked, looking at the fire.

"Yes, but I scorn it. Who can see pictures in furnaces?"

"Pictures in furnaces," Melody repeated uncertainly; but Awanda also scorned explaining herself again so soon.

The bath salts took fire and filled the room with a piney fragrance. A raindrop fell down the chimney and hissed on the coals. Melody couldn't have been sweeter, though she didn't have much to say. Instead of looking into the fire for pictures, she pulled the curtains apart so that she could look out into the rainy afternoon, across the sodden lawn to the blacktop road, lavender in the late light of the spring day.

She's a child of nature, Awanda thought. She can't bear to be shut away from the elements. The trappings of civilization silence her. Candlelight's artificial—that's why she objected to it. She's natural and I'm not.

In any case, she was silent, and for this reason Awanda started her record-playing earlier than she had planned. "The Dance of the Hours" was finished, and "Aloha, Farewell to Thee" was playing when Chuck Peters opened the front door. His curly hair had sparkles of rain on top of the waves, and his big round face was beaming.

"Hi, Awanda," he said. Then, looking at his wristwatch, he told Melody, "You said four-fifteen, and four-fifteen it is. How's that for promptness?"

Melody rose. She recovered her lost powers of conversation. She couldn't have thanked Awanda more effusively if she had been a ten-day house guest and the honoree of two hunt balls.

Awanda was too surprised to do more than make a gesture toward the uneaten food. Perhaps Melody didn't see the gesture. Chuck was the one who responded.

"Melody's watching her figure. Me, too," he added with a grin. "But nobody's watching mine." He filled his mouth and his pockets. "Awanda," he said, "you should have invited me in the first place."

Awanda knew that Chuck understood that she had been used; that he felt sorry for her and was trying to be kind. Under the circumstances, she didn't care for his kindness. What did she care whether the food was eaten or not? She hadn't planned on an afternoon of eating in the first place.

"What shall I tell your mother when she comes for you?" she asked Melody coldly.

"Oh, Mother's expecting Chuck to bring me home," Melody said.

"At four-fifteen?" Awanda asked.

Chuck was the one who answered. "She's expecting us at six, and we'll try not to disappoint her."

After they left, Awanda stood in the center of the room for a while, unmoving. She had no idea of deceiving her mother about the time Melody had left; though afterward she saw that it might appear to her mother that she had. Her first impulse was to destroy every outward sign of all her foolish romanticism. She blew out the candles, threw the brownies Chuck had left in the fireplace. Then, without planning that either, she ate every single caramel and tangerine herself, reset the phonograph to play "Aloha." Then she went to her room, locked her door, and lay down on her bed. She felt sick to her stomach.

She didn't see any of her family until ten o'clock the next morning. When she came out, no one said a word to her about Melody's visit; but she could tell that they knew about it and pitied her. It was still raining, and her father, since it was too wet to work on the ranch, was going into Los Angeles with her mother, to shop. He stood looking out at the downpour, waiting for her mother to finish dressing.

"Why don't you come with us, Awanda?" he asked. "We're planning on taking in a movie before we come home."

She would as soon think of taking a bath with her father and mother as going to a movie with them. Being at a movie with them was a sign to everyone that she had given up; and she hadn't. But even with a guarantee that not a living soul would see her with them, she wouldn't go. They had the wrong feelings about movies, and they had no tact about expressing their feelings. It killed her to accept an actor and his story, to believe in him, to live inside his dream, then to be wrenched outside the dream by some big display of logic from her father about repeater rifles being used before 1860, or some comment of her mother's about the actor's third wife or the perfectly obvious division between his real hair and his toupee. Why did they go to the movies if all they wanted to do was decide which was real hair and which false? Or to tell phony guns from authentic ones? She wanted to believe. So did Ben. That was one of the few things they agreed on. But Ben could sit calmly while their father and mother broke the movie down into bits of story and pieces of hair that didn't match. She couldn't do that. She wanted people to feel what she did—and if they didn't, it hurt her. She had either to keep her mouth shut and pretend or open it and argue. People liked her pretending self better than her arguing self, but she liked neither and dreamed of a time when (or was it some person with whom?) all pretending and arguing would be over.

"Is Ben going?" she asked her father.

"Not if I know anything about it," her mother said, coming from her bedroom hatted and gloved for the city. "Ben's not going to put a foot off this ranch until he's finished his homework."

"Well," said Awanda, choosing to pretend rather than argue, "I'd better stay home and study too."

"You don't have to go, Awanda," her mother said, trying to speak as sharply as if yesterday afternoon had never happened, "but don't pretend that you have to stay home to study."

From the way her mother spoke, you might think it was worse for her to get straight A's than for Ben to get straight C's and D's—except in what interested him, which was mighty little: Mathematics and History. And in a way, Awanda thought it was worse herself. It was too yielding of her to work hard on any subject given her. She was stubborn now, to make up for it. She didn't even say good-bye when they left the house.

As she watched them drive away, she thought, When your mother's dead, you'll be sorry for all the times you wouldn't say good-bye to her. But her mother wasn't dead yet, and if she started saying good-bye now, there was no telling where she would stop. Or could stop. She might tell her mother why she pretended she had to study and why she wouldn't go to the movies with them, and even, worst of all, what it was she hadn't given up yet about. She couldn't give herself away like that. Though life was certainly tame if someone didn't want to make discoveries about her; and to make them want to, she had to take some risks. She took the greatest risks with Ben. She had to, to get him to notice her at all.

Ben was in his room supposedly studying "Gareth and Lynette" in the *Idylls of the King*. She'd bet anything he wasn't doing it. There was too much lovemaking and not enough historical fact in "Gareth and Lynette." Though lovemaking, she supposed, was just as historical as treaties and war making, if you looked at it the right way.

The door to Ben's room was wide open. That was another difference between them. She had to close her door to be alone, but Ben could be alone anywhere. He was stooped over his desk like a real scholar, but not a scholar working on the *Idylls of the King*, which lay on the floor beside him. It was useless to wonder what. It was useless to wonder about Ben at all, because he was changing so fast. Last year he had been two inches shorter than she. This year he was two inches taller. Last year his hair had been white, his teeth too large for his mouth, and his mouth had no real shape. Now his hair had some color, even if it was hard to say what, his teeth had apparently shrunk, and his underlip met his upper lip in a firm line. Nevertheless, improved as he was, Awanda could still beat him in everything. Except his two favorite subjects. She could run faster, talk faster, and bat farther. Why, then, did this boy, whose accomplishments she couldn't admire, whose looks, as far as she was concerned, had been until lately a mess, fascinate her so? She stood gazing at his bent back, knowing that he knew she was there, but that if she stood there until doomsday he wouldn't turn around until he was ready.

There was a mystery somewhere in what she felt about Ben, which she couldn't understand. She didn't like his looks—and kept looking. She knew she could beat him in everything—but kept on wanting to do it again. She wouldn't want him to know her secret, not for the world—yet she kept trying to lure him into guessing it. She was thirteen months older than he—but she had nothing of an older sister's protective concern for a younger brother. "What is the secret of your fatal fascination, Benjamin?" she asked herself, not Ben.

A mockingbird, which had been sheltering from the rain in one of the palms along the driveway, flew down to Ben's window, hovered there for a second as if inspecting Ben from that angle, then darted away. None the wiser, Awanda thought. But the bird emboldened her. She went into Ben's room and leaned on his table.

"You aren't studying," she said.

"I'm not studying English," he corrected her. She looked down at his desk and saw that he was doing cryptograms again.

"If I win this week's contest," he said, "I get a round trip for two to Las Vegas."

"What would you do at Las Vegas?" she asked.

"I probably won't win," he said.

"If you aren't studying, I challenge you to a duel."

"I was just getting started."

"Listen," Awanda said, "I'm not begging you. I'm just saying that if you're willing, I'm willing."

She didn't know why he should be. His heart was never really in it, and she always beat him. And though dueling, as they practiced it, was no contest to the death, even the winner, as she knew, could suffer some painful blows before he won. She couldn't remember how or when their contests had started. Probably when Ben whittled dueling weapons from laths. They had never decided what their weapons should be called. At present, they were calling them swords, though in the past they had been rapiers, poinards, lances, and sabers. In the beginning, they had said they were "fencing," and why or when they had changed to "dueling," she had forgotten. Perhaps it was because they had begun to be willing to damage each other more painfully with their blows—though it was Ben, the halfhearted fighter and full-time loser, who always got the worst of it. She had twinges of conscience sometimes about winning from so good-natured a fighter. She sometimes wondered if Ben didn't wish he had never invented weapons and dueling and was back in the days of his unarmed innocence. They did have rules. Neither wanted to lose an ear or put out an eye. And chivalry demanded that certain regions of both be avoided. But chivalry and caution combined didn't prevent occasions when the fight had to be discontinued while a contestant recovered on a bale of hay. (Face down so that the tears wouldn't show.)

"Are you coming, or aren't you?" Awanda asked. Though she *said* she wasn't begging, she knew she was; she had to fight someone.

And she knew that Ben, with her mother's final words in his ears, "Be nice to Awanda today," was coming with her.

"OK," Ben said. "I'm stuck on this, anyway."

She hurried him out of the house before he had time to change his mind.

The rain had slackened, and the wind had picked up. They walked through a blowing wet curtain down the hillside to the building that was half-garage, half-barn. They did their dueling in the lower half, where hay for the cow was stored. They had more privacy there, and Awanda thought it was the kind of place where, in the days when duels were forbidden, men would secretly have fought. It was gloomy and musty. The wind blew through the cracks with a solemn desolate sound. Awanda's skin prickled. She might have been a real dueler, breaking the law and risking death.

Ben, besides providing the weapons, provided the rules. He kept the swords under a canvas cover on a rack he had made for them. He always handed Awanda her sword first.

"Do you find it in order?"

If she did, and she always did, he took down his sword and examined it.

Next he said, "Salute!" and they crossed swords lightly.

Then he said, "The oath," and, swords touching, they repeated together, "Caesar, we who are about to die salute you."

Finally he said, "On guard!" Then, with swords protecting their faces, he gave the order "Fight!"

Usually Awanda, who had not devised these preliminaries and thought little of them, was eager to get through them and to get at the real business of winning victories. They kept track of their encounters. So far there had been seventy-two, all of which she had won. But this morning, with circumstances perfect, rain falling, a mournful wind blowing, a big hurt that could be eased by suffering a smaller one, she was suddenly finished with fake duels, with half-hearted opponents who didn't care whether they won or lost, with easy victories. And particularly she was finished with pretending that her brother was a real opponent. He wasn't. He has no more a real opponent than a doll was a real baby. This was no more a real life-and-death encounter than playing house was being married.

She left the barn, running, and paid no attention to Ben calling after her, "What's the matter, Awanda? Are you mad, Awanda?"

Up at the house, as if the whole of spring vacation had been noth-ing but a preparation for it, she performed her desperate act. She went directly to the bookcase, opened the glass doors, and took out Ben's sacred book, the record book of the Yolo Indians. She sat down at the desk with it and opened it, as she had done dozens of times before. The book was another of Ben's mysteries. The Yolo Indians themselves were a mystery. Why twelve boys between the ages of thirteen and fifteen should form a new club, with Boy Scouts and Hi-Y's all around them, was a mystery. Why they should tax themselves twenty-five cents apiece to buy a record book of red leather and gray buckram was a deep mystery. But the deepest mystery of all was why they had made silent, nonwriting Ben their secretary. Though as things turned out he hadn't had to write a word. The Yolo Indians had ex-hausted all their strength in getting organized and in buying their record book. They had never had a meeting after they bought the book, and nothing had been recorded in it. That was its great temp-tation to Awanda. It was empty except for the words "Property of the Yolo Indians," and the names of the club members: Clarence Ross, Wilbur Marshburn, Cecil Pugh, John Buckmaster, Peter Mendez, Roy Leeper—oh, Awanda knew them all by heart. She had felt those fine empty white pages and smelled that leather and buckram binding and read through those names more times than she could remem-ber—and dreamed of putting *her* mark in it.

She had been tempted by the book about the same number of times that Ben had inspected it. Her father called it "Ben's Book of Life," because Ben would come in, take that book off its shelf, read its twelve names, and inspect its vacant pages like some old minister leafing through the family Bible for a suitable verse. It was all a mystery to *everyone*: the Indians, their book, and what they supposed their sec-retary could write in it, since they never met; or what Ben could write in it even if they did meet. A mystery to everyone but Ben, who knew exactly what he should do with the book: guard it. He belonged to a band of brothers, the Yolo Indians, and this was their joint and no doubt sole possession. It had cost them good money, required sacri-fices, and *he* was the one they had trusted with its keeping. He was worthy of the trust. He *kept* it: behind glass doors, dustless and inspected. He was dedicated to the job, and if the Yolos ever needed anything recorded, Ben and the book would be ready.

Awanda understood perfectly how Ben felt. But she also saw, clear as crystal this morning, that keeping a record book for the Yolo Indians was as foolish as dueling with your brother with make-believe swords. It had no meaning. The Yolos were not a real club. They never met, they had nothing to record. If they had had one meeting, if Ben had written as much as one word of his own, a non-Yolo word in it, Awanda would have respected the sign "Property of the Yolo Indians." She had waited a year. They had nothing to say. She had; though she didn't know why it had to be written in their book, or even what *the* word was. It was a terrible waste for that beautiful book to be behind glass doors unused. If she didn't write in it now, someday, years ahead, when she was an old-maid schoolteacher, her mother would take it down from its shelf, open it, and say, "Ben's Yolo Indians book! Remember how he used to guard it? Here is it, empty as the day they bought it. Could you find some use for it? For grades, perhaps?"

By the time her mother got around to saying that, she might be worse than an old maid; she might be dead. She couldn't wait. Beneath the names of the Yolo Indians, but on a line to herself, she wrote with a dark, determined, but trembling stroke, her own name: "Mary Awanda Tooley." Then, under her own name, she wrote very rapidly, surprising herself, so that she read what her hand had written as if both (hand and writing) belonged to someone else: "I am desperately in love."

She reread that amazing statement and was awed by its truth. It was *that* she hadn't given up about. She didn't know who he was, but he was someone. Somewhere. She had been finished for a long time with going to the movies with her father and mother, yesterday she had finished with lighting candles for girls, and today she was finished with make-believe duels with her brother.

She heard Ben come in and didn't try to hide the book. Not out of bravery, but because he'd have to see sooner or later. Ben didn't care *what* she wrote. She could've written baseball scores or multiplication tables, and he'd have been just as mad. She could've torn every page from the real Bible and spat on each one or walked naked before the Yolo Indians, and he wouldn't have been so mad. Such things would have been her own business. But the Yolo Indians record book was his business.

"You come on out to the barn," he said.

His face was so white his hair appeared to have darkened. His teeth were once again too big for his thin-lipped mouth.

"You stole something that didn't belong to you," he said, and he put the damaged book carefully back behind the glass doors.

She followed him out to the barn, pleasurably excited. Ben was finally stirred up. The fight would at least be real.

It was very real. There were no preliminaries, no oaths, no sword crossings, and no warnings. Ben simply picked up his sword and got in two hard broadside slaps, one across the shoulders and one across the cheek, while she was still waiting for the words "On guard!" She fought as hard as she could, and enjoyed it; at first, because it was real and because the outcome was in doubt. Then the outcome appeared not at all in doubt. She kept on without pleasure because she didn't know how to say "I give up." She never did say it. When her hand was too swollen to hold her sword any longer, Ben stopped.

"Are you sorry?" he asked.

"No," she said.

But since she couldn't pick up the sword she had dropped, the fight was over, anyway. Ben wasn't the kind of boy, even when he was in the right, to hit an unarmed person, even his sister.

She walked to the house by herself. Her face, in the bathroom mirror, surprised her. "He really won," she told herself, and the words somehow pleased her. She fixed up her face as best she could with ice water and cosmetics. Not so much to protect Ben from anything her father and mother would say as because she didn't want to talk to them about the fight. Or the book.

Her father and mother either saw nothing—and Ben had a few scratches of his own—or pretended to see nothing. She didn't mention the fight, and Ben, to her surprise, didn't mention his desecrated book.

Her father and mother had had a fine time. Her mother had bought a new Easter hat, and they had taken in a movie.

"Supposedly laid in Kentucky," her father said, at the dinner table, "but with eucalyptus trees and live oaks showing up on every ridge."

And her mother said that when the heroine heaved her bosom up and down, which was often, the upper part of her chest rose and fell like the tides, whereas her falsies, evidently attached to her foundation, remained solid and unmoving as concrete.

Awanda washed the dishes for her mother, then went to bed early. She had been asleep and awakened suddenly thinking, He tore my name from the book. If her name was gone, if it was no more than erased, she thought her life was ruined. She could, with a little saving, easily buy the Yolo Indians a new record book; but no one could replace what she had written. She couldn't even do it herself, by writing it there a second time.

She hurried into the living room and took the record book from the bookcase. The rain, which has been falling steadily all week, had stopped. The sky was clearing, and though smoky-edged clouds still ringed the moon, there was enough light at the front window for her to see that her name and her declaration still stood where she had placed them. She shut the book very solemnly. They would stay there, since Ben, who was no postponer, would have torn them out at once if that had been his intention.

The room smelled of yesterday's fire. The records she had stacked for playing were still out; "Aloha" was still on the turntable. Yesterday, she had supposed she could never again hear that word without suffering. "Aloha, farewell to thee," she said, smiling. She put the Yolo Indians book away and returned to her bed. She turned over a few times, then settled down comfortably in the midst of her bruises.

# *Reverdy*

I NEVER SEE asters without remembering her, never the haze of their pink and lavender blossoming as summer dies, but her name is in my heart: Reverdy, Reverdy.

I never say her name—not to anyone. When people ask about her, as they do occasionally even now, I say "she" and "her." "She is still gone." "We do not hear from her." "Yes, she was very beautiful," I say. But not her name.

Not Reverdy. That is buried deep, deep in my heart. Where the blood is warmest and thickest . . . where it has a sound to me like bells, or water running, or the doves whose voices in the evening wind are like smoke among the madrones and eucalyptus.

I have longed all these years to tell her how it was the night she left. You may scarcely believe it, but it is worse to have a good thing that is not true believed about you, than a bad. To be thanked for an act you meant to be harmful—every year those words sharpen until at last they cut like knives.

You mustn't think she was like me. She wasn't in the least. Not inside or out. She had dark hair like a cloud. Yes, really. It wasn't curly, but it didn't hang straight. It billowed out. And her face—oh, you mustn't think it was anything like mine. She had hazel eyes and a pointed chin. And you've seen lots of people, haven't you, with very live, animated faces and dead eyes? It was just the other way with Reverdy. Her face was always quiet, but her eyes were so alive they glowed. Oh, she was the most beautiful, most alive, and most loved girl in the world, and she was my sister.

I cannot bear for people to say we were alike. She was really good, and I was just a show-off.

Mother—she was better later, and gentler, but then she was bad, cruel and suspicious with Reverdy. Everybody loved Reverdy. Not just the boys. But Mother wouldn't see that. She always acted as if Reverdy were boy-crazy, as if Reverdy tried to entice the boys to her.

But it wasn't true. Reverdy never lifted a finger to a boy, though they were around her all the time from the day she was ten. Bringing her May baskets, or valentines, or ponies to ride.

And the big, tough boys liked her, too. When she was twelve and thirteen, big eighteen-year-olds would come over and sit on the steps and smoke and talk to Reverdy. They never said anything out of the way. I know because most of the time I was with them. Reverdy didn't care. She never wanted to be alone with them. Reverdy would listen to them until she got tired, then she'd say, "Good-bye for now." She'd always say, "Good-bye for now," and then she'd go out and play—maybe "Run, sheep, run"—with the little kids my age. And the little kids would all shout when Reverdy came out to play with them. If the game had been about to die, it would come to life again. If some of the kids had gone home, they'd yell, "Hey, Johnnie" or "Hey, Mary," or whoever it was, "Reverdy's going to play," and then every-one would come back, and in a minute or two the game would be better than ever.

I used to be awfully proud of being her sister. I don't know what I would have done without her. I was a terribly plain little frump—I wore glasses and had freckles. If I hadn't been Reverdy's sister, I'd have had to sit and play jacks by myself, until Joe came along. But boys would try to get Reverdy's attention by doing things for me. They'd say to her, "Does your sister want to ride on my handlebars?" And Reverdy would say, all glowing, happier than if she'd been asked, "Do you, Sister?" Of course I did, and when the boy came back, she'd ride with him just to thank him.

I don't know why people, why the boys, liked her so. Of course, she was beautiful, but I think it was more that she was so much— well, whatever she was at the moment; she never pretended. She talked with people when she wanted to, and when she got tired of them, she didn't stay on pretending, but said, "Good-bye for now," and left.

But Mother would never believe she wasn't boy-crazy, and I would hear her talking to Reverdy about girls who got in trouble, and how she'd rather see a daughter of hers in her grave. I didn't know what she was talking about, but it would make my face burn and scalp tingle just to hear her. She wouldn't talk sorrowfully or lovingly to

Reverdy, but with hate. It wasn't Reverdy she hated, but you couldn't tell that, looking at her. She would bend over Reverdy and shake her finger and there would be long ugly lines from her nose to her mouth, and her eyebrows would be drawn down until you could see the bony ridges they were supposed to cover, all bare and hard. It used to make me tremble to see her. Then Reverdy would get mad. I don't think she knew half the time what Mother was talking about, either—only that Mother was full of hate and suspicion. She'd wait until Mother had finished, then she'd go to the foothills for a walk, even if it was dark, and stay for a long time. And then Mother would think she was out with some boy again.

I remember one time my mother came to me and said, "Clare, I want you to tiptoe out to the arbor and see what's going on there. Reverdy's out there with Sam Foss, and I haven't heard a sound out of them for an hour or more."

The arbor was a kind of little bower covered with honeysuckle. There was only a tiny little door, and the honeysuckle strands hung so thick over it the arbor was a kind of dark, sweet-smelling cave. Reverdy and I used to play house there. I knew I ought to say I wouldn't go spying on Reverdy, but I wanted to please Mother, so I went creeping out toward the arbor, holding my breath, walking on my toes. I didn't know then—but I've found out since—you can't do a thing without becoming that thing. When I started out to look for Reverdy I was her little sister, loving her. But creeping that way, holding my breath, spying, I became a spy. My hands got heavy and hot and my mouth dry, and I wanted to see her doing . . . whatever it was Mother was fearful of.

And then when I got to the arbor and peeped in, I saw that Chummie, our ten-year-old brother, was there with them, and they were all practicing sign language. Deaf-and-dumb language was the rage with kids that summer, and there was that big Sam Foss sitting cross-legged, practicing sign language so hard he was sweating. They had oranges rolled until they were soft, and straws stuck in them to suck the juice out.

That's all they were doing. Practicing deaf-and-dumb language, and sucking oranges that way, playing they were bottles of pop. I guess they'd taken a vow not to talk, because nobody said a word. Even when Reverdy saw me peeping in, she didn't say anything, just spelled out, "Hello, Sister." But my hands felt so hot and swollen I couldn't spell a thing, and I just stood there and stared until I heard Mother call me to her, where she was standing strained and waiting on the back steps.

"They're playing sign language with Chummie," I told her.

"Is Chummie with them?" she asked, and her face relaxed and had a sort of shamed look on it, I thought.

I went in the house and put on the old dress I went swimming in, and floated around in the irrigation canal until supper was over, so I wouldn't have to sit and look across the table at Reverdy.

Things like that were always happening. I loved Reverdy more than anybody, and I hated Mother sometimes for spying and suspecting and lecturing. But I wanted people to love me. And especially you want your mother to love you—isn't that true? And no one loved me the way Reverdy was loved. I wasn't beautiful and spontaneous, I had to work hard and to good deeds to be loved. I couldn't be free the way Reverdy was. I was always thinking of the effect I was making. I couldn't say, "Good-bye for now," and let people go to hell if they didn't like me. I was afraid they'd never come back, and I'd be left . . . alone. But Reverdy didn't care. She liked being alone—and that's the reason people loved her, I guess.

One evening in October, when it was almost dark, I was coming home from the library, coasting across lots in the hot dry Santa Ana that had been blowing all day. Cool weather had already come, and then three days of this hot wind. Dust everywhere. Under your eye-lids, between your fingers, in your mouth. When we went to school in the morning the first thing we'd do would be to write our names in the dust on our desks. I had on a skirt full of pleats that evening, and I pulled the pleats out wide so the skirt made a sort of sail and the wind almost pushed me along. I watched the tumbleweeds blow-ing, and listening to the wind in the clump of eucalyptus by the barn, and felt miserable and gritty. Then I saw Reverdy walking up and down the driveway by the house, and I felt suddenly glad. Reverdy loved the wind, even Santa Ana's, and she was always out walking or running when the wind blew, if she didn't have any work to do. She liked to carry a scarf in her hand and hold it up in the wind so she could feel it tug and snap. When I saw Reverdy, I forgot how dusty and hot the wind was and remembered only how alive it was and how Reverdy loved it. I ran toward her, but she didn't wave or say a word, and when she reached the end of the driveway she turned her back on me and started walking toward the barn.

Before I had a chance to say a word to her, Mother came to the door and called to me to come in and not to talk to Reverdy. As soon as I heard her voice, before I could see her face, I knew there was some trouble—some trouble with Reverdy—and I knew what kind of trouble, too. I went in the house and shut the door. The sound of Reverdy's footsteps on the pepper leaves in the driveway outside stopped, and Mother put her head out the window and said, "You're to keep walking, Reverdy, and not stop. Understand? I want to hear footsteps and I want them to be brisk." Then she closed the window, though it was hard to do against the wind.

I stood with my face to the window and looked out into the dusty, windy dark where I could just see Reverdy in her white dress walking up and down, never stopping, her head bent, not paying any attention to the wind she loved. It made me feel sick to see her walking up and down there in the dusty dark like a homeless dog, while we were snug inside.

But Mother came over to the window and took the curtain out of my hand and put it back over the glass. Then she put her arm around my shoulders and pressed me close to her and said, "Mother's own dear girl who has never given her a moment's trouble."

That wasn't true. Mother had plenty of fault to find with me usually—but it was sweet to have her speak lovingly to me, to be cherished and appreciated. Maybe you can't understand that, maybe your family was always loving, maybe you were always dear little daughter, or maybe a big golden wonder-boy. But not me and not my mother. So try to understand how it was with me then, and how happy it made me to have Mother put her arms around me. Yes, I thought, I'm mother's comfort. And I forgot I couldn't make a boy look at me if I wanted to, and blamed Reverdy for not being able to steer clear of them the way I did. She just hasn't any consideration for any of us, I decided. Oh, I battened on Reverdy's downfall all right.

Then Father and Chummie came in, and Mother took Father away to the kitchen and talked to him there in a fast, breathless voice. I couldn't hear what she was saying, but I knew what she was talking about, of course. Chummie and I sat there in the dark. He whirled first one way and then another on the piano stool.

"What's Reverdy doing walking up and down outside there?" he asked.

"She's done something bad again," I told him.

Mother's voice got higher and higher, and Chummie said he'd have to go feed his rabbits, and I was left alone in the dark listening to her, and to Reverdy's footsteps on the pepper leaves. I decided to light the lights, but when I did—we had acetylene lights—the blue-white glare was so terrible I couldn't stand it. Not to sit alone in all that light and look at the dusty room and listen to the dry sound of the wind in the palms outside, and see Reverdy's books on the library table where she'd put them when she got home from school, with a big bunch of wilted asters laid across them. Reverdy always kept her room filled with flowers, and if she couldn't get flowers, she'd have leaves or grasses.

No, I couldn't stand that, so I turned out the lights and sat in the dark and listened to Reverdy's steps, not fast or light now, but heavy and slow—and I sat there and thought I was Mother's comforter, not causing her trouble like Reverdy.

Pretty soon I heard Mother and Father go outside, and then their voices beneath the window. Father was good, and he was for reason, but with Mother he lost his reason. He was just like me, I guess. He wanted Mother to love him, and because he did he would go out and say to Reverdy the things Mother wanted him to say.

Chummie came back from feeding his rabbits and sat with me in the dark room. Then I got the idea of a way to show Mother how much I was her comfort and mainstay, her darling younger daughter, dutiful and harmonious as hell. Mother wanted me and Chummie to be musical—she'd given up with Reverdy—but Chummie and I had taken lessons for years. Usually we kicked and howled at having to play; so I thought, If we play now, it will show Mother how thoughtful and reliable we are. It will cheer her up while she's out there in the wind talking to that bad Reverdy. Yes, she will think, I have one fine, dependable daughter anyway.

So I said to Chummie, "Let's play something for Mother." So he got out his violin, and we played that piece I've ever afterward hated. Over and over again, just as sweet as we could make it. Oh, I felt smug as hell as I played. I sat there on the piano stool with feet just so, and my hands just so, and played carefully, every note saying, "Mother's comfort. Mother's comfort. Played by her good, fine, reliable daughter."

We could hear Mother's high voice outside the window and Reverdy's low murmur now and then. Chummie finally got tired of playing—the music wasn't saying anything to him—and went out to the kitchen to get something to eat. I went too, but the minute I took a bite I knew I wasn't hungry, and Chummie and I both went to bed. I lay in bed a long time waiting to hear Mother and Reverdy come in, but there wasn't any sound but the wind.

I was asleep when Reverdy did come in. She sat down on the side of my bed, and it was just her sitting there that finally woke me. Then, when I was awake, she picked up my hand and began to press my fingertips one by one, and spoke in the sweetest, kindest voice. You'd never have thought to hear her that she had just spent four or five hours the way she did.

She said, "I'll never forget your playing for me, Sister. Never. Never. It was kind and beautiful of you. Just when I thought I was all alone, I heard you telling me not to be sad." Then she leaned over and kissed me and said, "Good night, now. I've put some asters in water for you. They're a little wilted but I think they'll be all right by morning. Go to sleep, now. I'll never forget, Clare."

If I could only have told her, if I could only have told her then. If I could have said to her, "I was playing for Mother, Reverdy. I guess I was jealous of your always having the limelight. I wanted to be first for once." If I could only have said, "I love you more than anything, Reverdy, but I have a mean soul," she would have put her cheek to mine and said, "Oh, Clare, what a thing to say."

But I couldn't do it, and next morning she was gone. And there on the table by my bed were the asters she had left for me, grown fresh overnight.

# Up a Tree

I CALLED HAROLD FOSDICK, the attorney, at about four o'clock. I thought of him because he was the one my mother had gone to see when I was fourteen or fifteen. I was afraid that attorneys, like bankers, might quit work early and that Mr. Fosdick would already have gone home.

"This is Eugenia Calloway," I said when his secretary answered. "I'd like to speak to Mr. Fosdick if he's in."

"Oh, Miss Calloway," his secretary said, with that special something in her voice I was beginning to be accustomed to hearing. "He's with a client just now, but I'll have him call back in a short time."

He called back at once. "Eugenia," he said.

He didn't really know me well enough to be calling me Eugenia. I'm almost nineteen years old, and so far as I know he's never seen me except for that one visit to his office. But I was glad to hear my first name. I'd been "Miss Calloway" all day, and I was glad to have someone speak to me as though I were a friend or a relation.

"What can I do for you, Eugenia?"

"Nothing, maybe," I said. "I'm just calling to ask you about my legal rights."

Mr. Fosdick was silent for a second or two. Then he said, "Ted Hughes is your father's lawyer, you know."

Of course I knew that. "I don't know Mr. Hughes personally," I said.

"You don't know me."

"I was with Mother that time when she came to see you. You were very nice to her."

Under different circumstances he might have said, "I'm always nice to the ladies." But the circumstances weren't different. "Your mother was an unusual woman, Eugenia." No one was going to contradict that. God knows I always thought so myself, and still do, though in a different way.

261

"All I want is some information. It might not even have to be from a lawyer."

"If I give it, it'll have to be from a lawyer, I'm afraid."

"Okay. What I want to know is, do I have to see all these reporters? Have they any legal right to question me? Have they any . . ."

Mr. Fosdick broke in, as if I were in court and testifying, "Legal right? They haven't even any *human* right."

"Then I'm not required to answer. . . ."

"Required to answer? Eugenia, you're not a child. You surely know a reporter is nothing but a man hunting news. He has no more right to ask you . . . about your mother's death . . . than he has to ask you . . . Well, he has no right. Spit in his eye."

"There's too many of them. I don't have that much spit. How can I keep them from pounding on the door?"

"Move away from there for the time being. I'd think you'd want to anyway."

I didn't want to move away from there. "Where would I go?"

"Don't you have any relatives?"

"You know who mother's relatives are. Out in Riverside County."

"Well, you wouldn't feel at home there. Where are your father's people?"

"Back east. If he has any. He never mentioned them."

"Move into town to a hotel. A hotel could protect you from intruders."

"I want to stay here. And I want reporters to stay away."

Mr. Fosdick was quiet for another few seconds. Then he said, "There's a lane runs into your place from the main road, isn't there? The house is at the back of the ranch?"

"You weren't ever out here, were you?"

"Not since you've lived there. But that ranch is a lot older than you are. How old do you think those eucalyptus trees are?"

I didn't want to talk about eucalyptus trees, so I didn't say anything.

"There should be a barricade, at the entrance to the lane. 'Private Property, Entrance Forbidden.' That would take care of the reporters."

"I don't know how to build a barricade."

"Isn't there anyone there with you?"

"Not unless you count the reporters."

"Well, they're not going to build you a barricade. That's a cinch."

"They're not here now. They've gone back to town to file their stories. Or to get something to eat. Anyway, I'm alone, now."

"I'll send my yardman right out. He'll build you a barricade and put up a sign. That should take care of the reporters. Have you already talked with a lot of them?"

"I've really only *talked* with one."

"Smith? The young fellow from the *Star*?"

"How did you know?"

"He's sympathetic. And nice looking. He's the one a girl *would* talk to. What did you say?"

"I don't remember, exactly. But quite a lot, I'm afraid."

Afraid? I *knew* I had talked to him a lot. I had been dying, it seemed, to talk to someone. Especially Smith, once I got started. Three days had gone by, and except for Mr. Hughes and the reporters there had been no one. Three days and all that wondering and remembering. Trying to put two and two together. And trying even harder not to put two and two together.

I read somewhere recently that a person at twelve has all the intelligence he is ever going to have. I believe it. I could have dealt with this at twelve just as well as I can now. Perhaps better. At twelve I knew exactly what was right and what was wrong. Or thought I did. Now I'm not so sure. Also I now know that it is easier to love the dead than the living. That confuses me. And I know that pity can bind you closer than love. You feel that you owe more to pity than you do to love. Love gives you joy; pity, pain. And isn't what pain says more to be trusted than what joy says? Pain says you have cancer. Joy says he loves you madly. You're prejudiced in favor of joy, aren't you?

Mr. Fosdick said, "Eugenia. Eugenia. Are you all right?"

"I'm okay. I was thinking."

"You've got plenty to think about. I grant you that. Look here, I'm coming out in the pickup with Tony. While he's putting up the barricade, I'd like to talk to you."

I was tired. "I've been talking all day, Mr. Fosdick."

"That's one of the reasons I want to see you. I'm a friend of Ted Hughes."

"I didn't say anything to hurt Mr. Hughes. Or Father."

"You said you didn't know *what* you had said."

"I don't *know* anything that could hurt Father. So it doesn't matter what I say."

"Have you seen your father?"

"Since he's in jail, you mean?"

"That's what I mean."

"No."

"Why not?"

"He said he'd rather not just yet."

"That's strange. Well, I'll be out in an hour. I've a man here I have to finish with. Then I'll pick up Tony and be right out."

"Okay."

"I'm not coming as a lawyer, you understand. I'm coming as a friend. As someone who knew your mother."

"Okay, I'll be here."

"Meanwhile, don't talk to any more reporters. Not even Smith. And don't let them clamber around that platform."

"You don't have to worry about that. The police are taking care of that. Mr. Fosdick?"

"Yes?"

"Do they have a right to keep me away from it?"

"Yes, they do."

"It's on our property. It's practically a part of my home."

"Well, it's a peculiar part now. I wouldn't think you'd want to go up there now. I'd think wild horses couldn't drag you. Now you stay put where you are, and I'll see you in an hour."

It was two hours. I knew it would be. The client would take more time than Mr. Fosdick had expected. It's fifteen miles between here and Santa Ana, where his office is, and when he got home he wouldn't be able to locate Tony at once. After that he'd have to buy lumber for the barricade. So I could just relax.

I had told myself and told myself to stop looking at Mother's picture. Stop peering over it with a magnifying glass like some mad old Sherlock Holmes. I had to use a magnifying glass because the picture was a snapshot, and though good of Mother, it wasn't very clear. It was good of Mother because it wasn't taken by Father. When he took a picture of her, she was self-conscious. She knew he didn't like her looks, and she was too proud to bridle and smile for him and try to look attractive and appealing. (What she was, I now see, was downright starkly beautiful.) This snapshot was probably taken by her brother, Uncle Eloy. I think the strand of leaves hanging over her head was part of the bougainvillea vine which covered the tank house at the Souza place. She knew Eloy liked her, so she was relaxed and smiling. Facing Father was like facing a firing squad for her.

The beautiful woman in the picture was a woman I had never seen before. When she was alive, she was like a painting, so close to me that all I could see were blobs of paint and brush strokes. Death had moved her far enough away so that I could see her true outline. She had a strong face, with high cheekbones, heavy brows, and a nose that was large, but neither sharp nor long. In the snapshot there is a shadowy smile at the corners of her mouth. Her face is manly but beautiful, like a tender Indian chief's, or a great resolute Egyptian queen's. Her hair, clipped together at the back, is hanging down like the switch tail of a black racing mare. She was thirty-eight when she died. Three days ago. I don't know how old she was when this picture was taken. Twenty-eight, perhaps. If Katharine Hepburn had a strong face and was madrone colored instead of pink and white, she'd look a lot like Mother.

I had been shoving the picture, after I looked at it, to the very back of the drawer of the library table, promising myself not to look at it ever again. I hadn't appreciated her when she was alive. What was I doing now, gazing and gazing? Pretty soon I would be kissing her picture and crying, "Never leave me, dear Mama. Forgive me, dear Mama." Now I put the picture and the glass on top of the table.

Okay. So I hadn't appreciated her when she was alive. Never thought of her as an Indian chief or an Egyptian queen in my life before. Thought of her instead as someone Father and I had put up with. If death taught me better, well, better late than never. Such thoughts wouldn't do Mother any harm now. And they might do me some good.

"Good-bye, Mother," I said. "I'll be back before dark."

This was as crazy as staring at her picture through a magnifying glass. Crazier. When Mother was alive I never told her anything. Father and I were in cahoots together. Talking to her seemed disloyal to him. And Mother never asked me any questions. Sometimes I resented this. Other mothers wanted to know what time their daughters got in and who they were out with and when was their last period. I wanted to be worried over a little. Maybe I was. But Mother never said so, and I wouldn't ask. So we were both lonely, I guess; though I had Father to talk to and she didn't.

It was a little after five when I went outside. In mid-October with daylight saving, the light is still strong, but beginning to slant, at that hour. It was unnaturally quiet and clear; Santa Ana weather, the hush before the strong dry wind blows up the canyon from the east. Our ranch is at the very edge of the Santa Ana canyon, beyond what used to be the town of Olive. Olive was just beyond Orange. But everything has run into everything else now in Southern California, and beginnings and endings are all mixed up.

Our ranch is still a ranch because Father, being a doctor, hasn't had to subdivide. He doesn't have to make money ranching. In fact, he can lose money ranching, and it helps his tax bracket. Though this isn't the reason he has kept the ranch.

The place began fifty years ago as an olive ranch. Most of the olive trees have been replaced by avocados now. The olive trees that are left are gnarled and scaley. But they bear good crops still, and Mother cured her own olives in big stone jars of brine.

It seemed lighter outside than it really was because our house was so dark. It was built about the time the olives were planted and has never been remodeled, except for the bathrooms and kitchen. It's old-style California with a screened porch on all four sides. That's one reason for the darkness, though it would have been dark anyway because of the redwood paneling inside. Old-time Californians liked it that way. That was the point, they thought, in coming indoors: get away from that hot glare. Being Easterners (not Mother, of course), their eyes weren't adjusted to so much sunshine. Around the house are all the trees the old-timers planted for shade and coolness, peculiar kinds that didn't grow back east. Pepper trees, with trunks gnarled as the olives. Peppers have tiny little dry red berries. When the wind blows a clump of pepper trees sounds like a tangle of rattlesnakes practicing buzzing. There are palms of every variety, of course. When a Santa Anna blows, the palm fronds clash against each other with the sound of scraping timbers.

At the east end of the ranch, next to what's left of the old grove, is a big double row of eucalyptus trees, planted fifty years ago as a windbreak. Everybody planted eucalyptus windbreaks in those days. Mostly they've been dug up or cut down now. They get in the way of subdivisions. People say they are dirty because they drop their limbs sometimes in storms. The few ranchers who are left don't like them because eucalyptus saps water from the soil. Father didn't have to worry about any of these things. So our windbreak still stands and is a landmark for miles around. It can even be seen from out at sea. Mother loved it. So do I. No other tree as large as the eucalyptus gives itself so easily to wind; or is so open to the sun. When the sun shines and a Santa Ana blows, a big eucalyptus shimmers and glitters like a bonfire of green-white diamonds.

I walked down toward the windbreak, slowly breathing in the sharp aromatic eucalyptus smell. In the old days people with lung disease were advised to live near a eucalyptus grove. Doctors thought the smell was healing. The Indians still pound up leaves to make a kind of poultice to use for chest colds. The trees don't smell medicinal to me: they smell fresh and free, like the old days Mother talked about and the open country she knew.

The platform was toward the south end of the row of trees. There were two policemen there. They sat on upended orange boxes, with a third box crosswise between, which they used as a card table. They had put their cards away when I came down that morning. I don't know whether it's against the rules for policemen to play cards when on duty or whether they were afraid I'd think they weren't paying proper respect for the dead.

I looked up at the trees at that end of the windbreak and at the platform. I didn't intend to go near the policemen again. They couldn't do me any good, and all I did was to make them uneasy. They sat at the foot of the ladder that leads up to the platform. The platform is built between two trees, seedlings, I suppose, which grow a few feet away from the double line of the real windbreak trees. Mother had it built six or seven years ago. I don't know who the Police Department thinks would want to go up there. I do, but they wouldn't expect me to want to. And I can get up there without using the ladder. I can shinny up to the platform between the two trees, and the police would never know I was there.

Police brutality? I don't suppose the most aggressive men are chosen to sit in olive groves to watch bird-watching platforms. These two men would look okay in checkered aprons baking cookies. They have their revolvers on the orange-box card table like old-time TV gamblers. I don't know what they would do if I started climbing the ladder. They're too portly to climb after me. Would they shoot me in the leg? That would be brutal but maybe they would consider it in the line of duty. Enjoy it, maybe; I don't know.

While I was watching them, one of the men stood, then picked up his pistol. "You're not allowed down here, fellow," he called. He put his pistol in his holster, but he had showed that he was armed and meant business.

"I'm not coming down there. I was looking for Miss Calloway."

"She's right here in front of you."

"I can see her now."

I recognized the voice. It was Smith, the man I'd talked too much to. I turned and walked back toward him.

"Hi, Smith," I said.

"I've got another name," he said.

"I know. Don or Ron or Jess or Steve. I don't want to know it."

"What makes you so mean to men?"

"I'm not mean to men."

"Just me?"

"You're a reporter, aren't you?"

But he was right. Brush them off at once, then you can console yourself by thinking, Well, what did you expect from someone you treated like that? No one's going to fall for a mean-mouth like you.

"Do you hate all reporters?"

"Of course not. I don't know all of them. But I talked too much to you."

"That's why I came out. To show you what I wrote."

"I don't want to see it."

"This isn't anything about the case. In this, it's what you told me about buzzards."

"Buzzards are in the case."

"I suppose they are. This is a special piece, though, just on them. It doesn't mention the case. I wanted to check some of the facts. I tried to quote you exactly."

"I'm in the case. How do you think you can be writing about me, and about buzzards, and make people think that's all you're talking about?"

"I don't suppose I can. I don't care, actually. I want it to be a good piece of writing about buzzards and about you."

"The *Star* is a lousy paper. If your piece is good, they won't use it."

"It can be good about buzzards. Buzzards aren't political. They're human interest."

"Human or inhuman?"

"I saw a piece of yours in the *Yucca*. It's not much good either."

"You're frank, anyway."

"I didn't mean what you wrote. I mean the *Yucca*."

"What do you expect? It doesn't pay. And it's conscientious. Somebody there reads every word I send them."

"Where else have you been published?"

"Nowhere. But twice in the *Yucca*. What do you read it for if it's no good?"

"I read everything. Would you like to hear the buzzard piece?"

"No."

"I'll read it to you, and if you don't like what you hear, you can walk off. It's nothing but what you told me."

He began reading before I could say a word.

" 'Buzzards live the year round in the eucalyptus windbreak at the east end of the Calloway property. They don't nest there. Their nests are in the rocky hills still farther east. But the eucalyptus windbreak is their home. They soar in at dusk after their days of hunting food are over. In October, for some reason naturalists don't understand, hundreds of buzzards congregate in one spot for a fly-in.' "

"I didn't say 'fly-in.' "

"I know you didn't."

"I would never say that. It sounds too cute."

"I'll take it out. 'The windbreak on the Calloway ranch is one of these congregating spots. The buzzards don't get together to mate or to hunt. They do nothing but fly in crisscrossing patterns, so tight you'd expect twenty collisions a minute. They miss by a feather's breadth.' "

"I didn't say that."

"I know you didn't."

"It's okay, though. It's the truth."

" 'It's a beautiful sight. They aren't flying to get anywhere. Or to kill anything. Just for joy. Just for pure joy. They don't even fly; they soar. In perfectly still afternoons, with no wind to support them, they find updrafts which send them, without their moving a wing, skyward. They fill the air with black scissors. All they cut in two is sky. All they snip off is joy.' "

"That's pretty fancy for the *Star*."

"You said it."

"Okay. What else did I say?"

"You said, 'A couple of hundred birds will decide at the same time to light. All of them at once will slide into and among the eucalyptus leaves and limbs where there isn't any opening to be seen. The trees seem to open up for them, the leaves to lift for them to enter, and the limbs to stiffen to hold them once they've landed.' "

" 'Leaves lift and limbs stiffen.' Sounds like Swinburne."

"You said it. There's only one more sentence. 'And all this without a sound.' "

I didn't intend to cry.

Smith said, "I didn't intend to make you cry."

"It's okay. I've wanted to and couldn't."

"Couldn't?"

"I didn't have the right. You don't have any right to cry for someone who's gone when you've wished a thousand times he was gone. *She* was gone. If you've wished she was gone, you should rejoice when she is gone."

"But you don't?"

"No. Of course not."

Smith gave me his handkerchief. "Why did the buzzards make you cry?"

They were floating homeward at that minute, sliding down the sky from the south to the trees.

"I never saw a buzzard until my mother spoke of them. I didn't hate them the way some people do; they just didn't exist for me. Mother would stand about where we are at twilight to watch them come home. I don't know how old I was when I first went out to stand beside her. She said they were beautiful. I told her they ate dead meat."

"So do we," she said.

"They eat rotten meat," I told her.

"They don't kill it."

"Neither do we."

"Somebody does for us."

"Somebody does for the buzzards."

"The buzzards don't pay them to do it. Nobody dies because of a buzzard."

"Is that why you like them?"

"That's one reason. Another is, they're beautiful."

"Beautiful?"

"Watch them fly."

I did and I saw that they were beautiful.

"And they're so quiet."

"Is that better than singing?"

"There's screaming and squawking, too. No one wants to be quiet but a buzzard."

"If you could be an animal, would you choose to be a buzzard?"

"I am an animal. We're all animals. The buzzards are good animals."

"May I put this in my piece?" Smith asked.

"No. You can't put anything else I say in the paper either. Otherwise I'm going in the house."

"I promise you. She sounds like a wonderful woman."

"She was."

"But you didn't like her?"

"No. I was ashamed of her."

"Because she was half Indian?"

"Partly. Most people thought she was Mexican. She didn't look Indian. Not like the Sobobas anyway. Have you ever seen a Soboba?"

"No. Not and know it, anyway."

"Well, look at me. Pudding shape, pudding face, pudding nose, pudding mouth. That's a Soboba."

Smith didn't contradict me. How could he? He said, "I never heard of a Soboba with red hair."

"No, I've got Calloway coloring and Soboba shape. It was just the other way with Mother. Soboba coloring and a face like her father's. It made her a beauty. But I didn't know it when she was alive. They called her a greaser at school. When you're ten years old, you hate having a greaser for a mother. She did queer things, too. She didn't like a lawn. She liked a yard she could sweep. So we don't have any grass. She didn't like to work inside. So she shelled peas and things like that sitting out in the yard. She washed out in the yard. Herself, I mean. She went fishing and brought fish home in a gunny sack."

"Where could she find any fish around here?"

"Down at Newport. She would sit all day on the pier along with kids and old men and Negroes."

"And your father didn't like this?"

"*I* didn't like it. I don't think it made any big difference to him."

"There must've been something that rubbed him the wrong way."

"I think he didn't like so much devotion."

"That's a queer thing not to like."

"Maybe you've never had too much."

"That's right. But I can't imagine not liking it."

"Polishing your shoes?"

"Okay with me."

"Waxing your car?"

"No complaints."

"Calling you to the phone when other women call?"

"Ideal."

"Well, doctors are different. They like something to fight. They wouldn't be doctors if they didn't. They want to fight and win. Mother was already *won*. She wasn't a challenge any more. She accepted Father completely no matter what he did. He was her husband, and what her husband did was right. I never heard her complain about anything."

"Even the women?"

"She was his *wife*. They weren't."

"What do you think?"

"I thought that Father and I were putting something over on Mother. 'Us Calloways.' That's the way I thought of Father and me. Us Calloways against the redskins. Mother was an outsider, and Father and I put up with her. I was trained that way. It began when I was too young to know what was going on. But I can remember when I was six, going along with Father to call on ladies. I had a nap or played with the puppies while he doctored the lady. That's what I thought he did."

"In a manner of speaking," Smith said, "I guess he did."

"What makes doctors so irresistible?"

"They aren't."

"Father was."

"He'd have been irresistible as a grocery clerk. If you look like a professional football player, you don't have to be a doctor."

"How do you know what he looks like?"

"There've been plenty of pictures of him in the papers. Besides, he took out my tonsils. *And* my appendix."

"You must've been a sickly kid."

"No, Doctors pushed such things when I was a kid. And my folks had the money."

"Father's way past stuff like that now."

"I know. Open-heart surgery and so forth. Why did he marry your mother if her devotion got on his nerves?"

"Me. I was on the way. *That* kind of devotion didn't get on his nerves, ever. He didn't know she had the other kind yet. He was a poor nobody and she was a beautiful Indian maiden. I don't *know* that. Maybe it was a shotgun wedding. Maybe her relatives out on the reservation threatened to bury him in an anthill. There would've been other women no matter who he married. Only, another wife would have divorced him. Mother wouldn't. She loved him. He was a fine man and her husband, and she was proud of him and proud to be his wife. And a woman expected a man to be manly."

" 'Being manly.' Is that what your mother called cheating?"

"She didn't *call* it anything. That's how I think she felt about it. He was her husband and it was for life."

"So your father had to . . ."

" 'Had to.' I didn't say a word about had to. I don't intend to talk about my father."

"You talk about your mother."

"She isn't in trouble. He is. Besides, she wouldn't want me to talk about him."

Smith said, "Maybe you *are* a Soboba."

"I told you I was the exact shape of a Soboba."

"Okay. Yes. You did. Okay. What about the buzzard piece?"

"What 'What about it'?"

"Is it okay with you?"

"Don't quote me."

"If I don't quote you. I don't have anything."

"You say what you want to say about buzzards, and I'll say what I want to say."

"A lot more people read the *Star* than will ever read the *Yucca*."

"You know what a lot of people want to read. I don't. You give it to them. But not Mother's buzzards. They're too good for a lot of people."

Mean-mouth again. But not to put Smith down. That's what I truly felt. The sun had set. To the west the sky was red and gold, and buzzards were silently sliding home to the trees. In the east the sky was pink, and against it Old Saddle Back was grape-bloom blue, but as solid looking as the big mountains, Baldy and Wilson. Smith was watching the buzzards, too.

"I'll give you a can of beer if you come up to the house." It was about the first invitation I'd ever given to a male since I was sixteen. I expected Smith to have a date in town. Instead, he said, "Okay, that would taste good."

We were halfway to the house when Mr. Fosdick turned into our lane, stopped to let Tony out and to put down the lumber for the barricade.

"There comes a man who told me not to talk to you," I said.

"I'd better be on my way then."

"You show me your buzzard piece, and I'll show you mine. If I ever write it," I said.

"It's a deal," Smith said. He started his car, but waited for Mr. Fosdick to drive in before he drove out.

I took Mr. Fosdick into the living room. I showed him to our best chair, the fumed-oak Morris with the brown corduroy cushions. It was old, but in a way it was modern because it had an adjustable four-position tilt-back. Mr. Fosdick didn't sit. He turned a full circle, like a man in a museum trying to make up his mind what to look at first. Then he took off his specs. When he did that, I remembered who he had reminded me of when Mother and I called on him. He hadn't changed a bit and he still looked like the same man: Woodrow Wilson. I had been studying American history then and had spent a whole week seeing Wilson's picture in the chapter on World War I. The horn-rimmed spectacles were wrong, of course, and with them off he looked more like the president.

"My God, my God," Mr. Fosdick said.

Mr. Fosdick used the name of God, Christ, Jesus, heaven, hell, the devil, and damnation very often. I wouldn't exactly call it cursing. It was more as if he felt himself the resident of a universe where there were more powers and personalities than were visible, and that this was his courteous way of letting them know that he was aware of them and was trying to include them in his life. He certainly included them in his conversation. In some ways it was embarrassing. I felt like an eavesdropper to someone praying. This shows how different it was from real profanity, which would have made me mad. I wouldn't care to be cursed. And there is no obscenity that disgusts me.

Mr. Fosdick patted his chair all over as if it were a horse before he sat down. "Jesus, sweet Jesus," he said. "I never expected to see a room like this again. I didn't know there was one like it left in California."

"What's so queer about it?"

"Mission furniture. Redwood paneling. Leaded-glass doors to the bookcases. Grass rug. Eucalyptus portieres between dining and living room. Clock held up by lions' heads. Why, hell, Eugenia, you must know all this. It surely hasn't been changed since the day Gene bought it."

"It hasn't."

"Why didn't he modernize it?"

"He didn't care. He wasn't here half the time. And Mother thought it was wonderful."

"After the reservation, I suppose it was. Why didn't you change it?"

"I didn't have the say around the house."

"Who did?"

"Around the house . . . Mother."

"Eugenia, I didn't come out here to talk about furniture. How are you? How're you feeling?"

"I don't know. I'm changing. I don't feel the same as I did at first."

"Do you remember the day you came to my office with your mother?"

"Yes. That's why I called you."

"I've never forgotten your mother. I never will. And not just because of that damned idea she had."

"It wasn't such a damned idea. And she had her way, finally."

"Not exactly, I wouldn't say."

"She got there. That was what she wanted. A book influenced her. Did she tell you that?"

"A lot of people told me that."

"Mother's whole life was changed by that book, about how Californians were buried."

"It was Americans, not just Californians."

"Americans. Mother didn't think it was fair that undertakers should make the rules about how persons were buried."

"Well, my God, who said anything about fair? But Christ Almighty, her ideas were a lot worse. Who could put up with thirty-foot platforms all over the country with dead bodies stretched out on them?"

"The Indians could."

"Not *her* Indians. The Sobobas never went in for anything like that."

"She was a half-breed. She didn't have to be tied down by what any one tribe did. All Indians were being discriminated against, she thought."

"Nobody's going to dispute that. If your poor mother were alive today, she could have people organized and burning down mortuaries so that Indians could have platform burial again. My God, they're tearing down whole universities now for less. Soul food and Swahili! Jesus, how do *they* stack up alongside something important like how your ancestors were buried?"

"Mother would never have done anything like that. Organized or torn down or burned down. She wouldn't even protest. She was shy. She was born to endure. She was afraid to go to your office that day without me."

"What good could you do her? You were nothing but a kid."

"I was Father's daughter. And I was white. And she thought I was smart. I know now that's what she thought. She saved every one of my report cards and every composition I ever wrote."

"You probably were smart. Probably *are*. You're Gene's daughter."

"I'm Mother's, too."

"She was plenty smart in her way. Except for that idea of hers that a lawyer would be able to fix it up so she could be on a platform and be eaten by buzzards instead of worms when she died."

"I would prefer it myself. Wouldn't you?"

"After I'm dead, I don't care what eats me.'

"She cared."

"What did your father think of all this?"

"He didn't say. Nothing, I suspect. He lived his life and she could live hers."

"Up a tree was okay with him?"

"I never heard him say it wasn't."

"What did he say when she had that platform built?"

"Nothing. It was for bird watching."

"Buzzard watching."

"They're birds. She watched them. So did I."

"Did your father ever climb up to that platform?"

"Not that I know of."

"He must've once."

"You believe that?"

"It's nothing I want to believe."

Mr. Fosdick puts his glasses back on, began to cry, and had to take them off. "I don't want to believe it. Gene was my friend. I'd a thousand times rather be where your mother is than where Gene is."

I watched Mr. Fosdick polish his glasses.

"Eugenia," he said, "you are one-hundred-percent Indian. Here your mother's dead, your father's in jail accused of her murder, and I'm the one doing the crying."

"I never was encouraged much to cry when I was young. Mother didn't believe in it, and Father was never around to notice. I'm sorry Mother's dead. But being in jail doesn't mean you're guilty."

"You don't get there without damned strong evidence that you belong there."

"They haven't much evidence against Father."

"Mrs. Crowther swears that Gene said on his way back to town that he'd see that his wife didn't cause them any more trouble."

"She never caused Father trouble."

"She wouldn't divorce him. That's trouble if you want to marry someone else."

"He didn't want to marry anyone else."

"Mrs. Crowther came out here with your father, and he told your mother . . . Well, you heard it all. You were here."

"When they started quarreling, I left."

"Your mother and your father?"

"Mother never quarreled with Father. Father and Mrs. Crowther."

"What were they quarreling about?"

"I don't know. I tried not to hear."

"Did your father threaten your mother?"

"No. But Mrs. Crowther did. Maybe Mrs. Crowther killed Mother."

"Mrs. Crowther has an alibi from the minute she got back into town. Your father hasn't."

"Maybe I killed her."

"Don't be blasphemous."

"There were times when I wished she was dead."

"Fortunately, you didn't tell anyone that. And fortunately, she wasn't found dead after you said it. Where did you go when you left the house?"

"I took my bedroll and went to spend the night in the hills."

"Alone?"

"Sure, alone. I'm no hippie."

"Did anyone see you?"

"I don't know. I didn't see anyone."

"When did you get home?"

"Next day. About noon."

"Was your mother here?"

"No."

"Weren't you alarmed?"

"No. I didn't ask her when I wanted to go someplace, and she didn't ask me."

"Where did you think she was?"

"Uncle Eloy's. Out by San Jacinto. That's where she goes when she leaves for a while. That was Sunday night. I phoned Uncle Eloy on Tuesday. He hadn't seen her."

"Then you called the police?"

"Yes."

"Why didn't you call your father?"

"I didn't know where to find him."

"Did you try his office?"

"They didn't know where to find him."

"And the police couldn't find her when they came?"

"No."

"But you did?"

"Later, yes."

"How did you know where to look?"

"I didn't. I went up there by chance."

"You didn't see your father carry her up there?"

"I wasn't here. I told you that. She was a big woman. How could he carry her up there kicking and screaming?"

"She didn't have to be kicking and screaming when he carried her up. Though he was a strong enough man to have done that if necessary."

"How did he kill her?"

"Who knows? What can you tell from bones that have been stripped bare? He knew that. And he knew that I'd come forward with evidence that some years ago she'd seen me about being buried on a platform."

"Buried on, not killed on."

"Okay. Buried. There must have been a lot of buzzards up around that platform for a couple of days. It's a wonder you didn't notice them."

"This is the time of year buzzards from all over come to these trees."

"To the trees, maybe, but not just to that platform. But you didn't see them?"

"I don't spend my entire time watching buzzards."

Mr. Fosdick took off his glasses again. I don't know why he wore them. When he seemed to want to see something particularly closely, he took them off. He leaned forward and looked at me as if I were a strange animal. Or a page of print in some language of which he knew only a few words. I was standing in front of him. I had never sat down since he came in. I felt more alert standing up. He had stopped swearing. I remembered that when Mother and I had gone to his office there had been no swearing. Perhaps he saved swearing for his social life, but when it came to business, he was all business.

"Did Ted Hughes send you here?" I asked. "Or maybe Mrs. Crowther?"

"You called *me*, remember?"

"I haven't said anything to hurt Father."

"You certainly haven't. I'll tell Ted that. Why don't you go up to see your father?"

"I told you that, don't you remember? He doesn't want to see me. He said he wouldn't talk to me if I came."

"You'd think he'd *want* to see you."

"He's probably ashamed of being in jail. How can they keep a man in jail just because of what some woman says? Probably she was trying to get even with some other woman when she said it."

"They couldn't keep him in jail. Except that the wife's dead, and he said she'd cause them no more trouble. And there's no other explanation. Is there?"

"Maybe not. But don't you feel sorry for him? His wife dead. And the woman he was going to marry, according to you, accusing him of murder. Don't you pity him?"

"My God, yes. He was my good friend. I've shed tears for him. That's more than I've seen you do."

"Well, he wasn't a very good father. Let's face it. He kept me from loving my mother."

"Eugenia, come home with me. This is no place for a girl to be staying alone after what's happened here."

"Nothing's happened here."

"You weren't here. Remember? So how do you know? Come home with me. My wife would be glad to have you. Clarice will be home from Pomona. She must be about your age."

"She's my age exactly. No, I don't like to be in town. This is home."

"Okay then. If you need me, phone, and I'll be right out. Tony's barricade should be up by now, and you shouldn't have any more trouble with reporters."

An hour or so after Mr. Fosdick left, I went down the back way to the south end of the windbreak. The Santa Ana that had been threatening was already beginning to blow a little. There was a small moon, short of full quarter by a night or so. I could've made the trip in pitch dark, but the pale moonshine plus the stars of a clear night made the way plain—besides making me feel more tranquil and peaceful than I had for days.

I could have climbed right up the ladder. One policeman was nowhere to be seen. The other, stretched out on his sleeping bag, was dozing. I was barefoot. Though I did not like to be called the daughter of a greaser, I liked to play at being a hundred percent old-time Indian, who could move noiselessly through a forest never slipping on a twig; and able to make an owl's soft hoot, absolutely owl-like, but recognizable as a signal, too. I gave the hoot then, to try out the cops, but the one I could see never so much as twitched.

So though I could have climbed the ladder, I wanted to go up the hard way, and out of sight, for practice. I wanted to see if I could still do it. People never expected me to be agile because I'm so stubby. They are mistaken. I am agile. I can put my head to the floor and look at you upside down and backward from between my legs, the way a baby can. A baby is not tall and thin either.

The way up to the platform, on the back side, without using the ladder and out of sight of the police, was by a mountain-climbing maneuver. You go between the two trees that hold the platform, back against one tree, feet against the other. The trees are exactly the right distance apart for inching up that way. It's no trick to reach the platform, but it's a little tricky getting onto it. For a second you hang by your arms thirty feet in the air.

The platform is about six by six. You can stretch full length on it, either direction. I lay down flat on it facing Saddle Back Mountain. There was enough of a Santa Ana blowing to rock the platform gently. Above were the dark forms of the buzzards roosting. They look so much smaller roosting than they do flying. They are mostly wing-spread and feathers. I have never held a live buzzard, but I think they would weigh less than a young chicken. Without feathers they would be almost nothing.

The last time I had been up to the platform I had used the ladder. There had been the first tiny thread of a new moon, which is shaped like a eucalyptus leaf. Mother believed, and so did I, that you will have bad luck if you don't see the new moon the first night it is in the sky. It is also discourteous not to give your attention to something that is making a start. I looked at the new moon that night, because I knew Mother would want me to; but I could not see much luck in it. I said to it, "Prosper, prosper, new moon," though I had never done that before and was disgusted when I had heard Mother, a grown woman, talk to the moon as if it were alive and had ears. It was a part of her queerness; and when you're young, the last thing you want is a queer mother, a mother who talks to the moon and puts fish in a gunnysack.

Somehow I had believed that the buzzards would be ceremonious when they stripped the flesh from bones set out for their feasting. Mother had talked that way, as if they were as dignified and professional as undertakers; only not hirelings. But they had scrambled her bones, pushed them every which way. In my mind I truly believe I thought they would arrange them as neatly as a corpse in a silk-lined casket. I expected to be able to lie down beside Mother, she on one side of the platform, I on the other, and together we would rest there and remember and decide what to do. She was not even all there. Some of her bones had been pushed to the ground. I went down and brought them all up. That was what she had wanted, to be in the sky, not on the ground. But there was no use trying to arrange them as they had been when they were covered with flesh. She wouldn't care about that, and, besides, I didn't know how to do it. The thin thread of a moon had left the sky by the time I got back on the platform. It was warm, and I stayed there all night, sometimes sleeping. I was asleep at first light, and it was the buzzards, creaking a little as they levered themselves upward, that awakened me. I lay perfectly still, wondering if they could tell that I was alive. They swooped low across the platform but never stopped. My flesh was alive and Mother's was gone. I went back to the house, and after a day had passed I phoned the police to tell them what I had discovered.

This was a different night. Mother's bones had gone to where she had never wanted them to go, to an undertaker's. But first she had been where she wanted to be. Father wouldn't let me talk to him, but I understood that, too. I didn't really want to talk to him or see him. I didn't care if the silence was between us forever. Except for him, I think I might have loved Mother *before* she died. Maybe not. Anyway, he had fixed it so the love I had once had for him had changed to pity.

I lay on the platform, the wind rising, the platform swaying rock-aby, and the cop who had been dozing snoring now, full out, tired of silly tree watching and of pretending that he *was* tree watching.

Out of habit, not thinking, I felt around to the back of the far eucalyptus where a limb had dropped off leaving a hole as deep as two hands and as wide as one. When I was learning to smoke, I had kept cigarettes there. Mother kept binoculars there, a pencil, a pad of paper. She wasn't just a buzzard lover. She wanted to remember what they did, how many were in the sky at once, and so forth, like Thoreau. I let my hand lie in there touching Mother's things that had meant nothing to me when she was alive. "Mother's bird-watching junk." And I could have been up there with her learning with her when she was alive. And I would have been, too, I think, except for Father, who made me *his* child and not hers. But above everything that she loved, birds, the new moon, me (I now believe), she loved Father.

I went back up to the platform very early the next morning. The cops were both there, not even pretending to watch. Sleeping like hounds, twitching and grumbling with dreams. I stayed quiet until sunup. Then I called down to them.

They hopped out of their sleeping bags with only their shorts and undershirts on. Before they grabbed for their pants, they grabbed for their holsters.

"Put on your pants and don't shoot," I said. "I'm Eugenia Calloway. I've found some of Mother's things up here I'd like to have."

"There is nothing up there," the first one who finished said. "That platform has been gone over with a fine-tooth comb."

"They're not on the platform."

"What are you doing up there?" the tall Sherlock Holmes–looking one said.

"I am being where Mother was."

"How did you get up there?"

"Climbed," I said.

They'd been sleeping like skunks, so what could they say? They had to say something.

"It's forbidden."

"Why?"

"That's none of our business. Or yours."

"I'm not trying to break the law. That's why I told you what I'd found. I could've sneaked it out."

"What did you find?"

"I didn't take the stuff out. What I can feel is Mother's binoculars."

"Out? What's it in?"

"A hole in the tree."

"You come on down," the boss cop said. I came down the ladder as if I'd gone up that way. Carefully, too, like a clumsy young lady. The plump cop, agile like me, did the climbing.

"I don't see anything," he called down.

"Feel around in back of the big tree," I told him.

He began to bring out objects—binoculars, pencil, notebook, a package of Life Savers, some Kleenex, and the big plastic bottle with just a few red capsules rattling around in the bottom.

Down on the ground, the two cops looked at their treasure trove, especially the plastic bottle.

"Is this medicine your mother took?"

"She didn't take any medicine that I know of."

"Seconal," said the tall man. "Sleeping pills. Did you ever see this before?"

"You don't have to answer," the plump cop assured me. "Anything you say can be used against you."

"We oughtn't to be saying anything ourselves."

"Nothing being said is official. This isn't a big city. We're all neighbors here, so to speak. This girl's father relieved me of a kidney stone once."

"I've seen the bottle before. It was in the medicine cabinet. Father took a sleeping pill sometimes when he'd been working too hard and was too strung up to sleep."

"Was it full or empty when you last saw it?"

"Almost full. Father was no drug addict. I don't think he took a pill once a month. You can ask him," I said.

The scholarly-looking cop, now that he had his pants and jacket on, was leafing through Mother's notebook. It was a plain flappy-backed twenty-five-cent book. The binoculars were expensive, but the notebook was small and cheap, big enough to hold buzzard facts, but small enough to fit snugly into the hole.

"Your mother was quite a buzzard authority," he said.

"Yes, she was."

He came to the last page that had been written on, about two-thirds of the way through the book. He stood staring at the page he had come to. The plump cop and I stepped closer to have a look. The page was blank except for two words. Three, if you count "good-bye" as two. It looked like mother's handwriting—and it didn't; her writing, if she was writing in the dark. Or was sick. The words were, "Good-bye. Hello."

"Everything else is buzzard stuff," the tall man said wonderingly, as if he had been reading a cookbook that suddenly started to print obituaries.

"I think we'd better get this into town," said the Dr. Watson of the two.

One should have stayed, I thought, to guard the platform if that was what they'd been doing. Maybe they thought the platform, wasn't so important any more. Whenever they thought, they got on their motorcycles, leaving me, their sleeping bags, and the buzzards stirred up by the noise of their cycles and circling wildly, alone in the clear early-morning air.

The funeral was three days later at ten in the morning. Mr. Olmstead came over at nine with a big spice cake his wife had made and four combs of honey. He kept bees and he always brought Mother honey because he said that without her trees his hives would be empty. Eucalyptus honey is a little strong, deep amber colored, but very good if you don't use too much. Mr. Olmstead looked like a Pilgrim Father, tall, wrinkled, and worn to the bone. He was a rancher trying to make a living ranching. He and Mrs. Olmstead and Mother liked each other. The Olmsteads were bee fanciers the way Mother was a buzzard fancier, and they made jokes when they got together, saying that they were going to talk about the "birds and the bees"; which of course they really did.

I suppose I showed my amazement at the amount of honey he'd brought. And the size of the spice cake.

"We thought you'd need it for the folks who'll come in for lunch after the funeral."

I hadn't planned to have folks in for lunch. "It don't need to be a sit-down affair," Mr. Olmstead said. "But your mother's relatives will be here, and they'd like to have a cup of coffee and talk, I expect."

And Mother would like them to. "It's better the way things have turned out," Mr. Olmstead said. "Not good. Nobody could say it's good to die at thirty-eight, but it's better this way. I'm glad for your sake."

"It's the way Mother wanted it," I said.

The funeral was just a graveside ceremony. Mother had been born a Catholic; I don't know how much she'd lived a Catholic—more than I knew, perhaps. Perhaps her sticking to Father had been as much a part of her Catholicism as anything else. Anyway, no matter what she was born or how she had lived, she was being buried a Catholic. And if you have to be taken down from the birds and the trees, that is a good way. The ceremony seemed bird-old; and the priests were black as buzzards and red-nosed in the chilly morning air.

The burial ground is an old one on the hillside beside the first adobe church in these parts. It's not much used any more. The tombstones bear the old Spanish and Mexican names Yorba, Sanchez, Ortega, Sepulveda, Novano. Now there would be a new name: Inez Souza Calloway.

There were twenty-seven people there. Half of them, almost, were Uncle Eloy's family. I stood with them. Uncle Eloy had got the whole Soboba works: squat body, round face, small steady eyes, dark skin. I stood as close to him as I could. He was a good man, a school-bus driver, and my mother had loved him dearly. When he took her picture, her love for him showed. The Olmsteads were there, of course. Smith was there. Mr. and Mrs. Fosdick. Father's lawyer.

Father never once looked at me. I looked straight at him. I wanted to catch his eye. I don't know what I would have said with my eyes had I had the chance. But I didn't get it. He kept his head bowed and his eyes on that box of bones. He knew why he was there instead of in jail; and he knew why she was there. Knowing these things, I suppose he couldn't look at me.

It didn't make me sad to have Mother's bones buried. Her flesh had gone where she wanted it to go. And I think she might even have been glad to have those old words said above her bones. After the casket was in the ground and the earth placed on top of it and the words about dust and earth and ashes had been said, I did what

Mr. Olmstead had suggested; I asked people to the house—the Olmsteads; Uncle Eloy's family; Mr. and Mrs. Fosdick. I didn't ask Smith, but he marched right along with Uncle Eloy's kids as if all that talk about buzzards had made him one of the tribe.

I didn't ask Father either. After everything was over, he did look at me. And I knew, from that one look, that he would never again set foot in that house. He walked away from the graveyard fast, so fast that his lawyer, Ted Hughes, who is shorter than he is, had to trot to keep up with him.

I looked one last time at the grave. After a Santa Ana has blown itself out in the fall, it often clouds up to rain. It was doing that now. The first fall rains in California are a benediction. Everyone loves them. "Rain, rain," I said, like Mother talking to the new moon.

My cousin Gertrude Souza was waiting for me. She is fourteen years old and about six inches taller than I am already. She wears miniskirts.

"I never saw anyone buried before," she said.

"Neither did I, Gertrude."

We walked toward the cars together, and she said, "We are first cousins."

"From now on," I promised her.

# There Ought to Be a Judge

THE GIRL WATCHED and listened, and afterward she remembered. At the time, it was nothing so much: a rainy night, a boy hunting for some people he had lost, and then, after drinking the whisky her father gave him, speaking of them. At the time, she only watched and listened; later, the lonesomeness set in.

It was a warm May night; at dusk there had been a light rain, and now at nine there were bursts of distant thunder. The windows were open, and the girl could smell the laid dust and the wet lilacs. It was the kind of night when young people think something should happen, and the girl let the new petticoat, in which she was setting insertion, lie on her lap while she listened; but there were only four sounds, and none of them said, "Now he comes," which is the sound for which girls listen. Her father's breathing was a steady noise, and the flick of turned pages in the book he read came regularly, too. Besides these there were the distant rumble of thunder and the wing flutter of two moths circling the lamp. Since no more was to be heard, the girl picked up her sewing and added to the room its final sound: that of the delicate clip clip of her thimble against the needle.

The boy entered without knocking. The room was a hotel sitting room, and there was no real need to knock, but most people did.

"Is this the Kokomo House?" he asked.

Her father looked up from his book. "That's what the sign says," he told the boy.

"Are you Jacob Suttle? The proprietor?"

"I am."

The girl could tell that her father was feeling a little testy, but the boy didn't seem to notice it. She saw at once that the boy had foreign blood of some kind; his black hair had that high gloss pure whites don't often have, and a penny laid against his skin would have been lost. He was a big fellow, but lean through the face so that the bones below his eyes caught the light.

He walked over to her father's chair and said, "Has a man by the name of Elias Overfield been here?"

Jacob Suttle closed his book on his finger. "No," he said, "there hasn't."

"Nor a girl by the name of Missouri Overfield? A tall girl with red-brown hair?"

"No. No Overfields, man or girl."

"Look it up," the boy said. "Look it up in your register. You might've forgotten. They came north. I figured they'd reach Kokomo the third night."

"Son," said Jacob Suttle, "there's been just five people stop here this week, all men and none Overfields. That's an unusual name, and I'd remember it."

"I figured they'd be here," the boy said, and the girl saw he was going to faint, but he managed to land in a chair instead of on the floor. The upper part of his body fell across the center table, and if her father hadn't snatched the lamp away, it would have been sent flying.

"Get the whisky, Hannah," Jacob Suttle said, but the boy sat up and said, "I'm all right."

"Do as I tell you, Hannah," her father said, and the girl brought the whisky bottle and two glasses, and her father poured three or four fingers in each glass. The boy held his glass in his hand for a while, staring at it, then tossed the drink down his throat as if he were pouring it out the window.

"That'll make you feel better, son," Jacob Suttle said. "That'll make you forget your troubles." But it didn't. It made him remember them.

"There ought to be some place in the land where there was a judge," he said, "who could tell you exactly what was right and what was wrong, and I would go to this man and tell him everything and let him judge."

"Well, son," Jacob Suttle told him, "I'm no judge of right and wrong, but you can tell me if you want to."

The boy poured himself another tote of whisky. "For three days," he said, "I've been thinking how a stove poker would feel in my hand and the sound it would make landing on that bony old head of his. One good big splintering sound, then the old fool would be quiet, keeping his mouth shut for the first time in his life. No more preaching for him and no more ruining my life."

The boy reached again for the whisky, but Jacob Suttle put the bottle on the floor. "You'd ought to think twice before you talk murder that way."

"Murder," said the boy. "If I could tell someone who knew right from wrong, he wouldn't call it murder."

"Listen, son," said Jacob Suttle, "I can see you're not used to whisky, and more 'n likely you're saying things you'll blame yourself for in the morning. Now I've got a room here where you can rest, and by daylight things'll look better."

"If you don't want to listen . . ." began the boy.

"What's your name, son?"

"Joseph Fane," the boy said.

"Joseph, if it'll ease your mind any, I want to listen."

Jacob Suttle took a match out of his vest pocket, put it where he'd left off reading, closed his book, and laid it on the table. The girl settled her needle along the edge of the insertion, folded the petticoat she was making, and listened.

"I'm the teacher at Maiden Creek," said Joseph Fane, and the girl understood that was a place the boy thought they'd know, and she saw it somewhere to the south, a white building shining in morning sunlight, and, inside, Joseph Fane, dark and grave, instructing his pupils.

"This was my first year. The Saturday before school opened, I was cleaning the place, tacking pictures on the wall, writing exercises on the board. When I'd finished, I walked down to the branch to wash up before going to my boarding place for supper. It was about sundown, and the sun slanted through the willows along the branch bottom. It'd been a hot afternoon; birds would tweet once or twice, but night bugs and tree toads hadn't opened up yet. I was washed and standing looking up at the school in the quiet when I heard hoofs in the beech mast along the woods trace.

"First I saw just a patch of white now and then as the horse came opposite a place bare of leaves, and finally the whole horse and the girl who was riding him. Missouri on Old Moon.

"Look," the boy asked, "do I sound drunk?"

"No," Jacob Suttle said, "I wouldn't say that."

He asked another question. "There's got to be a first time, hasn't there, that a man meets the girl he's going to love?"

Jacob Suttle nodded. "I wouldn't deny that."

"The first time," the boy said, "could be at an oyster supper and she sluicing out the oyster stew. Or hoeing corn with the evening sun shining through the little hairs on her arms. Or maybe he'll see her first walking down a dusty road at nightfall holding the hands of her little brothers, and calling to their old dog, who's run off to the wood lot. Those would be all good ways, but if a man could choose, how could he choose better than to see her come through green beech trees riding on a white horse?"

The girl listened for her father's answer, but Jacob Suttle said nothing, so, her heart beating fast to be speaking of love, she herself said, "Yes, that would be a good way," and she saw that the boy heard her voice with surprise, as if only then realizing there were three persons in the room.

"I walked up the rise," he said, "and met her before the school-house. I asked her to light down, but she wouldn't. She had to get back to cook her father's supper. They lived alone and he depended upon her. She told me she wanted to start school on Monday. She'd graduated last year from Maiden Creek but couldn't go off to school because of being her father's housekeeper. 'I hear you've got a box of new books,' she said. 'If it's agreeable to you, I'd like to go another year and study out of them.'

"I told her she could. I told her I'd give her special studies from these books so she wouldn't have to go over work past and done. So she thanked me and slewed fat Old Moon around and rode back down the trace the way she'd come."

I wonder, the girl thought, was she a person like me? If it had been me on Old Moon, would he be speaking of me now, saying she was a small thing with a big braid of yellow hair?

"I've covered many a page with poetry about Missouri," the boy went on, "but the first I ever wrote, that starts

> *She had the dark and windswept beauty*
> *of the hills from whence she came,*

is as good as any. There was something wild and free about Missouri's looks. Indoors, she'd always lounge against a window looking out, and outdoors, she'd always be lifting her eyes to the clouds or treetops. Her hair was brown, but under the sun it would light up like a bonfire, and her eyes were the color of the sand that lies in the bends of Rush Branch."

The girl leaned forward as if she were saying, Look, look, there are other ways of being pretty, too; but the boy went on about Missouri.

"There was nothing about her I didn't love—except her father, and for no good reason, and maybe what I say now is hindsight. He was a short man, wide as a door, with tow-colored whiskers. He was a good farmer and stock raiser, out early and late with his crops and beasts. He was a smooth talker, except that sometimes he'd put a word in a sentence that didn't make sense there. But discounting him, everything about Missouri was to my liking—every single thing— the way she had of taking up the carpets in her house and dousing out the whole place with hot lye water so's the house always smelled like clean-scrubbed wood, and the way her face would mirror what she was reading, so if you knew the book, you could always tell by her look what part she was at.

"And Missouri loved me and was to have married me this summer. And that," the boy said, "is enough to say of our lovemaking. A man's lovemaking is about all he's got in this world to call his own, for sure. I wouldn't tell more to help my cause with any judge in the land. If he couldn't see from what's been said how beautiful Missouri was and how I loved her, more wouldn't help."

The thunder was fading away; the moths, unable to kill themselves because the girl kept small pieces of screen on top of all her lamp chimneys to save them from the flame, still fluttered hopefully; a light gust of wind shook the roof.

Jacob Suttle looked across the table at the boy. "Nothing here," he said, "so far as I can see, to make you want to lay a stove poker across anybody's head."

"That's to come," the boy said. "Old Man Overfield always had a hankering after protracted meetings. He never went up front or made any manner of profession, but he'd sit on a back bench, and when the preacher said, 'Brethren, we've all sinned and falled short of the mark,' he'd groan and say, 'Amen to that, brother. Amen.'

"Did you ever hear of the revival preacher Jerd Smith?" the boy asked.

"I've heard the name," Jacob Suttle said.

"Last week Jerd Smith was holding meetings at Bethel. Old Man Overfield was set on going, and Missouri wanted to go, too. Missouri wasn't seeking salvation, but she likes to see people and to join in the singing. So on Wednesday night I drove them over in my buggy.

"The church was bulging with people, and we had to find seats nearer the front than I'd like. The big hanging lamps overhead were aswinging a little and that coming-going kind of light didn't make people's faces any prettier. Then out from a side door, tripping and treading, came this Jerd Smith, dressed in a black coat and wearing trousers so tight you could see his leg muscles work as he walked. His red hair was shoved straight back from his forehead, and his face was white like that of a man who is never in the sunlight. His eyes had a faraway look, as if he'd just come out of the Lord's presence and could barely see us here on earth yet. He leaned over the pulpit, and in a voice so quiet and gentle you had to strain your ears to hear it, he made some announcements.

"Everybody was sitting on their chair's edge looking up at him. Was this the man they'd heard about? The man who'd had more 'n one woman talking in tongues, and who'd leaned over an old farmer saying, 'Confess, brother, confess,' until the farmer'd owned up to a long-forgotten killing? He was that one, and they knew it and they judged him like a storm by the silence that comes before it.

"Then, still quiet, he gave out a song to sing, and he led it low and sad. Next he read his text, 'Repent ye, repent ye, for the kingdom of God is at hand,' slow and yearning at first and then bearing down so that the repent ye's clanged like a plowshare hitting stone. People were beginning to get the shakes now, some moaning, some crying out, others kneeling by their chairs with their faces hid.

"Mr. Suttle," the boy said, "it was in my mind to get out of there then, and I'd be willing to admit to any judge I did wrong not to do so. Something put it in my mind to clear out, but there I set and didn't break away, and that was wrong. Instead, I looked at Missouri,

and she was far away, the ruckus going over her head. But Old Overfield was leaning forward, his face red and his eyes popped out like a
man about to have a stroke. I laid my hand on his arm and opened
my mouth to ask him if he wouldn't like to go out for a breath of air,
but he pushed me off and said, 'Keep your hands off me. I ain't fit to
touch.'

"Then this Jerd Smith starts the song that ends up 'Why not now,'
and every time he said the word 'now' he tossed his songbook to the
ceiling, where it made a sharp crack like a drumbeat. Then he'd stop
his singing and tossing and say low and sweet, 'Why not now, friend?'

"It was when he was doing this that Old Man Overfield jumped to
his feet, grabbed Missouri by the arm, and before I could make a turn
to stop him, ran toward the front shouting as he went, 'Got to tell the
Lord. Got to lose my burden.' "

Jacob Suttle looked over at his daughter. "You go to bed, Hannah.
Get on, now. You should've been there an hour ago."

Hannah knew what her father was thinking: that the boy was going
to say something she shouldn't hear, and Joseph knew it, too. "What
do you take me for?" he asked in a voice curling out like a shaving.
"A man like Jerd Smith, rejoicing in sins? A man like Elias Overfield,
gone soft in the head? I'm not going to tell you what Old Man Overfield had to say. That old sin, long ago done, repented to till the poor
old coot wasn't the same as other men. No, sir, I've got no mind to
tell you what Old Overfield had to say. Too many people's already
heard that. No, sir. That belongs to Old Overfield. Ask him, if you've
got a mind to hear it."

Jacob Suttle said no more about going to bed, and the girl leaned
back in her chair.

"But I have got a mind," the boy went on, "to speak about Missouri. Her father led her up there under all those eyes and shouted
out the things he had to say. He was happy, I reckon, ranting and
foaming, and people hanging on his words, but my Missouri, she
who'd always held her head so high, never down-dropping or woebe-
gone, there she stood. And I was so near to her in feeling I could tell
how even her bones felt crushed, ready to mix themselves with earth,
never walk upright again, never answer to any certain name. What
her father was saying was like a dream to her, the way a sickness

when you're young's forgotten as soon as you put a foot out of bed. And there she had to stand while every person lived it all out again in her father's words.

"I tried to get to her, but they held me back, and finally a few came to their senses and tried to quiet the old man—but not Jerd Smith, not that preacher. He stood there, his white face twisting, saying, 'Praise God, praise God,' and it struck me that like as not one reason he liked preaching was because he could taste all manner of sin that way, without taking any blame himself.

"It was when he reached down to bring Missouri up to a place beside him on the platform—make a holy show, as they say, of her— that I broke away from those who were holding me. I don't have any idea what I was saying, but they yelled blasphemy at me, and some-body clunked me on the head.

"This was the last I knew. When I came to, the meeting was over and Missouri and her father were gone. And I don't blame Old Man Overfield, or Missouri for going with him. How'd they hold their heads up thereabouts again after what Overfield had confessed about the two of them. The man I blame is Jerd Smith—and if I don't find Missouri, he's got to answer to me. And there's no judge of right and wrong in any land who'll hold me to blame for what I'll do."

The boy stood, and Jacob Suttle rose, too, urging him to stay the night and take some rest, but the boy wouldn't hear of it. "I've got no time to lose," he said. "I've had word of a couple like Missouri and her father working northward. I'll head for Peru and maybe catch them there."

"What's to come of your school?" Jacob Suttle asked.

"The school?" the boy repeated, as if surprised that any thought should be given to it. "The country's full of schoolteachers, but I'm the one who loves Missouri." He picked up his carpetbag and walked, swaying a little, toward the door. The girl stood, her sewing in her hands, watching her father bid Joseph Fane farewell. Jacob Suttle came slowly back into the room, slowly turned down the lamp, then with a sound like a sigh, blew it out.

"Headin' for Peru," he said, "and nothing but two swallows of whisky to go on."

The girl heard him stop at the bottom stair. He spoke musingly, as if he had forgotten she was his daughter, as if she had become another person, a real person to him.

"Reckon he'll ever find her, Hannah?"

She answered him like a real person. "No," she said, "he'll never find her."

She stayed for a while stock-still in the warm darkness, then put her sewing on the table, took up a match from the cup beside the lamp, and went to the mirror which hung in the panel between the two windows. She lit the match and held it so that her face was reflected white and soft in the shadows. She had never before regarded herself so closely.

Was it a face that could be remembered? Did it lie like a pond lily upon the dark and shining surface of the mirror? Would he possibly remember it, saying another way would be to see her the first time, sitting small and quiet, her sewing in her lap, listening to the sounds of a May night?

Would he? She went to the still-open window and leaned out. There ought to be a judge, and he would surely see that she would never have left Joseph Fane. No matter what had been said or who had heard it, she would never once during her whole life have left his side.

# Gallup Poll

WHEN THE PRUNE SEASON is over, Nick and I go up to the city to look at the people. That is our real need, to let our prune-conscious minds see faces once more; remark on eyes and hands, observe the motions they make, the messages they convey; imagine the worlds they inhabit. Imagine the fog- and wind-swept apartments, the grassy peninsula estates, the sprawling homes of professors' families across the bay, all filled with people who have never seen an unpackaged prune.

After we check our bags, we go straight to the St. Francis cocktail room. Perhaps you've never been in it. It's really a funny room, though you don't notice that at first; at first, only the people and the soft lights and the drinks: Dubonnet rubies, Daiquiris like bleached emeralds, and rubies and topazes together in the Old Fashioneds.

You see yourself, too . . . after a long absence, in the very beginning you see, more than anything else, your own progress. The clusters of laughing people—women with their coats hanging carelessly over the red leather chairs; the men, papers folded, forgetting the headlines for thirty minutes. They're all there, but in the beginning strictly as background for you.

But after you've found your seat and are no longer a person arriving, you notice, once again, the room itself. The ceiling is the most peculiar, really. When first you look up at it, you have the feeling you might be on the wrong side of the bed, Beauty-rest mattress over you instead of under you. Then after the second drink you see what that ceiling is really like: it's like the lid of a de-luxe coffin. All that richness; you'll probably never see the like again until . . . Well, forget that.

"Old coffin lid over me again," I said to Nicky.

"Over us all," Nick said.

"Men don't know it, though," I told him. "Not the way women do."

Not the way I do. Some may, I suppose. Next to us were two men drinking wearily, their legs stretched out hampering traffic.

"I had a letter from Bob," one said. "He's at Fort Ord. Don't know how long he'll be there, though."

"How old is he now?"

"Twenty."

Beyond the two men were a man and a woman. They were so unaware of anyone except themselves that they invited inspection as a picture does; their intensity, their absorption in each other placed them on a plane emotionally remote from us, so that it was possible to watch them as if they were acting a scene from some formal and half-remembered play.

I went on to look at other people. I was greedy for faces, and before I went back to the prune trees I wanted to see them all, not just this one man and woman; or the three in uniform standing at the bar, or the girl with the dreaming face, or the sad, orating businessmen.

Nicky still stared at the engrossed couple.

"There's nothing so remarkable about those two," I told Nicky defensively.

The man was pleasant-looking, dark and young, you couldn't honestly say more—though his face was what women call "poetic." That doesn't mean he looked like Keats, or had Byron's proud, sultry front. It only means his face made you feel the way poetry does; as if you were hearing a voice you loved read, "O western wind, when wilt thou blow," or "My heart is like a singing bird."

The man was very young, twenty-two or -three at the most; he had on the uniform of a Navy flier, with those ribbons and stars that denote service, and perhaps awards, but which I can never interpret.

The woman—perhaps her face was poetic, too, though I don't ever remember hearing a man say that of a woman. Although they write poetry about women.

"There is the face," I said to Nick, "which could have launched the thousand ships."

Nick had been looking, too. "It has, it has," he repeated dreamily.

Well, yes . . . it had . . . but it could again. Couldn't it? Couldn't it?

"You don't call a woman in her thirties—even her middle thirties— old, do you, Nicky?"

My husband smiled at me. "No," he said. What else could he say? I'm thirty-eight. "That's the flower. The crown and flower, really. But it's fifteen years beyond twenty."

"Her hair—that color's real," I told him.

It was a kind of silver mist. Mist with the sun shining through it. Can you remember Jean Harlow? It was hair like that. She wore a black dress, plain, simple. That was right. It would have been a pity to distract the eye by a single ornament from the lines of her figure; but, though her dress was right, and hair and carriage distinctive, still there was something . . . disheveled about her.

The boy was doing the talking; she was doing the drinking. Not for the drink's sake, though.

"She drinks the way Mays chews gum," Nicky said.

I nodded. The boy was leaning toward her talking, talking, his dark mobile face flushed and intent. All his words were there in the room— only there were so many other words, too. I wished for some kind of word filter so that I could sort his out.

"She won't say yes, and she won't say no," Nicky said.

"They're talking about how it'll be when he's gone."

"She's not talking," Nicky reminded me.

"She's thinking, though. Thinking how it's going to be when he's gone. No phone ringing. No car in front of the house. Nothing but the letters."

Now and then the woman let the tips of her fingers touch the boy's brown wrist.

"She'd better cut that out," Nicky said.

She did. She leaned over and picked up her gold purse, opened it, and took from it what looked like a little leather engagement book. Slowly she began to tear out pages, easily and neatly, taking her time. The boy no more than glanced at what she was doing, then went on talking.

"He wouldn't care if she took down her hair and started combing it," I said.

Except when she took a drink (she used both hands for tearing out the pages), she tore out pages; and even while she drank, her free hand kept working on a loosened page.

"What's she up to?" Nicky said.

"I don't know. Maybe saying 'yes, no, yes, no.' Whichever the last page is will decide it."

She came to the last page. Then she took out a little silver pencil and began writing; on each page she wrote something—not a word, more than that, a sentence, maybe two. Not a single word, anyway. When she'd finish one page, she'd fold it neatly and write her sentence, or perhaps two, on the next. The boy finally reached over in a mechanical sort of way, his eyes still on the woman's face, and picked up one of the folded sheets. She unloosed it from his fingers and smiled at him. It was the sweetest smile, the first time I'd seen her smile since I'd been watching her. She wasn't tense any more; it was as if—oh, I don't know—as if there wasn't anything more to worry about. She spoke to the boy, evidently to ask for another drink, because he ordered another Martini—what she'd been drinking. The boy wasn't talking now, just watching her write, as if the movement of her hand was as beautiful to him as dancing, or flying.

"She's the French teacher at Balboa High School," Nicky said. "She's writing out exercises in the conjugations of irregular verbs for her classes tomorrow." He leaned back satisfied.

"What the hell," he said suddenly, sitting up straight.

She had left the table, the little pack of folded papers in her hand, and was passing them out, one to each person. She did it calmly and naturally, as if she were giving people napkins at a cocktail party. The people who got the pieces of paper unfolded them, read, stared at the woman, read again, fell into a buzz of talk.

The boy just watched her, completely bemused. Whatever she did was right with him.

Nicky acted bored. "Gallup Poll woman," he said. "Do you favor bombing Hanoi?"

I wasn't bored. I was afraid she was going to pass the papers only to the people on the left of her table. If she had done that—I don't know, I think I would have gone over to someone and asked to see his paper. I felt I had to see what she had written; but finally she started circling our way.

Nicky stopped pretending. "Oh Lord," he said, "I hope they hold out."

They did. She gave Nicky his first.

"Thank you," she said in a low voice.

"Thank you," she said to me as she put a slip in my hand. I looked at her closely. Her eyes were gray. She didn't seem to see me at all.

Nicky and I finished reading at the same time, and without a word exchanged slips. They were identical. Each read, "Will you please write here how old you think I am? Don't flatter me."

Nicky said, "Thirty-six."

"No." I told him. "No. Not a day over thirty-four. And don't write that. Can't you see what she's doing, Nick? She's said to herself, 'If they think, if the majority of them think, well, not more than five years older than he is, I'll say *yes*.' "

"Sure, I see that," Nick said. "That's why I'm going to write the truth. I'll give her the benefit of the doubt. I'll write thirty-four instead of thirty-six."

"Write twenty-five," I said. "That's all she needs to be happy. They'll go away, they'll be happy together. Just your making a change in one number, writing a two instead of a three can do that. Such a little thing to do to make a woman happy."

"Aren't you happy?"

"I am. I am happy. That's why I want her to be. Look at her."

She was sitting at her table with a numb, waiting look, drooping a little, as if frightened at what she had done.

Nick was counting. "She'll be happy, all right—if this poll can make her. There's twice as many women here as men. She'll get her vote, all right."

"Write thirty, anyway," I said.

Nicky didn't say anything. He just wrote. I wrote "Twenty-five." Then I crossed it out and wrote "Twenty-four."

One of the men at the table next to ours started collecting the papers. "No use keeping the poor girl in suspense," he said. I could see what he had written on his paper. "Thirty-four."

"He's jealous," I told Nicky. "he can't bear to think she'd prefer a boy."

"It's not that," Nicky said. "It's us versus that ceiling, versus that tufted lid, trying to hold it up, keeping it from closing down on us. All of us, the boy *and* the woman. Defying it, squeezing out one more hour."

The man made the rounds and put the little stack of papers, folded again, in front of the woman. She opened them slowly, as if afraid of what she might read, putting one to the left, one to the right of her glass. The stack on the right was soon much the higher. She didn't even bother to look at the last three or four slips, but leaned across the table, put her hand in the boy's. You wouldn't hear a word she said, of course, but what her lips said as she leaned toward the boy was, "Yes . . . yes . . . yes."

"They'll be in Reno by midnight," Nicky said mock glumly, as they left.

I laughed. "In spite of you."

Nicky put his hand in mind. "Not in spite of *me*," he said. "I wrote twenty-two."

That was overdoing it. I know our ten years' difference shows, but I couldn't have borne it if he hadn't given her a vote of confidence.

"Ceiling unlimited," Nick said, lifting his glass to the elaborate coffin lid.

I looked up, and it really did seem as if the lid had lifted, that there was more space and time to live in. "Here's to their happiness," I answered. "And ours," I added under my breath. It's not a subject Nicky likes me to harp on.

# Alive and Real

S EE WHAT THE CHILDREN are doing, will you, Meredith?"
Meredith Johnson sometimes had the unworthy suspicion that
his wife thought up useless little tasks for him simply because the sight of him comfortably established and at ease while she
still had work to do irritated her. Now, no sooner had he finished his
Sunday lawn mowing, fuchsia watering, and car washing, and settled
himself in his deep chair by the radio, prepared to read and listen,
than Alice called to him from the kitchen. After a little, above the
clatter of her preparation of their late lunch, she called again.

"Meredith," she said, "Meredith."

Meredith made a slight noise in his throat to let Alice know he had
heard her. Nothing, he hoped, either positive enough to commit him
to any action or so contradictory that it might precipitate a discussion
as to whether or not the children needed looking after. They didn't,
he was certain. They were six and eleven years old, and what harm
could possibly come to them on a twenty-acre suburban orange ranch,
he could not imagine. Had they lived in the city, or had the ranch
fronted on one of the busy boulevards, the situation would have been
different and no one, then, would have needed to remind him to keep
an eye on them; but the orange grove was as safe as, or safer than,
any wire-enclosed, sand-bottomed play yard, and besides, he had seen
Tim, Sara, and the three Benton kids less than half an hour before,
headed, with some contraption they had made, toward the arroyo at
the back of the ranch.

He had stood holding the hose with which he was sprinkling the
fuchsias and watched them until they, somehow aware of being
watched, had hastily put a tree row between themselves and him. He
thought he had never seen a picture that represented half so well
childlike innocence and that complete absorption that only children
can achieve as his two and the Benton three made, hurrying, brown-
legged and shining-haired, down the quiet tree rows. Earlier, the May

morning had been hazed over with a light shimmer of mist off the Pacific, but the sun had burned through it, leaving air, trees, even mockingbirds, towhees, and children—it seemed to him—unusually bright and fair.

The sun caught the fine spray from his hose and set it adazzle; hummingbirds darted toward it, uncertain whether it was flower or flood; drops hung from the hibiscus at the side door, more resplendent than jewels. The quiet Sunday morning lay like a calm hand upon the land. He, Alice, the children, the ranch, the morning itself, and the whole of their wonderfully lucky life together were, for the moment, caught up and suspended out of harm's way, a transparent and shining bubble.

Ordinarily, life was fragmentary. It was shreds and particles. It was tasks, obligations, worries, pleasures, all so mixed and, while each persisted, so sharp and pressing that one never caught sight of the whole life. Above all, it was not often that one was able to catch sight of oneself in the center of that small and satisfying world. The experience for Meredith Johnson was so unusual and so beautiful that he tried, by concentrating upon it, to prolong it. Remember, he told himself, remember. Remember the bubble, and inside it the five kids, your two lanky redheads and the Benton three, round and brown as buttons; remember the house and Alice in it, softly opening and shutting doors; remember the orchard, trim as a garden, and you yourself here sending this multicolored spray down onto the flowers. For a minute he was able to hold not only this vision of his own small world, but also the millions of others like it, stretching across the earth, all the beautiful, shining, private, early-morning bubbles of the earth's thousands of families. Then the children, with that sense of guilt that watching breeds in the watched, turned about suddenly, saw him, thrust whatever it was they were carrying in front of them, and darted behind a tree row.

The whole vision had broken down then. With that sudden movement, the fragments had returned; but even now, half an hour later, something of that feeling of wholeness still persisted, so that he wanted to sit quietly reflective, not go whooping about up and down the tree rows in order to be able to report to Alice whether the kids were playing the new game they had invented last week, called "I patent the jewels," or had reverted to their old stand-by of "run sheep run."

He cocked an ear toward the kitchen and heard Alice moving about there once more, rhythmically, refrigerator door opened, refrigerator door closed, faucet on, faucet off, and he thought he could perhaps get his radio on quietly enough not to bring her in. He knew exactly which station he wanted, so there need be no hunting, nothing but the preliminary click and the smooth voice of Austin Loomis gaining in power as the radio warmed.

He clicked his radio on, and though there was actually no way this could be done more quietly at one time than at another, this, he thought, is one of the quietest clicks I ever managed. As Loomis's voice poured smoothly into the sunlit living room, he gentled its accustomed resonance to a kitten's purr. The actual dropping of the bomb was some hour or more away, but Loomis was already there, already describing with his easy but never merely facile eloquence the island, the peaceful Pacific waters surrounding it, the disposition of the doomed ships, even the reactions of the tethered and probably doomed goats.

Meredith Johnson was privately (except that he sometimes mentioned the fact to Alice) of the opinion that he had a sharper visual imagination than most people, and now he thought he could not have seen better had he been there what Loomis was describing so vividly: the sparkle of light on the white crests of breaking waves, the flash of planes overhead, the dark impassive growth of the tropical island. And he was able to feel, too, the waiting tension of all those gathered there: the young men (the doers) and the old men (the planners).

He supposed that perhaps unconsciously his awareness of what day this was had made, by contrast, the felicity of his moment of seeing so great. As a day of wind and rain makes the hearthside snugger, so knowledge of that experiment half across the Pacific had enhanced his own feelings of peace and safety. After a time he scarcely listened to Austin Loomis's voice at all. The sonorous words became no more than a dark, forbidding weather of the kind best suited to make his surroundings assume their most cheerful aspect.

Outside the big picture window, the palm fronds moved with the gentle, homesick sound of a gate closing. Meredith, listening, remembered the farm in Kansas where he had been born. They had had a gate weighted with window pulleys there which had had just such a melancholy creak when closed or opened. He hadn't heard the creak of that gate for twenty-five years; and when he had, at the age of ten, the sound hadn't seemed in the least melancholy. It had been, instead, very cheerful, saying, "Someone is coming," and, hearing it, he had sped to a window, if it were winter; or if it were summer, to the gate itself. Now the dry complaint of the palm fronds, the squeak of the remembered date, the somber drone of massed planes, as Loomis enlivened his descriptions with some realistic sound effects, merged in Meredith's mind. Kansas, California, Bikini: they were all there together.

Listening and remembering, he had forgotten Alice, and she startled him when she came in from the kitchen, busy with her familiar postkitchen exercise of rubbing lotion onto her hands. She evidently had known all the time that he had not gone out to see about the children, for she glanced at him without surprise, then walked across to the picture window.

"Has it happened yet?" she asked.

Meredith had had no idea that Alice knew about the experiment.

"Half an hour more," he said, "if they're prompt."

Alice finished her hands and turned away from the window. "You'll just have time then to go out and see about the children." She sank down into the big chair by the window and let her head rest against the chair back.

"You tired, Alice?" Meredith asked.

She looked tired. She had a fair, oval face, which weariness easily smudged, and the soft skin appeared darkened now, almost dented, as if something in the day had bruised and hurt her.

"I don't know why I should be," she said. "I've put twelve cupcakes in the oven and one pot roast on the stove. Nothing in that to do in a healthy young woman." Alice smiled, and all the smudges were erased, and the dents were smoothed out. Then she sighed, leaned back again in the chair, and folded her hands, as if with one hand she carried sympathy to the other.

"I do wish you'd go check up on the kids, though," she said, not opening her eyes.

"I don't know what in the world you think could happen to them," Meredith told her. "They're far safer out there than . . ."

Alice interrupted him. "I'd much rather go myself than argue about it. It would be a lot easier."

"Okay, okay," Meredith said, and snapped off the radio.

Now that he was going, Alice was ready to give in a little, too.

"I admit it's just curiosity on my part," she said. "but they're up to something, Tim and Sara and those Benton kids."

"Up to something," Meredith repeated in the tone parents keep for that special something.

"Oh, no," Alice said, "nothing like that. It's just that they've got my curiosity aroused with all their mumbo-jumbo and darting around hiding stuff."

"Hiding stuff?" Meredith remembered how quickly the children had got out of sight whatever it was they carried that morning.

"Something they've been making," Alice said.

"Well, there's no harm in that," Meredith told her. "Kids are always having secrets."

"I don't think there is any *harm* in it," Alice said. "I'm just curious. But Sara thinks there's harm in it. She wouldn't say her prayers last night. She said, 'I'm too wicked to pray to the Lord, Mama.' And she wasn't a bit happy about it either. You know how much Sara likes praying to the Lord."

Meredith did know. Whether this was because the Lord, of all the people Sara knew, was the only one who never said, "Hush up for a minute, can't you, Sara?" he couldn't say, but Sara's nightly prayers were long and thorough.

"The poor kid," he said, and got to his feet. "They must really be up to something. I'll creep up on them."

"Oh, you don't need to creep," Alice told him. "They don't actually think we're able to see them, anyway. They'd carry this stuff they were working on—cardboard, strings, I don't know what all—about one-third hidden, right past me, as if either I couldn't see two feet beyond my nose or, if I could see, I wouldn't have sense enough to make out what they were up to."

"Maybe they're making kites," Meredith suggested.

"It'd take more than a kite to cut off those nightly talks of Sara's,"

Alice said. "No, it's something they think is wrong—but think we'll never catch on to. Because they don't believe we're actually real and alive. Us grown-ups," Alice explained, smiling at Meredith, "us parents."

Meredith stood up, slapped his thigh. "I'll teach those kids who's real and alive around here," he said. "I sure will."

"Well, hurry back," Alice told him, "or you'll miss it."

"Miss what?" Meredith had forgotten, for the moment.

"Oh," he said, remembering. "The big blast. Don't worry. I'll be back for that. I wouldn't miss it."

He went down the road for a distance before cutting in through the Benton orchard. In that way, without any creeping, he could come unobserved upon the children, where they did their usual playing, in the eucalyptus grove on the Benton side of the arroyo.

The day had turned very warm and still. He slowly walked down a tree row, sizing up the Benton crop as he went. It was lighter than his own, though there was not a thing in his own heavier set of oranges for which he could give himself credit. He and Benton had exactly the same kind of soil, sprayed, fertilized, and irrigated at the same time, in the same way. It was just a piece of luck. Still, he rejoiced in it somewhat. It was a part of the morning's special pleasantness. Just as when he had watched his kids and Benton's, earlier, he had thought, I'm glad mine are the rangy redheads instead of those brown dumplings of Benton's.

At the far edge of the Benton orchard he was brought up by a sound, a sound that rippled his scalp a little. Had he been walking through an African jungle instead of a California orange grove, he would have thought himself about to come upon a small but earnest band of savages, chanting grace before they popped the missionary into the pot. What he heard, and stood listening the better to hear, was not singing; but then it was not speech either. It was a chant, he supposed, a child's approximation of the liturgical and ritualistic; and it was not so much the raw, thin, naked sound of the children's uncertain voices as something in their voices that stiffened the beard on his unshaved Sunday face.

Standing there in the quiet orchard, listening, he thought, Maybe the kids are right; maybe I'm not real. Then he did what he had said he would do. He crept up on the children, moving from tree to tree, whatever noise he made covered by the sound of their own ungodly and barbaric nonsense. He stopped not six feet from the children and, peering from behind a big ragged eucalyptus, was able to see them all plainly. There they stood, the five of them, his own Tim facing the other four and acting as some kind of conductor, or master of ceremonies, for their chorus of gibberish—if it was gibberish, for Meredith had too much to take in all at once to be certain about every detail. First he heard the children, then he began to see them, and last of all to see the object toward which the children lifted their strained, attentive faces. Seeing it, his first thought was that they were playing at lynching a man, for suspended from the lowest limb of one of the small eucalyptus trees was a cardboard man, or something in the shape of a man anyway, something with a trunk and head, with two arms and two legs—but with a tail, too, and horns; sharp, curved, evil, and unfaunlike horns.

Meredith Johnson caught his breath. This was no man. This was the Prince of Darkness himself. The cloven-hoofed devil, the Black Prince risen to power. This was devil worship and these were his communicants. No wonder small Sara had given over praying to the Lord.

Tim had about his neck a sacerdotal scarf, and he intoned the services from a small black notebook, and his congregation answered with frightened conviction; Sara, her face white, hands clenched; twelve-year-old Joanie Benton, her eyes narrowed, skin taut across her cheekbones; the two younger Bentons, round eyed and sweating.

"Most holy devil," his congregation quavered in reply.

"Prince of Darkness."

"Prince of Darkness" came the shrill echo.

"Ruler of earth."

"Ruler of earth."

"And all above the earth." Tim's voice cracked here a little, and there was a slight break in the rhythm of the service, but the children whispered, "And all above the earth."

"Most holy devil."

Meredith gazed in pity. Perhaps it was funny, this devil worship, but he didn't think so, and it certainly wasn't funny to the kids. He remembered how, when he had been younger than Tim, he had himself made a brief trial of tree worship. The tree he had chosen had been a grisly old black locust, the sole tree left standing in what was called, because of it, the "tree field," on that distant Kansas farm. He had gone out at dusk, knelt down, and said, "Our tree which art on earth, hallowed be thy roots and branches, thy treedom come. . . ."

It had almost killed him, that prayer to the tree, and afterward he had been sick at his stomach and had lain on the ground and hoped that God would smite him so that the memory of his unfaithfulness might be blotted out. Still, it had been a trial he felt he must make, a thing he must find out about God and trees, no matter how much he suffered. And it hadn't been funny, and if what the kids were doing now was funny, then death was funny, and sin, and the worn-out heart, and the broken earth.

"Most holy devil," the children answered.

"In dust . . ."

"In dust . . ."

"We humble ourselves before thee."

In dust they humbled themselves, Tim leading them. They went down on their knees with the sudden bonelessness of children and laid their foreheads in the dust.

As the children so abased themselves, Meredith moved forward to say something, do something—just what, he was not sure, but something that would put an end to their painful play-acting.

What he did do he was not then, or ever afterward, able to account for; he was not able to understand what in himself or the day could possibly have prompted him to step behind that cardboard figure so that when the children lifted their heads from the dust, they saw not the harmless devil of their own construction but a new devil, a devil alive and real—one whose gaping mouth was filled with sharp white teeth and whose empty eye sockets framed eyes bright and menacing.

But unexplainable as it was, that was what he did, and that was why the children, his own two and the Benton three, screamed so on that fine Sunday afternoon.

# I'll Ask Him to Come Sooner

AT FIVE-THIRTY the pressure of the day in a sanatorium is at its greatest. The day's routine is over, but the night with its routine has not yet come, and there is left a bare, uninhabited space in which the mind cannot live with ease. It would seem, Flory thought, that all of us together, wishing, desiring ardently, could push the clock's hands ahead, could accelerate the sun—but no, the next hour and a half, when the sad day that began so long ago, in darkness, with the night nurse making her final rounds, is not yet ended, must be endured.

Flory's supper tray still rested on the bed, pinning the bedclothes across her thighs. She lay looking at the respectable curves they made. A year ago they were planks, two-by-fours, now they looked like young trees, solid and rounded. A year ago, she thought, I was sick, much sicker than I knew, but I was good, and I was believing—and now, whom do I believe in? Whom trust? Not myself, surely.

A year ago, far advanced tuberculosis had meant nothing to her. It simply sounded like the ultimate of its kind, and that of course was what she had always wanted in everything—A plus on her papers, jumbo olives, the forty-foot diving platform, fires that roared to the chimney top. When she had arrived at the Vineyard, she had felt infinitely scornful of those in bed with incipient TB, and those with moderately advanced cases were as dull as ditch water to her—tepid, tepid. She had believed the thing to do was to be desperately ill, hopeless indeed—go to bed, obey the doctor's orders, and get up cured. And by some miraculous chance, that was about the way she had done it. Oh, Jesus, she thought, how foolish and believing I was then, and how sick and how good.

The doors of the nurse's dining room began to bang. Bates never pretended that this TB business was anything but hell for all of them. Bates's attitude, indeed, was that the patients had a slightly better time than she, for they, by one exit or another, often escaped, got clear of the Vineyard Sanatorium completely, while she stayed on.

She trod in, a solid clump-clump. No tippy-toes or whispers for her. "Well, Miss Shaw," she said, "I see there wasn't any of this delicious meal you could resist. Stewed tomatoes, baked potatoes, tapioca pudding, all down the hatch. I thought Herman did a particularly good job on the tapioca tonight, didn't you? Every fish eye as transparent and rubbery as in life."

Flory wished she could say, "Bates, stay with me. Stay till seven. I need you, Bates, until a little after seven"—but she couldn't do that. The sanatorium recognized only physical needs. Bates would stay if she had a hemorrhage, or if her pleurisy needed taping; but this—this other didn't exist for Bates and the Vineyard.

"Bates," she said, "can't anything be done about the time from supper until seven? Couldn't it just be done away with, Bates? Couldn't we just eat our suppers and then have it night, time for bed lights and books?"

"That time," Bates said, matter of fact as ever, "is for you to rest in. That's what you're here for, Miss Shaw. Complete bed rest. No TV's then, no books, no writing—rest, and if you like that sort of thing, think."

But what about, Flory wondered. What are we to think about? Remembering is not for us—to recall a life other than this, the life we had before, when—Oh, no, no. It is too painful, it is scalding. And to plan. What can we plan? As far as the next X ray. That is as far as we can get in planning, and to do that takes a crazy optimism; we all die between X rays. There is only this world, this little private world of the sanatorium, of the present, that it is safe to think about. And it isn't safe for me any longer.

"What do you think about, Bates?" she asked.

"Well," said Bates, "I was thinking about the lobster I had last night at Lucca's—and about going home to Maine this summer."

"Remembering and planning," Flory said. "Remembering and planning."

"If you've finished with that tray, Miss Shaw," Bates said, "I'll take it along. This is Wednesday night, you know—husbands' night. I've got to get all the wives into their best bed jackets. The husbands will be here at seven sharp—all except Marguerite Delaney's; he'll be late, as usual, I suppose."

Flory laid her hand across her eyes and held her mouth firm.

Bates stood with the tray deftly balanced. "All you spinsters lie here and pine on Wednesday nights, I suppose, at the sounds of billing and cooing going on. But you're really damned lucky. Not a wife here doesn't have an eight o'clock temp on Wednesday evenings."

"Yes, that's right," Flory managed to say. "We lie here and pine, but we're damned lucky."

"You don't look it," Bates said, and went out, catching the screened door neatly with her toe so that it closed without sound. When she had gone, the heavy silence of the after-supper hour settled down like ashes about the sanatorium, until it was buried deep as any Pompeii. Soundless as any Pompeii, forgotten as any Pompeii.

Flory lay neatly in her bed, her supple brown hands on top of the blue spread, loose and easy, her breath coming evenly from the diaphragm, as she'd been taught, and tried to send her mind into paths where no pain lay. If any such be left to me, she thought. Through the great glassless windows of her room she could see the homeward-bound cars thread the boulevard of the valley below—black rods of movement, they were, from that height, like tubercle bacilli moving along some superbronchial tract. Must I see everything in terms of disease? she thought. And then for a moment, noting the homeward-bound cars, she saw her own apartment as it had been at five-thirty, when her workday had ended: the curtains, lifting, lifting in the languid little wind that blows down city streets at that hour; the sun gilding her books; a few petals dropped, while she had been away, from the apple blossoms her mother had brought in from the ranch. Her apartment—ah, but it was hers no more, the books packed, the flower bowls empty, stacked in some dusty box. She was gone out of that world of the living to this middle world, this place where you could look neither forward nor backward, this place where even the present had become intolerable to her, this September evening, this husbands' night.

When I first came, Flory thought, I believed in everything. When Dr. Hedges brought me my X rays and had to pull my blind down at the head of my bed so that I could see them properly, he always put his hand on my breast to balance himself—and I always decided it was an accident and was embarrassed for him. And when the janitor boy said he would put a special mixture on my floor for two dollars a month extra, I believed him and paid it.

I thought I would make friends here, too—yes, I believed even that. I knew no better. The first winter in the infirmary, where none of us ever left our beds, the others were only voices, only a variety of coughs. Then, when the rains were past and our beds were pushed onto the long porch, I saw the faces behind the called messages, the coughs choked down, the midnight crying.

Helen Morton, from Virginia, whose face was as soft, gentle, and dusky as her voice. Helene Broka, with her little snubbed-up hazelnut face, laughing, laughing, and saying, "You'd have thought they'd have thought of the sour grapes that would be picked here when they called this the Vineyard Sanatorium." And Laura, with her tender, eager brown eyes, who was determined to live. Laura, who was so reasonable, who never complained, drank twice the amount of milk required, and never once lifted the heavy bag of shot from her chest. But she didn't understand she wasn't living in a reasonable world, or fighting a reasonable disease. Felice, Laura's opposite, her red hair and feverish blue eyes blazing. "To hell with the rules," she'd say. "Where have they ever got us? What He most enjoys"—He wasn't God, but some power, evidently more powerful than God, who planted TB in people's lungs—"is to see us follow the rules, deny ourselves everything, and get worse and worse."

I didn't know any better than to make friends with them all, love them all. Then I got stronger and stronger—every picture better, sed rate going down and down, cavities closing—and every single advance was like a disloyalty to them; was like marching ahead and leaving wounded companions behind. They were happy for me, but there was a shadow in their eyes when they said the congratulatory words, as if I had selfishly grabbed something of which there wasn't enough to go around. No, they couldn't get well with me, but I had to die with each of them, each one.

And even then I didn't learn. When I left the infirmary, when I came here to Culbertson, when I could walk every noon to the dining hall for my dinner, then you would have thought, wouldn't you, that the time had come to be a little realistic, a little literal?

But no, then I had to talk with Marguerite, to long to do something for her. I walked by her room every day on my way to dinner. I noticed her first because of the beautiful bed jackets and dressing gowns she wore. All red—every shade of red; deep velvety reds, almost black; orange reds like changing leaves; pink reds like a cat's tongue. They were so beautiful and brilliant you hardly noticed the girl inside them. She was so pale it was almost as if she wasn't, and I wondered at her wearing them. Blood reds in a sanatorium where there is already too much sight of red. Usually she had her hair braided back from her face, but once in a while it lay uncombed on her pillow, a great fan-shape swirl of black silk. She used to smile at me as I went by, and then one day she said, "Hello," and I sat down for a minute to talk to her.

"I've been noticing your beautiful bed jackets," I said. "They're gorgeous. You must like red."

"No," she said in that little whispering voice she used not to stir up a cough, "it's my husband who likes red. I wear them for him. I hate red. You know how it is when you have fever—you like cool colors. Mist blue, mint green. Don't those colors sound good to you—and cool?"

"Yes," I said, and noticed her face had, already so early in the day, the transparent white of high fever. "But red's a good color for your hair."

"That's what Delaney says."

"Delaney?" I asked.

"My husband."

"That's an unusual name."

"Oh—it's his last name. His first name's . . . well, he doesn't like it . . . so everyone calls him Delaney. I wish Delaney could see you."

"Why?" I asked.

"Because you look so well. Delaney says it's foolish to stay here—that I'm thinner every time he sees me. But I think I ought to stay. The doctor says it's my only chance. Though I don't want to, of course. It would be a lot easier to give up and go home with Delaney. I worry about him."

"Isn't he well?" I wanted to know.

"Delaney, sick!" She started to laugh, but a cough stopped her. I tried not to see or listen as she used her sputum cup. "No, it's not that," she said. "He comes up every Wednesday night. You must have seen him—he has to walk by your room to get here."

"Maybe," I said, "but I wouldn't know him."

"He's the best-looking one," she said, and managed a little twinkle. I thought then that was just a thing wives say—here in the san, where a male anchor in the outside world might seem their only hold on reality. I didn't know it was the literal truth, an understatement. Not here alone, not here alone, Delaney, is your face most beautiful.

"You were pretty sick when you came here, weren't you?" she asked.

Yes. Yes. Now I knew what to say—exactly. When I first came, my greatest joy was to watch those fat, those stalwart ones walk down the path to the dining room and to be told the story of their progress—she came with two cavities; she had empyema for six months; she's had a thoracoplasty—and then, then to see them waddle and laugh. They were the articles of my faith.

"Yes," I told her, "yes, I was."

"How much did you weigh then?"

"A hundred and three."

That made her gasp. "Really," she said, "really. Were you a hemorrhage case?"

*She* was. I'd been told.

"Yes," I said, "yes, I was," and felt like a veteran with wound stripes.

"And now?"

"Nothing for a year."

"Not even streaking?"

"No, nothing."

Her little face, almond shaped, and pale, like an almond blanched, somehow became focused, concentrated itself, came forward out of hopelessness into living. I was her faith made manifest. Her belief, living, breathing, in a blue robe. "Stay here, get well." Ah, it could be done—it had been done.

"I wish Delaney could see you," she said again. "It's so hard to stay here when your husband wants you to come home. To think you should stay and yet . . ." She broke off. "But it wouldn't do any good to get well and then find out . . ." No, she couldn't say it. "It's so hard for Delaney to get up here. Wednesday nights are the only time he can come. He works every day, and Sunday he always plays golf. He has to think of his health, too, you know. Oh, it's awfully tedious for him, and sickness upsets him so."

I began to hate this Delaney. Crazy name. Upsetting Marguerite, dividing her mind, dressing her in red. Jesus, Jesus, I'd like to tell that handsome boy a thing or two, I thought.

How long afterward was it when I had my stiff neck? It doesn't matter. It was almost seven, I know, and I lay trying to lose myself in the movement of the leaf shadows across my white wall, anything so as not to look forward—into uncertainty—or backward—into the lost, when Bates came it.

"I'll massage your neck," she said. "I've got a few minutes. Why didn't you tell me? I wouldn't have known anything about it if Mrs. Delaney hadn't mentioned it."

"It's nothing," I said. "How's Marguerite this evening?"

"Worse every day," she said. "I've just finished helping her get ready to put on her act for her husband."

"Act?" I asked.

"You know—makeup, quilted red-velvet bed jacket, perfume, nails done. He wants his senses titillated. All five of them. And she's fool enough to want to do it for him."

She kneaded my neck with her hard fingers until I sweated with pain—but I was glad even for a stiff neck, some harmless pain which could be thought about without danger. At seven the husbands began to arrive—most of them had been waiting below at the gardener's cottage for the gates to open—and within five or six minutes there were no more footsteps on the graveled paths, only a murmur of conversation from the rooms about me, and an occasional baritone laugh, forced and abrupt.

Until suddenly there was a woman's sob, a great, heavy, racking cry, as if a sorrow had been held back until it had mounted into a wave no barrier could resist. Crying is no novelty here—even that anguished cry, I thought I had heard before.

"God damn that Delaney," Bates said.

"Is that Marguerite?" I asked. "Is he making her cry?"

"Yes," Bates said. "Making her cry as he does every Wednesday night by being late. She gets all dressed, and waits and waits. Listens to every footstep, sees the others go by. They only have an hour together anyway—and he's always fifteen to thirty minutes late. By the time he gets here, she's cried all her makeup off, is coughing so she has to use her sputum cup every other word. And Delaney doesn't like that, so he sits and looks at her coldly."

"Does his work keep him?" I asked. "Is there any reason?"

"No reason except his damn cursed selfishness," Bates said evenly. "He's some electric company official. Worked up from a lineman, Mrs. Delaney said. Used to shinny up poles. It's God's pity he didn't fall off one."

Every time Marguerite's crying quickened, Bates pinched my neck muscles harder—but I didn't mind. I felt just as she did.

Then a black Porsche came through the Vineyard gates and swung into a vacant place among the cars at the foot of the hill. A tall man jumped out, and by the time the car door slammed, he was up half a dozen steps.

"That's Delaney," Bates said. "Pretty early for him."

I sat up in bed; he had to walk past my window to get around the corner to Farnsworth, where Marguerite lay. After he climbed the steps, he was out of sight under the wisteria pergola until he came out just across from my room. It was August then, and the evening light, though it had lost all color, was as clear as shadowless water. Delaney came through it like a shadow himself, dark as night, dark as Marguerite. He was all in white, a white rough sweater, and white ducks, as if he'd been playing tennis. By some chance he was looking directly into this room, directly at me. He didn't smile or lower his eyes, but gazed and gazed—and so did I.

"Well," said Bates when he had passed, "selfish-looking bastard, isn't he?"

"Yes," I said. "Yes, he is." And he was. He had that fine, indrawn look of one who thinks of himself alone, a look of reality and concentration. None of himself was lost in regard for others, but all adhered closely about a central core of self-regard. Those who go about loving others, suffering for a cat smashed by a roadside, or a town bombed, or a man imprisoned, lose something of themselves. They spread themselves thin, loving—and suffering. Ah, but not Delaney, not Delaney; he was solid—solid and real. Solid in this separate world where almost everyone, through sympathy, loses his identity.

But I hated him, too. As much as Bates. Hated him for making Marguerite suffer. For I am a tubercular, and all tuberculars are, in a sense, in league together against those who are well.

Yes, I hated that easy, domineering stride, the black curly hair, the crooked nose, the long torso of the wrestler, the feet toeing in a little—even though these were the things I had always loved most in a man. I hated them in this selfish Delaney.

Wednesday evening after Wednesday evening I heard Marguerite crying—and Wednesday evening after Wednesday evening I saw this black Delaney come striding casually, giving me long, slow looks as he went by. And I gave him long looks in return, looks that said, You selfish beast, don't think that I don't see through you and scorn you— late to your wife and eying another woman as you come.

"Look," I said one night to Bates, when it was almost too dark to see Delaney go by. "Some night I'm going out and give Delaney a punch in the nose. Yes, I am. I'll give him another dent in that crooked nose of his. I'll trip him as he comes up the steps, push him over, and he can lie there in the dark with a broken leg and learn what it means to lie and suffer alone."

"You seem to think a lot about Delaney."

"No," I told her. "No, it's Marguerite I think about. I talk to her almost every day, you know. She cries so much. She's so thin. Someday, Bates, you'll go to her room and find only bones, bird-thin bones inside her long red robe. That's all you'll find, Bates. That and her long black hair. And it will be because none of us has cared enough to help her."

"Help her?" Bates asked. "How could we help her? I get her into her red bed jackets every Wednesday evening. I dampen her mascara. I brush her hair. I tell her to take it easy."

"It's not that, Bates," I said. "She'll die dolled up as fast as dowdy. Someone's got to tell Delaney to come sooner. That's what she can't bear—waiting for him. Lying there waiting for him. Thinking every step she hears is his, rising to it, brightening her eyes, all of her blood gone to her ears to listen—and then the footsteps going by. I'm going to ask him to come sooner, Bates. I've been thinking about it. I'm going to ask him."

And Bates said, "I can see you've been thinking about it—you tell it as if you were the one who was doing the waiting."

It was something to think about—and I had thought about it. How I would hear his car grind to a stop on the gravel, late. Hear the door bang, the footsteps of a man hurrying, whose weight never touches his heels, and how I would be hiding in the deep shadow of the pergola—gotten out of my room without a single nurse's missing me. How I would take the edges of his coat in my hands (he wore a coat now the nights were cooler). I would take the rough coat edges close enough to my mouth so that he could hear me whisper, "Listen, Delaney, you must come sooner." I thought about it a thousand times. I would do it for Marguerite. I never got further in my thinking than to say, "You must come sooner, Delaney." After that the picture blurred, the film broke.

But still I didn't do it—though every night I heard Marguerite cry, I said, "I'll ask him to come sooner." Then my new X ray showed no progress since the last one—fibrosis standing still; and next door in Olney the engineer from South America died. He'd only been here two months—and had malaria as well as tuberculosis—but he'd seemed well until his terminal hemorrhage. He waved to me when he sat up while the nurse made his bed. He'd sent me over some of his books and I'd sent him *Bliss* and *The Garden Party*, and I'd planned how, when we were both better—oh, yes, I was a little in love with him, not having said a word to him, having seen only his sun-blackened face, his sun-bleached hair. But you must love someone here, be real to someone besides yourself. Then, the whole of one night, the lights on in his room, the cars coming and going on the driveway below— and in the morning his mattress and pillows hanging out of a window in the sun. And that evening Marguerite crying and crying, waiting for Delaney's footsteps.

All week I thought about it. Death touching all about me, and I not lifting a finger to stop it, as apart from life as if it had already left me. So I said a week ago, "Tonight, tonight I'll tell him to come sooner." I was waiting in the pergola, just as I'd planned, deep in the shadows where the wisteria leaves are still thick overhead. I heard the car door slam and the footsteps springing just as I had known I would hear them; and just as I had known I would, I pulled his face down close so that I could whisper. "Delaney, you must come sooner." His hands against the small of my back were heavy, and when he held me close against him, he was as solid and real as I had known he would be, and his face against mine was as I had felt it before—in a dream, perhaps. "Sooner?" he said. "Sooner? It's you who are late. I've waited weeks."

There was a sound of cars on the driveway below. Flory sat up in bed. "Oh," she said. "Bates ought to stay with me tonight until a little after seven. I need her until after seven." But even while talking to herself, she was getting out of bed, getting into her dressing gown, and listening, listening for the sound the Porsche would make as it slid to a stop on the graveled parkway of the san.

# Hunting for Hoot Owls

I REMEMBER the exact hour at which George accomplished what he had set out to do two years before. We were living where we do now, in Saskatchewan. It was three-thirty on the afternoon of Thursday, October 28, 1958. In this latitude, at that hour and in that month, it was almost night and nearly winter. There was still light, of course, but it slanted in like the indirect lighting of modern homes with nothing visible to proclaim its source. It was a clear cool light, compact, as if shrunken by the cold. There were still a few bleached leaves on the willows down by the lake; not many, and the few that were left were dropping fast. There was no wind, and the leaves dropped straight down as if weighted with lead. It made me feel deaf to hear no sound when they landed.

I remember all this so distinctly, I suppose, because of what George said when he opened the door. I had been standing at the window of the living room (also bedroom, dining room, and, at the far end, kitchen) watching George come up the path from the spring. The lake, at the upper end, was freezing over, and, as it did so, more and more small animals came down to the spring to drink. The spring, too, would soon freeze, but meanwhile George had gone up after lunch to box it in so that for the time it lasted it would be a little clearer than what we had been drinking.

Even though I didn't then know what George was going to say when he came in, I gazed at him like a mind reader filled with premonitions. I mean I really looked at him. After thirty-five years of marriage, a wife only occasionally sees her husband. This doesn't mean that he's as unexciting as the furniture, any more than that he's one with the stars. It does mean that most eyes, after a certain amount of seeing husbands, be it of furniture or stars, no longer see with much curiosity or attention.

But I really saw George that afternoon, as he came up the pathway. It was the change of background that made him visible. In Southern

323

California amidst other schoolmen, George didn't stand out—but here under the immense gloomy trees, with the black lake behind him, George looked terribly human, noble even. Carrying his tools, whistling "Annie Laurie" under a sky threatening snow, ringed round by the trees which constantly watched us, George looked accomplished, and daring, to me.

George came in, put down saw, hammer, and the coffee can in which he had carried the nails. Then he took off his mackinaw and hung it on *its* peg beside the door. (*Its* peg because when you live in one room you have to be orderly; otherwise, socks turn up in the coffeepot, and the coffeepot turns up in bed. Such confusion may be exhilarating for the young, but at our age George and I find it ugly.) So the mackinaw went on *its* peg. Then George, like an Enoch Arden returning after a twenty-year absence, took a solemn searching around the room. Satisfied with his inspection, he went to the front window, folded his arms, and gazed out toward the lake.

"Agnes," he asked, "do you know what day this is?"

I knew. But I forestalled his saying the word I didn't want to hear. "Thursday, October 28, 1958," I told him.

George paid no attention to this. "Boxing in the spring was the last job I had in mind to do."

"Fine," I said, and hurried on. "Before I forget it, the Clasbys called. They want you to call back."

We have few neighbors, and the few are far away and mostly without phones. A phone call is an event.

George ignored the Clasby's call. He turned away from the window and faced me; and he was bound, I knew then, to say the word I didn't want to hear.

"Agnes," George said, "what I set out to do two years ago is now done. I am now a retired man."

Now that's a simple word, and I suppose it occurs at least once in every issue of every newspaper and magazine published in the United States. And I know, too, that there are plenty of wives who don't, for various reasons, like the sound of that word. Some don't want to live on less money. Others don't want to be excluded from the social affairs that hinge upon their husband's jobs. And almost all, after being conditioned for forty years to their husband's absence, are made nervous by the prospect of having to live with him again. And this is perfectly natural. What would husbands think if *wives* suddenly announced that they were retiring from their housekeeping jobs and would, hereafter, spend the day with him in the office? The prospect would make a lot of husbands very uneasy, and nothing a wife could say about "greater companionship" or "time for her to let up a bit" would reassure him. Office routines, he'd feel sure, would just go to hell. Well, the home has its routines, too.

None of these fears bothered me about George's retirement. Since the death of George's mother, money has been no problem for us. The social affairs a schoolman's job open to him are duties for his wife rather than pleasures. A schoolman's wife is accustomed to having the PTA ladies, Junior Rally Committees, Citizens' Advisory Councils, members of the Taxpayers' League, the Scholastic Society, the Latin Forum, and winning basketball teams around the house; so she, unlike other wives, is in no need of being rehabilitated for a life with others after forty years in solitary. She has been well prepared for togetherness. Retirement will simply cut down on the numbers.

What she isn't prepared for, or what I wasn't prepared for, when George announced at the age of fifty-eight that he intended to give up his job at the end of the year, was the picture this called up of George's past life. George didn't have to retire; his contract had three years to run; a committee of representative citizens had waited upon him asking him *not* to retire. Still he was determined to give up his job.

"I will finish out this year only," George told them, "and that ends it."

To me, it was as if he had said, "I will commit suicide in seven months." Not that life without work seems suicide to me. But to retire in your prime from your life's work? What does that say? It says that you haven't been with your life's work, that you've sold your life like a bag of groceries. Oh, it's the saddest thing in the world, I think, this desire men have to escape their jobs. Sadder than death or disease, because these come to us without our choosing; and our work, we have chosen. That's why I didn't want to hear George say the word. That word meant that George had suffered in his work. It meant that he'd made a bad bargain, underestimated his powers, or misunderstood them, miscalculated our needs. Forty years at the heart of his life gone by! George had traded his life for his living.

I suppose I should have been glad, this being so, to hear that George was escaping, that he was throwing off his chains. Instead, I couldn't bear to know that they had existed.

"Retirement," I said to George two years ago, "is death without burial."

"No," George said. "Retirement is resurrection after death."

Death! This gave me a sick feeling under the heart. George had complained on occasion. Who doesn't? I do, and I've loved my life as wife and housekeeper. But I had no idea that what he had been doing every day was something he longed to escape from.

I said, "George, wouldn't you feel downcast to discover that I've hated the housework, the cooking and cleaning and washing and bedmaking I've done all my life?"

"Yes," he said, "I would."

"It's the same for me with you."

"No, it isn't. Work's no curse for women."

"But it is for men?"

"Certainly. Didn't you ever read the Bible? Childbearing is woman's curse. And they've got a built-in retirement clause for that. Men have to decide for themselves when they're through."

"Women are *sad* to be through."

"Would you like to be pregnant now?"

"At my time of life . . ."

"Exactly the way I feel," George said, "at my time of life, still holding down a job."

We had had a vacation house on Lake McClintick for ten years and had spent at least a month there every summer. It was to this cabin George had planned to retire; and it was here, with the spring boxed in, that George had declared himself, on October 28, 1958, to be, in fact, and according to plan, retired.

Now this was certainly something for which I had been prepared. What George said was scarcely news; nevertheless, I felt shock, the same kind of shock I experienced when my mother, who had had a long sickness, finally died. I had expected her death for two years, but when she finally ceased to breathe I could not accept the change. Death, I knew all about; but not a world in which my own mother did not return me look for look. It was the same with George. After he said those words, though I was prepared for them, I felt as a woman might who sees her husband for the first time after he's entered a monastery. He looks the same, but he is not the same. He has renounced something. Now I don't want to romanticize the two of us, George and Agnes, into another Abelard and Héloïse. I hadn't lost George as Héloïse lost Abelard, but the man without a job was not the husband I had known.

I don't know what George felt that evening. I should have asked him. But the strangeness of his being without work embarrassed me. It didn't seem delicate to speak of it. Perhaps he expected a celebration of some kind, a ceremony even. He had refused the usual farewell retirement banquet at home. Perhaps this was the time for it. We had creamed chipped beef and hot soda biscuits that night for supper. Dessert was canned pears. Really a little less than I usually manage. We finished supper, did the usual chores, read a little, and went to bed. We forgot to call the Clasbys. That was the first night I imitated the hoot owls.

Since September these big downy birds, more silent in movement than snow, had begun, in the deepening cold of the autumn nights, to call each other from the treetops. Actually, I don't know whether they were in the tops of trees or not. I never saw one, except at dusk, when there is still as much green as black in the darkness, and then the owls were flying. You see them by chance when they glide overhead, noiseless as clouds. But in the night they make up for all this quiet evening gliding with a bombardment of hoots; and they *sound* then as if they were in the tops of trees. I don't know why they hoot; whether they are courting, or complaining of the cold, or simply conversing. They *are* conversing, whatever the subject. One owl calls, then waits for an answer before speaking again. The answer comes, and so the conversation goes on. The sound they make is deep and hollow. It seems mixed with feathers. They are doing, I suppose, what I had heard coyotes do in Southern California. But the coyote's voice is lean, filled with sand and dryness and the big stretch of the deserts. The owls sound northern and are hemmed in by the millions of trees, and their voices have the soft echoing roar that a sound-absorbent ceiling gives.

I knew George wasn't asleep on that first night of his official retirement. We sleep in a double bed, and he was too unmoving to be asleep. So I didn't have to worry about waking him. I hadn't known that I had been wanting to imitate a hoot owl; but surely I must have wanted to do so for a long, long time; otherwise it wouldn't have seemed so absolutely necessary and natural to shape my throat and make an accurate owl call. Nor such a relief to do so.

My success amazed me. Could I, if I had attempted it, have been doing this all my life? Had I, from the beginning, had this power? Not only was my imitation accurate, but it had carrying power; for after the same wait owl gives owl, I was, miracle of miracles, answered. I didn't press my luck, though. I was excited enough to have kept on hooting all night. But owls don't do that, I thought; and if I was going to imitate owls, I was determined to do it right.

Next morning, as if in recognition of all the night's other transformations, the earth itself was transformed. Snow had fallen, and yesterday's world had vanished. We were in the midst of something new. In any case, with the new snow, with my excitement over the discovery of my unexpected ability, I didn't think as much as I had expected to about George's altered state. Also, while we were still at the breakfast table, the Clasbys called again.

I answered, and Ed Clasby said they had intended running over to our place for a little advice, but since their car had broken down, could we come to their place? I wondered why we couldn't advise them on the phone, but Ed urged, "if it wasn't too much trouble," that we come over.

The Clasbys, Ed and Edie, were young people in their thirties with three stair-step children, one to five, and an older boy of nine. Ed worked at the motel at the other end of the lake, which put up sportsmen, mostly fishermen, during the season. The place closed the first of October, and I don't know what Ed had been accustomed to doing in the winter. It was about what he was going to do *this* winter that he wanted to see us.

I always had the feeling that the Clasbys should have lived someplace where it was warmer, where it mattered less if the glass fell out of a window or a shoe sole wore through. They needed some hounds under the porch and a jug of corn likker to pass round. The Clasbys themselves appeared to feel no lack of hounds, windowpanes, or jugs. No one could have been more hospitable. Everyone in Saskatchewan keeps a pot of coffee on the back of the stove all day long and puts a cup in your hand the minute you set a foot inside the door. But in no other home do you have to step across, around, and over such a welter of misplaced articles. (I take it that *anything* on the floor except rugs, furniture, and feet is misplaced.) And the Clasbys really welcome you.

There they stood in the midst of disaster, as any housekeeper judges disaster, able to concentrate on welcoming their guests. I accord them the same admiration I would give to persons carrying on in spite of cyclone and hurricane.

Ed Clasby put a cup in my hands before I could get my mittens off. Maybe Ed really does hail from the Deep South. When I try to recall his voice, I hear the sweet prolonged relish for his own words that characterizes Southerners.

"It sure was good of you folks to make a trip on a morning like this. Don't think I don't appreciate it. Cletus, ram another stick of firewood in the cookstove." Cletus was the nine-year-old.

Ed and Edie looked alike; rather as if, not too far back in the pedigree of each, there had been a seal—the furred sea animal, I mean. The three stair steps were the same. Only Cletus showed a lack of seal blood. Some of his extra-human, washed-out appearance was no doubt the result of being surrounded by all those soft brown eyes, masses of soft brown hair, and plump softly sloping shoulders. Cletus was built like an icicle made of skimmed milk. He had broomstraw hair and wore it jagged, like an Italian actress. He was perfectly silent, but completely present. Cletus, as it turned out, was the reason we were there.

Ed came right to the point. He had the offer from a brother-in-law to go in with him in the air-taxi service the brother-in-law was setting up. Not only would this be to Ed's financial advantage, but Ed considered himself a natural mechanic. Being separated from engines had been for him, he said, the same as a musician's being separated from his violin or a jockey from his horse. I could see that this might be so, for, as Ed talked, he was tinkering with something out of his car. His fingers knew it so well he could work and talk at the same time, the way some women can knit and talk. What he was working on was the reason the car wouldn't run. Magneto, carburetor, distributor? I don't know. Anyway, something fair-sized and detachable. He had started working outside the night before and had had the car pretty well stripped down when dark came. Then, during the night, the snowstorm! He had left everything out there, as was his habit with engines, he said, in apple-pie order. It wasn't any trick locating his distributor, if that was what it was; but the smaller things were another story, to hell and gone under six inches of snow. He couldn't rake or sweep the snow away, he said (maybe he just didn't want to be bothered), because he'd send cotter pins and spark plugs flying. I'm making up the names of these small objects out there under the snow. I could write Ed; or, if I didn't intend to keep this away from George until I've finished, ask him, and get the proper names. But I don't think it matters. Engines probably have hundreds of nameable small parts. So do human beings; but who bothers, in writing of men and women, with listing all of their bones, glands, and organs? This may be the machine age, but I don't feel inclined to do for an engine what I wouldn't do for a person.

In any case, the point is that most of those parts *were* still out there under the snow, and that when Ed wanted another he said, "Cletus, fetch me a right-handed swivel bar." And Cletus would go out, and in a few minutes return with whatever it was Ed had asked for. Or at least I judge so, for never once did Ed say, "Cletus, didn't you hear me say a *right-handed* swivel bar?" Ed just took whatever Cletus handed him and went on with his knitting. I didn't give any thought to what Cletus did outside, because, while he was running and fetching, Edie was talking to me about their problems and telling me why it was they had asked us over.

But George interrupted our conversation. He was standing at a window, looking out into the yard. "Excuse me, Mrs. Clasby," he said, "but I want Agnes to see something."

I went to him, and George said, "Look at that boy out there, Agnes."

The thermometer stood at twenty and there was no sun. But out there in the snow, with no coat on, Cletus was fishing around in the snow as calm as a boy on the seashore in midsummer. "Fish" is the wrong word. He wasn't fishing. First, he sized up the snow at his feet in a businesslike way, then he put his hand under it, made one or two delicate moves, and pulled up something. He never pulled up something and had a look at it. He looked, felt, pulled, and started for the house with what he had.

"He works like a surgeon, doesn't he?" George asked.

"More like a magician," I said, for I had my doubts, for all his boasting, that Ed had left the car's innards in any very predictable pattern, kidneys opposite each other, stomach in the middle, and so on.

"In any case," George said, as Cletus brought up something the size of a darning needle, "that's a remarkable performance we're watching."

In spite of the performance, when Ed and Edie got around to their reason for wanting to see us, George said he'd have to think it over. What they wanted was for us to take care of Cletus while Ed teamed up with his brother-in-law in the air-taxi business. The reasons they gave for wanting to leave Cletus with us were understandable and even humane. There were no schools at Lucknow, where they were going, and it seemed a pity to take Cletus out of school. And there was an even more understandable reason. Cletus was no child of theirs. He was not even a relation. Ed's brother had married a divorced woman with a child, Cletus. The mother had run away from Ed's brother; and Ed's brother, who didn't care after that whether he lived or died, died. And in a most unfortunate way. He walked, whether on purpose or not, into a saw in the plywood factory where he worked. He was cut in two, Ed said, lengthwise.

I was horrified to hear this told before Cletus; but it was evidently an old story to him. Runaway mother. Runaway father, too, for all we knew. Stepfather cut in two lengthwise. Cletus never turned a hair. His nonchalance was remarkable. I suppose if you were to survive with the Clasbys, you'd have to learn to be nonchalant about a number of things.

"The reason we turned to you folks," Ed Clasby said, "is because George was a schoolteacher and is dedicated to learning. He wouldn't care to see a bright boy like Cletus done out of an education."

"George is retired," I said quickly. It surprised me how glib I could be with that word when I thought it was advantageous to use it.

There was no use trying to outglib Ed Clasby. "You ain't retired, Agnes," he said. "And at Cletus's age, most of the looking after him would fall on your shoulders."

This was, of course, God's truth. But it wasn't a very handy time to admit it. I didn't have to. George hasn't been an administrator for thirty years for nothing. He doesn't get maneuvered into a corner easily.

"We'll think it over, Ed, and let you know. When you planning on leaving?"

"A week, at the longest. Sooner if the weather moderates."

"Don't think we don't appreciate the confidence you've shown in us, Ed," George told him. "But this isn't anything to go into half-cocked."

So we left, leaving poor little Cletus like a parcel of goods put up for sale and not taken. I didn't feel any enthusiasm myself about taking on the care of a young magician who could find needles in snow-drifts. But he was human and so was I. I tried not to catch his eye.

Though I could've told him that if he wanted to live with us, not to worry. George had already decided to take him in. When George intends to say no, he says it. When he intends to say yes, he postpones. The consequences of any yes are usually greater than the consequences of any no. George always wants to think his yeses over—even though he knows he's going to say them.

On the way home I said to George, "Where will he sleep?"

"The couch in the kitchen," George answered. "I'll fix up a screen to shut him off from us."

George didn't make the least pretense, with me, of needing time to think things over. "Clasby was right about one thing," he continued. "The bulk of the work will fall on you—or would, if I didn't do something about it. Which I will."

George began that very evening to do something about it. He washed the supper dishes. I couldn't have been more surprised if he had started knitting little bootees. I didn't know that George *could* wash dishes. It wasn't that George had had any theories about "man's work" and "woman's work." It was simply that in former times he hadn't been around at dishwashing time. George, at the sink, made me feel that I was living in a topsy-turvy world.

I went to bed thinking about the day's changes and wondering about the changes that were bound to come. I didn't hear any hoot owls, let alone *my* hoot owl. I was more asleep than awake when George, who had stayed up puttering around in his newly assumed role of housekeeper, said, "Agnes, why don't you answer?"

"Answer what?" I asked.

"Listen," he said.

I listened. Somewhere very near, on tree, or rooftree, an owl hooted.

"Your owl's come down for a little more talk," George said. "He's waiting for his nightly pillow talk."

As George said this, the owl on treetop, or rooftree, let loose with his long soft roll of sound. There was no reply from any other owl.

"He's talking to you, Agnes."

Now it's one thing, spontaneously and without forethought, to have imitated a hoot owl. It's another to do it the second time, and at the bidding of a listening and waiting audience. You feel self-conscious. You feel you'll fail. You feel you'll make a laughingstock of yourself. It's one thing to call up spirits from the vasty deep; it's another to have them answer; and still another to be required to converse with them while your family listens. My voice stuck in my throat.

"Go on, Minerva," George said. "Hoot. You started this."

Minerva, goddess of wisdom, owl on her shoulder! That about silenced me. But then the owl, in the cold of the deep northern night, called again. No doubt I imagined it. Nevertheless, I thought there was a waiting note in the sound. And what waits can be disappointed. I answered, and there was, without the customary pause, an immediate answer. I was truly in touch with something. I forgot that George was listening. And to do him justice, he never made another sound to remind me that he was. I talked to that bird as I'd never talked to a human. If you say, "Naturally, you never hooted to a human being, did you?" you miss the point. Certainly I never hooted to a human being. And certainly "hoot" is the name given to the sound I made. Nevertheless, and whatever name you give that sound, I was speaking. I was speaking to what was roofless and wild, to what lived in the night and saw in the dark and fed on the living. I was able to say what I had never been able to say back at the bridge parties and PTA's of Southern California. Nor to George himself, for that matter. George was listening now, but I wasn't speaking *to* him.

The conversation which I had started self-consciously ended naturally. When I had had my say, the owl had apparently had his. There was one distant call; then if he spoke again, his voice was indistinguishable from those of the other night criers.

Before I went to sleep again I had a moment's misgiving about Cletus. What was he going to think of living in a house with a woman who talked to hoot owls? Because I knew I would want to continue my conversation the next night. It was a moment's misgiving only. I was asleep in a wink, and the next thing I knew I was awake, smelling frying bacon and listening to the sough of cookstove and heater, both drawing briskly. George, who ordinarily never put a foot out of bed until he smelled coffee, *was* making himself over. And I needn't have worried about Cletus and hoot owls, as I learned later.

He came to stay with us at the end of the week. George had required less time than usual to think things over, and the weather had moderated, so that the Clasbys could be on their way earlier than they had anticipated. Cletus entered our lives like a daytime owl, blond, reflective, and outspoken. It was soon hard to believe that we had lived so much of our lives without him. He had only two disturbing habits. One, we could do nothing about. He was, as I said, outspoken. Well, he wasn't just outspoken. When he spoke out, he did so in words George and I never used. I don't mean that he was either saucy or dirty minded. He said what he thought and he used the words he knew.

As an example of saying what he thought, one night when George was washing and Cletus was drying the dishes, Cletus said, "Who had this job before you got me?"

This might have sounded, if you didn't know Cletus, as if he were saying, "How did you get along without me?" That wasn't Cletus's intent. Information was all he wanted—and George knew it.

"Agnes did the dishes before you came. Washed them *and* dried them."

"And worked at her job, too?"

What Cletus called my "job" was a hobby I'd taken up after George started doing the housework. Before I was married, I had kept scrapbooks. Not the usual scrapbooks of a girl in her teens: football programs, party invitations, hotel matchbooks. I was never interested in things like that. Instead, I kept clippings from magazines and newspapers, pictures of celebrities, quotations from speeches, reproductions of famous pictures. I know this sounds stuffy; and I probably was a stuffy girl. But that's the kind of scrapbook I kept. I really thought of them as providing a picture of my times, and myself as a kind of Samuel Pepys with a paste pot. Colossal egoist! But what young person isn't? Naturally, after I was married, I hadn't found time for my hobby. But I hadn't been able to resist collecting items either. I put these, loose, into cartons, and through all our moving about, I hung onto the cartons. Now, with winter shutting down, with the housework taken over by George, I got out my scrapbooks again. Though I hadn't had time to fill them, I had never been able to resist buying a fine scrapbook when I saw one on sale; thus everything was at hand for the resumption of my hobby. I had George move the large workbench he no longer needed, now that he had finished his carpentry work, inside. It was a fine big table, large enough to hold two or three scrapbooks at a time. And to my surprise I found that I now wanted to write captions for my pictures, as well as paste them in the books. I wanted to say what I *thought* about those pictures of people and past events. So there I would be, when Cletus got home from school, seated at my big table, busy with pen, scissors, and paste pot.

I suppose it did *look* like a job.

"She didn't work at her job before you came," George explained to Cletus. "She did all the housework."

"What was *your* job then?" Cletus asked.

"I was the head of some schools."

"Like Mrs. Longnecker?"

Mrs. Longnecker was the principal of the two-room school Cletus attended.

"Yes. Except I had a couple of dozen schools under me."

"Why did they fire you?"

"They didn't. I retired."

"Retired?" Cletus asked.

"I stopped working—permanently."

"You're working now," Cletus said, "doing the dishes." And George was, grunting away as he scoured a baking dish in which the macaroni and cheese had burned. "And she's got the real job," Cletus said, nodding toward me, writing at my big table.

"That's one way of looking at it," George agreed.

Cletus concluded that conversation. "Looks like you got me just in time for the drying."

This is an example of Cletus's outspokenness, but not of his vocabulary. It's not easy to give an example of that, because words of that kind are only recently written down; but what follows illustrates it to some degree; also his outspokenness.

George drives Cletus three miles, morning and evening, to catch the bus which takes him to school, and back. One evening while Cletus was outside getting an armload of wood, George told me, "Mrs. Longnecker gave Cletus a whack across the hand with a ruler today. Left a considerable welt."

I was surprised. Cletus, according to his friends, was teacher's pet. "Why would she do a thing like that?"

George laughed a little. "She's nervous this week."

"Nervous this week?"

"Cletus says she's having the grannies this week."

"The grannies?" For a minute the word made no more sense than Chinese. Then I caught on, and I don't know whether I was the more surprised at the old-fashioned word or at Cletus's up-to-date knowledge.

"For heaven's sake," I said, "where did Cletus dig up a backwoodsy word like that?"

"He's a pretty backwoodsy boy," George said.

"Well, how does he happen to know so much about grannies and nervous, then?"

"They both happen in the backwoods."

We didn't try to do anything about Cletus's vocabulary or his outspokenness. He'd got his bad words by copying people who used them. We decided he would get his good words the same way. But his second habit, we did try to do something about. He had to get up every night. Now under ordinary circumstances that would have been of no consequence one way or another. But our bathroom was a privy back of the house a hundred feet; and the temperatures were sinking toward zero. Cletus didn't mind this nightly trip. He made it without a word of complaint. George was the one who complained.

George valued his sleep. What with hoot-owl conversations to listen to at bedtime, together with early-morning rising, he didn't like being awakened just as he had fallen soundly asleep. The noise wasn't Cletus's fault. Cletus naturally had to put on shoes for the trip. The floor wasn't carpeted. The door stuck, then squeaked, then had to be banged to get it to close tight. All this was repeated in reverse order on the return trip, squeak, bang, clop, clop; plus the rattling of the springs as Cletus, after his frosty journey, shook a while before getting warmed up.

On the night George decided that there had to be a change, I, the usually sound sleeper, was awakened by sounds I couldn't at first identify. They were outside the house, a muffled banging, an unending stomping and yelling.

I awakened George. "What's that noise?"

"Cletus," he said without a moment's pause. "It must be Cletus. I fell asleep before he came back." George leaped from the bed, raised the window, and shouted, "Cletus, Cletus, are you all right?"

The banging stopped. "Hell, no." The answer was faint, but firm.

"What's the trouble?"

"I'm locked in."

The privy had a wooden latch on the outside as well as the inside, and this had somehow fallen into place when Cletus entered. I don't know how long he had been out there. Thank God nothing was frostbitten.

But that decided George. "The boy has to have his own chamber pot," he said.

"There isn't much privacy," I reminded George.

"There's enough," George said. "Besides, we can sleep right through that. I'll drive you in to town today and you can buy one."

We bought one, or I did; though such a thing wasn't, even in that backwoods country, easy to locate. I might have been asking for a bustle for all the understanding I received. Maybe there's a more up-to-date word for it now. Maybe I just ran into some delicate-minded clerks. I got one, finally, at a secondhand store, by pointing.

Anyway, George thought we would have a good night's sleep that night. No shoes, on or off. No floorboards squeaking. No bedsprings clattering. No doors banging. He had given Cletus a searchlight with a real lighthouse beam so that there would be no occasion for any stumbling about.

But I was wakened after a few hours' sleep by cold air flowing under the covers. George was sitting bolt upright, a hand over his eyes to shield them from the crisscrossing beams of that blinding searchlight of Cletus's.

"Cletus!" he called. "In God's name, what are you doing?"

"I'm hunting hoot owls."

"What?" George asked, louder than necessary, irritated because he believed he couldn't have heard aright.

"I'm hunting hoot owls," Cletus said again.

"There are no hoot owls in here."

"I'm hunting them outside, in the trees."

"You can't see them from inside," George told him.

"I can see their eyes," Cletus said. "They're looking down at us like tigers."

George, at that, lay down with a slap of his back against the mattress. He pulled the covers over his face, determined to sleep in spite of that searchlight. But Cletus turned it off at once and went back to bed himself.

Next morning he asked George if he should stop hunting hoot owls. "I was trying to be quiet," he said. "I didn't know the light would wake you up."

"No, you keep on," George said, sorry for the way he had yelled in the night. "I'll tie something over my eyes tonight."

That was three months ago. Since then George sent off for and received a "sleep mask," which shuts out every iota of light. Now he sleeps right through Cletus's nighttime hunts.

Soon after Cletus started this pastime of his (after all, he is only a little boy without parents, alone in the night), I got caught up with my scrapbooks—every loose item pasted in, every caption written. But by then I had the habit of sitting at this table working at my "job," as Cletus calls it. And since, with George taking over the household chores, there is no earthly reason why I shouldn't, here I sit from midmorning until midafternoon, indulging myself. I write all day; and when dusk comes, I have a chat with a hoot owl. And at night I'm wakened from my first sleep by a boy with elf locks, who sits on a chamber pot turning his flashlight hither and yon until the icicles on the eaves glitter like torches and he sees (he tells us) a circle of tiger eyes. What a life! Who on God's earth could have foreseen it? If I could have foreseen my life now, two years ago (not the reality, which is fine), but described in the words, "keep scrapbooks, talk to hoot owls, take in a boy with leaky kidneys," why, I would never have set foot out of Orange County.

And if George could have foreseen *his* life? He's growing herbs! Herbs! In a box in the kitchen window. Thyme, sweet marjoram, parsley, chives. Rue and rosemary, too, for all I know. He uses them in cooking. I never had patience, myself, in the old days, with women who took care of African violets—like mothers with nursing babies. Let alone *men* growing herbs. But why not? What I'm doing is queer enough.

Since I finished the scrapbooks, I've been writing this account of our life here. It's the last of March now. Often at noonday the icicles are dripping. George said there were signs of life in the spring he boxed over six months ago—on the day he said he had retired.

That's the name I gave this account when I finished it. "Retired." I wrote that word at the top of the first page and handed the document, pages stapled together, to George. "Read it," I said.

I was as uneasy as could be while he read. For all I knew, what I'd said about him might make him mad. Or, worse still, might simply bore him. He took it all fine. He chuckled once or twice. Once he looked up to say, "I wouldn't care to be present when the Clasbys read this."

"Unless you mail this to them, then nail them to a chair while they read, there's not much danger of that, is there?"

"No," George said, "I reckon not."

When he finished he said, "I've got just one suggestion. You've got the wrong title."

"What should it be?" I asked.

"Semiretired," he said.

I confess to feeling a little asperity when George said I had the wrong title. It would be a funny thing, wouldn't it, if I didn't know the right title for my own piece of writing? But "Semiretired" was actually nearer the facts.

I was about to tell George so when Cletus spoke up. This all happened, I've forgotten to say, on a Saturday afternoon just after lunch. We were sitting around in the sunlight and drip, enjoying the letup school people feel, even after they're retired, on the weekend.

"I've got a better title," Cletus said.

I didn't know Cletus had read it. Obviously, there isn't much privacy around here, and I hadn't put my pages away as I wrote. I left them on my "desk" with an iron on top of them for a paperweight. There weren't any secrets in it, nothing to hurt anyone's feelings, except, as George noted, maybe the Clasbys. So I didn't care if Cletus had read it, but I didn't know he had. I never saw him at it.

But if I answered Cletus a little tartly, it wasn't because he'd read it; it was because he, like George, thought he could, with a snap of the fingers, produce the perfect title.

"What is your suggestion, Cletus?" I asked.

"Change of Life." Cletus said it fast, so proud of what he'd hit upon, he couldn't wait to have us hear it.

There was no use pretending Cletus didn't know that he was dealing in *double-entendre*. He did. That's why he was so proud of the title. Not just the change in our way of living: George at the sink instead of going to his office; me at my desk instead of at the sink; but the other, too. One stone used and two birds dead, with that title.

There was no more point in chiding Cletus for knowing about such things than there is in rebuking a third grader who happens to understand algebra. The third grader's caught on early to what he's bound (unless he's dimwitted) to learn in time, anyway. The same was true of Cletus.

So I spoke only of the practical aspects of such a title. "That might be a good title if I'd written only about George and me, Cletus. But you're in the story, too. What's changed for you? Going to school, studying; life hasn't changed much for you."

"Yes, it has," Cletus said without a minute's thought. "There's one big change. Every night I hunt hoot owls. Hunting hoot owls! Last night I saw fifteen eyes, and me in the middle of the circle. That's a change for me. Hunting hoot owls."

That hit a chord. It went too deep to talk about. I got up and started to clear the table, which George, unusual for him, had let stand while he read.

"You two go on up and have a look at the spring," I said. "I want a vacation from my job. I want to wash dishes."

That night when Cletus sent his beam from window to window, I thought, "Hunting for Hoot Owls." But doesn't that leave George out? George, with his sleep mask on, and his herbs on the kitchen window, and calling me "Minerva" when I answer that first call at dusk? No, I thought, everything you search for doesn't have to hoot.

I got out of bed silently, and went carefully across the icy floor to Cletus. I kneeled down so that I could follow the light as he flashed it from tree to tree. He was right. We were encircled. They were there, whether we hunted them or not, greater than stars, because they lived, because they looked back and had voices with which to answer us.

I tiptoed over to my desk, crossed out the old title, and wrote in the new. Naturally, in the dark, I made a big scrawl of it. But next morning the very size of the words seemed to be a part of their truth; and neither George nor Cletus, when they saw them, had any further suggestions to make.

# Crimson Ramblers
# of the World, Farewell

THE OCTOBER MORNING, when thirteen-year-old Elizabeth Prescott opened her eyes, was sallow, like a faded suntan. October mornings in Southern California can be many different ways, but this was the way Elizabeth liked best, sunshine remembered but not present. There had been just enough rain in the night to stir up all the scents locked in the dust by summer's heat and dryness. Hundreds of smells, at the very least, sailed into her nose. It made her feel a little crazy, so many smells she could not name: castor bean she recognized, eucalyptus, wild tobacco, licorice, offbloom acacia, alfalfa, petunia, wet dirt, coffee perking for breakfast. But most of the scents she could not identify, sniff though she would.

Me, though, she thought triumphantly. I can smell me. I'm a real hound-nose. Though it was really no test, considering her hour-long lathering with rose-geranium soap before she had gone to bed. Her feet still felt withered from last night's soaking in the foot tub. She lifted the covers to look at them: wrinkled but lily white, like the feet of a dead knight.

She let the covers drop and thought, I wish I had somebody to smile at. Oh boy, I wish I could wake up and smile at somebody and not stop smiling all day long. I wish I could wake up and someone would look into smiling eyes and say, "Another beautiful day, darling." Someone who knew that she was willing to get up, eager to dedicate her whole day to silence, hard work, and smiling. I wish it would be Mother and she wouldn't yell "Get up," or even whisper it. I wish I could smile a message at Mother and have it recognized; if a smile collided with a smile, whammo, bango, there'd be a big crackup. Splinters of smiles, first crashing, then sparkling in the air like an explosion in a diamond mine, or maybe in a bombed mirror factory.

Well, I know someone, she thought, to smile at. I know Crimson Rambler Rice. Though she'd have to wait for school to smile at Crimson Rambler, and maybe by school time she wouldn't feel like smiling. At home things happened to stop smiles.

"I never knew anyone by the name of Rice who was any account," her mother had said.

Her mother had known lots of Rices, all amounting to less than a hill of beans. "And no puns intended either." So it was too much to expect that the one Rice her daughter had run across would be an exception to the rule.

"What does this Clarence Rice's father do?"

Elizabeth didn't know. What did that have to do with Clarence? Clarence? No one called him that. He had red hair and ran fast. When he'd started school in September, the kids had wanted to call him Red. He wouldn't let them.

"That's not my name."

"What's your name, Red?"

"Crimson Rambler."

"Why, Red?"

"Because my hair's crimson and I can ramble."

"Your hair's sure crimson, Red, but can you ramble?"

"Ramble round anything here."

So they had a track meet. Crimson Rambler (he said) Rice against the world. Everything on two feet he ran circles round. Dogs he kept up with (nobody had greyhounds at the Yorba Linda Grammar School). Ginny Todd's tomcat went past him like lightning past a hill. Then it climbed a tree.

"I'm no tree climber," Crimson Rambler said, "I never claimed that."

"How come you're a Crimson Rambler, then?" Elizabeth asked. "The crimson rambler is a climbing rose."

That decided the kids. If E. Prescott was against the Rambler, they were for him. She knew too much. No, that wasn't it. They didn't care how much she knew if only she'd keep it to herself. And she didn't, couldn't. Each morning on the way to school she rehearsed keeping it to herself. Then something like this would happen: Somebody who had *named* himself after a climber said he couldn't climb. So she had to point out the error.

"Crimson," the kids had said, just to show her, "you're a rambler, all right."

But Crimson Rambler didn't care how much she knew. He liked knowledge. He liked having his errors pointed out. He was a learner as well as a rambler. He liked her. He was the first boy who ever had—and shown it. He never said a loving word, but he didn't need to. He chose her first for every game; sat by her at lunchtime; when he passed the drawing paper he gave her more sheets than he gave anyone else; he never squirted anyone but her from the drinking fountain. And on Friday he had asked her to ride on Monday—this was Monday—on the handlebars of his bicycle. She had never ridden on any boy's handlebars, had never been asked before, had almost given up hoping.

Oh, Crimson Rambler! Thinking of his looks, she almost stopped smiling. They were too wonderful for smiles. Too ineluctable? Was that the word. Was it a *word*! Crimson Rambler's looks were one with all the stars and heavenly bodies and ancient gods. They were classical. When he smiled it was too sweet for the naked eye to endure. An expression at the corners of his mouth when he smiled said, All my strength and toughness and meanness (and he was strong and tough and mean) I am making sweet and gentle and quiet for you.

Oh Crimson Rambler Rice!

Who could she smile at now? Merv? Go smiling into Merv's room and say, "Brother, I forgive you everything?"

The trouble was she had nothing to forgive Merv. Mother was always saying, so that she and Howie could hear, "Merv is my favorite child." That was nothing to forgive Merv for. And there never *would* be anything to forgive Merv for and never any reason to smile at him either, because Merv wouldn't smile back. He wasn't mean or downcast, just too damn dead calm to smile.

Howie had something to forgive her for and she had something to forgive him for. "You'll never die of lockjaw," Howie had said to her.

That was something to forgive, and she was willing, but Howie was too mad at her to smile. She didn't blame Howie, though what she'd done had not been intended to hurt him. It had been intended to help him. The trouble was he didn't want help.

Mother had said, "Basil Cobb is teaching Howie dirty words." Howie was eight and Basil twelve.

"What kind of dirty words?"

"Never you mind. But you speak to him about it."

"Why can't Merv?"

"Merv wouldn't know what to say."

"I don't either."

"Something will come to you. It always does."

And it had. "Stop teaching my little brother dirty words."

"Like what, Movie Star Prescott?"

"Movie Star" was a thing she had to grin and bear. Because her name was Elizabeth and because she didn't look like a movie star, that's what mean kids called her.

"Like what?"

It was the first time in her life she'd been asked a question and had no answer. It was a humiliating thing to have to stand before a questioner wordless.

"Like what, Movie Star Prescott?"

She had no idea. She was ignorant as well as wordless.

"Like son of a bitch, Movie Star Prescott?"

So she slapped him. She knew it was a point of honor, when that was said, to fight. It was an aspersion cast upon your mother, and while you didn't have to fight for a brother, you had to fight for your mother. Otherwise you had a streak of yellow a yard wide. There were mothers, perhaps you wouldn't want to fight for. But not hers.

Everywhere I look I see beauty, she thought; perhaps it was a defect of her eyes, like seeing double. Could both Crimson Rambler Rice and her mother be as beautiful as she thought them? Her mother had the two prettiest things in the world for a woman: little black curls at the back of her neck, falling down from the pulled-up knot of hair; and color in her face that swept back and forth from shell pink to deepest rose depending upon how glad or mad she was.

Her mother was very mad and very red when she heard of the slapping. "You have humiliated Howie," she said.

There was no disputing this.

"Here comes Sistie to button up your little pantsies, Howie baby," Basil would yell every time Howie came out of the boy's lavatory. There was no use denying that such talk was humiliating; just as there was no use expecting an early-morning smile from Howie either.

That left her father and her mother; and she knew she was already in bad with Father. Her hour-long bath in the kitchen last night had been, as much as anything, to wash away her troubles.

After supper her father had said, "Elizabeth, I'd like to have a little talk with you."

His voice, her full name, Mother's leaving the room had all told her that what Father had to say was serious. It was just dusk. He sat in his chair in the living room. His white shirt was visible but his dark trousers had disappeared into the big dark chair, and the big dark chair was disappearing in evening's shadow, going under like a sinking ship.

She stood before her father wanting to help him. It was not easy for her father to criticize her. She knew that. What came as natural as breathing to her mother hurt her father. She wanted to please her mother; but her father she wanted to help. She loved him, and almost the only way she had of showing it was being loving and dutiful with Mother. It was a wordless compact she and her father had. "If you love me, make your mother happy." That was what he said without words and what she without words agreed to. Father had recognized a fact: happiness, for him, was making Mother happy.

He gave everything to his wife, including his daughter and his daughter's love. She never kissed her father, hugged him, sat upon his knee as other daughters did. She never dared and he didn't want her to; not because he didn't like kissing and hugging *and* her, but because Mother would love him more if he sacrificed such pleasures—handed them over as a gift to her. So the way to show her father she loved him was to be cool to him and do loving things for Mother.

Only, time and again she failed: was cross, snappy, mean, selfish, critical, disobedient, and sometimes downright snarling-yelling mad. She loved her mother for the same reasons her father did, probably: for her funny jokes, her beautiful looks, her wonderful pies; and especially the excitement of living either in a cyclone or a storm cellar; one or the other all the time.

But what her father didn't see was that it was easier for him to be always calm and courteous, loving, in deed as in fact, to Mother than for her. Mother thought he was the most wonderful person in the world; she never slapped him, told him to shut up, asked him to do unreasonable things, or said to other people in his hearing, "He is not my favorite husband," the way she did with her when she said, "Liz is not my favorite child."

Her father asked a lot of his daughter. He asked her to be just as loving to her mother as he was to his wife. He asked her to forgo her love for him and present it as a gift to Mother. Since she really did love Mother, this required a love almost stronger than a human being could generate. And it made all her failures with Mother almost too heavy to bear. She failed two people when she failed Mother.

Last night her father had been resting his face in his hands. His eyes were out of sight. Only his Masonic ring caught lights and blinked a lodge greeting at her. In the silence, and knowing she had another double failure of some kind to face, her hands began to sweat and her stomach went slowly round and round, winding itself into a smaller and smaller knot to make room for a bigger and bigger sorrow.

"Elizabeth, don't answer me now. I want you to think about what I have to say for a while, then answer. Are you willing?"

Was she willing? She was willing to think until her brains steamed. Already the skin was tightening across her cheekbones and her mouth was widening and narrowing as she prepared herself to think. If thinking could undo the day before's yelling madness with Mother, she would think her eyeballs out of their sockets and break her eardrums with the pressure of cogitation.

"Tell me, Father," she said urgently. The engine of her brain was running hard, but it needed a direction in which to go.

"Elizabeth, you're such a fine girl, such a fine, bright, strong girl."

This was terrible: that her father thought he had to *say* these things.

"Your mother . . ." He couldn't go on.

"I love Mother."

"I know you do."

"But I argue, contradict, disobey, act scornful. . . ."

"Elizabeth, I think I'd be the happiest man on earth if you could get on better with your mother. I'd not ask for a thing more in life."

"I promise. I promise. . . ."

"Don't," her father urged. "Go think about it."

Thinking about it had been the whole trouble. If she could have spoken at once and without thinking, all she would have said was, "Oh, Father, I'll try to be better."

What she'd said later was the same thing exactly, only she'd had time while she was washing dishes to feel more and more. And the more she felt, the more impossible it was to come right out and say it. "Father, I'll try to be better." That's all it was, the same thing said in a fancy roundabout way. And, fool that she was, she'd even thought her father might enjoy the fanciness. She had wanted to bare her heart, make eternal promises, tell him of her steely resolutions; but not in so many words. Thinking had told her how to say it—and not say it. And how to spare them both tears by roundaboutness.

She did a wonderful job on the dishes, dried her hands, combed her hair, and went to stand again before her father. He had vanished from sight now except for the white shirt, an iceberg on the dark water.

"Father?"

"Yes, Elizabeth."

"Father, I want you to know that whereas in the past you have had in this house a big, rough, unmannerly Airedale dog, growling and showing his teeth, he is now about to be replaced. . . ."

Her father interrupted her. "Elizabeth, what's this long story about dogs? What's it got to do with your attitude toward your mother?"

"Why, everything." But the story would explain that.

"Whereas," she started over, "you have had this big unmannerly Airedale in the house, in the future you will have a small gentle lap dog, quiet, well-behaved, gentle. . . ."

Her father had sprung to his feet as if stabbed.

"Stop it," he ordered. "If what you're trying to do is to give me a demonstration of what your mother has to put up with day in and day out, you've succeeded."

"Father, please let me . . ."

Her father fell back to this chair. "Enough is enough. Go play. Go study. Whatever you want. You haven't the least idea of what I was asking you."

And all the time the shoe was on the other foot. She knew what he was asking and he didn't, but he wouldn't hear any more. All of him had gone from sight; the iceberg had sunk. Did they sink? No, melt. And Father was crying, she knew that; like something which thinks that because it is out of sight it can't be heard.

"Twenty-four hours a day of this," he said as she left. "No wonder your mother's nerves are frazzled."

"Frazzled?" her mother asked, coming from wherever she'd been listening to the conversation. "Who said anything about frazzled? And what's wrong with trying to make yourself clear by giving examples? The Bible does it all the time."

Elizabeth couldn't believe her ears. Mother saying that she was Biblical! And it was partly true. That was what was so astounding about Mother. She didn't skate around on the surface. She plunged in deep.

"The Bible's full of comparisons. Fig trees and lilies and houses built on sand. What's wrong with big dogs and little dogs, if they make the meaning clearer?"

Mother's arm around her was not a dead weight like other arms she'd had round her: uncles and aunts and such old worn-out huggers. Mother's arm was as alive as a king snake, warm and nonpoisonous, clasping her lovingly.

She snuggled into its curve. "Be this way forever," she prayed. Nine months ago, on the last day of the year, her mother sat up with her until the hikers came at midnight for the trip to Old Baldy. She hadn't asked her mother. Hadn't told her that the last hour of the old year, with snow on the mountain in the morning of the new year was important. Mother *knew*. Her mother read her like a book. And sometimes clapped her shut like a book. And there was no way to stop that. She could only love the times she was read and pondered and understood.

She had taken her long bath to help her wash away her father's scolding; and her knowledge that her mother's arm that had cradled could be raised as quickly against her.

Things like that couldn't be washed away of course, but she had awakened smelling the October morning, thinking of Crimson Rambler and the bicycle ride, and smiling. And no one to smile at but herself. So she jumped out of bed and did so, in the mirror. It will be a better face, she thought, with time and suffering; though it would never be the small-boned, black-haired, pink-petaled face (the best kind of face, in her opinion) of her mother. But it was hers, and this was a day in her life and no one else's, and the day of her first ride on the handlebars of a boy's bicycle. No old twerp's; though whoever had asked her, she'd have accepted. She knew that. But fate had spared her, had made the first the best. Oh, Crimson Rambler Rice. Had he shined it, tied a ribbon on, lived Friday, Saturday, and Sunday waiting for this day? Was he smiling, too, as he got up, happy to see that it had rained in the night so that they could have a sweet-smelling dust-free ride?

She went to the window and looked out in the direction of the foothills where Crimson Rambler lived. The sallow light was pinker now. In the barley field meadowlarks were singing. A big unknown bird cleared the eucalyptus windbreak, then went up and up across the sky, straight and steady enough to be an airplane. No one had called her. From the kitchen, which was under her room—and which, as far as smells went, was practically in her room, her floor and the kitchen's ceiling being not only one and the same but with knot-holes—the coffee smell came up stronger and stronger. Someone was up and cooking.

"The household is astir," she told herself. The words excited her. The smile went inward. She began her morning dance, which was mostly running and jumping; but the jumps were enormous flights that carried her half across the room. I'll invite Crimson Rambler for a ride on my wings in exchange for his bicycle courtesy.

Then she was suddenly tired as well as excited and lay down quickly on the floor and lifted the rug for a peek through the biggest knothole at life in the kitchen. Usually her father got up first and started things going: coffee, water for the oatmeal, oven heating for the toast. Sometimes he shaved at the kitchen sink. Every month or so she remembered to have a peek, and he had never known it, busy whistling, slicing bacon, having a trial cup of coffee. It was a secret she had, and the kitchen was her secret garden and the knothole her gate to enter.

On her stomach, comfortably full length, she lay quietly eye-spying her way into her secret garden. At first she saw no one, though there on the stove was the coffeepot perking and the griddle smoking.

Somewhere she heard splashing and by getting a little way from the knothole she was able to see her father, stark naked, standing at the kitchen sink having a kind of sponge bath from the washbasin there. He was rinsing off his private parts, and though her every intention was to back away fast, her eye fitted itself to that knothole like a ball bearing to a socket; she gazed as if this were the sight she had been created to see. Her father sloshed and whistled. It was her mother, coming into the kitchen with her sixth sense of just where to look to catch her daughter at her worst, who looked up immediately through the knothole and deep into her daughter's eye. She didn't say a word. They stared at each other as if their eyes had fallen into a lock which someone else would have to break. Then, still without speaking a word, her mother left the room.

She was standing, with the rug back down, when her mother entered the room. Her mother still had on her nightgown. Her black hair was hanging down her shoulders; her cheeks were burning.

"Do you do this very often?"

"Do what?"

"Don't spar with me, Peeping Tom. Look down into the kitchen through your peephole?"

"I've looked before."

"Does your father know it?"

"I don't think so."

"Have you seen him naked before?"

"No."

"But you've been waiting for your chance?"

"No, I haven't."

"You weren't backing away very fast."

"I was going to. I was getting ready to."

"What do you have to do to get ready to stop looking at your naked father?"

"I don't know."

"What kind of a girl do you think you are, up to such tricks?"

"I don't know."

"Do you think Merv would do a thing like that?"

"No."

"You're right. He wouldn't. Merv is a clean, natural, decent boy.

He wouldn't stoop to spying on his naked mother. Or father. That is an unnatural act. You have heard of unnatural acts, haven't you?"

"Yes."

"Do you know what they are?"

"No."

"Spying on your naked father. That's an unnatural act."

"I didn't intend to."

"Flat on your face, eye glued to a peephole? Did somebody push you there?"

"No."

"No, no, no. Well, since you don't know, I'll tell you what you are. You are perverted. You have an unnatural interest in sex. And your own father! Your father was awake half the night worrying about you and your story to him about being some kind of a dog. Even though I tried to explain it. What kind of a daughter tells her father she's a dog? Tell me."

"Crazy, I guess."

"Do you know what a female dog is called?"

"Yes."

"What?"

"A bitch."

"Don't be one. I'm not going to tell your father about this. It would sicken him. But *I* know about it. And I am going to keep a close watch on you. Respect and obedience. That's all he wants from you. And with your tendencies, you'd better watch yourself when you get around *anything* with pants on."

At the bedroom door she said, "Wait until the rest of us have eaten. I don't think anyone would consider it a pleasure to eat with you this morning."

She didn't eat breakfast at all. she didn't go downstairs until her father had gone to work and her brothers had left for school.

When she came down the stairs her mother was waiting for her. "Elizabeth," she said, "I was upset, but what I said was for your own good. You're of an age now when you'll have to be careful. Guard yourself and your feelings."

Her mother put her arms around her and pressed her pink petal-cool cheek to hers, kissed her, as she sometimes did, on each eyelid, then stood in the door and waved until she went over the dip of the hill and out of sight.

The schoolyard was empty when she got there. She heard allegiance being pledged inside. Late was late, so she took an extra minute to inspect Crimson Rambler's bicycle; there it was on the rack, washed and polished and ready to go. Even the tires had been scrubbed. She tiptoed over to the bicycle and touched it. She felt daring. It was the next thing to touching Crimson Rambler himself. The bicycle was warm and smooth in the October sunlight, very bright, shining, and dust-free.

Even though Crimson Rambler Rice was two years older than she, over fifteen, actually, they were in the same room, and she had to walk in under his eyes. There was no use trying to smile. She wasn't happy that way any more, but she was excited, shaking even. She counted the steps to her desk and watched her feet to keep herself from staring at Crimson Rambler. But she saw him. She couldn't lower her eyelids far enough to hide even his clean sweatshirt or the comb marks in his freshly wet hair.

Arithmetic was first, and when Hank Simon passed the papers for this, he handed her a note, too. "Elizabeth" was printed on the outside in the big dashing way Crimson Rambler had. She opened it behind her arithmetic book.

It began "My sweetheart." That was all she read. "My sweetheart." That was really nauseating. She rose, surprising herself, and went with the note to the wastepaper basket at the front of the room. Then, looking straight at Crimson Rambler, she began to tear the note into tiny pieces. "Sweetheart"? Why, Crimson Rambler Rice, she thought, did you really think I could be anyone's sweetheart but mother's? I don't want a thing my mother doesn't give me, and anything anyone else gives me I'll give to her. Big old Crimson Rambler Rice, did you think you could win me away from my mother with your bicycle and silly notes? Did you think I'd fall for *anything* in pants? That shows how crazy you are, because people who've got any sense don't think much of girls like that. That shows you haven't got any standards to speak of, Crimson Rambler Rice, and I have.

The note, torn up, she let dribble in a little paper waterfall into the basket. Old silly Crimson Rambler and his "sweetheart"! Why, Mother, your merest loving glance means more to me than suggestive notes from boys.

Crimson Rambler stared at her, but she didn't care. By the time the last of his note had fallen into the basket, she'd stopped trembling. She walked back toward her desk feeling happy to have made it up to her mother for all her earlier wicked thoughts, feeling strong and calm. Feeling like her father, calm, helpful, and devoted.

She stopped at the desk of Fione Quigley, a sweet little girl who didn't understand decimals. "Slide over, Fione," she said. "I'll help you with your arithmetic."

She put her arm around Fione's shoulder and whispered, "It's the same as fractions, only another way of saying it."

She looked to see if Crimson Rambler was watching. He was. She gave him a long square look and with eyes said, Farewell, Crimson Rambler Rice. Never try to tempt me again.

# Night Piece for Julia

To BE ALONE in the night, to be cold, to be homeless, fleeing, perhaps: Julie had always feared these things.

Where was she? She couldn't be sure at first. Just outside Bentonville, perhaps. It was there she tried walking with her shoes off. Her pumps had cut into her heels until they were bleeding. But the icy gravel of the unpaved road hurt her feet more than the shoes. She stood still for a while without courage either to take another step forward or to force her cut feet back into her shoes. I always heard coldness numbed, she thought, but it doesn't; it hurts, too, and it makes the other hurt more. She could have walked in the half-frozen slush at the side of the road, but she still had a concern for her appearance that would not let her splash, stocking-footed, through the mud. Suddenly, almost spasmodically, she shoved her feet down into the shoes. The pain twisted her face. "I will think of them as outside myself," she said, "as if they were two animals, pets of mine that suffer." She laughed a little hysterically. My dogs, she thought. Why, other people have played this game. That's what soldiers say, and policemen, when they think they can't take another step. They say, "My dogs hurt," and walk right on. She looked down at her narrow feet in the rain-soaked, round-toed suède pumps, her ankles and insteps red through the gauzy stockings. "Poor dogs, *hundschen*," she said, "it is almost night. We'll rest soon."

She managed a few short stiff steps, then, with teeth grating, she swung into an approximation of her usual stride. The rain was turning to sleet, but the wind had veered so it was no longer in her face. She was so cold she could not tell whether the clothes under her coat were wet or not. She got her hand out of her glove and put it inside her coat, but it was so numb she couldn't tell wet from dry. Well, she thought, if I can't tell whether I'm wet or dry, what difference does it make?

It had been so dark all afternoon that the added darkness of night-fall was scarcely noticed. It only seemed to her that she could see less clearly than she had, as if her sight were tiring, too. She rubbed the back of her wet glove across her wet face, but still the sodden corn shocks that lined the road were gray and indistinct. In her effort to concentrate on something outside herself, she was a bird perched on the snake fence beside the road. She was almost as surprised as if it had been a child. "What are you doing out in weather like this?" she said.

She thought she'd been though the town before, but always quickly, in an auto. Two or three sentences would be said, and then, while their dust still lingered in the single block of stores that made up the town, they would have passed beyond it, onto the road between the cornfields. But walking, limping, whipped (words she had no knowl-edge of before now had meaning so intense she thought their look alone would always in the future hurt her) by the wind-driven sleet, she measured out the short distance by a scale that added infinity to them. She limped from sign to sign, from gas station to gas station. Without these means of marking her progress she could never have gone on. "I will just walk to the next station," she would say, and when she had reached it she would hobble on to one more. The road was empty of cars, the service stations tight shut, their glass opaque with condensed moisture. Their swinging signs rattled in the wind with a sound of chains.

By the time she reached the town it was full night. Lights were on in most of the stores and houses. She skirted the main highway, tak-ing a back street that paralleled it through town. She passed three or four shops, all closed; a dry-cleaning plant, a plumber's, a second-hand furniture store. The furniture store had one window set up as a bedroom, with a bird's-eye maple dresser, dressing table, and a bed of a kind fashionable in the early nineteen hundreds. She leaned against the window, where she was somewhat protected from the sleet, and looked at the bed. It had a cheap factory-made patchwork quilt on it and two pillows in lavender slips. It looked like heaven to Julia, a bed, something she had taken for granted every night of her life before. I'll have to ask someplace, she thought. I can't go on in this cold. I'll have to risk it. I'll die if I don't. She held her hands against the glass. The yellow light behind it made it look warm, but to her icy hands it was only an extension of ice.

She saw herself in the mirror of the dressing table and instinctively tried to tidy herself. Her face looked as hard and white as a stone, like something already frozen. In the mirror her gray eyes were black, her wet yellow hair gray. Her fingers were almost too numb to push the fallen strands of her hair back under her dark cap. She got her lipstick out of her pocket and tried to put lips onto the blue scar the cold had made of her mouth, but her fingers were too stiff for that precise work. She thought she looked sick and water soaked, but still neat. Now that she was ready to go on, she became aware again of her heels, throbbing with a pulse of pain that seemed to beat even in her eyes.

I'll stop at the first place, she thought. Everyone has to sleep. No one would refuse me on a night like this. She walked on painfully, unable to joke any longer about her feet. The sleet bit into her face like fire.

She went up the steps of the first house where she saw a woman behind the undrawn blinds. From the street she had looked motherly, a plump, aproned woman with gray hair. She came to the door at once when Julia knocked.

"Well?" she asked in a harsh accusing voice.

"I haven't any money," Julia said. "I'm sick. I've been walking all afternoon. Will you let me have a bed for the night?"

"I'll call the authorities," the woman said. "There's a place for girls like you." She turned as if to go to a phone.

"No, no," Julia cried. "I won't bother you. I'll get to where I was going. Thank you."

The woman shut the door before she could turn around. "I didn't think she would," Julia said to console herself. "I didn't really expect it."

She got out of town as she had come into it, only more painfully, with more frequent stops. I always heard it was easy to freeze to death, she thought. She was shuddering all over, uncontrollably, so that the shuddering racked and hurt her. All of her body ached, as her hand had ached when, as a child, she had held a piece of ice as long as she could for a dare. "If there were only a snowbank, a bed of white snow where I could lie down and die. I would rest myself in it. I would pull it over me. I would press my cheek to it." But with this wet, ice-splintered ground, she would have to go on until she fell.

She was about to climb the curve of a small stone bridge when she saw the flicker of a red light beneath it, a fire, a windbreak, something to protect her from the sleet. She stumbled off the road and tried to run down the incline toward the fire. It was small, but really burning. She cupped her numb hands over it. Not until some of the heat had penetrated her skin did she look up, see the face of the man who sat with his back braced against the opposite side of the culvert. She would have screamed, but a tide of slow cold horror rose in her throat, choking her.

Julia stretched her legs out along the warm smooth sheets and opened her eyes, saw the silver lights on the green ruffled curtains, the acacia spilling over the round bowl. "You almost overdid it tonight," she told herself. "You almost screamed then." She put her warm hand on the soft satin over her heart. It was jarred by her heartbeat. She had almost overdone it, but it had worked again. Remembering that imagined suffering, that formless face, she was able to turn, once again, toward her husband, lying beside her in the warm sweet-smelling bed.

"So," he said in the tone of one who has been waiting. When he moved his hands slowly over her shallow breasts, she scarcely winced.

# Live Life Deeply

A T NINE O'CLOCK Friday morning, the Courtneys, then almost
frantic over the disappearance of their fourteen-year-old
daughter, Elspeth, received a phone call from a man who
said his name was either Leighton D. or Creighton C. Hall. Ellie's
father, who had answered the phone, was too upset to hear well, and
the man at the other end of the wire was too upset, to judge by his
voice, to speak clearly.

"I didn't quite catch your name," Mr. Courtney said.

"Creighton C. Hall," the man repeated.

The Courtneys had phoned everyone they thought might have any
information concerning Ellie's whereabouts—friends, parents of friends,
teachers; but they knew, and had called, no Halls. Mr. Courtney was
going to tell Mr. Hall, who, he supposed, was calling on business, to
please phone back later, when Mr. Hall once again repeated his name
and added, "I'm calling from Merton Memorial Hospital."

Mr. Courtney knew at once, then, that Mr. Hall was calling about
Ellie.

"Is she badly hurt?" he asked anxiously.

But before he would continue, Mr. Hall wanted to make sure he
was talking to the right person. "Is this Ellie's father?" he asked. "Is
this John Courtney?"

"It is," Mr. Courtney answered, almost shouting in his impatience.
"How's Ellie?"

"She's fine," Mr. Hall said, "now."

"Was she badly hurt?" Mr. Courtney asked again.

"She wasn't hurt at all."

"What's she doing at the hospital then?"

"She's here with me," Mr. Hall said.

"With you?" Mr. Courtney asked. "What's the matter with you?"

"There's nothing the matter with me," said Mr. Hall. "I'm here
with my wife, who's having a baby."

At this minute Mrs. Courtney, who had been hanging onto her husband's arm trying to hear what was being said at the other end of the line and had caught little more than the word *hospital,* could stand the suspense no longer.

"John," she asked, "is Ellie in the hospital?"

"Just a minute, please," Mr. Courtney told Mr. Hall.

Then he turned to his wife. "She's at the hospital. But she's all right. There's nothing wrong with her. She's with a man named Hall."

"What's she doing with him?" Mrs. Courtney asked, not feeling much reassured.

"His wife's having a baby," Mr. Courtney explained, and returned to his conversation with Mr. Hall.

Mrs. Courtney didn't feel that this information actually explained much and, while she waited impatiently for her husband to finish talking, she tried to imagine a chain of circumstances that would have landed Ellie at Merton Memorial Hospital in the company of an expectant father and mother.

Because her husband was in the midst of irrigating the lemons, he had been up earlier than usual that morning, about five-thirty. He had noticed that Ellie was not in her bed on the sleeping porch as he went out to work and, though she did not ordinarily get up any sooner than was necessary to catch the school bus, he hadn't thought much of her absence. The morning had been particularly nice, warm and shimmering, and Ellie might have risen romantically early to see the sun rise. Or hear the birds sing. Or, for that matter, to wash her face in the morning dew. Ellie had been subject to an unusual number of unexplainable fourteen-year-old vagaries during the past month, it seemed to him. Anyway, he had said nothing about Ellie's absence to his wife until he returned to the house for breakfast. "Ellie back yet?" he had asked as he sat down at the table in the kitchen.

It was only then that Mrs. Courtney learned that Ellie had been gone since five-thirty—or at least since five-thirty. How much earlier, they had no way of knowing. Mrs. Courtney had walked down to the arroyo at the back of the ranch, one of Ellie's favorite spots; Mr. Courtney had tramped up the first slopes of the foothills north of the ranch; they had both shouted and called. There had been no response. Ellie missed her breakfast, then missed the bus. At eight o'clock the Courtneys began to phone, and were beginning, when Mr. Hall called at nine, to think of the police.

Mrs. Courtney had felt particularly uneasy because Ellie had put on at that hour of the morning (or earlier) not her school clothes or pair of shorts, but her very best outfit, her white Easter suit. This was Ellie's first suit, and she was unusually proud of it. Ellie didn't care whether her other clothes were on hangers or on the floor, but her suit she kept not only on a hanger, but in a clothes bag with two old, faded, but still faintly sweet sachets dangling across its shoulders. The fact that Ellie had worn her suit convinced Mrs. Courtney that her daughter's absence was something planned—not merely a spontaneous morning ramble that had somehow extended itself. But, spontaneous or planned, she didn't understand the Hall's connection with it.

The minute her husband hung up, she wanted to know everything and all at once.

"Take it easy, Gloria," Mr. Courtney said. "Ellie is there. She's not hurt in any way or sick. And she's with this Hall. That's all I know. We're going over to the hospital right away. To get her."

"Didn't this Hall explain anything to you?" Mrs. Courtney asked. "How he happened to have picked up a fourteen-year-old girl in the first place? I should think he'd feel duty-bound to make some explanation."

"I don't know that he did pick her up. Besides, Ellie didn't want him to call us at all. He was calling without her knowing it."

"That's what *he* said," Mrs. Courtney reminded her husband.

Mr. Courtney admitted that all he had heard was Mr. Hall's version of the affair. "Hall wasn't in any mood to talk at all," he defended him, "with his wife having a baby."

"You mean—she's in labor now?"

"That's what I gathered." Mr. Courtney, who was wearing a sleeveless undershirt, went into his bedroom, brought out a shirt, and began to unbutton it. "You going to wear what you've got on in to the hospital?" he asked. What Mrs. Courtney had on was a faded-denim slack suit.

"I don't suppose I should go at all," she said worriedly. "This call could be a hoax. It might be just a plan of Hall's to get us away from the house. I think I should stay here."

"Maybe you're right," Mr. Courtney said. "I'll call you the minute I get there. And you call me if anything happens here."

Mrs. Courtney, noticing her husband's mud-spattered khaki pants and heavy irrigation boots, had a momentary impulse to call him back to change. She was too anxious to have word at once from Ellie to really care how he looked, however, and she let him leave without a word about his appearance.

Merton Memorial Hospital was only six miles from the Courtney ranch, two miles outside the town of Tenant, where Ellie went to school. Mr. Courtney was there in ten minutes. Feeling as worried as any expectant father, he asked the way to the maternity ward of the first person he encountered inside the building.

"Third floor," he was told. "Waiting room's at the end of the hall. You can't miss it."

The waiting room had a door with a glass inset, and Mr. Courtney saw, before he entered it, that Ellie was not there. Its occupants were three men. The three men looked as if they might be members of three separate generations: a battered-looking, unshaven young man; a forty-year-old, pink and fresh-faced; an old fellow with his grizzled, shovel-shaped beard half hidden behind a copy of the *Rotarian*.

Mr. Courtney entered the little room, which was forbiddingly cheerful, with maple tavern chairs and bright hunting prints, and glanced doubtfully about.

"I'm looking for a Mr. Hall," he said. "Creighton C. Hall."

"That'd be me," the young fellow answered, stubbing out his half-smoked cigarette in a mound of other half-smoked cigarettes.

"Where's Ellie?" Mr. Courtney asked at once.

"She went out to get something to eat. She . . ."

"I told you I'd be right over," Mr. Courtney said, interrupting him. "She'd already gone when I called."

Mr. Courtney, anxious to discover what kind of a fellow his daughter was mixed up with, sat down beside Mr. Hall. Hall was young, twenty-two or -three, blond, with a smudge of darker whiskers and a manner half truculent, half worried.

"I wish you could have kept my daughter here until I came," Mr. Courtney said.

"Well, she hadn't had any breakfast or any supper or any sleep," Hall explained. "It was about time she ate."

This lack of supper and sleep was news to Mr. Courtney. "Where'd she go? I'll pick her up."

Mr. Hall shrugged. "I don't know where she went. She went with his wife. Ask him." He nodded across the room to where the middle-aged man sat facing them.

"Excuse me," Mr. Courtney said, "I believe my daughter went out with your wife to get something to eat. Do you happen to know where they went?"

"Haven't any more idea than a jackrabbit," the pink-faced man answered, obviously happy to relieve the tedium of waiting with talk. "We left home so early this morning my wife didn't get her coffee, so she was going to drive back into town for it. But I don't know where she'd go. We're just here because our daughter's having a baby. We don't know the town. Was that your little girl that went with my wife?"

"Well, I think so," Mr. Courtney said.

"She's a nice little girl. Looked kind of peaked, though, and when my wife said she was going out for coffee, Mr. Hall suggested the little girl go along. They'll be right back, I can assure you. My wife could hardly bear to tear herself away and, except for the coffee, wouldn't've. If my wife don't have her coffee by ten o'clock, she's atremble in every limb. You might say she's a coffee addict."

Creighton Hall gave Mr. Courtney a sardonic look and lit another cigarette. Mr. Courtney said, "It was kind of your wife to take my daughter with her," then quickly turned his chair so that he faced Mr. Hall. This put his back to the other man.

"Do you know Ellie?" he asked.

"Never saw her before this morning."

"Where was she then?"

"Reservoir Hill."

Reservoir Hill, besides being a hill and the location of the town of Tenant's water supply, was a kind of semipark, with a grove of eucalyptus trees, numerous shrubs, oleanders, redberries, Carpenteria,

Matalija poppies, and the like. There were, in addition, a few tables for picnickers and a couple of grills where steaks could be broiled and coffee made. Since the Hill was not more than four miles from their ranch, the Courtneys had eaten supper there more than once.

"What time was this? When you first saw her?"

"I didn't notice. Six, maybe, or maybe a little before."

"How'd *you* happen to be there at that hour?" Mr. Courtney asked, feeling suddenly suspicious.

"I was up there trying to make up my mind whether my wife should have this cesarean or not."

Mr. Courtney felt a sudden pricking of conscience. Here he was, interested only in Ellie, while this young fellow's wife was perhaps in a bad way.

"How *is* your wife?" he asked.

"I don't know. You can't find out anything around here. She's having it now."

"The cesarean?"

Hall nodded somberly.

"They say that's the easiest way." Mr. Courtney tried to reassure him. "No danger at all."

"Not when you've already been in labor thirty-six hours," Hall said. "Not when your heart's not any too good anyway. But God, it was just as bad the other way. Worse, it looked like to me, because it might last longer."

"What'd your wife want?"

"She wasn't in any condition to know what she wanted. All she *said* was, do whatever's cheapest."

"Didn't the doctors advise you?"

"You know doctors. They're not sticking their necks out. On the one hand, this seems our best course; on the other hand, it don't seem so good. It was all up to me."

"Well, it's hard lines," Mr. Courtney said. "I know."

"Ellie your only kid?"

Mr. Courtney nodded.

"I sure don't blame you. This is my last. My wife's never going through this again. Look at that old fellow down there," he said.

Mr. Courtney looked cautiously over his shoulder. The grizzled beard was now hidden behind a University of California bulletin. "These grandfathers take it pretty calm," he said.

"He's no grandfather," Hall said. "Well, he may be a grandfather, but he's not getting this kid secondhand. It's his own. His ninth."

Mr. Courtney could not refrain from another look.

"Took him three wives to do it, though," Hall said bitterly. Then, as a nurse came to the door, he leaped to his feet.

"Mr. Beamish," the nurse said, "your daughter's just presented you with a fine seven-pound granddaughter. Would you like to have a little peek at her?"

Mr. Beamish bustled up and out. At the door he turned back to say, "If my wife comes, tell her where I am."

Mr. Hall, still on his feet, called, "Nurse, nurse, how's my wife?" But the nurse either didn't hear him or didn't want to answer.

"Damned machines," he said, sitting down. "They got no more feeling than a tombstone." Then, as if he didn't like the sound of his final word, he hurried on. "Your wife have any trouble when your daughter was born?"

Mr. Courtney was glad to get back to Ellie. He sympathized with Hall but, actually, he scarcely knew any more about Ellie than he had when he left home.

"A little," he said. "but it turned out all right. It usually does. About Ellie, now—what was she doing up on Reservoir Hill at that hour of the morning? Did she tell you?"

Hall gave him a sharp, tough look. "Yeah, she told me."

Mr. Courtney waited.

"She was figuring out how she could do away with herself."

When he took his next breath, Mr. Courtney was aware of it. "Do away with herself?"

Hall paused as if he would give Mr. Courtney a chance to say once more that everything usually turned out all right; but Mr. Courtney said nothing. "Don't tell her I told you, though," Hall said. "She don't want you to know anything about it."

"But she told *you?*"

"Sure. I was feeling like hell and she was feeling like hell, so we told each other our troubles. She was walking around up there crying and I was sitting there darned near it. 'Sis,' I said, 'I don't know whether my wife's going to live or die. What's your trouble?' So she told me."

"I didn't know Ellie had any real troubles, not any real troubles."

"This isn't any real trouble," Hall said, "except to a kid. But right at present she thinks that her life's ruined. That she can't ever go back to school and so forth. So she wishes she were dead."

Mr. Courtney had been seeing the Reservoir. It was a deep gray-green pool with steep, concrete-lined sides. In the early morning a milky mist sometimes hung over it.

"But why?" he asked. "Why does she feel this way?"

"Because she thinks she's a laughingstock, and that's a thing a kid can't stand. And because a person she loved, and about worshiped, I guess, went and did this to her."

Mr. Courtney supposed he must have looked pretty stricken, for Hall said quickly, "It was one of her teachers. You know a Miss Fisher?"

Mr. Courtney nodded. Love and worship were the proper words, all right, for what Ellie felt for Miss Fisher. They lived, at home, on an everlasting diet of the remarkable Miss Fisher. They knew all about her wonderful voice (she had read poetry aloud to her classes), her vast knowledge, her sensitive perceptions (shadows by moonlight are much more beautiful than shadows by sunlight), her glorious hair (red), her fastidiousness (she always wore gloves and a hat, even when she went for the shortest stroll). Insofar as it was possible for a fourteen-year-old to model herself upon a thirty-five-year-old, Ellie had done so. And Ellie believed, her father thought, that Miss Fisher had, in return, some special regard for her.

"Yes," Mr. Courtney said. "I know she has a teacher named Fisher. And you're right. Ellie thinks she's wonderful."

"Well," Hall said, "that wonderful old bastard ought to have her neck wrung a couple of times."

"Why?" Mr. Courtney asked. "What's she done?"

"The kids hand these compositions in to her. Little short ones. Snapshots or something, they call them."

"Impressions."

"Yeah, impressions. Well, your kid wrote one that she was proud of. She really believed in this one. And when she walks into class, this Fisher has it all written out on the board. Then in a few well-chosen, witty words, she takes the skin right off your daughter, peels her right down naked before all those kids. Has everybody laughing their heads off to think anybody'd be such a damn fool as to write such stuff. Fisher doesn't say your daughter wrote it, but a couple of the kids know it, and they tell everyone, so now everybody's guying her and kidding her. She can't take two steps without being yelled at by somebody, and she thinks the great Fisher thinks she's a fool. So life's not worth living any more. See?"

Mr. Courtney saw, all right. "What was the piece about? Something kind of funny?"

"No, sir, it wasn't. I believe it myself and I think it's darned good. It's called 'Live Life Deeply.' That's what they yell at her now, she says. 'Come on and live life deeply,' they yell every time she sticks her head out a door. You want to read it?" Hall asked. "I got it here."

He took a much-folded piece of binder paper from his wallet. "I told Ellie I'd like to keep it. I wasn't kidding her either. I really would. It kind of fit my case this morning."

Mr. Courtney unfolded the single sheet of paper. It was pretty dirty and pretty tearstained. At the top in Ellie's large sturdy letters were the words, "Live Life Deeply. An Impression."

"Life," it began, "may be compared to a glorious sea and human beings to bathers. Some wade in ankle deep, some to their waists, and some all over. Let us not hesitate in the shallows of life, wet only to the ankles, but plunge bravely in. Let us live life deeply. Out where the breakers crash—"

Suddenly Mr. Courtney did not want to read any more of it. He refolded the sheet and handed it back to Hall. Hall put it in his wallet. "You see anything wrong with it?" he asked.

Mr. Courtney shook his head. "Not for fourteen."

"This Fisher made her stand up and try to tell what she meant by living life deeply and how it was different from living on the heights. All that crap."

Mr. Courtney groaned.

"Here they are now," Hall said.

Mr. Courtney turned around. It was a surprise to him to see Ellie looking, except that her suit was dirty and grass stained and she herself somewhat pale, about as usual. He had been so recently up at the Reservoir and in that classroom that he felt that he, at least, had changed. He got to his feet and started toward Ellie, but as he did so, a nurse, coming in behind her, called, "Mr. Hall, you're a papa," and Mr. Hall shot out in front of him.

"How's my wife?" he demanded.

"She's fine, just fine," the nurse said; then seeing the woman with Ellie added, "And you've got a sweet little granddaughter, Mrs. Beamish."

"What's mine?" Hall wanted to know.

"Daughter," the nurse said. "Eight pounds. Takes after Papa."

"Wowie!" Hall cried. "Come on, everybody. Meet Miss Hall."

"You know you just get a little peep at her through the glass," the nurse told him. "Just a wee little peep!"

"Sure, sure," Hall said. "I go to the movies. Come on, Ellie," he said, taking her hand. "Let's get the hell out of here." Hall and Ellie, half running, led the way down the corridor. Behind them, more sedately, followed Mrs. Beamish, Mr. Courtney, and the nurse.

Hall admired his daughter immensely. "She sure does look better than that little old red grandfather's kid, don't she?" he exulted.

The nurse explained that babies born by cesarean section were always whiter than others.

"Don't start belittling my daughter," Hall advised.

While Hall was peering and praising, Mr. Courtney remembered that he hadn't called his wife. "I'll be right back," he told Ellie, and hurried off to find a phone booth.

As soon as Mr. Courtney left, Hall said to Ellie, "I called your father. I told him all about it. I had to. I let him read that piece, too."

During the excitement of seeing the new baby, Ellie had had a little respite from her troubles. Now she felt their full weight returning to her.

"Look here," Hall said, "there was nothing wrong with that piece, if you meant it."

Ellie looked up at him inquiringly.

"I mean, were you a show-off? Just blowing your top to get a little attention? Just saying, live life deep, but not meaning it?"

"Oh, no," Ellie said sadly. "I meant it. That's the trouble."

"Trouble? What the hell!" Hall exclaimed. 'You're just where you wanted to be."

"Am I?" Ellie asked, struggling to see what Hall meant.

"Why, sure. You got your folks half nuts worrying about you, you've ruined your best dress, you're cutting school, the kids all yell at you, and the great Miss Fisher thinks you write tripe. What more do you want?"

Ellie was speechless.

"Well, maybe you didn't mean it," Hall said. "Maybe what you really want to do is wallow around all your life in a big chocolate sundae. Is that it?"

"Oh, no!" Ellie said.

"Well, OK then." Hall made a motion as if to give Ellie a friendly spank, evidently decided that she was not a big-enough girl for that, and ended up with a half-slap, half-pat to the cheek.

"Keep your chin up, kid," he said. "That's what I'm going to tell my daughter."

As soon as they were out of the hospital grounds, Ellie asked her father if she had to go back to school that afternoon.

"No," Mr. Courtney told her, "you don't. I finish irrigating tomorrow, and the next day we can leave. For a week, as far as I'm concerned. Go up to Yosemite. It'd be nice up there this time of year. How'd you like that?"

"I'd like it," Ellie said, "but I couldn't do it. I couldn't miss that much school. You know," she added, "I've got a good idea for an Impression for next week. I'm going to call it, 'A Morning in a Maternity Ward.' I don't see how anybody can yell that at me, do you?"

Ellie's father made a sudden, unintelligible sound, and Ellie turned to look at him. She couldn't bear to think that he was doing what it seemed he might be, and she looked quickly away—at the familiar countryside, which, because she was unaccustomed to seeing it in the middle of a school morning, was strange and exciting to her.

# Mother's Day

ALBAN, MY HUSBAND, and I had come down to spend the Mother's Day weekend with my widowed mother on her ranch south of Los Angeles. We found her too concerned over my Aunt El-Dora, however, to participate very whole-heartedly in any celebration in honor of her day. What my Aunt El-Dora was doing was neither illegal nor, as far as I could see, immoral. Still, it didn't sit well with Mother.

"Where is her pride?" she asked me.

I didn't know. And I didn't feel responsible in the way Mother did. Although I'm only five years younger than Aunt El-Dora, the pride of the aunt is not the concern of the niece.

Mother and I were in the dining room of the house that has been my mother's home since the death of her father-in-law. The afternoon was warm and we sat resting, cooling our arms on the dark walnut of the big pseudo-Spanish table, Mother at one end, I at the other. We had paused, for a minute or two we thought, in the dining room after washing the lunch dishes, on our way to more comfortable chairs in the living room, but after the custom of women we had lingered there. In the living room, the electric clock with the cathedral chimes sounded half past something.

Mother looked at her wristwatch. "Half past three," she said. "It's getting late." But neither of us moved.

Behind Mother were the French doors that open onto what is called in Southern California "an outdoor living room"—really, a greenhouse made of lathes and covered, in this case, with an enormous wisteria vine. Through the doors I could see Alban stretched full length in the canopied glider, reading the *Post* about Botts, the Earthworm Tractor fellow, and keeping time to the glider's creak with his stockinged toes. The *Post*, as he leafed through it, rustled gently, echoing the clatter of the palms along the driveway. Mockingbirds sang from habit. Their hearts were not in it. Only at dusk do they really lift their voices. The air was heavy with the scent of the wisteria vine, which was in full bloom, and of the Valencia groves, which were in bloom, too, and added their fragrance to that of the wisteria. Strong though they were, heavy and musky and sweet, these scents did not enter Mother's thickly curtained, heavily carpeted room very freely. Mother wants to be indoors or out; she likes definite boundaries. That's one reason she was troubled about El-Dora. The boundaries about El-Dora seemed wavering and uncertain.

"Right here in the shadow of the church, too," she lamented.

"It would have to be a pretty long shadow," I told her. "El-Dora being a mile and a half down the road from the church." I meant it for a joke; my intention was to lighten the talk.

"You know what I mean," Mother said, unsmiling.

I did indeed. The churches of the Temple Brethren cast longer, darker shadows than those of any other denomination. I know. I, too, am a Temple Brother, like Mother, like El-Dora. Or at least like El-Dora *was*.

Outside the creak of the glider had ceased.

"Why don't you take Alban a glass of lemonade?" Mother asked.

Mother is always alert to find ways in which I can please Alban. She was happy when Alban came courting. I think she was afraid I might be an old maid. I know she didn't think me very attractive as a girl. It hurt me then, but I understand it better now. She didn't like her own looks and I was her spit and image. If you don't like your own looks, it is irritating, I suppose, to see them popping out at you on unexpected occasions and from unexpected angles. Mirrors you can avoid, but a young daughter has to be with you at least part of the time. Who made Mother think she was unattractive? Not my father. Father and Mother never came home from anyplace, church, or party, that he didn't say, "Ethel, you were far and away the best-looking woman there." He would stand off, cocking his head as if to truly assess her, then repeat after this deliberate scanning, "Far and away. Far and away."

And it was the truth. He wasn't simply reassuring her, or flattering her. What she thinks now of the face we have in common I don't know. Someday I'm going to ask her. I looked at her against the light of the French windows: head, with its puff of gunmetal hair, not gray but ash blond darkened, held to one side as she listened for the sound of the glider to announce that Alban was once more at ease. Her pink lips were full and pleasant over her teeth, which have a slight outward slant; her eyes, big and shining, are sea blue and flecked as that blue always is with green. And all of her, from the gunmetal hair to the finger mangled in a corn chopper when she was a girl, alive and shining in spite of her sixty years. I don't know how the Temple Brethren ever caught her. They didn't, of course. She was born one, just as I was.

Anyway, that's my face, too, minus twenty-five years. And while I admit, as I read recently, that no woman with a long upper lip can be *pretty*, still we're not as plain as Mother thinks. But the habit, early formed, of compensating to Alban for my lack of beauty still persists. I got the pitcher of lemonade from the refrigerator, poured a glass, and took it to him.

The lathe house under its canopy of blossoming wisteria was a big purple cave. So beautiful! I felt loving toward the whole human race simply to think that it was capable of developing a vine like the wisteria and of training it over a support like a lathe house so that for a week or two in spring there would exist a room lined with amethysts and scented like honey. The light was lavender colored. Bees seemed to be hanging in the air. And over all the dry, homesick rustle of palms along the driveway.

"It's like being in a big, sweet purple cave," I told Alban.

He was deep in his story and didn't hear me. He drained the glass, put it down, and said, "Your mother's never happy unless she's feeding someone, is she?"

"I wouldn't say never."

He shook the seeds in the bottom of the glass. "Got any more?"

"Lots more," I said, and fetched the pitcher.

"I knew he'd like it," my mother told me as I went out with it.

When I had reseated myself at my end of the table, she began to speak again of Aunt El-Dora. "Go down and see her, Merlin. You're of El-Dora's generation. She'll listen to you."

El-Dora . . . Merlin . . . Those names tell you something—a good deal, perhaps—about the women of my generation. We are the El-Doras, Merlins, La Fays, Valoes, Vernices, Lu Renes. And we are the daughters of the Ethels, the Rachels, the Hannahs, the Graces. They made their gestures of protest in naming us. Gave us the burden of their unrealized dreams.

El-Dora's mother, Rachel, was my grandfather's sister. Great-aunt Rachel had had seven children before moving at the age of forty-five to Southern California. The youngest of that pre-California group was ten. No one, probably not Aunt Rachel herself, had expected any more. Then in three years, three more: Royal, Carmencita, and El-Dora. Thus an aunt so near my own age.

"What do you want me to say, Mother?"

"Her pride . . ." Mother began again.

"After all," I reminded Mother, "he *is* her husband. It's her legal and moral—"

"Legal, perhaps," my mother interrupted me, "but not moral."

There was no use arguing. Instead, I listened to the tu-rooing of the doves that had once belonged to my grandfather but that on his death had been freed and now lived, such as had escaped boys and hawks and cats, in the eucalyptus trees at the back of the grove. Mother listened, too, and in remembering Grandfather thought, I suppose, of his sister, El-Dora's mother.

"I'm glad Aunt Rachel isn't here to see El-Dora now."

"Would she make El-Dora punish her, I wonder, the way she used to?"

My mother put her hand to her eyes as if to shut out an unpleasant sight. "I never liked that. I'm sure it was wrong."

"The first time I saw it was at the mock wedding."

"Mock wedding? I don't remember any mock wedding."

"Remember" is always a magic word, but especially when mother and daughter use it. Years ago they saw the same thing—or, rather, the same event happened before their eyes—and now, twenty years later, they discover that each saw something entirely different from the other. The mother tells her story; the daughter tells. What each saw is unbelievable. What each missed is unbelievable. Put the two stories together, and there, perhaps, is the real event. But who can say what the real event is?

Mother remembered the mock wedding after I had described it. But she hadn't been there; she had only heard about it. It happened while Caprice—Caprice is my younger sister—and I were visiting Grandfather Webster in this very house. One afternoon we walked down the oiled road between the orange groves to play with Aunt Rachel's children.

"Do you remember," I asked my mother, "that we used to have the second story of Aunt Rachel's tank house for a playhouse?"

My mother nodded. "I do remember. El-Dora is living there now."

"Living there? How can she?"

"She's renting the front house. And the tank house has been fixed up. The pump and tank were taken out years ago. It's really very attractive. The only place hereabouts where you can see over the groves now they've grown so high."

Usually, because of the engine for the pump and the smell of whatever it was they burned in it—distillate or kerosene—we played ship in the tank house when I was a child. Crew below with the pump and engine, passengers upstairs. But that day El-Dora told us the minute we arrived that we were going to play bride and groom.

"The trouble was," I told Mother, "there wasn't a suitable groom."

"There still isn't," my mother said, her face in a twinkle grown flinty and condemning.

"Oh, Mother!" I exclaimed. I hated to see her like this, and in a flash her face had changed once more. Back was the pink-mouthed, loving mother, and I longed to make amends for my unfair thoughts of a minute before. Happy to have her back and loving, I said, my voice soft with the pleasant thing I had remembered, "I remember I wore that natural linen dress you had embroidered so beautifully for me."

"Oh, pshaw," Mother said.

"I remember how proud I was of it, starting out for El-Dora's that afternoon."

Mother was beginning to remember, too. "I can see you and Caprice starting out for Aunt Rachel's that afternoon. I can see you both now, plain as day, and I remember thinking Caprice looked awfully-wispy and washed-out beside you."

"Oh, Mother!" I said. Twenty-five years and still pleased by that. And not a word of truth in it. Caprice is and was a real beauty, about as wispy and washed-out as a cherry tree in full bloom. But I loved remembering that dress. I had felt good in it. I was a chubby girl, and the skirt had been full enough for me to move comfortably. And it had smelled good, that linen fabric, like freshly mowed lawns or newly baled hay.

"Mother, has linen changed in the way it smells?"

"I think it has. I think it's something they do to preshrink it—or make it wrinkle resistant."

"I used to think that dress smelled like Ireland."

"Perhaps it did, dear."

I was remembering more and more: the roses with which El-Dora had decorated the playroom—Gold of Ophir, opal colored and cinnamon sweet. She had made a wedding veil of a lace curtain, and a wedding dress from one of Aunt Rachel's white nightgowns. There was a wedding bouquet of nasturtiums made spray style, and even a big bowl of pink champagne.

"Champagne!" Mother exclaimed when I told her this. "Why, that's impossible."

I had thought of it as champagne for so long that I had almost forgotten it *was* impossible. It was actually lemonade colored with beet juice and frothed with bicarbonate of soda. I don't know why it didn't make us sick. What it did was make us drunk—beautifully, beautifully drunk, at first; then fighting drunk later on.

"We got drunk as lords on it."

"Drunk as lords! Why, Merlin!"

"Except for that there would never have been a fight."

We were drunk on pink lemonade, and from drunkenness we went easily to blows. El-Dora had tried to make me be the groom. It was ridiculous to have a bride twice as big as the groom, I thought, but El-Dora was set on being a bride. She had an old suit of Royal's for me to wear, with a fancy vest and a boutonniere, and though I wanted to be the bride myself, to please El-Dora I began to put on the groom's suit. But it was too tight for me. I wasn't built for boy's clothes. It hurt me and I could see how silly I looked in it.

"I'm not going to be any old groom," I told El-Dora.

"Oh, yes, you are," she said, and began rebuttoning the button I was unbuttoning.

"I won't!" I yelled.

"You will!" she yelled, pushing me back into the suit I was tearing myself out of. The end of that was blows, of course. El-Dora slapped me and I cried. Bellowed, I suppose. Anyway, Aunt Rachel heard and came running.

When she was told what had happened, she said, "El-Dora, you have done wrong. You have made me suffer. Now I want you to show all your friends just how you make your mother suffer when you do wrong." So she forced El-Dora to hit her over and over again.

My mother groaned when I told her this. Then after a few minutes' silence she asked in a voice I could scarcely hear, "Did she have El-Dora use a switch—or something?"

"No. Her hand."

"Where?" Mother whispered.

"The face."

"Slapping?"

"Yes. El-Dora had slapped me, you know."

Mother rubbed her hands over her own face. After a while she said, "How could Aunt Rachel *make* a big fifteen-year-old girl do that . . . if she didn't want to? I couldn't have forced you—under any circumstances—to do such a thing, could I?"

"I don't know. If you had trained me to do that since I was little—perhaps."

"But at fifteen . . . couldn't El-Dora have revolted?"

"Maybe at fifteen she didn't want to."

"You mean she enjoyed hitting her own mother?"

"She hit her pretty hard."

This was such a terrible thought to my mother she propped her elbows on the table and rested her face in her hands as if something had given way inside her. So we sat in silence for some time, she with her face in her hands, I looking beyond her to where Alban lay in the glider. Whether it was our silence or the fact that he had finished both his story and the lemonade I don't know. Anyway, Alban came in then, carrying the empty pitcher. He put it on the table, looked at me, looked at Mother, then said, "Something bothering you ladies on this fine afternoon?"

"We were talking about Aunt El-Dora."

Alban pulled out a chair and sat down. "She in trouble again?"

"Mother thinks so."

"Well, my conscience is clear. I tried to keep her on the straight and narrow the one chance I had."

Mother lifted her face from her hands. "When was this, Alban?"

"I told you about it at the time, Mother," I said.

But *Alban* had never told her about it.

"When El-Dora decided to leave her first husband—what was his name?" Alban asked.

"Vergil," Mother supplied.

"When she decided to leave Vergil, she came to see me at my office. They were living up north then, and El-Dora offered to sell me a lot of her personal belongings, cheap. She wanted to raise some quick money."

"Did you buy them?" Mother asked, out of courtesy, for now that she had been reminded she surely remembered my telling her of El-Dora's call on Alban.

"Not I. In the first place, they were not things we had any use for. In the second place, I wasn't going to have any part in encouraging her to leave a respectable hard-working man like Vergil to take up with an unknown quantity like that tramp printer. And how right I was."

Mother nodded. "I know. El-Dora came home after that broke up. She used to come down here and cry on my shoulder until she found Walt."

"Well, what's wrong now? Does she want to divorce Walt now?"

"Oh, no. The shoe's on the other foot . . . now."

"Walt wants to divorce her?"

"No, I mean the shoe's on the other foot because she *ought* to want to divorce him. Or at least she ought not to want to live with him. She *couldn't* live with him if she had any pride."

Alban pursed his lips and cocked his head. "Walt stepping out on her?"

"Worse than that, much worse."

I could see Alban wondering what Mother would consider worse than that. He started to say something, then changed his mind and waited for Mother to explain.

"Walt's living with another woman."

"You mean he's left El-Dora?"

"He's left her for five days of the week. He lives with this woman down at Indio, where his job is five days of the week. Then he comes up here on Friday nights and lives with El-Dora."

"Maybe she doesn't know anything about it," Alban said. "The wife's always the last one to know anything about it, they say."

"She knows about it, all right."

"Well, maybe she likes it," Alban suggested. "Maybe two days of Walt is enough."

"She does not like it," Mother said with dignity. "She is eating her heart out. She begins crying the minute he leaves her Sunday evening and she doesn't stop crying until Thursday when she starts planning for his return. It's disgusting. But she won't listen to a word of criticism of Walt. She says she loves him and he's her husband and if she can't be with him seven days a week then she is happy to be with him two days a week. Is it legal to live that way, Alban? You know something about the law."

"El-Dora certainly isn't doing anything illegal. Walt's her husband and she's got every legal right to live with him when she can."

"But that woman in Indio? Isn't El-Dora helping her break the law? Isn't that collusion or something?"

Alban smiled. "I don't think you could prove very easily that living with your husband is encouraging him to take up with another woman. It could work out that way, of course, but legally you wouldn't have much of a case."

"Anyway, it's immoral," Mother repeated. "Oh, something has just broken in El-Dora. Something has just given away. She's too soft. If she'd put her foot down and tell Walt he either had to stay home or get out, he'd stay home. But she won't do it. 'Walt has to do whatever he wants to,' she says. 'Joie's a lot younger than I am. I can't blame Walt for being attracted to her.' "

"Joie this Indio dame?" Alban asked.

Mother nodded. " 'Joie's got a beautiful voice,' El-Dora says, 'and Walt's always loved music.' Where's her spunk? Why doesn't she have some faith in herself?"

"El-Dora's a good-looking woman," Alban admitted.

"Well, why doesn't she stand up for her rights, then?"

"Oh, Mother, there aren't any rights in love."

My mother turned on me impatiently. "I know your views, Merlin. Just now I'm talking to Alban. She ought to say to Walt, 'Leave that woman or leave me!' Oughtn't she, Alban?"

"She's afraid he might do it, Mother."

Mother threw her hands in the air. "Oh, I give up. In your own way, Merlin, you're as bad as El-Dora. But I do think you ought to go down and call on her anyway. Even if you won't back me up."

Alban said, "No reason why we can't do that, is there, Merlin?"

"Thank God, Alban," Mother exclaimed, "that in you we have a man who has never given us a moment's worry."

Alban made some slight sound—laugh, snort, sigh. I couldn't say which. Then he repeated his invitation. "It's a nice hour for a walk. Let's go down to see El-Dora, Merlin."

Mother decided it. She got up from the table. "Good," she said. "Bring El-Dora back with you. Sunday evening's the mournful time for her. I'll fry a chicken for supper—we'll stir up a little merriment."

"This is your day, Mother Webster," Alban said. "You're supposed to be taking it easy, not cooking up meals for lovesick relatives."

"A mother is never more happy than when looking after the welfare of her brood," Mother said.

This was unusually unctuous talk for Mother, though a kind she often falls into with Alban. As if embarrassed by it, she hurried at once to the kitchen and was already bustling about with supper preparations when Alban and I started out for El-Dora's.

The evening couldn't have been prettier. There was just enough duskiness to soften all outlines: orange trees were big green tents and the verbena that covered the ground between the road and the groves was a Persian carpet. It was a road I'd known all my life, the very one I'd walked down to attend the mock wedding. Then, of course, time had been forever and I hadn't bothered to look at things like trees and flowers. Now time was half used up for me and I knew it and I took in what I could while I could. And it was all so beautiful. I wanted Alban and me to do something about it together. What, I don't know, since Alban certainly wasn't going to talk about it, and would only listen grudgingly if I began to speak about what he called "Merlin's beauties of nature."

But a man and a woman shouldn't walk separated through such things, should they? Walk down a road at evening not touching? I wanted to put my hand out to Alban. Take hold of him, touch him, tell him.

I don't suppose it can be a fact that Alban has sharper elbows, knees, Adam's apple, fingertips, and so on, than other men? That there is something harsh, dry, twiglike, and painful about all these projections, members of the body, whatever is the proper name for them? It cannot be, in fact, true, yet the truth is I've often been hurt by them, and my impression on reaching out to Alban is of running into some kind of thorny growth. But the evening's beauty was too much to endure alone, so I put my arm through his. Though I didn't risk saying anything. Just lifted my head in a motion that included and commented.

So thus thornily linked and without a word we walked down the road to Aunt Rachel's house, and past it, down the driveway to the tank house where El-Dora now lived. The tank house stood in the center of a half-dozen pepper trees, and its big shingled tower rose through and above the lacy fronds of the pepper trees like a lighthouse tower above waves. Lights were already on, and the top section of the Dutch door was open to let in the evening's sweetness and coolness. And Walt was still there. At the far side of the room he sat in a rocking chair, reading. El-Dora was a foot or two from him, stirring something on the stove. Between stirs she would come over, lean against Walt's shoulder, and read with him. Once she brought a spoonful of whatever she was cooking for him to taste. Once he laughed, then read aloud to her the passage that had made him laugh. When she went back to the stove, she held onto his hand and he let his arm stretch full length so the link wouldn't be broken. Both were smiling. I don't mean a grin; their expressions hadn't much to do with their mouths being open or their teeth showing. But what lies behind a smile, the feeling that curves the mouth and bares the teeth, that look was on—or perhaps the word is "behind"—their faces.

Alban and I stood staring through the screen of pepper-tree branches like any Peeping Toms, convinced that this was no time to come calling but unable or unwilling to tear ourselves away from what we saw. I can't speak for what Alban thought. What I thought was, So this is marriage. I'd been *in* it for sixteen years, but I'd never seen it before; never seen before "the matrimonial state" as apart from two married people together, which is just a quantity, not a quality.

But the surface we were looking at wasn't all. The moment of parting was near when the clasping hand would unclasp and Walt would go back to Joie and her sweet songs. The touching was real for itself, but for El-Dora, anyway, there was desperation in it. She hovered, she touched, fed, listened, in agony. I could feel it. Her heart was breaking. And *your* heart, I reminded myself, is not breaking. It was some consolation.

Alban brought me to my senses. He touched my arm with his sharp-ended fingers and we went tiptoeing out of that yard like people leaving a church service. Once onto the road, we walked along silently. I didn't try to take Alban's arm again. My thoughts were given over to El-Dora's situation, with losing Walt, and I didn't hear Alban when he spoke.

"What did you say?" I asked.

Alban replied in a harsh voice. "What I said was, 'All that and Joie, too.' "

I was startled. I had thought only of El-Dora's misery and I had taken for granted that that was what Alban had been thinking of. The fact that Alban had not been concerned about El-Dora at all, had just thought how well off Walt was, stopped me in my tracks.

Alban stopped also and faced me. "Why did you do it?" he asked.

I didn't know what he was talking about.

"Why were you and your mother so set on catching me? Two big, good-looking women closing in on one poor puny nineteen-year-old? Why did you do it?"

I said, "I was only nineteen, too." But I thought, Good-looking? Then, all so unnecessary.

"I didn't intend to close in on you, Alban."

"I know it. I scarcely figured in the plan."

We stood facing each other under the darkening sky. Alban reached out a hand to me, patted me two or three times, very gently for Alban. "Forget it, Merlin. It was a long time ago."

We walked home, serenaded by the mockingbirds, which are night singers, as I've said.

Mother had decked the table as if for a party. In the center was an angel-food cake decorated with sweet peas. Candles in mother's best cut-glass holders were already lit. The room was filled with the smell of frying chicken.

Mother's face fell when she came out of the kitchen and saw that we were alone. "Where's El-Dora?"

When I told her that Walt was still there and that we hadn't wanted to disturb them, she was silent for a while, then said, "I blame El-Dora's mother for all this. I place the blame squarely on Aunt Rachel for the unnatural life her daughter is leading. She broke the girl's spirit."

She stopped abruptly. It is one of Mother's rules not to bore Alban with troubles—hers or mine. She hurried into the kitchen and came back at once with some pretty, fruity drink—nonalcoholic, of course.

"Alban," she cried, "I've made something better for you than you had this afternoon."

"It will have to be good then," Alban answered very politely, taking a glass.

When each had his glass, Mother said, "Let's drink to Alban."

But Alban wouldn't have it that way. "This is your day, Mother Webster, not mine. Let's drink to Mother's Day."

Mother, who knew nothing about the etiquette of toasts, drained her glass with us. As we put our empty glasses back on the tray, the palms were clattering again with what I suppose is their true sound— a sound of the desert, of dryness and loneliness and vast infertile wastes of sand. But here amidst our irrigated groves and in our stucco bungalows we have long since learned to associate that sound with home.

# The Heavy Stone

W HEN FRANCES REDMOND returned from the florist with the lilies, the choir was just leaving the church. Their final practice before Easter was over. All had gone well, and the singers, now homeward bound, were content with themselves, Mr. Donner, their director, and the holy season. They were preparing to celebrate. Two or three of the choir members stopped to admire the lilies, which Frances had in the back of the station wagon, but only Mr. Donner volunteered to help her carry them into the church. Frances was a little amazed to see him clasp his fine white hands about the rough clay pots, for she had heard it said that Mr. Donner was so proud of his hands, which he displayed conspicuously when directing the choir, that he would use them for no rough work whatsoever, and that for even ordinary chores he protected them with cotton gloves.

After Mr. Donner left and before she began placing the lilies along the edge of the choir loft, Frances brought them all together in a gardenlike clump in front of the altar. They had cost much more than she had expected, forty-eight dollars for the twelve, and what she would use for money during the next weeks at school she didn't know. Still, because they were so beautiful and because Joel had been so fond of lilies, she didn't regret buying them. They were a wonderfully stately flower, proud and mysterious. Like the church itself, she thought.

With a delicate stroke she touched the pin-point diamond frosting of one of the lilies. She thought of herself as a lover of flowers, but she knew she was not; not in any such way, certainly, as her brother Joel had been. At ten, Joel had been growing lilies from seed, a difficult accomplishment even for a grown gardener. On his eighteenth birthday he had sent her yellow violets picked on the green hills back of Fort Ord. And on the day he had been killed his friend had written them that Joel had in his breast pocket a handful of native wild cyclamen, the shooting stars of California's early spring.

It was this love of Joel's for flowers that had first suggested to Frances that she decorate the church in his memory at Eastertime. It was not by any means her sole reason for the undertaking, but it was the easiest to explain and the one she mentioned first to her mother.

Her mother had been pleased, but matter-of-fact. "Dear," she had said, "this isn't anything you'll be able to do just hit or miss, you know. It will have to be done properly and be ready on time. And it will be a great deal of work."

"Nobody asked Joel what he wanted to do in the army," she had replied. "He had to do whatever he was told to do, and no questions asked. I'm no better than Joel. I can do what needs to be done."

"I know," her mother told her, "but someone had always taken care of the church decorations before. It's nothing you really must do."

"That's the trouble," Frances said. "I've always let someone else do the work and I've just enjoyed and admired. This time I want to do the work."

This time, though she had not been able to say so to her mother, she hoped to feel herself close to Joel in doing, as he had done, work to which she wasn't accustomed. And because it would be work with flowers, which Joel had loved, and for an occasion that celebrated the triumph of life over death, she hoped, too, that she might be able to lighten the pain that, since Joel's death, had rested like a heavy stone upon her heart.

"And Frances," her mother had said finally, "decorating the church for Easter isn't a thing to do with set teeth. A grim duty to undertake because it needs to be done and somebody has to do it."

"Oh, Mother!" she had exclaimed. "Do you think you have to tell me that?"

How could anything connected with Joel be done in any way except with love? Since his death she had been trying very hard to be more like him—and that meant being more loving. In decorating the church, she wanted to express her growing likeness to her brother. And though she had not been able to make all this clear to her mother, for neither of them was yet able to speak of Joel at any length without breaking down, her mother understood her purposes sufficiently to arrange with Dr. Emmons, their pastor, for her to undertake the work.

Leaning over the lilies, taking deep breaths of their fragrance, which seemed somehow golden to Frances, like the powder in their throats, she was very happy she *had* undertaken it. Everything was going well. She had been working all day and was bone tired, but there wasn't much left to do. The worst had been putting the yellow Spanish broom, which she had gathered in the hills back of town, on the ledges under the high, arched windows. That had been a job for a monkey, not a human being. To do this she had had to balance dangerously and uncertainly on top of a wobbling stepladder, and now in the small of her back she could feel her muscles trembling like frayed ropes. Placing the cheesecloth, which she had died purple and bordered with fleurs-de-lis cut from gilt paper, over the expanse of gray cold plaster behind the choir loft had taken acrobatics which were almost beyond her, too.

Her plan had been to frame the choir loft, which was above and behind the altar and pulpit, with a foot-high hedge of lily-studded greenery. The greenery part had been simple: manzanita branches brought down from the hills. What had not been simple, what in any other circumstances she would have called absolutely hellish, was putting the chicken wire, which was to provide the framework for the branches, in place. She did, finally, get it in place, but only because she had been willing to struggle on, in spite of a torn dress and bleeding hands. But the wire was firmly attached now, and it held up the gray-green manzanita, so that the choir would appear to rise for its singing from a formal garden of clipped hedges and nodding lilies. Still touching the lilies, still bending over them, Frances reviewed what was yet to be done. Almost nothing: place the lilies behind the choir-loft hedge so that they would nod over it; put the tall candles in the two gold-and-crystal candelabra she had brought from home; tie the great floral cross, sheathed with creamy stock and banded with golden lilies, to the railing in front of the choir loft. That was all.

All her exasperation and weariness began to leave her. She could see the church as it would be when every frond and flower was in place, the candles lighted, and the lilies, spraying outward from the arms of the cross, promised Easter joy to all. She felt very happy, very loving, and very near Joel. This was how Joel would feel if he were here working, she thought.

Contentedly she began to sing the song the choir had been practicing. "Hallelujah, Christ is risen. Gone is now the heavy stone."

"Those are the words," somebody said, and Frances whirled about to see Mrs. Askew, the choir's first soprano, walking noiselessly down the aisle.

"Oh! Mrs. Askew," she exclaimed. "I didn't hear you."

"As I was saying," Mrs. Askew continued, "those are the words, all right, but I've never heard that tune before. I should think that melody would have been dinned into you after all the practices you've listened to, Frances. Hallelujah, Christ is risen. Gone is now the heavy stone," Mrs. Askew sang in her high flawless voice, so that Frances felt as if she were having a private Easter service of her own. "It's a perfectly simple, easy melody."

"I know," Frances said, humbly. "I can't sing."

Then, to hide her embarrassment at having been overheard, she said, "I love lilies, don't you, Mrs. Askew? Don't you think they look just like the spirit of Easter?"

"They'd look like the spirit of Christmas or the spirit of the Fourth of July, I guess, if we used them then," said Mrs. Askew. She bent over one of the lilies, shaking her head at what she saw. "Look at this! Turning brown on the edges already. Where'd you get these, Frances?"

"Rossi's," said Frances proudly. Rossi's was the "right" place to buy flowers.

"That explains it," said Mrs. Askew with conviction. "Here's one about to drop its head already." The head of the lily Mrs. Askew was pointing to looked perfectly secure and fresh to Frances, but Mrs. Askew was evidently right. She had only to bend it back and forth a few times before it fell off, dropped to the floor, spraying some of its golden powder onto Mrs. Askew's black pumps. She bent to flick it off with her handkerchief.

"That Rossi's," she said irritably.

Frances felt humiliated. She had gone to the best and most expensive florist and had bought the most expensive lilies. This was something on which she could not possibly have tried to economize. "I thought Rossi's was good," she faltered. "And I particularly reminded them that the lilies were for the church."

"Frances Redmond," Mrs. Askew exclaimed, "you didn't go and do that?"

"Why, yes," said Frances, "I did. I was proud that they were for the church."

"You didn't tell them *what* church?"

"Of course," said Frances.

"Well, that *does* explain it."

"Explain what?" Frances asked, bewildered.

"These poor, fading, second-rate lilies."

"Are . . . are Rossi's known for poor lilies?"

Mrs. Askew snorted. "Rossi's is known for very fine lilies, and they all go to Mr. Rossi's own church. I bet he's laughing his head off right now at wishing this sorry bunch of stuff on us while *his* church will have lilies four feet high and six to a stem." Mrs. Askew loosened another petal and let it fall to the floor. "Falling to pieces already! You poor child. You were certainly taken in."

Frances could not believe such a thing, not of Mr. Rossi, who was round and fat and had seemed kind. He had given her a daphne cluster for her coat when she left, and had wished her success with her decorating and a happy Easter. "Mr. Rossi would never think of such a thing," she declared warmly. "He helped me pick out the lilies himself."

Mrs. Askew laughed dryly. "I can well believe it."

"Not for Easter," protested Frances, "not for a church, he wouldn't do such a thing. Nobody could."

"Why, that's nothing," Mrs. Askew assured her. "Our church always gets its flowers of Eby's. The Ebys belong here, and I for one would be good and sore at Charley Eby if he didn't send his second-rate stuff to some other church and save his first-rate stuff for us. That's nothing more than sound merchandising and sticking by those who stick by you. It's the way businesses are run?"

"But Easter isn't a business?" Frances protested.

"Selling lilies is a business," said Mrs. Askew with finality, "and Pete Rossi did a good stroke of business when he got rid of these.

You weren't figuring on just leaving them huddled together here, were you, Frances?"

"No," said Frances, though she was almost ashamed to admit she had any plans at all for the lilies, so much diminished were they in her eyes by Mrs. Askew's disparagement. "I had planned to put them on the edge of the choir loft back of the hedge. The idea was," she explained doubtfully, "to make it look as if the choir were singing in a garden."

"Garden?" said Mrs. Askew shortly. "If it were a garden, you wouldn't catch me singing in it. Bugs, drafts, poor acoustics, and any Tom, Dick, or Harry who wanted, listening! But looking like a garden is something else. I'll carry a couple of pots up for you, if you like. My gloves are either up there or I've lost them."

Frances carried two pots herself, and when these, with Mrs. Askew's two, were placed behind the manzanita hedge some of the pleasure she had first felt in the lilies, and had lost while listening to Mrs. Askew, returned. "What do you think?" she asked shyly. "Will they do?"

Mrs. Askew pursed her lips thoughtfully. "Well, since you've asked my honest opinion, Frances, I think the hedge is a little too high. I've heard many a member of this congregation say that they liked to see, as well as hear, the choir. They don't care about disembodied voices. If that was all they were after, they'd stay home and listen to their record players. They want to see us as well as hear. Of course, nothing would suit any of *us* better than to be absolutely out of sight. But I don't think, in a case like this, we have a right to consult our own selfish wishes. So for that reason I'd try to find some way to lower these lilies. Here're my gloves," she said, spying them under the chair she had occupied at practice.

"Lower them or maybe bank 'em around the pulpit," she advised from the back of the church, on her way out. "That's my advice."

There wasn't any way to lower the lilies. They had either to rest on the ledge where they were or be done away with altogether. Frances placed them all as she had planned. Perhaps now and then a lily would obscure someone's view of a singer, but, she thought irritably, I don't believe people are as crazy about seeing the choir sing as Mrs.

Askew thinks. I know I'd far rather look at a lily than Mrs. Askew, and I bet other people would, too. She walked to the back of the church. From there the choir loft looked truly gardenlike, with the lilies lifting their creamy trumpets above the bank of green, and she decided they should stay.

She did not know how to get the large flowered cross attached to the railing of the choir loft without the janitor Mr. Leggett's help. But since he had been so cross about the extra work she had already caused him, she attempted it herself. By seven o'clock it was firmly in place, and there wasn't a leaf or flower petal left on the floor or a pew cushion out of place. She seated herself in the back row for a final check on her handiwork. In the peaceful orderly room, much of the pleasure she had had in planning the decorations returned. She wished she could light the candles, but was afraid to do so.

There was nothing whatever that still needed doing, she decided, unless she righted one of the sprays of larkspur which was hanging unevenly from the shallow, tripod-supported bowl in front of the pulpit.

I wish I hadn't seen that, she thought, but she got up and put the spray back in place. "There," she said, "stay put, now."

As she talked to the flowers, or to Joel, or perhaps to herself because she was so tired, she heard a gentle thudding on the swinging doors which opened out of the main vestibule into church.

"Come in," she called, and two old ladies whose faces she had often seen in church, but whose names she could not remember, came hesitantly through the doors.

"We wouldn't interrupt you for anything," one said, "but we do want to see what you've done."

"You're not interrupting at all," Frances told them. "I've finished."

"We meant the conversation."

Frances laughed. "I was talking to the flowers. Telling them not to go slipping and sliding about."

"Yes," they agreed. "They are hard to manage sometimes. In that shallow bowl, especially."

Frances walked to the back of the church and stood close to the two women, one square and rather tall, the other short and round. Both were gray and spectacled and both wore blue-and-white print dresses buttoning down the front. She remembered that they were sisters, the tall one a Mrs. Something, and the short round one a Miss Something, but Miss or Mrs. what, she simply could not think.

"I'm Frances Redmond," she told them, hoping they would say who they were, but they continued to gaze about, wordlessly. "I've been decorating the church."

"Yes, we heard you were."

"How do you think it looks?" Frances asked, hoping for a morsel of praise.

"It looks lovely, dear. Lovely and up-to-date," the short sister said.

"Up-to-date?" Frances repeated, wondering what was up-to-date about lilies and crosses and armloads of Spanish broom.

"Nothing old-fashioned," the tall sister explained. "And all those lilies! Lilies are so dear this Easter. How did you ever persuade the Finance Committee to let you spend so much money?"

Frances didn't quite know how to answer. "I bought them myself," she said finally.

The two sisters looked at each other. "Well, that explains a good deal," the tall one said. She turned to Frances. "That was sweet of you, dear, very unselfish of you to share your bounty with us. You mustn't forget, though, that the Bible says that it is harder for a camel to pass through a needle's eye than for a rich man to enter Heaven!"

Frances was not quite sure what was being said to her, though she felt uneasy about its import. And all possible answers seemed awkward to her. If she said, "I pauperized myself to buy them, practically," it would sound as if she were asking praise for her sacrifice. And if she didn't say that, it would sound as if she were admitting that she was rich, which was certainly not true. She did not even like to use the word "rich" in church, where other things were so much more important. With a sudden inspiration as to how the truth might be told and the word avoided, she said, "I guess I won't have any trouble getting through the needle's eye."

The sisters gave each other another look, and the plump one said gently, "None of us can speak with any certainty of such matters, dear. Though we may all hope."

"Oh, I didn't mean that," Frances said intensely. "I could never mean that." This was the worst that had yet happened to her, that anyone should think her so smug and stupid. "That was the furthest thing from my mind. What I meant was . . ." But the sisters were uninterested in what she meant. They were interested only in the decorations, and when they had inspected these closely they were ready to go.

"Thank you, dear," the round sister said. "It was very sweet of you to let a couple of old ladies have a close peek at what you've done."

And the tall one added, "Yes, we're on the shelf now, Clara and I. But we're still interested in what the younger generation has to offer, even if we can't keep up with them. Everything you have done, dear, has the modern touch. I think your cross is especially modern. We would never have thought of that, would we, Clara?"

"Modern?" faltered Frances. "How do you mean, modern?"

"Oh, I don't know. Just modern. That band of gold lilies, for instance. And the flowers spraying out that way. Not like the poor old rugged cross of our day. But then, our day has passed. Thank you, dear, for giving us a little preview."

After the sisters left, Frances tried to see the cross through their eyes, but it was impossible. In the empty, quiet church it looked timeless to her, simple and beautiful, frothed over with the foam of its white flowers, splashed with the gold lilies.

When she got home she told her mother about the two old ladies. " 'So modern, so modern,' they kept saying," she said, between bites of the cold chicken and hot cocoa which her mother had insisted she eat.

"Well, there's nothing wrong with modern, is there?" her mother asked.

"There is when you say it the way she said it. 'It's very modern, isn't it, Clara?' "

"Oh," said her mother. "Clara and Emma!"

"Do you know them, Mother?"

"Yes."

"Well, they don't think much of your daughter or her decorations. Why're they so interested in decorations, anyway?"

But her mother, instead of answering, suddenly noticed her empty cocoa cup. "Have some more cocoa, Frances," she urged.

"I'll take it upstairs with me," Frances said, lifting the filled cup.

"I feel damaged. I bet I climbed up and down that stepladder a thousand times."

"Do you want me to call you in the morning?" her mother asked. "With the first service at nine, you'd better be there at eight-thirty, hadn't you?"

Frances yawned, wanted to stretch, but couldn't with the cup in her hand. "Better call me at seven-thirty. I want to get there in time to see if anything's fallen to pieces during the night." She gave her mother's shoulder a squeeze with her free hand. "It looks nice, Mama. You'll be proud of it."

Next morning she blinked sleepily up at her mother. "It can't be seven-thirty already," she said.

"It isn't," her mother said, "but Dr. Emmons wants to talk to you."

"Here?" she said, sitting up, half awake.

"Oh, no, not here. On the phone."

Frances ran out into the hall in her pajamas. "Darn! I bet something's gone to pieces."

"Dr. Emmons?" she said.

"Good morning, Frances," Dr. Emmons said. "First of all, Frances, I want to thank you for the beautiful piece of work you've done. It's given me much pleasure. I've just returned from a little tour of inspection with Mrs. Askew and Mr. Donner, and I can't tell you how the sight of your beautiful flowers has heartened me."

Frances relaxed. Nothing had collapsed, no one had stepped on a forgotten thumbtack, Mr. Leggett hadn't complained of extra leaves to sweep up. It was Easter morning. Through the open door she could see the sun, yellow as lily pollen on her bedroom floor. Already, from those churches with early services, the Easter bells were beginning to peal.

"Thank you, Dr. Emmons," she said happily. "I loved doing it."

"There is one little thing, Frances," Dr. Emmons went on, "or, rather, to be strictly truthful, two. Mrs. Askew feels the choir is somewhat hidden by your decorations. Mrs. Askew has been our soloist for ten years, and I'm sure you want her to be happy as much as I do."

"Oh, yes, Dr. Emmons!" said Frances.

"I've told Mrs. Askew, that if you agreed, four or five inches might be clipped from the top of the hedge. The choir has worked hard, and it is quite understandable that they want to convey their Easter message face to face with their neighbors. But only you, my dear Frances, can do any cutting, and then only if you really want to. What do you think?"

"I'll be right over and do it," Frances said.

"Well, if you think best, Frances. It's a matter wholly for you to decide. The other little thing is this. Mr. Donner says a goodly number of our nonmusical members follow the music by watching him direct rather than by listening. And he hates particularly to disappoint them this morning when so much of the service will be musical. Can you hear me, Frances?"

"Yes," said Frances, "I can."

"Mr. Donner thinks that the removal of just a few of the more exuberant sprays from the cross, Frances, would be all that was necessary."

"Yes," said Frances.

"You quite understand, don't you, Frances, that all this is absolutely up to you? You've created a beautiful effect, and no one but you is to touch it. In case you do want to make any changes, however, Mr. Donner will wait at the church for a half hour so that he can tell you which are the sprays that need cutting."

"Tell him I'll be there," said Frances.

She repeated the conversation to her mother as she hurriedly washed and dressed. Mrs. Redmond brought a cup of coffee up to her, and Frances tried to hold it with one hand and comb her hair with the other.

"You understand, don't you, Frances," her mother said solicitously, "that this sort of thing is bound to happen where a number of people are involved? No matter how perfect the result, it's bound to disappoint someone."

"Of course," said Frances, giving up the hair combing. "I wasn't born yesterday."

"You've worked so hard," her mother said. "I don't you to be hurt by someone who thinks the arrangement could be better."

Frances put down her cup. "Mother," she said, "I'm not the least hurt. I don't care a whoop about what you call my arrangements. I really don't."

She jumped up from the bench in front of the dressing table. She really didn't give a whoop about the arrangements. If someone, if anyone, had suggested other flowers, other plans, she would not have cared in the least. Sunflowers instead of lilies, crowns instead of fleur-de-lis, anchors instead of crosses.What did hurt, what hurt so hard that she could not speak of it, could not really look at it, but must work fast enough to keep it out of sight, was the reason . . . the reason . . . back of every objection, of every need for change . . . of . . . But she would not let the reason emerge, she would not let it come between her and Easter, between her and Joel, between her and love.

"Hurt," she told her mother. "It's nothing more than a few little mechanical things. What kind of a daughter do you think you've got, anyway, not to be able to take a little criticism? Me, I'm sensible."

She clapped her hat on her uncombed hair, stuffed bobby pins, necklace, stockings, and makeup into her bag, laid her cheek against her mother's, and said, "Look, Ma, I'm strong stuff."

Her mother leaned over the banister as she ran downstairs. "Frances, you're not thinking of going in to church on Easter morning bare-legged and with your hair streaming down your back, are you?"

Frances paused at the front door. "I'll finish up in the ladies' rest room after I've done the clipping and changing. Don't worry, I'll look fine for the Easter parade."

The clipping and changing were not much. Mrs. Askew had the hedge marked like a lady's skirt for shortening. Clip off the tops of the manzanita bushes, sweep up the resultant mess, and that job was finished. The hedge, in her opinion, lost its natural look by this operation, but the choir would now be able to sing in utmost visibility. And anyway, what did it matter how high an artificial hedge was? Not at all, of course.

Mr. Donner was there to point out the changes he wanted made on the cross. Most of the band of golden lilies would have to go, and much of that froth of white she had so admired. This work required more delicacy and precision than trimming the hedge, and Frances, in her nervous hurry to be done in time, was not able to do it well. Meaning to take only one spray of stock, she loosened others. Trying to get at one lily, she broke off two or three, until finally, when she had finished, the cross had become ragged and partial: sagging where it should have been upright, pocked with losses where it should have been complete and firm. But Mr. Donner was content. He was not now obscured in his directing by the cross, and he clasped Frances's hand heartily with both his fine white ones.

"Good girl," he said. "Nice cooperative child! Now run and put yourself in order."

Frances did run, because the church was already beginning to fill with people. She had left her handbag in the ladies' room, which opened out of the main vestibule. Now she hurried in, locked the door behind her, rinsed her face and hands, put on her stockings, and started on her hair. She finally got it up, and her hat on, but she looked so frightful she took her hat off and started all over again. Then, just as she was in the middle of this second attempt, she remembered the candles. They were unlighted! They must be lit, and she hadn't spoken to a soul about them. It would be to pitiful for them to stand there shedding no light amidst the flowers and music, while the beautiful words were sung and spoken.

In spite of her half-combed hair, she ran out into the vestibule, now filled with people. She searched for someone she knew and finally caught the eye of Mr. Sewell, one of the ushers. She beckoned frantically to him, and Mr. Sewell abandoned, with apologies, the couple he had been ready to guide to a pew, and came to her.

"Oh! Mr. Sewell," Frances said, "I forgot the candles. They went completely out of my mind. They must be lit. Have you any matches?"

Mr. Sewell looked at her half-combed hair dubiously, as if he were afraid she wanted to run, hatless, through the congregation to light the candles herself. But she didn't. She didn't care who lit them. Just so they were lit.

"That's all been taken care of," Mr. Sewell assured her briskly. "At the beginning of the choral prelude, two ushers in blue suits are going to march down and light them. One down either aisle. Make a nice little ceremony of it."

"Oh! Fine," said Frances, "fine! I had forgotten it completely."

"It's all taken care of," Mr. Sewell assured her. "I planned it my-self."

Frances stepped back into the ladies' room and started once more on her hair. It went up better, now that all her responsibilities were taken care of. She got her hat on just right, with the ribbons falling over her collar in back as they should, and, thank goodness, she hadn't forgotten her gloves.

She was ready to leave, had her hand on the doorknob even, when from the organ there came the first strong triumphant notes, followed by a silence in which she could hear, in the vestibule, the slight shuf-fling sound of the two ushers in blue suits getting into step before proceeding down their separate aisles for the candle lighting.

Then the organ became triumphant, the choir lifted its voice in the hymn of joy, the very doorknob in Frances's hand trembled with the force of the music. This was the hour for which she had waited, for which she had worked, the hour of love that would restore and re-unite, the hour of the resurrection. "Hallelujah, Christ is risen," sang the choir. "Gone is now the heavy stone."

She stepped out into the vestibule. Mrs. Askew was singing. Mr. Donner, hands white as lilies, was not obscured by the cross as he conducted. The two sisters had been given a back seat. The cross, less modern than it had been, still did not make them smile. Were Mr. Rossi's lilies really beginning to brown? Dr. Emmons's glasses sparkled in the morning light. The two ushers stately and square in suits that seemed to match trod in time to the music toward the candles.

Frances ran back into the ladies' room, the music following her. "Gone is now the heavy stone."

She dropped to her knees and laid her cheek against the cool enamel pedestal of the washbasin. When she was able to stop crying, she tiptoed back into the vestibule and out of the church. Outside the church she heard the last of the singing: "Christ is risen."

# 99.6

NURSE WILLIAMS came for the lunch tray. She was cheerful and crackling. "A fine lunch," she said. "I always say there is no one who can equal Graham in making a pudding! And you have eaten everything. That is fine."

The woman in bed did not trouble to tell her that the taste of food meant nothing to her. The doctors had told her that she must eat to get well. Then she would eat: no matter what the food was, no matter how it tasted, she would never send a crumb back. She was determined to get well. She was determined to live. So long as there remained a single word she had never read, a single tree she had never seen, she would live. But she knew better than to attempt to convey any of this to the nurse. Instead, she asked her, and waited for the answer with breath barely sliding out of her lungs before she called it back, "It's going to be warm today, isn't it?"

The nurse considered. There had been a high fog that morning, and shreds of it were still caught in the eucalyptus on the hills. But the sun had come through, and a pale and watery light fell on the administration building below them.

"Oh, no," she said, shaking her head. "It won't warm up this afternoon. Too much fog this morning. Well, have a good rest, Mrs. Kent." And off she went with the tray, limber-legged and bustling.

Mrs. Kent thought bitterly: If I were a nurse, I would learn the answers people wanted and give them to them. It is going to be hot, and if my temperature's up a little it will be the heat. It is folly for doctors to say that bodily temperature doesn't vary with the weather. If you put a kettle over the fire it gets hot, doesn't it? I shall expect a little rise this afternoon, because of the heat.

No reading or writing was permitted for a half hour after lunch. For that half hour one merely digested—and thought. And when the half hour was over, rest period began, and for two hours one rested—and thought. Then at three, temperatures were taken and faces

397

washed. It was for three Mrs. Kent waited. It was for that hour she awakened in the morning. Yet, in the morning she had other interests: could read her paper, open her mail. But the thought of three o'clock was there behind all, distorting and embittering all, though not until now, after lunch, did it begin to displace all else. Each morning she entered an open space, a space in which there was room for many things, but as the day wore on, it narrowed like a funnel. Now, after lunch, there was yet room for her to move upright, though she was cramped; but from that time on, the funnel contracted very rapidly until she was lying flat, writhing toward the opening, burning, burning, encompassed by the hot bright metal of the funnel's spout. At three she emerged; sad, despairing perhaps, but not bound.

Mrs. Kent half sat up in bed. Thus raised, she could see herself in the mirror on the wall opposite. Behind her cheekbones, behind her eyes, she could feel a tide of warmth. But her face, reflected in the mirror, looked white and cool.

If only it would stay that way. Perhaps it would. She put her hand to her cheek, but the cheek was hot. Not so hot, however, as some days, she thought. She lay back with a stir of hope; perhaps there would be no flush today. Three months ago that word had only pleasant connotations for her: "the flush of hope," "the flush of youth." Now it meant but one thing: "the hectic flush of the dying consumptive." Sometime, years ago, she had read that phrase, and it had meant nothing to her; six words in some story. How had she been able to read with no horrible start, no coagulation of blood, no premonition of doom, these terrible words? Yet, premonitions there may have been, for the words had stayed with her. She could even remember the book in which she had first read them, a book called *English Orphans*; a silly book she had gulped down when she was ten or eleven years old. There was a girl in the book named Rose, a headstrong girl who would not obey her mother. She was a vain girl, too, and she went to a party in a snowstorm with only a scarf about her shoulders and light dancing slippers on her feet. But she was punished for her wayward ways. She began to cough, she had a hectic flush, she died.

Mrs. Kent turned her top pillow over so that she might have the cool side against her shoulders. She carefully pushed her hair back so that it did not touch her cheeks, keep from her whatever air was stirring. At the top of each cheek, she could feel a round spot burning, burning. She could feel waves of heat given off by those discs of fire. She could feel the spots growing in circumference, until they would cover her entire face. But she reminded herself that this had little to do with temperature, for one day when her flush had been deepest and most painful, her temperature had been almost normal. This was unpleasant, it was hateful, but it meant nothing.

All footsteps had ceased. It was after one. Rest period. She made an effort to direct her mind to matters beyond her sickness. But what else matters, she thought. My temperature tells me how I progress. It tells me whether I am living or dying. It is the only real thing. What is past is mine no more and my temperature will tell me whether or not I have a future. Why do people say to me, "But you have always done so many things. Your memories must be a great comfort." In books, authors who have never known a sick day have their heroines, sick to death, luxuriate in their memories. My memories burn and scald me. Had I never known any other life, then I would never have known the bitterness of renunciation. Blot out my memory! Let me forget that I have a husband, a child, work. Let my body forget that it ever sprung into the air, cleft a wave, or clambered up a rock. Clean my mind of torturing memories—then this routine of death may be bearable.

We all overdramatize our ills, I suppose. Or do we? Even Keats: "That is arterial blood. It is my death warrant." Ah, but it was! Katherine Mansfield leaped from her bed to say, "Hark, hark, the lark at heaven's gate sings," and, with the consumptive's beautiful feeling for contrast, had a hemorrhage, and all of her beautiful words were blotted out forever.

Mrs. Kent raised herself in bed that she might look at her face again. The flush spread to ear and jawbone, a satiny purplish mask. Her eyes were bright and large; bright and large like a bunny's eyes when it is lifted by its long soft ears, and the stick that is to crush the delicate bones of its head is poised above it. And yet people cried, "How well you look, Marianne. Anyone can tell that with that fine color there's little wrong with you." Anyone who knows anything can tell a block away I'm consumptive.

The handbook said, "Many nervous girls and women may have a

temperature for months after all activity has stopped." I'm nervous. This temperature probably means nothing. I may not even have any today. Ninety-nine and six-tenths yesterday. That's nothing, really nothing. It doesn't go on the doctor's chart until it's over 99.6. That's only a degree. Many a child goes to school with that temperature. And it's so hot today. The heat really accounts for four-tenths of a degree. If it weren't for the heat, my temperature would probably be only 99.2. And for many people, for sensitive, emotional people, 99 is normal. That only gives me two-tenths of a degree of fever. And what's two-tenths of a degree? Many thermometers have more than that much error! They incline to err with age. Oh, if I only had a new thermometer; this old one has the habit of rising; the mercury mounts before I get it near my mouth. If I were to lift it now and look at it, I would see that it had already risen. This is the hour it triumphs. It waits for three o'clock so that it can see me tremble. When I hold it in my mouth, my heart beats so that it is jarred by every thud. It shan't have that satisfaction today. I don't care if it reads 99.6; that's just the heat and my nervousness.

Why do I delude myself so? It is fever, fever. My eyelids are hot against my eyes. My armpits are dry; the back of my neck burns. It is fever. "You must fight, Marianne," they say. How fight fever? What cool thought can quench a fire? Let green waves with their heavy, cool weight fall upon me, bathe me with the foam of many waves, and still, deep in me, this coal would burn. Let snow fall upon me, let it be blown against my body by a bleak, icy wind, let all earth be held in a black frost, rigid as iron, and still my body would pulse with heat. Let me lie naked, face down, upon an iceberg floating in a frozen sea, and my hot breast would melt the ice beneath me.

"You must fight, Marianne!" I cannot fight this flame. I am fevered and I must die. I shall be consumed. They say truly, "She has consumption," for I am being consumed. Cranmer offered his hand to the flame first because it was a traitor. My whole body has betrayed me. I offer it to the flames. Burn and blacken, lick flesh from bones and turn bones to powder, and then at last a wind will blow through the powder and I shall be cool.

Oh, God, forgive my thoughts. Let me not burn. Give me a normal temperature for just a day, and tomorrow I shall not mind the fever

again. Just today, just as a sign I make some progress. That is not
much to ask, God. Most people have it and never thank you, and, oh!
God, I will thank you forever. I will praise your blessed name through
eternity. I will be an ever-vocal witness of your loving kindness. If it
couldn't be 98.6, then 99. I do not ask the impossible, God. I do not
ask that I have no fever, only that it will be a little better than yesterday, as a sign that this will pass away. Oh, I do not fear. I have asked
in faith. I shall be better today. This is perhaps the turning point, I
shall remember that from this day, all went better.

"It's not bad today, is it, Miss Williams?"

"Not bad at all, Mrs. Kent. The same as yesterday, 99.6."

# The Day of the Hawk

The doctor said that if I could watch "something die, without flinching," I could consider myself well again. Something, he said, that "needed to die, that had to be killed in the course of events."

I told him I didn't think that made much difference. The "needing to die" part. The agony of salt isn't any easier for the silvery slug because the gardener says it needs to die, and kerosene and flame aren't any more soothing to ants because their death is a good riddance. Oh, God, in what agony will they wave their little hands! No, if I'm to watch something die, it won't matter whether it needs to die or not; what we feel doesn't affect an animal's feelings. The lamb isn't reassured when it sees the knife at its throat by the thought that it is needed for chops. No, I think more clearly about this than does Uncle Doc, for all that I'm the patient and he's the doctor. He could learn some things from me.

I think I can do it, though. I've accepted death—it has to be. But if I am to look at something die, it had as well be a lark as a pig. It's all one to them whether they die for our sport or our good. I know I can do it. I've made progress in the last six months, I'm sure, and I shall take the first opportunity to prove it to Uncle Doc. Jim will be so glad if I can, for things couldn't have gone on much longer as they were. That I can admit this shows that I *have* made progress. Jim is so strong and reasonable that my weakness has been harder for him to bear than it would be for most men.

*Friday, February 17*

The weather has been stormy, so I have stayed in my room all day, reading and writing. Jim says that if he were the doctor, he'd take pen and paper from me. He says that I write, write, write, brooding over old and past things, and that this makes me more neurotic. But he's wrong. Really, it's just the other way around. I *am* young, and, as Jim says, my life is before me; but there have been sad happenings in the past, and though I do make an effort, my mind goes over and over them, and I think, If only I had done this or that, how different everything might be.

And as I think I'm back again to the moment when the decision had to be made, without knowing it my fingernails go into my palms, and all my body is rigid with effort. But when I write down these speculations and remorses, it eases my mind; it's out of my mind then, down here, and I need not think just how it all came about; and if I want to justify myself for saying yes, I can look back here and see how then it seemed the only thing to do. I can read it here, as if it had happened to some other woman; and I can understand how it happened to me.

Nothing I planned as a girl have I been able to carry out; except that I still write in my journal each day—and have for ten years. I like to look at the journals; there are twenty of them, quite a long row. Well, I've produced something.

*Sunday, February 19*

And still it rains. Not heavily, but there have been gusts all day. Jim has been playing golf even so. He is not fond of golf, but he says it helps him meet the right men, and there's nothing he wouldn't do to advance himself. He told me that when he married me, and it's been true.

Before he left he wanted to know when I was going to get out and put the doctor's advice to the test. I'm willing to any time. I want to, really want to; but Jim agreed it might be foolish venturing out into this rain.

Though it isn't a cold rain. California rains in February aren't cold, ever. Elinor was in this afternoon with a great bunch of yellow violets she had picked on Hunter's Hill. They were wet from the rain, and so sweet; sweeter and richer than blue violets, because yellow is a richer color than blue. Smelling them didn't seem enough; there was no depth of satisfaction in that! I wanted to bite them, to taste spring in them, to press them hard against my breast.

But when I did this, and rocked in delight to feel them so cool and fresh against my skin, Elinor said, "Stop that."

Once you've been ill, everyone wants you to be calm and repressed. Jim is always telling me to walk more slowly, for instance; but then, he did this even before we were married. But the violets were lovely, and I put them in a brown jug Mother used for cream when Elinor and I were girls at home. I put the jug on the windowsill, and it was almost as if the rain outside were falling on the violets. A green-and-yellow ladybug, shaped like a raindrop, crawled up the pane from the flowers. I raised the window and put it outside, for it's of use somewhere for pollinization. It made sense to put it outside.

Elinor and I talked of old times: how poor we were then and how happy, too. Elinor is happy now, for she is getting ahead with her painting. She looked beautiful, with her pale cool cheeks and black hair.

She said, "Do you remember how we used to plan to make a name together? You writing books, I illustrating them? The first one was going to be 'Thimble Farm.' Do you remember you said you were going to know all there was to know in this world?"

I told her I remembered, but that then I thought I could know all things in my mind from books and from observation. I didn't know of a knowledge to be got through veins and nerves and muscles. I didn't know anything about a knowledge that could thicken one's blood with sorrow.

Elinor cried out, "Oh, let's not talk of now, Sylvia. You've been sick. Let's think about our days at home. You were loud and cheerful then. Always clowning. Do you remember the dance you used to do to the 'Blue Danube'? Newspapers for wings, footstools for hedges? Then you would be a spring-intoxicated butterfly, you said, and fly about. How Mother used to laugh. You were fat, then, you know, and not at all graceful. When I would tell you you were fat, you'd say you were a 'pinguid pismire,' and when I said you were loud, you'd say you were a 'cachinnating cockalorum.' You did love big words."

So she talked on and on, laughing and smoking and putting her ashes in her pocket like a boy. I knew what she was trying to do, for she kept glancing at me out of the corner of her eye, and she looked pleased when I smiled. But there is no need for that sort of thing with me any more. I'm quite reconciled and content.

I enjoyed the talk of our days at home with Mother for its own sake, not because it was distracting. I hadn't remembered for a long time that I used to be able to milk; or that I could squirt a stream right into Tabby's mouth. And how once, when Elinor and I were delivering milk at night, we got frightened and sang "God will take care of you, o'er all the way, through all the day" all the way home. It was Sunday night, and they heard us at church and thought we were sacrilegious, but we were really earnest and prayerful.

We were laughing and admiring the colors of the afterglow through the eucalyptus, a beautiful wintry green flecked with burnished gold and rose, when Jim came in. We had forgotten to turn on the lights, and only Elinor's cigarette gleamed from where she sat in the window seat.

Jim switched on the light and said, "No moping in the dark, girls." Though it wasn't dark yet. Then he said to me, "How's my pet? Haven't been smoking, have you?"

Jim thinks smoking is unwomanly, as well as dangerous in other ways. I hadn't, so Jim began to tell us about his golf. He had played with Mr. Nathan. He could have beaten him, but he said Nathan would enjoy playing with him more next time if he let him win. Elinor left before he had time to finish. Jim called her a "little devil," and she says she hates diminutives.

*Monday, February 20*

"My room really has for me a touch of fairy. Is there anything better than my room. Anything outside?" Katherine Mansfield said that, and I feel it, too. My room isn't beautiful, but it holds so many things I love; my books, my pictures, my little ticking clock. My candles waiting to burn for me. And, sitting here on my window seat, I can see old Skytop, with its head in the clouds this morning, and the Santa Ana looks as if it had a fair stream of water in it after last night's rain. The sky is clearing now, though, and I think I'll go out this afternoon. I've been inside for months, and there's no longer any need of it. Uncle Doc is right. I'm ready to live an unsheltered life.

The talk with Elinor yesterday afternoon has made me think again of how this all came about. All would have been different, I suppose, if I had never met Jim—or never married him. But once I had met him I think I never considered anything else. Oh! I cannot analyze my actions. Though I ask myself a thousand times, Why! I can never answer. I can only see myself doing what I did as if compelled.

I suppose Elinor's yellow violets brought it all to mind again. I was picking violets on Hunter's Hill when I first met Jim. I had gone up on a Sunday afternoon late. After reading and writing all day, I wanted fresh air more than I wanted violets, but the hill was covered, and they were so beautiful I couldn't resist picking them.

When I had my hands full I went to the little round palm-covered summerhouse on top of the hill to rest and watch the valley lights come on. Jim was there. He had been there all afternoon studying. I had seen him before, of course, and had even spoken to him in the newspaper office. He was the new man in Meyer Feldstrom's office. I thought he was—I still think he is—the most beautiful man I've ever seen. I have often tried to describe him in order to discover why this particular face is, for me, so compelling. What it has—not just a beauty of line and coloring, of black hair and eyes, and clean fine jawline, and a nose not blurred with flesh—is a definite promise of compassionate intelligence. It moved me then, as it does now, and then I had no reason in the world not to be happy that he liked me.

We talked in the summerhouse for some time that evening. He said, I remember, that the social notes I wrote for the paper were the best social notes he had ever read. He knew my Uncle Horace, the editor. He knew my Uncle Doc.

I don't know whether it was then, or later, he told me of his life. He was almost thirty then. He had been poor, not as Elinor and I were poor, but living in squalor and misery, with a lazy, unambitious family about him. He had rid himself of them, and by denial and hard work and absolutely ruthless determination had finished college and passed his bar examinations. And every step since then had been toward an advancement. Belleview isn't a large place, but Feldstrom is known all over the state, and next year Jim takes Meyer's place when he goes to Washington. All this is only the beginning, Jim says, and I know he's right.

I suspect it was partly because of his ambition and determination that he appealed to me. I dream so much, and carry so little through myself. I don't know why he wanted to marry me. I didn't, even then, do the things he likes a woman to. I wasn't pretty. Or not very. Of course my being related to everyone for miles about was some help to him. Anyway, we did marry. I was wild to marry him, hating the delay of getting clothes and household things together.

Elinor cried all through the ceremony, and when she took my flowers she said, "You damned idiot," but the minister thought she said, "God bless you," and smiled on her.

### Tuesday, February 21

The rain is over, I'm sure. The fragrance of the lilies under my window determines me to go out this afternoon. I haven't set my foot on earth for six months, and then before that I was in bed for three months. Uncle Doc was here this morning to see if I had been out yet and had followed his advice. I told him no, but that I was going this afternoon.

Then he said, "Remember, Sylvia, avoid nothing. You cannot change anything. You must either accept life as it is or continue to hide here in your room as you have done for six months. That isn't living: to sit here on the window seat and peer out at life like some old, half-blind owl, and write in your book that the sun shines, or it doesn't."

Oh! Uncle Doc is good for me, and what he says is true.

Then he said, "Sylvia, you've never talked to me of what lay behind your trouble. I know the outlines, of course, and it isn't out of any curiosity I ask you, but for your own sake. Until you can talk of this thing, put it away from you in words, the seeds of it are still deep in you, and though you think you give it no nourishment, it will grow in spite of you."

I told him I could not talk of it, not to him even; not even though I knew he was right; I knew he was a thousand times right.

"Well, Sylvia," he said, "you know what you can do, though I know what's best for you to do. Could you write it in your book, Sylvia? Write it all out for me? Then when I've read it, perhaps we can talk."

I didn't tell him I would, I couldn't promise. But I think I can and that it will help. To write here has helped with everything else; and I hope that when I see the words written out, saying that this I did, and this, it will be as if another woman, and not I, had been responsible for those actions. But even if for Uncle Doc I'm able to write the facts, they won't be true. Not in all the lines of every book in the world can the truth of what I felt night after night after night, and day after day, be recorded.

When I told Jim, he said, "In God's name, why didn't you take care?" Just that, nothing else. I shall never forget these words. I said, "What difference can two months make?" He said, "It makes all the difference in the world to my image and to the way your family is going to think of me." I said, "We're married. No one's going to pay any attention to a baby a month or two early." He said, "There's no need to take a chance on that. I'll arrange things."

Jim respected you so much, Uncle Doc, he didn't want me to breathe a word of it to you. "There's no use dragging him into it. I'll make the arrangements, and no one will be the wiser." He made the arrangements, and I did as he said; and we were all wiser and sadder.

I don't need to tell you the rest, Uncle Doc. I was sick then, and you came. As long as I was sick, everything was all right. I could think of nothing but the pain. And I believed I would die, too. Oh, I longed to die. But you know that I got better, and finally you brought me home, and soon I was as strong as ever.

It wasn't until the day of the hawk, was it, Uncle Doc, that you knew, about the other? I had known for a long time, but until then I had kept it hidden from everyone. At first I myself did not understand what compelled me to act as I did. And then I knew and justified my actions to myself. I had to do what I did. It was the only retribution I could make—I must help all living things to stay alive. Now nothing more must die because of me, and perhaps many things that would have died, except for me, would live.

I was busy all those early days after I came home from the hospital, busy and happy and crafty, that Jim might not know. Oh, it took time and patience. There were the bees caught in the gum of a diseased tree, alive and fighting, but doomed to die. I saved them all. I gave them hours of life they would not otherwise have had.

When the water ran low in the reservoir, carp and catfish were left half exposed to the air, floundering and dying. I saved them, too. It was backbreaking work carrying them in a bucket of water to put in a ditch that hadn't gone dry. But I did it, and all the thanks I wanted was in the eyes of those fish, as they looked at me with gratitude when I dropped them in the water. They blessed me with their eyes and forgave me my sin.

But it wasn't only animals: it was plants as well, for they are tender and living, and they can suffer and die even as we. If ivy was choking out a violet, I must dig it up and plant it where it might live. A strand of honeysuckle vine had worked under the telephone wire where it ran around the corner of the house, and was growing yellow and pinched. It would soon have died, but I saved it, and it bloomed with heavier blossom than it ever had before. Pale new grass pushed itself from beneath heavy boards that were holding it down. I lifted the boards to give the grass a taste of the sun. But when the boards were lifted, clay-colored sow bugs ran about in dismay. The sun which brought life to the grass brought death to them, so I carried them to a damp darkness where they might live.

I know now that I cannot do as I did then, but I cannot but believe that what I did then was right; that a virtue bloomed in me then that I do not now have; that if all were made as I was then, this world would know a happiness it has long forgotten.

Yes, Uncle Doc, I am reconciled, though I cannot say that those days were wrong. I was very close to all living things then, and though it meant agony to me whenever they suffered, I rejoiced when they triumphed and lived. I helped thousands of animals and plants. I kept a record; each night I wrote down what I had been able to do during the day, for it seemed to me then as if there were a scale and on one side was my sin, heavy, black, horrible, and on the other were all the soft, velvet-throated flowers and the animals with their wary, tolerant eyes, which except for me would be dead, sunk into formless pulp. Each night I added to the living side of the scales what I had saved during the day: perhaps only a hairy spider, or a big-eyed wasp, but always the other side weighed heavier and sometimes I feared I could never balance it. And I never have, for a thousand lives saved cannot replace one life taken.

All this time, though, you, and Jim, too, knew I was unwell and strange. You didn't know until the day of the hawk, did you, that I was "unbalanced," as Jim said. You remember that I cried out that that was just the word, "unbalanced," and that I must work day and night until the scales balanced again. When Jim said that, I believed the scales I saw were visible to all, and all saw that my sin was so heavy and black that the scales kicked the beam.

Do you remember the day of the hawk, Uncle Doc? You and Elinor and Jim and I had driven over the hills through the barley fields east of town. The barley was waist high and bearded, but blue-green yet, and not ready for the bailer. I asked Jim to stop so that we could watch the wind waves in the barley, and the cloud shadows that swept like ships across it. While we sat watching, a hawk flew low, and there was a movement, not of the wind in the barley. I knew the hawk was hanging over a rabbit or a squirrel that had run into the barley to hide. But there were patches of thin barley, and all at once the hawk swooped down, and I knew that the next minute it would have its talons in soft flesh and fur. So, before any of you could stop me, I was through the barbed-wire fence, and into the barley, screaming and waving my arms. But I had hesitated a minute too long, and the hawk dropped on the bunny. Can you forget that rabbit's cry as it felt the hawk's talons enter its flesh, a thin, clear, child-like cry of anguish and surprise?

Then I was overwhelmed to think that once more I had failed, and that death had come again through me, and I forgot to be crafty and secret, and cried and screamed. I was determined not to go home, but to sit there on the little hill that overlooked the barley field and save whatever else came there for shelter. I lay on my face and clung to the rocks, for Jim tried by force to make me leave. It was then that Jim called me unbalanced. That was the day you knew at last, and the day you finally took me away.

I never told you the reason for the day of the hawk until now; and now you will understand that it was right for me to do as I did, and that only in that way could I expiate my sin. But in the hospital where you took me, and in these months here at home, I have seen that I cannot go on as I was. I am reconciled to bearing the burden of what I did. I accept death. I tried to be a god and to give life. Now that is past, and I shall do as you say, Uncle Doc. I shall go outside. I shall have Jim's friends here again. I want his smile and praise. Uncle Doc, you will not for my sake show to Jim any of that hostility for him I feel you sometimes have? Oh, do not, for I want his kindness; more, much more than that, more than I can easily write.

Now I have told you everything, and I am glad, glad you asked it of me. You share the heaviness now, and my heart is much lighter for that sharing. The rain is over, Uncle Doc. I shall call Elinor and ask her to walk with me this afternoon. You shall have this tomorrow to read; then let us never speak of it again. It will still be a dark thing, but behind me.


*Tuesday, 4:00 p.m.*

Elinor has just left: she wouldn't go with me. But Jim is home now changing his clothes. We're going to walk through the orchard; see if the rain caused much washing. I think the cover crop held the soil, though; there's little mud on the road.

There should be some tangerines left on the two trees at the far end of the ranch. I think no one has been back there for weeks.

I have on my brown boots and pants and my green sweater and cap. I've admired myself in the mirror for ten minutes. I look so strong and hearty. I look a very mountaineer whose boots cover miles every day. My face looked aback at me from the mirror like anybody's face, friendly, and even, yes, good.

Oh! I am happy, happy! In spite of Elinor and what she said this afternoon. I told her I was going out; that Uncle Doc thought I was able to and should. She was glad about that, but she wanted me to leave Jim and live with her and Mother. She has never liked or appreciated Jim, never. I do not know why, for he has always been kind and gallant to her. She was bitter and urgent, walking about the room, rearranging my books and pictures and not knowing what she did. Her mouth got thin and straight, as it does when she's in earnest, and her cheeks burned.

She said, "Sylvia, remember the old days. We can bring them back." I wouldn't listen to her. She said, "Sylvia, you can't bring it off without help. You won't get it. Forgive me, Sylvia, but come home with me."

I told her I couldn't leave Jim. She was angry when she left, not even "Good-bye," and her gloves and books forgotten on the table.

I hear Jim's door close and his heavy steps; he, too, has changed into his boots. So, we leave the house, and its darkness, and we go out into the orchard.

*September*

So long since I have written here. Uncle Doc brought me my book weeks ago, but I could not bear to open it. I boasted of my happiness and virtue. Oh, God, I claimed them for my own. One must never do that. Perhaps if I had not, I wouldn't have lost them. But I lost them, I lost them in a minute, in less than a minute, between dusk and dark. The sun went down, with the heel of my boot I put out the light, and its scream was red, red on the black clouds. Red, red on the windows. Red in Jim's eyes, red on the heel of my boot. Red and shrill, pain screamed red and shrill, and then was quiet. Gray, nasty pulpy death. I put out the light. I brought gray, pulpy death again. I killed. I killed.

Jim said, "Kill it."

It came out of its hole, half drowned, and its fur was streaked with mud and it shivered with the cold.

It cried, "Save me." It cried, "Give me life."

Jim kicked it with his boot, and he called to me, "Step on that damned gopher!"

I longed to please him. This was my test. I stepped, and its bones crackled like thunder and its cry was like lightning through the thunder.

My boot was the end of the world for it. It lifted its eyes to my face and asked for life. I trod it down to the dust, down to join my son. I sent him a playmate.

My son will say to him, "Do you know my mother?"

And he will answer, "Death is your mother. Murder is her name. And she is red, red and dripping in heavy boots."

Oh, murder is my name, murder is my name, and I am red that all shall know.

# Like Visitant of Air

THE GREAT EQUINOCTIAL STORMS were past, but heavy rain still fell. The greasy swells of the Atlantic were indented by multitudinous wind-driven drops. In England, as far north as Yorkshire, rain was sprayed down the mouths of wide chimneys and hissed for a second on well-fed fires.

Through all of October the New England coast was pelted with the loose, not very cold rain of early fall. In Boston, in Cambridge, the cobblestones were drenched and lumbering cart horses put down their feet warily; gutters were fluid and eaves musical. There was so much rain that what the ear noticed was not the constant gurgle and splash, but its cessation.

Moss was especially green in the northern niches of the stone walls about Concord. Emerson, in his study, harkened with pleasure to the cheerful drumming; Minott got out his fishing tackle and came home in the evening, wet, but with a goodly string of pickerel.

Thoreau, at Walden, leaned back in his hard chair and listened attentively. He left the page before him on his little slant-topped desk half-filled. His ear, attuned to the music of the telegraph wire and the owl's cry, to the dry rustle of scrub-oak leaves and the surf-like sound of the draft in his stove, heard much in the rain others missed.

It was water, it was wet, it was rain. The sounds said more than that to Thoreau. He knew the pools and ponds, the creeks and rills and marshes it was filling now; he knew the roots that sucked thirstily, the summer-dried nests that swelled as if with life beneath the day-long downpour.

He noted the wind's veering, its increase in velocity. His big nose picked up through the cabin's unplastered walls the spicy scent of wet and wind-bruised sassafras.

He walked to the door, and, opening it, looked out into the dark wet night. It was late. In Concord all lights were out. In Emerson's home, in Channing's, in Cyrus Hubbard's, all slept, or lay unsleeping listening to the constant long liquid chuckle of the rain. He thrust a hand out into the stormy night in order to come at the rain more nakedly.

He had a sudden longing to step out into the rain, to walk toward someone, to walk to someone, come bone-drenched to someone and enter; to be known and dried, and say without preamble what the rain, its sound and meaning, were to him. His muscled and adroit hand closed about the water his palm held.

Where go? To whom speak? In Concord no one listened for his footsteps. He closed the door. In the light of his well-trimmed lamp rainwater glistened on his brown hand. He looked down at his half-written page . . . and yet, there was someone to whom he spoke. He wrote for someone, his words were for some ear.

He pulled out his chair, picked up his pen and held it poised, listening, then laid it down.

On the table lay the books. On the hearth burned the fire, meager but ruddy, not less alive for being small. It was afternoon if you looked at the clock, night if darkness counted.

In the doorway of the room Anne stood, twilight and order laced together like a poem for her reading. An ordered beauty. To know, oh! not to know, that was to presume, but to believe, that for one evening, at least, they were safe, that nothing could take the books, the small fire, the windows neatly set away from them; to believe that for one evening nothing could interrupt their words; no screaming, no stumbling, no sobbing. And that there would be no dying away into silence until a suitable ending had been reached. The framed, the metered, the musical, the self-contained: these they would make and these would endure beyond flesh.

Anne was the poet; the room, that night, was poetry to her of a kind her soft and well-intentioned words could never make real. She stood on the poem's threshold; it was pain not to enter.

The room was taut with perfection; a pin-point tension lay across it like the film with which a brimming glass protects its flood. It seemed, perhaps, as if she would never enter, but stand, always outside, regarding.

Yet the hand as well as the eye loves order, and she walked down into the room and touched the three stacks of books that waited on the table: Charlotte's the highest; Emily's a single book and writing block; her own, which made her smile, books and papers, needles and folded cloth, and thimble atop it all like a dome or minaret. "My little writing housewife," Emily had called her.

She paced from hearth to window the way the three were used to pace together. She straightened the hearthrug, which, angled by inches from the horizontal, was setting the room awry. Now the room was perfect, nothing lacking, spare and warm and clean; shining like holiness, and twice as reassuring. This was what Emily had said.

She pressed her hand against the window. Glass could not stop the wind's cold force; what her hand felt was, beyond the glass, buffeting Emily's whole body as she tramped the moors.

"Anne," said Charlotte, coming into the room with her quick unquiet steps, her hurried household rustle which echoed the wind, "stand away from those draughts. Or put on a shawl."

"Emily's walking in the wind," said Anne.

"She's dressed for it," said Charlotte. And then with her implacable rectitude, "At least I hope she is."

"It's so late," said Anne. "I'd be afraid out this time of night. I'd think she'd come in when night comes."

"Oh, Emily . . . Emily," said Charlotte, her dark solicitous face both loving and chagrined. "She'll stay out later, I don't doubt. I've gone and angered her."

"Angered?" asked Anne.

"Come," said Charlotte, "let's poke up the fire. Let's not be so cautious. Let's send a few sparks up the chimney."

She laid her arms across Anne's shoulders. Together they paced the stretch from window to fire. Charlotte rattled the grate with energy. "Throw on another chunk, Anne. Let's have a blaze . . . let's remember tonight. Emily's got her wind. Let's us have a fire. If I choose fire and Emily the wind, what do you choose, Anne?"

"The sea," said Anne softly. "I've always loved it. And flowers, too," she said. "May I choose two, Charlotte?"

"Throw on another piece," said Charlotte, poking fiercely. "Yes, I give you flowers and the sea. I keep fire," she said.

"Emily'll want rain, too," said Anne. "And some place to see the wind and rain from. She'll want the moors to go with them."

"All right." Charlotte stood with her back to the blazing fire. "Wind, rain, the moors. That makes three for Emily. You take three now."

"The sea. Flowers." Anne thought. "Love," she added.

"That's not the same," Charlotte objected. "You changed the category. That's noumenon, not phenomenon."

"All the same," said Anne, "I take it. Flowers, the sea, love."

"Oh, Anne, Anne," said Charlotte. "Here we stand talking. Here we stand choosing. As if we could choose. Do you ever think where we are, Anne? The moors hanging over us, the graveyard below. Lost between them. No one knows we live or breathe. No one ever will know. And you choose love. Who is there to love? Have you seen a face? Heard a voice?"

"I didn't mean it that way, not just that way."

"Why not?" asked Charlotte, leaning forward, so that her thin sallow face was rosy in the light. "Why not? We have a right to. We have talent here. We have great talent here, worthy to be loved and great enough for honor."

"Loving-kindness," said Anne, "was what . . ."

"Loving-kindness," said Charlotte scornfully. "That's due to all. That's duty." She stood away from the table where she was leaning. She trod the few steps before the fireplace as if the fire she had chosen burned in her heart. "I think of something beyond loving-kindness. I think of Emily," she said. "Do you think loving-kindness her just dessert?"

"She never spoke," said Anne, "of wanting . . ."

"She never will speak," said Charlotte. "The hills can molder, these tombstones rot"—Charlotte's dark head flashed hillward and graveward—"before she'll speak. But she will write . . . she does write."

"Charlotte," said Anne, "you didn't . . ."

"I did," said Charlotte somberly. "I did, and she is angry . . . and if she should stay out all night . . . if she should catch her death out there . . . and I suffer because of it . . . forever—still, what I did was right."

"Right," said Anne. "It was her private book."

"You knew about it?"

Yes was the only answer, but Anne would only nod her head.

"Why?" asked Charlotte. "Why would she not tell me? Why only you?"

"You would do something about it," Anne said. "You would talk about it."

"I will," said Charlotte. "I will do something about it. I will talk about it. Emily is a genius."

Anne started up from her stool. Genius—that was a solemn word, and Charlotte used words carefully.

"Did you read them all, Charlotte?"

"Every one."

"What did she say to you?"

"About six words . . . thief . . . Peeping Tom."

"They were hers, her soul."

"It is a great soul. It has no right to hide. Here in this house, by this fire, even, lines no other woman could have written." Charlotte was rigidly quiet when she became excited. "She can imagine greatly, write lines so wild and melancholy, so terse and vigorous, no man alive can equal them. But she's a woman . . . she will write in a private book . . . walk on the moor, and all will be lost."

Anne said, "You write, too, Charlotte."

"I do," said Charlotte. "I mean to make it known. But I cannot do what Emily does. I see this world. Emily sees beyond. I can tell you how the wind sounds round the corner of this house. Emily hears how it sounded before there was ever a house for it to touch. She shall be known, too."

"Charlotte," asked Anne, "even if she does not want it?"

"She does want it," said Charlotte fiercely. "Why did she not destroy them? Why did she copy them carefully? Writing's not just the hand moving. It's speaking to someone, somewhere. Emily shall have her chance to see to whom she's speaking."

Anne went to Charlotte. She pressed her hand against the two veins that sharply throbbed on Charlotte's forehead. "I have a book of poems, too," she said. "Will you read them, Charlotte?"

Charlotte, trusted, was fierce no longer. "See, Anne, I told you this is a night to remember."

"They aren't like Emily's," said Anne.

"Oh, no," said Charlotte. "How could they be? You aren't like Emily. They'll be good and sweet."

"But not great."

"Goodness and sweetness are great," said Charlotte. "They'll be in a book all together." She leaned toward the fire as if reading them there. "Think of it, Anne. The three of us together."

The wind had died away from its steady blowing, but sudden explosive gusts still rattled the shutters. "It's coming on to rain again," said Charlotte. "Listen."

"Emily'll be in now," said Anne. "She won't leave us worrying."

Keeper growled in the entryway. "Emily," called Charlotte.

Anne's eyes waited for Emily. She came in quietly. There were drops of rain on her brown hair. She closed the door quickly behind her so that no wind could have entered the room; still there was something like wind and like autumn in the room now that she was there. Anne gazed at her sister. When she is on the moors, she is the wind. She does not just listen to it; she cries with it, she swoops with it . . . she can't be expected to stop all of a sudden.

Perfection in a room. Polished, with curtains and chairs; a wooden wall with glass set in it; a hole bricked up in one wall for a fire; dishes to eat from; and a needle to pull thread through a cloth . . . But the wind will blow it all away. Let all housewifely things vanish! While she watched Emily, the walls irked Anne; they fretted her. Let them blow away; perhaps then she, too, could hear the wind, as it had sounded before it ever blew near the dusted and neatly kept corners of a house.

Emily leaned against the mantel, tall and supple, one hand extended toward the fire. "It's warming up outside," she said, "now that it's begun to rain."

We'll talk of the weather now, Anne thought; but no, Charlotte would not.

"Emily," she said, "I'm sorry if I pained you. I'm not sorry I read your poems. It was my duty, and I'm thankful every hour that I chanced on that book. I think it was put in my way. I think there was Providence in it."

Emily inclined her head toward the hand that rested on the mantel and sniffed at a piece of gorse she'd brought in with her. She seemed still to be where it had been.

"Emily," said Charlotte, "you must work at them. They must be copied. I have plans. They don't belong to you. They belong to the world."

"The world," said Emily, and threw her piece of gorse into the fire. Anne watched it curl there. It was almost as if Emily herself were burning. "They belong to me. They did belong to me," she said. She picked up her book and writing block from the table.

"Where are you going?" Charlotte asked.

"To my room," said Emily.

Charlotte sprang from her chair. "You've just come in, you're cold. I must go read to Papa, anyway. Stay, stay. I won't be here to annoy you." She took her own stack of belongings under her arm. At the door she turned back. "Bonnie love," Charlotte said; but Anne saw no change in Emily's face as the door closed behind Charlotte.

Emily replaced her things, then whistled Keeper in from the hall. She sat before the fire, one arm about his neck.

"She said," said Anne, explaining Charlotte, "you were a genius."

Emily stroked Keeper's knobby ears, and when she stopped, Keeper's nose nudged her into stroking again.

"She said," Anne went on, "you had a right to find the person for whom those words were written." She hesitated before Emily's indifference. She said, "The one to whom your heart spoke had a right to hear your words."

"How could poems be written," asked Emily, "to someone unknown?"

"You know someone?" asked Anne.

Emily laughed. She had a better laugh, Anne thought, than anyone else in this house; neither thin, nor sharp, nor wild. "Which curate?" Emily asked. "Perhaps the little man who sells us writing paper? Or that schoolmaster Charlotte reveres? Annie, Annie."

"She said it isn't only the *hand* that writes."

"It isn't, it isn't," said Emily.

" 'The heart speaking'—those were Charlotte's words."

"That's fanciful," Emily said.

"We chose three things while you were out."

"For me, too?" asked Emily.

"For you," Anne told her. "The wind, the moors, rain."

Emily was silent.

"For me, flowers, the sea, love. I meant loving-kindness, but Charlotte thought not."

Emily looked up from the fire and said nothing.

"She said there was in this house that which was worthy of love and honor."

"Let it stay here," said Emily violently, clutching Keeper's scruff so sharply he growled. "Let it stay here. There is one who hears. I shall never find him. There is one in whose ear my words would be like his own. I shall never know him. Every syllable I say he would say yes to. He exists. He is not fancy. He lives. This wind blows to him, this rain sounds to him as it does to me. His step would match mine. These walls would mean as little to him as they do to me. Listen," she said.

The rain was being slapped against the house; there was no sound any longer of drops, but of water heavy as a wave against the side of a ship.

"That is real. He is real. Charlotte is mistaken. There is no one else to hear or who cares to hear. Love and honor," she said, "I have nothing to sell for them. They are a gift."

Anne watched her sister. She spoke as if she saw; she looked as if she communed, as if behind the wind, beyond the rain, there was a voice that answered, an ear that heard.

Anne waited a long time before she spoke again. "Charlotte said this would be a night to remember."

Emily, half reclining on Keeper, lay back, her eyes on the fire that had begun to burn low.

"Who will remember?" she asked.

At Walden, Thoreau, who had for a long time sat motionless, listening to the ceaseless autumnal drumming, glanced back over what he had been writing: *"this afternoon . . . shall I go down this long hill*

*in the rain? . . . I ask myself. And I say to myself, Yes, roam far
. . . you are really free. The noble life is continuous and unremitting
. . . live with a longer radius . . . Dismiss prudence. . . ."*

He picked up his pen, dipped it in ink and wrote again. *"Remember
only what is promised. Make the day light you and night hold a
candle."*

He remembered the night outside, unlit and candleless; he heard
the wind and rain. Alone he listened, alone he spoke. He opened his
door once more, once more thrust his hand out into the darkness,
and spoke with great urgency. "Where are you?" he said. "Where are
you?"

# The Condemned Librarian

LOUISE MCKAY, M.D., the librarian at Beaumont High School, sent me another card today. It was on the wickerwork table, where Mother puts my snack, when I got home from teaching. This afternoon the snack was orange juice and graham crackers, the orange juice in a plain glass, so that the deepness, the thickness of the color was almost like a flame inside a hurricane lamp. The graham crackers were on a blue willowware plate, and it just so happened that Dr. McKay's card was Van Gogh's "Sunflowers." It was a perfect still life, the colors increasing in intensity through the pale sand of the wickerwork table to the great bong (I want to say), for I swear I could hear it, of Van Gogh's flaming sunflowers. I looked at the picture Mother had composed for me (I don't doubt) for some time before I read Dr. McKay's card.

Dr. McKay sends me about four cards a year—not at any particular season, Christmas, Easter, or the like. Her sentiments are not suited to such festivals. Usually her message is only a line or two: "Why did you do it?" or "Condemned, condemned, condemned." Something very dramatic and always on a postcard, so that the world at large can read it if it chooses. Mother shows her perfect tact by saying nothing if she does read. Perhaps she doesn't; though a single sentence in a big masculine hand is hard to miss. Except for her choice of the Van Gogh print, which showed her malice, Dr. McKay's message this afternoon was very mild—for her. "I am still here, which will no doubt make you happy."

Apart from the fact that anyone interested in the welfare of human beings generally would want her there (or at least not practicing in a hospital), it does make me happy. This evening when I pulled down the flag, I was somehow reassured, standing there in the schoolyard with the cold north wind blowing the dust in my face, to think that over there on the other side of the mountains Louise McKay was

423

ending her day, too. Take away the mountains and fields and we might be gazing into each other's eyes.

I sat down in my room with the juice my mother had squeezed—we hate substitutes—and looked at the card and remembered when I had first seen that marching handwriting. Everything else about her has changed, but not that. I saw it first on the card she gave me telling me of my next date with her. From the moment I arrived at Oakland State, I started hearing about Dr. Louise McKay. She was a real campus heroine, though for no real reason. Except that at a teachers college, with no football heroes, no faculty members with off-campus reputations, the craving for superiority must satisfy itself on the material at hand, however skimpy. And for a student body made up of kids and middle-aged teachers come to Oakland from the lost little towns of mountain and desert, I suppose it was easy to think of Dr. McKay as heroic or fascinating or accomplished.

I was different, though. I was neither middle-aged nor a kid. I was twenty-six years old and I had come to Oakland expecting something. I had had choices. I had made sacrifices to get there, sacrifices for which no "heroic" lady doctor, however "fascinating," "well dressed" (I can't remember all the phrases used about her now), could be a substitute.

I had a very difficult time deciding to go to Oakland State. I had taught at Liberty School for six years and I loved that place. It was "beautiful for situation," as the Bible says, located ten miles out of town in the rolling semidry upland country where the crop was grain, not apricots and peaches. It was a one-room school, and I was its only teacher. It stood in the midst of this sea of barley and oats like an island. In winter and spring this big green sea of ripening grain rolled and tossed about us—all but crested and broke—all but, though never quite. In a way, this was irritating.

For half the year at Liberty there were no barley waves to watch, only the close-cut stubble of reaped fields and the enormous upthrust of the San Jacinto Mountains beyond. Color was my delight then. I used to sit out in the schoolyard at noon or recess and paint. A former teacher had discarded an old sleigh-back sofa, had it put out in the yard halfway between the school and the woodshed. It stood amidst the volunteer oats and mustard like a larger growth. It seemed planted in earth. In the fall when Santa Anas blew, tumbleweeds piled up about it. I don't know how long it had been there when I arrived, but it had taken well to its life in the fields; its legs balanced, its springs stayed inside the upholstery, and the upholstery itself still kept some of its original cherry tones. There I sat—when I wasn't playing ball with the kids—like a hunter, hidden in a game blind; only my game wasn't lions and tigers, it was the whole world, so to speak: the mountains, the grain fields, the kids, the schoolhouse itself. I sat there and painted.

Oh, not well. I've never said that, ever. Never claimed that for a minute. And it's easy to impress children and country people who think it's uncanny if you can draw an apple that looks like an apple. And I could do much more than that. I could make mountains that looked like mountains, children who looked like children. How that impressed the parents! So I had gotten in the habit of being praised, though from no one who counted, no one who knew. I had been sensibly brought up by my mother, taught to evaluate these plaudits rightly. I understood that my schoolyard talent didn't make me a Bonheur or Cassatt. Even so, there was nothing else I had ever wanted to do. This schoolteaching was just a way of making money, of helping my mother, who was a widow.

So, because of the time I had for painting and because of the gifts Liberty School had for my eyes, I had six happy years. I sat like a queen on that sofa in the grass while the meadowlarks sang and the butcherbirds first caught their lunches, then impaled their suppers, still kicking, on the barbed-wire fence. I didn't paint all the time, of course. Kids learned to read there. At the end of the sixth year there was only one eighth grader who could beat me in mental arithmetic. I was the acknowledged champion at skin-the-cat and could play adequately any position on the softball team.

There was not much left to learn at Liberty, and I began, I don't know how, to feel that learning, not teaching, was my business.

In the middle of my sixth year I had to put a tarpaulin over the sofa. A spring broke through the upholstery, a leg crumbled. After that I had to prop it on a piece of stove wood. That spring I noticed for the first time that the babies of age six I had taught my first year were developing Adam's apples or busts. Girls who had been thirteen

and fourteen my first year came back to visit Liberty School, married
and with babies in their arms.

"You haven't changed," they would tell me. "Oh, it's a real anchor
to find you here, just the same."

Their husbands, who were often boys my own age, twenty-four or
twenty-five, treated me like an older woman. I might have been their
mother, or mother-in-law. I was the woman who had taught their
wives. I don't think I looked so much old then as ageless. I've taken
out some of the snaps of that year, pictures taken at school. My face,
in a way, looks as young as my pupils'; in other ways, as old as Mt.
Tahquitz. It looks back at me with the real stony innocence of a face
in a coffin—or a cradle.

At Thanksgiving time I was to be out of school three days before
the holiday, so that I could have a minor operation. When I left school
on Friday, Mary Elizabeth Ross, one of my fourth graders, clasped
me fondly and said, "May I be the first to hold your baby when you
get back from the hospital?"

She wouldn't believe it when I told her I was going to the hospital
because I was sick, not to get a baby, and she cried when I came
back to school empty-armed.

That I noticed these things showed my restlessness. It might have
passed, I might have settled in to a lifetime on that island, except
that at Christmas I hung some of my paintings with my pupils' pictures at the annual Teachers' Institute exhibit. They caused a stir,
and I began foolishly to dream of painting full time, of going to a big
city, Los Angeles or San Francisco, where I would take a studio and
have lessons. I didn't mention the idea to anyone, scarcely to myself.
When anyone else suggested such a thing to me, I pooh-poohed it.
"Me, paint? Don't be funny."

But I dreamed of it; the less I said, the more I dreamed; and the
more I dreamed, the less possible talking became. I didn't paint much
that winter, but I moved through those months with the feel of a
paintbrush in my hand. I could feel, way up in my arm, the strokes I
would need to make to put Tahquitz, dead white against the green
winter sky on canvas, put it there so people could see how it really
floated, that great peak, was hung aloft there like a giant ship against
the sky. But I didn't say a word to anyone about my plans, not even

to the School Board when I handed in my resignation at Easter. I hadn't lost my head entirely. I told them I was going to "study." I didn't say what. They thought education, of course.

The minute I had resigned, I was filled with fear. I sat on my three-legged sofa amidst the waves of grain that never crested and shivered until school was out. I had undoubtedly been a fool; not only was I without money, but where would I find anything as good as what I had? Everything began to say "stay." I would enter my room at night (the one in which I now write), which my mother kept so exquisitely, books ranged according to size and color, the white bedspread at once taut and velvety, the blue iris in a fan-shaped arc in a brown bowl— and I was a part of that composition. If I walked out, the composition collapsed. And outside, I, too, was a fragment. I would stand there asking myself, "Where will you find anything better?"

There was never any answer.

I could only find something different, and possibly worse. So why go? I had seen myself as a lady Sherwood Anderson, locking the factory door behind me and walking down the tracks toward freedom and self-expression. I could dream that dream but I was afraid to act it. I would stand in my perfectly neat bedroom and frighten myself with pictures of my next room, far away, sordid, with strangers on each side. Fear was in my chest like a stone that whole spring. I had no talent, I was gambling everything on an egotistical attention-seeking whim. It was perfectly natural to have done so, but my misery finally drove me to talking with my mother. It was perfectly natural, she assured me, to want a change of scene and occupation. Who didn't occasionally? But why run away to big cities and studios? Why wouldn't the perfectly natural, perfectly logical thing (since I'd already resigned) be to go to Oakland State and study for my Secondary Credential? The minute I, or Mother—I don't remember which of us—thought of this way out, I was filled with bliss, real bliss. I would get away, go to a real city, be surrounded with people devoted to learning, but not risk everything.

I heard about Dr. Louise McKay from the minute I arrived on the campus. She was, as I've said, a kind of college heroine, though it was hard to understand why. What had she done that was so remarkable? She had been a high-school librarian, and had become a doctor.

What's so extraordinary about that? The girls, and by that I mean the women students—for many of them were teachers themselves, well along in their thirties and forties, or even fifties—the girls always spoke about Louise McKay's change of profession as if it were a Lazaruslike feat; as if she had practically risen from the dead. People are always so romantic about doctors, and it's understandable, I suppose, dealing as they do with life and death. But Louise McKay! The girls talked about her as if what she'd done had been not only romantic, but also heroic.

In the first place, they emphasized her age. Forty-two! To me at twenty-six that didn't, of course, seem young. Still, it was silly to go on about her as if she were a Grandma Moses of medicine—and as if medicine itself were not, quite simply, anything more than doctoring people; saying, "This ails you" and "I think this pill will help you." They spoke of doctoring as if it were as hazardous as piloting a jet plane. And they spoke of Louise McKay's size, "that tiny, tiny thing," as if she'd been a six-year-old, praising her for her age and her youth at one and the same time. Her size, they said, made it seem as if the child-examining-doll game were reversed; as if doll took out stethoscope and examined child. She was that tiny and dainty, they said, that long-lashed and pink-cheeked. They exclaimed over her clothes, too. They were delightful in themselves, but particularly so because they emphasized the contrast between her profession and her person. She was a scientist and might have been expected to wear something manly and practical—or something dowdy. She did neither. They'd all been to her for their physical examinations—somehow I'd never been scheduled for that—and could give a complete inventory of her chic wardrobe. I saw her only once before I called on her professionally in December. I didn't see many people, as a matter of fact, at Oakland State, in any capacity, except professional.

True, I was studying. Not that the work was difficult—or interesting either. History of Education, Principles of Secondary Education, Classroom Management, Curriculum Development. But the books were better than the people. Had I lived out there on my three-legged sofa with children and nature too long? Or was there something really wrong with the people in teachers colleges? Anyway, I had no friends, and the nearer I got to a Secondary Credential, the less I wanted it. But I wanted something—miserably, achingly, wretchedly, I wanted something. Whether or not this longing, this sense of something lost, had anything to do with the illness that came upon me toward the end of December, I don't know. I attributed this illness at first to the raw damp bay weather after my lifetime in the warmth and dryness of the inland foothills; I thought that my lack of routine, after days of orderly teaching, might be responsible, and, finally, after I had adopted a routine and had stayed indoors out of the mists and fogs and the discomfort persisted, I told myself that everyone as he grew older lost some of his early exuberant health. I was no longer in my first youth, and thus, "when my health began to fail"—I thought of it in that way rather than as having any specific ailment—accounted for my miseries. I had always been impatient with the shufflings and snufflings, the caution on stairs and at the table of the no-longer-young. I thought they could do better if they tried. No I began to understand that they couldn't do better and that they probably were trying. I was trying. I couldn't do better. I panted on the hills and puffed on the library steps. I leaned against handrails, I hawked and spat and harrumphed like any oldster past his prime. I did what I could to regain the well-being of my youth. I took long walks to get back my lost wind, ate sparingly, plunged under tingling showers.

By the end of December I felt so miserable I decided to see Dr. McKay at the infirmary. So many new things had been discovered about glands and vitamins, about toxins and antitoxins, that one pill a day was possibly all that stood between me and perfect health. I had the feeling, as people do who have always been well, that a doctor commands a kind of magic—can heal with a glance. Even Dr. McKay, this little ex-librarian, a doll of a woman, with her big splashy earrings and high-heeled shoes and expensive perfumes, could cast a spell of health upon me.

That was the first time I'd ever seen Louise McKay close. My first thought was, She looks every inch her age. She had dark hair considerably grayed, there were lines about her eyes, and her throat muscles were somewhat slack. My second thought was, Why doesn't she admit it? I was dressed more like a middle-aged woman than she. Of course, since she had on a white surgeon's coat, all that could be seen of her "personal attire" was the three or four inches of brown tweed skirt beneath it. But she wore red, very high-heeled shell pumps. Her hair was set in a modified page boy, ends turned under in a soft roll, with a thick, rather tangly fringe across her forehead. It was a somewhat advanced hairstyle for that year—certainly for a middle-aged doctor. Her eyebrows, which were thick and dark, had been obviously shaped by plucking, and her fingernails were painted coral. She was smiling when I came in. She had considerable color in her face for a dark-haired woman, and she sat at a desk with flowers and pictures on it—not family pictures, but little prints of famous paintings.

She said, looking at her appointment calendar, which had my name on it, "Miss McCullars?"

I said, "Yes."

Then she said, "I see we have something in common." She meant our Scotch names of course, but out of some contrariness which I find hard to explain now, I pretended not to understand, so that she had to explain her little joke to me. But then, it wasn't very funny. She discovered, in looking through her files, that I hadn't had the usual physical examination on entering college.

"Why not?" she asked.

"I didn't get a notice to come," I said, "so I just skipped it."

"It would've helped," she told me, "to have that record now to check against. Just what seems to be the trouble?"

"It's probably nothing. I'm probably just the campus hypochondriac."

"That role's already filled."

I didn't feel well even then, though the stimulation of the talk and of seeing the famous Dr. McKay did make me forget some of my miseries. So I began that afternoon what I always continued in her office—an impersonation of high-spirited, head-tossing health. I don't know why. It wasn't a planned or analyzed action. It just happened that the minute I opened her office door I began to act the part of a person bursting with vitality and health. There I was, practically dying on my feet, as it was later proved, but hiding the fact by every device

I could command. What did I think I was doing? The truth is, I wasn't thinking at all.

"I must say you don't look sick," she admitted. Then she began to ask me about my medical history.

"I don't have any medical history. Except measles at fifteen."

"Was there some specific question you wanted to ask me? Some problem?"

So she thought I was one of those girls? Or one of her worshipers just come in to marvel.

"I don't feel well."

"What specifically?"

"Oh—aches and pains."

"Where?"

"Oh—here, there, and everywhere."

"We'll run a few tests, and I'll examine you. The nurse will help you get undressed."

When it was over, she said, "Is your temperature ordinarily a little high?"

"I don't know. I never take it."

"You have a couple of degrees now."

"Above or below normal?"

A little of her school-librarian manner came out. "Are you trying to be funny?"

I wasn't in the least.

"A fever is always above normal."

"What does it mean to have a fever?"

"An infection of some sort."

"It could be a tooth? A tonsil?"

"Yes, it could be. I want to see you tomorrow at ten."

I remember my visit next morning very well. The acacia trees were in bloom, and Dr. McKay's office was filled with their dusty honeybee scent. Dr. McKay was still in street clothes—a blouse, white, high-necked, but frothy with lace and semitransparent, so that you saw more lace beneath. As if she were determined to have everything, I thought: age and youth, practicality and ornamentation, science and femininity. You hero of the campus, I thought, ironically. But she rebuked us schoolteachers by the way she dressed and held herself—and lived, I expected; she really did. And I, I rebuked her in turn, for our hurt honor.

"How do you feel this morning?" she asked.

What did she think to uncover in me? A crybaby and complainer, she standing there in her lovely clothes and I in my dress sun-faded from the Liberty schoolyard?

"Fine," I told her, "I feel fine."

How I felt was her business to discover, wasn't it, not mine to tell? If I knew exactly how I felt, and why, what would've been the use of seeing a doctor? Besides, once again in her office I was stimulated by her presence so that my miseries when not there seemed quite possibly something I had imagined.

"I wanted to check your temperature this morning," she told me.

She sat me down on a white stool, put a thermometer in my mouth, then, while we waited, asked me questions which she thought I could answer with a nod of the head.

"You like teaching? You want to go on with it? You have made friends here?"

She was surprised when she took the thermometer from my mouth. After looking at it thoughtfully, she shook it down and said, "Morning temperature, too."

"You didn't expect that?"

"No, frankly, I didn't."

"Why not?"

"In the kind of infection I suspected you had, a morning temperature isn't usual."

I didn't ask what infection she suspected. I had come to her office willing to be thumped, X-rayed, tested in any way she thought best. I was willing to give her samples of sputum or urine, to cough when told to cough, say ahhh or hold my breath while she counted ten. Whatever she told me to do I would do. But she had turned doctor, not I. If she was a doctor, not a librarian, now was her chance to prove it. Here I was with my fever, come willingly to her office. Let her tell me its cause.

For the next month, Dr. McKay lived, so far as I was concerned, the life of a medical detective, trying to find the villain behind the temperature. The trouble was that the villain's habits differed from day to day. It was as if a murderer had a half-dozen different thumb-prints, and left now one, now another, behind him. One day much temperature, the next day none. Dr. McKay eliminated villain after villain: malaria, tonsillitis, rheumatic fever, infected teeth. And while she found disease after disease which I did not have, I grew steadily worse. By May about the only time I ever felt well was while I was in Dr. McKay's office. Entering it was like going onto a stage. How-ever near I might have been to collapse before that oak door opened, once inside it I was able to play with perfect ease my role of health. I was unable, actually, to do anything else. I assumed health when I entered her office, as they say Dickens, unable to stand without sup-port, assumed health when he walked out before an audience.

It was nothing I planned. I couldn't by an act of will have feigned exuberance and well-being, gone to her office day after day con-sciously to play the role of Miss Good Health of 1940, could I? No, something unconscious happened the minute I crossed that thresh-old, something electric—and ironic. I stood, sat, stooped, reclined, breathed soft, breathed hard, answered questions, flexed my mus-cles, exposed my reflexes for Dr. McKay with vigor and pleasure—and irony. Especially irony. I was sick, sick, falling apart, crumbling, dying on my feet, and I knew it. And this woman, this campus hero whose province it was to know it, was ignorant of the fact. I didn't know what ailed me and wasn't supposed to. She was. It was her business to know.

In the beginning, tuberculosis had been included among the other suspected diseases. But the nontubercular fever pattern, the absence of positive sputum, the identical sounds of the lungs when percussed all had persuaded Dr. McKay that the trouble lay elsewhere. I did not speculate at all about my sickness. I had never been sick before, or even, for that matter, known a sick person. For all I knew, I might have elephantiasis or leprosy, and when Dr. McKay began once again to suspect tuberculosis, I was cooperative and untroubled. She was going to give me what she called a "patch test." Whether this is still used, I don't know. The test then consisted of the introduction of a small number of tubercle baclli to a patch of scraped skin. If, after a day or two, there was no "positive" reaction, no inflammation of the skin, one was thought to have no tubercular infection.

On the day Dr. McKay began this test she used the word "tuberculosis" for the first time. I had experienced when I entered her office that afternoon my usual heightening of well-being, what amounted to a real gaiety.

"So you still don't give up?" I asked when she announced her plan for the new test. "Still won't admit that what you have on your hands is a hypochondriac?"

It was a beautiful afternoon in late May. School was almost over for the year. Students drifted past the window walking slowly homeward, relishing the sunshine and the blossoming hawthorn, their faces lifted to the light. Cubberly and Thorndyke and Dewey given the go-by for an hour or two. Some of this end-of-the-year, lovely-day quiet came into my interview with Dr. McKay. Though it had started with my usual high-spirited banter, I stopped that. It seemed inappropriate. I experienced my usual unusual well-being, but there was added to it that strange, quiet, listening tenderness which marks the attainment of a pinnacle of some kind.

Dr. McKay stood before her window, her surgeon's jacket off—I was her last patient for the day—in her usual frothy blouse, very snow white against the rose red of the hawthorn trees.

She turned away from the window and said to me, "You aren't a hypochondriac."

She shook her head. "I don't know." Then she explained the patch test to me.

"Tuberculosis?" I asked. "And no hectic flush, no graveyard cough, no skin and bones?"

The words were still bantering, possibly, but the tone had changed, tender, tender, humorous, and fondling; the battle—if there had been one—over; and the issue, whatever it was, settled. "In spite of all that, this test?"

"In spite of all that," she said.

She did the scraping deftly. I watched her hands, and while I doubt that there is any such thing as a "surgeon's hands," Dr. McKay's didn't look like a librarian's either, marked by fifteen years of mucilage pots, library stamps, and ten-cent fines. I could smell her perfume and note at close range the degree to which she defied time and the expected categories.

"Come back Monday at the same time," she told me when she had finished.

"What do you expect Monday?" I asked.

"I'm no prophet," she answered. "If I were . . ." She didn't finish her sentence.

We parted like comrades who have been together on a long and dangerous expedition. I don't know what she felt or thought—that she had really discovered, at last, the cause of my illness, perhaps. What I felt is difficult to describe. Certainly my feelings were not those of the usual patient threatened with tuberculosis. Instead, I experienced a tranquillity I hadn't known for a long time. I felt like a lover and a winner, triumphant but tranquil. I knew there would be no positive reaction to the skin test. Beyond that I didn't think.

I was quite right about the reaction. Dr. McKay was completely professional Monday afternoon; buttoned up in her jacket, stethoscope hanging about her neck. I entered her office feeling well, but strange. My veins seemed bursting with blood or triumph. I looked out the window and remembered where I had been a year ago. Breathing was difficult, but in the past months I had learned to live without breathing. I wore a special dress that afternoon because I thought the occasion special. I wouldn't be seeing Dr. McKay again. It was made of white men's-shirting Madras and had a deep scooped neckline, bordered with a ruffle.

"How do you feel?" Dr. McKay asked, as she always did, when I entered.

"Out of this world," I told her.

"Don't joke," she said.

"I wasn't. It's the truth. I feel wonderful."

"Let's have a look at the arm."

"You won't find anything."

"How do you know? Did you peek?"

"No, I didn't, but you won't find anything."

"I'll have a look anyway."

There was nothing, just as I'd known. Not a streak of pink even.

Nothing but the marks of the adhesive tape to distinguish one arm from the other. Dr. McKay looked and looked. She touched the skin and pinched it.

"Okay," she said, "you win."

"What do you mean I win? You didn't want me to be infected, did you?"

"Of course not,"

"I told you all along I was a hypochondriac."

"Okay, Miss McCullars," she said again, "you win." She sat down at her desk and wrote something on my record sheet.

"What's the final verdict?" I asked.

She handed the sheet to me. What she had written was "TB patch test negative. Fluctuating temperature due to neurotic causes."

"So I won't need to come back?"

"No."

"Nor worry about my lungs?"

"No."

Then with precise timing, as if that were the cue for which for almost six months I had been waiting, I had, there in Dr. McKay's office, my first hemorrhage. A hemorrhage from the lungs is always frightening, and this was a very bad one and my first. They got me to the infirmary at once, but there behind me in Dr. McKay's office was the card stained with my blood and saying that nothing ailed me. I was not allowed to speak for twenty-four hours, and my thought, once the hemorrhaging had stopped, was contained in two words, which ran through my mind, over and over again. "I've won. I've won." What had I won? Well, for one thing, I'd won my release from going on with my work for that Secondary Credential. All that could be forgotten, and forgotten also the need to leave Liberty at all. I could go back there, back to my stranded sofa and the school library and the mountains, blue over the green barley.

When at the end of twenty-four hours I was permitted to whisper, Dr. Stegner, the head physician at Oakland State, came to see me.

"When did you first see Dr. McKay?" he asked.

"In December."

"What course of treatment did she prescribe?"

"Not any. She didn't know what was wrong with me."

"Did she ever X-ray you?"

"No."

This, I began to learn, was the crux of the case against Dr. McKay. For there was one. She should have X-rayed me. She should have known that in cases of far advanced tuberculosis, and that was what I had, the already deeply infected system pays no attention to the introduction of one or two more bacilli. All of its forces are massed elsewhere—there are no guards left to repulse border attacks of unimportant skirmishers. But by this time my mother had arrived, alert, knowledgeable, and energetic.

"My poor little girl," she said, "this woman doctor has killed you."

I wasn't dead yet, but as I heard the talk around me I began to understand that in another year or two I might very well be so. And listening to my mother's talk, I began to agree with her. Dr. McKay had robbed me not only of health, but also of a promising career—I had been poised upon the edge of something unusual. I was training myself for service. I had remarkable talents. And now all was denied me, and for this denial I could blame Dr. McKay. I did. She had cut me down in midcareer through her ignorance. What did the campus think of its hero now? For the campus had heard of Dr. McKay's mistake. And the Board of Regents! My mother said it was her duty; that she owed the steps she was taking to some other poor girl who might suffer as I had through Dr. McKay's medical incompetence. I thought it was a matter for her to decide, and besides, I was far too ill to have or want any say in such decisions. I was sent, as soon as I was able to be moved, to a sanatorium near my home in Southern California.

I had been there four months when I saw Dr. McKay again. At the beginning of the visiting hour on the first Saturday in October, the nurse on duty came to my room.

"Dr. McKay to see you," she said.

I had no chance to refuse to see her—though I don't know that I would have refused if I'd had the chance—for Dr. McKay followed the nurse into the room and sat down by my bed.

She had changed a good deal; she appeared little, nondescript, and mousy. She had stopped shaping her eyebrows and painting her nails. I suppose I had changed, too. With the loss of my fever, I had lost also all my show of exuberance and life. I lay there in the hospital bed looking, I knew, as sick as I really was. We stared at each other without words for a time.

Then I said, to say something, for she continued silent, "How are things at Oakland State this year?"

"I'm not at Oakland State. I was fired."

I hadn't known it. I was surprised and dismayed, but for a heartbeat—in a heartbeat—I experienced a flash of that old outrageous exultation I had known in her office. I was, in spite of everything, for a second, well and strong and tender in victory. Though what my victory was, I sick and she fired, I couldn't have told.

"I'm sorry," I said. I was. It is a pitiful thing to be out of work.

"Don't lie," she said.

"I am not lying," I told her.

She didn't contradict me. "Why did you do it?" she asked me.

"Do what?" I said, at first really puzzled. Then I remembered my mother's threats. "I had nothing to do with it. Even if I'd wanted to, I was too sick. You know that. I had no idea you weren't in Oakland this year."

"I don't mean my firing—directly. I mean that long masquerade. I mean that willingness to kill yourself, if necessary, to punish me. I tell you a doctor of fifty years' experience would've been fooled by you. Why? I'd never seen you before. I wanted nothing but good for you. Why did you do it? Why?"

"I don't know what you mean."

"What had I ever done to you? Lost there in that dark library, dreaming of being a doctor, saving my money and finally escaping. How had I harmed or threatened you that you should be willing to risk your life to punish me?"

Dr. McKay had risen and was walking about the room, her voice, for one so small, surprisingly loud and commanding. I was afraid a nurse would come to ask her to be quiet. Yet I hesitated myself to remind her to speak more quietly.

"Well," she said, "you have put yourself in a prison, a fine narrow prison. Elected it of your own free will. And that's all right for you, if you wanted a prison. But you had no right to elect it for me, too. That

was murderous. Really murderous." I began to fear that she was losing control of herself, and tried to ask questions that would divert her
mind from the past.

"Where are you practicing, now?" I asked.

She stopped her pacing and stood over me. "I am no longer in
medicine," she said. "I'm the librarian in the high school at Beaumont."

"That's not where you were before?"

"No, it's much smaller and hotter."

"It's only thirty miles—as the crow flies—from Liberty, where I
used to teach. I'm going back there as soon as I'm well. It was a
mistake to leave it." She said nothing.

"I really love Liberty," I said, "and teaching. The big fields of barley, the mountains. There was an old sofa in the schoolyard, where I
used to sit. It was like a throne. I thought for a while I wanted to get
away from there and try something else. But that was all a crazy
dream. All I want to do now is get back."

"I wish you could have discovered that before you came to Oakland."

I ignored this. "Don't you love books?"

"I had better love books," she said, and left the room.

As it happened, I've never seen her again, though I get these cards.
I didn't go back to Liberty four years later—when I was able again to
teach. I got this other school, but somehow the magic I had felt earlier with the children, I felt no longer. An outdated little schoolroom
with the windows placed high so that neither teacher nor pupils could
see out; a dusty schoolyard; and brackish water. The children I teach
now look so much like their predecessors that I have the illusion of
living in a dream, of being on a treadmill teaching the same child the
same lesson through eternity. Outside on the school grounds, my
erstwhile throne, the sofa, does not exist. The mountains, of course,
are still there—a great barrier at the end of the valley.

Just across the mountains are Beaumont and Dr. McKay; and I am
sometimes heartened, standing on the packed earth of the schoolyard
in the winter dusk, as she suggested, to think of her reshelving her
books, closing the drawer of her fine-till, at the same hour. We can't
all escape; some of us must stay home and do the homely tasks, how-

ever much we may have dreamed of painting or doctoring. "You have the company," I tell myself, looking toward her across the mountains. Then I get into my car to drive into town, where my mother has all this loveliness waiting for me; a composition, once again, that really includes me.

# Child of the Century

MARY PUTNAM YOUNG died in the town of Merritt, California, on June 16, 1947, at the age of seventy-eight. She was buried three days later at ten in the morning in Rose Hill Cemetery. By two that afternoon, her son and only child, Oliver Putnam Young, aged forty-seven, was in the law office of King, Flaherty, and King in search of legal advice.

Maurice Flaherty, brother-in-law of the older King and uncle of the younger, a man about Oliver's age, came out of an inner office to see him. "I'm sorry about your mother," he said. The two men had grown up together in Merritt and knew each other well. "I couldn't get to the funeral, but Jane intended to go."

"Yes," said Oliver, "she did go. I saw her there."

Though Flaherty was surprised to have Oliver come in so soon after the funeral, he bethought himself of something suitable to say. "No matter how old we are, these things always hit us hard," he said. After this statement he waited a moment for some response. When none was forthcoming, he continued. "Well, Oliver, what can I do for you? Something about your mother's will?" Although Oliver had managed Young's Drugstore for twenty-five years, his mother had retained its ownership.

"No," said Oliver, "it's nothing about Mother. It's about me."

"You?" asked Flaherty with surprise.

"I'd like some legal advice about my birth."

"About your birth?" Flaherty repeated. The afternoon was warm, and he seemed quite unable to concentrate, staring in a bemused fashion at two mud daubers as they wove a pattern of indecision about the open window of the stuffy little room.

"You know when I was born," Oliver said. "The day it was."

Oliver didn't remember the day, of course, but remembered the September afternoon when he had first been told of that day. He had been playing in the backyard, making corrals for his herds of animals. He had a flock of innumerable sow bugs, almost as many lady-bugs, five grasshoppers, two stinkbugs, one potato bug, and four flies. He had removed the wings from the flies, and they were quite as tractable and earthbound as the sow bugs and far more so than the ladybugs and grasshoppers, which came and went at will over the dirt walls of the corrals he had built.

"Come in, Oliver dear," his mother called.

"I can't," he called back.

"Can't?" asked Mrs. Young, surprised. "Can't isn't a word my little boy knows."

Oliver sometimes had the confused feeling—he had never got over it—that there were two Olivers: himself and the other Oliver, who was his mother's little boy.

"I can't," he yelled again. "All my bugs will get away."

"Bugs!" exclaimed Mrs. Young. "Bugs aren't things my little boy would play with."

"I am," Oliver, the Oliver who was not his mother's little boy, shouted.

"Come here at once," his mother ordered.

He went reluctantly onto the porch and saw that his mother had a pitcher of lemonade and a plate of cookies on the wicker porch table, as if she expected company. "Mother," he protested, "all my bugs will run away."

"Animals that belong to my little boy," his mother assured him, "will not run away."

They had, though, Oliver remembered. All of them except the sow bugs, which he had not cared for anyway, and the flies, which were dead.

"Wash your hands and face and put on a clean blouse," his mother told him. "I've something important to talk to my little boy about."

He washed and washed, until he reached the comfortable stage of having forgotten what he was washing for. Then he pleasantly prac-ticed opening his eyes under water and, tiring of that, scooped water into one ear and tilted his head to see if it would run out the other. His mother came and put an end to these experiments. She dried him, buttoned him into one of his best blouses, and sat him on a chair by the wicker table. When he had finished eating his two oatmeal cookies and had drained his glass of lemonade, his mother pulled his chair closer to hers and pointed to the large scrapbook she held on her lap.

"Do you know what book this is, Oliver?"

"No," he said.

"Read what it says," his mother told him.

Though he was only six, Oliver had been sent to school when he was five and could read after a fashion. Haltingly, he pronounced the words printed on the cover of the scrapbook. "The Baby of the Century."

"Do you know who the Baby of the Century is, Oliver?" his mother asked.

"No," said Oliver.

His mother then opened the scrapbook and, pointing to a large, time-yellowed newspaper picture of a baby, said, "Read this, Oliver." With her forefinger, she guided his eyes to the proper line.

"Oliver Putnam Young, Baby of the Century," he read.

"My little boy, Baby of the Century," his mother said.

It was then, at that moment, Oliver sometimes thought, that the heaviness of after years had first descended upon him; there on the porch, looking at this picture and hearing the peculiar, throbbing note in his mother's voice.

He had even attempted to escape what was personal in the situation by speaking not of the baby, but of the century. What a century was he had no idea, unless perhaps an animal, something like a centipede. "What is a century?" he asked.

"A century," his mother told him, "is a period of a hundred years, and you, Oliver, were born at the exact minute the twentieth century was born."

"Were you born in the twentieth century, too, Mother?"

"Oh, no," his mother said. "I represent the nineteenth century; but you, Oliver, are the twentieth century."

The two mud daubers in the offices of King, Flaherty, and King hovered about the upper slats of the Venetian blind covering the top half of the window. Maurice Flaherty shooed at them, but they paid no attention to him.

"You remember when I was born?" Oliver asked.

"I sure do," Maurice Flaherty answered. "The stroke of midnight, January first, nineteen-hundred."

That was the truth—not ten minutes or even ten seconds before or after, but exactly on the stroke of the hour, so that his first wail had mingled with the sounds of the bells, guns, whistles, firecrackers, and pounded milk pans with which the residents of Merritt were celebrating the arrival of the new century.

The fact that his birth had occurred at this hour had seemed, first to his mother and then later, unhappily, to Oliver himself, significant, a portent of something. But of what? Oliver's mother had taken for granted that it was a portent of success for her son, and of no ordinary success either. Her little boy, who had been born on January 1, 1900, would, she felt, equal in some way the promise of the new century.

She early searched her son for intimations of the direction in which this success would lie; but the "Century Baby," as the newspapers had called him, was in no way unusual. In appearance, he was a large-headed, silky-haired, tallow-colored baby, and he became a medium-headed, silky-haired, tallow-colored boy. The little boy, as later the grown man, had shallow, saucer-shaped indentations at the temples, and when he was troubled, which was often, a forked vein like a plum-colored tree spread across the center of his forehead. His silky, straw-colored hair did not, even as he grew older, develop enough body to permit him to sweep it upward into a pompadour of the kind other boys his age were wearing, and though he became a large boy for his age, he did not become a strong one. He was willing, even anxious, to excel in games; but his muscles were soft and spongy, and they did not, however much he willed it, respond so quickly and reliably as those of other boys born on less auspicious dates.

This troubled him, but it did not trouble his mother. She had no idea that a child sent into the world simultaneously with the twentieth century was destined to become a mere jumper, runner, or ball tosser. Indeed, the fact that Oliver was incompetent at games convinced her anew that he was no ordinary boy and that Fate was looking after her own—making certain that hours which might otherwise have been wasted in tree climbing and ball tossing would be free for training of another sort. But of what sort?

It was of this training that Oliver's mother spoke on the afternoon she first showed him her Baby of the Century scrapbook. She had noticed that he occasionally hummed. When they were downtown, he would stop to listen to the Salvation Army band, and once she had seen him waving his arms in time to "Three Little Blackberries," a gramophone record of his grandfather's. It seemed very likely that the Baby of the Century was destined to become a great artist, and since no artist, to her mind, was so great as a violin virtuoso, she had begun to see Oliver against a backdrop of velvet curtains, silky hair falling over his fragile temples, bow arm lifted.

"Would my little boy like to play the violin?" she asked.

This question had seemed to Oliver to lead away from the Baby of the Century talk, which embarrassed and depressed him, and in his relief he at once said, "Yes."

"I thought so!" his mother exclaimed joyously. She ran into the house and brought out a violin of a size suitable for a six-year-old. "There," she said, handing the instrument to Oliver, who took it gingerly in his arms. "Always remember this hour, Oliver, the hour when you first began to make music." And then, more practically, "On Saturday, Professor Schuyler will come to give my little boy a lesson."

Professor Schuyler came for four years and three months. Then he departed. On the day of the Professor's departure, Saturday, December 17, 1910, he entered the Youngs' living room singing the song Oliver had heard him sing for four years and three months. It began "O Lily up and Lily down and lay them on the side wheels," and went on Oliver knew not how, for this was all the Professor had ever sung.

"How is our young Paganini today?" the Professor asked that December afternoon. Sometimes he asked, "How is our young Ole Bull?" and other times, "How is our young Mozart?"

But Oliver did not mind. He knew the Professor asked these questions because of the set of books about the lives of great musicians his mother had bought. Oliver had not minded either the four long years of practice. They had given him an excuse for avoiding what was even more painful than the music lessons—the games in which he could not excel; they had made his mother happy, and they had brought the Professor, who interested him and never called him Child of the Century.

The Professor was a tall man with a dark, seamed face. Each Saturday he drove to the Youngs' in a buggy drawn by a dapple gray horse. In the whip socket of the buggy, the Professor carried the butt end of a broken whip. Oliver had never seen him use this stump on his horse; but sometimes, after a lesson, the Professor would linger for a few minutes in his buggy meditatively scratching his back with the whip stump.

The Professor quite often spread a large handkerchief over his face while he listened to Oliver practice. Once when Oliver's mother had discovered him thus, he had said, without so much as lifting a corner of the handkerchief to provide himself a peephole, "The ears resent the eyes." Hearing this, Mrs. Young had tiptoed from the room.

There were times, however, when Professor Schuyler did not have Oliver practice at all, but played for the whole of the lesson period. He would stand, on these occasions, by the front window, his eyes on the rise and fall of the green or sallow grass in the vacant lot across the street, while Oliver listened to the sounds cascading from his violin. Oliver did not associate these sounds with music. They reached him simply as feeling, as an audible expression of the heaviness that almost continuously filled his chest and was the result both of his love for his mother and of his conviction that, in spite of everything he could do, he was a disappointment to her.

About his own playing, Oliver had a variety of feelings; but what he most often felt was despair. He simply could not make the notes he saw before him come forth from his violin as music. Some barrier in his hands or mind, or both, prevented it. Still, no one reproved him—neither his mother nor Professor Schuyler—and playing on the afternoon of December 17, 1910, Oliver was consoled by a thought that had often consoled him before; perhaps his terrible sense of failure and insufficiency was the true sign of the great artist. Perhaps it was with just such a feeling that Mozart had practiced. Perhaps what he felt about his playing was exactly what a Child of the Century, destined to be a great violinist, should feel.

The lesson that afternoon went worse than usual. Professor Schuyler early retired to his handkerchief; but Oliver, even without those black eyes upon him, was unable to put three notes together properly. He stumbled, misplayed, broke down completely, started over.

Finally, after producing a whining, sniggering sound so strange as to rouse the Professor from behind his covering, Oliver, out of his embarrassment and despair, cried, "Mozart—Mozart was pretty mad, too, I guess, when he made mistakes like that."

At that name, Professor Schuyler leaped to his feet and attempted to throw his handkerchief to the floor. But it would not throw; it floated. "Mozart," he said. "Mozart. As long as it was your mama who had these ideas, it didn't matter; but if you've got them, too, it's time to call a halt." Professor Schuyler then took Oliver's violin, threw it into the fireplace on top of the smoldering eucalyptus logs, broke the bow over his knee, and sent it to join the blazing instrument. "Boy," he said sternly, "you can no more play the violin than a pig can sing. And while there's no harm I can see in a pig's trying to sing, calling himself a nightingale is another matter entirely, conducive to craziness in the world, and a sign it's time to call a halt."

That afternoon Oliver heard for the first—and last—time the next line of the Professor's song. "O Lily up and Lily down," the Professor sang, "and lay them on the side wheels, the river feels the boat go round but that's not what the boat feels." Gently he closed the front door behind him, climbed into his buggy, scratched himself briefly, and drove away forever.

After that, everything was better for a while. Oliver's mother, naturally, was angry with Professor Schuyler for destroying her son's violin. However, she was able to recover some of its cost by refusing to pay him for Oliver's final lessons. She had nothing to say to Oliver except that, since there were no competent teachers in the neighborhood, she was afraid he would have to give up his musical training.

The next two years, Oliver's twelfth and thirteenth, were, he afterward thought, the happiest of his life. He was permitted, for the most part, to do as he liked, and there was very little, or at least he heard very little, Child of the Century talk. The Youngs at that time lived near an arroyo, which, dammed at one end by a Pacific Electric embankment, held during the winter and spring months a considerable body of water. From this pond Oliver fished up tadpoles, water dogs, even an occasional small turtle. These he kept in glass jars on the back porch, and he enjoyed standing before them in a kind of pleasant stupor, watching their easy, fluid movements.

One evening, shortly after his twelfth birthday, he caught a small green snake by the pond side. He took it to the house to place with the other inhabitants of his menagerie. While he was arranging its home on the back porch, he heard his mother speak from the kitchen to some unseen guest in the living room. "Oliver, you know," she said, "is going to be a great scientist."

There was some reply Oliver could not make out. Then his mother went on, "I was so foolish for a while, so old-fashioned. I hampered my boy so. I was determined he should be a violinist, but his heart was just not in it. At heart he really has never been anything but a scientist. Exactly what we should have expected of a child of this century, of course."

Hearing these words, Oliver lost all pleasure in his thin, coiling snake. The old heaviness, the old responsibility began once again to fill his chest. He started to tiptoe from the porch; but his mother, catching sight of him, called him back.

She was delighted when she saw what he had in his hand and hurried them, unhappy snake and boy, to meet her caller. "See!" she cried. "What did I tell you? A born scientist!"

Oliver was not a born scientist; but except for the nervousness and self-consciousness his mother's expectations aroused in him, he might, by unrelenting effort, have made himself a scientist of sorts. But the burden of this expectation, coupled with his barely average ability, kept him below average in all his science classes in high school. And it was this poor scholastic record, together with his unhappiness and sense of failure, that caused him, in 1917, to enlist in the army. Since he was underage, it was necessary for him to have his parents' permission. He had expected his mother to weep, protest, perhaps even refuse her permission. Instead, she was pleased and enthusiastic.

"I had hoped my boy would want to do this," she told him. She placed her hand on his soft, light hair—she had to reach up to do this now—as if she were bestowing a benediction. "This is a crusade, Oliver, a holy task of liberation. Perhaps it was for this you were born."

Mrs. Young kissed Oliver and sent him forth. But she was unable to believe that he had been born to serve as a pharmacist's assistant in a hospital in New Jersey, or that his work was of much importance in the holy task of liberation. His destiny must still lie ahead.

Oliver went home from the army at nineteen, large, rather slope-shouldered, with attentive, watchful eyes. He felt he was missing something, and the strain of looking for it showed in his eyes and in the frequency with which the plum-colored tree spread across his forehead. He enrolled at the state university and, because he could think of nothing better to do, continued as a science major. His two years in the army had not improved him as a student, and the accident in which he was hurt was the result of some volunteer experimentation he was carrying on in the hope of persuading his chemistry professor to raise his grade. He lost the thumb and forefinger of his left hand, and for a time it was thought he would also lose his life.

When he began to recover, his mother sat by his bedside and traced with her gentle fingers the espaliered vein on his forehead. "Science is dangerous, Oliver," she said in her gentle, surprised voice. "My boy might have been blown up, destroyed. He wasn't born for that. Promise me, Oliver, that you will give up science. I had no idea that science was so dangerous."

Oliver gave up not only science, but also college. He had lost two years in the army; he lost another year as a result of his accident. When he was well enough to be up and about, he entered, at the age of twenty-one, his father's drugstore as his assistant.

Because of his illness, perhaps, his mother seemed content, at the time, for him to be so employed. Since Oliver did not dislike the work, his discontent was inexplicable. Then, to his unhappy consternation, he discovered that the hope that, during his younger years, his mother had cherished for him had become a part of his own makeup. He would have supposed that his many disappointments would have cured him of his mother's disease of hope. As an artist, he had ended with his violin blazing like any piece of kindling in the fireplace; as a soldier, with the neat pills rolling out from under his trained and obedient thumb; as a scientist, with a part of his hand lost.

Were these experiences not enough to prevent him from beginning anew a search for some means of expressing his uniqueness? What uniqueness had he other than the date of his birth and the persistence of his mother's belief in him? Yet these, evidently, were enough. The only difference was that in him his mother's disease took a new course. He no longer expected to find in the outer world any sign of the uniqueness of Oliver Putnam Young. His kingdom would be interior, known only to himself and one other. It would be a kingdom of love.

It was natural that, as he was dreaming of love, love soon particularized itself. When Pauline Mercer came into the drugstore with her bronze-and-rose skin, her short, daring haircut, her air of being at home in the world, she was immediately dearer to him than anything he had dreamed. Though the dreaming he had done, filled as it was with shreds of Tennyson and Mrs. Browning, scenes from *The Ordeal of Richard Feverel*, remembered snatches of his mother's conversation, conditioned the manner of his loving.

Afterward it seemed to him that nothing he had said or done for the whole of the time he knew Pauline Mercer had any connection with what he wanted to do or say, but only with the pattern of loving his dream had formed.

For his first date with Pauline, he rented at the local garage the largest and fanciest car available. He did not consider his father's model worthy of either Pauline or his dream. He was unfamiliar with the big car and drove it awkwardly and self-consciously. The front seat was bisected, and he and Pauline sat far removed from each other, formal and dignified, like chauffeur and footman in a vehicle conveying royalty. Pauline somehow got the idea that the car belonged to Oliver's father; and since in Oliver's dream a young man's father would own such a car, Oliver let her think so.

For the rest of the ride his mind tossed about, alternating between two courses of action equally impossible: persuading his father to buy a car of similar make or admitting to Pauline that he had, for all practical purposes, lied. While he was still painfully concerned with this problem, they passed a carnival, a gay eruption of glitter and sound into the spring night.

"Let's stop," Pauline cried, clasping Oliver's arm with both hands.

This pressure made Oliver tremble, and for a minute he let himself think of the pleasures of the carnival: the Ferris wheel, the chute-the-chutes, the photographer's booth—all permitting, if not requiring, that the escort's arm be about the girl. But his dream of love would permit nothing so unpremeditated and simply pleasurable. He was taking Pauline to a hotel for dinner, the proper place for the beginning of a stately and romantic courtship.

He drove into Los Angeles, where, unused to city traffic, he so entangled himself at an intersection that a policeman had to extricate him. In an effort to impress Pauline, he talked back and was given a ticket. From then on, his stomach, out of nervousness, rumbled violently. To his sensitive ear, its reverberations were audible above all the city's sounds. To muffle this internal clamor, he tooted the horn whenever an internal spasm seemed imminent. He thus arrived at the Ambassador in a burst of horn blowing. The doorman came to the car at a brisk trot, anticipating, after so precipitate a summons, a large tip. When he received none at all, he turned away muttering.

The Ambassador's dining room frightened Oliver. He had never eaten in so luxurious a place, and he had no idea what to do: how to get rid of his hat and overcoat, how to get a table, what to do when he did get one. Because it seemed uncourageous to hang diffidently upon the fringes of the crowded dining room, waiting to be noticed, he took his hat and coat in one hand, grasped Pauline's elbow sharply with the other, and made for an empty table. He was turned back by a waiter, who rid himself of a day-long accumulation of spleen by speaking to Oliver as if he were something contemptible, a beetle he would crush.

They were seated, finally, near the doors to the kitchen, where the uproar of cooking and serving made conversation difficult. This was a blessing for Oliver, since what he had to say, following the pattern of his dream, was foolish. The menu arrived. One-third of it he could not read; two-thirds he could not pronounce. With a little finger, pink and curling as a newly boiled shrimp, he pointed to various items. After these had arrived and he had eaten of them, Oliver felt better, though filled with a gnawing shame for his mistakes and ineptitudes. He sat silent amid the din, his maimed hand exposed on the table.

Pauline touched it with gentle fingers. "That must keep you from doing a lot of things you'd like to do," she said.

Oliver, who was sensitive about his hand, removed it from the table. "Yes," he said. Then, with evasive melancholy, "One thing in particular."

"What is it?" Pauline asked. "Something you wanted terribly to do?"

"Something I could do," he said, pensively understating.

"Don't you like to talk about it, Oliver?"

"I never have talked about it to anyone else," he said, truthfully enough.

"Because it makes you sad?"

Oliver nodded. "But you're different."

"What what it, Oliver?"

"Play the violin," Oliver answered, emerging, to his own consternation but according to the dictates of his dream, as hero and thwarted artist.

"Oh, Oliver!" Pauline's bronze and rose became rosier with sympathy. "How terrible!"

Oliver said nothing.

"Could you—could you—play well?"

Oliver nodded. "They'd told me so," he said. Then suddenly, above the clamor of china, "My old teacher used to call me a young Mozart. He was only joking, of course."

The words Oliver heard himself speaking could not have surprised him more had they been issued from the empty air beside him. "You fool, you fool," he told himself. "You darn fool. Can't you even tell the truth?" No, he could not; or, rather, he was. He was telling the truth of a world in which he had spent more time than in Merritt; he was telling the truth of the Child of the Century, of that other Oliver, his mother's boy.

"Oh, Oliver," Pauline said again. "How did it happen? Or can you bear to think of it?"

Oliver looked desolate, but managed to speak. "Research," he said.

"Chemical research?"

Oliver nodded.

"About the war?"

"Ultimately," Oliver answered.

For a moment there was a lull in the kitchen clatter, and the music of the dance orchestra spread across the dining room. It lapped about them, warm as a summer tide and as unlasting. Oliver rested for a second on its cresting surface. Then the tide ebbed, ran backward, exposed the kitchen behind them, the bill on the table, the falseness of everything he had said.

On the way back to Merritt, Oliver was too occupied with his remembrance of this falseness to proceed according to dream. When he left Pauline, out of his natural, unplanned misery, he kissed her.

Next evening, carrying the most elaborate box of chocolates in stock at Young's Drugstore, he called at the Mercer home. Pauline and her thirteen-year-old brother, Stanley, were in the backyard pumping in a swing, which hung from the scaly branch of an old pepper tree. After they got the swing to its maximum height and then let it die, Stanley, a well-trained young brother, remembered he had a date.

Pauline, who had been standing in the swing, now sat in it and, swaying gently, looked up at Oliver's package. "Merchandise!" she exclaimed.

Oliver handed her the box of chocolates. "Can you ever forgive me?" he asked.

"Forgive you?" Pauline said, surprised. "Forgive you for what?"

This generosity shook Oliver. "For kissing you." He went on earnestly, "I want you to know that I respect you just as much as if you hadn't let me, and that I know you're not in the habit of letting a fellow kiss you on his first date." This was a thoroughly planned speech, and Oliver expected good results.

Instead, Pauline jumped to a standing position in the swing and began to pump furiously. Oliver could see her white underpants, or at least the blue embroidery around the edges, but he realized that this display was in no way coquettish.

"Beat it," Pauline yelled. "Go on, get away from here, you goop. Go on home."

In spite of this bad beginning, Pauline went with him for more than a year. Oliver continued to make awkward, impetuous love and to retreat from this lovemaking with self-hate because it did not fit the pattern he had earlier laid down. He was lost between two worlds, unable to be one thing or another, still hunting the kingdom of love wherein the uniqueness of Oliver Putnam Young might find expression. He knew well enough that Pauline was the person who should inhabit this kingdom with him and that every day he made it more impossible for her to do so.

In the summer of 1922, Oliver bought his car, a new, fashionable roadster. One August evening, after a movie in Merritt, he and Pauline sat parked on the rim of the reservoir in the hills behind the town.

"I don't know why you put up with me," Oliver said morosely.

"I don't know either," Pauline answered lightly. "You're an awful goop."

"No, honestly," said Oliver, "why do you?"

"I guess it's because sometimes I think there's something kind of neat and sweet about you, Oliver, way down deep inside, where I don't see it very often. But I think, maybe, if I wait long enough, it will get to be all of you."

"Neat and sweet?" asked Oliver. "What do you mean by that?"

Pauline couldn't or wouldn't say, and that very evening Oliver convinced her, finally and completely, that this neatness and sweetness, whatever it was, was deep inside him, indeed, and that no matter how long she waited it would never be all of him. They sat for some time not talking, listening to the plop of carp and catfish in the waters below them, watching the headlights of cars swing like luminous antennae up the incline leading to the reservoir.

Pauline took a cigarette from her purse. She tapped it, with newly gained competence, against the back of her hand. "Give me a light," she said.

"I've asked you not to smoke, Pauline," Oliver told her reproachfully. He had. The girl he had imagined himself wooing, the girl of whom he had read and heard his mother speak and about whom he could quote snatches of poetry, did not smoke.

"So you have," said Pauline. She struck a match on the side of her Oxford and lighted the cigarette.

"Throw that thing away!" Oliver ordered.

Pauline's response was to inhale to so deeply that tears filled her eyes. But she was laughing when she said, "Try and make me."

Oliver took her wrist and said, "All right, I will. Drop that thing." It had started as fun; but once it had started, Oliver had to win. The man dominated. That was part of the dream. "Drop it," he said, increasing his pressure on her wrist.

Pauline was still laughing. "Who says so?" she asked. She reached over quickly with her hand and got hold of the cigarette, holding its burning end toward her palm. "Fooled you," she said.

Oliver grasped her hand and turned her fingers inward, so that the live coal of the cigarette, very rosy and pretty in the darkness of the summer night, came nearer and nearer the flesh of her palm. "Drop that cigarette," he said, "or you'll be burned."

Pauline had stopped laughing. "You can't make me. There is nothing in this world you can make me do, Oliver."

Oliver forced the cigarette closer to her palm. "I can," he said. "I can, too."

As the live coal touched her hand, Pauline lunged backward, but did not let go of the cigarette.

"Drop it! Drop it," Oliver first commanded, then pleaded.

But Pauline would not drop it. Her fingers gripped the cigarette as if it were a dear possession her hand would hold firmly, even in death.

"Drop it," begged Oliver.

Pauline said nothing. There was a peculiar smell in the car, and Oliver suddenly released his pressure on Pauline's fingers, jumped out of the car, and ran to the edge of the reservoir. There he washed his face, and more especially his hands, over and over again in the cool water. He let the water slide between his fingers and across his palms as if he were the one who had been burned. When he went back to the car, Pauline was gone.

She never spoke to him again. He saw her next day on the street in Merritt, her hand elaborately bandaged. He tried to stop her, to ask her forgiveness; but she looked at him without a flicker of recognition. When he phoned her, she hung up. One day outside Young's Drugstore, he detained her with a hand on her arm while he begged her to forgive him, to talk to him. She stood quietly enough, unresponsive as a lamppost, looking downward. When Oliver saw that she was looking at a white, puckered, craterlike scar on the palm of her hand, he never again attempted to stop her or speak to her.

The next year, September 18, 1923, he married Loretta Olsen, a tall blond girl, thin and shy, but with a slow, pleasant smile. As the falseness of his dream had spoiled him for Pauline, so Pauline had spoiled him for Loretta. He continually asked Loretta to be what she could not: careless, jaunty, easygoing, unself-conscious. He asked her, in fact, to be Pauline. Asking this, he missed all of what she had: her quiet humor, loyalty, sensitiveness. He wanted none of these things.

He wanted Pauline. Without Pauline, he began to pity himself; he, Oliver Putnam Young, with no place to bestow his uniqueness, no one with whom to share that kingdom of love for which he had been born and in which he was to find the meaning of his life.

In 1924, Oliver's father died and Oliver's first child, a daughter, was born. Oliver's mother asked that the child receive her name, and though Loretta thought Mary Loretta was a pretty name and gave her mother-in-law sufficient recognition, the baby was called Mary Putnam.

Oliver's mother no longer spoke directly to him of her expectations for him. But her belief was unshaken. Oliver often heard her speak to her namesake, as the child grew older, of the remarkable circumstances of his birth and of what it portended. It was obvious, however, that she was reconciled to the fact that her son might not distinguish himself as she had long anticipated.

Oliver, during the twelve years, 1924 to 1936, which saw the birth of his children, began to wonder if it was not his destiny to be a father. To live in these young people, to guide and educate them so they would be an ornament to the age in which they lived—what greater task could any man have? But he was too self-centered to find expression in the life of any other human being, even a child of his own. The hope the date of his birth and his mother's belief had grafted on him could not be fulfilled vicariously. He must himself do something, be something, continue his search for a means of saying whatever it was he had been born to say.

About the time his oldest child, Mary, was fourteen, the boy, Oliver Junior, twelve, and the baby, Paula, two, Oliver made an important decision. He decided that the mistake he had made in his search was this: he had expected that his gift, whatever it was, would find its expression in conjunction with others. As a violinist, he had been dependent on an audience; as inhabitant of the kingdom of love, on a woman; as a father, on his children.

It was the strangeness to him of his own children, his inability to express himself in or through them, that finally opened his eyes. Why had he not understood from the beginning that his gift was a lonely one? Not only one that would never have outward recognition, but also one that would exist and develop without reference to other human beings. An interior grace, needing for a stage only his own soul; for approbation, nothing more than the plaudits of his own conscience. Integrity, compassion, unselfish high-mindedness—these, he told himself, had always been the world's highest goals, and he had been a fool to content himself with lower.

No wonder he had failed in his earlier efforts! The goals he had chosen had all been unworthy of him. Now, expecting nothing more— or less—than the development of his spiritual nature, he would be free of the fear of disappointment in the world. What did it now matter if to undiscerning eyes he appeared to be no more than the small-town proprietor of a small-town drugstore? He would know better.

For a time, Oliver had a brief resurgence of hope. But it was very brief. He discovered, in the first place, that he was in a bad business for the practice of probity and the development of his spiritual nature. His customers were in the habit of buying over and sometimes under the counter at Young's Drugstore articles not congruent with that practice or that development. At first, Oliver resolutely removed these articles from his stock. When he began to lose valued customers, he realized that, however much he might desire a sphere of spiritual isolation where he could grow toward perfection, in his work he was tied to his customers. He replaced the articles, divorced himself spiritually from the drug business, and withdrew into a larger world. But the events of the larger world came seeping inward to invade his security. His son suddenly was taken ill and died.

Oliver's mother never recovered from the shock of her grandson's death, though her final illness was much later and of short duration. Oliver was called to her bedside on the afternoon of Thursday, the twelfth of June, and she died on the night of the sixteenth. As he sat by her bed during those five days, he was aghast at the unspoken accusations he directed toward her. There she lay, once so lovely and commanding, now gaunt, broken, without power, almost without speech. It was the time, if ever, for a son's compassion and love. Instead, Oliver thought: You put a burden upon me that I should never have been asked to bear. You expected too much of me, and you expected the wrong things. You put one set of ideas in my head, while you built up, before I was born, a world in which none of those ideas would work. You are to blame for it all.

His mother, as if she had heard him speak, opened her eyes. "Oliver," she said in her weak, loving voice, "my son."

"Yes, Mother," said Oliver.

His mother made a movement of her hand in his direction, and Oliver took her hand in his. It was a cluster of fragile bones against his plump palm.

"My boy," she said tremulously, "never forget—when you were born—or what I expected of you—will always expect. You won't forget, will you, Oliver?"

"No, Mother," said Oliver. But in his mind he was saying: Die, die. Release me. Let me go in peace. Let me be free of the burden of your expectations.

And when, three days later, his mother did die, he felt nothing but a wonderful lightness and well-being. Never forget when I was born! he exulted. Never forget what you expected of me! That is exactly what I'm going to do at the first possible minute. Forget the whole thing.

During his mother's funeral service, he said to himself again and again, "Free, free." The emotion this word gave him was so great and obvious that people mistook it for the sorrow he did not feel. For reasons of decency, he lingered after his mother's interment, speaking to her friends and relatives.

An old lady about his mother's age said to him, "I'm your mother's second cousin, Jennie Rideout. You don't remember me, but I'll never forget you. You were born on the stroke of midnight, January first, nineteen-hundred. 'Baby of the Century,' they called you. Your mother expected great things of you. We all did."

Oliver walked away from her without a word, drove his family home, had a bite to eat, and went at once to Maurice Flaherty's office.

Flaherty repeated the words with relish. "The stroke of midnight! The Baby of the Century! Right here in the flesh!"

"I intend to change all that," said Oliver.

Flaherty was a black Irishman, red-cheeked in the afternoon. "What is it you want changed? The flesh?" he asked, tapping Oliver's paunch.

Oliver drew away irritably. Now that there was only this one matter to be taken care of, he was impatient of delay. He pushed aside Flaherty's hand. "What I want changed," he said, "is the date of my birth."

Flaherty sat down on the edge of the heavy, golden-oak table and looked up at his friend. "What would you like?" he asked ironically. "About twelve years removed? Oliver Putnam Young, born in 1912 and now thirty-five. Is that what you want?"

"Don't be a fool," Oliver said. "All I want is that January first, nineteen-hundred business killed. Put me back a day; put me forward a day. That's all I ask."

Flaherty cocked his head. "You know I can't do that, Oliver."

"Why can't you? Fix it up so I will never again have to write, 'Oliver Putnam Young, January first, nineteen-hundred,' and hear some fool say, 'If it isn't the Child of the Century himself.' Make it legal. Authorize it, notarize it, witness it, whatever it takes."

"It can't be done," Flaherty said.

"Why can't it? People have their names changed every day. What's the difference?"

"The name," said Flaherty, "is a matter of chance. The birth is an actual happening in time."

"It's a matter of chance, too," Oliver argued, "most of the time."

"Now, look here," said Flaherty, "I know law. I've practiced for a quarter of a century, and there is no possible way a birth date can be changed. That I'm certain of."

Oliver bleakly fingered his empurpled forehead. "I'm stuck, then, am I?" he asked.

Flaherty stood up. "Insofar as your birth date goes," he said, "you are stuck."

Without another word, Oliver turned, opened the frosted-glass, gilt-inscribed door, and went out. Flaherty watched his friend's shadowed outline diminish down the corridor.

# Flow Gently, Sweet Aspirin

I N FRONT OF a fire in the tan stucco house sat Tom and Laureen Ashe. It was April outside; the locust was full of pink blossoms and looked, Laureen said, like a ghost blushing, but inside it was cold. Tom was so busy planning a program for Public Schools Week to make Oilinda high-school conscious that Laureen had to tend the fire. She had just shoved a eucalyptus chunk into the fireplace, and was going outside to sniff its smoke, when the phone rang.

She ran to answer it, though she supposed it was only some youngster calling Tom about his Chemistry assignment, but it was Aggie Merton, the principal's wife. Laureen was surprised, since Mrs. Merton didn't, as a rule, do more than nod pleasantly to the wives of the faculty men and say good afternoon in a slow, soft bubble of a voice that threatened to founder before it cleared her chin. Mrs. Merton by no means confined her social activities to the education pool, but swam in Oilinda's best circles. Mrs. Hollingsworth, the banker's wife, Mrs. Hertz, the wife of Oilinda's leading doctor, and Mrs. Lammereaux, the widow of a railroad president, were her friends and members of her bridge club.

Even the telephone was powerless to detonate Mrs. Merton's bubbles.

"I wonder, Mrs. Ashe," she said, "if you could take Mrs. Hollingsworth's place Friday afternoon at my bridge club?"

Laureen was, naturally, pleased to hear this, but decided not to show it too much. "I'd love to, Mrs. Merton," she said, "but you know I have my harp lesson on Friday afternoons." Just as well let her know I have a cultural interest, Laureen thought.

"Of course, Mrs. Ashe, no one realizes more than I the need of routine. I haven't been an educator's wife for twenty-five years for nothing, you know, but there are times—" The sentence broke off while bubbles of sound that were not quite words continued to curve delicately against Laureen's ear.

460

"You're quite right, Mrs. Merton," Laureen said. "I really can't resist. I'll be very happy to come."

Laureen pranced back to Tom and the fire. "Hey, Tom," she asked, "why's Angie Merton such a social knockout? She's got a figure like a pouter pigeon, and she goes whoo, whoo, just like a pigeon, too."

Tom laid down his writing board and put a cigarette in his mouth. "It's the owl who goes whoo, whoo," he said. His cigarette wagged with each word. "You jealous, Laurie? You want to be the local Mrs. Astor?"

"Well, it wouldn't hurt you any," Laureen said, "if I got to be the darling of the local banking circle. Might distract attention from your subversive activities."

Tom threw his cigarette, unlighted, into the fireplace. "Subversive activities, hell. Listen, I make one speech to the Twenty-Thirtians, to define, mind you, to define—clarify, not advocate—and—" He took another cigarette from his frayed pack and began singing one of his infinite parodies, his usual response to a situation he thought couldn't be helped with words.

> *Jesus, I am all confusion*
> *Pure unbounded chaos I.*
> *Fix in me some stern compulsion*
> *Let me be thy right-hand guy.*

"OK, OK," Laureen stopped him. "But it wouldn't. And I am."

"What d'you mean you are?" Tom asked.

"That was Mrs. Merton on the phone. She wants me to play bridge with her club on Friday."

"Yeah? Going to go?"

"What do you think?"

"I don't know. You don't like bridge much, do you?"

"No, I don't like bridge, but I'd play every afternoon until school's out if I thought it would help you get the vice-principalship." Laureen sat on the arm of Tom's chair and let her long bob fan out against his shoulder. "And you're going to need help if you keep dallying with that teachers' union stuff," she said somberly.

"So I've got a campaign manager," Tom said. "What's my platform?"

"Don't joke. You know that if Andrews gets the Toluma principalship, you're the logical man for his job. You're the only man in the school with your Ph.D. for one thing."

"Looky, kid. That's not the way it's done. Merton wants a vice-principal who can handle discipline for him. OK. I fit there all right. And he wants someone who can take care of curriculum revision. OK again. That's up my alley. But he wants, first of all, somebody the Presbyterians like, and the Rotarians, and the American Legion. And the DAR. And I'm not so sure he'll think I'm a peg who'll fit all those holes."

"I'll bet you, though, Tom, that Mrs. Merton wouldn't be inviting me to this party if they weren't considering you. Why should she? She's never asked any of the other teachers' wives."

"What makes you think Mrs. Merton's the power behind the throne?"

"Nobody could look as much like Abe Lincoln as Ellsworth Merton does without being a figurehead. Now could he really, Tom?"

Tom laughed. "Don't let Ellie's rustic pose fool you. Under his linsey-woolsey the wheels are going round plenty fast. Why d'you want me to get the vice-principalship anyway, Laurie? There's a lot of grief in cracking down on kids. Andrews says that's the reason he has his hat in the ring at Toluma. 'I've had enough of vice-principalships,' he says. 'I'll take the head job, now, if I can get it—handle teachers and finances and let someone else go through the kids' lockers for pot and pornography.' Why d'you want to let me in for all that, Laurie?"

"Why?" Laureen asked. "I'll tell you why. For the two thousand dollars extra you'll get." But the minute she said it, she knew it wasn't that. That sure round sum. It wasn't the two thousand dollars; it was the dreams—dreams of what the two thousand dollars would do. But she shied away from the word *dreams,* too. That was what she called Tom's plans, Tom's efforts. "Dreams. Visions. Wishful thinking." "A teachers' union," Tom would say, and use the words *security* and *cooperation* and *equity.* And she would answer, "Dreams, dreams. The thing to do is to think of yourself."

Was it just a case of her dreams against Tom's? A white woolen dressing gown and the harp paid for—against Tom's nice-sounding words? Her dream, the white woolen dressing gown, would keep her warm on a rainy Sunday, or a windy morning—and Tom's dreams, could you warm yourself with an ideal, snuggle up cozily to a hope?

"Two thousand dollars," she repeated firmly. "Maybe we could move out of this concrete box. I could go to the city for lessons."

Tom looked at her with delight. He thinks I'm just like a kid wanting things for Christmas, like a princess in a fairy tale complaining of a pea under her mattress, Laureen decided. It tickles him to look into a mind so different from his own. Her heart melted with kindness. She started to say, "What's your dream?" but let the breath she had drawn in for the words seep out in a sigh. She knew. No use hearing that Twenty-Thirty speech over again. No use having her own dream obscured.

During the week that followed she spent a good deal of time thinking about what she should wear to Mrs. Merton's. Not her best, she decided, as if this were the party of her life. The night before, she tried on her black jersey with the new drawnwork collar her mother had sent her. When she saw in the mirror how the color set off her ash blond hair, and the way the material outlined her slender, curving figure, she decided on it at once.

"Hey, Tom," she called from the doorway of their bedroom, "is this the ticket?"

Tom was sitting before the fire rubbing olive oil into Trudle, their shepherd. He turned toward her, but continued rubbing the dog. "Tom, tell me," she said, "is this better than my green silk?" She swayed back against the door frame, breasts arched, one bent knee advanced.

Tom rolled his eyes and began to sing, "Let me to thy bosom fly, where I—"

Laureen stopped him. "If it's the last thing I ever do, Tom Ashe, I'm going to teach you to give a reasonable answer to a reasonable question, and leave off this damned singing."

Tom filled his cupped hand with oil before he answered her. "That means learning to ask reasonable questions you know, Laurie."

After the party, Laureen was sure the dress had been just right. She had left Mrs. Merton's a little early, while the others were still sitting around the bridge tables eating candied almonds and salted pine nuts. She had decided it would be thoughtful to leave a little early on her first afternoon with them, so that they could have an opportunity to pool opinions about her. And, too, she was impatient to get home, tell Tom what Mrs. Merton had said about the vice-principalship.

Her head ached, but she walked so fast in spite of it that the quiet evening air flowed past her face like a breeze. Suddenly she slackened her pace. Tom's at that meeting, she thought, and heaven knows when he'll get home, and here I am, speeding along as if spring would give me a hotfoot if I slowed down. She walked slowly for a while, trying to be a young woman appreciating a spring landscape. "Slowly walking, sweetly savoring," she said, but it didn't make it true. "The acacias are like trees of yellow pollen made by the bees, and the grass burns like flame in the vacant lots." It was no use. There weren't any words with which she could pin the spring evening to her consciousness. She was just a young woman walking through a spring landscape, and all her savoring was of what she had to tell Tom. Neither her headache nor her desire not to get home before Tom could keep her from hurrying. The meadowlarks sang their evening notes, clear as shadowless water, and the cars of men coming home from work turned into home driveways, but Laureen heard neither.

Tom, Tom, she thought, it's in the bag. Aggie's giving you a big build-up. You should have heard how she introduced me. "I want you to meet Dr. Ashe's wife," she'd said. "Dr. Ashe is on Ellsworth's faculty, you know. We're very proud of him. No doubt you've read of his work in developing new techniques in remedial reading." You wouldn't have thought that she knew the words, would you? But she knew them, she's learned them. She's building you up. She put me at her table for tea. Andrews has Toluma, Tom. Aggie said so, and she said, "We need a young, progressive man to take Andrews's place." That's you, Tom. "Progressive," she said, "not radical. Not one of these men who is more interested in getting teachers organized than in teaching." You might have thought she knew where you were this afternoon. Oh, Tom, Tom, why will you? But I covered you beautifully. "Whatever teachers do is of interest to Tom," I said. "He believes it is impossible to deal successfully with what you don't understand." That was the best I could do, seeing that she might know exactly where you were. She "ah, yes-ed" that, but then she bubbled, "It would be best—wouldn't it, dear Mrs. Ashe?—if he avoided even the appearance—" The bubble broke then. You know how it does, and she said, "But I'm sure I can leave that to you, Mrs. Ashe." And I said, "Yes, you can," and I meant it, Tom—if I'm not too late.

Laureen pulled off her little flowered turban and rubbed her hand across her forehead, but the ache in her head needed more than rubbing to cure it. Venus was shining now, a golden lantern, and the western hills were already dark. If only Tom would be home, Laureen thought. All I want in this world is two aspirin and Tom to be home when I get there. That's not much to want. Until she rounded the big live oak at the corner of Madrona she wouldn't be able to see the house. She walked past it with her eyes shut, and then, opening them suddenly, she saw Tom's car in front of the house, the light on in their bedroom.

She was out of breath when she opened the front door.

"Tom, Tom," she called.

"Here," he answered from the bathroom. "I'm washing up."

She went into their bedroom and lay down across the bed, kicking off her pumps and putting the cool pillow across her forehead. "Bring me a couple of aspirin when you come out, will you, Tom?"

"Soon as I dry," he said. "Got a headache?"

"Lousy. Just started though." She was tired now of the long story she had rehearsed for Tom. She wanted only to tell him quickly, and find out quickly. "Andrews got Toluma all right," she called.

"Yeah?" Tom answered, his voice revealing nothing.

"And the vice-principalship is yours—if you want it enough."

"What do you mean, want it enough?" She heard him take one foot down from the edge of the bathtub, put the other one up.

"You can't have it and this union stuff, too. They don't go together. Aggie said so. You'll have to make up your mind, Tom," she said with sudden intensity, sitting up, so that the pain in her head boomed. "What did you do this afternoon? Tell me. I can't bear to wait."

Laureen listened so hard her head seemed to throb in unison with the soft backward and forward swish of Tom's towel. Swish—throb, swish—throb. Just so he doesn't start some cockeyed parody. If he does that I'll know it's all over, his name signed, his word given.

"Tom," she called. "You'll rub your skin off. I'm waiting for those aspirin."

"OK, Laurie." Tom came out in slippers and shorts, with a glass of water in one hand and the aspirin bottle in the other. Laurie held out her hand, and he tipped two aspirin into her palm. But she couldn't swallow them, they wouldn't help her until she knew. "You didn't sign anything this afternoon, did you? You didn't commit yourself, did you, Tom?"

Tom dropped the aspirin bottle on the bed, took the two aspirin out of her hand, popped them into her mouth, and held the glass of water to her lips while he sang:

> *Flow gently, sweet aspirin,*
> *Between her pale flanks,*
> *Flow gently, sweet aspirin*
> *A-down her fair banks.*

Laurie swallowed the aspirin and lay back on the bed with the pillow across her eyes again. For a minute she was lost and sad; her dream was gone, and she didn't know her way about in Tom's dream yet—maybe she never would. But then, somehow, she had a strange feeling of happiness, not very strong, not very definite—like a splinter of light slipping under a blind into a dark room. But it was there.

She lifted one hand and waved her fingers gently.

"What's the matter, Laurie?" Tom asked. "What're you doing?"

"Waving good-bye to the vice-principal," Laurie said.

# The Second (or Perhaps Third) Time Round

WHEN I WAS SIXTEEN, I had never been kissed. I also kept survival lists. At that time I saw no connection between the two facts. Not being kissed doesn't need to be explained. Everyone, at some time or other in his life, hasn't been. At sixteen I thought it showed on me like a harelip or a leg brace. I went around trying to *look* kissed. When anyone said, "Sweet sixteen and never been kissed," I thought he meant me. I couldn't do anything about being sixteen, or about not being kissed—at least there wasn't anything I then knew to do—but I did try not to be sweet. At this I was an off-and-on success.

Not being kissed at sixteen was harder for me to endure than it otherwise would have been because Ramona, my twelve-year-old sister, had been. She had had boy friends since she was ten. She had big boys of fifteen hanging around her from whom I would have been proud to have a glance. They treated me like Ramona's old-maid aunt. My brother Neddie was only sixteen months younger than I. When we were together where people didn't know us, I sidled up to him in a way I hoped onlookers would think romantic. To this day Neddie still sits across the room from me when we visit. That year of sidling has made him permanently wary.

Naturally, I didn't tell anyone how I felt about not being kissed; or even that I hadn't been. The omission shamed me. I didn't mention the survival lists either, though I'm not sure why. Perhaps I knew instinctively that people are drawn to the expenders, not the hoarders, of life. Perhaps my motives were even worse; perhaps I thought I had discovered the only life belt on a sinking vessel.

I remember the very first item that went on that list. "Never climb a shaley mountain with a sharp-ended Madrone stick for a cane." I wrote this down after reading of the death of a seventeen-year-old boy. He had been climbing a shaley mountain, using a sharp-ended Madrone stick for a cane. He slipped. The Madrone stick pierced his

jugular vein. In twenty minutes he was dead. This was obviously a
death that could easily be avoided. "Never climb a shaley mountain,"
etc.

My survival lists were made up of such reminders, ways in which
to avoid dying unnecessarily. There were, clearly, deaths you could
not prevent by taking care. There were sicknesses for which you
couldn't be vaccinated; there were acts of God, which couldn't be
anticipated, earthquakes and tidal waves and mad dogs. With such,
my lists had nothing to do. But the papers were filled with accounts
of people who, except for some one foolish act, would still be alive.
Sherwood Anderson, for instance: "A bit of a toothpick lodged in a
tidbit, eaten by him at a farewell cocktail party, perforated his intes-
tine and he was taken from the ship in a dying condition at Ceylon."
That piece of information resulted in the second injunction on my
survival list. "Never eat a tidbit in which a bit of toothpick has been
lodged."

A lady doing her washing with her long hair hanging was scalped
by her electric wringer. Into my survival notebook went, "Never do a
washing with long hair hanging."

A man who had a patented fling-up garage door flung it up insecurely and had his skull crushed when the door came down on him
as he turned to reenter his car. "Never raise a patented fling-up door
insecurely."

I was an expert on what not to do to live. If God wanted me to die,
he would have to take the full responsibility. It wasn't going to be
accidental, the result of any stupidity of mine. My lists told me what
not to do in three hundred and eleven situations, ranging from what
not to do while washing clothes and garaging cars to what not to do
while swimming at neap tide and exercising stallions. I knew how to
avoid being killed while hunting abalone, crossing railroad bridges,
taking baths, and lighting gas ovens. I was as near immortality as
thinking will ever get you. I couldn't help noting, with satisfaction,
the deaths of poor nonthinkers in situations where I would have sur-
vived. Nevertheless, I was far from happy.

At sixteen the connection, now so obvious, between these lists and
not being kissed, was not apparent to me. I think it may have crossed
my mind that keeping lists of ways to survive was not a very stirring

activity. It was nothing I could boast of when other girls told of crawling in windows at 2:00 A.M. so that their parents wouldn't know they had been out. But that the list-making, itself, was the result of a feverish determination to postpone death until I had lived (as I understood living at sixteen) never occurred to me. I didn't realize that other girls were so busy dating, dancing, and kissing that the thought of death never entered their heads. Outside of a full life at home and at school (and these are activities a sixteen-year-old can dispose of with one hand), I hadn't a thing to do with my imagination but to anticipate kissing and plan to survive. Kissing was scarce and death everywhere; so, until my real life began, survival was my full-time job. Then, when my real life showed signs of getting underway, the long wait had made me so nervous and diffident I missed my first chance.

George Phelps phoned to ask me if I would go with him to see Ronald Colman in *Beau Geste*. To my horror, I found myself saying no. After waiting so many years for that invitation, my pride wouldn't permit me to say yes. I was like a beggar who has overestimated, not his need, but his humility. When he hears the dime he has waited for so long at last rattle in his tin cup, he flings it back in the donor's face. So I with George. "I'm going to be busy Friday night, George."

I was. Crying. George Phelps was a perfectly presentable boy, and when I wouldn't go with him to see *Beau Geste* he had asked Mary Beth Turley, a girl who wasn't too nervous to say yes. I spent the evening thinking of the good time they were having and wondering whether or not I would ever have another invitation. Opportunity, they said, knocked only once. This, perhaps, was the history of old maids: they had failed to answer that first knock. My fate was perhaps already sealed. "Sweet sixteen and never been kissed" was simply the threshold of my disaster. Nothing would have changed at sour sixty. On that night I made up my mind that if opportunity ever did knock again, I would say yes, no matter what shape it took or name it had.

Incredibly, in two weeks' time there was another knock. It was as my mother had said. For each girl there is an international date line, and boys know when girls have crossed it. When they're *ready*. My mother propounded this theory to cheer me when I was downcast.

On the other hand, if she thought I was settling into spinsterhood spinelessly, she didn't shrink from picturing for me the wasteland that lay ahead. She had been a girl like Ramona. She had been married at seventeen; a daughter without boyfriends seemed pitiful to her, if not defective. *She* had no intention, whatever I had, of letting me miss that second knock.

I was amazed that it was Gene French who asked me. There wasn't a thing wrong with him; he was a big, olive-skinned boy, a minor athlete and well-known ladies man. He had been going with girls since he was thirteen. The idea of a date with him scared me to death. I would have preferred a boy I could feel a little sorry for, someone who stuttered or was cross-eyed. When I had vowed to say yes to whoever asked me next, I had imagined such a one, not a Gene French.

I did everything I could think of to prepare myself for the occasion. I washed my hair every day for a week before the date. I had read that absolute cleanliness is irresistible. I lived, for that week, almost entirely on lemon juice. I understood that this gave the skin a transparency that was irresistible. Maybe. What lemon juice gave me was something resembling ringworm. And the daily hair-washing made my fine blond hair stand on end, as if electrified.

My mother took charge of me. The situation evidently looked hopeless. Otherwise the idea of taking charge would never have occurred to her, nor would I have permitted it. Mama was a slapdash dresser herself. She subdued her own hair with a curling iron. If she ran out of handkerchiefs, she grabbed up a napkin. There were more pins than stitches in her clothes. Nevertheless, a crisis, I knew, gave her unsuspected powers. I really believed that she could win the Singer Sewing Machine contest for the best-dressed woman in America if she thought it necessary to do so.

She took me, hopeless, out of the room I shared with Ramona, plunked me down on the bench in front of the bird's-eye-maple dressing table in her and my father's room and began to work on me. Desperation made her great. By sheer will power, plus a lot of backcombing and some curling, she forced my hair to adhere hair to hair, and to take on shape. Hairpins, caught in the web of her back-combing, stayed put. She cut off the end of her own switch and plumped up a flat spot with it. She made spit curls, and kept them in place with a mixture of sugar and water. When she had finished with me no one could say I didn't have a hairdo.

Next she tackled my complexion. She worked on it with her own cake powder, applied with a damp sponge. As she swabbed away on my lemon-juice-scarred face, I grew calmer. I watched what she was doing with the detachment one gives a window washer or floor waxer. The sight of her slow circular gestures was mesmerizing. Added to sight was the feel of the cool damp sponge. I was the canvas that receives the paint, as well as the eye that watches the picture grow.

On that evening (it was May) I cannot remember (though I sat staring into a mirror in which her face, as well as mine, was reflected) once seeing my mother's face. She was nothing but hands for me. I know what she looked like, of course. Thirty-four, thin as a rail, big blue-green eyes, long fingers (the nail of one damaged in a corn sheller), a voice trembling with life. I didn't, at sixteen, care for her looks. She would never have had her picture used in an advertisement for Mother's Home-baked Bread. She didn't look like a mother. No gray hairs, no bosom to speak of, no rosy cheeks, no spectacles. She didn't, most of the time, even *act* like a mother. She wasn't acting like a mother in helping me get ready for my date. She never played roles. She was being herself, and what she was doing for me she would have done for anyone. She was against spinsterhood, and the unhappiness that she supposed accompanied it, on principle.

She treated me like a daughter in one respect though. And I loved it. She remembered with me. I don't think there was anyone else to whom she would have told her wondering tales of her youth. Certainly there was no one else to whom I listened as I listened to her. Partly, I suppose, because what had happened to her and her mother, seemed also to have happened to me; but mostly because her vivid, emotional way of telling took hold of my imagination.

"I remember," she said, as she sponged the powder onto my face, "a time when Mama helped *me* dress for a meeting with your father."

My grandmother had died when I was nine. I had some memories of her, but she was, for the most part, not a grandmother I remembered but my mother's mother; and my mother's ambivalence about her mother made Grandma an enigma my mind loved to tussle with.

"I had been at home getting over a bout of typhoid fever," my mother said. "You and Neddie were both born, and I was expecting Ramona. I was a sight. Half my hair had fallen out. I was skin and bones, except where Ramona was beginning to show. And I was tired in every bone. Your father was driving down from Noblesville to pick us up. I looked forward to seeing your father, but not enough to take any pains in dressing up for him. I was just too run-down to care. I wasn't going to put on a corset or curl my hair or take off my house slippers. I was just going to meet him in my Mother Hubbard and let him see what I'd been through. What I wanted was sympathy, not admiration. Mama put a stop to all that. I might want pity—and for all I know she may have thought I deserved pity—but she wasn't going to have me looking pitiful for my husband.

" 'You get out of those bedclothes,' she told me, 'before Herbie arrives. What do you want him to think you are—an invalid?'

"That's exactly what I felt like, but Mama march-timed me out of my dressing sacque and house slippers and into a corset and a dress that really fit, in jig time. She plumped up my corset cover with a couple of handkerchiefs. She pinned in the seams of my dress until what curves I had showed. She doused me with Hoyt's cologne. She pinked-up my cheeks with juice from a red geranium. When she finished with me, she said, 'Now you don't look quite so much like something the cats dragged in,' and she sent me downstairs to wait for Herbie, while she took care of you and Neddie. She'd worn me out with her prinking. I went downstairs thinking it would be a good thing if I'd faint and teach her a lesson. But when I saw your father's eyes light up, I forgot to faint. And I don't know that I ever did thank Mama for what she did for me that day—and did in spite of me. And I must've worn *her* out, because I was so determined not to be beautified, I bucked like a steer the whole time she worked on me. Then I left her to look after you and Neddie without a thought while I went down to meet my beau."

"Beau?" I asked. "He was your husband, wasn't he?"

"He greeted me like a beau," Mama said.

While my mother was telling me this story, I was remembering with her; but remembering, also, something she had forgotten: this whole experience as seen by her at another time. I couldn't remember then, and can't now, where or when I had heard it. I had been present when that dressing, then twelve years past, took place. But what my mother felt while her mother decked her out, I couldn't, of course, have known. To whom did my mother tell what she had felt? To *her* sister, when I was present but supposedly too young to understand or remember? To me, myself, when little, did my mother, in one of her frequent attempts to figure out *her* mother, tell this story? Someone she could talk to, but who couldn't ask questions and wouldn't remember? I don't know. The source of that knowledge is a mystery to me. But I had the knowledge. And it was more vivid and real to me than the version I listened to as my mother helped me to get ready for my date with Gene French. Did the story, as I had heard it first, seem true because I had heard it first? Because I was younger and more impressionable? Because my mother, in her first telling, had been more vehement and impassioned? And truthful? Did this second account strike me (without my knowing it) as being watered down with the kindness with which we remember the dead?

I don't know. But what I first heard, and believed, even while hearing the second version, was a different story entirely, though everything that happened was the same. My mother had had typhoid. She had gone home to stay with her mother and father while she convalesced. She was longing to see her husband, as true a husband as ever lived, but handsome, so that other women were forever casting sheep's eyes at him. He was a true husband, but he needed a wife by his side. In addition to wanting to see her husband, Mama was eager to leave her mother's home. She had outgrown her mother's ways of doing things. Living with two small children had made her more tolerant of disorder than her mother. Trying once again to be a daughter had shown her how completely she had become a wife.

The day her husband was to come for her, she was still weak from her sickness and tired easily. Nevertheless, she had taken pains with her hair, sadly thinned because of the fever. She had put on a new lavender-sprigged challis dressing sacque. She had saved it for this very occasion. It matched, or almost matched, her purple kid house shoes. She wore her hand-carved ivory beads. She didn't mind looking a little like an invalid, since she felt herself still to be one. Herbie might as well know from the outset that she wasn't absolutely robust yet.

Mama had stretched out on her bed after she had finished dressing for a catnap before my father arrived. There was a six-hour ride behind a couple of jogging horses, and with two run-about children to look after, ahead of her. She would need every bit of strength she could summon.

She had just fallen asleep when she was awakened by her mother.

"Mama, what's wrong?" she asked.

"What's wrong?" her mother, whose name was Mary Frances, repeated. "Molly, don't you know Herbie's due here in a half an hour?"

"I know it, Mama."

"Then why aren't you dressing?"

"I am dressing, Mama."

"Molly, you're not thinking of letting Herbie catch sight of you in that getup?"

"What's wrong with it? I thought it looked nice." She showed her mother how shoes and dressing sacque matched, and how nicely the cream of the ivory beads set off the lavender sprigs.

"I grant you," her mother said, "it's nice enough for a sickroom. But for greeting a husband, no. Herbie's going to get the idea he's saddled with an invalid; you've had so many sick spells since Neddie was born. You'll feel a lot better yourself if you get into something that looks a little more like traveling and a little less like cod-liver oil and morning sickness. Now, come on. Up with you, and we'll have you looking more like what Herbie is expecting to see."

Mama and her mother were I think opposites in many ways. But they had a connecting link: dreams. They were both dreamers. The difference was Mama's dreams solaced her; her mother's spurred her on. Mary Frances was a dreamer who *did*. She was a small, round, black-haired woman. She flew like a bee and sometimes like a bullet around her lanky, freckled-faced, slow-moving husband. And around her lanky, milk-skinned, dreaming daughter. Mary Frances was a planner; she looked ahead, foresaw, organized. She had Mama, as she had said she would, up and out of that dressing sacque in a trice.

When Mama complained, "I just don't think I can stand a corset. It shuts off my breath," her mother said, "Nonsense, it'll give you support." When Mama objected, "Mother, Herbie knows I'm flat-chested," she said, "That don't mean he won't like the *look* of a curve or two in the right spot."

It was while her mother was plumping out her bosom with a couple of rouched-up handkerchiefs that it came over Mama, like cold water lapping her clear to her armpits, what her mother was doing, what she was deliberately doing. She was making sure she wouldn't be saddled with a daughter whose husband couldn't stomach any more invalidism; a somicky, sickly woman, always trailing around in sickroom clothes, a passel of children at her heels and a pain somewhere in her innards. Mama's ways hadn't set any better with her mother than her mother's ways had set with Mama. Mama could *hear* her mother thinking: A handsome man like Herbie, with girls laying themselves out to catch his attention, can't be blamed if he begins noticing them; particularly if his wife won't put herself out a little for him. Herbie Chalmers don't have the most stable blood in his veins to begin with. He's done very well so far. But if Molly don't take a few pains, she'll find herself without a husband. And I'll find myself starting in where I was twenty-five years ago, and a second brood of young ones to bring up.

That's what Mama heard her mother thinking. She knew that was what was in her mother's mind as surely as if her mother had spoken the words. She didn't have to hear the words. Every act of her mother's spoke them. She felt like flesh being decked out for the auction block. You can expect that from an auctioneer. But to have yourself made attractive, seductive if possible, by your own mother for reasons of ridding herself of you—how would that strike you? It made Mama sick at heart and it made her furious. All right, if that was what her mother feared, she would cooperate completely. She threw herself into the deck-out job wholeheartedly. Her body, which had been cold, flamed as if with a return of her fever. She urged her mother to lace the corset tighter, to make her false bosoms larger, to rat her hair more preposterously, to color her cheeks a brighter red. Her mother was delighted.

"You'll never be sorry you made the effort," she told her daughter.

Mama hated the idea that she and Father weren't united by something more lasting than colors and curves. She despised the thought of consciously baiting a trap to hold him. She was heartsick to learn that her mother wouldn't be happy to have her only daughter with her, under whatever circumstances, for the rest of her days. She walked down the stairs, when Father came, determined never again so long as she lived to suggest to her mother by so much as a fleeting visit the possibility that she might remain to be a burden. She walked down the stairs hating Father, too; seeing him through her mother's eyes, saying to him in her mind: If flesh is what you value, take a look. I haven't got much, but this is the best I can do with what I've got.

This is the story as I first heard it; and I couldn't help wondering, as my mother told it for the second time, and in such a different way, why it had changed. But it was good for me to have something to wonder about besides myself and what Gene French would think of me. How I would look. What I would say. I had a real puzzle to divert me. Not one that required immediate solving, but one that filled the back of my mind where panic lay, whenever I began to think too closely about the hours ahead. It never occurred to me to say to my mother, "When I heard this story before, it was different." I didn't, first of all, because of the hurry. I didn't want to slow Mama down in the work that had to be done on me, with an analysis of her own past. But since I never did ask her, there must have been another reason. Perhaps I was too delicate minded to want to bring back to her mind an ugly story, when a kinder one had taken its place. Perhaps I didn't want a $2+2=4$ story. I really wanted to wonder. My mother had always been a mystery to me. I didn't want the mystery cleared up. I didn't want to see through her.

In any case, I didn't then, or ever, ask her any questions. Then I was too busy. It was almost time for Gene French to arrive, and I still wasn't dressed. I hurried cold fingered and dry mouthed, after my mother finished my hair and complexion, into my clothes. My mother loaned me a Georgette blouse of hers, through which the pink ribbons of my camisole showed seductively. She had bought me my first pair of high-heeled shoes. When all preparations were over, I certainly looked ready for something—though I'm not sure it was a date with a high-school boy.

Gene French should have known I had never been out with a boy before. And knowing that, he should have planned a different kind of date. He should have taken me to a movie or a party, or someplace where there was something to watch and people to listen to, besides ourselves. Maybe what he planned to do was neck, and my appearance, towering hairdo, enameled complexion, transparent waist, high heels, made him feel he would be tackling a store-window dummy. Maybe my frozen high-and-mighty air, with which I tried to cover up my trembling fear, convinced him that I thought he was a toad. Whatever the reason, we sat in his car, with the greatest distance possible between us, both absolutely mute.

Going to a soda fountain was probably supposed to wind up the date, not start it. But in desperation, stuck with a speechless mannequin, Gene French was forced to play his trump card early. It won him no tricks, but it did hasten things. In the car we couldn't see ourselves. The confectionery was lined with mirrors. We could see ourselves, both mute, and me preposterously turned out. We could also see other people, laughing, talking, having a good time. I watched myself and others. But I still could not say a word. I felt like the man in "The Pit and the Pendulum," doomed but powerless to free himself.

When we went out to the car again, I was able to croak, "Thank you," to Gene.

This sign of life encouraged him. He tried to start a conversation. "I'm glad you liked the sodas. I didn't know whether we should go to the Cardinal awhile, or to the Poinsettia. Most of the kids hang out down at the Card. But they serve really punk ice cream down there, they never heard of putting whipped cream on their sodas, and you have to scream to make yourself heard. 'I scream for ice cream.' That's their motto down at the Card, and they really mean it. If you want ice cream, go to the Poinsettia. If you want to scream, what's the point going anywhere? I can scream anywhere, can't you?"

"No," said I, and Gene waited for me to say why. I couldn't say why.

He didn't try again. He started the car, and when I saw which way he was headed, I felt desperate. He was taking me home. It was a sweet moonlit May night, and I had been away from home for no more than an hour. He wasn't going the longest way around and he wasn't taking it slowly. Get it over with, he was telling himself. Get rid of this zombie.

I lived five miles out of town on a ranch. At the rate we were traveling we would be there in five minutes. To get to our house you had to turn off the main road and go down a lane to the back of the twenty acres, where my father had built our house.

When Gene made the turn off the main road, I said, or more likely screamed, "Stop!" I don't think, after all I had suffered, and after all my unsuccessful efforts to speak, that, when at last I did so, I could have managed a natural tone. And I scared Gene. He turned off the car like a shot. "Are you sick?" he asked.

"Sick, sick, sick," I said, like a modern comedian. I couldn't speak at all without exaggeration and overemphasis.

"What's the matter?" he asked.

"This," I said. I took off my shoes and threw them out the window. I dug the makeshift rat out of my hair and threw it after them.

"You think this is the real me, don't you?" I accused him. "This horrible painted" (liquid powder was white paint, wasn't it), "yes, painted creature. This dressed-up man-bait. This false-haired" (I threw a few hairpins out the window), "high-heeled, nitwitted whore. You did, didn't you? You were taken in. You had no idea that behind all this falseness, all this cheapness, was me. It's *not* me. It has nothing to do with me. It's my mother. She made me go out this way. She wants me to be attractive to men. I hate it."

I was, literally, raving. I had no idea, when I started to speak, what I would say, or where my words would lead me. But once I heard what my words said, they convinced me. I was a victim. I was not really a tongue-tied, unpopular, graceless dolt. I was a princess in disguise, and my mother had fabricated the disguise.

I began to take down my hair. It was quite a job, what with pins, combs, back-coming, sugar and water. But getting out that home-made rat had wobbled my hairdo on its foundations and opened up a fissure through which I could work. I don't know what a girl can do today that will equal the intimacy taking down your hair had in my girlhood. She can take off all her clothes, but I doubt that that seems so much intimate, as daring. Well, letting down your hair was daring, too. You took your hair down in your bedroom. You took it down as a preparation for going to bed. It was associated with everything you shouldn't do with a boy. I knew this perfectly well. My hands trembled. But acting was now as compulsive as silence had been. Gene French was all that stood between me and being an old maid. Combs and hairpins and invisible nets flew out the window. Gene French must've been scared out of his wits. If I had been doing all this symbolic disrobing outside the car, I'm sure he would have driven off and left me. But he couldn't very well shove me out. Or get out himself and run. And perhaps he was curious.

When my waist-long mop of blond hair was at last down, I pushed it back and turned to face Gene French in the moonlight.

"Look," I bade him, "here is the real me."

God knows what I looked like, shoeless, hair swinging, there in the moonlight, incoherent with fear and frustration and disappointment. And determination. But, thank God, Gene French knew what to do. He kissed me.

I had anticipated that kiss for so long and worked so hard for it that when, finally, it arrived, I couldn't feel it. I don't suppose I could have felt a branding iron that evening. I had had to anesthetize myself in order to do what I did: revile my mother, throw off my clothing, perform the getting-ready-for-bed act. I couldn't come out of ether fast enough to feel. Besides, the kiss, as a physical act to savor, hadn't been what I was concentrating on getting. I had been concentrating on the kiss as diploma, or certificate or passport. After you got these things, you found uses for them. So I graduated that night and got my diploma signed several times over. I was certified kissable.

I had to creep into the house, such was my disorder, then emerge from my bedroom and pretend that I had actually been getting ready for bed. Next morning I had to get up before dawn and retrieve from down the lane my discarded gear.

I never again added a single item to my survival lists. It didn't seem to me that so many people were dying needlessly as had formerly been the case. If they were, I just didn't see the accounts of their deaths; or if I did, they didn't seem, any longer, to concern me. They didn't worry me. I didn't even worry about the picture I had painted to Gene French of my mother, as a mercenary old madam, dressing her daughter like merchandise. I didn't worry as to whether it was true or not true. My mother was happy. Gene French asked me for other dates; and once he had broken the ice, so did other boys. And my mother thought she was responsible for it all. Maybe she was.

What I really wish is that the three of us, my grandmother, Mary Frances, my mother, Molly, and I, Rosellen, could sit down together and talk over those bygone hours of dressing. The two who are dead and I. What really took place? What were the two mothers doing? And would the two daughters change anything their mothers did?

I'm willing to let things stand.